The Blight

The Blight

Shayol Ghul

Mountains of Dhoom

Fal Dara

SALDAEA

KANDOR

ARAFEL

SHIENAR

Aiel Waste

Tar Valon

Dragonmount

CAIRHIEN

The Spine of the World

Rivers

ANDOR

Caemlyn

MURANDY

LDAN

ALTARA

ILLIAN

TEAR

INN

SEA    OF    STORMS

# THE
# GREAT
# HUNT

THE WHEEL OF TIME
by Robert Jordan

*The Eye of the World*
*The Great Hunt*

# THE GREAT HUNT

## ROBERT JORDAN

TOR
*fantasy*

A TOM DOHERTY ASSOCIATES BOOK
NEW YORK

This book was printed on acid-free paper.

THE GREAT HUNT

Copyright © 1990 by Robert Jordan

A Tor Book
Published by Tom Doherty Associates, Inc.
49 West 24th Street
New York, N.Y. 10010

Maps by Thomas Canty
Interior illustrations by Matthew C. Nielsen
Cover painting by Darrell Sweet

ISBN: 0-812-50971-4 (pbk)

Library of Congress Cataloging-in-Publication Data

Jordan, Robert.
The great hunt / Robert Jordan.
p.     cm.
Sequel to: The eye of the world.
ISBN 0-312-85140-5 (hbk)
I. Title.
PS3560.07617G74      1990
813'.54—dc20                                                    90-11128
                                                                      CIP

Printed in the United States of America

First edition: November 1990

0   9   8   7   6   5   4   3   2   1

This book is dedicated to Lucinda Culpin, Al Dempsey, Tom Doherty, Susan England, Dick Gallen, John Jarrold, the Johnson City Boys (Mike Leslie, Kenneth Loveless, James D. Lund, Paul R. Robinson), Karl Lundgren, the Montana Gang (Eldon Carter, Ray Grenfell, Ken Miller, Rod Moore, Dick Schmidt, Ray Sessions, Ed Wildey, Mike Wildey, and Sherman Williams), William McDougal, Louisa Cheves Popham Raoul, Ted and Sydney Rigney, Robert A. T. Scott, Bryan and Sharon Webb, and Heather Wood.

They came to my aid when God walked across the water, and the true Eye of the World passed over my house.

—Robert Jordan
Charleston, SC
February 1990

# CONTENTS

*And it shall come to pass that what men made shall be shattered, and the Shadow shall lie across the Pattern of the Age, and the Dark One shall once more lay his hand upon the world of man. Women shall weep and men quail as the nations of the earth are rent like rotting cloth. Neither shall anything stand nor abide . . .*

*Yet one shall be born to face the Shadow, born once more as he was born before and shall be born again, time without end. The Dragon shall be Reborn, and there shall be wailing and gnashing of teeth at his rebirth. In sackcloth and ashes shall he clothe the people, and he shall break the world again by his coming, tearing apart all ties that bind. Like the unfettered dawn shall he blind us, and burn us, yet shall the Dragon Reborn confront the Shadow at the Last Battle, and his blood shall give us the Light. Let tears flow, O ye people of the world. Weep for your salvation.*

—*from* **The Karaethon Cycle: The Prophecies of the Dragon,**
as translated by Ellaine Marise'idin Alshinn,
Chief Librarian at the Court of Arafel,
in the Year of Grace 231 of the New Era, the Third Age

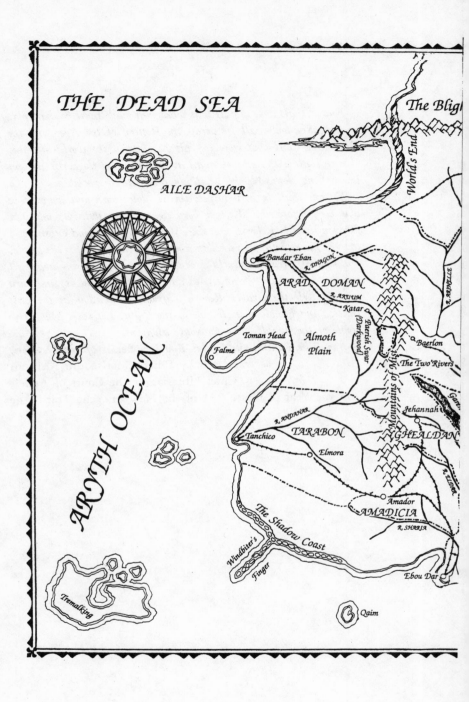

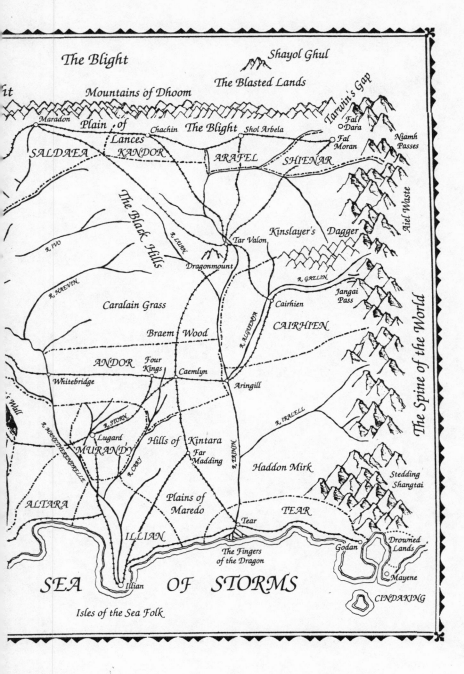

# PROLOGUE

## *In the Shadow*

The man who called himself Bors, at least in this place, sneered at the low murmuring that rolled around the vaulted chamber like the soft gabble of geese. His grimace was hidden by the black silk mask that covered his face, though, just like the masks that covered the hundred other faces in the chamber. A hundred black masks, and a hundred pairs of eyes trying to see what lay behind them.

If one did not look too closely, the huge room could have been in a palace, with its tall marble fireplaces and its golden lamps hanging from the domed ceiling, its colorful tapestries and intricately patterned mosaic floor. If one did not look too closely. The fireplaces were cold, for one thing. Flames danced on logs as thick as a man's leg, but gave no heat. The walls behind the tapestries, the ceiling high above the lamps, were undressed stone, almost black. There were no windows, and only two doorways, one at either end of the room. It was as if someone had intended to give the semblance of a palace reception chamber but had not cared enough to bother with more than the outline and a few touches for detail.

Where the chamber was, the man who called himself Bors did not know, nor did he think any of the others knew. He did not like to think about where it might be. It was enough that he had been summoned. He did not like to think about that, either, but for such a summons, even he came.

He shifted his cloak, thankful that the fires were cold, else it would have been too hot for the black wool draping him to the floor. All his clothes were black. The bulky folds of the cloak hid the stoop he used to disguise his height, and bred confusion as to whether he was thin or thick. He was not the only one there enveloped in a tailor's span of cloth.

Silently he watched his companions. Patience had marked much of his life. Always, if he waited and watched long enough, someone made a mistake. Most of the men and women here might have had the same philosophy; they watched, and listened silently to those who had to speak. Some people could not bear waiting, or silence, and so gave away more than they knew.

Servants circulated through the guests, slender, golden-haired youths proffering wine with a bow and a wordless smile. Young men and young women alike, they wore tight white breeches and flowing white shirts. And male and female alike, they moved with disturbing grace. Each looked more than a mirror image of the others, the boys as handsome as the girls were beautiful. He doubted he could distinguish one from another, and he had an eye and a memory for faces.

A smiling, white-clad girl offered her tray of crystal goblets to him. He took one with no intention of drinking; it might appear untrusting—or worse, and either could be deadly here—if he refused altogether, but anything could be slipped into a drink. Surely some among his companions would have no objections to seeing the number of their rivals for power dwindle, whomever the unlucky ones happened to be.

Idly he wondered whether the servants would have to be disposed of after this meeting. *Servants hear everything.* As the serving girl straightened from her bow, his eye caught hers above that sweet smile. Blank eyes. Empty eyes. A doll's eyes. Eyes more dead than death.

He shivered as she moved gracefully away, and raised the goblet to his lips before he caught himself. It was not what had been done to the girl that chilled him. Rather, every time he thought he detected a weakness in those he now served, he found himself preceded, the supposed weakness cut out with a ruthless precision that left him amazed. And worried. The first rule of his life had always been to search for weakness, for every weakness was a chink where he could probe and pry and influence. If his current masters, his masters for the moment, had no weakness. . . .

Frowning behind his mask, he studied his companions. At least there was plenty of weakness there. Their nervousness betrayed them, even those who had sense enough to guard their tongues. A stiffness in the way this one held himself, a jerkiness in the way that one handled her skirts.

A good quarter of them, he estimated, had not bothered with disguise beyond the black masks. Their clothes told much. A woman standing before a gold-and-crimson wall hanging, speaking softly to a figure—impossible to say whether it was man or woman—cloaked and hooded in gray. She had obviously chosen the spot because the colors of the tapestry set off her garb. Doubly foolish to draw attention to herself, for her scarlet dress, cut low in the bodice to show too much flesh and high at the hem to display golden slippers, marked her from Illian, and a woman of wealth, perhaps even of noble blood.

Not far beyond the Illianer, another woman stood, alone and admirably silent. With a swan's neck and lustrous black hair falling in waves below her waist, she kept her back to the stone wall, observing everything. No nervousness there, only serene self-possession. Very admirable, that, but her coppery skin and her creamy, high-necked gown—leaving nothing but her hands uncovered, yet clinging and only just barely opaque, so that it hinted at everything and revealed nothing—marked her just as clearly of the first blood of Arad Doman. And unless the man who called himself Bors missed his guess entirely, the wide golden bracelet on her left wrist bore her House symbols. They would be for her own House; no Domani bloodborn would bend her stiff pride enough to wear the sigils of another House. Worse than foolishness.

A man in a high-collared, sky-blue Shienaran coat passed him with a wary, head-to-toe glance though the eyeholes of his mask. The man's carriage named him soldier; the set of his shoulders, the way his gaze never rested in one place for long, and the way his hand seemed ready to dart for a sword that was not there, all proclaimed it. The Shienaran wasted little time on the man who called himself Bors; stooped shoulders and a bent back held no threat.

The man who called himself Bors snorted as the Shienaran moved on, right hand clenching and eyes already studying elsewhere for danger. He could read them all, to class and country. Merchant and warrior, commoner and noble. From Kandor and Cairhien, Saldaea and Ghealdan. From every nation and nearly every people. His nose wrinkled in sudden disgust. Even a Tinker, in bright green breeches and a virulent yellow coat. *We can do without* those *come the Day.*

The disguised ones were no better, many of them, cloaked and shrouded as they were. He caught sight, under the edge of one dark robe, of the silver-worked boots of a High Lord of Tear, and under another a glimpse of golden lion-head spurs, worn only by high officers in the Andoran Queen's Guards. A slender fellow—slender even in a floor-dragging black robe and an anonymous gray cloak caught with a plain silver pin—watched from the shadows of his deep cowl. He could be anyone, from anywhere . . . except for the six-pointed star tattooed on the web between thumb and forefinger of his right hand. One of the Sea Folk then, and a look at his left hand would show the marks of his clan and line. The man who called himself Bors did not bother to try.

Suddenly his eyes narrowed, fixing on a woman enveloped in black till nothing showed but her fingers. On her right hand rested a gold ring in the shape of a serpent eating its own tail. Aes Sedai, or at least a woman trained in Tar Valon by Aes Sedai. None else would wear that ring. Either way made no difference to him. He looked away before she could notice his watching, and almost immediately he spotted another woman swathed from head to toe in black and wearing a Great Serpent ring. The two witches gave no sign that they knew each other. In the White Tower they sat like spiders in the middle of a web, pulling the strings that made kings and queens dance, meddling. *Curse them all to death eternal!* He realized that he was grinding his teeth. If numbers must dwindle—and they must, before the Day—there were some who would be missed even less than Tinkers.

A chime sounded, a single, shivering note that came from everywhere at once and cut off all other sounds like a knife.

The tall doors at the far end of the chamber swung open, and two Trollocs stepped into the room, spikes decorating the black mail that hung to their knees. Everyone shied back. Even the man who called himself Bors.

Head and shoulders taller than the tallest man there, they were a stomach-turning blend of man and animal, human faces twisted and altered. One had a heavy, pointed beak where his mouth and nose should have been, and feathers covered his head instead of hair. The other walked on hooves, his face pushed out in a hairy muzzle, and goat horns stuck up above his ears.

Ignoring the humans, the Trollocs turned back toward the door and bowed, servile and cringing. The feathers on the one lifted in a tight crest.

A Myrddraal stepped between them, and they fell to their knees. It was garbed in black that made the Trollocs' mail and the humans' masks seem bright, garments that hung still, without a ripple, as it moved with a viper's grace.

The man who called himself Bors felt his lips drawing back over his teeth, half snarl and half, he was shamed to admit even to himself, fear. It had its face uncovered. Its pasty pale face, a man's face, but eyeless as an egg, like a maggot in a grave.

The smooth white face swiveled, regarding them all one by one, it seemed. A visible shiver ran through them under that eyeless look. Thin, bloodless lips quirked in what might almost have been a smile as, one by one, the masked ones tried to press back into the crowd, milling to avoid that gaze. The Myrddraal's look shaped them into a semicircle facing the door.

The man who called himself Bors swallowed. *There will come a day, Half-man. When the Great Lord of the Dark comes again, he will choose his new Dreadlords, and you will cower before them. You will cower before men. Before me! Why doesn't it speak? Stop staring at me, and speak!*

"Your Master comes." The Myrddraal's voice rasped like a dry snake skin crumbling. "To your bellies, worms! Grovel, lest his brilliance blind and burn you!"

Rage filled the man who called himself Bors, at the tone as much as the words, but then the air above the Halfman shimmered, and the import drove home. *It can't be! It can't. . . !* The Trollocs were already on their bellies, writhing as if they wanted to burrow into the floor.

Without waiting to see if anyone else moved, the man who called himself Bors dropped facedown, grunting as he bruised himself on the stone. Words sprang to his lips like a charm against danger—they were a charm, though a thin reed against what he feared—and he heard a hundred other voices, breathy with fear, speaking the same against the floor.

"The Great Lord of the Dark is my Master, and most heartily do I serve him to the last shred of my very soul." In the back of his mind a voice chattered with fear. *The Dark One and all the Forsaken are bound. . . .* Shivering, he forced it to silence. He had abandoned that voice long since. "Lo, my Master is death's Master. Asking nothing do I serve against the Day of his coming, yet do I serve in the sure and certain hope of life everlasting." *. . . bound in Shayol Ghul, bound by the Creator at the moment of creation. No, I serve a different master now.* "Surely the faithful shall be exalted in the land, exalted above the unbelievers, exalted above thrones, yet do I serve humbly against the Day of his Return." *The hand of the Creator shelters us all, and the Light protects us from the Shadow. No, no! A different master.* "Swift come the Day of Return. Swift come the Great Lord of the Dark to guide us and rule the world forever and ever."

The man who called himself Bors finished the creed panting, as if he had run ten miles. The rasp of breath all around told him he was not the only one.

"Rise. All of you, rise."

The mellifluous voice took him by surprise. Surely none of his companions, lying on their bellies with their masked faces pressed to the mosaic tiles, would have spoken, but it was not the voice he expected from. . . . Cautiously, he raised his head enough to see with one eye.

The figure of a man floated in the air above the Myrddraal, the hem of his blood-red robe hanging a span over the Halfman's head. Masked in blood-red, too. Would the Great Lord of the Dark appear to them as a man? And masked, besides? Yet the Myrddraal, its very gaze fear, trembled and almost cowered where it stood in the figure's shadow. The man who called himself Bors grasped for an answer his mind could contain without splitting. One of the Forsaken, perhaps.

That thought was only a little less painful. Even so, it meant the Day of the Dark One's return must be close at hand if one of the Forsaken was free. The Forsaken, thirteen of the most powerful wielders of the One Power in an Age filled with powerful wielders, had been sealed up in Shayol Ghul along with the Dark One, sealed away from the world of men by the Dragon and the Hundred Companions. And the backblast of that sealing had tainted the male half of the True Source; and all the male Aes Sedai, those cursed wielders of the Power, went mad and broke the world, tore it apart like a pottery bowl smashed on rocks, ending the Age of Legends before they died, rotting while they still lived. A fitting death for Aes Sedai, to his mind. Too good for them. He regretted only that the women had been spared.

Slowly, painfully, he forced the panic to the back of his mind, confined it and held it tight though it screamed to get out. It was the best he could do. None of those on their bellies had risen, and only a few had even dared raise their heads.

"Rise." There was a snap in the red-masked figure's voice this time. He gestured with both hands. "Stand!"

The man who called himself Bors scrambled up awkwardly, but halfway to his feet, he hesitated. Those gesturing hands were horribly burned, crisscrossed by black fissures, the raw flesh between as red as the figure's robes. *Would the Dark One appear so? Or even one of the Forsaken?* The eyeholes of that blood-red mask swept slowly across him, and he straightened hastily. He thought he could feel the heat of an open furnace in that gaze.

The others obeyed the command with no more grace and no less fear in their rising. When all were on their feet, the floating figure spoke.

"I have been known by many names, but the one by which you shall know me is Ba'alzamon."

The man who called himself Bors clamped his teeth to keep them from chattering. Ba'alzamon. In the Trolloc tongue, it meant Heart of the Dark, and even unbelievers knew it was the Trolloc name for the Great Lord of the Dark. He Whose Name Must Not Be Uttered. Not the True Name, Shai'tan, but still forbidden. Among those gathered here, and others of their kind, to sully either with a human tongue was blasphemy. His breath whistled through his nostrils, and all around him he could hear others

panting behind their masks. The servants were gone, and the Trollocs as
well, though he had not seen them go.

"The place where you stand lies in the shadow of Shayol Ghul." More
than one voice moaned at that; the man who called himself Bors was not
sure his own was not among them. A touch of what might almost be called
mockery entered Ba'alzamon's voice as he spread his arms wide. "Fear not,
for the Day of your Master's rising upon the world is near at hand. The Day
of Return draws nigh. Does it not tell you so that I am here, to be seen by
you favored few among your brothers and sisters? Soon the Wheel of Time
will be broken. Soon the Great Serpent will die, and with the power of that
death, the death of Time itself, your Master will remake the world in his
own image for this Age and for all Ages to come. And those who serve me,
faithful and steadfast, will sit at my feet above the stars in the sky and rule
the world of men forever. So have I promised, and so shall it be, without
end. You shall live and rule forever."

A murmur of anticipation ran through the listeners, and some even took
a step forward, toward the floating, crimson shape, their eyes lifted, rap-
turous. Even the man who called himself Bors felt the pull of that promise,
the promise for which he had dealt away his soul a hundred times over.

"The Day of Return comes closer," Ba'alzamon said. "But there is much
yet to do. Much to do."

The air to Ba'alzamon's left shimmered and thickened, and the figure of
a young man hung there, a little lower than Ba'alzamon. The man who
called himself Bors could not decide whether it was a living being or not.
A country lad, by his clothes, with a light of mischief in his brown eyes
and the hint of a smile on his lips, as if in memory or anticipation of a
prank. The flesh looked warm, but the chest did not move with breath, the
eyes did not blink.

The air to Ba'alzamon's right wavered as if with heat, and a second
country-clad figure hung suspended a little below Ba'alzamon. A curly-
haired youth, as heavily muscled as a blacksmith. And an oddity: a battle
axe hung at his side, a great, steel half-moon balanced by a thick spike.
The man who called himself Bors suddenly leaned forward, intent on an
even greater strangeness. A youth with yellow eyes.

For the third time air solidified into the shape of a young man, this time
directly under Ba'alzamon's eye, almost at his feet. A tall fellow, with eyes
now gray, now almost blue as the light took them, and dark, reddish hair.
Another villager, or farmer. The man who called himself Bors gasped. Yet
another thing out of the ordinary, though he wondered why he should
expect anything to be ordinary here. A sword swung from the figure's belt,
a sword with a bronze heron on the scabbard and another inset into the

long, two-handed hilt. *A village boy with a heron-mark blade? Impossible!*
*What can it mean? And a boy with* yellow *eyes.* He noticed the Myrddraal
looking at the figures, trembling; and unless he misjudged entirely, its
trembling was no longer fear, but hatred.

Dead silence had fallen, silence that Ba'alzamon let deepen before he
spoke. "There is now one who walks the world, one who was and will be,
but is not yet, the Dragon."

A startled murmur ran through his listeners.

"The Dragon Reborn! We are to kill him, Great Lord?" That from the
Shienaran, hand grasping eagerly at his side where his sword would hang.

"Perhaps," Ba'alzamon said simply. "And perhaps not. Perhaps he can
be turned to my use. Sooner or later it will be so, in this Age or another."

The man who called himself Bors blinked. *In this Age or another? I*
*thought the Day of Return was near. What matter to me what happens in another*
*Age if I grow old and die waiting in this one?* But Ba'alzamon was speaking
again.

"Already a bend is forming in the Pattern, one of many points where he
who will become the Dragon may be turned to my service. Must be turned!
Better that he serve me alive than dead, but alive or dead, serve me he
must and will! These three you must know, for each is a thread in the
pattern *I* mean to weave, and it will be up to you to see that they are
placed as I command. Study them well, that you will know them."

Abruptly all sound was gone. The man who called himself Bors shifted
uneasily, and saw others doing the same. All but the Illianer woman, he
realized. With her hands spread over her bosom as if to hide the rounded
flesh she exposed, eyes wide, half frightened and half ecstatic, she was
nodding eagerly as though to someone face-to-face with her. Sometimes she
appeared to give a reply, but the man who called himself Bors heard not a
word. Suddenly she arched backwards, trembling and rising on her toes.
He could not see why she did not fall, unless something unseen held her.
Then, just as abruptly, she settled back to her feet and nodded again,
bowing, shivering. Even as she straightened, one of the women wearing a
Great Serpent ring gave a start and began nodding.

*So each of us hears his own instructions, and none hears another's.* The man
who called himself Bors muttered in frustration. If he knew what even one
other was commanded, he might be able to use the knowledge to advantage, but this way. . . . Impatiently he waited for his turn, forgetting
himself enough to stand straight.

One by one the gathering received their orders, each walled in silence yet
still giving tantalizing clues, if only he could read them. The man of the
Atha'an Miere, the Sea Folk, stiffening with reluctance as he nodded. The

Shienaran, his stance bespeaking confusion even while he acquiesced. The second woman of Tar Valon giving a start, as of shock, and the gray-swathed figure whose sex he could not determine shaking its head before falling to its knees and nodding vigorously. Some underwent the same convulsion as the Illianer woman, as if pain itself lifted them to toe tips.

"Bors."

The man who called himself Bors jerked as a red mask filled his eyes. He could still see the room, still see the floating shape of Ba'alzamon and the three figures before him, but at the same time all he could see was the red-masked face. Dizzy, he felt as if his skull were splitting open and his eyes were being pushed out of his head. For a moment he thought he could see flames through the eyeholes of the mask.

"Are you faithful . . . Bors?"

The hint of mocking in the name sent a chill down his backbone. "I am faithful, Great Lord. I cannot hide from you." *I am* faithful! *I swear it!*

"No, you cannot."

The certainty in Ba'alzamon's voice dried his mouth, but he forced himself to speak. "Command me, Great Lord, and I obey."

"Firstly, you are to return to Tarabon and continue your *good* works. In fact, I command you to redouble your efforts."

He stared at Ba'alzamon in puzzlement, but then fires flared again behind the mask, and he took the excuse of a bow to pull his eyes away. "As you command, Great Lord, so shall it be."

"Secondly, you will watch for the three young men, and have your followers watch. Be warned; they are dangerous."

The man who called himself Bors glanced at the figures floating in front of Ba'alzamon. *How can I do that? I can see them, but I can't see anything except his* face. His head felt about to burst. Sweat slicked his hands under his thin gloves, and his shirt clung to his back. "Dangerous, Great Lord? Farmboys? Is one of them the—"

"A sword is dangerous to the man at the point, but not to the man at the hilt. Unless the man holding the sword is a fool, or careless, or unskilled, in which case it is twice as dangerous to him as to anyone else. It is enough that I have told you to know them. It is enough that you obey me."

"As you command, Great Lord, so shall it be."

"Thirdly, regarding those who have landed at Toman Head, and the Domani. Of this you will speak to no one. When you return to Tarabon. . . ."

The man who called himself Bors realized as he listened that his mouth was sagging open. The instructions made no sense. *If I knew what some of the others were told, perhaps I could piece it together.*

Abruptly he felt his head grasped as though by a giant hand crushing his temples, felt himself being lifted, and the world blew apart in a thousand starbursts, each flash of light becoming an image that fled across his mind or spun and dwindled into the distance before he could more than barely grasp it. An impossible sky of striated clouds, red and yellow and black, racing as if driven by the mightiest wind the world had ever seen. A woman—a girl?—dressed in white receded into blackness and vanished as soon as she appeared. A raven stared him in the eye, *knowing* him, and was gone. An armored man in a brutal helm, shaped and painted and gilded like some monstrous, poisonous insect, raised a sword and plunged to one side, beyond his view. A horn, curled and golden, came hurtling out of the far distance. One piercing note it sounded as it flashed toward him, tugging his soul. At the last instant it flashed into a blinding, golden ring of light that passed through him, chilling him beyond death. A wolf leaped from the shadows of lost sight and ripped out his throat. He could not scream. The torrent went on, drowning him, burying him. He could barely remember who he was, or what he was. The skies rained fire, and the moon and stars fell; rivers ran in blood, and the dead walked; the earth split open and fountained molten rock. . . .

The man who called himself Bors found himself half crouching in the chamber with the others, most watching him, all silent. Wherever he looked, up or down or in any direction, the masked face of Ba'alzamon overwhelmed his eyes. The images that had flooded into his mind were fading; he was sure many were already gone from memory. Hesitantly, he straightened, Ba'alzamon always before him.

"Great Lord, what—?"

"Some commands are too important to be known even by he who carries them out."

The man who called himself Bors bent almost double in his bow. "As you command, Great Lord," he whispered hoarsely, "so shall it be."

When he straightened, he was alone in silence once more. Another, the Taren High Lord, nodded and bowed to someone none else saw. The man who called himself Bors put an unsteady hand to his brow, trying to hold on to something of what had burst through his mind, though he was not completely certain he wanted to remember. The last remnant flickered out, and suddenly he was wondering what it was that he was trying to recall. *I know there was something, but what? There* was *something! Wasn't there?* He rubbed his hands together, grimacing at the feel of sweat under his gloves, and turned his attention to the three figures hanging suspended before Ba'alzamon's floating form.

The muscular, curly-haired youth; the farmer with the sword; and the lad with the look of mischief on his face. Already, in his mind, the man who called himself Bors had named them the Blacksmith, the Swordsman, and the Trickster. *What is their place in the puzzle?* They must be important, or Ba'alzamon would not have made them the center of this gathering. But from his orders alone they could all die at any time, and he had to think that some of the others, at least, had orders as deadly for the three. *How important are they?* Blue eyes could mean the nobility of Andor—unlikely in those clothes—and there were Borderlanders with light eyes, as well as some Tareni, not to mention a few from Ghealdan, and, of course. . . . No, no help there. But *yellow* eyes? *Who* are *they? What* are *they?*

He started at a touch on his arm, and looked around to find one of the white-clad servants, a young man, standing by his side. The others were back, too, more than before, one for each of the masked. He blinked. Ba'alzamon was gone. The Myrddraal was gone, too, and only rough stone was where the door it had used had been. The three figures still hung there, though. He felt as if they were staring at him.

"If it please you, my Lord Bors, I will show you to your room."

Avoiding those dead eyes, he glanced once more at the three figures, then followed. Uneasily he wondered how the youth had known what name to use. It was not until the strange carved doors closed behind him and they had walked a dozen paces that he realized he was alone in the corridor with the servant. His brows drew down suspiciously behind his mask, but before he could open his mouth, the servant spoke.

"The others are also being shown to their rooms, my Lord. If you please, my Lord? Time is short, and our Master is impatient."

The man who called himself Bors ground his teeth, both at the lack of information and at the implication of sameness between himself and the servant, but he followed in silence. Only a fool ranted at a servant, and worse, remembering the fellow's eyes, he was not sure it would do any good. *And how did he know what I was going to ask?* The servant smiled.

The man who called himself Bors did not feel at all comfortable until he was back in the room where he had waited on first arriving, and then not much. Even finding the seals on his saddlebags untouched was small comfort.

The servant stood in the hallway, not entering. "You may change to your own garments if you wish, my Lord. None will see you depart here, nor arrive at your destination, but it may be best to arrive already properly clothed. Someone will come soon to show you the way."

Untouched by any visible hand, the door swung shut.

The man who called himself Bors shivered in spite of himself. Hastily he undid the seals and buckles of his saddlebags and pulled out his usual cloak. In the back of his mind a small voice wondered if the promised power, even the immortality, was worth another meeting like this, but he laughed it down immediately. *For that much power, I would praise the Great Lord of the Dark under the Dome of Truth.* Remembering the commands given him by Ba'alzamon, he fingered the golden, flaring sun worked on the breast of the white cloak, and the red shepherd's crook behind the sun, symbol of his office in the world of men, and he almost laughed. There was work, great work, to be done in Tarabon, and on Almoth Plain.

# CHAPTER 1

## *The Flame of Tar Valon*

The Wheel of Time turns, and Ages come and pass leaving memories that become legend, then fade to myth, and are long forgot when that Age comes again. In one Age, called the Third Age by some, an Age yet to come, an Age long past, a wind rose in the Mountains of Dhoom. The wind was not the beginning. There are neither beginnings nor endings to the turning of the Wheel of Time. But it was a beginning.

Born among black, knife-edged peaks, where death roamed the high passes yet hid from things still more dangerous, the wind blew south across the tangled forest of the Great Blight, a forest tainted and twisted by the touch of the Dark One. The sickly sweet smell of corruption faded by the time the wind crossed that invisible line men called the border of Shienar, where spring flowers hung thick in the trees. It should have been summer by now, but spring had been late in coming, and the land had run wild to catch up. New-come pale green bristled on every bush, and red new growth tipped every tree branch. The wind rippled farmers' fields like verdant ponds, solid with crops that almost seemed to creep upward visibly.

The smell of death was all but gone long before the wind reached the stone-walled town of Fal Dara on its hills, and whipped around a tower of the fortress in the very center of the town, a tower atop which two men seemed to dance. Hard-walled and high, Fal Dara, both keep and town,

never taken, never betrayed. The wind moaned across wood-shingled rooftops, around tall stone chimneys and taller towers, moaned like a dirge.

Stripped to the waist, Rand al'Thor shivered at the wind's cold caress,
and his fingers flexed on the long hilt of the practice sword he held. The
hot sun had slicked his chest, and his dark, reddish hair clung to his head
in a sweat-curled mat. A faint odor in the swirl of air made his nose twitch,
but he did not connect the smell with the image of an old grave fresh-
opened that flashed through his head. He was barely aware of odor or image
at all; he strove to keep his mind empty, but the other man sharing the
tower top with him kept intruding on the emptiness. Ten paces across, the
tower top was, encircled by a chest-high, crenellated wall. Big enough and
more not to feel crowded, except when shared with a Warder.

Young as he was, Rand was taller than most men, but Lan stood just as
tall and more heavily muscled, if not quite so broad in the shoulders. A
narrow band of braided leather held the Warder's long hair back from his
face, a face that seemed made from stony planes and angles, a face unlined
as if to belie the tinge of gray at his temples. Despite the heat and exertion,
only a light coat of sweat glistened on his chest and arms. Rand searched
Lan's icy blue eyes, hunting for some hint of what the other man intended.
The Warder never seemed to blink, and the practice sword in his hands
moved surely and smoothly as he flowed from one stance to another.

With a bundle of thin, loosely bound staves in place of a blade, the
practice sword would make a loud clack when it struck anything, and leave
a welt where it hit flesh. Rand knew all too well. Three thin red lines
stung on his ribs, and another burned his shoulder. It had taken all his
efforts not to wear more decorations. Lan bore not a mark.

As he had been taught, Rand formed a single flame in his mind and
concentrated on it, tried to feed all emotion and passion into it, to form a
void within himself, with even thought outside. Emptiness came. As was
too often the case of late it was not a perfect emptiness; the flame still
remained, or some sense of light sending ripples through the stillness. But
it was enough, barely. The cool peace of the void crept over him, and he
was one with the practice sword, with the smooth stones under his boots,
even with Lan. All was one, and he moved without thought in a rhythm
that matched the Warder's step for step and move for move.

The wind rose again, bringing the ringing of bells from the town.
*Somebody's still celebrating that spring has finally come.* The extraneous thought
fluttered through the void on waves of light, disturbing the emptiness, and
as if the Warder could read Rand's mind, the practice sword whirled in
Lan's hands.

For a long minute the swift *clack-clack-clack* of bundled lathes meeting filled the tower top. Rand made no effort to reach the other man; it was all he could do to keep the Warder's strikes from reaching him. Turning Lan's blows at the last possible moment, he was forced back. Lan's expression never changed; the practice sword seemed alive in his hands. Abruptly the Warder's swinging slash changed in mid-motion to a thrust. Caught by surprise, Rand stepped back, already wincing with the blow he knew he could not stop this time.

The wind howled across the tower . . . and trapped him. It was as if the air had suddenly jelled, holding him in a cocoon. Pushing him forward. Time and motion slowed; horrified, he watched Lan's practice sword drift toward his chest. There was nothing slow or soft about the impact. His ribs creaked as if he had been struck with a hammer. He grunted, but the wind would not allow him to give way; it still carried him forward, instead. The lathes of Lan's practice sword flexed and bent—ever so slowly, it seemed to Rand—then shattered, sharp points oozing toward his heart, jagged lathes piercing his skin. Pain lanced through his body; his whole skin felt slashed. He burned as though the sun had flared to crisp him like bacon in a pan.

With a shout, he threw himself stumbling back, falling against the stone wall. Hand trembling, he touched the gashes on his chest and raised bloody fingers before his gray eyes in disbelief.

"And what was that fool move, sheepherder?" Lan grated. "You know better by now, or should unless you have forgotten everything I've tried to teach you. How badly are you—?" He cut off as Rand looked up at him.

"The wind." Rand's mouth was dry. "It—it pushed me! It. . . . It was solid as a wall!"

The Warder stared at him in silence, then offered a hand. Rand took it and let himself be pulled to his feet.

"Strange things can happen this close to the Blight," Lan said finally, but for all the flatness of the words he sounded troubled. That in itself was strange. Warders, those half-legendary warriors who served the Aes Sedai, seldom showed emotion, and Lan showed little even for a Warder. He tossed the shattered lathe sword aside and leaned against the wall where their real swords lay, out of the way of their practice.

"Not like that," Rand protested. He joined the other man, squatting with his back against the stone. That way the top of the wall was higher than his head, protection of a kind from the wind. If it was a wind. No wind had ever felt . . . solid . . . like that. "Peace! Maybe not even *in* the Blight."

"For someone like you. . . ." Lan shrugged as if that explained everything. "How long before you leave, sheepherder? A month since you said you were going, and I thought you'd be three weeks gone by now."

Rand stared up at him in surprise. *He's acting like nothing happened!*
Frowning, he set down the practice sword and lifted his real sword to his
knees, fingers running along the long, leather-wrapped hilt inset with a
bronze heron. Another bronze heron stood on the scabbard, and yet another
was scribed on the sheathed blade. It was still a little strange to him that
he had a sword. Any sword, much less one with a blademaster's mark. He
was a farmer from the Two Rivers, so far away, now. Maybe far away
forever, now. He was a shepherd like his father—*I was a shepherd. What am
I now?*—and his father had given him a heron-marked sword. *Tam is my
father, no matter what anybody says.* He wished his own thoughts did not
sound as if he was trying to convince himself.

Again Lan seemed to read his mind. "In the Borderlands, sheepherder, if
a man has the raising of a child, that child is his, and none can say different."

Scowling, Rand ignored the Warder's words. It was no one's business
but his own. "I want to learn how to use this. I need to." It had caused
him problems, carrying a heron-marked sword. Not everybody knew what
it meant, or even noticed it, but even so a heron-mark blade, especially in
the hands of a youth barely old enough to be called a man, still attracted
the wrong sort of attention. "I've been able to bluff sometimes, when I
could not run, and I've been lucky, besides. But what happens when I can't
run, and I can't bluff, and my luck runs out?"

"You could sell it," Lan said carefully. "That blade is rare even among
heron-mark swords. It would fetch a pretty price."

"No!" It was an idea he had thought of more than once, but he rejected
it now for the same reason he always had, and more fiercely for coming
from someone else. *As long as I keep it, I have the right to call Tam father. He
gave it to me, and it gives me the right.* "I thought any heron-mark blade was
rare."

Lan gave him a sidelong look. "Tam didn't tell you, then? He must
know. Perhaps he didn't believe. Many do not." He snatched up his own
sword, almost the twin of Rand's except for the lack of herons, and
whipped off the scabbard. The blade, slightly curved and single-edged,
glittered silvery in the sunlight.

It was the sword of the kings of Malkier. Lan did not speak of it—he
did not even like others to speak of it—but al'Lan Mandragoran was Lord
of the Seven Towers, Lord of the Lakes, and uncrowned King of Malkier.
The Seven Towers were broken now, and the Thousand Lakes the lair of
unclean things. Malkier lay swallowed by the Great Blight, and of all the
Malkieri lords, only one still lived.

Some said Lan had become a Warder, bonding himself to an Aes Sedai, so he could seek death in the Blight and join the rest of his blood. Rand had indeed seen Lan put himself in harm's way seemingly without regard for his own safety, but far beyond his own life and safety he held those of Moiraine, the Aes Sedai who held his bond. Rand did not think Lan would truly seek death while Moiraine lived.

Turning his blade in the light, Lan spoke. "In the War of the Shadow, the One Power itself was used as a weapon, and weapons were made with the One Power. Some weapons *used* the One Power, things that could destroy an entire city at one blow, lay waste to the land for leagues. Just as well those were all lost in the Breaking; just as well no one remembers the making of them. But there were simpler weapons, too, for those who would face Myrddraal, and worse things the Dreadlords made, blade to blade.

"With the One Power, Aes Sedai drew iron and other metals from the earth, smelted them, formed and wrought them. All with the Power. Swords, and other weapons, too. Many that survived the Breaking of the World were destroyed by men who feared and hated Aes Sedai work, and others have vanished with the years. Few remain, and few men truly know what they are. There have been legends of them, swollen tales of swords that seemed to have a power of their own. You've heard the gleemen's tales. The reality is enough. Blades that will not shatter or break, and never lose their edge. I've seen men sharpening them—playing at sharpening, as it were—but only because they could not believe a sword did not need it after use. All they ever did was wear away their oilstones.

"Those weapons the Aes Sedai made, and there will never be others. When it was done, war and Age ended together, with the world shattered, with more dead unburied than there were alive and those alive fleeing, trying to find some place, any place, of safety, with every second woman weeping because she'd never see husband or sons again; when it was done, the Aes Sedai who still lived swore they would never again make a weapon for one man to kill another. Every Aes Sedai swore it, and every woman of them since has kept that oath. Even the Red Ajah, and they care little what happens to any male.

"One of those swords, a plain soldier's sword"—with a faint grimace, almost sad, if the Warder could be said to show emotion, he slid the blade back into its sheath—"became something more. On the other hand, those made for lord-generals, with blades so hard no bladesmith could mark them, yet marked already with a heron, those blades became sought after."

Rand's hands jerked away from the sword propped on his knees. It toppled, and instinctively he grabbed it before it hit the floorstones. "You mean Aes Sedai made this? I thought you were talking about *your* sword."

"Not all heron-mark blades are Aes Sedai work. Few men handle a sword with the skill to be named blademaster and be awarded a heron-mark blade, but even so, not enough Aes Sedai blades remain for more than a handful to have one. Most come from master bladesmiths; the finest steel men can make, yet still wrought by a man's hands. But that one, sheepherder . . . that one could tell a tale of three thousand years and more."

"I can't get away from them," Rand said, "can I?" He balanced the sword in front of him on scabbard point; it looked no different than it had before he knew. "Aes Sedai work." *But Tam gave it to me. My* father *gave it to me.* He refused to think of how a Two Rivers shepherd had come by a heron-mark blade. There were dangerous currents in such thoughts, deeps he did not want to explore.

"Do you really want to get away, sheepherder? I'll ask again. Why are you not gone, then? The sword? In five years I could make you worthy of it, make you a blademaster. You have quick wrists, good balance, and you don't make the same mistake twice. But I do not have five years to give over to teaching you, and you do not have five years for learning. You have not even one year, and you know it. As it is, you will not stab yourself in the foot. You hold yourself as if the sword belongs at your waist, sheepherder, and most village bullies will sense it. But you've had that much almost since the day you put it on. So why are you still here?"

"Mat and Perrin are still here," Rand mumbled. "I don't want to leave before they do. I won't ever—I might not see them again for—for years, maybe." His head dropped back against the wall. "Blood and ashes! At least they just think I'm crazy not to go home with them. Half the time Nynaeve looks at me like I'm six years old and I've skinned my knee, and she's going to make it better; the other half she looks like she's seeing a stranger. One she might offend if she looks too closely, at that. She's a Wisdom, and besides that, I don't think she's ever been afraid of anything, but she. . . ." He shook his head. "And Egwene. Burn me! She knows why I have to go, but every time I mention it she looks at me, and I knot up inside and. . . ." He closed his eyes, pressing the sword hilt against his forehead as if he could press what he was thinking out of existence. "I wish. . . . I wish. . . ."

"You wish everything could be the way it was, sheepherder? Or you wish the girl would go with you instead of to Tar Valon? You think she'll give up becoming an Aes Sedai for a life of wandering? With you? If you put it to her in the right way, she might. Love is an odd thing." Lan sounded suddenly weary. "As odd a thing as there is."

"No." It was what he had been wishing, that she would want to go with him. He opened his eyes and squared his back and made his voice firm.

"No, I wouldn't let her come with me if she did ask." He could not do that to her. *But Light, wouldn't it be sweet, just for a minute, if she said she wanted to?* "She gets muley stubborn if she thinks I'm trying to tell her what to do, but I can still protect her from that." He wished she were back home in Emond's Field, but all hope of that had gone the day Moiraine came to the Two Rivers. "Even if it means she does become an Aes Sedai!" The corner of his eye caught Lan's raised eyebrow, and he flushed.

"And that is all the reason? You want to spend as much time as you can with your friends from home before they go? That's why you're dragging your feet? You know what's sniffing at your heels."

Rand surged angrily to his feet. "All right, it's Moiraine! I wouldn't even be here if not for her, and she won't as much as talk to me."

"You'd be dead if not for her, sheepherder," Lan said flatly, but Rand rushed on.

"She tells me . . . tells me horrible things about myself"—his knuckles whitened on the sword. *That I'm going to go mad and die!*—"and then suddenly she won't even say two words to me. She acts as if I'm no different than the day she found me, and that smells wrong, too."

"You want her to treat you like what you are?"

"No! I don't mean that. Burn me, I don't know what I mean half the time. I don't want that, and I'm scared of the other. Now she's gone off somewhere, vanished . . ."

"I told you she needs to be alone sometimes. It isn't for you, or anyone else, to question her actions."

". . . without telling anybody where she was going, or when she'd be back, or even if she would be back. She has to be able to tell me something to help me, Lan. Something. She has to. If she ever comes back."

"She's back, sheepherder. Last night. But I think she has told you all she can. Be satisfied. You've learned what you can from her." With a shake of his head, Lan's voice became brisk. "You certainly aren't learning anything standing there. Time for a little balance work. Go through Parting the Silk, beginning from Heron Wading in the Rushes. Remember that that Heron form is only for practicing balance. Anywhere but doing forms, it leaves you wide open; you can strike home from it, if you wait for the other man to move first, but you'll never avoid his blade."

"She *has* to be able to tell me something, Lan. That wind. It wasn't natural, and I don't care how close to the Blight we are."

"Heron Wading in the Rushes, sheepherder. And mind your wrists."

From the south came a faint peal of trumpets, a rolling fanfare slowly growing louder, accompanied by the steady *thrum-thrum-THRUM-thrum* of drums. For a moment Rand and Lan stared at each other, then the drums drew them to the tower wall to stare southward.

The city stood on high hills, the land around the city walls cleared to ankle height for a full mile in all directions, and the keep covered the highest hill of all. From the tower top, Rand had a clear view across the chimneys and roofs to the forest. The drummers appeared first from the trees, a dozen of them, drums lifting as they stepped to their own beat, mallets whirling. Next came trumpeters, long, shining horns raised, still calling the flourish. At that distance Rand could not make out the huge, square banner whipping in the wind behind them. Lan grunted, though; the Warder had eyes like a snow eagle.

Rand glanced at him, but the Warder said nothing, his eyes intent on the column emerging from the forest. Mounted men in armor rode out of the trees, and women ahorseback, too. Then a palanquin borne by horses, one before and one behind, its curtains down, and more men on horseback. Ranks of men afoot, pikes rising above them like a bristle of long thorns, and archers with their bows held slanted across their chests, all stepping to the drums. The trumpets cried again. Like a singing serpent the column wound its way toward Fal Dara.

The wind flapped the banner, taller than a man, straight out to one side. As big as it was, it was close enough now for Rand to see clearly. A swirl of colors that meant nothing to him, but at the heart of it, a shape like a pure white teardrop. His breath froze in his throat. The Flame of Tar Valon.

"Ingtar's with them." Lan sounded as if his thoughts were elsewhere. "Back from his hunting at last. Been gone long enough. I wonder if he had any luck?"

"Aes Sedai," Rand whispered when he finally could. All those women out there. . . . Moiraine was Aes Sedai, yes, but he had traveled with her, and if he did not entirely trust her, at least he knew her. Or thought he did. But she was only one. So many Aes Sedai together, and coming like this, was something else again. He cleared his throat; when he spoke, his voice grated. "Why so many, Lan? Why any at all? And with drums and trumpets and a banner to announce them."

Aes Sedai were respected in Shienar, at least by most people, and the rest respectfully feared them, but Rand had been in places where it was different, where there was only the fear, and often hate. Where he had grown up, some men, at least, spoke of "Tar Valon witches" as they would speak of the Dark One. He tried to count the women, but they kept no ranks or order, moving their horses around to converse with one another or with whoever was in the palanquin. Goose bumps covered him. He had traveled with Moiraine, and met another Aes Sedai, and he had begun to think of himself as worldly. Nobody ever left the Two Rivers, or almost nobody, but he had. He had seen things no one back in the Two Rivers had ever laid eyes on, done things they had only dreamed of, if they had dreamed so far. He had seen a queen and met the Daughter-Heir of Andor, faced a Myrddraal and traveled the Ways, and none of it had prepared him for this moment.

"Why so many?" he whispered again.

"The Amyrlin Seat's come in person." Lan looked at him, his expression as hard and unreadable as a rock. "Your lessons are done, sheepherder." He paused then, and Rand almost thought there was sympathy on his face. That could not be, of course. "Better for you if you were a week gone." With that the Warder snatched up his shirt and disappeared down the ladder into the tower.

Rand worked his mouth, trying to get a little moisture. He stared at the column approaching Fal Dara as if it really were a snake, a deadly viper. The drums and trumpets sang, loud in his ears. The Amyrlin Seat, who ordered the Aes Sedai. *She's come because of me.* He could think of no other reason.

They knew things, had knowledge that could help him, he was sure. And he did not dare ask any of them. He was afraid they had come to gentle him. *And afraid they haven't, too,* he admitted reluctantly. *Light, I don't know which scares me more.*

"I didn't mean to channel the Power," he whispered. "It was an accident! Light, I don't want anything to do with it. I swear I'll never touch it again! I swear it!"

With a start, he realized that the Aes Sedai party was entering the city gates. The wind swirled up fiercely, chilling his sweat like droplets of ice, making the trumpets sound like sly laughter; he thought he could smell an opened grave, strong in the air. *My grave, if I keep standing here.*

Grabbing his shirt, he scrambled down the ladder and began to run.

# CHAPTER
# 2

## *The Welcome*

The halls of Fal Dara keep, their smooth stone walls sparsely decorated with elegantly simple tapestries and painted screens, bustled
with news of the Amyrlin Seat's imminent arrival. Servants in
black-and-gold darted about their tasks, running to prepare rooms or carry
orders to the kitchens, moaning that they could not have everything ready
for so great a personage when they had had no warning. Dark-eyed warriors, their heads shaven except for a topknot bound with a leather cord,
did not run, but haste filled their steps and their faces shone with an
excitement normally reserved for battle. Some of the men spoke as Rand
hurried past.

"Ah, there you are, Rand al'Thor. Peace favor your sword. On your way
to clean up? You'll want to look your best when you are presented to the
Amyrlin Seat. She'll want to see you and your two friends as well as the
women, you can count on it."

He trotted toward the broad stairs, wide enough for twenty men abreast,
that led up to the men's apartments.

"The Amyrlin herself, come with no more warning than a pack peddler.
Must be because of Moiraine Sedai and you southerners, eh? What else?"

The wide, iron-bound doors of the men's apartments stood open, and
half jammed with top-knotted men buzzing with the Amyrlin's arrival.

"Ho, southlander! The Amyrlin's here. Come for you and your friends, I suppose. Peace, what honor for you! She seldom leaves Tar Valon, and she's never come to the Borderlands in my memory."

He fended them all off with a few words. He had to wash. Find a clean shirt. No time to talk. They thought they understood, and let him go. Not a one of them knew a thing except that he and his friends traveled in company with an Aes Sedai, that two of his friends were women who were going to Tar Valon to train as Aes Sedai, but their words stabbed at him as if they knew everything. *She's come for me.*

He dashed through the men's apartments, darted into the room he shared with Mat and Perrin . . . and froze, his jaw dropping in astonishment. The room was filled with women wearing the black-and-gold, all working purposefully. It was not a big room, and its windows, a pair of tall, narrow arrowslits looking down on one of the inner courtyards, did nothing to make it seem larger. Three beds on black-and-white tiled platforms, each with a chest at the foot, three plain chairs, a washstand by the door, and a tall, wide wardrobe crowded the room. The eight women in there seemed like fish in a basket.

The women barely glanced at him, and went right on clearing his clothes—and Mat's and Perrin's—out of the wardrobe and replacing them with new. Anything found in the pockets was put atop the chests, and the old clothes were bundled up carelessly, like rags.

"What are you doing?" he demanded when he caught his breath. "Those are my clothes!" One of the women sniffed and poked a finger through a tear in the sleeve of his only coat, then added it to the pile on the floor.

Another, a black-haired woman with a big ring of keys at her waist, set her eyes on him. That was Elansu, *shatayan* of the keep. He thought of the sharp-faced woman as a housekeeper, though the house she kept was a fortress and scores of servants did her bidding. "Moiraine Sedai said all of your clothes are worn out, and the Lady Amalisa had new made to give you. Just keep out of our way," she added firmly, "and we will be done the quicker." There were few men the *shatayan* could not bully into doing as she wished—some said even Lord Agelmar—and she plainly did not expect any trouble with one man young enough to be her son.

He swallowed what he had been going to say; there was no time for arguing. The Amyrlin Seat could be sending for him at any minute. "Honor to the Lady Amalisa for her gift," he managed, after the Shienaran way, "and honor to you, Elansu Shatayan. Please, convey my words to the Lady Amalisa, and tell her I said, heart and soul to serve." That ought to satisfy the Shienaran love of ceremony for both women. "But now if you'll pardon me, I want to change."

"That is well," Elansu said comfortably. "Moiraine Sedai said to remove all the old. Every stitch. Smallclothes, too." Several of the women eyed him sideways. None of them made a move toward the door.

He bit his cheek to keep from laughing hysterically. Many ways were different in Shienar from what he was used to, and there were some to which he would never become accustomed if he lived forever. He had taken to bathing in the small hours of the morning, when the big, tiled pools were empty of people, after he discovered that at any other time a woman might well climb into the water with him. It could be a scullion or the Lady Amalisa, Lord Agelmar's sister herself—the baths were one place in Shienar where there was no rank—expecting him to scrub her back in return for the same favor, asking him why his face was so red, had he taken too much sun? They had soon learned to recognize his blushes for what they were, and not a woman in the keep but seemed fascinated by them.

*I might be dead or worse in another hour, and they're waiting to see me blush!* He cleared his throat. "If you'll wait outside, I will pass the rest out to you. On my honor."

One of the women gave a soft chortle, and even Elansu's lips twitched, but the *shatayan* nodded and directed the other women to gather up the bundles they had made. She was the last to leave, and she paused in the doorway to add, "The boots, too. Moiraine Sedai said everything."

He opened his mouth, then closed it again. His boots, at least, were certainly still good, made by Alwyn al'Van, the cobbler back in Emond's Field, and well broken in and comfortable. But if giving up his boots would make the *shatayan* leave him alone so he could go, he would give her the boots, and anything else she wanted. He had no time. "Yes. Yes, of course. On my honor." He pushed on the door, forcing her out.

Alone, he dropped onto his bed to tug off his boots—they *were* still good, a little worn, the leather cracked here and there, but still wearable and well broken-in to fit his feet—then hastily stripped off, piling everything atop the boots, and washed at the basin just as quickly. The water was cold; the water was always cold in the men's apartments.

The wardrobe had three wide doors carved in the simple Shienaran manner, suggesting more than showing a series of waterfalls and rocky pools. Pulling open the center door, he stared for a moment at what had replaced the few garments he had brought with him. A dozen high-collared coats of the finest wool and as well cut as any he had ever seen on a merchant's back or a lord's, most embroidered like feastday clothes. A dozen! Three shirts for every coat, both linen and silk, with wide sleeves and tight cuffs. Two cloaks. Two, when he had made do with one at a time all his life. One cloak was plain, stout wool and dark green, the other deep blue with a stiff-standing collar embroidered in gold with herons . . . and high on the left breast, where a lord would wear his sign. . . .

His hand drifted to the cloak of its own accord. As if uncertain what they would feel, his fingers brushed the stitching of a serpent curled almost into a circle, but a serpent with four legs and a lion's golden mane, scaled in crimson and gold, its feet each tipped with five golden claws. His hand jerked back as if burned. *Light help me! Was it Amalisa had this made, or Moiraine? How many saw it? How many know what it is, what it means? Even one is too many. Burn me, she's trying to get me killed. Bloody Moiraine won't even talk to me, but now she's given me bloody fine new clothes to die in!*

A rap at the door sent him leaping half out of his skin.

"Are you done?" came Elansu's voice. "Every stitch, now. Perhaps I had better. . . ." A creak as if she were trying the knob.

With a start Rand realized he was still naked. "I'm done," he shouted. "Peace! Don't come in!" Hurriedly he gathered up what he had been wearing, boots and all. "I'll bring them!" Hiding behind the door, he opened it just wide enough to shove the bundle into the arms of the *shatayan.* "That's everything."

She tried to peer through the gap. "Are you sure? Moiraine Sedai said everything. Perhaps I had better just look—"

"It's everything," he growled. "On my honor!" He shouldered the door shut in her face, and heard laughter from the other side.

Muttering under his breath, he dressed hurriedly. He would not put it past any of them to find some excuse to come bulling in anyway. The gray breeches were snugger than he was used to, but still comfortable, and the shirt, with its billowy sleeves, was white enough to satisfy any goodwife in Emond's Field on laundry day. The knee-high boots fit as if he had worn them a year. He hoped it was just a good cobbler, and not more Aes Sedai work.

All of these clothes would make a pack as big as he was. Yet, he had grown used to the comfort of clean shirts again, of not wearing the same breeches day after day until sweat and dirt made them as stiff as his boots, then wearing them still. He took his saddlebags from his chest and stuffed what he could into them, then reluctantly spread the fancy cloak out on the bed and piled a few more shirts and breeches on that. Folded with the dangerous sigil inside and tied with a cord looped so it could be slung on a shoulder, it looked not much different from the packs he had seen carried by other young men on the road.

A peal of trumpets rolled through the arrowslits, trumpets calling the fanfare from outside the walls, trumpets answering from the keep towers.

"I'll pick out the stitching when I get a chance," he muttered. He had

seen women picking out embroidery when they had made a mistake or
changed their mind on the pattern, and it did not look very hard.

The rest of the clothes—most of them, in fact—he stuffed back into the
wardrobe. No need to leave evidence of flight to be found by the first
person to poke a head in after he went.

Still frowning, he knelt beside his bed. The tiled platforms on which the
beds rested were stoves, where a small fire damped down to burn all night
could keep the bed warm through the worst night in a Shienaran winter.
The nights were still cooler than he was used to this time of year, but
blankets were enough for warmth now. Pulling open the firebox door, he
took out a bundle he could not leave behind. He was glad Elansu had not
thought anyone would keep clothes in there.

Setting the bundle atop the blankets, he untied one end and partially
unfolded it. A gleeman's cloak, turned inside out to hide the hundreds of
patches that covered it, patches in every size and color imaginable. The
cloak itself was sound enough; the patches were a gleeman's badge. Had
been a gleeman's badge.

Inside nestled two hard leather cases. The larger held a harp, which he
never touched. *The harp was never meant for a farmer's clumsy fingers, boy.* The
other, long and slim, contained the gold-and-silver chased flute he had
used to earn his supper and bed more than once since leaving home. Thom
Merrilin had taught him to play that flute, before the gleeman died. Rand
could never touch it without remembering Thom, with his sharp blue eyes
and his long white mustaches, shoving the bundled cloak into his hands
and shouting for him to run. And then Thom had run himself, knives
appearing magically in his hands as if he were performing, to face the
Myrddraal that was coming to kill them.

With a shiver, he redid the bundle. "That's all over with." Thinking of
the wind on the tower top, he added, "Strange things happen this close to
the Blight." He was not sure he believed it, not the way Lan had apparently meant it. In any case, even without the Amyrlin Seat, it was past
time for him to be gone from Fal Dara.

Shrugging into the coat he had kept out—it was a deep, dark green, and
made him think of the forests at home, Tam's Westwood farm where he
had grown up, and the Waterwood where he had learned to swim—he
buckled the heron-mark sword to his waist and hung his quiver, bristling
with arrows, on the other side. His unstrung bow stood propped in the
corner with Mat's and Perrin's, the stave two hands taller than he was. He
had made it himself since coming to Fal Dara, and besides him, only Lan
and Perrin could draw it. Stuffing his blanketroll and his new cloak
through the loops on his bundles, he slung the pair from his left shoulder,

tossed his saddlebags atop the cords, and grabbed the bow. *Leave the sword-arm free,* he thought. *Make them think I'm dangerous. Maybe* somebody *will.*

Cracking the door revealed the hall all but empty; one liveried servant dashed by, but he never so much as glanced at Rand. As soon as the man's rapid footfalls faded, Rand slipped out into the corridor.

He tried to walk naturally, casually, but with saddlebags on his shoulder and bundles on his back, he knew he looked like what he was, a man setting out on a journey and not meaning to come back. The trumpets called again, sounding fainter here inside the keep.

He had a horse, a tall bay stallion, in the north stable, called the Lord's Stable, close by the salley gate that Lord Agelmar used when he went riding. Neither the Lord of Fal Dara nor any of his family would be riding today, though, and the stable might be empty except for the stableboys. There were two ways to reach the Lord's Stable from Rand's room. One would take him all the way around the keep, behind Lord Agelmar's private garden, then down the far side and through the farrier's smithy, likewise certainly empty now, to the stableyard. Time enough that way for orders to be given, for a search to start, before he reached his horse. The other was far shorter; first across the outer courtyard, where even now the Amyrlin Seat was arriving with another dozen or more Aes Sedai.

His skin prickled at the thought; he had had more than enough of Aes Sedai for any sane lifetime. One was too many. All the stories said it, and he knew it for fact. But he was not surprised when his feet took him toward the outer courtyard. He would never see legendary Tar Valon—he could not afford that risk, now or ever—but he might catch a glimpse of the Amyrlin Seat before he left. That would be as much as seeing a queen. *There can't be anything dangerous in just looking, from a distance. I'll keep moving and be gone before she ever knows I was there.*

He opened a heavy, iron-strapped door onto the outer courtyard and stepped out into silence. People forested the guardwalk atop every wall, top-knotted soldiers, and liveried servants, and menials still in their muck, all pressed together cheek by jowl, with children sitting on shoulders to look over their elders' heads or squeezing in to peer around waists and knees. Every archers' balcony was packed like a barrel of apples, and faces even showed in the narrow arrowslits in the walls. A thick mass of people bordered the courtyard like another wall. And all of them watched and waited in silence.

He pushed his way along the wall, in front of the smithies and fletchers' stalls that lined the court—Fal Dara was a fortress, not a palace, despite its size and grim grandeur, and everything about it served that end—apologizing quietly to the people he jostled. Some looked around with a frown, and a few gave a second stare to his saddlebags and bundles, but none broke the silence. Most did not even bother to look at who had bumped past them.

He could easily see over the heads of most of them, enough to make out clearly what was going on in the courtyard. Just inside the main gate, a line of men stood beside their horses, sixteen of them. No two wore the same kind of armor or carried the same sort of sword, and none looked like Lan, but Rand did not doubt they were Warders. Round faces, square faces, long faces, narrow faces, they all had the look, as if they saw things other men did not see, heard things other men did not hear. Standing at their ease, they looked as deadly as a pack of wolves. Only one other thing about them was alike. One and all they wore the color-shifting cloak he had first seen on Lan, the cloak that often seemed to fade into whatever was behind it. It did not make for easy watching or a still stomach, so many men in those cloaks.

A dozen paces in front of the Warders, a row of women stood by their horses' heads, the cowls of their cloaks thrown back. He could count them, now. Fourteen. Fourteen Aes Sedai. They must be. Tall and short, slender and plump, dark and fair, hair cut short or long, hanging loose down their backs or braided, their clothes were as different as the Warders' were, in as many cuts and colors as there were women. Yet they, too, had a sameness, one that was only obvious when they stood together like this. To a woman, they seemed ageless. From this distance he would have called them all young, but closer he knew they would be like Moiraine. Young-seeming yet not, smooth-skinned but with faces too mature for youth, eyes too knowing.

*Closer? Fool! I'm too close already! Burn me, I should have gone the long way.* He pressed on toward his goal, another iron-bound door at the far end of the court, but he could not stop looking.

Calmly the Aes Sedai ignored the onlookers and kept their attention on the curtained palanquin, now in the center of the courtyard. The horses bearing it held as still as if ostlers stood at their harness, but there was only one tall woman beside the palanquin, her face an Aes Sedai's face, and she paid no mind to the horses. The staff she held upright before her with both hands was as tall as she, the gilded flame capping it standing above her eyes.

Lord Agelmar faced the palanquin from the far end of the court, bluff and square and face unreadable. His high-collared coat of dark blue bore the three running red foxes of the House Jagad as well as the stooping black hawk of Shienar. Beside him stood Ronan, age-withered but still tall; three foxes carved from red avatine topped the tall staff the *shambayan* bore.

Ronan was Elansu's equal in ordering the keep, *shambayan* and *shatayan,* but Elansu left little for him except ceremonies and acting as Lord Agelmar's secretary. Both men's topknots were snow-white.

All of them—the Warders, the Aes Sedai, the Lord of Fal Dara, and his *shambayan*—stood as still as stone. The watching crowd seemed to hold its breath. Despite himself, Rand slowed.

Suddenly Ronan rapped his staff loudly three times on the broad paving stones, calling into the silence, "Who comes here? Who comes here? Who comes here?"

The woman beside the palanquin tapped her staff three times in reply. "The Watcher of the Seals. The Flame of Tar Valon. The Amyrlin Seat."

"Why should we watch?" Ronan demanded.

"For the hope of humankind," the tall woman replied.

"Against what do we guard?"

"The shadow at noon."

"How long shall we guard?"

"From rising sun to rising sun, so long as the Wheel of Time turns."

Agelmar bowed, his white topknot stirring in the breeze. "Fal Dara offers bread and salt and welcome. Well come is the Amyrlin Seat to Fal Dara, for here is the watch kept, here is the Pact maintained. Welcome."

The tall woman drew back the curtain of the palanquin, and the Amyrlin Seat stepped out. Dark-haired, ageless as all Aes Sedai were ageless, she ran her eyes over the assembled watchers as she straightened. Rand flinched when her gaze crossed him; he felt as if he had been touched. But her eyes passed on and came to rest on Lord Agelmar. A liveried servant knelt at her side with folded towels, steam still rising, on a silver tray. Formally, she wiped her hands and patted her face with a damp cloth. "I offer thanks for your welcome, my son. May the Light illumine House Jagad. May the Light illumine Fal Dara and all her people."

Agelmar bowed again. "You honor us, Mother." It did not sound odd, her calling him son or him calling her Mother, though comparing her smooth cheeks to his craggy face made him seem more like her father, or even grandfather. She had a presence that more than matched his. "House Jagad is yours. Fal Dara is yours."

Cheers rose on every side, crashing against the walls of the keep like breaking waves.

Shivering, Rand hurried toward the door to safety, careless of whom he bumped into now. *Just your bloody imagination. She doesn't even know who you are. Not yet. Blood and ashes, if she did. . . .* He did not want to think of what would have happened if she knew who he was, what he was. What would happen when she finally found out. He wondered if she had had

anything to do with the wind atop the tower; Aes Sedai could do things
like that. When he pushed through that door and slammed it shut behind
him, muting the roar of welcome that still shook the courtyard, he heaved
a relieved sigh.

The halls here were as empty as the others had been, and he all but ran.
Out across a smaller courtyard, with a fountain splashing in the center,
down yet another corridor and out into the flagstoned stableyard. The
Lord's Stable itself, built into the wall of the keep, stood tall and long,
with big windows here inside the walls, and horses kept on two floors. The
smithy across the courtyard stood silent, the farrier and his helpers gone to
see the Welcome.

Tema, the leathery-faced head groom, met him at the wide doors with a
deep bow, touching his forehead and then his heart. "Spirit and heart to
serve, my Lord. How may Tema serve, my Lord?" No warrior's topknot
here; Tema's hair sat on his head like an inverted gray bowl.

Rand sighed. "For the hundredth time, Tema, I am not a lord."

"As my Lord wishes." The groom's bow was even lower this time.

It was his name that caused the problem, and a similarity. Rand al'Thor.
Al'Lan Mandragoran. For Lan, according to the custom of Malkier, the
royal "al" named him King, though he never used it himself. For Rand,
"al" was just a part of his name, though he had heard that once, long ago,
before the Two Rivers was called the Two Rivers, it had meant "son of."
Some of the servants in Fal Dara keep, though, had taken it to mean he was
a king, too, or at least a prince. All of his argument to the contrary had
only managed to demote him to lord. At least, he thought it had; he had
never seen quite so much bowing and scraping, even with Lord Agelmar.

"I need Red saddled, Tema." He knew better than to offer to do it
himself; Tema would not let Rand soil his hands. "I thought I'd spend a
few days seeing the country around the town." Once he was on the big bay
stallion's back, a few days would see him at the River Erinin, or across the
border into Arafel. *They'll never find me then.*

The groom bent himself almost double, and stayed bent. "Forgive, my
Lord," he whispered hoarsely. "Forgive, but Tema cannot obey."

Flushing with embarrassment, Rand took an anxious look around—there
was no one else in sight—then grabbed the man's shoulder and pulled him
upright. He might not be able to stop Tema and a few others from acting
like this, but he could try to stop anyone else from seeing it. "Why not,
Tema? Tema, look at me, please. Why not?"

"It is commanded, my Lord," Tema said, still whispering. He kept
dropping his eyes, not afraid, but ashamed that he could not do what Rand
asked. Shienarans took shame the way other people took being branded a

thief. "No horse may leave this stable until the order is changed. Nor any stable in the keep, my Lord."

Rand had his mouth open to tell the man it was all right, but instead he licked his lips. "No horse from any stable?"

"Yes, my Lord. The order came down only a short time ago. Only moments." Tema's voice picked up strength. "All the gates are closed as well, my Lord. None may enter or leave without permission. Not even the city patrol, so Tema has been told."

Rand swallowed hard, but it did not lessen the feeling of fingers clutching his windpipe. "The order, Tema. It came from Lord Agelmar?"

"Of course, my Lord. Who else? Lord Agelmar did not speak the command to Tema, of course, nor even to the man who did speak to Tema, but, my Lord, who else could give such a command in Fal Dara?"

*Who else?* Rand jumped as the biggest bell in the keep bell tower let out a sonorous peal. The other bells joined in, then bells from the town.

"If Tema may be bold," the groom called above the reverberations, "my Lord must be very happy."

Rand had to shout back to be heard. "Happy? Why?"

"The Welcome is finished, my Lord." Tema's gesture took in the bell tower. "The Amyrlin Seat will be sending for my Lord, and my Lord's friends, to come to her, now."

Rand broke into a run. He just had time to see the surprise on Tema's face, and then he was gone. He did not care what Tema thought. *She will be sending for me now.*

# CHAPTER
## 3

### *Friends and Enemies*

Rand did not run far, only as far as the sally gate around the corner from the stable. He slowed to a walk before he got there, trying to appear casual and unhurried.

The arched gate was closed tight. It was barely big enough for two men to ride through abreast, but like all the gates in the outer wall, it was covered with broad strips of black iron, and locked shut with a thick bar. Two guards stood before the gate in plain conical helmets and plate-and-mail armor, with long swords on their backs. Their golden surcoats bore the Black Hawk on the chest. He knew one of them slightly, Ragan. The scar from a Trolloc arrow made a white triangle against Ragan's dark cheek behind the bars of his face-guard. The puckered skin dimpled with a grin when he saw Rand.

"Peace favor you, Rand al'Thor." Ragan almost shouted to be heard over the bells. "Do you intend to go hit rabbits over the head, or do you still insist that club is a bow?" The other guard shifted to stand more in front of the gate.

"Peace favor you, Ragan," Rand said, stopping in front of them. It was an effort to keep his voice calm. "You know it's a bow. You've seen me shoot it."

"No good from a horse," the other guard said sourly. Rand recognized him, now, with his deep-set, almost-black eyes that never seemed to blink. They peered from his helmet like twin caves inside another cave. He supposed there could be worse luck for him than Masema guarding the gate, but he was not sure how, short of a Red Aes Sedai. "It's too long," Masema added. "I can shoot three arrows with a horsebow while you loose one with that monster."

Rand forced a grin, as if he thought it was a joke. Masema had never made a joke in his hearing, nor laughed at one. Most of the men at Fal Dara accepted Rand; he trained with Lan, and Lord Agelmar had him at table, and most important of all, he had arrived at Fal Dara in company with Moiraine, an Aes Sedai. Some seemed unable to forget his being an outlander, though, barely saying two words to him, and then only if they had to. Masema was the worst of those.

"It's good enough for me," Rand said. "Speaking of rabbits, Ragan, how about letting me out? All this noise and bustle is too much for me. Better to be out hunting rabbits, even if I never see one."

Ragan half turned to look at his companion, and Rand's hopes began to lift. Ragan was an easygoing man, his manner belying his grim scar, and he seemed to like Rand. But Masema was already shaking his head. Ragan sighed. "It cannot be, Rand al'Thor." He gave a tiny nod toward Masema as if to explain. If it were up to him alone. . . . "No one is to leave without a written pass. Too bad you did not ask a few minutes ago. The command just came down to bar the gates."

"But why would Lord Agelmar want to keep *me* in?" Masema was eyeing the bundles on Rand's back, and his saddlebags. Rand tried to ignore him. "I'm his guest," he went on to Ragan. "By my honor, I could have left anytime these past weeks. Why would he mean this order for me? It is Lord Agelmar's order, isn't it?" Masema blinked at that, and his perpetual frown deepened; he almost appeared to forget Rand's packs.

Ragan laughed. "Who else could give such an order, Rand al'Thor? Of course, it was Uno who passed it to me, but whose order could it have been?"

Masema's eyes, fixed on Rand's face, did not blink. "I just want to go out by myself, that's all," Rand said. "I'll try one of the gardens, then. No rabbits, but at least there won't be a crowd. The Light illumine you, and peace favor you."

He walked away without waiting for an answering blessing, resolving not to go near any of the gardens on any account. *Burn me, once the ceremonies are done there could be Aes Sedai in any of them.* Aware of Masema's eyes on his back—he was sure it was Masema—he kept his pace normal.

Suddenly the bells stopped ringing, and he skipped a step. Minutes were passing. A great many of them. Time for the Amyrlin Seat to be shown to her chambers. Time for her to send for him, to start a search when he was not found. As soon as he was out of sight of the salley gate, he began to run again.

Near the barracks' kitchens, the Carters' Gate, where all the foodstuffs for the keep were brought in, stood closed and barred, behind a pair of soldiers. He hurried past, across the kitchen yard, as if he had never meant to stop.

The Dog Gate, at the back of the keep, just high enough and wide enough for one man on foot, had its guards, too. He turned around before they saw him. There were not many gates, even as big as the keep was, but if the Dog Gate was guarded, they all would be.

Perhaps he could find a length of rope. . . . He climbed one of the stairs to the top of the outer wall, to the wide parapet with its crenellated walls. It was not comfortable for him, being so high and exposed if that wind came again, but from there he could see across the tall chimneys and sharp roofs of the town all the way to the city wall. Even after nearly a month, the houses still looked odd to his Two Rivers eyes, eaves reaching almost to the ground as if the houses were all wood-shingled roof, and chimneys angled to let heavy snow slide past. A broad, paved square surrounded the keep, but only a hundred paces from the wall lay streets full of people going about their daily business, aproned shopkeepers out under the awnings in front of their shops, rough-clothed farmers in town to buy and sell, hawkers and tradesmen and townspeople gathered in knots, no doubt to talk about the surprise visit from the Amyrlin Seat. He could see carts and people flowing through one of the gates in the town wall. Apparently the guards there had no orders about stopping anyone.

He looked up at the nearest guardtower; one of the soldiers raised a gauntleted hand to him. With a bitter laugh, he waved back. Not a foot of the wall but was under the eyes of guards. Leaning through an embrasure, he peered down past the slots in the stone for setting hoardings, down the sheer expanse of stone to the drymoat far below. Twenty paces wide and ten deep, faced with stone polished slippery smooth. A low wall, slanted to give no hiding place, surrounded it to keep anyone from falling in by accident, and its bottom was a forest of razor-sharp spikes. Even with a rope to climb down and no guards watching, he could not cross that. What served to keep Trollocs out in the last extreme served just as well to keep him in.

Suddenly he felt weary to the bone, drained. The Amyrlin Seat was there, and there was no way out. No way out, and the Amyrlin Seat there. If she knew he was there, if she had sent the wind that had seized him, then she was already hunting him, hunting with an Aes Sedai's powers. Rabbits had more chance against his bow. He refused to give up, though. There were those who said Two Rivers folk could teach stones and give lessons to mules. When there was nothing else left, Two Rivers people hung on to their stubbornness.

Leaving the wall, he wandered through the keep. He paid no mind to where he went, so long as it was nowhere he would be expected. Not anywhere near his room, nor any of the stables, nor any gate—Masema might risk Uno's tongue to report him trying to leave—nor garden. All he could think of was keeping away from *any* Aes Sedai. Even Moiraine. She *knew* about him. Despite that, she had done nothing against him. *So far. So far as you know. What if she's changed her mind? Maybe she sent for the Amyrlin Seat.*

For a moment, feeling lost, he leaned against the corridor wall, the stone hard under his shoulder. Eyes blank, he stared at a distant nothing and saw things he did not want to see. *Gentled. Would it be so bad, to have it all over? Really over?* He closed his eyes, but he could still see himself, huddling like a rabbit with nowhere left to run, and Aes Sedai closing round him like ravens. *They almost always die soon after, men who've been gentled. They stop wanting to live.* He remembered Thom Merrilin's words too well to face that. With a brisk shake, he hurried on down the hall. No need to stay in one place until he was found. *How long till they find you anyway? You're like a sheep in a pen. How long?* He touched the sword hilt at his side. *No, not a sheep. Not for Aes Sedai or anybody else.* He felt a little foolish, but determined.

People were returning to their tasks. A din of voices and clattering pots filled the kitchen that lay nearest the Great Hall, where the Amyrlin Seat and her party would feast that night. Cooks and scullions and potboys all but ran at their work; the spit dogs trotted in their wicker wheels to turn the spitted meats. He made his way quickly through the heat and steam, through the smells of spices and cooking. No one spared him a second glance; they were all too busy.

The back halls, where the servants lived in small apartments, were stirring like a kicked antheap as men and women scurried to don their best livery. Children did their playing in corners, out of the way. Boys waved wooden swords, and girls played with carved dolls, some announcing that *hers* was the Amyrlin Seat. Most of the doors stood open, doorways blocked only by beaded curtains. Normally, that meant whoever lived there was open to visitors, but today it simply meant the residents were in a hurry. Even those who bowed to him did so with hardly a pause.

Would any of them hear, when they went to serve, that he was being sought, and speak of seeing him? Speak to an Aes Sedai and tell her where to find him? The eyes that he passed suddenly appeared to be studying him slyly, and to be weighing and considering behind his back. Even the children took on sharper looks in his mind's eye. He knew it was just his imagination—he was sure it was; it had to be—but when the servants' apartments were behind him, he felt as if he had escaped before a trap could spring shut.

Some places in the keep were empty of people, the folk who normally worked there released for the sudden holiday. The armorer's forge, with all the fires banked, the anvils silent. Silent. Cold. Lifeless. Yet somehow not empty. His skin prickled, and he spun on his heel. No one there. Just the big square tool chests and the quenching barrels full of oil. The hair on the back of his neck stirred, and he whipped round again. The hammers and tongs hung in their places on the wall. Angrily he stared around the big room. *There's nobody there. It's just my imagination. That wind, and the Amyrlin; that's enough to make me imagine things.*

Outside in the armorer's yard, the wind swirled up around him momentarily. Despite himself he jumped, thinking it meant to catch him. For a moment he smelled the faint odor of decay again, and heard someone behind him laughing slyly. Just for a moment. Frightened, he edged in a circle, peering warily. The yard, paved with rough stone, was empty except for him. *Just your bloody imagination!* He ran anyway, and behind him he thought he heard the laughter again, this time without the wind.

In the woodyard, the presence returned, the sense of someone there. The feel of eyes peering at him around tall piles of split firewood under the long sheds, darting glances over the stacks of seasoned planks and timbers waiting on the other side of the yard for the carpenter's shop, now closed up tight. He refused to look around, refused to think of how one set of eyes could move from place to place so fast, could cross the open yard from the firewood shed to the lumbershed without even a flicker of movement that he could see. He was sure it was one set of eyes. *Imagination. Or maybe I'm going crazy already.* He shivered. *Not yet. Light, please not yet.* Stiff-backed, he stalked across the woodyard, and the unseen watcher followed.

Down deep corridors lit only by a few rush torches, in storerooms filled with sacks of dried peas or beans, crowded with slatted racks heaped with wrinkled turnips and beets, or stacked with barrels of wine and casks of salted beef and kegs of ale, the eyes were always there, sometimes following him, sometimes waiting when he entered. He never heard a footstep but his own, never heard a door creak except when he opened and closed it, but the eyes were there. *Light, I am going crazy.*

Then he opened another storeroom door, and human voices, human laughter, drifted out to fill him with relief. There would be no unseen eye here. He went in.

Half the room was stacked to the ceiling with sacks of grain. In the other half a thick semicircle of men knelt in front of one of the bare walls. They all seemed to wear the leather jerkins and bowl-cut hair of menials. No warriors' topknots, no livery. No one who might betray him accidentally. *What about on purpose?* The rattle of dice came through their soft murmurs, and somebody let out a raucous laugh at the throw.

Loial was watching them dice, rubbing his chin thoughtfully with a finger thicker than a big man's thumb, his head almost reaching the rafters nearly two spans up. None of the dicers gave him a glance. Ogier were not exactly common in the Borderlands, or anywhere else, but they were known and accepted here, and Loial had been in Fal Dara long enough to excite little comment. The Ogier's dark, stiff-collared tunic was buttoned up to his neck and flared below the waist over his high boots, and one of the big pockets bulged and sagged with the weight of something. Books, if Rand knew him. Even watching men gamble, Loial would not be far from a book.

In spite of everything, Rand found himself grinning. Loial often had that effect on him. The Ogier knew so much about some things, so little about others, and he seemed to want to know everything. Yet Rand could remember the first time he ever saw Loial, with his tufted ears and his eyebrows that dangled like long mustaches and his nose almost as wide as his face—saw him and thought he was facing a Trolloc. It still shamed him. Ogier and Trollocs. Myrddraal, and things from the dark corners of midnight tales. Things out of stories and legends. That was how he had thought of them before he left Emond's Field. But since leaving home he had seen too many stories walking in the flesh ever to be so sure again. Aes Sedai, and unseen watchers, and a wind that caught and held. His smile faded.

"All the stories are real," he said softly.

Loial's ears twitched, and his head turned toward Rand. When he saw who it was, the Ogier's face split in a grin, and he came over. "Ah, there you are." His voice was a deep bumblebee rumble. "I did not see you at the Welcome. That was something I had not seen before. Two things. The Shienaran Welcome, and the Amyrlin Seat. She looks tired, don't you think? It cannot be easy, being Amyrlin. Worse than being an Elder, I suppose." He paused, with a thoughtful look, but only for a breath. "Tell me, Rand, do you play at dice, too? They play a simpler game here, with only three dice. We use four in the *stedding*. They won't let me play, you know. They just say, 'Glory to the Builders,' and will not bet against me. I don't think that's fair, do you? The dice they use *are* rather small"—he frowned at one of his hands, big enough to cover a human head—"but I still think—"

Rand grabbed his arm and cut him off. *The Builders!* "Loial, Ogier built Fal Dara, didn't they? Do you know any way out except by the gates? A crawl hole. A drain pipe. Anything at all, if it's big enough for a man to wiggle through. Out of the wind would be good, too."

Loial gave a pained grimace, the ends of his eyebrows almost brushing his cheeks. "Rand, Ogier built Mafal Dadaranel, but that city was destroyed in the Trolloc Wars. This"—he touched the stone wall lightly with broad fingertips—"was built by men. I can sketch a plan of Mafal Dadaranel—I saw the maps, once, in an old book in Stedding Shangtai—but of Fal Dara, I know no more than you. It *is* well built, though, isn't it? Stark, but well made."

Rand slumped against the wall, squeezing his eyes shut. "I need a way out," he whispered. "The gates are barred, and they won't let anyone pass, but I need a way out."

"But why, Rand?" Loial said slowly. "No one here will hurt you. Are you all right? Rand?" Suddenly his voice rose. "Mat! Perrin! I think Rand is sick."

Rand opened his eyes to see his friends straightening up out of the knot of dicers. Mat Cauthon, long-limbed as a stork, wearing a half smile as if he saw something funny that no one else saw. Shaggy-haired Perrin Aybara, with heavy shoulders and thick arms from his work as a blacksmith's apprentice. They both still wore their Two Rivers garb, plain and sturdy, but travel-worn.

Mat tossed the dice back into the semicircle as he stepped out, and one of the men called, "Here, southlander, you can't quit while you're winning."

"Better than when I'm losing," Mat said with a laugh. Unconsciously he touched his coat at the waist, and Rand winced. Mat had a dagger with a ruby in its hilt under there, a dagger he was never without, a dagger he could not be without. It was a tainted blade, from the dead city of Shadar Logoth, tainted and twisted by an evil almost as bad as the Dark One, the evil that had killed Shadar Logoth two thousand years before, yet still lived among the abandoned ruins. That taint would kill Mat if he kept the dagger; it would kill him even faster if he put it aside. "You'll have another chance to win it back." Wry snorts from the kneeling men indicated they did not think there was much chance of that.

Perrin kept his eyes down as he followed Mat across to Rand. Perrin always kept his eyes down these days, and his shoulders sagged as if he carried a weight too heavy even for their width.

"What's the matter, Rand?" Mat asked. "You're as white as your shirt. Hey! Where did you get those clothes? You turning Shienaran? Maybe I'll buy myself a coat like that, and a fine shirt." He shook his coat pocket, producing a clink of coins. "I seem to have luck with the dice. I can hardly touch them without winning."

"You don't have to buy anything," Rand said tiredly. "Moiraine had all our clothes replaced. They're burned already for all I know, all but what you two are wearing. Elansu will probably be around to collect those, too, so I'd change fast if I were you, before she takes them off your back." Perrin still did not look up, but his cheeks turned red; Mat's grin deepened, though it looked forced. They too had had encounters in the baths, and only Mat tried to pretend it did not matter. "And I'm not sick. I just need to get out of here. The Amyrlin Seat is here. Lan said . . . he said with her here, it would have been better for me if I were gone a week. I need to leave, and all the gates are barred."

"He said that?" Mat frowned. "I don't understand. He'd never say *anything* against an Aes Sedai. Why now? Look, Rand, I don't like Aes Sedai any more than you do, but they aren't going to do anything to us." He lowered his voice to say that, and looked over his shoulder to see if any of the gamblers was listening. Feared the Aes Sedai might be, but in the Borderlands, they were far from being hated, and a disrespectful comment about them could land you in a fight, or worse. "Look at Moiraine. She isn't so bad, even if she is Aes Sedai. You're thinking like old Cenn Buie telling his tall tales back home, in the Winespring Inn. I mean, she hasn't hurt us, and they won't. Why would they?"

Perrin's eyes lifted. Yellow eyes, gleaming in the dim light like burnished gold. *Moiraine hasn't hurt us?* Rand thought. Perrin's eyes had been as deep a brown as Mat's when they left the Two Rivers. Rand had no idea how the change had come about—Perrin did not want to talk about it, or about very much of anything since it happened—but it had come at the same time as the slump in his shoulders, and a distance in his manner as if he felt alone even with friends around him. Perrin's eyes and Mat's dagger. Neither would have happened if they had not left Emond's Field, and it was Moiraine who had taken them away. He knew that was not fair. They would probably all be dead at Trollocs' hands, and a good part of Emond's Field as well, if she had not come to their village. But that did not make Perrin laugh the way he used to, or take the dagger from Mat's belt. *And me? If I was home and still alive, would I still be what I am now? At least I wouldn't be worrying about what the Aes Sedai are going to do to me.*

Mat was still looking at him quizzically, and Perrin had raised his head enough to stare from under his eyebrows. Loial waited patiently. Rand could not tell them why he had to stay away from the Amyrlin Seat. They did not know what he was. Lan knew, and Moiraine. And Egwene, and Nynaeve. He wished none of them knew, and most of all he wished Egwene did not, but at least Mat and Perrin—and Loial, too—believed he was still the same. He thought he would rather die than let them know, than see the hesitation and worry he sometimes caught in Egwene's eyes, and Nynaeve's, even when they were trying their best.

"Somebody's . . . watching me," he said finally. "Following me. Only. . . . Only, there's nobody there."

Perrin's head jerked up, and Mat licked his lips and whispered, "A Fade?"

"Of course not," Loial snorted. "How could one of the Eyeless enter Fal Dara, town or keep? By law, no one may hide his face inside the town walls, and the lamplighters are charged with keeping the streets lit at night so there isn't a shadow for a Myrddraal to hide in. It could not happen."

"Walls don't stop a Fade," Mat muttered. "Not when it wants to come in. I don't know as laws and lamps will do any better." He did not sound like someone who had half thought Fades were only gleemen's tales less than half a year before. He had seen too much, too.

"And there was the wind," Rand added. His voice hardly shook as he told what had happened on the tower top. Perrin's fists tightened until his knuckles cracked. "I just want to leave here," Rand finished. "I want to go south. Somewhere away. Just somewhere away."

"But if the gates are barred," Mat said, "how do we get out?"

Rand stared at him. "We?" He had to go alone. It would be dangerous for anyone near him, eventually. He would be dangerous, and even Moiraine could not tell him how long he had. "Mat, you know you have to go to Tar Valon with Moiraine. She said that's the only place you can be separated from that bloody dagger without dying. And you know what will happen if you keep it."

Mat touched his coat over the dagger, not seeming to realize what he was doing. "'An Aes Sedai's gift is bait for a fish,'" he quoted. "Well, maybe I don't want to put the hook in my mouth. Maybe whatever she wants to do in Tar Valon is worse than if I don't go at all. Maybe she's lying. 'The truth an Aes Sedai tells is never the truth you think it is.'"

"You have any more old sayings you want to rid yourself of?" Rand asked. "'A south wind brings a warm guest, a north wind an empty house'? 'A pig painted gold is still a pig'? What about, 'talk shears no sheep'? 'A fool's words are dust'?"

"Easy, Rand," Perrin said softly. "There is no need to be so rough."

"Isn't there? Maybe I don't want you two going with me, always hanging around, falling into trouble and expecting me to pull you out. You ever think of that? Burn me, did it ever occur to you I might be tired of always having you there whenever I turn around? Always there, and I'm tired of it." The hurt on Perrin's face cut him like a knife, but he pushed on relentlessly. "There are some here think I'm a lord. A lord. Maybe I like that. But look at you, dicing with stablehands. When I go, I go by myself. You two can go to Tar Valon or go hang yourselves, but I leave here alone."

Mat's face had gone stiff, and he clutched the dagger through his coat till his knuckles were white. "If that is how you want it," he said coldly. "I thought we were. . . . However you want it, al'Thor. But if I decide to leave at the same time you do, I'll go, and you can stand clear of me."

"Nobody is going anywhere," Perrin said, "if the gates are barred." He was staring at the floor again. Laughter rolled from the gamblers against the wall as someone lost.

"Go or stay," Loial said, "together or apart, it doesn't matter. You are all three *ta'veren*. Even I can see it, and I don't have that Talent, just by what happens around you. And Moiraine Sedai says it, too."

Mat threw up his hands. "No more, Loial. I don't want to hear about that anymore."

Loial shook his head. "Whether you hear it or not, it is still true. The Wheel of Time weaves the Pattern of the Age, using the lives of men for thread. And you three are *ta'veren,* centerpoints of the weaving."

"No more, Loial."

"For a time, the Wheel will bend the Pattern around you three, whatever you do. And whatever you do is more likely to be chosen by the Wheel than by you. *Ta'veren* pull history along behind them and shape the Pattern just by being, but the Wheel weaves *ta'veren* on a tighter line than other men. Wherever you go and whatever you do, until the Wheel chooses otherwise you will—"

"No more!" Mat shouted. The men dicing looked around, and he glared at them until they bent back to their game.

"I am sorry, Mat," Loial rumbled. "I know I talk too much, but I did not mean—"

"I am not staying here," Mat told the rafters, "with a bigmouthed Ogier and a fool whose head is too big for a hat. You coming, Perrin?" Perrin sighed, and glanced at Rand, then nodded.

Rand watched them go with a stick caught in his threat. *I must go alone. Light help me, I have to.*

Loial was staring after them, too, eyebrows drooping worriedly. "Rand, I really didn't mean to—"

Rand made his voice harsh. "What are you waiting for? Go on with them! I don't see why you're still here. You are no use to me if you don't know a way out. Go on! Go find your trees, and your precious groves, if they haven't all been cut down, and good riddance to them if they have."

Loial's eyes, as big as cups, looked surprised and hurt, at first, but slowly they tightened into what almost might be anger. Rand did not think it could be. Some of the old stories claimed Ogier were fierce, though they never said how, exactly, but Rand had never met anyone as gentle as Loial.

"If you wish it so, Rand al'Thor," Loial said stiffly. He gave a rigid bow and stalked away after Mat and Perrin.

Rand slumped against the stacked sacks of grain. *Well,* a voice in his head taunted, *you did it, didn't you. I had to,* he told it. *I will be dangerous just to be around. Blood and ashes, I'm going to go mad, and. . . . No! No, I won't! I will not use the Power, and then I won't go mad, and. . . . But I can't risk it. I can't, don't you see?* But the voice only laughed at him.

The gamblers were looking at him, he realized. All of them, still kneeling against the wall, had turned to stare at him. Shienarans of any class were almost always polite and correct, even to blood enemies, and Ogier were never any enemies of Shienar. Shock filled the gamblers' eyes. Their faces were blank, but their eyes said what he had done was wrong. Part of him thought they were right, and that drove their silent accusation deep. They only looked at him, but he stumbled out of the storeroom as if they were chasing him.

Numbly he went on through the storerooms, hunting a place to secrete himself until some traffic was allowed through the gates again. Then he could hide in the bottom of a victualer's cart, maybe. If they did not search the carts on the way out. If they did not search the storerooms, search the whole keep for him. Stubbornly he refused to think about that, stubbornly concentrated on finding a safe place. But every place he found—a hollow in a stack of grain sacks, a narrow alley along the wall behind some wine barrels, an abandoned storeroom half filled with empty crates and shadows—he could imagine searchers finding him there. He could imagine that unseen watcher, whoever it was—or whatever—finding him there, too. So he hunted on, thirsty and dusty and with cobwebs in his hair.

And then he came out into a dimly torch-lit corridor, and Egwene was creeping along it, pausing to peer into the storerooms she passed. Her dark hair, hanging to her waist, was caught back with a red ribbon, and she wore a goose-gray dress in the Shienaran fashion, trimmed in red. At the sight of her, sadness and loss rolled over him, worse than when he had chased Mat and Perrin and Loial away. He had grown up thinking he would marry Egwene one day; they both had. But now. . . .

She jumped when he popped out right in front of her, and her breath caught loudly, but what she said was, "So there you are. Mat and Perrin told me what you did. And Loial. I know what you're trying to do, Rand, and it is plain foolish." She crossed her arms under her breasts, and her big, dark eyes fixed him sternly. He always wondered how she managed to seem to be looking down at him—she did it at will—although she was only as tall as his chest, and two years younger besides.

"Good," he said. Her hair suddenly made him angry. He had never seen a grown woman with her hair unbraided until he left the Two Rivers. There, every girl waited eagerly for the Women's Circle of her village to say she was old enough to braid her hair. Egwene certainly had. And here she was with her hair loose except for a ribbon. *I want to go home and can't, and she can't wait to forget Emond's Field.* "You go away and leave me alone, too. You don't want to keep company with a shepherd anymore. There are plenty of Aes Sedai here for you to moon around, now. And don't tell any of them you saw me. They're after me, and I don't need you helping them."

Bright spots of color bloomed in her cheeks. "Do you think I would—"

He turned to walk away, and with a cry she threw herself at him, flung her arms around his legs. They both tumbled to the stone floor, his saddlebags and bundles flying. He grunted when he hit, sword hilt digging into his side, and again when she scrabbled up and plopped herself down on his back as if he were a chair. "My mother," she said firmly, "always told me the best way to learn to deal with a man was to learn to ride a mule. She said they have about equal brains most of the time. Sometimes the mule is smarter."

He raised his head to look over his shoulder at her. "Get off me, Egwene. Get off! Egwene, if you don't get off"—he lowered his voice ominously—"I'll do something to you. You know what I am." He added a glare for good measure.

Egwene sniffed. "You wouldn't, if you could. You would not hurt anybody. But you can't, anyway. I know you cannot channel the One Power whenever you want; it just happens, and you cannot control it. So you are not going to do anything to me or anybody else. I, on the other hand, have been taking lessons with Moiraine, so if you don't listen to some sense, Rand al'Thor, I might just set your breeches on fire. I can manage that

much. You keep on as you are and see if I cannot." Suddenly, for just a
moment, the torch nearest them on the wall flared up with a roar. She gave
a squeak and stared at it, startled.

Twisting around, he grabbed her arm, pulled her off his back, and sat
her against the wall. When he sat up himself, she was sitting there across
from him, rubbing her arm furiously. "You really would have, wouldn't
you?" he said angrily. "You're fooling with things you don't understand.
You could have burned both of us to charcoal!"

"Men! When you cannot win an argument, you either run away or resort
to force."

"Hold on there! Who tripped who? Who sat on who? And you threatened—tried!—to—" He raised both hands. "No, you don't. You do this
to me all the time. Whenever you realize the argument isn't going the way
you want, suddenly we are arguing about something else completely. Not
this time."

"I am not arguing," she said calmly, "and I am not changing the subject, either. What is hiding except running away? And after you hide,
you'll run away for true. And what about hurting Mat, and Perrin, and
Loial? And me? I know why. You're afraid you will hurt somebody even
worse if you let them stay near you. If you don't do what you shouldn't,
then you do not have to worry about hurting anybody. All this running
around and striking out, and you don't even know if there's a reason. Why
should the Amyrlin, or any Aes Sedai but Moiraine, even know you exist?"

For a moment he stared at her. The longer she spent with Moiraine and
Nynaeve, the more she took on their manner, at least when she wanted to.
They were much alike at times, the Aes Sedai and the Wisdom, distant and
knowing. It was disconcerting coming from Egwene. Finally he told her
what Lan had said. "What else could he mean?"

Her hand froze on her arm, and she frowned with concentration.
"Moiraine knows about you, and she hasn't done anything, so why should
she now? But if Lan. . . ." Still frowning, she met his eyes. "The storerooms are the first place they will look. If they do look. Until we find out if
they are looking, we need to put you somewhere they would never think of
searching. I know. The dungeon."

He scrambled to his feet. "The dungeon!"

"Not in a cell, silly. I go there some evenings to visit Padan Fain.
Nynaeve does, too. No one will think it odd if I go early today. In truth,
with everybody looking to the Amyrlin, no one will even notice us."

"But, Moiraine. . . ."

"She doesn't go the dungeons to question Master Fain. She has him brought to her. And she has not done that very much for weeks. Believe me, you will be safe there."

Still, he hesitated. Padan Fain. "Why do you visit the peddler, anyway? He's a Darkfriend, admitted out of his own mouth, and a bad one. Burn me, Egwene, he brought the Trollocs to Emond's Field! The Dark One's hound, he called himself, and he has been sniffing on my trail since Winternight."

"Well, he is safe behind iron bars now, Rand." It was her turn to hesitate, and she looked at him almost pleading. "Rand, he has brought his wagon into the Two Rivers every spring since before I was born. He knows all the people I know, all the places. It's strange, but the longer he has been locked up, the easier in himself he has become. It's almost as if he is breaking free of the Dark One. He laughs again, and tells funny stories, about Emond's Field folk, and sometimes about places I never heard of before. Sometimes he is almost like his old self. I just like to talk to somebody about home."

*Since I've been avoiding you,* he thought, *and since Perrin's been avoiding everybody, and Mat's been spending all his time gambling and carousing.* "I shouldn't have kept to myself so much," he muttered, then sighed. "Well, if Moiraine thinks it's safe enough for you, I suppose it is safe enough for me. But there's no need for you to be mixed in it."

Egwene got to her feet and concentrated on brushing off her dress, avoiding his eye.

"Moiraine *has* said it's safe? Egwene?"

"Moiraine Sedai has never told me I could not visit Master Fain," she said carefully.

He stared at her, then burst out, "You never asked her. She doesn't know. Egwene, that's stupid. Padan Fain's a Darkfriend, and as bad as ever a Darkfriend was."

"He is locked in a cage," she said stiffly, "and I do not have to ask Moiraine's permission for everything I do. It is a little late for you to start worrying about doing what an Aes Sedai thinks, isn't it? Now, are you coming?"

"I can find the dungeon without you. They are looking for me, or will be, and it won't do you any good to be found with me."

"Without me," she said dryly, "you'll likely trip over your own feet and fall in the Amyrlin Seat's lap, then confess everything while trying to talk your way out of it."

"Blood and ashes, you ought to be in the Women's Circle back home. If

men were all as fumble-footed and helpless as you seem to think, we'd
never—"

"Are you going to stand here talking until they do find you? Pick up
your things, Rand, and come with me." Not waiting for an answer, she
spun around and started off down the hall. Muttering under his breath, he
reluctantly obeyed.

There were few people—servants, mainly—in the back ways they took,
but Rand had the feeling that they all took special notice of him. Not
notice of a man burdened for a journey, but of *him,* Rand al'Thor in particular. He knew it was his imagination—he hoped it was—but even so,
he felt no relief when they stopped in a passageway deep beneath the keep,
before a tall door with a small iron grill set in it, as thickly strapped with
iron as any in the outer wall. A clapper hung below the grill.

Through the grill Rand could see bare walls, and two top-knotted soldiers sitting bareheaded at a table with a lamp on it. One of the men was
sharpening a dagger with long, slow strokes of a stone. His strokes never
faltered when Egwene rapped with the clapper, a sharp clang of iron on
iron. The other man, his face flat and sullen, looked at the door as if
considering before he finally rose and came over. He was squat and stocky,
barely tall enough to look through the cross-hatched bars.

"What do you want? Oh, it's you again, girl. Come to see your
Darkfriend? Who's that?" He made no move to open the door.

"He's a friend of mine, Changu. He wants to see Master Fain, too."

The man studied Rand, his upper lip quivering back to bare teeth. Rand
did not think it was supposed to be a smile. "Well," Changu said finally.
"Well. Tall, aren't you? Tall. And fancy dressed for your kind. Somebody
catch you young in the Eastern Marches and tame you?" He slammed back
the bolts and yanked open the door. "Well, come in if you're coming." He
took on a mocking tone. "Take care not to bump your head, my Lord."

There was no danger of that; the door was tall enough for Loial. Rand
followed Egwene in, frowning and wondering if this Changu meant to
make some sort of trouble. He was the first rude Shienaran Rand had met;
even Masema was only cold, not really rude. But the fellow just banged the
door shut and rammed the heavy bolts home, then went to some shelves
beyond the end of the table and took one of the lamps there. The other
man never ceased stropping his knife, never even looked up from it. The
room was bare except for the table and benches and shelves, with straw on
the floor and another iron-bound door leading deeper in.

"You'll want some light, won't you," Changu said, "in there in the dark
with your Darkfriend friend." He laughed, coarse and humorless, and lit
the lamp. "He's waiting for you." He thrust the lamp at Egwene, and

undid the inner door almost eagerly. "Waiting for you. In there, in the dark."

Rand paused uneasily at the blackness beyond, and Changu grinning behind, but Egwene caught his sleeve and pulled him in. The door slammed, almost catching his heel; the latch bars clanged shut. There was only the light of the lamp, a small pool around them in the darkness.

"Are you sure he'll let us out?" he asked. The man had never even looked at his sword or bow, he realized, never asked what was in his bundles. "They aren't very good guards. We could be here to break Fain free for all he knows."

"They know me better than that," she said, but she sounded troubled, and she added, "They seem worse every time I come. All the guards do. Meaner, and more sullen. Changu told jokes the first time I came, and Nidao never even speaks anymore. But I suppose working in a place like this can't give a man a light heart. Maybe it is just me. This place does not do my heart any good, either." Despite her words, she drew him confidently into the black. He kept his free hand on his sword.

The pale lamplight showed a wide hall with flat iron grills to either side, fronting stone-walled cells. Only two of the cells they passed held prisoners. The occupants sat up on their narrow cots as the light struck them, shielding their eyes with their hands, glaring between their fingers. Even with their faces hidden, Rand was sure they were glaring. Their eyes glittered in the lamplight.

"That one likes to drink and fight," Egwene murmured, indicating a burly fellow with sunken knuckles. "This time he wrecked the common room of an inn in the town single-handed, and hurt some men badly." The other prisoner wore a gold-embroidered coat with wide sleeves, and low, gleaming boots. "He tried to leave the city without settling his inn bill"—she sniffed loudly at that; her father was an innkeeper as well as Mayor of Emond's Field—"nor paying half a dozen shopkeepers and merchants what he owed."

The men snarled at them, guttural curses as bad as any Rand had heard from merchants' guards.

"They grow worse every day, too," she said in a tight voice, and quickened her step.

She was enough ahead of him when they reached Padan Fain's cell, at the very end, that Rand was out of the light entirely. He stopped there, in the shadows behind her lamp.

Fain was sitting on his cot, leaning forward expectantly as if waiting, just as Changu had said. He was a bony, sharp-eyed man, with long arms and a big nose, even more gaunt now than Rand remembered. Not gaunt from the dungeon—the food here was the same as the servants ate, and not even the worst prisoner was shorted—but from what he had done before coming to Fal Dara.

The sight of him brought back memories Rand would just as soon have done without. Fain on the seat of his big peddler's wagon wheeling across the Wagon Bridge, arriving in Emond's Field the day of Winternight. And on Winternight the Trollocs came, killing and burning, hunting. Hunting three young men, Moiraine had said. *Hunting me, if they only knew it, and using Fain for their trail hound.*

Fain stood at Egwene's approach, not shielding his eyes or even blinking at the light. He smiled at her, a smile that touched only his lips, then raised his eyes above her head. Looking straight at Rand, hidden in the blackness behind the light, he pointed a long finger at him. "I feel you there, hiding, Rand al'Thor," he said, almost crooning. "You can't hide, not from me, and not from them. You thought it was over, did you not? But the battle's never done, al'Thor. They are coming for me, and they're coming for you, and the war goes on. Whether you live or die, it's never over for you. Never." Suddenly he began to chant.

"Soon comes the day all shall be free.
Even you, and even me.
Soon comes the day all shall die.
Surely you, but never I."

He let his arm fall, and his eyes rose to stare intently at an angle up into the darkness. A crooked grin twisting his mouth, he chuckled deep in his throat as if whatever he saw was amusing. "Mordeth knows more than all of you. Mordeth knows."

Egwene backed away from the cell until she reached Rand, and only the edge of the light touched the bars of Fain's cell. Darkness hid the peddler, but they could still hear his chuckles. Even unable to see him, Rand was sure Fain was still peering off at nothing.

With a shiver, he pried his fingers off his sword hilt. "Light!" he said hoarsely. "This is what you call being like he used to be?"

"Sometimes he's better, and sometimes worse." Egwene's voice was unsteady. "This is worse—much worse than usual."

"What is he seeing, I wonder. He's mad, staring at a stone ceiling in the dark." *If the stone weren't there, he'd be looking straight at the women's apartments. Where Moiraine is, and the Amyrlin Seat.* He shivered again. "He's mad."

"This was not a good idea, Rand." Looking over her shoulder at the cell, she drew him away from it and lowered her voice as if afraid Fain might overhear. Fain's chuckles followed them. "Even if they don't look here, I cannot stay here with him like this, and I do not think you should, either. There is something about him today that. . . ." She drew a shaky breath. "There is one place even safer from search than here. I did not mention it before because it was easier to get you in here, but they will never look in the women's apartments. Never."

"The women's. . . ! Egwene, Fain may be mad, but you're madder. You can't hide from hornets in a hornets' nest."

"What better place? What is the one part of the keep no man will enter without a woman's invitation, not even Lord Agelmar? What is the one place no one would ever think to look for a man?"

"What is the one place in the keep sure to be full of Aes Sedai? It is crazy, Egwene."

Poking at his bundles, she spoke as if it were all decided. "You must wrap your sword and bow in your cloak, and then it will look as if you are carrying things for me. It should not be too hard to find you a jerkin and a shirt that isn't so pretty. You will have to stoop, though."

"I told you, I won't do it."

"Since you're acting stubborn as a mule, you should take right to playing my beast of burden. Unless you would really rather stay down here with him."

Fain's laughing whisper came through the black shadows. "The battle's never done, al'Thor. Mordeth knows."

"I'd have a better chance jumping off the wall," Rand muttered. But he unslung his bundles and set about wrapping sword and bow and quiver as she had suggested.

In the darkness, Fain laughed. "It's never over, al'Thor. Never."

# CHAPTER
## 4

### Summoned

A lone in her rooms in the women's apartments, Moiraine adjusted the shawl, embroidered with curling ivy and grapevines, on her shoulders and studied the effect in the tall frame mirror standing in a corner. Her large, dark eyes could appear as sharp as a hawk's when she was angry. They seemed to pierce the silvered glass, now. It was only happenstance that she had had the shawl in her saddlebags when she came to Fal Dara. With the blazing white Flame of Tar Valon centered on the wearer's back and long fringe colored to show her Ajah—Moiraine's was as blue as a morning sky—the shawls were seldom worn outside Tar Valon, and even there usually only inside the White Tower. Little in Tar Valon besides a meeting of the Hall of the Tower called for the formality of the shawls, and beyond the Shining Walls a sight of the Flame would send too many people running, to hide or perhaps to fetch the Children of the Light. A Whitecloak's arrow was as fatal to an Aes Sedai as to anyone else, and the Children were too wily to let an Aes Sedai see the bowman before the arrow struck, while she still might do something about it. Moiraine had certainly never expected to wear the shawl in Fal Dara. But for an audience with the Amyrlin, there were proprieties to observe.

She was slender and not at all tall, and smooth-cheeked Aes Sedai agelessness often made her appear younger than she was, but Moiraine had a commanding grace and calm presence that could dominate any gathering. A manner ingrained growing up in the Royal Palace of Cairhien had been heightened, not submerged, by still more years as an Aes Sedai. She knew she might need every bit of it today. Yet much of the calm was on the surface, today. *There must be trouble, or she would not have come herself,* she thought for at least the tenth time. But beyond that lay a thousand questions more. *What trouble, and who did she choose to accompany her? Why here? Why now? It cannot be allowed to go wrong now.*

The Great Serpent ring on her right hand caught the light dully as she touched the delicate golden chain fastened in her dark hair, which hung in waves to her shoulders. A small, clear blue stone dangled from the chain, in the middle of her forehead. Many in the White Tower knew of the tricks she could do using that stone as a focus. It was only a polished bit of blue crystal, just something a young girl had used in her first learning, with no one to guide her. That girl had remembered tales of *angreal* and even more powerful *sa'angreal*—those fabled remnants of the Age of Legends that allowed Aes Sedai to channel more of the One Power than any could safely handle unaided—remembered and thought some such focus was required to channel at all. Her sisters in the White Tower knew a few of her tricks, and suspected others, including some that did not exist, some that had shocked her when she learned of them. The things she did with the stone were simple and small, if occasionally useful; the kind a child would imagine. But if the wrong women had accompanied the Amyrlin, the crystal might put them off balance, because of the tales.

A rapid, insistent knocking came at the chamber door. No Shienaran would knock that way, not at anyone's door, but least of all hers. She remained looking into the mirror until her eyes stared back serenely, all thought hidden in their dark depths. She checked the soft leather pouch hanging at her belt. *Whatever troubles brought her out of Tar Valon, she will forget them when I lay this trouble before her.* A second thumping, even more vigorous than the first, sounded before she crossed the room and opened the door with a calm smile for the two women who had come for her.

She recognized them both. Dark-haired Anaiya in her blue-fringed shawl, and fair-haired Liandrin in her red. Liandrin, not only young-seeming but young and pretty, with a doll's face and a small, petulant mouth, had her hand raised to pound again. Her dark brows and darker eyes were a sharp contrast to the multitude of pale honey braids brushing her shoulders, but the combination was not uncommon in Tarabon. Both women were taller than Moiraine, though Liandrin by less than a hand.

Anaiya's blunt face broke into a smile as soon as Moiraine opened the door. That smile gave her the only beauty she would ever have, but it was enough; almost everyone felt comforted, safe and special, when Anaiya smiled at them. "The Light shine on you, Moiraine. It's good to see you again. Are you well? It has been so long."

"My heart is lighter for your presence, Anaiya." That was certainly true; it was good to know she had at least one friend among the Aes Sedai who had come to Fal Dara. "The Light illumine you."

Liandrin's mouth tightened, and she gave her shawl a twitch. "The Amyrlin Seat, she requires your presence, Sister." Her voice was petulant, too, and cold-edged. Not for Moiraine's sake, or not solely; Liandrin always sounded dissatisfied with something. Frowning, she tried to look over Moiraine's shoulder into the room. "This chamber, it is warded. We cannot enter. Why do you ward against your sisters?"

"Against all," Moiraine replied smoothly. "Many of the serving women are curious about Aes Sedai, and I do not want them pawing through my rooms when I am not here. There was no need to make a distinction until now." She pulled the door shut behind her, leaving all three of them in the corridor. "Shall we go? We must not keep the Amyrlin waiting."

She started down the hallway with Anaiya chatting at her side. Liandrin stood for a moment staring at the door as if wondering what Moiraine was hiding, then hurried to join the others. She bracketed Moiraine, walking as stiffly as a guard. Anaiya merely walked, keeping company. Their slippered footsteps fell softly on thick-woven carpets with simple patterns.

Liveried women curtsied deeply as they passed, many more deeply than they would have for the Lord of Fal Dara himself. Aes Sedai, three together, and the Amyrlin Seat herself in the keep; it was more honor than any woman of the keep had ever expected in her lifetime. A few women of noble Houses were out in the halls, and they curtsied, too, which they most certainly would not have done for Lord Agelmar. Moiraine and Anaiya smiled and bowed their heads to acknowledge each reverence, from servant or noble equally. Liandrin ignored them all.

There were only women here, of course, no men. No Shienaran male above the age of ten would enter the women's rooms without permission or invitation, although a few small boys ran and played in the halls here. They knelt on one knee, awkwardly, when their sisters dropped deep curtsies. Now and then Anaiya smiled and ruffled a small head as she passed.

"This time, Moiraine," Anaiya said, "you have been gone from Tar Valon too long. Much too long. Tar Valon misses you. Your sisters miss you. And you are needed in the White Tower."

"Some of us must work in the world," Moiraine said gently. "I will leave the Hall of the Tower to you, Anaiya. Yet in Tar Valon, you hear more of what occurs in the world than I. Too often I outrun what happens where I was yesterday. What news have you?"

"Three more false Dragons." Liandrin bit the words off. "In Saldaea, Murandy, and Tear false Dragons ravage the land. The while, you Blues smile and talk of nothing, and try to hold on to the past." Anaiya raised an eyebrow, and Liandrin snapped her mouth shut with a sharp sniff.

"Three," Moiraine mused softly. For an instant her eyes gleamed, but she masked it quickly. "Three in the last two years, and now three more at once."

"As the others were, these will be dealt with also. This male vermin and any ragtag rabble who follow their banners."

Moiraine was almost amused by the certainty in Liandrin's voice. Almost. She was too aware of the realities, too aware of the possibilities. "Have a few months been enough for you to forget, Sister? The last false Dragon all but tore Ghealdan apart before his army, ragtag rabble or not, was defeated. Yes, Logain is in Tar Valon by now, gentled and safe, I suppose, but some of our sisters died to overpower him. Even one sister dead is more loss than we can bear, but Ghealdan's losses were much worse. The two before Logain could not channel, yet even so the people of Kandor and Arad Doman remember them well. Villages burned and men dead in battle. How easily can the world deal with three at one time? How many will flock to their banners? There has never been a shortage of followers for any man claiming to be the Dragon Reborn. How great will the wars be this time?"

"It isn't so grim as that," Anaiya said. "As far as we know, only the one in Saldaea can channel. He has not had time to attract many followers, and sisters should already be there to deal with him. The Tarens are harrying their false Dragon and his followers through Haddon Mirk, while the fellow in Murandy is already in chains." She gave a short, wondering laugh. "To think the Murandians, of all people, would deal with theirs so quickly. Ask, and they do not even call themselves Murandians, but Lugarders, or Inishlinni, or this or that lord's or lady's man. Yet for fear one of their neighbors would take the excuse to invade, the Murandians leaped on their false Dragon almost as soon as he opened his mouth to proclaim himself."

"Still," Moiraine said, "three at the same time cannot be ignored. Has any sister been able to do a Foretelling?" It was a slight chance—few Aes Sedai had manifested any part of that Talent, even the smallest part, in centuries—so she was not surprised when Anaiya shook her head. Not surprised, but a little relieved.

They reached a juncture of hallways at the same time as the Lady

Amalisa. She dropped a full curtsy, bowing deep and spreading her pale green skirts wide. "Honor to Tar Valon," she murmured. "Honor to Aes Sedai."

The sister of the Lord of Fal Dara required more than a nod of the head. Moiraine took Amalisa's hands and drew her to her feet. "You honor us, Amalisa. Rise, Sister."

Amalisa straighted gracefully, with a flush on her face. She had never as much as been to Tar Valon, and to be called Sister by an Aes Sedai was heady even for someone of her rank. Short and of middle years, she had a dark, mature beauty, and the color in her cheeks set it off. "You honor me too greatly, Moiraine Sedai."

Moiraine smiled. "How long have we known each other, Amalisa? Must I now call you my Lady Amalisa, as if we had never sat over tea together?"

"Of course not." Amalisa smiled back. The strength evident in her brother's face was in hers, too, and no less for the softer line of cheek and jaw. There were those who said that as hard and renowned a fighter as Agelmar was, he was no better than an even match for his sister. "But with the Amyrlin Seat here. . . . When King Easar visits Fal Dara, in private I call him *Magami,* Little Uncle, as I did when I was a child and he gave me rides on his shoulder, but in public it must be different."

Anaiya *tsked.* "Sometimes formality is necessary, but men often make more of it than they must. Please, call me Anaiya, and I will call you Amalisa, if I may."

From the corner of her eye, Moiraine saw Egwene, far down the side hall, disappearing hurriedly around a corner. A stooped shape in a leather jerkin, head down and arms loaded with bundles, shambled at her heels. Moiraine permitted herself a small smile, quickly masked. *If the girl shows as much initiative in Tar Valon,* she thought wryly, *she will sit in the Amyrlin Seat one day. If she can learn to control that initiative. If there is an Amyrlin Seat left on which to sit.*

When she turned her attention back to the others, Liandrin was speaking.

". . . and I would welcome the chance to learn more of your land." She wore a smile, open and almost girlish, and her voice was friendly.

Moiraine schooled her face to stillness as Amalisa extended an invitation to join her and her ladies in her private garden, and Liandrin accepted warmly. Liandrin made few friends, and none outside the Red Ajah. *Certainly never outside the Aes Sedai. She would sooner make friends with a man, or a Trolloc.* Moiraine was not sure Liandrin saw much difference between men and Trollocs. She was not sure any of the Red Ajah did.

Anaiya explained that just now they must attend the Amyrlin Seat. "Of course," Amalisa said. "The Light illumine her, and the Creator shelter her. But later, then." She stood straight and bowed her head as they left her.

Moiraine studied Liandrin as they walked, never looking at her directly. The honey-haired Aes Sedai was staring straight ahead, rosebud lips pursed thoughtfully. She appeared to have forgotten Moiraine and Anaiya both. *What is she up to?*

Anaiya seemed not to have noticed anything out of the ordinary, but then she always managed to accept people both as they were and as they wanted to be. It constantly amazed Moiraine that Anaiya dealt as well as she did in the White Tower, but those who were devious always seemed to take her openness and honesty, her acceptance of everyone, as cunning devices. They were always caught completely off balance when she turned out to mean what she said and say what she meant. Too, she had a way of seeing to the heart of things. And of accepting what she saw. Now she blithely resumed speaking of the news.

"The word from Andor is both good and bad. The street riots in Caemlyn died down with the coming of spring, but there is still talk, too much talk, blaming the Queen, and Tar Valon as well, for the long winter. Morgase holds her throne less securely than she did last year, but she holds it still, and will so long as Gareth Bryne is Captain-General of the Queen's Guards. And the Lady Elayne, the Daughter-Heir, and her brother, the Lord Gawyn, have come safely to Tar Valon for their training. There was some fear in the White Tower that the custom would be broken."

"Not while Morgase has breath in her body," Moiraine said.

Liandrin gave a little start, as if she had just awakened. "Pray that she continues to have breath. The Daughter-Heir's party was followed to the River Erinin by the Children of the Light. To the very bridges to Tar Valon. More still camp outside Caemlyn, for the chance of mischief, and inside Caemlyn still are those who listen."

"Perhaps it is time Morgase learned a little caution," Anaiya sighed. "The world is becoming more dangerous every day, even for a queen. Perhaps especially for a queen. She was ever headstrong. I remember when she came to Tar Valon as a girl. She did not have the ability to become a full sister, and it rankled in her. Sometimes I think she pushes her daughter because of that, whatever the girl chooses."

Moiraine sniffed disdainfully. "Elayne was born with the spark in her; it was not a matter of choosing. Morgase would not risk letting the girl die from lack of training if all the Whitecloaks in Amadicia were camped outside Caemlyn. She would command Gareth Byrne and the Queen's Guards to cut a path through them to Tar Valon, and Gareth Byrne would do it if he had to do it alone." *But she still must keep the full extent of the girl's potential secret. Would the people of Andor knowingly accept Elayne on the Lion Throne after Morgase if they knew? Not just a queen trained in Tar Valon according to custom, but a full Aes Sedai?* In all of recorded history there had been only a handful of queens with the right to be called Aes Sedai, and the few who let it be known had all lived to regret it. She felt a touch of sadness. But too much was afoot to spare aid, or even worry, for one land and one throne. "What else, Anaiya?"

"You must know that the Great Hunt of the Horn has been called in Illian, the first time in four hundred years. The Illianers say the Last Battle is coming"—Anaiya gave a little shiver, as well she might, but went on without a pause—"and the Horn of Valere must be found before the final battle against the Shadow. Men from every land are already gathering, all eager to be part of the legend, eager to find the Horn. Murandy and Altara are on their toes, of course, thinking it's all a mask for a move against one of them. That is probably why the Murandians caught their false Dragon so quickly. In any case, there will be a new lot of stories for the bards and gleemen to add to the cycle. The Light send it is only new stories."

"Perhaps not the stories they expect," Moiraine said. Liandrin looked at her sharply, and she kept her face still.

"I suppose not," Anaiya said placidly. "The stories they least expect will be exactly the ones they will add to the cycle. Beyond that, I have only rumor to offer. The Sea Folk are agitated, their ships flying from port to port with barely a pause. Sisters from the islands say the Coramoor, their Chosen One, is coming, but they won't say more. You know how close-mouthed the Atha'an Miere are with outsiders about the Coramoor, and in this our sisters seem to think more as Sea Folk than Aes Sedai. The Aiel appear to be stirring, too, but no one knows why. No one ever knows with the Aiel. At least there is no evidence they mean to cross the Spine of the World again, thank the Light." She sighed and shook her head. "What I would not give for even one sister from among the Aiel. Just one. We know too little of them."

Moiraine laughed. "Sometimes I think you belong in the Brown Ajah, Anaiya."

"Almoth Plain," Liandrin said, and looked surprised that she had spoken.

"Now that truly *is* rumor, Sister," Anaiya said. "A few whispers heard as we were leaving Tar Valon. There may be fighting on Almoth Plain, and perhaps Toman Head, as well. I say, may be. The whispers were faint. Rumors of rumors. We left before we could hear more."

"It would have to be Tarabon and Arad Doman," Moiraine said, and shook her head. "They have squabbled over Almoth Plain for nearly three hundred years, but it has never come to open blows." She looked at Liandrin; Aes Sedai were supposed to throw off all their old loyalties to lands and rulers, but few did so completely. It was hard not to care for the land of your birth. "Why would they now—?"

"Enough of idle talk," the honey-haired woman broke in angrily. "For you, Moiraine, the Amyrlin waits." She took three quick strides ahead of the others and threw open one of a pair of tall doors. "For you, the Amyrlin will have no idle talk."

Unconsciously touching the pouch at her waist, Moiraine went past Liandrin through the doorway, with a nod as if the other woman were holding the door for her. She did not even smile at the white flash of anger on Liandrin's face. *What is the wretched girl up to?*

Brightly colored carpets covered the anteroom floor in layers, and the room was pleasantly furnished with chairs and cushioned benches and small tables, the wood simply worked or just polished. Brocaded curtains sided the tall arrowslits to make them seem more like windows. No fires burned in the fireplaces; the day was warm, and the Shienaran chill would not come until nightfall.

Fewer than half a dozen of the Aes Sedai who had accompanied the Amyrlin were there. Verin Mathwin and Serafelle, of the Brown Ajah, did not look up at Moiraine's entrance. Serafelle was intently reading an old book with a worn, faded leather cover, handling its tattered pages carefully, while plump Verin, sitting cross-legged beneath an arrowslit, held a small blossom up to the light and made notes and sketches in a precise hand in a book balanced on her knee. She had an open inkpot on the floor beside her, and a small pile of flowers on her lap. The Brown sisters concerned themselves with little beside seeking knowledge. Moiraine sometimes wondered if they were really aware of what was going on in the world, or even immediately around them.

The three other women already in the room turned, but they made no effort to approach Moiraine, only looked at her. One, a slender woman of the Yellow Ajah, she did not know; she spent too little time in Tar Valon to know all the Aes Sedai, although their numbers were no longer very great. She was acquainted with the two remaining, however. Carlinya was as pale of skin and cold of manner as the white fringe on her shawl, the exact opposite in every way of dark, fiery Alanna Mosvani, of the Green, but they both stood and stared at her without speaking, without expression. Alanna sharply snugged her shawl around her, but Carlinya made no move at all. The slender Yellow sister turned away with an air of regret.

"The Light illumine you all, Sisters," Moiraine said. No one answered.

She was not sure Serafelle or Verin had even heard. *Where are the others?*
There was no need for them all to be there—most would be resting in their
rooms, freshing from the journey—but she was on edge now, all the questions she could not ask running through her head. None of it showed on
her face.

The inner door opened, and Leane appeared, without her gilt-flamed
staff. The Keeper of the Chronicles was as tall as most men, willowy and
graceful, still beautiful, with coppery skin and short, dark hair. She wore a
blue stole, a hand wide, instead of a shawl, for she sat in the Hall of the
Tower, though as Keeper, not to represent her Ajah.

"There you are," she said briskly to Moiraine, and gestured to the door
behind her. "Come, Sister. The Amyrlin Seat is waiting." She spoke naturally in a clipped, quick way that never changed, whether she was angry or
joyful or excited. As Moiraine followed Leane in, she wondered what emotion the Keeper was feeling now. Leane pulled the door to behind them; it
banged shut with something of the sound of a cell door closing.

The Amyrlin Seat herself sat behind a broad table in the middle of the
carpet, and on the table rested a flattened cube of gold, the size of a travel
chest and ornately worked with silver. The table was heavily built, its legs
stout, but it seemed to squat under a weight two strong men would have
had trouble lifting.

At the sight of the golden cube Moiraine had difficulty keeping her face
unruffled. The last she had seen of it, it had been safely locked in
Agelmar's strongroom. On learning of the Amyrlin Seat's arrival she had
meant to tell her of it herself. That it was already in the Amyrlin's posses-
sion was a trifle, but a worrisome trifle. Events could be outpacing her.

She swept a deep curtsy and said formally, "As you called me, Mother,
so have I come." The Amyrlin extended her hand, and Moiraine kissed her
Great Serpent ring, no different from that of any other Aes Sedai. Rising,
she made her tone more conversational, but not too much so. She was
aware of the Keeper standing behind her, beside the door. "I hope you had
a pleasant journey, Mother."

The Amyrlin had been born in Tear, of a simple fisherman's family, not
a noble House, and her name was Siuan Sanche, though very few had used
that name, or even thought of it, in the ten years since she had been raised
from the Hall of the Tower. She was the Amyrlin Seat; that was the whole
of it. The broad stole on her shoulders was striped in the colors of the seven
Ajahs; the Amyrlin was of all Ajahs and of none. She was only of medium
height, and handsome rather than beautiful, but her face held a strength
that had been there before her elevation, the strength of the girl who had
survived the streets of the Maule, Tear's port district, and her clear blue

gaze had made kings and queens, and even the Captain Commander of the Children of the Light, drop their eyes. Her own eyes were strained, now, and there was a new tightness to her mouth.

"We called the winds to speed our vessels up the Erinin, Daughter, and even turned the currents to our aid." The Amyrlin's voice was deep, and sad. "I have seen the flooding we caused in villages along the river, and the Light only knows what we have done to the weather. We will not have endeared ourselves by the damage we've done and the crops we may have ruined. All to reach here as quickly as possible." Her eyes strayed to the ornate golden cube, and she half lifted a hand as if to touch it, but when she spoke it was to say, "Elaida is in Tar Valon, Daughter. She came with Elayne and Gawyn."

Moiraine was conscious of Leane standing to one side, quiet as always in the presence of the Amyrlin. But watching, and listening. "I am surprised, Mother," she said carefully. "This is no time for Morgase to be without Aes Sedai counsel." Morgase was one of the few rulers to openly admit to an Aes Sedai councilor; almost all had one, but few admitted it.

"Elaida insisted, Daughter, and queen or not, I doubt Morgase is a match for Elaida in a contest of wills. In any case, perhaps this time she did not wish to be. Elayne has potential. More than I have ever seen before. Already she shows progress. The Red sisters are swollen up like puff-fish with it. I don't think the girl leans to their way of thinking, but she is young, and there is no telling. Even if they don't manage to bend her, it will make little difference. Elayne could well be the most powerful Aes Sedai in a thousand years, and it is the Red Ajah who found her. They have gained much status in the Hall from the girl."

"I have two young women with me in Fal Dara, Mother," Moiraine said. "Both from the Two Rivers, where the blood of Manetheren still runs strong, though they do not even remember there was once a land called Manetheren. The old blood sings, Mother, and it sings loudly in the Two Rivers. Egwene, a village girl, is at least as strong as Elayne. I have seen the Daughter-Heir, and I know. As for the other, Nynaeve was the Wisdom in their village, yet she is little more than a girl herself. It says something of her that the women of her village chose her Wisdom at her age. Once she gains conscious control of what she now does without knowing, she will be as strong as any in Tar Valon. With training, she will shine like a bonfire beside the candles of Elayne and Egwene. And there is no chance these two will choose the Red. They are amused by men, exasperated by them, but they do like them. They will easily counter whatever influence the Red Ajah gains in the White Tower from finding Elayne."

The Amyrlin nodded as if it were all of no consequence. Moiraine's eyebrows lifted in surprise before she caught herself and smoothed her features. Those were the two main concerns in the Hall of the Tower, that fewer girls who could be trained to channel the One Power were found every year, or so it seemed, and that fewer of real power were found. Worse than the fear in those who blamed Aes Sedai for the Breaking of the World, worse than the hatred from the Children of the Light, worse even than the workings of Darkfriends, were the sheer dwindling of numbers and the lessening of abilities. The corridors of the White Tower were sparsely populated where once they had been crowded, and what could once be done easily with the One Power could now be done only with difficulty, or not at all.

"Elaida had another reason for coming to Tar Valon, Daughter. She sent the same message by six different pigeons to make sure I received it—and to whom else in Tar Valon she sent pigeons, I can only guess—then came herself. She told the Hall of the Tower that you are meddling with a young man who is *ta'veren,* and dangerous. He was in Caemlyn, she said, but when she found the inn where he had been staying, she discovered you had spirited him away."

"The people at that inn served us well and faithfully, Mother. If she harmed any of them. . . ." Moiraine could not keep the sharpness out of her voice, and she heard Leane shift. One did not speak to the Amyrlin Seat in that tone; not even a king on his throne did.

"You should know, Daughter," the Amyrlin said dryly, "that Elaida harms no one except those she considers dangerous. Darkfriends, or those poor fool men who try to channel the One Power. Or one who threatens Tar Valon. Everyone else who isn't Aes Sedai might as well be pieces on a stones board as far as she is concerned. Luckily for him, the innkeeper, one Master Gill as I remember, apparently thinks much of Aes Sedai, and so answered her questions to her satisfaction. Elaida actually spoke well of him. But she spoke more of the young man you took away with you. More dangerous than any man since Artur Hawkwing, she said. She has the Foretelling sometimes, you know, and her words carried weight with the Hall."

For Leane's sake, Moiraine made her voice as meek as she could. That was not very meek, but it was the best she could do. "I have three young men with me, Mother, but none of them is a king, and I doubt very much if any of them even dreams of uniting the world under one ruler. No one has dreamed Artur Hawkwing's dream since the War of the Hundred Years."

"Yes, Daughter. Village youths, so Lord Agelmar tells me. But one of them is *ta'veren.*" The Amyrlin's eyes strayed to the flattened cube again.

"It was put forward in the Hall that you should be sent into retreat for contemplation. This was proposed by one of the Sitters for the Green Ajah, with the other two nodding approval as she spoke."

Leane made a sound of disgust, or perhaps frustration. She always kept in the background when the Amyrlin Seat spoke, but Moiraine could understand the small interruption this time. The Green Ajah had been allied with the Blue for a thousand years; since Artur Hawkwing's time, they had all but spoken with one voice. "I have no desire to hoe vegetables in some remote village, Mother." *Nor will I, whatever the Hall of the Tower says.*

"It was further proposed, also by the Greens, that your care during your retreat should be given to the Red Ajah. The Red Sitters tried to appear surprised, but they looked like fisher-birds who knew the catch was unguarded." The Amyrlin sniffed. "The Reds professed reluctance to take custody of one not of their Ajah, but said they would accede to the wishes of the Hall."

Despite herself, Moiraine shivered. "That would be . . . most unpleasant, Mother." It would be worse than unpleasant, much worse; the Reds were never gentle. She put the thought of it firmly to one side, to deal with later. "Mother, I cannot understand this apparent alliance between the Greens and the Reds. Their beliefs, their attitudes toward men, their views of our very purposes as Aes Sedai, are completely opposite. A Red and a Green cannot even talk to each other without coming to shouts."

"Things change, Daughter. I am the fifth in a row raised to the Amyrlin Seat from the Blue. Perhaps they feel that is too many, or that the Blue way of thinking no longer suffices in a world full of false Dragons. After a thousand years, many things change." The Amyrlin grimaced and spoke as if to herself. "Old walls weaken, and old barriers fall." She shook herself, and her voice firmed. "There was yet another proposal, one that still smells like week-old fish on the jetty. Since Leane is of the Blue Ajah and I came from the Blue, it was put forward that sending two sisters of the Blue with me on this journey would give the Blue four representatives. Proposed in the Hall, to my face, as if they were discussing repairing the drains. Two of the White Sitters stood against me, and two Green. The Yellow muttered among themselves, then would not speak for or against. One more saying nay, and your sisters Anaiya and Maigan would not be here. There was even some talk, open talk, that I should not leave the White Tower at all."

Moiraine felt a greater shock than on hearing that the Red Ajah wanted her in their hands. Whatever Ajah she came from, the Keeper of the Chronicles spoke only for the Amyrlin, and the Amyrlin spoke for all Aes Sedai and all Ajahs. That was the way it had always been, and no one had ever suggested otherwise, not in the darkest days of the Trolloc Wars, not when Artur Hawkwing's armies had penned every surviving Aes Sedai inside Tar Valon. Above all, the Amyrlin Seat was the Amyrlin Seat. Every Aes Sedai was pledged to obey her. No one could question what she did or where she chose to go. This proposal went against three thousand years of custom and law.

"Who would dare, Mother?"

The Amyrlin Seat's laugh was bitter. "Almost anyone, Daughter. Riots in Caemlyn. The Great Hunt called without any of us having a hint of it until the proclamation. False Dragons popping up like redbells after a rain. Nations fading, and more nobles playing at the Game of Houses than at any time since Artur Hawkwing cut all their plottings short. And worst of all, every one of us knows the Dark One is stirring again. Show me a sister who does not think the White Tower is losing its grip on events, and if she is not Brown Ajah, she is dead. Time may be growing short for all of us, Daughter. Sometimes I think I can almost feel it growing shorter."

"As you say, Mother, things change. But there are still worse perils outside the Shining Walls than within."

For a long moment the Amyrlin met Moiraine's gaze, then nodded slowly. "Leave us, Leane. I would talk to my Daughter Moiraine alone."

There was only a moment's hesitation before Leane said, "As you wish, Mother." Moiraine could feel her surprise. The Amyrlin gave few audiences without the Keeper present, especially not to a sister she had reason to chastise.

The door opened and closed behind Leane. She would not say a word in the anteroom of what had occurred inside, but the news that Moiraine was alone with the Amyrlin would spread through the Aes Sedai in Fal Dara like wildfire through a dry forest, and the speculation would begin.

As soon as the door closed the Amyrlin stood, and Moiraine felt a momentary tingle in her skin as the other woman channeled the One Power. For an instant, the Amyrlin Seat seemed to her to be surrounded by a nimbus of bright light.

"I don't know that any of the others have your old trick," the Amyrlin Seat said, lightly touching the blue stone on Moiraine's forehead with one finger, "but most of us have some small tricks remembered from childhood. In any event, no one can hear what we say now."

Suddenly she threw her arms around Moiraine, a warm hug between old friends; Moiraine hugged back as warmly.

"You are the only one, Moiraine, with whom I can remember who I was. Even Leane always acts as if I had *become* the stole and the staff, even when we are alone, as if we'd never giggled together as novices. Sometimes I wish we still were novices, you and I. Still innocent enough to see it all as a gleeman's tale come true, still innocent enough to think we would find men—they would be princes, remember, handsome and strong and gentle?—who could bear to live with women of an Aes Sedai's power. Still innocent enough to dream of the happy ending to the gleeman's tale, of living our lives as other women do, just with more than they."

"We are Aes Sedai, Siuan. We have our duty. Even if you and I had not been born to channel, would you give it up for a home and a husband, even a prince? I do not believe it. That is a village goodwife's dream. Not even the Greens go so far."

The Amyrlin stepped back. "No, I would not give it up. Most of the time, no. But there have been times I envied that village goodwife. At this moment, I almost do. Moiraine, if anyone, even Leane, discovers what we plan, we will both be stilled. And I can't say they would be wrong to do it."

# CHAPTER
## 5

## *The Shadow in Shienar*

Stilled. The word seemed to quiver in the air, almost visible. When it was done to a man who could channel the Power, who must be stopped before madness drove him to the destruction of all around him, it was called gentling, but for Aes Sedai it was stilling. Stilled. No longer able to channel the flow of the One Power. Able to sense *saidar*, the female half of the True Source, but no longer having the ability to touch it. Remembering what was gone forever. So seldom had it been done that every novice was required to learn the name of each Aes Sedai since the Breaking of the World who had been stilled, and her crime, but none could think of it without a shudder. Women bore being stilled no better than men did being gentled.

Moiraine had known the risk from the first, and she knew it was necessary. That did not mean it was pleasant to dwell on. Her eyes narrowed, and only the gleam in them showed her anger, and her worry. "Leane would follow you to the slopes of Shayol Ghul, Siuan, and into the Pit of Doom. You cannot think she would betray you."

"No. But then, would she think it betrayal? Is it betrayal to betray a traitor? Do you never think of that?"

"Never. What we do, Siuan, is what must be done. We have both known it for nearly twenty years. The Wheel weaves as the Wheel wills, and you and I were chosen for this by the Pattern. We are a part of the Prophecies, and the Prophecies must be fulfilled. Must!"

"The Prophecies must be fulfilled. We were taught that they will be, and must be, and yet that fulfillment is treason to everything else we were taught. Some would say to everything we stand for." Rubbing her arms, the Amyrlin Seat walked over to peer through the narrow arrowslit at the garden below. She touched the curtains. "Here in the women's apartments they hang draperies to soften the rooms, and they plant beautiful gardens, but there is no part of this place not purpose-made for battle, death, and killing." She continued in the same pensive tone. "Only twice since the Breaking of the World has the Amyrlin Seat been stripped of stole and staff."

"Tetsuan, who betrayed Manetheren for jealousy of Elisande's powers, and Bonwhin, who tried to use Artur Hawkwing for a puppet to control the world and so nearly destroyed Tar Valon."

The Amyrlin continued her study of the garden. "Both of the Red, and both replaced by Amyrlin from the Blue. The reason there has not been an Amyrlin chosen from the Red since Bonwhin, and the reason the Red Ajah will take any pretext to pull down an Amyrlin from the Blue, all wrapped neatly together. I have no wish to be the third to lose the stole and the staff, Moiraine. For you, of course, it would mean being stilled and put outside the Shining Walls."

"Elaida, for one, would never let me off so easily." Moiraine watched her friend's back intently. *Light, what has come over her? She has never been like this before. Where is her strength, her fire?* "But it will not come to that, Siuan."

The other woman went on as if she had not spoken. "For me, it would be different. Even stilled, an Amyrlin who has been pulled down cannot be allowed to wander about loose; she might be seen as a martyr, become a rallying point for opposition. Tetsuan and Bonwhin were kept in the White Tower as servants. Scullery maids, who could be pointed to as cautions as to what can happen to the mightiest. No one can rally around a woman who must scrub floors and pots all day. Pity her, yes, but not rally to her."

Eyes blazing, Moiraine leaned her fists on the table. "Look at me, Siuan. Look at me! Are you saying that you want to give up, after all these years, after all we have done? Give up, and let the world go? And all for fear of a switching for not getting the pots clean enough!" She put into it all the scorn she could summon, and was relieved when her friend spun to face her. The strength was still there, strained but still there. Those clear blue eyes were as hot with anger as her own.

"I remember which of the two of us squealed the loudest when we were switched as novices. You had lived a soft life in Cairhien, Moiraine. Not like working a fishing boat." Abruptly Siuan slapped the table with a loud crack. "No, I am not suggesting giving up, but neither do I propose to watch everything slide out of our hands *while I can do nothing!* Most of my troubles with the Hall stem from you. Even the Greens wonder why I haven't called you to the Tower and taught you a little discipline. Half the sisters with me think you should be handed over to the Reds, and if that happens, you will wish you were a novice again, with nothing worse to look forward to than a switching. Light! If any of them remember we were friends as novices, I'd be there beside you.

"We had a plan! A plan, Moiraine! Locate the boy and bring him to Tar Valon, where we could hide him, keep him safe and guide him. Since you left the Tower, I have had only two messages from you. Two! I feel as if I'm trying to sail the Fingers of the Dragon in the dark. One message to say you were entering the Two Rivers, going to this village, this Emond's Field. Soon, I thought. He's found, and she'll have him in hand soon. Then word from Caemlyn to say you were coming to Shienar, to Fal Dara, not Tar Valon. Fal Dara, with the Blight almost close enough to touch. Fal Dara, where Trollocs raid and Myrddraal ride as near every day as makes no difference. Nearly twenty years of planning and searching, and you toss all our plans practically in the Dark One's face. Are you mad?"

Now that she had stirred life in the other woman, Moiraine returned to outward calm, herself. Calm, but firm insistence, too. "The Pattern pays no heed to human plans, Siuan. With all our scheming, we forgot what we were dealing with. *Ta'veren.* Elaida is wrong. Artur Paendrag Tanreall was never this strongly *ta'veren.* The Wheel will weave the Pattern around this young man as *it* wills, whatever our plans."

The anger left Amyrlin's face, replaced by white-faced shock. "It sounds as if *you* are saying we might as well give up. Do *you* now suggest standing aside and watching the world burn?"

"No, Siuan. Never standing aside." *Yet the world will burn, Siuan, one way or another, whatever we do. You could never see that.* "But we must now realize that our plans are precarious things. We have even less control than we thought. Perhaps only a fingernail's grip. The winds of destiny are blowing, Siuan, and we must ride them where they take us."

The Amyrlin shivered as if she felt those winds icy on the back of her neck. Her hands went to the flattened cube of gold, blunt, capable fingers finding precise points in the complex designs. Cunningly balanced, the top lifted back to reveal a curled, golden horn nestled within a space designed to hold it. She lifted the instrument and traced the flowing silver script, in the Old Tongue, inlaid around the flaring mouth.

"'The grave is no bar to my call,'" she translated, so softly she seemed to be speaking to herself. "The Horn of Valere, made to call dead heroes back from the grave. And prophecy said it would only be found just in time for the Last Battle." Abruptly she thrust the Horn back into its niche and closed the lid as if she could no longer bear the sight of it. "Agelmar pushed it into my hands as soon as the Welcome was done. He said he was afraid to go into his own strongroom any longer, with it there. The temptation was too great, he said. To sound the Horn himself and lead the host that answered its call north through the Blight to level Shayol Ghul itself and put an end to the Dark One. He burned with the ecstasy of glory, and it was that, he said, that told him it was not to be him, must not be him. He could not wait to be rid of it, yet he wanted it still."

Moiraine nodded. Agelmar was familiar with the Prophecy of the Horn; most who fought the Dark One were. "'Let whosoever sounds me think not of glory, but only of salvation.'"

"Salvation." The Amyrlin laughed bitterly. "From the look in Agelmar's eyes, he didn't know whether he was giving away salvation or rejecting the condemnation of his own soul. He only knew he had to be rid of it before it burned him up. He has tried to keep it secret, but he says there are rumors in the keep already. I do not feel his temptation, yet the Horn still makes my skin crawl. He will have to take it back into his strongroom until I leave. I could not sleep with it even in the next room." She rubbed frown lines from her forehead and sighed. "And it was not to be found until just before the Last Battle. Can it be that close? I thought, hoped, we would have more time."

"The Karaethon Cycle."

"Yes, Moiraine. You do not have to remind me. I've lived with the Prophecies of the Dragon as long as you." The Amyrlin shook her head. "Never more than one false Dragon in a generation since the Breaking, and now three loose in the world at one time, and three more in the past two years. The Pattern demands a Dragon because the Pattern weaves toward Tarmon Gai'don. Sometimes doubt fills me, Moiraine." She said it musingly, as if wondering at it, and went on in the same tone. "What if Logain was the one? He could channel, before the Reds brought him to the White Tower, and we gentled him. So can Mazrim Taim, the man in Saldaea. What if it is him? There are sisters in Saldaea already; he may be taken by now. What if we have been wrong since the start? What happens if the Dragon Reborn is gentled before the Last Battle even begins? Even prophecy can fail if the one prophesied is slain or gentled. And then we face the Dark One naked to the storm."

"Neither of them is the one, Siuan. The Pattern does not demand *a*

Dragon, but the one true Dragon. Until he proclaims himself, the Pattern will continue to throw up false Dragons, but after that there will be no others. If Logain or the other were the one, there would be no others."

"'For he shall come like the breaking dawn, and shatter the world again with his coming, and make it anew.' Either we go naked in the storm, or cling to a protection that will scourge us. The Light help us all." The Amyrlin shook herself as if to throw off her own words. Her face was set, as though bracing for a blow. "You could never hide what you were thinking from me as you do from everyone else, Moiraine. You have more to tell me, and nothing good."

For answer Moiraine took the leather pouch from her belt and upended it, spilling the contents on the table. It appeared to be only a heap of fragmented pottery, shiny black and white.

The Amyrlin Seat touched one bit curiously, and her breath caught. "*Cuendillar.*"

"Heartstone," Moiraine agreed. The making of *cuendillar* had been lost at the Breaking of the World, but what had been made of heartstone had survived the cataclysm. Even those objects swallowed by the earth or sunk in the sea had survived; they must have. No known force could break *cuendillar* once it was complete; even the One Power directed against heartstone only made it stronger. Except that some power *had* broken this.

The Amyrlin hastily assembled the pieces. What they formed was a disk the size of a man's hand, half blacker than pitch and half whiter than snow, the colors meeting along a sinuous line, unfaded by age. The ancient symbol of Aes Sedai, before the world was broken, when men and women wielded the Power together. Half of it was now called the Flame of Tar Valon; the other half was scrawled on doors, the Dragon's Fang, to accuse those within of evil. Only seven like it had been made; everything ever made of heartstone was recorded in the White Tower, and those seven were remembered above all. Siuan Sanche stared at it as she would have at a viper on her pillow.

"One of the seals on the Dark One's prison," she said finally, reluctantly. It was those seven seals over which the Amyrlin Seat was supposed to be Watcher. The secret hidden from the world, if the world ever thought of it, was that no Amyrlin Seat had known where any of the seals were since the Trolloc Wars.

"We know the Dark One is stirring, Siuan. We know his prison cannot stay sealed forever. Human work can never match the Creator's. We knew he has touched the world again, even if, thank the Light, only indirectly. Darkfriends multiply, and what we called evil but ten years ago seems almost caprice compared with what now is done every day."

"If the seals are already breaking. . . . We may have no time at all."

"Little enough. But that little may be enough. It will have to be."

The Amyrlin touched the fractured seal, and her voice grew tight, as if she were forcing herself to speak. "I saw the boy, you know, in the court-yard during the Welcome. It is one of my Talents, seeing *ta'veren*. A rare Talent these days, even more rare than *ta'veren,* and certainly not of much use. A tall boy, a fairly handsome young man. Not much different from any young man you might see in any town." She paused to draw breath. "Moiraine, he blazed like the sun. I've seldom been afraid in my life, but the sight of him made me afraid right down to my toes. I wanted to cower, to howl. I could barely speak. Agelmar thought I was angry with him, I said so little. That young man . . . he's the one we have sought these twenty years."

There was a hint of question in her voice. Moiraine answered it. "He is."

"Are you certain? Can he. . . ? Can he . . . channel the One Power?"

Her mouth strained around the words, and Moiraine felt the tension, too, a twisting inside, a cold clutching at her heart. She kept her face smooth, though. "He can." A man wielding the One Power. That was a thing no Aes Sedai could contemplate without fear. It was a thing the whole world feared. *And I will loose it on the world.* "Rand al'Thor will stand before the world as the Dragon Reborn."

The Amyrlin shuddered. "Rand al'Thor. It does not sound like a name to inspire fear and set the world on fire." She gave another shiver and rubbed her arms briskly, but her eyes suddenly shone with a purposeful light. "If he is the one, then we truly may have time enough. But is he safe here? I have two Red sisters with me, and I can no longer answer for Green or Yellow, either. The Light consume me, I can't answer for any of them, not with this. Even Verin and Serafelle would leap on him the way they would a scarlet adder in a nursery."

"He is safe, for the moment."

The Amyrlin waited for her to say more. The silence stretched, until it was plain she would not. Finally the Amyrlin said, "You say our old plan is useless. What do you suggest now?"

"I have purposely let him think I no longer have any interest in him, that he may go where he pleases for all of me." She raised her hands as the Amyrlin opened her mouth. "It was necessary, Siuan. Rand al'Thor was raised in the Two Rivers, where Manetheren's stubborn blood flows in every vein, and his own blood is like rock beside clay compared to Man-etheren's. He must be handled gently, or he will bolt in any direction but the one we want."

"Then we'll handle him like a newborn babe. We'll wrap him in swaddling clothes and play with his toes, if that's what you think we need. But to what immediate purpose?"

"His two friends, Matrim Cauthon and Perrin Aybara, are ripe to see the world before they sink back into the obscurity of the Two Rivers. If they can sink back; they are *ta'veren,* too, if lesser than he. I will induce them to carry the Horn of Valere to Illian." She hesitated, frowning. "There is . . . a problem with Mat. He carries a dagger from Shadar Logoth."

"Shadar Logoth! Light, why did you ever let them get near that place. Every stone of it is tainted. There isn't a pebble safe to carry away. Light help us, if Mordeth touched the boy. . . ." The Amyrlin sounded as though she were strangling. "If that happened, the world would be doomed."

"But it did not, Siuan. We do what we must from necessity, and it was necessary. I have done enough so that Mat will not infect others, but he had the dagger too long before I knew. The link is still there. I had thought I must take him to Tar Valon to cure it, but with so many sisters present, it might be done here. So long as there are a few you can trust not to see Darkfriends where there are none. You and I and two others will suffice, using my *angreal.*"

"Leane will do for one, and I can find another." Suddenly the Amyrlin Seat gave a wry grin. "The Hall wants that *angreal* back, Moiraine. There are not very many of them left, and you are now considered . . . unreliable."

Moiraine smiled, but it did not touch her eyes. "They will think worse of me before I am done. Mat will leap at the chance to be so big a part of the legend of the Horn, and Perrin should not be hard to convince. He needs something to take his mind off his own troubles. Rand knows what he is—some of it, at least; a little—and he is afraid of it, naturally. He wants to go off somewhere alone, where he cannot hurt anyone. He says he will never wield the Power again, but he fears not being able to stop it."

"As well he might. Easier to give up drinking water."

"Exactly. And he wants to be free from Aes Sedai." Moiraine gave a small, mirthless smile. "Offered the chance to leave Aes Sedai behind and still stay with his friends a while longer, he should be as eager as Mat."

"But how is he leaving Aes Sedai behind? Surely you must travel with him. We can't lose him now, Moiraine."

"I cannot travel with him." *It is a long way from Fal Dara to Illian, but he has traveled almost as far already.* "He must be let off the leash for a time. There is no help for it. I have had all of their old clothes burned. There has been too much opportunity for some shred of what they were wearing to have fallen into the wrong hands. I will cleanse them before they leave;

they will not even realize it has been done. There will be no chance they can be tracked that way, and the only other threat of that kind is locked away here in the dungeon." The Amyrlin, midway in nodding approval, gave her a questioning look, but she did not pause. "They will travel as safely as I can manage, Siuan. And when Rand needs me in Illian, I will be there, and I will see that it is he who presents the Horn to the Council of Nine and the Assemblage. I will see to everything in Illian. Siuan, the Illianers would follow the Dragon, or Ba'alzamon himself, if he came bearing the Horn of Valere, and so will the greater part of those gathered for the Hunt. The true Dragon Reborn will not need to gather a following before nations move against him. He will begin with a nation around him and an army at his back."

The Amyrlin dropped back into her chair, but immediately leaned forward. She seemed caught between weariness and hope. "But *will* he proclaim himself? If he's afraid. . . . The Light knows he should be, Moiraine, but men who name themselves as the Dragon *want* the power. If he does not. . . ."

"I have the means to see him named Dragon whether he wills it or not. And even if I somehow fail, the Pattern itself will see him named Dragon whether he wills it or not. Remember, he is *ta'veren*, Siuan. He has no more control over his fate than a candle wick has over the flame."

The Amyrlin sighed. "It's risky, Moiraine. Risky. But my father used to say, 'Girl, if you won't take a chance, you'll never win a copper.' We have plans to make. Sit down; this won't be done quickly. I will send for wine and cheese."

Moiraine shook her head. "We have been closeted alone too long already. If any did try listening and found your Warding, they will be wondering already. It is not worth the risk. We can contrive another meeting tomorrow." *Besides, my dearest friend, I cannot tell you everything, and I cannot risk letting you know I am holding anything back.*

"I suppose you are right. But first thing in the morning. There's so much I have to know."

"The morning," Moiraine agreed. The Amyrlin rose, and they hugged again. "In the morning I will tell you everything you need to know."

Leane gave Moiraine a sharp look when she came out into the anteroom, then darted into the Amyrlin's chamber. Moiraine tried to put on a chastened face, as if she had endured one of the Amyrlin's infamous upbraidings—most women, however strong-willed, returned from those big-eyed and weak-kneed—but the expression was foreign to her. She looked more angry than anything else, which served much the same purpose. She was only vaguely aware of the other women in the outer room; she thought some had gone and others come since she went in, but she barely looked at them. The hour was growing late, and there was much to be done before the morning came. Much, before she spoke to the Amyrlin Seat again.

Quickening her step, she moved deeper into the keep.

The column would have made an impressive sight under the waxing moon, moving through the Tarabon night to the jangle of harness, had there been anyone to see it. A full two thousand Children of the Light, well mounted, in white tabards and cloaks, armor burnished, with their train of supply wagons, and farriers, and grooms with the strings of remounts. There were villages in this sparsely forested country, but they had left roads behind, and stayed clear of even farmers' crofts. They were to meet . . . someone . . . at a flyspeck village near the northern border of Tarabon, at the edge of Almoth Plain.

Geofram Bornhald, riding at the head of his men, wondered what it was all about. He remembered too well his interview with Pedron Niall, Lord Captain Commander of the Children of the Light, in Amador, but he had learned little there.

*"We are alone, Geofram,"* the white-haired man had said. *His voice was thin and reedy with age. "I remember giving you the oath . . . what . . . thirty-six years ago, it must be, now."*

*Bornhald straightened. "My Lord Captain Commander, may I ask why I was called back from Caemlyn, and with such urgency? A push, and Morgase could be toppled. There are Houses in Andor that see dealing with Tar Valon as we do, and they were ready to lay claim to the throne. I left Eamon Valda in charge, but he seemed intent on following the Daughter-Heir to Tar Valon. I would not be surprised to learn the man has kidnapped the girl, or even attacked Tar Valon." And Dain, Bornhald's son, had arrived just before Bornhald was recalled. Dain was full of zeal. Too much zeal, sometimes. Enough to fall in blindly with whatever Valda proposed.*

*"Valda walks in the Light, Geofram. But you are the best battle commander among the Children. You will assemble a full legion, the best men you can find, and take them into Tarabon, avoiding any eyes attached to a tongue that may speak. Any such tongue must be silenced, if the eyes see."*

*Bornhald hesitated. Fifty Children together, or even a hundred, could enter any land without question, at least without open question, but an entire legion. . . . "Is it war, my Lord Captain Commander? There is talk in the streets. Wild rumors, mainly, about Artur Hawkwing's armies come back." The old man did not speak. "The King. . . ."*

*"Does not command the Children, Lord Captain Bornhald." For the first time there was a snap in the Lord Captain Commander's voice. "I do. Let the King sit in*

*his palace and do what he does best. Nothing. You will be met at a village called Alcruna, and there you will receive your final orders. I expect your legion to ride in three days. Now go, Geofram. You have work to do."*

*Bornhald frowned. "Pardon, my Lord Captain Commander, but who will meet me? Why am I risking war with Tarabon?"*

*"You will be told what you must know when you reach Alcruna." The Lord Captain Commander suddenly looked more than his age. Absently he plucked at his white tunic, with the golden sunburst of the Children large on the chest. "There are forces at work beyond what you know, Geofram. Beyond what even you can know. Choose your men quickly. Now go. Ask me no more. And the Light ride with you."*

Now Bornhald straightened in his saddle, working a knot out of his back. *I am getting old,* he thought. A day and a night in the saddle, with two pauses to water the horses, and he felt every gray hair on his head. He would not even have noticed a few years ago. *At least I have not killed any innocents.* He could be as hard on Darkfriends as any man sworn to the Light—Darkfriends must be destroyed before they pulled the whole world under the Shadow—but he wanted to be sure they *were* Darkfriends first. It had been difficult avoiding Taraboner eyes with so many men, even in the backcountry, but he had managed it. No tongues had needed to be silenced.

The scouts he had sent out came riding back, and behind them came more men in white cloaks, some carrying torches to ruin the night vision of everyone at the head of the column. With a muttered curse, Bornhald ordered a halt while he studied those who came to meet him.

Their cloaks bore the same golden sunburst on the breast as his, the same as every Child of the Light, and their leader even had golden knots of rank below it equivalent to Bornhald's. But behind their sunbursts were red shepherd's crooks. Questioners. With hot irons and pinchers and dripping water the Questioners pulled confession and repentance from Darkfriends, but there were those who said they decided guilt before ever they began. Geofram Bornhald was one who said it.

*I have been sent here to meet Questioners?*

"We have been waiting for you, Lord Captain Bornhald," the leader said in a harsh voice. He was a tall, hook-nosed man with the gleam of certainty in his eyes that every Questioner had. "You could have made better time. I am Einor Saren, second to Jaichim Carridin, who commands the Hand of the Light in Tarabon." The Hand of the Light—the Hand that dug out truth, so they said. They did not like the name Questioners. "There is a bridge at the village. Have your men move across. We will talk in the inn. It is surprisingly comfortable."

"I was told by the Lord Captain Commander himself to avoid all eyes."

"The village has been . . . pacified. Now move your men. *I* command, now. I have orders with the Lord Captain Commander's seal, if you doubt."

Bornhald suppressed the growl that rose in his throat. Pacified. He wondered if the bodies had been piled outside the village, or if they had been thrown into the river. It would be like the Questioners, cold enough to kill an entire village for secrecy and stupid enough to throw the bodies into the river to float downstream and trumpet their deed from Alcruna to Tanchico. "What I doubt is why I am in Tarabon with two thousand men, Questioner."

Saren's face tightened, but his voice remained harsh and demanding. "It is simple, Lord Captain. There are towns and villages across Almoth Plain with none in authority above a mayor or a Town Council. It is past time they were brought to the Light. There will be many Darkfriends in such places."

Bornhald's horse stamped. "Are you saying, Saren, that I've brought an entire legion across most of Tarabon in secrecy to root a few Darkfriends out of some grubby villages?"

"You are here to do as you are told, Bornhald. To do the work of the Light! Or are you sliding from the Light?" Saren's smile was a grimace. "If battle is what you seek, you may have your chance. The strangers have a great force on Toman Head, more than Tarabon and Arad Doman together may be able to hold, even if they can stop their own bickering long enough to work together. If the strangers break through, you will have all the fighting you can handle. The Taraboners claim the strangers are monsters, creatures of the Dark One. Some say they have Aes Sedai to fight for them. If they *are* Darkfriends, these strangers, they will have to be dealt with, too. In their turn."

For a moment, Bornhald stopped breathing. "Then the rumors are true. Artur Hawking's armies have returned."

"Strangers," Saren said flatly. He sounded as if he regretted having mentioned them. "Strangers, and probably Darkfriends, from wherever they came. That is all we know, and all you need to know. They do not concern you now. We are wasting time. Move your men across the river, Bornhald. I will give you your orders in the village." He whirled his horse and galloped back the way he had come, his torchbearers riding at his heels.

Bornhald closed his eyes to hasten the return of his night sight. *We are being used like stones on a board.* "Byar!" He opened his eyes as his second appeared at his side, stiffening in his saddle before the Lord Captain. The gaunt-faced man had almost the Questioner's light in his eyes, but he was a good soldier despite. "There is a bridge ahead. Move the legion across the river and make camp. I will join you as soon as I can."

He gathered his reins and rode in the direction the Questioner had taken. *Stones on a board. But who is moving us? And why?*

Afternoon shadows gave way to evening as Liandrin made her way through the women's apartments. Beyond the arrowslits, darkness grew and pressed on the light from the lamps in the corridor. Twilight was a troubled time for Liandrin of late, that and dawn. At dawn the day was born, just as twilight gave birth to night, but at dawn, night died, and at twilight, day. The Dark One's power was rooted in death; he gained power from death, and at those times she thought she could feel his power stirring. Something stirred in the half dark, at least. Something she almost thought she could catch if she turned quickly enough, something she was sure she could see if she looked hard enough.

Serving women in black-and-gold curtsied as she passed, but she did not respond. She kept her eyes fixed straight ahead, and did not see them.

At the door she sought, she paused for a quick glance up and down the hall. The only women in sight were servants; there were no men, of course. She pushed open the door and went in without knocking.

The outer room of the Lady Amalisa's chambers was brightly lit, and a blazing fire on the hearth held back the chill of the Shienaran night. Amalisa and her ladies sat about the room, in chairs and on the layered carpets, listening while one of their number, standing, read aloud to them. It was *The Dance of the Hawk and the Hummingbird,* by Teven Aerwin, which purported to set forth the proper conduct of men toward women and women toward men. Liandrin's mouth tightened; she certainly had not read it, but she had heard as much as she needed about it. Amalisa and her ladies greeted each pronouncement with gales of laughter, falling against each other and drumming their heels on the carpets like girls.

The reader was the first to become aware of Liandrin's presence. She cut off with a surprised widening of her eyes. The others turned to see what she was staring at, and silence replaced laughter. All but Amalisa scrambled to their feet, hastily smoothing hair and skirts.

The Lady Amalisa rose gracefully, with a smile. "You honor us with your presence, Liandrin. This is a most pleasant surprise. I did not expect you until tomorrow. I thought you would want to rest after your long jour—"

Liandrin cut her off sharply, addressing the air. "I will speak to the Lady Amalisa alone. All of you will leave. Now."

There was a moment of shocked silence, then the other women made their goodbyes to Amalisa. One by one they curtsied to Liandrin, but she did not acknowledge them. She continued to stare straight ahead at nothing, but she saw them, and heard. Honorifics offered with breathy unease at the Aes Sedai's mood. Eyes falling when she ignored them. They squeezed past her to the door, pressing back awkwardly so their skirts did not disturb hers.

As the door closed behind the last of them, Amalisa said, "Liandrin, I do not underst—"

"Do you walk in the Light, my daughter?" There would be none of that foolishness of calling her sister here. The other woman was older by some years, but the ancient forms would be observed. However long they had been forgotten, it was time they were remembered.

As soon as the question was out of her mouth, though, Liandrin realized she had made a mistake. It was a question guaranteed to cause doubt and anxiety, coming from an Aes Sedai, but Amalisa's back stiffened, and her face hardened.

"That is an insult, Liandrin Sedai. I am Shienaran, of a noble House and the blood of soldiers. My line has fought the Shadow since before there *was* a Shienar, three thousand years without fail or a day's weakness."

Liandrin shifted her point of attack, but she did not retreat. Striding across the room, she took the leather-bound copy of *The Dance of the Hawk and the Hummingbird* from the mantelpiece and hefted it without looking at it. "In Shienar above other lands, my daughter, the Light must be precious, and the Shadow feared." Casually she threw the book into the fire. Flames leaped as if it were a log of fat-wood, thundering as they licked up the chimney. In the same instant every lamp in the room flared, hissing, so fiercely did they burn, flooding the chamber with light. "Here above all. Here, so close to the cursed Blight, where corruption waits. Here, even one who thinks he walks in the Light may still be corrupted by the Shadow."

Beads of sweat glistened on Amalisa's forehead. The hand she had raised in protest for her book fell slowly to her side. Her features still held firm, but Liandrin saw her swallow, and her feet shift. "I do not understand, Liandrin Sedai. Is it the book? It is only foolishness."

There was a faint quaver in her voice. *Good.* Glass lamp mantles cracked as the flames leaped higher and hotter, lighting the room as bright as unsheltered noon. Amalisa stood as stiff as a post, her face tight as she tried not to squint.

"It is you who are foolish, my daughter. I care nothing for books. Here, men enter the Blight, and walk in its taint. In the very Shadow. Why wonder you that that taint may seep into them? Whether or not against their will, still it may seep. Why think you the Amyrlin Seat herself has come?"

"No." It was a gasp.

"Of the Red am I, my daughter," Liandrin said relentlessly. "I hunt all men corrupted."

"I don't understand."

"Not only those foul ones who try the One Power. All men corrupted. High and low do I hunt."

"I don't. . . ." Amalisa licked her lips unsteadily and made a visible effort to gather herself. "I do not understand, Liandrin Sedai. Please. . . ."

"High even before low."

"No!" As if some invisible support had vanished, Amalisa fell to her knees, and her head dropped. "Please, Liandrin Sedai, say you do not mean Agelmar. It cannot be him."

In that moment of doubt and confusion, Liandrin struck. She did not move, but lashed out with the One Power. Amalisa gasped and gave a jerk, as if she had been pricked with a needle, and Liandrin's petulant mouth perked in a smile.

This was her own special trick from childhood, the first learned of her abilities. It had been forbidden to her as soon as the Mistress of Novices discovered it, but to Liandrin that only meant one more thing she needed to conceal from those who were jealous of her.

She strode forward and pulled Amalisa's chin up. The metal that had stiffened her was still there, but it was baser metal now, malleable to the right pressures. Tears trickled from the corners of Amalisa's eyes, glistening on her cheeks. Liandrin let the fires die back to normal; there was no longer any need for such. She softened her words, but her voice was as unyielding as steel.

"Daughter, no one wants to see you and Agelmar thrown to the people as Darkfriends. I will help you, but you must help."

"H-help you?" Amalisa put her hands to her temples; she looked confused. "Please, Liandrin Sedai, I don't . . . understand. It is all so. . . . It's all. . . ."

It was not a perfect ability; Liandrin could not force anyone to do what she wanted—though she had tried; oh, how she had tried. But she could open them wide to her arguments, make them want to believe her, want more than anything to be convinced of her rightness.

"Obey, daughter. Obey, and answer my questions truthfully, and I promise that no one will speak of you and Agelmar as Darkfriends. You will not be dragged naked through the streets, to be flogged from the city if the people do not tear you to pieces first. I will not let this happen. You understand?"

"Yes, Liandrin Sedai, yes. I will do as you say and answer you truly."

Liandrin straightened, looking down at the other woman. The Lady

Amalisa stayed as she was, kneeling, her face as open as a child's, a child waiting to be comforted and helped by someone wiser and stronger. There was a rightness about it to Liandrin. She had never understood why a simple bow or curtsy was sufficient for Aes Sedai when men and women knelt to kings and queens. *What queen has within her my power?* Her mouth twisted angrily, and Amalisa shivered.

"Be easy in yourself, my daughter. I have come to help you, not to punish. Only those who deserve it will be punished. Truth only, speak to me."

"I will, Liandrin Sedai. I will, I swear it by my House and honor."

"Moiraine came to Fal Dara with a Darkfriend."

Amalisa was too frightened to show surprise. "Oh, no, Liandrin Sedai. No. That man came later. He is in the dungeons now."

"Later, you say. But it is true that she speaks often with him? She is often in company with this Darkfriend? Alone?"

"S-sometimes, Liandrin Sedai. Only sometimes. She wishes to find out why he came here. Moiraine Sedai is—" Liandrin held up her hand sharply, and Amalisa swallowed whatever else she had been going to say.

"By three young men Moiraine was accompanied. This I *know.* Where are they? I have been to their rooms, and they are not to be found."

"I—I do not know, Liandrin Sedai. They seem nice boys. Surely you don't think they are Darkfriends."

"Not Darkfriends, no. Worse. By far more dangerous than Darkfriends, my daughter. The entire world is in danger from them. They must be found. You will command your servants to search the keep, and your ladies, and yourself. Every crack and cranny. To this, you will see personally. Personally! And to no one will you speak of it, save those I name. None else may know. None. From Fal Dara in secrecy these young men must be removed, and to Tar Valon taken. In utter secrecy."

"As you command, Liandrin Sedai. But I do not understand the need for secrecy. No one here will hinder Aes Sedai."

"Of the Black Ajah you have heard?"

Amalisa's eyes bulged, and she leaned back away from Liandrin, raising her hands as though to shield herself from a blow. "A v-vile rumor, Liandrin Sedai. V-vile. There are n-no Aes Sedai who s-serve the Dark One. I do not believe it. You must believe me! Under the Light, I s-swear I do not believe it. By my honor and my House, I swear. . . ."

Coolly Liandrin let her go on, watching the last remaining strength leach out of the other woman with her own silence. Aes Sedai had been known to become angry, very angry, with those who even mentioned the Black Ajah much less those who said they believed in its hidden existence.

After this, with her will already weakened by that little childhood trick, Amalisa would be as clay in her hands. After one more blow.

"The Black Ajah is *real,* child. Real, and here within Fal Dara's walls." Amalisa knelt there, her mouth hanging open. The Black Ajah. Aes Sedai who were also Darkfriends. Almost as horrible to learn the Dark One himself walked Fal Dara keep. But Liandrin would not let up now. "Any Aes Sedai in the halls you pass, a Black sister could be. This I swear. I cannot tell you which they are, but my protection you can have. If in the Light you walk and me obey."

"I will," Amalisa whispered hoarsely. "I will. Please, Liandrin Sedai, please say you will protect my brother, and my ladies. . . ."

"Who deserves protection I will protect. Concern yourself with yourself, my daughter. And think only of what I have commanded of you. Only that. The fate of the world rides on this, my daughter. All else you must forget."

"Yes, Liandrin Sedai. Yes. Yes."

Liandrin turned and crossed the room, not looking back until she reached the door. Amalisa was still on her knees, still watching her anxiously. "Rise, my Lady Amalisa." Liandrin made her voice pleasant, with only a hint of the mocking she felt. *Sister, indeed! Not one day as a novice would she last. And power to command she has.* "Rise." Amalisa straightened in slow, stiff jerks, as if she had been bound hand and foot for hours. As she finally came upright, Liandrin said, the steel back in full strength, "And if you fail the world, if you fail me, that wretched Darkfriend in the dungeon will be your envy."

From the look on Amalisa's face, Liandrin did not think failure would come from any lack of effort on her part.

Pulling the door shut behind her, Liandrin suddenly felt a prickling across her skin. Breath catching, she whirled about, looking up and down the dimly lit hall. Empty. It was full night beyond the arrowslits. The hall was empty, yet she was sure there had been eyes on her. The vacant corridor, shadowy between the lamps on the walls, mocked her. She shrugged uneasily, then started down the hall determinedly. *Fancies take me. Nothing more.*

Full night already, and there was much to do before dawn. Her orders had been explicit.

Pitch-blackness covered the dungeons whatever the hour, unless someone brought in a lantern, but Padan Fain sat on the edge of his cot, staring into the dark with a smile on his face. He could hear the other two prisoners grumbling in their sleep, muttering in nightmares. Padan Fain was waiting for something, something he had been awaiting for a long time. For too long. But not much longer.

The door to the outer guardroom opened, spilling in a flood of light, darkly outlining a figure in the doorway.

Fain stood. "You! Not who I expected." He stretched with a casualness he did not feel. Blood raced through his veins; he thought he could leap over the keep if he tried. "Surprises for everyone, eh? Well, come on. The night's getting old, and I want some sleep sometime."

As a lamp came into the cell chamber, Fain raised his head, grinning at something, unseen yet felt, beyond the dungeon's stone ceiling. "It isn't over yet," he whispered. "The battle's never over."

# CHAPTER
# 6

## Dark Prophecy

The farmhouse door shook under furious blows from outside; the heavy bar across the door jumped in its brackets. Beyond the window next to the door moved the heavy-muzzled silhouette of a Trolloc. There were windows everywhere, and more shadowy shapes outside. Not shadowy enough, though. Rand could still make them out.

*The windows,* he thought desperately. He backed away from the door, clutching his sword before him in both hands. *Even if the door holds, they can break in the windows. Why aren't they trying the windows?*

With a deafening metallic screech, one of the brackets pulled partly away from the doorframe, hanging loose on nails ripped a finger's width out of the wood. The bar quivered from another blow, and the nails squealed again.

"We have to stop them!" Rand shouted. *Only we can't. We can't stop them.* He looked around for a way to run, but there was only the one door. The room was a box. Only one door, and so many windows. "We have to do something. Something!"

"It's too late," Mat said. "Don't you understand?" His grin looked odd on a bloodless pale face, and the hilt of a dagger stood out from his chest, the ruby that capped it blazing as if it held fire. The gem had more life than his face. "It's too late for us to change anything."

"I've finally gotten rid of them," Perrin said, laughing. Blood streamed down his face like a flood of tears from his empty sockets. He held out red hands, trying to make Rand look at what he held. "I'm free, now. It's over."

"It's never over, al'Thor," Padan Fain cried, capering in the middle of the floor. "The battle's never done."

The door exploded in splinters, and Rand ducked away from the flying shards of wood. Two red-clad Aes Sedai stepped through, bowing their master in. A mask the color of dried blood covered Ba'alzamon's face, but Rand could see the flames of his eyes through the eyeslits; he could hear the roaring fires of Ba'alzamon's mouth.

"It is not yet done between us, al'Thor," Ba'alzamon said, and he and Fain spoke together as one, "For you, the battle is never done."

With a strangled gasp Rand sat up on the floor, clawing his way awake. It seemed he could still hear Fain's voice, as sharp as if the peddler were standing beside him. *It's never over. The battle's never done.*

Bleary-eyed, he looked around to convince himself that he was still hidden away where Egwene had left him, bedded down on a pallet in a corner of her room. The dim light of a single lamp suffused the room, and he was surprised to see Nynaeve, knitting in a rocking chair on the other side of the lone bed, its covers still in place. It was night outside.

Dark-eyed and slender, Nynaeve wore her hair in a fat braid, pulled over one shoulder and hanging almost to her waist. She had not given up on home. Her face was calm, and she seemed aware of nothing except her knitting as she rocked gently. The steady *click-click* of her knitting needles was the only sound. The rug silenced the rocking chair.

There had been nights of late when he had wished for a carpet on the cold stone floor of his room, but in Shienar men's rooms were always bare and stark. The walls here had two tapestries, mountain scenes with waterfalls, and flower-embroidered curtains alongside the arrowslits. Cut flowers, white morningstars, stood in a flat, round vase on the table by the bed, and more nodded in glazed white sconces on the walls. A tall mirror stood in a corner, and another hung over the washstand, with its blue-striped pitcher and bowl. He wondered why Egwene needed two mirrors; there was none in his room, and he did not miss it. There was only one lamp lit, but four more stood around the room, which was nearly as large as the one he shared with Mat and Perrin. Egwene had it alone.

Without looking up, Nynaeve said, "If you sleep in the afternoon, you can't expect to sleep at night."

He frowned, though she could not see it. At least, he thought she could not. She was only a few years older than he, but being Wisdom added fifty years of authority. "I needed a place to hide, and I was tired," he said, then quickly added, "I didn't just come here. Egwene invited me into the women's apartments."

Nynaeve lowered her knitting and gave him an amused smile. She was a pretty woman. That was something he would never have noticed back home; one just did not think of a Wisdom that way. "The Light help me, Rand, you are becoming more Shienaran every day. Invited into the women's apartments, indeed." She sniffed. "Any day now, you'll start talking about your honor, and asking peace to favor your sword." He colored, and hoped she did not notice in the dim light. She eyed his sword, its hilt sticking out of the long bundle beside him on the floor. He knew she did not approve of the sword, of any sword, but she said nothing about it for once. "Egwene told me why you need a place to hide. Don't worry. We will keep you hidden from the Amyrlin, or from any other Aes Sedai, if that is what you want."

She met his eyes and jerked hers away, but not before he saw her uneasiness. Her doubt. *That's right, I can channel the Power. A man wielding the One Power! You ought to be helping the Aes Sedai hunt me down and gentle me.*

Scowling, he straightened the leather jerkin Egwene had found for him and twisted around so he could lean back against the wall. "As soon as I can, I will hide in a cart, or sneak out. You won't have to hide me long." Nynaeve did not say anything; she fixed on her knitting, making an angry sound when she dropped a stitch. "Where is Egwene?"

She let the knitting fall onto her lap. "I don't know why I am even trying tonight. I can't keep track of my stitches for some reason. She has gone down to see Padan Fain. She thinks seeing faces he knows might help him."

"Mine certainly did not. She ought to stay away from him. He's dangerous."

"She wants to help him," Nynaeve said calmly. "Remember, she was training to be my assistant, and being a Wisdom is not all predicting the weather. Healing is part of it, too. Egwene has the desire to heal, the need to. And if Padan Fain is so dangerous, Moiraine would have said something."

He barked a laugh. "You didn't ask her. Egwene admitted it, and I can just see you asking permission for anything." Her raised eyebrow wiped the laugh off his face. He refused to apologize, though. They were a long way from home, and he did not see how she could go on being Wisdom of Emond's Field if she was going to Tar Valon. "Have they started to search for me, yet? Egwene is not sure they will, but Lan says the Amyrlin Seat is here because of me, and I think I'll take his opinion over hers."

For a moment Nynaeve did not answer. Instead she fussed with her skeins of yarn. Finally she said, "I am not sure. One of the serving women came a little while ago. To turn down the bed, she said. As if Egwene would be going to sleep already, with the feast for the Amyrlin tonight. I sent her away; she didn't see you."

"Nobody turns your bed down for you in the men's quarters." She gave him a level look, one that would have set him stammering a year ago. He shook his head. "They wouldn't use the maids to look for me, Nynaeve."

"When I went to the buttery for a cup of milk earlier, there were too many women in the halls. Those who are attending the feast should have been getting dressed, and the others should either have been helping them or getting ready to serve, or to. . . ." She frowned worriedly. "There's more than enough work for everybody with the Amyrlin here. And they were not just here in the women's apartments. I saw the Lady Amalisa herself coming out of a storeroom near the buttery with her face all over dust."

"That's ridiculous. Why would she be part of a search? Or any of the women, for that matter. They'd be using Lord Agelmar's soldiers, and the Warders. And the Aes Sedai. They must just be doing something for the feast. Burn me if I know what a Shienaran feast takes."

"You are a woolhead, sometimes, Rand. The men I saw didn't know what the women were doing either. I heard some of them complaining about having to do all the work by themselves. I know it makes no sense that they were looking for you. None of the Aes Sedai seemed to be taking any interest. But Amalisa was not readying herself for the feast by dirtying her dress in a storeroom. They were looking for something, something important. Even if she began right after I saw her, she would barely have time to bathe and change. Speaking of which, if Egwene doesn't come back soon, she'll have to choose between changing and being late."

For the first time, he realized that Nynaeve was not wearing the Two Rivers woolens he was used to. Her dress was pale blue silk, embroidered in snowdrop blossoms around the neck and down the sleeves. Each blossom centered on a small pearl, and her belt was tooled in silver, with a silver buckle set with pearls. He had never seen her in anything like that. Even feastday clothes back home might not match it.

"You're going to the feast?"

"Of course. Even if Moiraine had not said I should, I would never let her think I was. . . ." Her eyes lit up fiercely for a moment, and he knew what she meant. Nynaeve would never let anyone think she was afraid, even if she was. Certainly not Moiraine, and especially not Lan. He hoped she did not know he was aware of her feelings for the Warder.

After a moment her gaze softened as it fell on the sleeve of her dress. "The Lady Amalisa gave me this," she said so softly he wondered if she was speaking to herself. She stroked the silk with her fingers, outlining the embroidered flowers, smiling, lost in thought.

"It's very pretty on you, Nynaeve. You're pretty tonight." He winced as soon as he said it. Any Wisdom was touchy about her authority, but Nynaeve was touchier than most. The Women's Circle back home had always looked over her shoulder because she was young, and maybe because she was pretty, and her fights with the Mayor and the Village Council had been the stuff of stories.

She jerked her hand away from the embroidery and glared at him, brows lowering. He spoke quickly to forestall her.

"They can't keep the gates barred forever. Once they are opened, I will be gone, and the Aes Sedai will never find me. Perrin says there are places in the Black Hills and the Caralain Grass you can go for days without seeing a soul. Maybe—maybe I can figure out what to do about. . . ." He shrugged uncomfortably. There was no need to say it, not to her. "And if I can't, there'll be no one to hurt."

Nynaeve was silent for a moment, then she said slowly, "I am not so sure, Rand. I can't say you look like more than another village boy to me, but Moiraine insists you are *ta'veren,* and I don't think she believes the Wheel is finished with you. The Dark One seems—"

"Shai'tan is dead," he said harshly, and abruptly the room seemed to lurch. He grabbed his head as waves of dizziness sloshed through him.

"You fool! You pure, blind, idiotic fool! Naming the Dark One, bringing his attention down on you! Don't you have enough trouble?"

"He's dead," Rand muttered, rubbing his head. He swallowed. The dizziness was already fading. "All right, all right. Ba'alzamon, if you want. But he's dead; I saw him die, saw him burn."

"And I wasn't watching you when the Dark One's eye fell on you just now? Don't tell me you felt nothing, or I'll box your ears; I saw your face."

"He's dead," Rand insisted. The unseen watcher flashed through his head, and the wind on the tower top. He shivered. "Strange things happen this close to the Blight."

"You *are* a fool, Rand al'Thor." She shook a fist at him. "I *would* box your ears for you if I thought it would knock any sense—"

The rest of her words were swallowed as bells crashed out ringing all over the keep.

He bounded to his feet. "That's an alarm! They're searching. . . ." *Name the Dark One, and his evil comes down on you.*

Nynaeve stood more slowly, shaking her head uneasily. "No, I don't think so. If they are searching for you, all the bells do is warn you. No, if it's an alarm, it is not for you."

"Then what?" He hurried to the nearest arrowslit and peered out.

Lights darted through the night-cloaked keep like fireflies, lamps and torches dashing here and there. Some went to the outer walls and towers, but most of those that he could see milled through the garden below and the one courtyard he could just glimpse part of. Whatever had caused the alarm was inside the keep. The bells fell silent, unmasking the shouts of men, but he could not make out what they were calling.

*If it isn't for me. . . .* "Egwene," he said suddenly. *If he's still alive, if there's any evil, it's supposed to come to me.*

Nynaeve turned from looking through another arrowslit. "What?"

"Egwene." He crossed the room in quick strides and snatched his sword and scabbard free of the bundle. *Light, it's supposed to hurt me, not her.* "She's in the dungeon with Fain. What if he's loose somehow?"

She caught him at the door, grabbing his arm. She was not as tall as his shoulder, but she held on like iron. "Don't be a worse goat-brained fool than you've already been, Rand al'Thor. Even if this doesn't have anything to do with you, the women are looking for something! Light, man, this is the women's apartments. There will be Aes Sedai out there in the halls, likely as not. Egwene will be all right. She was going to take Mat and Perrin with her. Even if she met trouble, they would look after her."

"What if she couldn't find them, Nynaeve? Egwene would never let that stop her. She would go alone, the same as you, and you know it. Light, I told her Fain is dangerous! Burn me, I told her!" Pulling free, he jerked open the door and dashed out. *Light burn me, it's supposed to hurt me!*

A woman screamed at the sight of him, in a laborer's coarse shirt and jerkin with a sword in his hand. Even invited, men did not go armed in the women's apartments unless the keep was under attack. Women filled the corridor, serving women in the black-and-gold, ladies of the keep in silks and laces, women in embroidered shawls with long fringes, all talking loudly at the same time, all demanding to know what was happening. Crying children clung to skirts everywhere. He plunged through them, dodging where he could, muttering apologies to those he shouldered aside, trying to ignore their startled stares.

One of the women in a shawl turned to go back into her room, and he saw the back of her shawl, saw the gleaming white teardrop in the middle of her back. Suddenly he recognized faces he had seen in the outer courtyard. Aes Sedai, staring at him in alarm, now.

"Who are you? What are you doing here?"

"Is the keep under attack? Answer me, man!"

"He's no soldier. Who is he? What's happening?"

"It's the young southland lord!"

"Someone stop him!"

Fear pushed his lips back, baring his teeth, but he kept moving, and tried to move faster.

Then a woman came out into the hall, face-to-face with him, and he stopped in spite of himself. He recognized that face above the rest; he thought he would remember it if he lived forever. The Amyrlin Seat. Her eyes widened at the sight of him, and she started back. Another Aes Sedai, the tall woman he had seen with the staff, put herself between him and the Amyrlin, shouting something at him that he could not make out over the increasing babble.

*She knows. Light help me, she knows. Moiraine told her.* Snarling, he ran on. *Light, just let me make sure Egwene's safe before they.* . . . He heard shouting behind him, but he did not listen.

There was enough turmoil around him out in the keep. Men running for the courtyards with swords in hand, never looking at him. Over the clamor of alarm bells, he could make out other noises, now. Shouts. Screams. Metal ringing on metal. He had just time to realize they were the sounds of battle—*Fighting? Inside Fal Dara?*—when three Trollocs came dashing around a corner in front of him.

Hairy snouts distorted otherwise human faces, and one of them had ram's horns. They bared teeth, raising scythe-like swords as they sped toward him.

The hallway that had been full of running men a moment before was empty now except for the three Trollocs and himself. Caught by surprise, he unsheathed his sword awkwardly, tried Hummingbird Kisses the Honeyrose. Shaken at finding Trollocs in the heart of Fal Dara keep, he did the form so badly Lan would have stalked off in disgust. A bear-snouted Trolloc evaded it easily, bumping the other two off stride for just an instant.

Suddenly there were a dozen Shienarans rushing past him at the Trollocs, men half dressed in finery for the feast, but swords at the ready. The bear-snouted Trolloc snarled as it died, and its companions ran, pursued by shouting men waving steel. Shouts and screams filled the air from everywhere.

*Egwene!*

Rand turned deeper into the keep, running down halls empty of life, though now and again a dead Trolloc lay on the floor. Or a dead man.

Then he came to a crossing of corridors, and to his left was the tail end of a fight. Six top-knotted men lay bleeding and still, and a seventh was dying. The Myrddraal gave its sword an extra twist as it pulled the blade

free of the man's belly, and the soldier screamed as he dropped his sword
and fell. The Fade moved with viperous grace, the serpent illusion
heightened by the armor of black, overlapping plates that covered its chest.
It turned, and that pale, eyeless face studied Rand. It started toward him,
smiling a bloodless smile, not hurrying. It had no need to hurry for one
man alone.

He felt rooted where he stood; his tongue stuck to the roof of his mouth.
The look of the Eyeless is fear. That was what they said along the Border.
His hands shook as he raised his sword. He never even thought of assuming
the void. *Light, it just killed seven armed soldiers together. Light, what am I
going to do. Light!*

Abruptly the Myrddraal stopped, its smile gone.

"This one is mine, Rand." Rand gave a start as Ingtar stepped up beside
him, dark and stocky in a yellow feastday coat, sword held in both hands.
Ingtar's dark eyes never left the Fade's face; if the Shienaran felt the fear of
that gaze, he gave no sign. "Try yourself on a Trolloc or two," he said
softly, "before you face one of these."

"I was coming down to see if Egwene is safe. She was going to the
dungeon to visit Fain, and—"

"Then go see to her."

Rand swallowed. "We'll take it together, Ingtar."

"You aren't ready for this. Go see to your girl. Go! You want Trollocs to
find her unprotected?"

For a moment Rand hung there, undecided. The Fade had raised its
sword, for Ingtar. A silent snarl twisted Ingtar's mouth, but Rand knew it
was not fear. And Egwene could be alone in the dungeon with Fain, or
worse. Still he felt ashamed as he ran for the stairs that led underground.
He knew a Fade's look could make any man afraid, but Ingtar had conquered the dread. His stomach still felt knotted.

The corridors beneath the keep were silent, and feebly lit by flickering,
far-spaced lamps on the walls. He slowed as he came closer to the dungeons, creeping as silently as he could on his toes. The grate of his boots on
the bare stone seemed to fill his ears. The door to the dungeons stood
cracked open a handbreadth. It should have been closed and bolted.

Staring at the door, he tried to swallow and could not. He opened his
mouth to call out, then shut it again quickly. If Egwene was in there and
in trouble, shouting would only warn whoever was endangering her. Or
whatever. Taking a deep breath, he set himself.

In one motion he pushed the door wide open with the scabbard in his
left hand and threw himself into the dungeon, tucking his shoulder under
to roll through the straw covering the floor and come to his feet, spinning

this way and that too quickly to get a clear picture of the room, looking desperately for anyone who might attack him, looking for Egwene. There was no one there.

His eyes fell on the table, and he stopped dead, breath and even thought freezing. On either side of the still-burning lamp, as if to make a centerpiece, sat the heads of the guards in two pools of blood. Their eyes stared at him, wide with fear, and their mouths gaped in a last scream no one could hear. Rand gagged and doubled over; his stomach heaved again and again as he vomited into the straw. Finally he managed to pull himself erect, scrubbing his mouth with his sleeve; his throat felt scraped raw.

Slowly he became aware of the rest of the room, only half seen and not taken in during his hasty search for an attacker. Bloody lumps of flesh lay scattered through the straw. There was nothing he could recognize as human except the two heads. Some of the pieces looked chewed. *So that's what happened to the rest of their bodies.* He was surprised at the calmness of his thoughts, almost as if he had achieved the void without trying. It was the shock, he knew vaguely.

He did not recognize either of the heads; the guards had been changed since he was there earlier. He was glad for that. Knowing who they were, even Changu, would have made it worse. Blood covered the walls, too, but in scrawled letters, single words and whole sentences splashed on every which way. Some were harsh and angular, in a language he did not know, though he recognized Trolloc script. Others he could read, and wished he could not. Blasphemies and obscenities bad enough to make a stablehand or a merchant's guard go pale.

"Egwene." Calmness vanished. Shoving his scabbard through his belt, he snatched the lamp from the table, hardly noticing when the heads toppled over. "Egwene! Where are you?"

He started toward the inner door, took two steps, and stopped, staring. The words on the door, dark and glistening wetly in the light of his lamp, were plain enough.

WE WILL MEET AGAIN ON TOMAN HEAD.
IT IS NEVER OVER, AL'THOR.

His sword dropped from a hand suddenly numb. Never taking his eyes off the door, he bent to pick it up. Instead he grabbed a handful of straw and began scrubbing furiously at the words on the door. Panting, he scrubbed until it was all one bloody smear, but he could not stop.

"What do you do?"

At the sharp voice behind him, he whirled, stooping to seize his sword.

A woman stood in the outer doorway, back stiff with outrage. Her hair was like pale gold, in a dozen or more braids, but her eyes were dark, and sharp on his face. She looked not much older than he, and pretty in a sulky way, but there was a tightness to her mouth he did not like. Then he saw the shawl she had wrapped tightly around her, with its long, red fringe.

*Aes Sedai. And Light help me, she's Red Ajah.* "I. . . . I was just. . . . It's filthy stuff. Vile."

"Everything must be left exactly as it is for us to examine. Touch nothing." She took a step forward, peering at him, and he took one back. "Yes. Yes, as I thought. One of those with Moiraine. What do you have to do with this?" Her gesture took in the heads on the table and the bloody scrawl on the walls.

For a minute he goggled at her. "Me? Nothing! I came down here to find. . . . Egwene!"

He turned to open the inner door, and the Aes Sedai shouted, "No! You will answer me!"

Suddenly it was all he could do to stand up, to keep holding the lamp and his sword. Icy cold squeezed at him from all sides. His head felt caught in a frozen vise; he could barely breathe for the pressure on his chest.

"Answer me, boy. Tell me your name."

Involuntarily he grunted, trying to answer against the chill that seemed to be pressing his face back into his skull, constricting his chest like frozen iron bands. He clenched his jaws to keep the sound in. Painfully he rolled his eyes to glare at her through a blur of tears. *The Light burn you, Aes Sedai! I won't say a word, the Shadow take you!*

"Answer me, boy! Now!"

Frozen needles pierced his brain with agony, grated into his bones. The void formed inside him before he even realized he had thought of it, but it could not hold out the pain. Dimly he sensed light and warmth somewhere in the distance. It flickered queasily, but the light was warm, and he was cold. Distant beyond knowing, but somehow just within reach. *Light, so cold. I have to reach . . . what? She's killing me. I have to reach it, or she'll kill me.* Desperately he stretched toward the light.

"What is going on here?"

Abruptly the cold and the pressure and the needles vanished. His knees sagged, but he forced them stiff. He would not fall to his knees; he would not give her the satisfaction. The void was gone, too, as suddenly as it had come. *She* was *trying to kill me.* Panting, he raised his head. Moiraine stood in the doorway.

"I asked what is going on here, Liandrin," she said.

"I found this boy here," the Red Aes Sedai replied calmly. "The guards are murdered, and here he is. One of yours. And what are you doing here, Moiraine? The battle is above, not here."

"I could ask the same of you, Liandrin." Moiraine looked around the room with only a slight tightening of her mouth for the charnel. "Why *are* you here?"

Rand turned away from them, awkwardly shoved back the bolts on the inner door and pulled it open. "Egwene came down here," he announced for anyone who cared, and went in, holding his lamp high. His knees kept wanting to give way; he was not sure how he stayed on his feet, only that he had to find Egwene. "Egwene!"

A hollow gurgle and a thrashing sound came from his right, and he thrust the lamp that way. The prisoner in the fancy coat was sagging against the iron grille of his cell, his belt looped around the bars and then around his neck. As Rand looked, he gave one last kick, scraping across the straw-covered floor, and was still, tongue and eyes bulging out of a face gone almost black. His knees almost touched the floor; he could have stood anytime he wanted to.

Shivering, Rand peered into the next cell. The big man with the sunken knuckles huddled in the back of his cell, eyes as wide as they could open. At the sight of Rand, he screamed and twisted around, clawing frantically at the stone wall.

"I won't hurt you," Rand called. The man kept on screaming and digging. His hands were bloody, and his scrabblings streaked across dark, conjealed smears. This was not his first attempt to dig through the stone with his bare hands.

Rand turned away, relieved that his stomach was already empty. But there was nothing he could do for either of them. "Egwene!"

His light finally reached the end of the cells. The door to Fain's cell stood open, and the cell was empty, but it was the two shapes on the stone in front of the cell that made Rand leap forward and drop to his knees between them.

Egwene and Mat lay sprawled bonelessly, unconscious . . . or dead. With a flood of relief he saw their chests rise and fall. There did not seem to be a mark on either of them.

"Egwene? Mat?" Setting the sword down, he shook Egwene gently. "Egwene?" She did not open her eyes. "Moiraine! Egwene's hurt! And Mat!" Mat's breathing sounded labored, and his face was deathly pale. Rand felt almost like crying. *It was supposed to hurt me. I named the Dark One. Me!*

"Do not move them." Moiraine did not sound upset, or even surprised. The chamber was suddenly flooded with light as the two Aes Sedai entered. Each balanced a glowing ball of cool light, floating in the air above her hand.

Liandrin marched straight down the middle of the wide hall, holding her skirts up out of the straw with her free hand, but Moiraine paused to look at the two prisoners before following. "There is nothing to do for the one," she said, "and the other can wait."

Liandrin reached Rand first and began to bend toward Egwene, but Moiraine darted in ahead of her and laid her free hand on Egwene's head. Liandrin straightened with a grimace.

"She is not badly hurt," Moiraine said after a moment. "She was struck here." She traced an area on the side of Egwene's head, covered by her hair; Rand could see nothing different about it. "That is the only injury she has taken. She will be all right."

Rand looked from one Aes Sedai to the other. "What about Mat?" Liandrin arched an eyebrow at him and turned to watch Moiraine with a wry expression.

"Be quiet," Moiraine said. Fingers still lying on the area where she said Egwene had been hit, she closed her eyes. Egwene murmured and stirred, then lay still.

"Is she. . . ?"

"She is sleeping, Rand. She will be well, but she must sleep." Moiraine shifted to Mat, but here she only touched him for a moment before drawing back. "This is more serious," she said softly. She fumbled at Mat's waist, pulling his coat open, and made an angry sound. "The dagger is gone."

"What dagger?" Liandrin asked.

Voices suddenly came from the outer room, men exclaiming in disgust and anger.

"In here," Moiraine called. "Bring two litters. Quickly." Someone in the outer room raised a cry for litters.

"Fain is gone," Rand said.

The two Aes Sedai looked at him. He could read nothing on their faces. Their eyes glittered in the light.

"So I see," Moiraine said in a flat voice.

"I told her not to come. I told her he was dangerous."

"When I came," Liandrin said in a cold voice, "he was destroying the writing in the outer chamber."

He shifted uneasily on his knees. The Aes Sedai's eyes seemed alike, now. Measuring and weighing him, cool and terrible.

"It—it was filth," he said. "Just filth." They still looked at him, not speaking. "You don't think I. . . . Moiraine, you can't think I had anything to do with—with what happened out there." *Light, did I? I named the Dark One.*

She did not answer, and he felt a chill that was not lessened by men rushing in with torches and lamps. Moiraine and Liandrin let their glowing balls wink out. The lamps and torches did not give as much light; shadows sprang up in the depths of the cells. Men with litters hurried to the figures lying on the floor. Ingtar led them. His topknot almost quivered with anger, and he looked eager to find something on which to use his sword.

"So the Darkfriend is gone, too," he growled. "Well, it's the least of what has happened this night."

"The least even here," Moiraine said sharply. She directed the men putting Egwene and Mat on the litters. "The girl is to be taken to her room. She needs a woman to watch in case she wakes in the night. She may be frightened, but more than anything else she needs sleep, now. The boy. . . ." She touched Mat as two men lifted his litter, and pulled her hand back quickly. "Take him to the Amyrlin Seat's chambers. Find the Amyrlin wherever she is, and tell her he is there. Tell her his name is Matrim Cauthon. I will join her as soon as I am able."

"The Amyrlin!" Liandrin exclaimed. "You think to have the Amyrlin as Healer for your—your pet? You are mad, Moiraine."

"The Amyrlin Seat," Moiraine said calmly, "does not share your Red Ajah prejudices, Liandrin. She will Heal a man without need of a special use for him. Go ahead," she told the litter bearers.

Liandrin watched them leave, Moiraine and the men carrying Mat and Egwene, then turned to stare at Rand. He tried to ignore her. He concentrated on scabbarding his sword and brushing off the straw that clung to his shirt and breeches. When he raised his head, though, she was still studying him, her face as blank as ice. Saying nothing, she turned to consider the other men thoughtfully. One held the body of the hanged man up while another worked to unfasten the belt. Ingtar and the others waited respectfully. With a last glance at Rand, she left, head held like a queen.

"A hard woman," Ingtar muttered, then seemed surprised that he had spoken. "What happened here, Rand al'Thor?"

Rand shook his head. "I don't know, except that Fain escaped somehow. And hurt Egwene and Mat doing it. I saw the guardroom"—he shuddered—"but in here. . . . Whatever it was, Ingtar, it scared that fellow bad enough that he hung himself. I think the other one's gone mad from seeing it."

"We are all going mad tonight."

"The Fade . . . you killed it?"

"No!" Ingtar slammed his sword into its sheath; the hilt stuck up above his right shoulder. He seemed angry and ashamed at the same time. "It's out of the keep by now, along with the rest of what we could not kill."

"At least you're alive, Ingtar. That Fade killed seven men!"

"Alive? Is that so important?" Suddenly Ingtar's face was no longer angry, but tired and full of pain. "We had it in our hands. In our hands! And we lost it, Rand. Lost it!" He sounded as if he could not believe what he was saying.

"Lost what?" Rand asked.

"The Horn! The Horn of Valere. It's gone, chest and all."

"But it was in the strongroom."

"The strongroom was looted," Ingtar said wearily. "They did not take much, except for the Horn. What they could stuff in their pockets. I wish they had taken everything else and left that. Ronan is dead, and the watchmen he had guarding the strongroom." His voice became quiet. "When I was a boy, Ronan held Jehaan Tower with twenty men against a thousand Trollocs. He did not go down easily, though. The old man had blood on his dagger. No man can ask more than that." He was silent for a moment. "They came in through the Dog Gate, and left the same way. We put an end to fifty or more, but too many escaped. Trollocs! We've never before had Trollocs inside the keep. Never!"

"How could they get in through the Dog Gate, Ingtar? One man could stop a hundred there. And all the gates were barred." He shifted uneasily, remembering why. "The guards would not have opened it to let anybody in."

"Their throats were cut," Ingtar said. "Both good men, and yet they were butchered like pigs. It was done from inside. Someone killed them, then opened the gate. Someone who could get close to them without suspicion. Someone they knew."

Rand looked at the empty cell where Padan Fain had been. "But that means. . . ."

"Yes. There are Darkfriends inside Fal Dara. Or were. We will soon know if that's the case. Kajin is checking now to see if anyone is missing. Peace! Treachery in Fal Dara keep!" Scowling, he looked around the dungeon, at the men waiting for him. They all had swords, worn over feastday clothes, and some had helmets. "We aren't doing any good here. Out! Everyone!" Rand joined the withdrawal. Ingtar tapped Rand's jerkin. "What is this? Have you decided to become a stableman?"

"It's a long story," Rand said. "Too long to tell here. Maybe some other time." *Maybe never, if I'm lucky. Maybe I can escape in all this confusion. No, I can't. Not until I know Egwene's all right. And Mat. Light, what will happen to him without the dagger?* "I suppose Lord Agelmar's doubled the guard on all the gates."

"Tripled," Ingtar said in tones of satisfaction. "No one will pass those gates, from inside or out. As soon as Lord Agelmar heard what had happened, he ordered that no one was to be allowed to leave the keep without his personal permission."

*As soon as he heard. . . ?* "Ingtar, what about before? What about the earlier order keeping everyone in?"

"Earlier order? What earlier order? Rand, the keep was not closed until Lord Agelmar heard of this. Someone told you wrong."

Rand shook his head slowly. Neither Ragan nor Tema would have made up something like that. And even if the Amyrlin Seat had given the order, Ingtar would have to know of it. *So who? And how?* He glanced sideways at Ingtar, wondering if the Shienaran was lying. *You really are going mad if you suspect Ingtar.*

They were in the dungeon guardroom, now. The severed heads and the pieces of the guards had been removed, though there were still red smears on the table and damp patches in the straw to show where they had been. Two Aes Sedai were there, placid-looking women with brown-fringed shawls, studying the words scrawled on the walls, careless of what their skirts dragged through in the straw. Each had an inkpot in a writing-case hung at her belt and was making notes in a small book with a pen. They never even glanced at the men trooping through.

"Look here, Verin," one of them said, pointing to a section of stone covered with lines of Trolloc script. "This looks interesting."

The other hurried over, picking up reddish stains on her skirt. "Yes, I see. A much better hand than the rest. Not a Trolloc. Very interesting." She began writing in her book, looking up every so often to read the angular letters on the wall.

Rand hurried out. Even if they had not been Aes Sedai, he would not have wanted to remain in the same room with anyone who thought reading Trolloc script written in human blood was "interesting."

Ingtar and his men stalked on ahead, intent on their duties. Rand dawdled, wondering where he could go now. Getting back into the women's apartments would not be easy without Egwene to help. *Light, let her be all right. Moiraine* said *she'd be all right.*

Lan found him before he reached the first stairs leading up. "You can go back to your room, if you want, sheepherder. Moiraine had your things fetched from Egwene's room and taken to yours."

"How did she know. . . ?"

"Moiraine knows a great many things, sheepherder. You should understand that by now. You had better watch yourself. The women are all talking about you running through the halls, waving a sword. Staring down the Amyrlin, so they say."

"Light! I am sorry they're angry, Lan, but I *was* invited in. And when I heard the alarm . . . burn me, Egwene was down here!"

Lan pursed his lips thoughtfully; it was the only expression on his face. "Oh, they're not angry, exactly. Though most of them think you need a strong hand to settle you down some. Fascinated is more like it. Even the Lady Amalisa can't stop asking questions about you. Some of them are starting to believe the servants' tales. They think you're a prince in disguise, sheepherder. Not a bad thing. There is an old saying here in the Borderlands: 'Better to have one woman on your side than ten men.' The way they are talking among themselves, they're trying to decide whose daughter is strong enough to handle you. If you don't watch your step, sheepherder, you will find yourself married into a Shienaran House before you realize what has happened." Suddenly he burst out laughing; it looked odd, like a rock laughing. "Running through the halls of the women's apartments in the middle of the night, wearing a laborer's jerkin and waving a sword. If they don't have you flogged, at the very least they'll talk about you for years. They have never seen a male as peculiar as you. Whatever wife they chose for you, she'd probably have you the head of your own House in ten years, and have you thinking you had done it yourself, besides. It is too bad you have to leave."

Rand had been gaping at the Warder, but now he growled, "I have been trying. The gates are guarded, and no one can leave. I tried while it was still daylight. I couldn't even take Red out of the stable."

"No matter, now. Moiraine sent me to tell you. You can leave anytime you want to. Even right now. Moiraine had Agelmar exempt you from the order."

"Why now, and not earlier? Why couldn't I leave before? Was she the one who had the gates barred then? Ingtar said he knew nothing about any order to keep people in before tonight."

Rand thought the Warder looked troubled, but all he said was, "When someone gives you a horse, sheepherder, don't complain that it isn't as fast as you'd like."

"What about Egwene? And Mat? Are they really all right? I can't leave until I know they're all right."

"The girl is fine. She'll wake in the morning, and probably not even remember what happened. Blows to the head are like that."

"What about Mat?"

"The choice is up to you, sheepherder. You can leave now, or tomorrow, or next week. It's up to you." He walked away, leaving Rand standing there in the corridor deep under Fal Dara keep.

# CHAPTER 7

## Blood Calls Blood

As the litter carrying Mat left the Amyrlin Seat's chambers, Moiraine carefully rewrapped the *angreal*—a small, age-darkened ivory carving of a woman in flowing robes—in a square of silk and put it back into her pouch. Working together with other Aes Sedai, merging their abilities, channeling the flow of the One Power to a single task, was tiring work under the best conditions, even with the aid of an *angreal*, and working through the night without sleep was not the best conditions. And the work they had done on the boy had not been easy.

Leane directed the litter bearers out with sharp gestures and a few crisp words. The two men kept ducking their heads, nervous at being around so many Aes Sedai at once, and one of them the Amyrlin herself, never mind that the Aes Sedai had been using the Power. They had waited in the corridor, squatting against the wall while the work was done, and they were anxious to be gone from the women's apartments. Mat lay with his eyes closed and his face pale, but his chest rose and fell in the even rhythm of a deep sleep.

*How will this affect matters?* Moiraine wondered. *He is not necessary with the Horn gone, and yet....*

The door closed behind Leane and the litter bearers, and the Amyrlin drew an unsteady breath. "A nasty business that. Nasty." Her face was smooth, but she rubbed her hands together as if she wanted to wash them.

"But quite interesting," Verin said. She had been the fourth Aes Sedai the Amyrlin had chosen for the work. "It is too bad we do not have the dagger so the Healing could be complete. For all we did tonight, he will not live long. Months, perhaps, at best." The three Aes Sedai were alone in the Amyrlin's chambers. Beyond the arrowslits dawn pearled
the sky.

"But he will have those months, now," Moiraine said sharply. "And if it can be retrieved, the link can still be broken." *If it can be retrieved. Yes, of course.*

"It can still be broken," Verin agreed. She was a plump, square-faced woman, and even with the Aes Sedai gift of agelessness, there was a touch of gray in her brown hair. That was her only sign of age, but for an Aes Sedai it meant she was very old indeed. Her voice held steady, though, matching her smooth cheeks. "He has been linked to the dagger a long time, however, as a thing like that must be reckoned. And he will be linked longer yet, whether it is found or not. He may already be changed beyond the reach of full Healing, even if no longer enough to contaminate others. Such a small thing, that dagger," she mused, "but it will corrupt whoever carries it long enough. He who carries it will in turn corrupt those who come in contact with him, and they will corrupt still others, and the hatred and suspicion that destroyed Shadar Logoth, every man and woman's hand turned against every other, will be loose in the world again. I wonder how many people it can taint in, say, a year. It should be possible to calculate a reasonable approximation."

Moiraine gave the Brown sister a wry look. *Another danger confronts us, and she sounds as if it is a puzzle in a book. Light, the Browns truly are not aware of the world at all.* "Then we must find the dagger, Sister. Agelmar is sending men to hunt those who took the Horn and slew his oathmen, the same who took the dagger. If one is found, the other will be."

Verin nodded, but frowned at the same time. "Yet, even if it is found, who can return it safely? Whoever touches it risks the taint if they handle it long. Perhaps in a chest, well wrapped and padded, but it would still be dangerous to those nearby for any great time. Without the dagger itself to study, we cannot be sure how much it must be shielded. But you saw it and more, Moiraine. You dealt with it, enough for that young man to survive carrying it and to stop him infecting others. You must have a good idea of how strong its influence is."

"There is one," Moiraine said, "who can retrieve the dagger without being harmed by it. One whom we have shielded and buffered against that taint as much as anyone can be. Mat Cauthon."

The Amyrlin nodded. "Yes, of course. He can do it. If he lives long enough. The Light only knows how far it will be carried before Agelmar's men find it. If they do find it. And if the boy dies first . . . well, if the dagger is loose that long, we have another worry." She rubbed her eyes tiredly. "I think we must find this Padan Fain, too. Why is this Darkfriend important enough for them to risk what they did to rescue him? Much easier for them just to steal the Horn. Still risky as a winter gale in the Sea of Storms, coming into the very keep like that, but they compounded their risk to free this Darkfriend. If the Lurks think he is that important"—she paused, and Moiraine knew she was wondering if it truly was still only the Myrddraal giving commands—"then so must we."

"He must be found," Moiraine agreed, hoping that none of the urgency she felt showed, "but it is likely he will be found with the Horn."

"As you say, Daughter." The Amyrlin pressed fingers to her lips to stifle a yawn. "And now, Verin, if you will excuse me, I will just say a few words to Moiraine and then sleep a little. I suppose Agelmar will insist on feasting tonight since last night was spoiled. Your help was invaluable, Daughter. Please remember, say nothing of the nature of the boy's hurt to anyone. There are some of your sisters who would see the Shadow in him instead of a thing men made on their own."

There was no need to name the Red Ajah. And perhaps, Moiraine thought, the Reds were no longer the only ones of whom it was necessary to be wary.

"I will say nothing, of course, Mother." Verin bowed, but made no move toward the door. "I thought you might wish to see this, Mother." She pulled a small notebook, bound in soft, brown leather, from her belt. "What was written on the walls in the dungeon. There were few problems with translation. Most was the usual—blasphemy and boasting; Trollocs seem to know little else—but there was one part done in a better hand. An educated Darkfriend, or perhaps a Myrddraal. It could be only taunting, yet it has the form of poetry, or song, and the sound of prophecy. We know little of prophecies from the Shadow, Mother."

The Amyrlin hesitated only a moment before nodding. Prophecies from the Shadow, dark prophecies, had an unfortunate way of being fulfilled as well as prophecies from the Light. "Read it to me."

Verin ruffled through the pages, then cleared her throat and began in a calm, level voice.

"Daughter of the Night, she walks again.
The ancient war, she yet fights.
Her new lover she seeks, who shall serve her and die, yet serve still.
Who shall stand against her coming?
The Shining Walls shall kneel.
Blood feeds blood.
Blood calls blood.
Blood is, and blood was, and blood shall ever be.

The man who channels stands alone.
He gives his friends for sacrifice.
Two roads before him, one to death beyond dying, one to life eternal.
Which will he choose? Which will he choose?
What hand shelters? What hand slays?
Blood feeds blood.
Blood calls blood.
Blood is, and blood was, and blood shall ever be.

Luc came to the Mountains of Dhoom.
Isam waited in the high passes.
The hunt is now begun. The Shadow's hounds now course, and kill.
One did live, and one did die, but both are.
The Time of Change has come.
Blood feeds blood.
Blood calls blood.
Blood is, and blood was, and blood shall ever be.

The Watchers wait on Toman's Head.
The seed of the Hammer burns the ancient tree.
Death shall sow, and summer burn, before the Great Lord comes.
Death shall reap, and bodies fail, before the Great Lord comes.
Again the seed slays ancient wrong, before the Great Lord comes.
Now the Great Lord comes.
Now the Great Lord comes.
Blood feeds blood.
Blood calls blood.
Blood is, and blood was, and blood shall ever be.
Now the Great Lord comes."

There was a long silence when she finished.

Finally the Amyrlin said, "Who else has seen this, Daughter? Who knows of it?"

"Only Serafelle, Mother. As soon as we had copied it down, I had men scrub the walls. They didn't question; they were eager to be rid of it."

The Amyrlin nodded. "Good. Too many in the Borderlands can puzzle out Trolloc script. No need to give them something else to worry over. They have enough."

"What do you make of it?" Moiraine asked Verin in a careful voice. "Is it prophecy, do you think?"

Verin tilted her head, peering at her notes in thought. "Possibly. It has the form of some of the few dark prophecies we know. And parts of it are clear enough. It could still be only a taunt, though." She rested a finger on one line. "'Daughter of the Night, she walks again.' That can only mean Lanfear is loose again. Or someone wants us to think she is."

"That would be something to worry us, Daughter," the Amyrlin Seat said, "if it were true. But the Forsaken are still bound." She glanced at Moiraine, looking troubled for an instant before she schooled her features. "Even if the seals *are* weakening, the Forsaken are still bound."

Lanfear. In the Old Tongue, Daughter of the Night. Nowhere was her real name recorded, but that was the name she had taken for herself, unlike most of the Forsaken, who had been named by those they betrayed. Some said she had really been the most powerful of the Forsaken, next to Ishamael, the Betrayer of Hope, but had kept her powers hidden. Too little was left from that time for any scholar to say for certain.

"With all the false Dragons that are appearing, it is not surprising someone would try to bring Lanfear into it." Moiraine's voice was as unruffled as her face, but inside herself she roiled. Only one thing for certain was known of Lanfear beside the name: before she went over to the Shadow, before Lews Therin Telamon met Ilyena, Lanfear had been his lover. *A complication we do not need.*

The Amyrlin Seat frowned as if she had had the same thought, but Verin nodded as if it were all just words. "Other names are clear, too, Mother. Lord Luc, of course, was brother to Tigraine, then the Daughter-Heir of Andor, and he vanished in the Blight. Who Isam is, or what he has to do with Luc, I do not know, however."

"We will find out what we need to know in time," Moiraine said smoothly. "There is no proof as yet that this is prophecy." She knew the name. Isam had been the son of Breyan, wife of Lain Mandragoran, whose attempt to seize the throne of Malkier for her husband had brought the Trolloc hordes crashing down. Breyan and her infant son had both vanished when the Trollocs overran Malkier. And Isam had been blood kin to Lan.

*Or is blood kin? I must keep this from him, until I know how he will react. Until we are away from the Blight. If he thought Isam were alive. . . .*

"'The Watchers wait on Toman Head,'" Verin went on. "There are a few who still cling to the old belief that the armies Artur Hawkwing sent across the Aryth Ocean will return one day, though after all this time. . . ." She gave a disdainful sniff. "The Do Miere A'vron, the Watchers Over the Waves, still have a . . . community is the best word, I suppose . . . on Toman Head, at Falme. And one of the old names for Artur Hawkwing was Hammer of the Light."

"Are you suggesting, Daughter," the Amyrlin Seat said, "that Artur Hawkwing's armies, or rather their descendants, might actually return after a thousand years?"

"There are rumors of war on Almoth Plain and Toman Head," Moiraine said slowly. "And Hawkwing sent two of his sons, as well as armies. If they did survive in whatever lands they found, there could well be many descendants of Hawkwing. Or none."

The Amyrlin gave Moiraine a guarded look, obviously wishing they were alone so she could demand to know what Moiraine was up to. Moiraine made a soothing gesture, and her old friend grimaced at her.

Verin, with her nose still buried in her notes, noticed none of it. "I don't know, Mother. I doubt it, though. We know nothing at all of those lands Artur Hawkwing set out to conquer. It's too bad the Sea Folk refuse to cross the Aryth Ocean. They say the Islands of the Dead lie on the other side. I wish I knew what they meant by that, but that accursed Sea Folk closemouthedness. . . ." She sighed, still not raising her head. "All we have is one reference to 'lands under the Shadow, beyond the setting sun, beyond the Aryth Ocean, where the Armies of Night reign.' Nothing there to tell us if the armies Hawkwing sent were enough by themselves to defeat these 'Armies of the Night,' or even to survive Hawkwing's death. Once the War of the Hundred Years started, everyone was too intent on carving out their own part of Hawkwing's empire to spare a thought for his armies across the sea. It seems to me, Mother, that if their descendants still lived, and if they ever intended to return, they would not have waited so long."

"Then you believe it is not prophecy, Daughter?"

"Now, 'the ancient tree,'" Verin said, immersed in her own thoughts. "There have always been rumors—no more than that—that while the nation of Almoth still lived, they had a branch of *Avendesora,* perhaps even a living sapling. And the banner of Almoth was 'blue for the sky above, black for the earth below, with the spreading Tree of Life to join them.' Of course, Taraboners call themselves the Tree of Man, and claim to be descended from rulers and nobles in the Age of Legends. And Domani claim descent from those who made the Tree of Life in the Age of Legends. There are other possibilities, but you will note, Mother, that at least three center around Almoth Plain and Toman Head."

The Amyrlin's voice became deceptively gentle. "Will you make up your mind, Daughter? If Artur Hawkwing's seed is *not* returning, then this is not prophecy and it doesn't matter a rotted fish head what ancient tree is meant."

"I can only give you what I know, Mother," Verin said, looking up from her notes, "and leave the decision in your hands. I believe the last of Artur Hawkwing's foreign armies died long ago, but because I believe it does not make it so. The Time of Change, of course, refers to the end of an Age, and the Great Lord—"

The Amyrlin slapped the tabletop like a thunderclap. "I know very well who the Great Lord is, Daughter. I think you had better go now." She took a deep breath, and took hold of herself visibly. "Go, Verin. I do not want to become angry with you. I do not want to forget who it was had the cooks leave sweetcakes out at night when I was a novice."

"Mother," Moiraine said, "there is nothing in this to suggest prophecy. Anyone with a little wit and a little knowledge could put together as much, and no one has ever said Myrddraal do not have a sly wit."

"And of course," Verin said calmly, "the man who channels must be one of the three young men traveling with you, Moiraine."

Moiraine stared in shock. *Not aware of the world? I* am *a fool.* Before she realized what she was doing, she had reached out to the pulsing glow she always felt there waiting, to the True Source. The One Power surged along her veins, charging her with energy, muting the sheen of Power from the Amyrlin Seat as she did the same. Moiraine had never before even thought of wielding the Power against another Aes Sedai. *We live in perilous times, and the world hangs in the balance, and what must be done, must be done. It must. Oh, Verin, why did you have to put your nose in where it does not belong?*

Verin closed her book and slipped it back behind her belt, then looked from one woman to the other. She could not but be aware of the nimbus surrounding each of them, the light that came from touching the True Source. Only someone trained in channeling herself could see the glow, but there was no chance of any Aes Sedai missing it in another woman.

A hint of satisfaction settled on Verin's face, but no sign that she realized she had hurled a lightning bolt. She only looked as if she had found another piece that fit in a puzzle. "Yes, I thought it must be so. Moiraine could not do this alone, and who better to help than her girlhood friend who used to sneak down with her to snitch sweetcakes." She blinked. "Forgive me, Mother. I should not have said that."

"Verin, Verin." The Amyrlin shook her head wonderingly. "You accuse your sister—and me?—of. . . . I won't even say it. And you are worried that you've spoken too familiarly to the Amyrlin Seat? You bore a hole in the boat and worry that it's raining. Think what you are suggesting, Daughter."

*It is too late for that, Siuan,* Moiraine thought. *If we had not panicked and reached for the Source, perhaps then. . . . But she is sure, now.* "Why are you telling us this, Verin?" she said aloud. "If you believe what you say, you should be telling it to the other sisters, to the Reds in particular."

Verin's eyes widened in surprise. "Yes. Yes, I suppose I should. I hadn't thought of that. But then, if I did, you would be stilled, Moiraine, and you, Mother, and the man gentled. No one has ever recorded the progression in a man who wields the Power. When does the madness come, exactly, and how does it take him? How quickly does it grow? Can he still function with his body rotting around him? For how long? Unless he is gentled, what will happen to the young man, whichever he is, will happen whether or not I am there to put down the answers. If he is watched and guided, we should be able to keep some record with reasonable safety, for a time, at least. And, too, there is *The Karaethon Cycle.*" She calmly returned their startled looks. "I assume, Mother, that he *is* the Dragon Reborn? I cannot believe you would do this—leave walking free a man who can channel—unless he was the Dragon."

*She thinks only of the knowledge,* Moiraine thought wonderingly. *The culmination of the direst prophecy the world knows, perhaps the end of the world, and she cares only about the knowledge. But she is still dangerous, for that.*

"Who else knows of this?" The Amyrlin's voice was faint, but still sharp. "Serafelle, I suppose. Who else, Verin?"

"No one, Mother. Serafelle is not really interested in anything that someone hasn't already set down in a book, preferably as long ago as possible. She thinks there are enough old books and manuscripts and fragments scattered about, lost or forgotten, to equal ten times what we have gathered in Tar Valon. She feels certain there is enough of the old knowledge still there to be found for—"

"Enough, Sister," Moiraine said. She loosed her hold on the True Source, and after a moment felt the Amyrlin do the same. It was always a loss to feel the Power draining away, like blood and life pouring from an open wound. A part of her wanted to hold on, but unlike some of her sisters, she made it a point of self-discipline not to grow too fond of the feeling. "Sit down, Verin, and tell us what you know and how you found it out. Leave out nothing."

As Verin took a chair—with a look to the Amyrlin for permission to sit in her presence—Moiraine watched her sadly.

"It is unlikely," Verin began, "that anyone who hasn't studied the old records thoroughly would notice anything except that you were behaving oddly. Forgive me, Mother. It was nearly twenty years ago, with Tar Valon besieged, that I had my first clue, and that was only. . . .

*Light help me, Verin, how I loved you for those sweetcakes, and for your bosom to weep on. But I will do what I must do. I will. I must.*


Perrin peered around the corner at the retreating back of the Aes Sedai. She smelled of lavender soap, though most would not have scented it even close up. As soon as she turned out of sight, he hurried for the infirmary door. He had already tried to see Mat once, and that Aes Sedai—Leane, he had heard somebody call her—had nearly snapped his head off without even looking around to see who he was. He felt uneasy around Aes Sedai, especially if they started looking at his eyes.

Pausing at the door to listen—he could hear no footsteps down the corridor either way, and nothing on the other side of the door—he went in and closed it softly behind him.

The infirmary was a long room with white walls, and the entrances to archers' balconies at either end let in lots of light. Mat was in one of the narrow beds that lined the walls. After last night, Perrin had expected most of the beds to have men in them, but in a moment he realized the keep was full of Aes Sedai. The only thing an Aes Sedai could not cure by Healing was death. To him, the room smelled of sickness anyway.

Perrin grimaced when he thought of that. Mat lay still, eyes closed, hands unmoving atop his blankets. He looked exhausted. Not sick really, but as if he had worked three days in the fields and only now laid down to rest. He smelled . . . wrong, though. It was nothing Perrin could put a name to. Just wrong.

Perrin sat down carefully on the bed next to Mat's. He always did things carefully. He was bigger than most people, and had been bigger than the other boys as long as he could remember. He had had to be careful so he would not hurt someone accidentally, or break things. Now it was second nature to him. He liked to think things through, too, and sometimes talk them over with somebody. *With Rand thinking he's a lord, I can't talk to him, and Mat certainly isn't going to have much to say.*

He had gone into one of the gardens the night before, to think things through. The memory still made him a little ashamed. If he had not gone, he would have been in his room to go with Egwene and Mat, and maybe he could have kept them from being hurt. More likely, he knew, he would be in one of these beds, like Mat, or dead, but that did not change the way he felt. Still, he had gone to the garden, and it was nothing to do with the Trolloc attack that was worrying him now.

Serving women had found him sitting there in the dark, and one of the Lady Amalisa's attendants, the Lady Timora. As soon as they came upon him, Timora sent one of the others running, and he had heard her say, "Find Liandrin Sedai! Quickly!"

They had stood there watching him as if they had thought he might vanish in a puff of smoke like a gleeman. That had been when the first alarm bell rang, and everybody in the keep started running.

"Liandrin," he muttered now. "Red Ajah. About all they do is hunt for men who channel. You don't think she believes I'm one of those, do you?" Mat did not answer, of course. Perrin rubbed his nose ruefully. "Now I'm talking to myself. I don't need that on top of everything else."

Mat's eyelids fluttered. "Who. . . ? Perrin? What happened?" His eyes did not open all the way, and his voice sounded as if he were still mostly asleep.

"Don't you remember, Mat?"

"Remember?" Mat sleepily raised a hand toward his face, then let it fall again with a sigh. His eyes began to drift shut. "Remember Egwene. Asked me . . . go down . . . see Fain." He laughed, and it turned into a yawn. "She didn't ask. Told me. . . . Don't know what happened after. . . ." He smacked his lips, and resumed the deep, even breathing of sleep.

Perrin leaped to his feet as his ears caught the sound of approaching footsteps, but there was nowhere to go. He was still standing there beside Mat's bed when the door opened and Leane came in. She stopped, put her fists on her hips, and looked him slowly up and down. She was nearly as tall as he was.

"Now you," she said, in tones quiet yet brisk, "are almost a pretty enough boy to make me wish I was a Green. Almost. But if you've disturbed my patient . . . well, I dealt with brothers almost as big as you before I went to the Tower, so you needn't think those shoulders will help you any."

Perrin cleared his throat. Half the time he did not understand what women meant when they said things. *Not like Rand. He always knows what to say to the girls.* He realized he was scowling and wiped it away. He did not want to think about Rand, but he certainly did not want to upset an

Aes Sedai, especially one who was beginning to tap her foot impatiently. "Ah . . . I didn't disturb him. He's still sleeping. See?"

"So he is. A good thing for you. Now, what are you doing in here? I remember chasing you out once; you needn't think I don't."

"I only wanted to know how he is."

She hesitated. "He is sleeping is how he is. And in a few hours, he will get out of that bed, and you'll think there was never anything wrong with him."

The pause made his hackles rise. She was lying, somehow. Aes Sedai never lied, but they did not always tell the truth, either. He was not certain what was going on—Liandrin looking for him, Leane lying to him—but he thought it was time he got away from Aes Sedai. There was nothing he could do for Mat.

"Thank you," he said. "I'd better let him sleep, then. Excuse me."

He tried to slide around her to the door, but suddenly her hands shot out and grabbed his face, tilting it down so she could peer into his eyes. Something seemed to pass through him, a warm ripple that started at the top of his head and went to his feet, then came back again. He pulled his head out of her hands.

"You're as healthy as a young wild animal," she said, pursing her lips. "But if you were born with those eyes, I am a Whitecloak."

"They're the only eyes I ever had," he growled. He felt a little abashed, speaking an Aes Sedai in that tone, but he was as surprised as she when he took her gently by the arms and lifted her to one side, setting her down again out of his way. As they stared at each other, he wondered if his eyes were as wide with shock as hers. "Excuse me," he said again, and all but ran.

*My eyes. My Light-cursed eyes!* The morning sunlight caught his eyes, and they glinted like burnished gold.

Rand twisted on his bed, trying to find a comfortable position on the thin mattress. Sunlight streamed through the arrowslits, painting the bare stone walls. He had not slept during the remainder of the night, and tired as he was, he was sure he could not sleep now. The leather jerkin lay on the floor between his bed and the wall, but aside from that he was fully dressed, even to his new boots. His sword stood propped beside the bed, and his bow and quiver rested in a corner across the bundled cloaks.

He could not rid himself of the feeling that he should take the chance Moiraine had given him and leave immediately. The urge had been with him all night. Three times he had risen to go. Twice he had gone as far as opening the door. The halls had been empty except for a few servants doing late chores; the way had been clear. But he had to know.

Perrin came in, head down and yawning, and Rand sat up. "How is Egwene? And Mat?"

"She's asleep, so they tell me. They wouldn't let me into the women's apartments to see her. Mat is—" Suddenly Perrin scowled at the floor. "If you're so interested, why haven't you gone to see him yourself? I thought you were not interested in us anymore. You said you weren't." He pulled open his door of the wardrobe and began rummaging for a clean shirt.

"I did go to the infirmary, Perrin. There was an Aes Sedai there, that tall one who's always with the Amyrlin Seat. She said Mat was asleep, and I was in the way, and I could come back some other time. She sounded like Master Thane ordering the men at the mill. You know how Master Thane is, all full of snap and do it right the first time, and do it right now."

Perrin did not answer. He just shucked off his coat and pulled his shirt off over his head.

Rand studied his friend's back for a moment, then dug up a laugh. "You want to hear something? You know what she said to me? The Aes Sedai in the infirmary, I mean. You saw how tall she is. As tall as most men. A hand taller, and she could almost look me in the eyes. Well, she stared me up and down, and then she muttered, 'Tall, aren't you? Where were you when I was sixteen? Or even thirty?' And then she laughed, as if it was all a joke. What do you think of that?"

Perrin finished tugging on a clean shirt and gave him a sidelong look. With his burly shoulders and thick curls, he made Rand think of a hurt bear. A bear that did not understand why had he been hurt.

"Perrin, I'm—"

"If you want to make jokes with Aes Sedai," Perrin broke in, "that's up to you. My Lord." He began stuffing his shirttail into his breeches. "I don't spend much time being—witty; is that the word?—witty with Aes Sedai. But then, I'm only a clumsy blacksmith, and I might be in some-body's way. My Lord." Snatching his coat from the floor, he started for the door.

"Burn me, Perrin, I'm sorry. I was afraid, and I thought I was in trou-ble—maybe I was; maybe I still am, I don't know—and I didn't want you and Mat to be in it with me. Light, all the women were looking for me last night. I think that's part of the trouble I'm in. I think so. And Lian-drin. . . . She. . . ." He threw up his hands. "Perrin, believe me, you don't want any part of this."

Perrin had stopped, but he stood facing the door and only turned his head enough for Rand to see one golden eye. "Looking for you? Maybe they were looking for all of us."

"No, they were looking for me. I wish they hadn't been, but I know better."

Perrin shook his head. "Liandrin wanted me, anyway, I know. I heard."

Rand frowned. "Why would she. . . ? It doesn't change anything. Look, I opened my mouth and said what I shouldn't. I did not mean it, Perrin. Now, please, would you tell me about Mat?"

"He's asleep. Leane—that's the Aes Sedai—said he would be on his feet in a few hours." He shrugged uncomfortably. "I think she was lying. I know Aes Sedai never lie, not so you can catch them, but she was lying, or keeping something back." He paused, looking at Rand sideways. "You didn't mean all that? We will leave here together? You, and me, and Mat?"

"I can't, Perrin. I can't tell you why, but I really do have to go by myse— Perrin, wait!"

The door slammed behind his friend.

Rand fell back on the bed. "I can't tell you," he muttered. He pounded his fist on the side of the bed. "I can't." *But you can go now,* a voice said in the back of his head. *Egwene's going to be all right, and Mat will be up and around in an hour or two. You can go now. Before Moiraine changes her mind.*

He started to sit up when a pounding on the door made him leap to his feet. If it was Perrin come back, he would not knock. The pounding came again.

"Who is it?"

Lan strode in, pushing the door to behind him with his boot heel. As usual, he wore his sword over a plain coat of green that was nearly invisible in the woods. This time, though, he had a wide, golden cord tied high around his left arm, the fringed ends hanging almost to his elbow. On the knot was pinned a golden crane in flight, the symbol of Malkier.

"The Amyrlin Seat wants you, sheepherder. You can't go like that. Out of that shirt and brush your hair. You look like a haystack." He jerked open the wardrobe and began pawing through the clothes Rand meant to leave behind.

Rand stood stiff where he was; he felt as though he had been hit in the head with a hammer. He had expected it, of course, in a way, but he had been sure he would be gone before the summons came. *She knows. Light, I'm sure of it.* "What do you mean, she wants me? I'm leaving, Lan. You were right. I am going to the stable right now, get my horse, and leave."

"You should have done that last night." The Warder tossed a white silk shirt onto the bed. "No one refuses an audience with the Amyrlin Seat, sheepherder. Not the Lord Captain Commander of the Whitecloaks himself. Pedron Niall might spend the trip planning how to kill her, if he could do it and get away, but he would come." He turned around with one of the high-collared coats in his hands and held it up. "This one will do." Tangled, long-thorned briars climbed each red sleeve in a thick, gold-embroidered line, and ran around each cuff. Golden herons stood on the collars, which were edged with gold. "The color is right, too." He seemed to be amused at something, or satisfied. "Come on, sheepherder. Change your shirt. Move."

Reluctantly Rand pulled the coarse wool workman's shirt over his head. "I'll feel a fool," he muttered. "A silk shirt! I never wore a silk shirt in my life. And I never wore so fancy a coat, either, even on a feastday." *Light, if Perrin sees me in that. . . . Burn me, after all that fool talk about being a lord, if he sees me in that, he'll never listen to reason.*

"You can't go before the Amyrlin Seat dressed like a groom fresh out of the stables, sheepherder. Let me see your boots. They'll do. Well, get on with it, get on with it. You don't keep the Amyrlin waiting. Wear your sword."

"My sword!" The silk shirt over his head muffled Rand's yelp. He yanked it the rest of the way on. "In the women's apartments? Lan, if I go for an audience with the Amyrlin Seat—the Amyrlin Seat!—wearing a sword, she'll—"

"Do nothing," Lan cut him off dryly. "If the Amyrlin is afraid of you—and it's smarter for you to think she isn't, because I don't know anything that could frighten that woman—it won't be for a sword. Now remember, you kneel when you go before her. One knee only, mind," he added sharply. "You're not some merchant caught giving short weight. Maybe you had better practice it."

"I know how, I think. I saw how the Queen's Guards knelt to Queen Morgase."

The ghost of a smile touched the Warder's lips. "Yes, you do it just as they did. That will give them something to think about."

Rand frowned. "Why are you telling me this, Lan? You're a Warder. You're acting as if you are on my side."

"I am on your side, sheepherder. A little. Enough to help you a bit." The Warder's face was stone, and sympathetic words sounded strange in that rough voice. "What training you've had, I gave you, and I'll not have you groveling and sniveling. The Wheel weaves us all into the Pattern as it wills. You have less freedom about it than most, but by the Light, you can still face it on your feet. You remember who the Amyrlin Seat is, sheepherder, and you show her proper respect, but you do what I tell you, and you look her in the eye. Well, don't stand there gaping. Tuck in your shirt."

Rand shut his mouth and tucked in his shirt. *Remember who she is? Burn me, what I wouldn't give to forget who she is!*

Lan kept up a running flow of instructions while Rand shrugged into the red coat and buckled on his sword. What to say and to whom, and what not to say. What to do, and what not. How to move, even. He was not sure he could remember it all—most of it sounded odd, and easy to forget—and he was sure whatever he forgot would be just the thing to make the Aes Sedai angry with him. *If they aren't already. If Moiraine told the Amyrlin Seat, who else did she tell?*

"Lan, why can't I just leave the way I planned? By the time she knew I was not coming, I'd be a league outside the walls and galloping."

"And she'd have trackers after you before you had gone two. What the Amyrlin wants, sheepherder, she gets." He adjusted Rand's sword belt so the heavy buckle was centered. "What I do is the best I can for you. Believe it."

"But why all this? What does it mean? Why do I put my hand over my heart if the Amyrlin Seat stands up? Why refuse anything but water—not that I want to eat a meal with her—then dribble some on the floor and say 'The land thirsts'? And if she asks how old I am, why tell her how long it is since I was given the sword? I don't understand half of what you've told me."

"Three drops, sheepherder, don't pour it. You *sprinkle* three drops only. You can understand later so long as you remember now. Think of it as upholding custom. The Amyrlin will do with you as she must. If you believe you can avoid it, then you believe you can fly to the moon like Lenn. You can't escape, but maybe you can hold your own for a while, and perhaps you can keep your pride, at least. The Light burn me, I am probably wasting my time, but I've nothing better to do. Hold still." From his pocket the Warder produced a long length of wide, fringed golden cord and tied it around Rand's left arm in a complicated knot. On the knot he fastened a red-enameled pin, an eagle with its wings spread. "I had that made to give you, and now is as good a time as any. That will make them think." There was no doubt about it, now. The Warder was smiling.

Rand looked down at the pin worriedly. *Caldazar.* The Red Eagle of Manetheren. "A thorn to the Dark One's foot," he murmured, "and a bramble to his hand." He looked at the Warder. "Manetheren's long dead and forgotten, Lan. It's just a name in a book, now. There is only the Two Rivers. Whatever else I am, I'm a shepherd and a farmer. That's all."

"Well, the sword that could not be broken was shattered in the end, sheepherder, but it fought the Shadow to the last. There is one rule, above all others, for being a man. Whatever comes, face it on your feet. Now, are you ready? The Amyrlin Seat waits."

With a cold knot in the pit of his belly, Rand followed the Warder into the hall.

# CHAPTER 8

## The Dragon Reborn

Rand walked stiff-legged and nervous at first, beside the Warder. *Face it on your feet.* It was easy for Lan to say. He had not been summoned by the Amyrlin Seat. He was not wondering if he would be gentled before the day was done, or worse. Rand felt as if he had something caught in his throat; he could not swallow, and he wanted to, badly.

The corridors bustled with people, servants going about their morning chores, warriors wearing swords over lounging robes. A few young boys carrying small practice swords stayed near their elders, imitating the way they walked. No sign remained of the fighting, but an air of alertness clung even to the children. Grown men looked like cats waiting for a pack of rats.

Ingtar gave Rand and Lan a peculiar look, almost troubled, opening his mouth, then saying nothing as they passed him. Kajin, tall and lean and sallow, pumped his fists over his head and shouted, *"Tai'shar Malkier! Tai'shar Manetheren!"* True blood of Malkier. True blood of Manetheren.

Rand jumped. *Light, why did he say that? Don't be a fool,* he told himself. *They all know about Manetheren here. They know every old story, if it has fighting in it. Burn me, I have to take a rein on myself.*

Lan raised his fists in reply. *"Tai'shar Shienar!"*

If he made a run for it, could he lose himself in the crowd long enough to reach his horse? *If she sends trackers after me. . . .* With every step he grew more tense.

As they approached the women's apartments, Lan suddenly snapped, "Cat Crosses the Courtyard!"

Startled, Rand instinctively assumed the walking stance as he had been taught, back straight but every muscle loose, as if he hung from a wire at the top of his head. It was a relaxed, almost arrogant, saunter. Relaxed on the outside; he certainly did not feel it inside. He had no time to wonder what he was doing. They rounded the last corridor in step with each other.

The women at the entrance to the women's apartments looked up calmly as they came closer. Some sat behind slanted tables, checking large ledgers and sometimes making an entry. Others were knitting, or working with needle and embroidery hoop. Ladies in silks kept this watch, as well as women in livery. The arched doors stood open, unguarded except for the women. No more was needed. No Shienaran man would enter uninvited, but any Shienaran man stood ready to defend that door if needed, and he would be aghast at the need.

Rand's stomach churned, harsh and acid. *They'll take one look at our swords and turn us away. Well, that's what I want, isn't it? If they turn us back, maybe I can still get away. If they don't call the guards down on us.* He clung to the stance Lan had given him as he would have to a floating branch in a flood; holding it was the only thing that kept him from turning tail and running.

One of the Lady Amalisa's attendants, Nisura, a round-faced woman, put aside her embroidery and stood as they came to a stop. Her eyes flickered across their swords, and her mouth tightened, but she did not mention them. All the women stopped what they were doing to watch, silent and intent.

"Honor to you both," Nisura said, bowing her head slightly. She glanced at Rand, so quickly he was almost not sure he had seen it; it reminded him of what Perrin had said. "The Amyrlin Seat awaits you." She motioned, and two other ladies—not servants; they were being honored—stepped forward for escorts. The women bowed, a hair more than Nisura had, and motioned them through the archway. They both gave Rand a sidelong glance, then did not look at him again.

*Were they looking for all of us, or just me? Why all of us?*

Inside, they got the looks Rand expected—two men in the women's apartments where men were rare—and their swords caused more than one raised eyebrow, but none of the women spoke. The two men left knots of conversation in their path, soft murmurs too low for Rand to make out.

Lan strode along as if he did not even notice. Rand kept pace behind their escorts and wished he could hear.

And then they reached the Amyrlin Seat's chambers, with three Aes Sedai in the hall outside the door. The tall Aes Sedai, Leane, held her golden-flamed staff. Rand did not know the other two, one of the White Ajah and one Yellow by their fringe. He remembered their faces, though, staring at him as he had run through these same halls. Smooth Aes Sedai faces, with knowing eyes. They studied him with arched eyebrows and pursed lips. The women who had brought Lan and Rand curtsied, handing them over to the Aes Sedai.

Leane looked Rand over with a slight smile. Despite the smile, her voice had a snap to it. "What have you brought the Amyrlin Seat today, Lan Gaidin? A young lion? Better you don't let any Greens see this one, or one of them will bond him before he can take a breath. Greens like to bond them young."

Rand wondered if it was really possible to sweat inside your skin. He felt as if he was. He wanted to look at Lan, but he remembered this part of the Warder's instructions. "I am Rand al'Thor, son of Tam al'Thor, of the Two Rivers, which once was Manetheren. As I have been summoned by the Amyrlin Seat, Leane Sedai, so do I come. I stand ready." He was surprised that his voice did not shake once.

Leane blinked, and her smile faded to a thoughtful look. "This is supposed to be a shepherd, Lan Gaidin? He was not so sure of himself this morning."

"He is a man, Leane Sedai," Lan said firmly, "no more, and no less. We are what we are."

The Aes Sedai shook her head. "The world grows stranger every day. I suppose the blacksmith will wear a crown and speak in High Chant. Wait here." She vanished inside to announce them.

She was only gone a few moments, but Rand was uncomfortably aware of the eyes of the remaining Aes Sedai. He tried to return their gaze levelly, the way Lan had told him to, and they put their heads together, whispering. *What are they saying? What do they know? Light, are they going to gentle me? Was that what Lan meant about facing whatever comes?*

Leane returned, motioning Rand to go in. When Lan started to follow, she thrust her staff across his chest, stopping him. "Not you, Lan Gaidin. Moiraine Sedai has a task for you. Your lion cub will be safe enough by himself."

The door swung shut behind Rand, but not before he heard Lan's voice, fierce and strong, but low for his ear alone. *"Tai'shar Manetheren!"*

Moiraine sat to one side of the room, and one of the Brown Aes Sedai he had seen in the dungeon sat to the other, but it was the woman in the tall chair behind the wide table who held his eyes. The curtains had been partially drawn over the arrowslits, but the gaps let in enough light behind her to make her face hard to see clearly. He still recognized her, though. The Amyrlin Seat.

Quickly he dropped to one knee, left hand on sword hilt, right fist pressed to the patterned rug, and bowed his head. "As you have summoned me, Mother, so have I come. I stand ready." He lifted his head in time to see her eyebrows rise.

"Do you now, boy?" She sounded almost amused. And something else he could not make out. She certainly did not look amused. "Stand up, boy, and let me have a look at you."

He straightened and tried to keep his face relaxed. It was an effort not to clench his hands. *Three Aes Sedai. How many does it take to gentle a man? They sent a dozen or more after Logain. Would Moiraine do that to me?* He met the Amyrlin Seat's look eye to eye. She did not blink.

"Sit, boy," she said finally, gesturing to a ladder-back chair that had been pulled around squarely in front of the table. "This will not be short, I fear."

"Thank you, Mother." He bowed his head, then, as Lan had told him, glanced at the chair and touched his sword. "By your leave, Mother, I will stand. The watch is not done."

The Amyrlin Seat made an exasperated sound and looked at Moiraine. "Have you let Lan at him, Daughter? This will be difficult enough without him picking up Warder ways."

"Lan has been teaching all the boys, Mother," Moiraine replied calmly. "He has spent a little more time with this one than the others because he carries a sword."

The Brown Aes Sedai shifted on her chair. "The Gaidin are stiff-necked and proud, Mother, but useful. I would not be without Tomas, as you would not lose Alric. I have even heard a few Reds say they sometimes wish for a Warder. And the Greens, of course. . . ."

The three Aes Sedai were all ignoring him, now. "This sword," the Amyrlin Seat said. "It appears to be a heron-mark blade. How did he come by that, Moiraine?"

"Tam al'Thor left the Two Rivers as a boy, Mother. He joined the army of Illian, and served in the Whitecloak War and the last two wars with Tear. In time he rose to be a blademaster and the Second Captain of the Companions. After the Aiel War, Tam al'Thor returned to the Two Rivers with a wife from Caemlyn and an infant boy. It would have saved much, had I known this earlier, but I know it now."

Rand stared at Moiraine. He knew Tam had left the Two Rivers and come back with an outlander wife and the sword, but the rest. . . . *Where did you learn all that? Not in Emond's Field. Unless Nynaeve told you more than she's ever told me. An infant boy. She doesn't say his son. But I am.*

"Against Tear." The Amyrlin Seat frowned slightly. "Well, there was blame enough on both sides in those wars. Fool men who would rather fight than talk. Can you tell if the blade is authentic, Verin?"

"There are tests, Mother."

"Then take it and test it, Daughter."

The three women were not even looking at him. Rand stepped back, gripping the hilt hard. "My father gave this sword to me," he said angrily. "Nobody is taking it from me." It was only then that he realized Verin had not moved from her chair. He looked at them in confusion, trying to recover his equilibrium.

"So," the Amyrlin Seat said, "you have some fire in you besides whatever Lan put in. Good. You will need it."

"I am what I am, Mother," he managed smoothly enough. "I stand ready for what comes."

The Amyrlin Seat grimaced. "Lan *has* been at you. Listen to me, boy. In a few hours, Ingtar will leave to find the stolen Horn. Your friend, Mat, will go with him. I expect that your other friend—Perrin?—will go, also. Do you wish to accompany them?"

"Mat and Perrin are going? Why?" Belatedly he remembered to add a respectful, "Mother."

"You know of the dagger your friend carried?" A twist of her mouth showed what she thought of the dagger. "That was taken, too. Unless it is found, the link between him and the blade cannot be broken completely, and he will die. You can ride with them, if you want. Or you can stay here. No doubt Lord Agelmar will let you remain as a guest as long as you wish. I will be leaving today, as well. Moiraine Sedai will accompany me, and so will Egwene and Nynaeve, so you will stay alone, if you stay. The choice is yours."

Rand stared at her. *She is saying I can go as I want. Is that what she brought me here for? Mat is dying!* He glanced at Moiraine, sitting impassively with her hands folded in her lap. She looked as if nothing in the world could concern her less than where he went. *Which way are you trying to push me, Aes Sedai? Burn me, but I'll go another. But if Mat's dying. . . . I can't abandon him. Light, how are we going to find that dagger?*

"You do not have to make the choice now," the Amyrlin said. She did not seem to care, either. "But you will have to choose before Ingtar leaves."

"I will ride with Ingtar, Mother."

The Amyrlin Seat nodded absently. "Now that that is dealt with, we can move on to important matters. I know you can channel, boy. What do you know?"

Rand's mouth fell open. Caught up in worrying about Mat, her casual words hit him like a swinging barn door. All of Lan's advice and instructions went spinning. He stared at her, licking his lips. It was one thing to think she knew, entirely another to find out she really did. The sweat finally seeped out on his forehead.

She leaned forward in her seat, waiting for his answer, but he had the feeling she wanted to lean back. He remembered what Lan had said. *If she's afraid of you.* . . . He wanted to laugh. If *she* was afraid of *him.*

"No, I can't. I mean . . . I didn't do it on purpose. It just happened. I don't want to—to channel the Power. I won't ever do it again. I swear it."

"You don't want to," the Amyrlin Seat said. "Well, that's wise of you. And foolish, too. Some can be taught to channel; most cannot. A few, though, have the seed in them at birth. Sooner or later, they wield the One Power whether they want to or not, as surely as roe makes fish. You will continue to channel, boy. You can't help it. And you had better *learn* to channel, learn to control it, or you will not live long enough to go mad. The One Power kills those who cannot control its flow."

"How am I supposed to learn?" he demanded. Moiraine and Verin just sat there, unruffled, watching him. *Like spiders.* "How? Moiraine claims she can't teach me anything, and I don't know how to learn, or what. I don't want to, anyway. I want to stop. Can't you understand that? To stop!"

"I told you the truth, Rand," Moiraine said. She sounded as if they were having a pleasant conversation. "Those who could teach you, the male Aes Sedai, are three thousand years dead. No Aes Sedai living can teach you to touch *saidin* any more than you could learn to touch *saidar.* A bird cannot teach a fish to fly, nor a fish teach a bird to swim."

"I have always thought that was a bad saying," Verin said suddenly. "There are birds that dive and swim. And in the Sea of Storms are fish that fly, with long fins that stretch out as wide as your outstretched arms, and beaks like swords that can pierce. . . ." Her words trailed off and she became flustered. Moiraine and the Amyrlin Seat were staring at her without expression.

Rand took the interruption to try to regain some control of himself. As Tam had taught him long ago, he formed a single flame in his mind and fed his fears into it, seeking emptiness, the stillness of the void. The flame seemed to grow until it enveloped everything, until it was too large to contain or imagine any longer. With that it was gone, leaving in its place a sense of peace. At its edges, emotions still flickered, fear and anger like black blotches, but the void held. Thought skimmed across its surface like pebbles across ice. The Aes Sedai's attention was only off him for a moment, but when they turned back his face was calm.

"Why are you talking to me like this, Mother?" he asked. "You should be gentling me."

The Amyrlin Seat frowned and turned to Moiraine. "Did Lan teach him this?"

"No, Mother. He had it from Tam al'Thor."

"Why?" Rand demanded again.

The Amyrlin Seat looked him straight in the eye and said, "Because you are the Dragon Reborn."

The void rocked. The world rocked. Everything seemed to spin around him. He concentrated on nothing, and the emptiness returned, the world steadied. "No, Mother. I can channel, the Light help me, but I am not Raolin Darksbane, nor Guaire Amalasin, nor Yurian Stonebow. You can gentle me, or kill me, or let me go, but I will not be a tame false Dragon on a Tar Valon leash."

He heard Verin gasp, and the Amyrlin's eyes widened, a gaze as hard as blue rock. It did not affect him; it slid off the void within.

"Where did you hear those names?" the Amyrlin demanded. "Who told you Tar Valon pulls the lines on *any* false Dragon?"

"A friend, Mother," he said. "A gleeman. His name was Thom Merrilin. He's dead, now." Moiraine made a sound, and he glanced at her. She claimed Thom was not dead, but she had never offered any proof, and he could not see how any man could survive grappling hand-to-hand with a Fade. The thought was extraneous, and it faded away. There was only the void and the oneness now.

"You are not a false Dragon," the Amyrlin said firmly. "You are the true Dragon Reborn."

"I am a shepherd from the Two Rivers, Mother."

"Daughter, tell him the story. A *true* story, boy. Listen well."

Moiraine began speaking. Rand kept his eyes on the Amyrlin's face, but he heard.

"Nearly twenty years ago the Aiel crossed the Spine of the World, the Dragonwall, the only time they have ever done so. They ravaged through Cairhien, destroyed every army sent against them, burned the city of Cairhien itself, and fought all the way to Tar Valon. It was winter and snowing, but cold or heat mean little to an Aiel. The final battle, the last that counted, was fought outside the Shining Walls, in the shadow of Dragonmount. In three days and three nights of fighting, the Aiel were turned back. Or rather they turned back, for they had done what they came to do, which was to kill King Laman of Cairhien, for his sin against the Tree. It is then that my story begins. And yours."

*They came over the Dragonwall like a flood. All the way to the Shining Walls.* Rand waited for the memories to fade, but it was Tam's voice he heard, Tam sick and raving, pulling up secrets from his past. The voice clung outside the void, clamoring to get in.

"I was one of the Accepted, then," Moiraine said, "as was our Mother, the Amyrlin Seat. We were soon to be raised to sisterhood, and that night we stood attendance on the then Amyrlin. Her Keeper of the Chronicles, Gitara Moroso, was there. Every other full sister in Tar Valon was out Healing as many wounded as she could find, even the Reds. It was dawn. The fire on the hearth could not keep the cold out. The snow had finally stopped, and in the Amyrlin's chambers in the White Tower we could smell the smoke of outlying villages burned in the fighting."

*Battles are always hot, even in the snow. Had to get away from the stink of death.* Tam's delirious voice clawed at the empty calm inside Rand. The void trembled and shrank, steadied, then wavered again. The Amyrlin's eyes bored at him. He felt sweat on his face again. "It was all a fever-dream," he said. "He was sick." He raised his voice. "My name is Rand al'Thor. I am a shepherd. My father is Tam al'Thor, and my mother was—"

Moiraine had paused for him, but now her unchanging voice cut him off, soft and relentless. "*The Karaethon Cycle,* the Prophecies of the Dragon, says that the Dragon will be reborn on the slopes of Dragonmount, where he died during the Breaking of the World. Gitara Sedai had the Foretelling sometimes. She was old, her hair as white as the snow outside, but when she had the Foretelling, it was strong. The morning light through the windows was strengthening as I handed her a cup of tea. The Amyrlin Seat asked me what news there was from the field of battle. And Gitara Sedai started up out of her chair, her arms and legs rigid, trembling, her face as if she looked into the Pit of Doom at Shayol Ghul, and she cried out, 'He is born again! I feel him! The Dragon takes his first breath on the slope of Dragonmount! He is coming! He is coming! Light help us! Light help the world! He lies in the snow and cries like the thunder! He burns like the sun!' And she fell forward into my arms, dead."

*Slope of the mountain. Heard a baby cry. Gave birth there alone, before she died. Child blue with the cold.* Rand tried to force Tam's voice away. The void grew smaller. "A fever-dream," he gasped. *I couldn't leave a child.* "I was born in the Two Rivers." *Always knew you wanted children, Kari.* He pulled his eyes away from the Amyrlin's gaze. He tried to force the void to hold.

He knew that was not the way, but it was collapsing in him. *Yes, lass. Rand is a good name.* "I—am—Rand—al'Thor!" His legs trembled.

"And so we knew the Dragon was Reborn," Moiraine went on. "The Amyrlin swore us to secrecy, we two, for she knew not all the sisters would see the Rebirth as it must be seen. She set us to searching. There were many fatherless children after that battle. Too many. But we found a story, that one man had found an infant on the mountain. That was all. A man and an infant boy. So we searched on. For years we searched, finding other clues, poring over the Prophecies. 'He will be of the ancient blood, and raised by the old blood.' That was one; there were others. But there are many places where the old blood, descended from the Age of Legends, remains strong. Then, in the Two Rivers, where the old blood of Manetheren seethes still like a river in flood, in Emond's Field, I found three boys whose namedays were within weeks of the battle at Dragonmount. And one of them can channel. Did you think Trollocs came after you just because you are *ta'veren?* You are the Dragon Reborn."

Rand's knees gave way; he dropped to a squat, hands slapping the rug to catch himself from falling on his face. The void was gone, the stillness shattered. He raised his head, and they were looking at him, the three Aes Sedai. Their faces were serene, smooth as unruffled ponds, but their eyes did not blink. "My father is Tam al'Thor, and I was born. . . ." They stared at him, unmoving. *They're lying. I am not . . . what they say! Some way, somehow, they're lying, trying to use me.* "I will not be used by you."

"An anchor is not demeaned by being used to hold a boat," the Amyrlin said. "You were made for a purpose, Rand al'Thor. 'When the winds of Tarmon Gai'don scour the earth, he will face the Shadow and bring forth Light again in the world.' The Prophecies must be fulfilled, or the Dark One will break free and remake the world in his image. The Last Battle is coming, and you were born to unite mankind and lead them against the Dark One."

"Ba'alzamon is dead," Rand said hoarsely, and the Amyrlin snorted like a stablehand.

"If you believe that, you are as much a fool as the Domani. Many there believe he is dead, or say they do, but I notice they still won't risk naming him. The Dark One lives, and he is breaking free. You will face the Dark One. It is your destiny."

*It is your destiny.* He had heard that before, in a dream that had maybe not been entirely a dream. He wondered what the Amyrlin would say if she knew Ba'alzamon had spoken to him in dreams. *That's done with. Ba'alzamon is dead. I saw him die.*

Suddenly it came to him that he was crouching like a toad, huddling under their eyes. He tried to form the void again, but voices whirled through his head, sweeping away every effort. *It is your destiny. Babe lying in the snow. You are the Dragon Reborn. Ba'alzamon is dead. Rand is a good name, Kari. I will not be used!* Drawing on his own native stubbornness, he forced himself back upright. *Face it on your feet. You can keep your pride, at least.* The three Aes Sedai watched with no expression.

"What. . . ." With an effort he steadied his voice. "What are you going to do to me?"

"Nothing," the Amyrlin said, and he blinked. It was not the answer he had expected, the one he had feared. "You say you want to accompany your friend with Ingtar, and you may. I have not marked you out in any way. Some of the sisters may know you are *ta'veren,* but no more. Only we three know who you truly are. Your friend Perrin will be brought to me, as you were, and I will visit your other friend in the infirmary. You may go as you will, without fear that we will set the Red sisters on you."

*Who you truly are.* Anger flared up in him, hot and corrosive. He forced it to stay inside, hidden. "Why?"

"The Prophecies must be fulfilled. We let you walk free, knowing what you are, because otherwise the world we know will die, and the Dark One will cover the earth with fire and death. Mark me, not all Aes Sedai feel the same. There are some here in Fal Dara who would strike you down if they knew a tenth of what you are, and feel no more remorse than for gutting a fish. But then, there are men who've no doubt laughed with you who would do the same, if they knew. Have a care, Rand al'Thor, Dragon Reborn."

He looked at each of them in turn. *Your Prophecies are no part of me.* They returned his gaze so calmly it was hard to believe they were trying to convince him he was the most hated, the most feared man in the history of the world. He had gone right through fear and come out the other side in some place cold. Anger was all that kept him warm. They could gentle him, or burn him to a crisp where he stood, and he no longer cared.

A part of Lan's instructions came back to him. Left hand on the hilt, he twisted the sword behind him, catching the scabbard in his right, then bowed, arms straight. "By your leave, Mother, may I depart this place?"

"I give you leave to go, my son."

Straightening, he stood there a moment longer. "I will not be used," he told them. There was a long silence as he turned and left.

The silence stretched on in the room after Rand left until it was broken by a long breath from the Amyrlin. "I cannot make myself like what we just did," she said. "It was necessary, but. . . . Did it work, Daughters?"

Moiraine shook her head, just the slightest movement. "I do not know. But it *was* necessary, and is."

"Necessary," Verin agreed. She touched her forehead, then peered at the dampness on her fingers. "He is strong. And as stubborn as you said, Moiraine. Much stronger than I expected. We may have to gentle him after all before. . . ." Her eyes widened. "But we cannot, can we? The Prophecies. The Light forgive us for what we are loosing on the world."

"The Prophecies," Moiraine said, nodding. "Afterwards, we will do as we must. As we do now."

"As we must," the Amyrlin said. "Yes. But when he learns to channel, the Light help us all."

The silence returned.

There was a storm coming. Nynaeve felt it. A big storm, worse than she had ever seen. She could listen to the wind, and hear what the weather would be. All Wisdoms claimed to be able to do that, though many could not. Nynaeve had felt more comfortable with the ability before learning it was a manifestation of the Power. Any woman who could listen to the wind could channel, though most were probably as she had been, unaware of what she was doing, getting it only in fits and starts.

This time, though, something was wrong. Outside, the morning sun was a golden ball in a clear blue sky, and birds sang in the gardens, but that was not it. There would have been nothing to listening to the wind if she could not foretell the weather before the signs were visible. There was something wrong with the feeling this time, something not quite the way it usually was. The storm felt distant, too far off for her to feel at all. Yet it felt as if the sky above should have been pouring down rain, and snow, and hail, all at the same time, with winds howling to shake the stones of the keep. And she could feel the good weather, too, lasting for days yet, but that was muted under the other.

A bluefinch perched in an arrowslit like a mockery of her weather sense, peering into the hallway. When it saw her, it vanished in a flash of blue and white feathers.

She stared at the spot where the bird had been. *There is a storm, and there isn't. It means something. But what?*

Far down the hall full of women and small children she saw Rand striding away, his escort of women half running to keep up. Nynaeve nodded firmly. If there was a storm that was not a storm, he would be the center of it. Gathering her skirts, she hurried after him.

Women with whom she had grown friendly since coming to Fal Dara tried to speak to her; they knew Rand had come with her and that they were both from the Two Rivers, and they wanted to know why the Amyrlin had summoned him. *The Amyrlin Seat!* Ice in the pit of her belly, she broke into a run, but before she left the women's apartments, she had lost him around too many corners and beyond too many people.

"Which way did he go?" she asked Nisura. There was no need to say who. She heard Rand's name in the conversation of the other women clustered around the arched doors.

"I don't know, Nynaeve. He came out as fast as if he had Heartsbane himself at his heels. As well he might, coming here with a sword at his belt. The Dark One should be the least of his worries after that. What is the world coming to? And him presented to the Amyrlin in her chambers, no less. Tell me, Nynaeve, is he really a prince in your land?" The other women stopped talking and leaned closer to listen.

Nynaeve was not sure what she answered. Something that made them let her go on. She hurried away from the women's apartments, head swiveling at every crossing corridor to look for him, fists clenched. *Light, what have they done to him? I should have gotten him away from Moiraine somehow, the Light blind her. I'm his Wisdom.*

*Are you,* a small voice taunted. *You've abandoned Emond's Field to fend for itself. Can you still call yourself their Wisdom?*

*I did not abandon them,* she told herself fiercely. *I brought Mavra Mallen up from Deven Ride to look after matters till I get back. She can deal well enough with the Mayor and the Village Council, and she gets on well with the Women's Circle.*

*Mavra will have to get back to her own village. No village can do without its Wisdom for long.* Nynaeve cringed inside. She had been gone months from Emond's Field.

"I am the Wisdom of Emond's Field!" she said aloud.

A liveried servant carrying a bolt of cloth blinked at her, then bowed low before scurrying off. By his face he was eager to be anywhere else.

Blushing, Nynaeve looked around to see if anyone had noticed. There were only a few men in the hall, engrossed in their own conversations, and some women in black-and-gold going about their business, giving her a bow or curtsy as she passed. She had had that argument with herself a hundred times before, but this was the first time it had come to talking to herself out loud. She muttered under her breath, then pressed her lips firmly together when she realized what she was doing.

She was finally beginning to realize her search was futile when she came on Lan, his back to her, looking down on the outer courtyard through an arrowslit. The noise from the courtyard was all horses and men, neighing and shouting. So intent was Lan that he did not, for once, seem to hear her. She hated the fact that she could never sneak up on him, however softly she stepped. She had been accounted good at woodscraft back in Emond's Field, though it was not a skill in which many women took any interest.

She stopped in her tracks, pressing her hands to her stomach to quiet a flutter. *I ought to dose myself with rannel and sheepstongue root,* she thought sourly. It was the mixture she gave anyone who moped about and claimed they were sick, or behaved like a goose. Rannel and sheepstongue root would perk you up a little, and did no harm, but mainly it tasted horrible, and the taste lasted all day. It was a perfect cure for acting the fool.

Safe from his eyes, she studied the length of him, leaning against the stone and fingering his chin as he studied what was going on below. *He's too tall, for one thing, and old enough to be my father, for another. A man with a face like that would have to be cruel. No, he's not that. Never that.* And he was a king. His land was destroyed while he was a child, and he would not claim a crown, but he was a king, for that. *What would a king want with a village woman? He's a Warder, too. Bonded to Moiraine. She has his loyalty to death, and ties closer than any lover, and she has him. She has everything I want, the Light burn her!*

He turned from the arrowslit, and she whirled to go.

"Nynaeve." His voice caught and held her like a noose. "I wanted to speak to you alone. You always seem to be in the women's apartments, or in company."

It took an effort to face him, but she was sure her features were calm when she looked up at him. "I'm looking for Rand." She was not about to admit to avoiding him. "We said all we need to say long ago, you and I. I shamed myself—which I will not do again—and you told me to go away."

"I never said—" He took a deep breath. "I told you I had nothing to offer for brideprice but widow's clothes. Not a gift any man could give a woman. Not a man who can call himself a man."

"I understand," she said coolly. "In any case, a king does not give gifts to village women. And this village woman would not take them. Have you seen Rand? I need to talk to him. He was to see the Amyrlin. Do you know what she wanted with him?"

His eyes blazed like blue ice in the sun. She stiffened her legs to keep from stepping back, and met him glare for glare.

"The Dark One take Rand al'Thor and the Amyrlin Seat both," he grated, pressing something into her hand. "I will make you a gift and you will take it if I have to chain it around your neck."

She pulled her eyes away from his. He had a stare like a blue-eyed hawk when he was angry. In her hand was a signet ring, heavy gold and worn with age, almost large enough for both her thumbs to fit through. On it, a crane flew above a lance and crown, all carefully wrought in detail. Her breath caught. The ring of Malkieri kings. Forgetting to glare, she lifted her face. "I cannot take this, Lan."

He shrugged in an offhand way. "It is nothing. Old, and useless, now. But there are those who would know it when they saw it. Show that, and you will have guestright, and help if you need it, from any lord in the Borderlands. Show it to a Warder, and he will give aid, or carry a message to me. Send it to me, or a message marked with it, and I will come to you, without delay and without fail. This I swear."

Her vision blurred at the edges. *If I cry now, I will kill myself.* "I can't. . . . I do not want a gift from you, al'Lan Mandragoran. Here, take it."

He fended off her attempts to give the ring back to him. His hand enveloped hers, gentle but firm as a shackle. "Then take it for my sake, as a favor to me. Or throw it away, if it displeases you. I've no better use for it." He brushed her cheek with a finger, and she gave a start. "I must go now, Nynaeve *mashiara*. The Amyrlin wishes to leave before midday, and there is much yet to be done. Perhaps we will have time to talk on the journey to Tar Valon." He turned and was gone, striding down the hall.

Nynaeve touched her cheek. She could still feel where he had touched her. *Mashiara*. Beloved of heart and soul, it meant, but a love lost, too. Lost beyond regaining. *Fool woman! Stop acting like a girl with her hair still not braided. It's no use letting him make you feel. . . .*

Clutching the ring tightly, she turned around, and jumped when she found herself face-to-face with Moiraine. "How long have you been there?" she demanded.

"Not long enough to hear anything I should not have," the Aes Sedai replied smoothly. "We *will* be leaving soon. I heard that. You must see to your packing."

Leaving. It had not penetrated when Lan said it. "I will have to say goodbye to the boys," she muttered, then gave Moiraine a sharp look. "What have you done to Rand? He was taken to the Amyrlin. Why? Did you tell her about—about. . . ?" She could not say it. He was from her own village, and she was just enough older than he to have looked after him a time or two when he was little, but she could not even think about what he had become without her stomach twisting.

"The Amyrlin will be seeing all three, Nynaeve. *Ta'veren* are not so common that she would miss the chance to see three together in one place. Perhaps she will give them a few words of encouragement, since they are riding with Ingtar to hunt those who stole the Horn. They will be leaving about the time we do, so you had better hurry with any farewells."

Nynaeve dashed to the nearest arrowslit and peered down at the outer courtyard. Horses were everywhere, pack animals and saddle horses, and men hurrying about them, calling to each other. The only clear space was where the Amyrlin's palanquin stood, its paired horses waiting patiently without any attendants. Some of the Warders were out there, looking over their mounts, and on the other side of the courtyard, Ingtar stood with a knot of Shienarans around him in armor. Sometimes a Warder or one of Ingtar's men crossed the paving stones to exchange a word.

"I should have gotten the boys away from you," she said, still looking out. *Egwene, too, if I could do it without killing her. Light, why did she have to be born with this cursed ability?* "I should have taken them back home."

"They are more than old enough to be off apron strings," Moiraine said dryly. "And you know very well why you could never do that. For one of them, at least. Besides, it would mean leaving Egwene to go to Tar Valon alone. Or have you decided to forgo Tar Valon yourself? If your own use of the Power is not schooled, you will never be able to use it against me."

Nynaeve spun to face the Aes Sedai, her jaw dropping. She could not help it. "I don't know what you are talking about."

"Did you think I did not know, child? Well, as you wish it. I take it that you *are* coming to Tar Valon? Yes, I thought so."

Nynaeve wanted to hit her, to knock away the brief smile that flashed across the Aes Sedai's face. Aes Sedai had not been able to wield power openly since the Breaking, much less the One Power, but they plotted and manipulated, pulled strings like puppetmasters, used thrones and nations like stones on a stones board. *She wants to use me, too, somehow. If a king or a queen, why not a Wisdom? Just the way she's using Rand. I'm no child, Aes Sedai.*

"What are you doing with Rand, now? Have you not used him enough? I don't know why you have not had him gentled, now the Amyrlin's here with all those other Aes Sedai, but you must have a reason. It must be some plot you're hatching. If the Amyrlin knew what you were up to, I wager she'd—"

Moiraine cut her off. "What possible interest could the Amyrlin have in a shepherd? Of course, if he were brought to her attention in the wrong way, he might be gentled, or even killed. He is what he is, after all. And there is much anger about last night. Everyone is looking for whom to blame." The Aes Sedai fell silent, and let the silence stretch. Nynaeve stared at her, grinding her teeth.

"Yes," Moiraine said finally, "much better to let a sleeping lion sleep. Best you see to your packing, now." She moved off in the direction Lan had gone, seeming to glide across the floor.

Grimacing, Nynaeve swung her fist back against the wall; the ring dug at her palm. She opened her hand to look at it. The ring seemed to heat her anger, focus her hate. *I will* learn. *You think because you know, you can escape me. But I will learn better than you think, and I will pull you down for what you've done. For what you've done to Mat, and to Perrin. For Rand, the Light help him and the Creator shelter him. Especially for Rand.* Her hand closed around the heavy circlet of gold. *And for me.*

Egwene watched the liveried maid folding her dresses into a leather-covered travel chest, still a little uncomfortable, even after nearly a month's practice, with someone else doing what she could very well have done herself. They were such beautiful dresses, all gifts from the Lady Amalisa, just like the gray silk riding dress she wore, though that was plain except for a few white morningstar blossoms worked on the breast. Many of the dresses were much more elaborate. Any one of them would shine at Sunday, or at Bel Tine. She sighed, remembering that she would be in Tar Valon for the next Sunday, not Emond's Field. From the little Moiraine had told her of novice training—almost nothing, really—she expected she might not be home for Bel Tine, in the spring, or even the Sunday after that.

Nynaeve put her head into the room. "Are you ready?" She came the rest of the way in. "We must be down in the courtyard soon." She wore a riding dress, too, in blue silk with red loversknots on the bosom. Another gift from Amalisa.

"Nearly, Nynaeve. I am almost sorry to be going. I don't suppose we'll have many chances in Tar Valon to wear the nice dresses Amalisa gave us." She gave an abrupt laugh. "Still, Wisdom, I won't miss being able to bathe without looking over my shoulder the whole time."

"Much better to bathe alone," Nynaeve said briskly. Her face did not change, but after a moment her cheeks colored.

Egwene smiled. *She's thinking about Lan.* It was still odd to think of Nynaeve, the Wisdom, mooning after a man. She did not think it would be wise to put it to Nynaeve in quite that way, but of late, sometimes the Wisdom acted as strangely as any girl who had set her heart on a particular man. *And one who doesn't have enough sense to be worthy of her, at that. She loves him, and I can see he loves her, so why can't he have sense enough to speak up?*

"I don't think you should call me Wisdom any longer," Nynaeve said suddenly.

Egwene blinked. It was not required, exactly, and Nynaeve never insisted on it unless she was angry, or being formal, but this. . . . "Why ever not?"

"You are a woman, now." Nynaeve glanced at her unbraided hair, and Egwene resisted the urge to hurriedly twist it into a semblance of a braid. Aes Sedai wore their hair any way they wanted, but wearing hers loose had become a symbol of starting on a new life. "You are a woman," Nynaeve repeated firmly. "We are two women, a long way from Emond's Field, and it will be longer still before we see home again. It will be better if you simply call me Nynaeve."

"We will see home again, Nynaeve. We will."

"Don't try to comfort the Wisdom, girl," Nynaeve said gruffly, but she smiled.

There was a knock at the door, but before Egwene could open it, Nisura came in, agitation all over her face. "Egwene, that young man of yours is trying to come into the women's apartments." She sounded scandalized. "And wearing a sword. Just because the Amyrlin let him enter that way. . . . Lord Rand should know better. He is causing an uproar. Egwene, you must speak to him."

"Lord Rand," Nynaeve snorted. "That young man is growing too big for his breeches. When I get my hands on him, I'll lord him."

Egwene put a hand on Nynaeve's arm. "Let me speak to him, Nynaeve. Alone."

"Oh, very well. The best of men are not much better than house-broken." Nynaeve paused, and added half to herself, "But then, the best of them are worth the trouble of housebreaking."

Egwene shook her head as she followed Nisura into the hall. Even half a year before, Nynaeve would never have added the second part. *But she'll never housebreak Lan.* Her thoughts turned to Rand. Causing an uproar, was he? "Housebreak him?" she muttered. "If he hasn't learned manners by this time, I'll skin him alive."

"Sometimes that is what it takes," Nisura said, walking quickly. "Men are never more than half-civilized until they're wedded." She gave Egwene a sidelong glance. "Do you intend to marry Lord Rand? I do not mean to pry, but you are going to the White Tower, and Aes Sedai seldom wed— none but some of the Green Ajah, that I've ever heard, and not many of them—and. . . ."

Egwene could supply the rest. She had heard the talk in the women's apartments about a suitable wife for Rand. At first it had caused stabs of jealousy, and anger. He had been all but promised to her since they were children. But she was going to be an Aes Sedai, and he was what he was. A man who could channel. She could marry him. And watch him go mad, watch him die. The only way to stop it would be to have him gentled. *I can't do that to him. I can't!* "I do not know," she said sadly.

Nisura nodded. "No one will poach where you have a claim, but you are going to the Tower, and he will make a good husband. Once he has been trained. There he is."

The women gathered around the entrance to the women's apartments, both inside and out, were all watching three men in the hallway outside. Rand, with his sword buckled over his red coat, was being confronted by Agelmar and Kajin. Neither of them wore a sword; even after what had happened in the night, these were still the women's apartments. Egwene stopped at the back of the crowd.

"You understand why you cannot go in," Agelmar was saying. "I know that things are different in Andor, but you do understand?"

"I didn't try to go in." Rand sounded as if he had explained all this more than once already. "I told the Lady Nisura I wanted to see Egwene, and she said Egwene was busy, and I'd have to wait. All I did was shout for her from the door. I did not try to enter. You'd have thought I was naming the Dark One, the way they all started in on me."

"Women have their own ways," Kajin said. He was tall for a Shienaran, almost as tall as Rand, lanky and sallow. His topknot was black as pitch. "They set the rules for the women's apartments, and we abide by them even when they are foolish." A number of eyebrows were raised among the women, and he hastily cleared his throat. "You must send a message in if you wish to speak to one of the women, but it will be delivered when they choose, and until it is, you must wait. That is our custom."

"I have to see her," Rand said stubbornly. "We're leaving soon. Not soon enough for me, but I still have to see Egwene. We will get the Horn of Valere and the dagger back, and that will be the end of it. The end of it. But I want to see her before I go." Egwene frowned; he sounded odd.

"No need to be so fierce," Kajin said. "You and Ingtar will find the Horn, or not. And if not, then another will retrieve it. The Wheel weaves as the Wheel wills, and we are but threads in the Pattern."

"Do not let the Horn seize you, Rand," Agelmar said. "It can take hold of a man—I know how it can—and that is not the way. A man must seek duty, not glory. What will happen, will happen. If the Horn of Valere is meant to be sounded for the Light, then it will be."

"Here is your Egwene," Kajin said, spotting her.

Agelmar looked around, and nodded when he saw her with Nisura. "I will leave you in her hands, Rand al'Thor. Remember, here, her words are law, not yours. Lady Nisura, do not be too hard on him. He only wished to see his young woman, and he does not know our ways."

Egwene followed Nisura as the Shienaran woman threaded her way through the watching women. Nisura inclined her head briefly to Agelmar

and Kajin; she pointedly did not include Rand. Her voice was tight. "Lord
Agelmar. Lord Kajin. He should know this much of our ways by now, but
he is too big to spank, so I will let Egwene deal with him."

Agelmar gave Rand a fatherly pat on the shoulder. "You see. You will
speak with her, if not exactly in the way you wished. Come, Kajin. We
have much to see to yet. The Amyrlin still insists on. . . ." His voice
trailed away as he and the other man left. Rand stood there, looking at
Egwene.

The women were still watching, Egwene realized. Watching her as well
as Rand. Waiting to see what she would do. *So I'm supposed to deal with him,
am I?* Yet she felt her heart going out to him. His hair needed brushing.
His face showed anger, defiance, and weariness. "Walk with me," she told
him. A murmur started up behind them as he walked down the hall beside
her, away from the women's apartments. Rand seemed to be struggling
with himself, hunting for what to say.

"I've heard about your . . . exploits," she said finally. "Running
through the women's apartments last night with a sword. Wearing a sword
to an audience with the Amyrlin Seat." He still said nothing, only walked
along frowning at the floor. "She didn't . . . hurt you, did she?" She could
not make herself ask if he had been gentled; he looked anything but gentle,
but she had no idea what a man looked like afterwards.

He gave a jerk. "No. She didn't. . . . Egwene, the Amyrlin. . . ." He
shook his head. "She didn't hurt me."

She had the feeling he had been going to say something else entirely.
Usually she could ferret out whatever he wanted to hide from her, but
when he really wanted to be stubborn, she could more easily dig a brick
out of a wall with her fingernails. By the set of his jaw, he was at his most
stubborn right now.

"What did she want with you, Rand?"

"Nothing important. *Ta'veren.* She wanted to see *ta'veren.*" His face softened as he looked down at her. "What about you, Egwene? Are you all
right? Moiraine said you would be, but you were so still. I thought you
were dead, at first."

"Well, I'm not." She laughed. She could not remember anything that
had happened after she had asked Mat to go to the dungeons with her, not
until waking in her own bed that morning. From what she had heard of the
night, she was almost glad she could not remember. "Moiraine said she
would have left me a headache for being foolish if she could have Healed
the rest and not that, but she couldn't."

"I told you Fain was dangerous," he muttered. "I told you, but you
wouldn't listen."

"If that's the way you are going to talk," she said firmly, "I will give you back to Nisura. She won't talk to you the way I am. The last man who tried to push his way into the women's apartments spent a month up to his elbows in soapy water, helping with the women's laundry, and he was only trying to find his betrothed and make up an argument. At least he knew enough not to wear his sword. The Light knows what they'd do to you."

"Everybody wants to do something to me," he growled. "Everybody wants to use me for something. Well, I won't be used. Once we find the Horn, and Mat's dagger, I'll never be used again."

With an exasperated grunt, she caught his shoulders and made him face her. She glared up at him. "If you don't start talking sense, Rand al'Thor, I swear I will box your ears."

"Now you sound like Nynaeve." He laughed. As he looked down at her, though, his laughter faded. "I suppose—I suppose I'll never see you again. I know you have to go to Tar Valon. I know that. And you'll become an Aes Sedai. I am done with Aes Sedai, Egwene. I won't be a puppet for them, not for Moiraine, or any of them."

He looked so lost she wanted to put his head on her shoulder, and so stubborn she really did want to box his ears. "Listen to me, you great ox. I *am* going to be an Aes Sedai, and I'll find a way to help you. I will."

"The next time you see me, you will likely want to gentle me."

She looked around hastily; they were alone in their stretch of the hall. "If you don't watch your tongue, I will not be able to help you. Do you want everyone to know?"

"Too many know already," he said. "Egwene, I wish things were different, but they aren't. I wish. . . . Take care of yourself. And promise me you won't choose the Red Ajah."

Tears blurred her vision as she threw her arms around him. "You take care of yourself," she said fiercely into his chest. "If you don't, I'll— I'll. . . ." She thought she heard him murmur, "I love you," and then he was firmly unwrapping her arms, gently moving her away from him. He turned and strode away from her, almost running.

She jumped when Nisura touched her arm. "He looks as if you set him a task he won't enjoy. But you mustn't let him see you cry over it. That negates the purpose. Come. Nynaeve wants you."

Scrubbing her cheeks, Egwene followed the other woman. *Take care of yourself, you wool-headed lummox. Light, take care of him.*

# CHAPTER
# 9

## *Leavetakings*

The outer courtyard was in ordered turmoil when Rand finally
reached it with his saddlebags and the bundle containing the harp
and flute. The sun climbed toward midday. Men hurried around
the horses, tugging at saddle girths and pack harness, voices raised. Others
darted with last-minute additions to the packsaddles, or water for the men
working, or dashed off to fetch something just remembered. But everyone
seemed to know exactly what they were doing and where they were going.
The guardwalks and archers' balconies were crowded again, and excitement
crackled in the morning air. Hooves clattered on the paving stones. One of
the packhorses began kicking, and stablemen ran to calm it. The smell of
horses hung thick. Rand's cloak tried to flap in the breeze that rippled the
swooping-hawk banners on the towers, but his bow, slung across his back,
held it down.

From outside the open gates came the sounds of the Amyrlin's pikemen
and archers forming up in the square. They had marched around from a
side gate. One of the trumpeters tested his horn.

Some of the Warders glanced at Rand as he walked across the courtyard;
a few raised eyebrows when they saw the heron-mark sword, but none
spoke. Half wore the cloaks that were so queasy-making to look at. Man-
darb, Lan's stallion, was there, tall, and black, and fierce-eyed, but the

man himself was not, and none of the Aes Sedai, none of the women, were in evidence yet either. Moiraine's white mare, Aldieb, stepped daintily beside the stallion.

Rand's bay stallion was with the other group on the far side of the courtyard, with Ingtar, and a bannerman holding Ingtar's Gray Owl banner, and twenty other armored men with lances tipped with two feet of steel, all mounted already. The bars of their helmets covered their faces, and golden surcoats with the Black Hawk on the chest hid their plate-and-mail. Only Ingtar's helmet had a crest, a crescent moon above his brow, points up. Rand recognized some of the men. Rough-tongued Uno, with a long scar down his face and only one eye. Ragan and Masema. Others who had exchanged a word, or played a game of stones. Ragan waved to him, and Uno nodded, but Masema was not the only one who gave him a cold stare and turned away. Their packhorses stood placidly, tails swishing.

The big bay danced as Rand tied his saddlebags and bundle behind the high-cantled saddle. He put his foot in the stirrup and murmured, "Easy, Red," as he swung into the saddle, but he let the stallion frisk away some of his stable-bound energy.

To Rand's surprise, Loial appeared from the direction of the stables, riding to join them. The Ogier's hairy-fetlocked mount was as big and heavy as a prime Dhurran stallion. Beside it, all the other animals looked the size of Bela, but with Loial in the saddle, the horse seemed almost a pony.

Loial carried no weapon that Rand could see; he had never heard of any Ogier using a weapon. Their *stedding* were protection enough. And Loial had his own priorities, his own ideas of what was needed for a journey. The pockets of his long coat had a telltale bulge, and his saddlebags showed the square imprints of books.

The Ogier stopped his horse a little way off and looked at Rand, his tufted ears twitching uncertainly.

"I didn't know you were coming," Rand said. "I'd think you would have had enough of traveling with us. This time there's no telling how long it will be, or where we will end up."

Loial's ears lifted a little. "There was no telling when I first met you, either. Besides, what held then, holds now. I can't let the chance pass to see history actually weave itself around *ta'veren*. And to help find the Horn. . . ."

Mat and Perrin rode up behind Loial and paused. Mat looked a little tired around the eyes, but his face wore a bloom of health.

"Mat," Rand said, "I'm sorry for what I said. Perrin, I didn't mean it. I was being stupid."

Mat only glanced at him, then shook his head and mouthed something to Perrin that Rand could not hear. Mat had only his bow and quiver, but Perrin also wore his axe at his belt, with its big half-moon blade balanced by a thick spike.

"Mat? Perrin? Really, I didn't—" They rode on toward Ingtar.

"That is not a coat for traveling, Rand," Loial said.

Rand glanced down at the golden thorns climbing his crimson sleeve and grimaced. *Small wonder Mat and Perrin still think I'm putting on airs.* On returning to his room he had found everything already packed and sent on. All of the plain coats he had been given were on the packhorses, so the servants said; every coat left in the wardrobe was at least as ornate as the one he wore. His saddlebags held nothing in the way of clothes but a few shirts, some wool stockings, and a spare pair of breeches. At least he had removed the golden cord from his sleeve, though he had the red eagle pin in his pocket. Lan had meant it for a gift, after all.

"I'll change when we stop tonight," he muttered. He took a deep breath. "Loial, I said things to you I should not have, and I hope you'll forgive me. You have every right to hold them against me, but I hope you won't."

Loial grinned, and his ears stood up. He moved his horse closer. "I say things I should not all the time. The Elders always said I spoke an hour before I thought."

Suddenly Lan was at Rand's stirrup, in his gray-green scaled armor that would make him all but disappear in forest or darkness. "I need to talk to you, sheepherder." He looked at Loial. "Alone, if you please, Builder." Loial nodded and moved his big horse away.

"I don't know if I should listen to you," Rand told the Warder. "These fancy clothes, and all those things you told me, they didn't help much."

"When you can't win a big victory, sheepherder, learn to settle for the small ones. If you made them think of you as something more than a farmboy who'll be easy to handle, then you won a small victory. Now be quiet and listen. I've only time for one last lesson, the hardest. Sheathing the Sword."

"You've spent an hour every morning making me do nothing but draw this bloody sword and put it back in the scabbard. Standing, sitting, lying down. I think I can manage to get it back in the sheath without cutting myself."

"I said listen, sheepherder," the Warder growled. "There will come a time when you must achieve a goal at all costs. It may come in attack or in defense. And the only way will be to allow the sword to be sheathed in your own body."

"That's crazy," Rand said. "Why would I ever—?"

The Warder cut him off. "You will know when it comes, sheepherder, when the price is worth the gain, and there is no other choice left to you. That is called Sheathing the Sword. Remember it."

The Amyrlin appeared, striding across the crowded courtyard with Leane and her staff, and Lord Agelmar at her shoulder. Even in a green velvet coat, the Lord of Fal Dara did not look out of place among so many armored men. There was still no sign of the other Aes Sedai. As they went by, Rand caught part of their conversation.

"But, Mother," Agelmar was protesting, "you've had no time to rest from the journey here. Stay at least a few days more. I promise you a feast tonight such as you could hardly get in Tar Valon."

The Amyrlin shook her head without breaking stride. "I cannot, Agelmar. You know I would if I could. I had never planned to remain long, and matters urgently require my presence in the White Tower. I should be there now."

"Mother, it shames me that you come one day and leave the next. I swear to you, there will be no repetition of last night. I have tripled the guard on the city gates as well as the keep. I have tumblers in from the town, and a bard coming from Mos Shirare. Why, King Easar will be on his way from Fal Moran. I sent word as soon as. . . ."

Their voices faded as they crossed the courtyard, swallowed up by the din of preparation. The Amyrlin never as much as glanced in Rand's direction.

When Rand looked down, the Warder was gone, and nowhere to be seen. Loial brought his horse back to Rand's side. "That is a hard man to catch and hold, isn't he, Rand? He's not here, then he's here, then he's gone, and you don't see him coming or going."

*Sheathing the Sword.* Rand shivered. *Warders must all be crazy.*

The Warder the Amyrlin was speaking to suddenly sprang into his saddle. He was at a dead gallop before he reached the wide-standing gates. She stood watching him go, and her stance seemed to urge him to go faster.

"Where is he headed in such a hurry?" Rand wondered aloud.

"I heard," Loial said, "that she was sending someone out today, all the way to Arad Doman. There is word of some sort of trouble on Almoth Plain, and the Amyrlin Seat wants to know exactly what. What I don't understand is, why now? From what I hear, the rumors of this trouble came from Tar Valon with the Aes Sedai."

Rand felt cold. Egwene's father had a big map back at home, a map Rand had pored over more than once, dreaming before he found out what the dreams were like when they came true. It was old, that map, showing some lands and nations the merchants from outside said no longer existed, but Almoth Plain was marked, butting against Toman Head. *We will meet again on Toman Head.* It was all the way across the world he knew, on the Aryth Ocean. "It has nothing to do with us," he whispered. "Nothing to do with me."

Loial appeared not to have heard. Rubbing the side of his nose with a finger like a sausage, the Ogier was still peering at the gate where the Warder had vanished. "If she wanted to know, why not send someone before she left Tar Valon? But you humans are always sudden and excitable, always jumping around and shouting." His ears stiffened with embarrassment. "I *am* sorry, Rand. You see what I mean about speaking before I think. I'm rash and excitable sometimes myself, as you know."

Rand laughed. It was a weak laugh, but it felt good to have something to laugh at. "Maybe if we lived as long as you Ogier, we'd be more settled." Loial was ninety years old; by Ogier standards, not old enough by ten years to be outside the *stedding* alone. That he had gone anyway was proof, he maintained, of his rashness. If Loial was an excitable Ogier, Rand thought most of them must be made of stone.

"Perhaps so," Loial mused, "but you humans do so much with your lives. We do nothing but huddle in our *stedding.* Planting the groves, and even the building, were all done before the Long Exile ended." It was the groves Loial held dear, not the cities men remembered the Ogier for building. It was the groves, planted to remind Ogier Builders of the *stedding,* that Loial had left his home to see. "Since we found our way back to the *stedding,* we. . . ." His words trailed off as the Amyrlin approached.

Ingtar and the other men shifted in their saddles, preparing to dismount and kneel, but she motioned them to stay as they were. Leane stood at her shoulder, and Agelmar a pace back. From his glum face, he appeared to have given up trying to convince her to remain longer.

The Amyrlin looked at them one by one before she spoke. Her gaze stayed on Rand no longer than on any other.

"Peace favor your sword, Lord Ingtar," she said finally. "Glory to the Builders, Loial Kiseran."

"You honor us, Mother. May peace favor Tar Valon." Ingtar bowed in his saddle, and the other Shienarans did, too.

"All honor to Tar Valon," Loial said, bowing.

Only Rand, and his two friends on the other side of the party, stayed upright. He wondered what she had said to them. Leane's frown took in all three of them, and Agelmar's eyes widened, but the Amyrlin took no notice.

"You ride to find the Horn of Valere," she said, "and the hope of the world rides with you. The Horn cannot be left in the wrong hands, especially in Darkfriend hands. Those who come to answer its call, will come whoever blows it, and they are bound to the Horn, not to the Light."

There was a stir among the listening men. Everyone believed that those heroes called back from the grave would fight for the Light. If they could fight for the Shadow, instead. . . .

The Amyrlin went on, but Rand was no longer listening. The watcher was back. The hair stirred on the back of his neck. He peered up at the packed archers' balconies overlooking the courtyard, at the rows of people jammed along the guardwalks atop the walls. Somewhere among them was the set of eyes that had followed him unseen. The gaze clung to him like dirty oil. *It can't be a Fade, not here. Then who? Or what?* He twisted in his saddle, pulling Red around, searching. The bay began to dance again.

Suddenly something flashed across in front of Rand's face. A man passing behind the Amyrlin cried out and fell, a black-fletched arrow jutting from his side. The Amyrlin stood calmly looking at a rent in her sleeve; blood slowly stained the gray silk.

A woman screamed, and abruptly the courtyard rang with cries and shouts. The people on the walls milled furiously, and every man in the courtyard had his sword out. Even Rand, he was surprised to realize.

Agelmar shook his blade at the sky. "Find him!" he roared. "Bring him to me!" His face went from red to white when he saw the blood on the Amyrlin's sleeve. He fell to his knees, head bowed. "Forgive, Mother. I have failed your safety. I am ashamed."

"Nonsense, Agelmar," the Amyrlin said. "Leane, stop fussing over me and see to that man. I've cut myself worse than this more than once cleaning fish, and he needs help now. Agelmar, stand up. Stand up, Lord of Fal Dara. You have not failed me, and you have no reason for shame. Last year in the White Tower, with my own guards at every gate and Warders all around me, a man with a knife came within five steps of me. A Whitecloak, no doubt, though I've no proof. Please stand up, or I will be shamed." As Agelmar slowly rose, she fingered her sliced sleeve. "A poor shot for a Whitecloak bowman, or even a Darkfriend." Her eyes flickered up to touch Rand's. "If it was at me he aimed." Her gaze was gone before he could read anything on her face, but he suddenly wanted to dismount and hide.

*It wasn't aimed at her, and she knows it.*

Leane straightened from where she had been kneeling. Someone had laid a cloak over the face of the man who had taken the arrow. "He is dead, Mother." She sounded tired. "He was dead when he struck the ground. Even if I had been at his side. . . ."

"You did what you could, Daughter. Death cannot be Healed."

Agelmar moved closer. "Mother, if there are Whitecloak killers about, or Darkfriends, you must allow me to send men with you. As far as the river, at least. I could not live if harm came to you in Shienar. Please, return to the women's apartments. I will see them guarded with my life until you are ready to travel."

"Be at ease," she told him. "This scratch will not delay me a moment. Yes, yes, I will gladly accept your men as far as the river, if you insist. But I will not let this delay Lord Ingtar a moment, either. Every heartbeat counts until the Horn is found again. Your leave, Lord Agelmar, to order your oathmen?"

He bowed his head in assent. At that moment he would have given her Fal Dara had she asked.

The Amyrlin turned back to Ingtar and the men gathered behind him. She did not look at Rand again. He was surprised to see her smile suddenly.

"I wager Illian does not give its Great Hunt of the Horn so rousing a send-off," she said. "But yours is the true Great Hunt. You are few, so you may travel quickly, yet enough to do what you must. I charge you, Lord Ingtar of House Shinowa, I charge all of you, find the Horn of Valere, and let nothing bar your way."

Ingtar whipped his sword from his back and kissed the blade. "By my life and soul, by my House and honor, I swear it, Mother."

"Then ride."

Ingtar swung his horse toward the gate.

Rand dug his heels into Red's flanks and galloped after the column already disappearing through the gates.

Unaware of what had occurred within, the Amyrlin's pikemen and archers stood walling a path from the gates to the city proper, the Flame of Tar Valon on their chests. Her drummers and trumpeters waited near the gates, ready to fall in when she left. Behind the rows of armored men, people packed the square in front of the keep. Some cheered Ingtar's banner, and others no doubt thought this was the start of the Amyrlin Seat's departure. A swelling roar followed Rand across the square.

He caught up with Ingtar where low-eaved houses and shops stood to either side, and more people thickly lined the stone-paved street. Some of them cheered, too. Mat and Perrin had been riding at the head of the column with Ingtar and Loial, but the two of them fell back when Rand joined them. *How am I ever going to apologize if they won't stay near me long enough for me to say anything? Burn me, he doesn't* look *like he's dying.*

"Changu and Nidao are gone," Ingtar said abruptly. He sounded cold

and angry, but shaken, too. "We counted every head in the keep, alive or
dead, last night and again this morning. They are the only ones not accounted for."

"Changu was on guard in the dungeon yesterday," Rand said slowly.

"And Nidao. They had the second watch. They always stayed together,
even if they had to trade or do extra duty for it. They were not on guard
when it happened, but. . . . They fought at Tarwin's Gap, a month gone,
and saved Lord Agelmar when his horse went down with Trollocs all
around him. Now this. Darkfriends." He drew a deep breath. "Everything
is breaking apart."

A man on horseback forced his way through the throng lining the street
and joined in behind Ingtar. He was a townsman, by his clothes, lean,
with a lined face and graying hair cut long. A bundle and waterbottles
were lashed behind his saddle, and a short-bladed sword and a notched
sword-breaker hung at his belt, along with a cudgel.

Ingtar noticed Rand's glances. "This is Hurin, our sniffer. There was no
need to let the Aes Sedai know about him. Not that what he does is wrong,
you understand. The King keeps a sniffer in Fal Moran, and there's another
in Ankor Dail. It's just that Aes Sedai seldom like what they do not understand, and with him being a man. . . . It's nothing to do with the Power,
of course. Aaaah! You tell him, Hurin."

"Yes, Lord Ingtar," the man said. He bowed low to Rand from his
saddle. "Honor to serve, my Lord."

"Call me Rand." Rand stuck out his hand, and after a moment Hurin
grinned and took it.

"As you wish, my Lord Rand. Lord Ingtar and Lord Kajin don't mind a
man's ways—and Lord Agelmar, of course—but they say in the town
you're an outland prince from the south, and some outland lords are strict
for every man in his place."

"I'm not a lord." *At least I'll get away from that, now.* "Just Rand."

Hurin blinked. "As you wish, my Lor—ah—Rand. I'm a sniffer, you
see. Been one four years this Sunday. I never heard of such a thing before
then, but I hear there's a few others like me. It started slow, catching bad
smells where nobody else smelled anything, and it grew. Took a whole year
before I realized what it was. I could smell violence, the killing and the
hurting. Smell where it happened. Smell the trail of those who did it.
Every trail's different, so there's no chance of mixing them up. Lord Ingtar
heard of it, and took me in his service, to serve the King's justice."

"You can smell violence?" Rand said. He could not help looking at the
man's nose. It was an ordinary nose, not large, not small. "You mean you
can really follow somebody who, say, killed another man? By smell?"

"I can that, my Lor—ah—Rand. It fades with time, but the worse the violence, the longer it lasts. Aiie, I can smell a battlefield ten years old, though the trails of the men who were there are gone. Up near the Blight, the trails of the Trollocs almost never fade. Not much to a Trolloc but killing and hurting. A fight in a tavern, though, with maybe a broken arm . . . that smell's gone in hours."

"I can see where you wouldn't want Aes Sedai to find out."

"Ah, Lord Ingtar was right about the Aes Sedai, the Light illumine them—ah—Rand. There was one in Cairhien once—Brown Ajah, but I swear I thought she was Red before she let me go—she kept me a month trying to find out how I do it. She didn't like not knowing. She kept muttering, 'Is it old come again, or new?' and staring at me until you would have thought I *was* using the One Power. Almost had me doubting myself. But I haven't gone mad, and I don't *do* anything. I just smell it."

Rand could not help remembering Moiraine. *Old barriers weaken. There is something of dissolution and change about our time. Old things walk again, and new things are born. We may live to see the end of an Age.* He shivered. "So we'll track those who took the Horn with your nose."

Ingtar nodded. Hurin grinned proudly, and said, "We will that—ah— Rand. I followed a murderer to Cairhien, once, and another all the way to Maradon, to bring them back for the King's justice." His grin faded, and he looked troubled. "This is the worst ever, though. Murder smells bad, and the trail of a murderer stinks with it, but this. . . ." His nose wrinkled. "There were men in it last night. Darkfriends, must be, but you can't tell a Darkfriend by smell. What I'll follow is the Trollocs, and the Halfmen. And something even worse." He trailed off, frowning and muttering to himself, but Rand could hear it. "Something even worse, the Light help me."

They reached the city gates, and just beyond the walls Hurin lifted his face to the breeze. His nostrils flared, then he gave a snort of disgust. "That way, my Lord Ingtar." He pointed south.

Ingtar looked surprised. "Not toward the Blight?"

"No, Lord Ingtar. Faugh!" Hurin wiped his mouth on his sleeve. "I can almost taste them. South, they went."

"She was right, then, the Amyrlin Seat," Ingtar said slowly. "A great and wise woman, who deserves better than me to serve her. Take the trail, Hurin."

Rand turned and peered back through the gates, up the street to the keep. He hoped Egwene was all right. *Nynaeve will look after her. Maybe it's better this way, like a clean cut, too quick to hurt till after it's done.*

He rode after Ingtar and the Gray Owl banner, south. The wind was making up, and cold against his back despite the sun. He thought he heard laughter in it, faint and mocking.

The waxing moon lit the humid, night-dark streets of Illian, which still rang with celebration left over from daylight. In only a few more days, the Great Hunt of the Horn would be sent forth with pomp and ceremony that tradition claimed dated to the Age of Legends. The festivities for the Hunters had blended into the Feast of Teven, with its famed contests and prizes for gleemen. The greatest prize of all, as always, would go for the best telling of *The Great Hunt of the Horn*.

Tonight the gleemen entertained in the palaces and mansions of the city, where the great and mighty disported themselves, and the Hunters come from every nation to ride out and find, if not the Horn of Valere itself, at least immortality in song and story. They would have music and dancing, and fans and ices to dispel the year's first real heat, but carnival filled the streets, too, in the moon-bright muggy night. Every day was a carnival, until the Hunt departed, and every night.

People ran past Bayle Domon in masks and costumes bizarre and fanciful, many showing too much flesh. Shouting and singing they ran, a half dozen together, then scattered pairs giggling and clutching each other, then twenty in a raucous knot. Fireworks crackled in the sky, gold and silver bursts against the black. There were almost as many Illuminators in the city as there were gleemen.

Domon spared little thought for fireworks, or for the Hunt. He was on his way to meet men he thought might be trying to kill him.

He crossed the Bridge of Flowers, over one of the city's many canals, into the Perfumed Quarter, the port district of Illian. The canal smelled of too many chamber pots, with never a sign that there had ever been flowers near the bridge. The quarter smelled of hemp and pitch from the shipyards and docks, and sour harbor mud, all of it made fiercer by heated air that seemed nearly damp enough to drink. Domon breathed heavily; every time he returned from the northcountry he found himself surprised, for all he had been born there, at the early summer heat in Illian.

In one hand he carried a stout cudgel, and the other hand rested on the hilt of the short sword he had often used in defending the decks of his river trader from brigands. No few footpads stalked these nights of revelry, where the pickings were rich and most were deep in wine.

Yet he was a broad, muscular man, and none of those out for a catch of gold thought him rich enough, in his plain-cut coat, to risk his size and his cudgel. The few who caught a clear glimpse of him, when he passed through light spilling from a window, edged back till he was well past.

Dark hair that hung to his shoulders and a long beard that left his upper lip bare framed a round face, but that face had never been soft, and now it was set as grimly as if he meant to batter his way through a wall. He had men to meet, and he was not happy about it.

More revelers ran past singing off-key, wine mangling their words. *"The Horn of Valere," my aged grandmother!* Domon thought glumly. *It be my ship I do want to hang on to. And my life, Fortune prick me.*

He pushed into an inn, under a sign of a big, white-striped badger dancing on its hind legs with a man carrying a silver shovel. Easing the Badger, it was called, though not even Nieda Sidoro, the innkeeper, knew what the name meant; there had always been an inn of the name in Illian.

The common room, with sawdust on the floor and a musician softly strumming a twelve-stringed bittern in one of the Sea Folk's sad songs, was well lighted and quiet. Nieda allowed no commotion in her place, and her nephew, Bili, was big enough to carry a man out with either hand. Sailors, dockworkers, and warehousemen came to the Badger for a drink and maybe a little talk, for a game of stones or darts. The room was half full now; even men who liked quiet had been lured out by carnival. The talk was soft, but Domon caught mentions of the Hunt, and of the false Dragon the Murandians had taken, and of the one the Tarens were chasing through Haddon Mirk. There seemed to be some question whether it would be preferable to see the false Dragon die, or the Tarens.

Domon grimaced. *False Dragons! Fortune prick me, there be no place safe these days.* But he had no real care for false Dragons, any more than for the Hunt.

The stout proprietress, with her hair rolled at the back of her head, was wiping a mug, keeping a sharp eye on her establishment. She did not stop what she was doing, or even look at him, really, but her left eyelid drooped, and her eyes slanted toward three men at a table in the corner. They were quiet even for the Badger, almost somber, and their bell-shaped velvet caps and dark coats, embroidered across the chest in bars of silver and scarlet and gold, stood out among the plain dress of the other patrons.

Domon sighed and took a table in a corner by himself. *Cairhienin, this time.* He took a mug of brown ale from a serving girl and drew a long swallow. When he lowered the mug, the three men in striped coats were standing beside his table. He made an unobtrusive gesture, to let Nieda know that he did not need Bili.

"Captain Domon?" They were all three nondescript, but there was an air about the speaker that made Domon take him for their leader. They did not appear to be armed; despite their fine clothes, they looked as if they did not need to be. There were hard eyes in those so very ordinary faces. "Captain Bayle Domon, of the *Spray*?"

Domon gave a short nod, and the three sat down without waiting for an invitation. The same man did the talking; the other two just watched, hardly blinking. *Guards,* Domon thought, *for all their fine clothes. Who do he be to have a pair of guards to look over him?*

"Captain Domon, we have a personage who must be brought from Mayene to Illian."

"*Spray* be a river craft," Domon cut him off. "Her draft be shallow, and she has no the keel for deep water." It was not exactly true, but close enough for landsmen. *At least it be a change from Tear. They be getting smarter.*

The man seemed unperturbed at the interruption. "We had heard you were giving up the river trade."

"Maybe I do, and maybe no. I have no decided." He had, though. He would not go back upriver, back to the Borderlands, for all the silk shipped in Taren bottoms. Saldaean furs and ice peppers were not worth it, and it had nothing to do with the false Dragon he had heard of there. But he wondered again how anyone knew. He had not spoken of it to anyone, yet the others had known, too.

"You can coast to Mayene easily enough. Surely, Captain, you would be willing to sail along the shoreline for a thousand gold marks."

Despite himself, Domon goggled. It was four times the last offer, and that had been enough to make a man's jaw drop. "Who do you want me to fetch for that? The First of Mayene herself? Has Tear finally forced her all the way out, then?"

"You need no names, Captain." The man set a large leather pouch on the table, and a sealed parchment. The pouch clinked heavily as he pushed them across the table. The big red wax circle holding the folded parchment shut bore the many-rayed Rising Sun of Cairhien. "Two hundred on account. For a thousand marks, I think you need no names. Give that, seal unbroken, to the Port Captain of Mayene, and he will give you three hundred more, and your passenger. I will hand over the remainder when your passenger is delivered here. So long as you have made no effort to discover that personage's identity."

Domon drew a deep breath. *Fortune, it be worth the voyage if there be never another penny beyond what be in that sack.* And a thousand was more money than he would clear in three years. He suspected that if he probed a little more, there would be other hints, just hints, that the voyage involved hidden dealings between Illian's Council of Nine and the First of Mayene. The First's city-state was a province of Tear in all but name, and she would no doubt like Illian's aid. And there were many in Illian who said it was time for another war, that Tear was taking more than a fair share of the trade on the Sea of Storms. A likely net to snare him, if he had not seen three like it in the past month.

He reached to take the pouch, and the man who had done all the talking caught his wrist. Domon glared at him, but he looked back undisturbed.

"You must sail as soon as possible, Captain."

"At first light," Domon growled, and the man nodded and released his hold.

"At first light, then, Captain Domon. Remember, discretion keeps a man alive to spend his money."

Domon watched the three of them leave, then stared sourly at the pouch and the parchment on the table in front of him. Someone wanted him to go east. Tear or Mayene, it did not matter so long as he went east. He thought he knew who wanted it. *And then again, I have no a clue to them.* Who could know who was a Darkfriend? But he knew that Darkfriends had been after him since before he left Marabon to come back downriver. Darkfriends and Trollocs. Of that, he was sure. The real question, the one he had not even a glimmer of an answer for, was why?

"Trouble, Bayle?" Nieda asked. "You do look as if you had seen a Trolloc." She giggled, an improbable sound from a woman her size. Like most people who had never been to the Borderlands, Nieda did not believe in Trollocs. He had tried telling her the truth of it; she enjoyed his stories, and thought they were all lies. She did not believe in snow, either.

"No trouble, Nieda." He untied the pouch, dug a coin out without looking, and tossed it to her. "Drinks for everyone till that do run out, then I'll give you another."

Nieda looked at the coin in surprise. "A Tar Valon mark! Do you be trading with the witches now, Bayle?"

"No," he said hoarsely. "That I do not!"

She bit the coin, then quickly snugged it away behind her broad belt. "Well, it be gold for that. And I suspect the witches be no so bad as some make them out, anyway. I'd no say so much to many men. I know a money changer who do handle such. You'll no have to give me another, with as few as be here tonight. More ale for you, Bayle?"

He nodded numbly, though his mug was still almost full, and she trundled off. She was a friend, and would not speak of what she had seen. He sat staring at the leather pouch. Another mug was brought before he could make himself open it enough to look at the coins inside. He stirred them with a callused finger. Gold marks glittered up at him in the lamplight, every one of them bearing the damning Flame of Tar Valon. Hurriedly he tied the bag. Dangerous coins. One or two might pass, but so many would say to most people exactly what Nieda thought. There were Children of the Light in the city, and although there was no law in Illian against dealing with Aes Sedai, he would never make it to a magistrate if the Whitecloaks heard of this. These men had made sure he would not simply take the gold and stay in Illian.

While he was sitting there worrying, Yarin Maeldan, his brooding, stork-like second on *Spray,* came into the Badger with his brows pulled down to his long nose and stood over the captain's table. "Carn's dead, Captain."

Domon stared at him, frowning. Three others of his men had already been killed, one each time he refused a commission that would take him east. The magistrates had done nothing; the streets were dangerous at night, they said, and sailors a rough and quarrelsome lot. Magistrates seldom troubled themselves with what happened in the Perfumed Quarter, as long as no respectable citizens were injured.

"But this time I did accept them," he muttered.

"'Tisn't all, Captain," Yarin said. "They worked Carn with knives, like they wanted him to tell them something. And some more men tried to sneak aboard *Spray* not an hour gone. The dock watch ran them off. Third time in ten days, and I never knew wharf rats to be so persistent. They like to let an alarm die down before they try again. And somebody tossed my room at the Silver Dolphin last night. Took some silver, so I'd think it was thieves, but they left that belt buckle of mine, the one set with garnets and moonstones, lying right out in plain sight. What's going on, Captain? The men are afraid, and I'm a little nervous myself."

Domon reared to his feet. "Roust the crew, Yarin. Find them and tell them *Spray* sails as soon as there do be men enough aboard to handle her." Stuffing the parchment into his coat pocket, he snatched up the bag of gold and pushed his second out the door ahead of him. "Roust them, Yarin, for I'll leave any man who no makes it, standing on the quay as he is."

Domon gave Yarin a shove to start him running, then stalked off toward the docks. Even footpads who heard the clinking of the pouch he carried steered clear of him, for he walked now like a man going to do murder.

There were already crewmen scrambling aboard *Spray* when he arrived, and more running barefoot down the stone quay. They did not know what he feared was pursuing him, or even that anything did pursue him, but they knew he made good profits, and after the Illianer way, he gave shares to the crew.

*Spray* was eighty feet long, with two masts, and broad in the beam, with room for deck cargo as well as in the holds. Despite what Domon had told the Cairhienin—if they had been Cairhienin—he thought she could stand the open water. The Sea of Storms was quieter in the summer.

"She'll have to," he muttered, and strode below to his cabin.

He tossed the sack of gold on his bed, built neatly against the hull like everything else in the stern cabin, and dug out the parchment. Lighting a lantern, hanging in its swivel from the overhead, he studied the sealed document, turning it as if he could read what was inside without opening it. A rap on the door made him frown.

"Come."

Yarin stuck his head in. "They're all aboard but three I couldn't find, Captain. But I've spread the word through every tavern, hell, and crib in the quarter. They'll be aboard before it's light enough to start upriver."

"*Spray* do sail now. To sea." Domon cut off Yarin's protests about light and tides, and *Spray* not being built for the open sea. "Now! *Spray* can clear the bars at dead low tide. You've no forgotten how to sail by the stars, have you? Take her out, Yarin. Take her out now, and come back to me when we be beyond the breakwater."

His second hesitated—Domon never let a tricky bit of sailing pass without him on deck giving orders, and taking *Spray* out in the night would be all of that, shallow draft or no—then nodded and vanished. In moments the sounds of Yarin shouting orders and bare feet thumping on the decks overhead penetrated Domon's cabin. He ignored them, even when the ship lurched, catching the tide.

Finally he lifted the mantle of the lantern and stuck a knife into the flame. Smoke curled up as oil burned off the blade, but before the metal could turn red, he pushed charts out of the way and pressed the parchment flat on his desk, working the hot steel slowly under the sealing wax. The top fold lifted.

It was a simple document, without preamble or salutation, and it made sweat break out on his forehead.

*The bearer of this is a Darkfriend wanted in Cairhien for murders and other foul crimes, least among them, theft from Our Person. We call upon you to seize this man and all things found in his keeping, to the smallest. Our representative will come to carry away what he has stolen from Us. Let all he possesses, save what We claim, go to you as reward for taking him. Let the vile miscreant himself be hanged immediately, that his Shadow-spawned villainy no longer taint the Light.*

> *Sealed by Our Hand*
> *Galldrian su Riatin Rie*
> *King of Cairhien*
> *Defender of the Dragonwall*

In thin red wax below the signature were impressed the Rising Sun seal of Cairhien and the Five Stars of House Riatin.

"Defender of the Dragonwall, my aged grandmother," Domon croaked. "Fine right the man do have to call himself that any longer."

He examined the seals and signature minutely, holding the document close to the lamp, with his nose all but brushing the parchment, but he could find no flaw in the one, and for the other, he had no idea what Galldrian's hand looked like. If it was not the King himself who had signed it, he suspected that whoever had had made a good imitation of Galldrian's scrawl. In any case, it made no real difference. In Tear, the letter would be instantly damning in the hands of an Illianer. Or in Mayene, with Taren influence so strong. There was no war now, and men from either port came and went freely, but there was as little love for Illianers in Tear as the other way round. Especially with an excuse like this.

For a moment he thought of putting the parchment into the lantern's flame—it was a dangerous thing to have, in Tear or Illian or anywhere he could imagine—but finally he tucked it carefully into a secret cubbyhole behind his desk, concealed by a panel only he knew how to open.

"My possessions, eh?"

He collected old things, as much as he could living on shipboard. What he could not buy, because it was too expensive or too large, he collected by seeing and remembering. All those remnants of times gone, those wonders scattered around the world that had first pulled him aboard a ship as boy. He had added four to his collection in Maradon this last trip, and it had been then that the Darkfriend pursuit began. And Trollocs, too, for a time. He had heard that Whitebridge had been burned to the ground right after he sailed from there, and there had been rumors of Myrddraal as well as Trollocs. It was that, all of it together, that had first convinced him he was not imagining things, that had had him on guard when that first odd commission was offered, too much money for a simple voyage to Tear, and a thin tale for a reason.

Digging into his chest, he set out on the desk what he had bought in Maradon. A lightstick, left from the Age of Legends, or so it was said. Certainly no one knew the making of them any longer. Expensive, that, and rarer than an honest magistrate. It looked like a plain glass rod, thicker than his thumb and not quite as long as his forearm, but when held in the hand it glowed as brightly as a lantern. Lightsticks shattered like glass, too; he had nearly lost *Spray* in the fire caused by the first he had owned. A small, age-dark ivory carving of a man holding a sword. The fellow who sold it claimed if you held it long enough you started to feel warm. Domon never had, and neither had any of the crew he let hold it, but it was old, and that was enough for Domon. The skull of a cat as big as a lion, and so old it was turned to stone. But no lion had ever had fangs, almost tusks, a foot long. And a thick disk the size of a man's hand, half white and half black, a sinuous line separating the colors. The shopkeeper in Maradon had said it was from the Age of Legends, thinking he lied, but Domon had haggled only a little before paying, because he recognized what the shopkeeper did not: the ancient symbol of Aes Sedai from before the Breaking of the World. Not a safe thing to have, precisely, but neither a thing to be passed up by a man with a fascination for the old.

And it was heartstone. The shopkeeper had never dared add that to what he thought were lies. No riverfront shopkeeper in Maradon could afford even one piece of *cuendillar*.

The disk felt hard and smooth in his hand, and not at all valuable except for its age, but he was afraid it was what his pursuers were after. Light-sticks, and ivory carvings, and even bones turned to stone, he had seen other times, other places. Yet even knowing what they wanted—if he did know—he still had no idea why, and he could no longer be sure who his pursuers were. Tar Valon marks, and an ancient Aes Sedai symbol. He scrubbed a hand across his lips; the taste of fear lay bitter on his tongue.

A knock at the door. He set the disk down and pulled an unrolled chart over what lay on his desk. "Come."

Yarin entered. "We're beyond the breakwater, Captain."

Domon felt a flash of surprise, then anger with himself. He should never have gotten so engrossed that he failed to feel *Spray* lifting on the swells. "Make west, Yarin. See to it."

"Ebou Dar, Captain?"

*No far enough. No by five hundred leagues.* "We'll put in long enough for me to get charts and top the water barrels, then we do sail west."

"West, Captain? Tremalking? The Sea Folk are tight with any traders but their own."

"The Aryth Ocean, Yarin. Plenty of trade between Tarabon and Arad Doman, and hardly a Taraboner or Domani bottom to worry about. They do no like the sea, I have heard. And all those small towns on Toman Head, every one holding itself free of any nation at all. We can even pick up Saldaean furs and ice peppers brought down to Bandar Eban."

Yarin shook his head slowly. He always looked at the dark side, but he was a good sailor. "Furs and peppers'll cost more there than running up-river for them, Captain. And I hear there's some kind of war. If Tarabon and Arad Doman are fighting, there may be no trade. I doubt we'll make much off the towns on Toman Head alone, even if they are safe. Falme's the largest, and it is not big."

"The Taraboners and the Domani have always squabbled over Almoth Plain and Toman Head. Even if it has come to blows this time, a careful man can always find trade. West, Yarin."

When Yarin had gone topside, Domon quickly added the black-and-white disk to the cubbyhole, and stowed the rest back in the bottom of his chest. *Darkfriends or Aes Sedai, I'll no run the way they want me. Fortune prick me, I'll no.*

Feeling safe for the first time in months, Domon went on deck as *Spray* heeled to catch the wind and put her bow west into the night-dark sea.

# CHAPTER 10

## *The Hunt Begins*

Ingtar set a fast pace for the beginning of a long journey, fast enough that Rand worried a little about the horses. The animals could keep up the trot for hours, but there was still most of the day ahead, and likely days more beyond that. The way Ingtar's face was set, though, Rand thought he might intend to catch those who had stolen the Horn in the first day, in the first hour. Remembering his voice when he swore his oath to the Amyrlin Seat, Rand would not have been surprised. He kept his mouth shut, though. It was Lord Ingtar's command; as friendly as he had been to Rand, he still would not appreciate a shepherd giving advice.

Hurin rode a pace behind Ingtar, but it was the sniffer who led them south, pointing the way for Ingtar. The land was rolling, forested hills, thick with fir and leatherleaf and oak, but the path Hurin set led almost straight as an arrow, never wavering except to go around a few of the taller hills, where the way was clearly quicker around than over. The Gray Owl banner rippled in the wind.

Rand tried to ride with Mat and Perrin, but when Rand let his horse drop back to them, Mat nudged Perrin, and Perrin reluctantly galloped to the head of the column with Mat. Telling himself there was no point riding at the back by himself, Rand rode back to the front. They fell to the rear again, Mat again urging Perrin.

*Burn them. I only want to apologize.* He felt alone. It did not help that he knew it was his own fault.

Atop one hill, Uno dismounted to examine ground churned by hooves. He poked at some horse droppings and grunted. "Bloody well moving fast, my Lord." He had a voice that sounded as if he were shouting when he was just speaking. "We've not made up an hour on them. Burn me, we may have lost a flaming hour. They'll kill their bloody horses, the way they're going." He fingered a hoofed track. "No horse, that. Bloody Trolloc. Some flaming goat feet over there."

"We will catch them," Ingtar said grimly.

"Our horses, my Lord. Does no good to ride them into the bloody ground before we do catch up, my Lord. Even if they do kill their horses, bloody Trollocs can keep going longer than horses."

"We will catch them. Mount, Uno."

Uno looked at Rand with his one eye, then shrugged and climbed into his saddle. Ingtar took them down the far slope at a run, half sliding all the way to the bottom, and galloped up the next.

*Why did he look at me that way,* Rand wondered. Uno was one of those who had never shown much friendliness toward him. It was not like Masema's open dislike; Uno was not friendly with anyone except a few veterans as grizzled as himself. *Surely* he *doesn't believe that tale about me being a lord.*

Uno spent his time studying the country ahead, but when he caught Rand looking at him, he gave back stare for stare, and never said a word. It did not mean much. He would stare Ingtar in the eye, too. That was Uno's way.

The path chosen by the Darkfriends— *And what else,* Rand wondered; Hurin kept muttering about "something worse"—who had stolen the Horn never came close to any village. Rand saw villages, from one hilltop to another, with a mile or more of up-and-down country between, but there was never one close enough to make out the people in the streets. Or close enough for those people to make out a party heading south. There were farms, too, with low-eaved houses and tall barns and smoking chimneys, on hilltops and on hillsides and in the bottoms, but never one close enough for the farmer to have seen their quarry.

Eventually even Ingtar had to realize that the horses could not keep on as they were going. Rand heard muttered curses, and Ingtar pounded his thigh with a gauntleted fist, but finally he ordered everyone to dismount. They trotted, leading their horses, uphill and down, for a mile, then mounted and rode again. Then it was down again and trot. Trot a mile, then ride a mile. Trot, then ride.

Rand was surprised to see Loial grinning when they were down on the ground, toiling up a hill. The Ogier had been uneasy about riding and horses when they first met, preferring to trust to his own feet, but Rand thought he had long gotten over that.

"Do you like to run, Rand?" Loial laughed. "I do. I was the fastest in Stedding Shangtai. I outran a horse, once."

Rand only shook his head. He did not want to waste breath on talk. He looked for Mat and Perrin, but they were still at the back, too many men between for Rand to make them out. He wondered how the Shienarans could manage this in their armor. Not a one of them slowed or voiced a complaint. Uno did not even look as if he were breaking a sweat, and the bannerman never let the Gray Owl waver.

It was a quick pace, but twilight began to close without any sight of those they hunted except their tracks. At last, reluctantly, Ingtar called a halt to make camp for the night in the forest. The Shienarans went about getting fires started and setting picket-lines for the horses with a smooth economy of effort born of long experience. Ingtar posted six guards, in pairs, for the first watch.

Rand's first order of business was finding his bundle in the wicker panniers from the packhorses. It was not hard—there were few personal bundles among the supplies—but when he had it open, he let out a shout that brought every man in the camp erect with sword in hand.

Ingtar came running. "What is it? Peace, did someone get through? I did not hear the guards."

"It's these coats," Rand growled, still staring at what he had unpacked. One coat was black, embroidered with silver thread, the other white worked in gold. Both had herons on the collars, and both were at least as ornate as the scarlet coat he was wearing. "The servants told me I had two good, serviceable coats in here. Look at them!"

Ingtar sheathed his sword over his shoulder. The other men began to settle back down. "Well, they are serviceable."

"I can't wear these. I can't go around dressed like this all the time."

"You can wear them. A coat's a coat. I understand Moiraine Sedai herself saw to your packing. Maybe Aes Sedai do not exactly understand what a man wears in the field." Ingtar grinned. "After we catch these Trollocs, perhaps we'll have a feast. You will be dressed for it, at least, even if the rest of us are not." He strolled back to where the cook fires were already burning.

Rand had not moved since Ingtar mentioned Moiraine. He stared at the coats. *What is she doing? Whatever it is, I will not be used.* He bundled everything together again and stuffed the bundle back into the pannier. *I can always go naked,* he thought bitterly.

Shienarans took turns at the cooking when they were in the field, and Masema was stirring the kettle when Rand returned to the fires. The smell of a stew made from turnips, onions, and dried meat settled over the camp. Ingtar was served first, and then Uno, but everyone else stood in line however they happened to come. Masema slopped a big ladle of stew on Rand's plate; Rand stepped back quickly to keep from getting the overflow on his coat, and made room for the next man while sucking a burned thumb. Masema stared at him, with a fixed grin that never reached his eyes. Until Uno stepped up and cuffed him.

"We didn't bloody bring enough for you to be spilling it on the flaming ground." The one-eyed man looked at Rand and left. Masema rubbed his ear, but his glare followed Rand.

Rand went to join Ingtar and Loial, sitting on the ground under a spreading oak. Ingtar had his helmet off, on the ground beside him, but otherwise he was fully armored. Mat and Perrin were already there, eating hungrily. Mat gave a broad sneer at Rand's coat, but Perrin barely looked up, golden eyes shining in the half-light from the fires, before bending back to his plate.

*At least they didn't leave this time.*

He sat cross-legged on the other side of Ingtar from them. "I wish I knew why Uno keeps looking at me. It's probably this bloody coat."

Ingtar paused thoughtfully around a mouthful of stew. Finally he said, "Uno no doubt wonders if you are worthy of a heron-mark blade." Mat snorted loudly, but Ingtar went on unperturbed. "Do not let Uno upset you. He would treat Lord Agelmar like a raw recruit if he could. Well, perhaps not Agelmar, but anyone else. He has a tongue like a file, but he gives good advice. He should; he's been campaigning since before I was born. Listen to his advice, don't mind his tongue, and you will do all right with Uno."

"I thought he was like Masema." Rand shoveled stew into his mouth. It was too hot, but he gulped it down. They had not eaten since leaving Fal Dara, and he had been too worried to eat that morning. His stomach rumbled, reminding him it was past time. He wondered if telling Masema he liked the food would help. "Masema acts like he hates me, and I don't understand it."

"Masema served three years in the Eastern Marches," Ingtar said. "At Ankor Dail, against the Aiel." He stirred his stew with his spoon, frowning. "I ask no questions, mind. If Lan Dai Shan and Moiraine Sedai want to say you are from Andor, from the Two Rivers, then you are. But Masema can't get the look of the Aiel out of his head, and when he sees you. . . ." He shrugged. "I ask no questions."

Rand dropped his spoon in the plate with a sigh. "Everybody thinks I'm somebody I am not. I am from the Two Rivers, Ingtar. I grew tabac with—with my father, and tended his sheep. That is what I am. A farmer and shepherd from the Two Rivers."

"He's from the Two Rivers," Mat said scornfully. "I grew up with him, though you'd never know it now. You put this Aiel nonsense in his head on top of what's already there, and the Light knows what we'll have. An Aiel lord, maybe."

"No," Loial said, "he has the look. You remember, Rand, I remarked on it once, though I thought it was just because I didn't know you humans well enough then. Remember? 'Till shade is gone, till water is gone, into the Shadow with teeth bared, screaming defiance with the last breath, to spit in Sightblinder's eye on the Last Day.' You remember, Rand."

Rand stared at his plate. *Wrap a shoufa around your head, and you would be the image of an Aielman.* That had been Gawyn, brother to Elayne, the Daughter-Heir of Andor. *Everybody thinks I'm somebody I'm not.*

"What was that?" Mat asked. "About spitting in the Dark One's eye."

"That's how long the Aiel say they'll fight," Ingtar said, "and I don't doubt they will. Except for peddlers and gleemen, Aiel divide the world in two. Aiel, and enemies. They changed that for Cairhien five hundred years ago, for some reason no one but an Aiel could understand, but I do not think they will ever do so again."

"I suppose not," Loial sighed. "But they do let the Tuatha'an, the Traveling People, cross the Waste. And they don't see Ogier as enemies, either, though I doubt any of us would want to go out into the Waste. Aiel come to Stedding Shangtai sometimes to trade for sung wood. A hard people, though."

Ingtar nodded. "I wish I had some as hard. Half as hard."

"Is that a joke?" Mat laughed. "If I ran a mile wearing all the iron you're wearing, I would fall down and sleep a week. You've done it mile after mile all day."

"Aiel are hard," Ingtar said. "Man and woman, hard. I've fought them, and I know. They will run fifty miles, and fight a battle at the end of it. They're death walking, with any weapon or none. Except a sword. They will not touch a sword, for some reason. Or ride a horse, not that they need to. If you have a sword, and the Aielman has his bare hands, it is an even fight. If you're good. They herd cattle and goats where you or I would die of thirst before the day was done. They dig their villages into huge rock spires out in the Waste. They've been there since the Breaking, near enough. Artur Hawkwing tried to dig them out and was bloodied, the only major defeats he ever suffered. By day the air in the Aiel Waste shimmers with heat, and by night it freezes. And an Aiel will give you that blue-eyed stare and tell you there is no place on earth he would rather be. He won't be lying, either. If they ever tried to come out, we would be hard-pressed to stop them. The Aiel War lasted three years, and that was only four out of thirteen clans."

"Gray eyes from his mother doesn't make him an Aiel," Mat said.

Ingtar shrugged. "As I said, I ask no questions."

When Rand finally settled down for the night, his head hummed with unwanted thoughts. *Image of an Aielman. Moiraine Sedai wants to say you're from the Two Rivers. Aiel ravaged all the way to Tar Valon. Born on the slopes of Dragonmount. The Dragon Reborn.*

"I will not be used," he muttered, but sleep was a long time coming.

Ingtar broke camp before the sun was up in the morning. They had breakfasted and were riding south while the clouds in the east were still red with sunrise to come and dew still hung on the leaves. This time Ingtar put out scouts, and though the pace was hard, it was no longer horse-killing. Rand thought maybe Ingtar had realized they were not going to do it all in a day. The trail still led south, Hurin said. Until, two hours after the sun rose, one of the scouts came galloping back.

"Abandoned camp ahead, my Lord. Just on that hilltop there. Must have been at least thirty or forty of them there last night, my Lord."

Ingtar put spurs to horse as if he had been told the Darkfriends were still there, and Rand had to keep pace or be trampled by the Shienarans who galloped up the hill behind him.

There was not much to see. The cold ashes of campfires, well hidden in the trees, with what looked like the remnants of a meal tossed in them. A refuse heap too near the fires and already buzzing with flies.

Ingtar kept the others back, and dismounted to walk through the camp-site with Uno, examining the ground. Hurin rode the circumference of the site, sniffing. Rand sat his stallion with the other men; he had no desire for any closer look at a place where Trollocs and Darkfriends had camped. And a Fade. *And something worse.*

Mat scrambled up the hill afoot and stalked into the campsite. "Is this what a Darkfriend camp looks like? Smells a bit, but I can't say it looks any different from anybody else's." He kicked at one of the ash heaps, knocking out a piece of burned bone, and stooped to pick it up. "What do Darkfriends eat? Doesn't look like a sheep bone, or a cow."

"There was murder done here," Hurin said mournfully. He scrubbed at his nose with a kerchief. "Worse than murder."

"There were Trollocs here," Ingtar said, looking straight at Mat. "I suppose they got hungry, and the Darkfriends were handy." Mat dropped the blackened bone; he looked as if he were going to be sick.

"They are not going south any longer, my Lord," Hurin said. That took everyone's attention. He pointed back, to the northeast. "Maybe they've decided to break for the Blight after all. Go around us. Maybe they were just trying to put us off by coming south." He did not sound as if he believed it. He sounded puzzled.

"Whatever they were trying," Ingtar snarled, "I'll have them now. Mount!"

Little more than an hour later, though, Hurin drew rein. "They changed again, my Lord. South again. And they killed someone else here."

There were no ashes there, in the gap between two hills, but a few minutes' search found the body. A man curled up and stuffed under some bushes. The back of his head was smashed in, and his eyes still bulged with the force of the blow. No one recognized him, though he was wearing Shienaran clothes.

"We'll waste no time burying Darkfriends," Ingtar growled. "We ride south." He suited his own words almost before they were out of his mouth.

The day was the same as the day before had been, though. Uno studied tracks and droppings, and said they had gained a little ground on their quarry. Twilight came with no sight of Trollocs or Darkfriends, and the next morning there was another abandoned camp—and another murder done, so Hurin said—and another change of direction, this time to the northwest. Less than two hours on that track found another body, a man with his skull split open by an axe, and another change of direction. South again. Again gaining ground, by Uno's reading of the tracks. Again seeing nothing but distant farms until nightfall. And the next day was the same, changes in direction, murders and all. And the next.

Every day brought them a little closer behind their prey, but Ingtar fumed. He suggested cutting straight across when the trail changed direction of a morning—surely they would come on the trail heading south again, and gain more time—and before anyone could speak, he said it was a bad idea, in case this once the men they hunted did not turn south. He urged everyone to greater speed, to start earlier and ride till full dark. He reminded them of the charge the Amyrlin Seat had given them, to recover the Horn of Valere, and let nothing bar their way. He spoke of the glory they would have, their names remembered in story and history, in gleemen's tales and bards' songs, the men who found the Horn. He talked as if he could not stop, and he stared down the trail they followed as if his hope of the Light lay at the end of it. Even Uno began to look at him askance.

And so they came to the River Erinin.

It could not properly be called a village at all, to Rand's mind. He sat
his horse among the trees, peering up at half a dozen small houses with
wood-shingled roofs and eaves almost to the ground, on a hilltop overlooking the river beneath the morning sun. Few people passed this way. It was
only a few hours since they had broken camp, but past time for them to
have found the remains of the Darkfriends' resting place if the pattern held.
They had seen nothing of the sort, however.

The river itself was not much like the mighty Erinin of story, here so far
toward its source in the Spine of the World. Perhaps sixty paces of swift
water to the far bank, lined with trees, and a barge-like ferry on a thick
rope spanning the distance. The ferry sat snugged against the other side.

For once the trail had led straight to human habitation. Straight to the
houses on the hill. No one moved on the single dirt street around which
the dwellings clustered.

"Ambush, my Lord?" Uno said softly.

Ingtar gave the necessary orders, and the Shienarans unlimbered their
lances, sweeping around to encircle the houses. At a hand signal from
Ingtar they galloped between the houses from four directions, thundering
in with eyes searching, lances ready, dust rising under their hooves. Nothing moved but them. They drew rein, and the dust began to settle.

Rand returned to his quiver the arrow he had nocked, and slung his bow
on his back again. Mat and Perrin did the same. Loial and Hurin had just
waited there where Ingtar had left them, watching uneasily.

Ingtar waved, and Rand and the others rode up to join the Shienarans.

"I don't like the smell of this place," Perrin muttered as they came
among the houses. Hurin gave him a look, and he stared back until Hurin
dropped his eyes. "It smells wrong."

"Bloody Darkfriends and Trollocs went straight through, my Lord,"
Uno said, pointing to a few tracks not chopped to pieces by the Shienarans.
"Straight through to the goat-kissing ferry, which they bloody left on the
other side. Blood and bloody ashes! We're flaming lucky they didn't cut it
adrift."

"Where are the people?" Loial asked.

Doors stood open, curtains flapped at open windows, but no one had
come out for all the thunder of hooves.

"Search the houses," Ingtar commanded. Men dismounted and ran to
comply, but they came back shaking their heads.

"They're just gone, my Lord," Uno said. "Just bloody gone, burn me.
Like they'd picked up and decided to flaming walk away in the middle of

the bloody day." He stopped suddenly, pointing urgently to a house behind Ingtar. "There's a woman at that window. How I bloody missed
her. . . ." He was running for the house before anyone else could move.

"Don't frighten her!" Ingtar shouted. "Uno, we need information. The
Light blind you, Uno, don't frighten her!" The one-eyed man disappeared
through the open door. Ingtar raised his voice again. "We will not harm
you, good lady. We are Lord Agelmar's oathmen, from Fal Dara. Do not be
afraid! We will not harm you."

A window at the top of the house flew up, and Uno stuck his head out,
staring around wildly. With an oath he pulled back. Thumps and clatters
marked his passage back, as if he were kicking things in frustration. Finally
he appeared from the doorway.

"Gone, my Lord. But she was there. A woman in a white dress, at the
window. I saw her. I even thought I saw her inside, for a moment, but
then she was gone, and. . . ." He took a deep breath. "The house is
empty, my Lord." It was a measure of his agitation that he did not curse.

"Curtains," Mat muttered. "He's jumping at bloody curtains." Uno
gave him a sharp look, then returned to his horse.

"Where did they go?" Rand asked Loial. "Do you think they ran off
when the Darkfriends came?" *And Trollocs, and a Myrddraal. And Hurin's
something worse. Smart people, if they ran as hard as they could.*

"I fear the Darkfriends took them, Rand," Loial said slowly. He grimaced, almost a snarl with his broad nose like a snout. "For the Trollocs."
Rand swallowed and wished he had not asked; it was never pleasant to
think on how Trollocs fed.

"Whatever was done here," Ingtar said, "our Darkfriends did it. Hurin,
was there violence here? Killing? Hurin!"

The sniffer gave a start in his saddle and looked around wildly. He had
been staring across the river. "Violence, my Lord? Yes. Killing, no. Or not
exactly." He glanced sideways at Perrin. "I've never smelled anything exactly like it before, my Lord. But there was hurting done."

"Is there any doubt they crossed over? Have they doubled back again?"

"They crossed, my Lord." Hurin looked uneasily at the far bank. "They
crossed. What they did on the other side, though. . . ." He shrugged.

Ingtar nodded. "Uno, I want that ferry back on this side. And I want
the other side scouted before we cross. Just because there was no ambush
here doesn't mean there will not be one when we are split by the river.
That ferry does not look big enough to carry us all in one trip. See to it."

Uno bowed, and in moments Ragan and Masema were helping each
other out of their armor. Stripped down to breechclouts, with a dagger
stuck behind in the small of the back, they trotted to the river on horse-

men's bowed legs and waded in, beginning to work their way hand over hand along the thick rope along which the ferry ran. The cable sagged enough in the middle to put them in the river to their waists, and the current was strong, pulling them downstream, yet in less time than Rand expected they were hauling themselves over the slatted sides of the ferry. Drawing their daggers, they disappeared into the trees.

After what seemed like forever, the two men reappeared and began pulling the ferry slowly across. The barge butted against the bank below the village, and Masema tied it off while Ragan trotted up to where Ingtar waited. His face was pale, the arrow scar on his cheek sharp, and he sounded shaken.

"The far bank. . . . There is no ambush on the far bank, my Lord, but. . . ." He bowed deeply, still wet and shivering from his excursion. "My Lord, you must see for yourself. The big stoneoak, fifty paces south from the landing. I cannot say the words. You must see it yourself."

Ingtar frowned, looking from Ragan to the other bank. Finally, he said, "You have done well, Ragan. Both of you have." His voice became more brisk. "Find these men something to dry themselves on from the houses, Uno. And see if anybody left water on for tea. Put something hot into them, if you can. Then bring the second file and the pack animals over." He turned to Rand. "Well, are you ready to see the south bank of the Erinin?" He did not wait for an answer, but rode down to the ferry with Hurin and half the lancers.

Rand hesitated only a moment before following. Loial went with him. To his surprise, Perrin rode down ahead of them, looking grim. Some of the lancers, making gruff jokes, dismounted to haul on the rope and walk the ferry over.

Mat waited until the last minute, when one of the Shienarans was untying the ferry, before he kicked his horse and crowded aboard. "I have to come sooner or later, don't I?" he said, breathless, to no one in particular. "I have to find it."

Rand shook his head. With Mat looking as healthy as he ever had, he had almost forgotten why he was along. *To find the dagger. Let Ingtar have the Horn. I just want the dagger for Mat.* "We will find it, Mat."

Mat scowled at him—with a sneering glance for his fine red coat—and turned away. Rand sighed.

"It will all come right, Rand," Loial said quietly. "Somehow, it will."

The current took the ferry as it was hauled out from the bank, tugging it against the cable with a sharp creak. The lancers were odd ferrymen, walking the deck in helmets and armor, with swords on their backs, but they took the ferry out into the river well enough.

"This is how we left home," Perrin said suddenly. "At Taren Ferry. The ferrymen's boots clunking on the deck, and the water gurgling around the ferry. This is how we left. It will be worse, this time."

"How can it be worse?" Rand asked. Perrin did not answer. He searched the far bank, and his golden eyes almost seemed to shine, but not with eagerness.

After a minute, Mat asked, "How can it be worse?"

"It will be. I can smell it," was all Perrin would say. Hurin eyed him nervously, but then Hurin seemed to be eyeing everything nervously since they had left Fal Dara.

The ferry bumped against the south bank with a hollow thud of stout planks against hard clay, almost under overhanging trees, and the Shienarans who had been hauling on the rope mounted their horses, except for two Ingtar told to take the ferry back over for the others. The rest followed Ingtar up the bank.

"Fifty paces to a big stoneoak," Ingtar said as they rode into the trees. He sounded too matter-of-fact. If Ragan could not speak of it. . . . Some of the soldiers eased the swords on their backs, and held their lances ready.

At first Rand thought the figures hanging by their arms from the thick gray limbs of the stoneoak were scarecrows. Crimson scarecrows. Then he recognized the two faces. Changu, and the other man who had been on guard with him. Nidao. Eyes staring, teeth bared in a rictus of pain. They had lived a long time after it began.

Perrin made a sound in his throat, nearly a growl.

"As bad as ever I've seen, my Lord," Hurin said faintly. "As bad as ever I've smelled, excepting the dungeon at Fal Dara that night."

Frantically Rand sought the void. The flame seemed to get in the way, the queasy light fluttering in time with his convulsive swallows, but he pushed on until he had wrapped himself in emptiness. The queasiness pulsed in the void with him, though. Not outside, for once, but inside. *No wonder, looking at this.* The thought skittered across the void like a drop of water on a hot griddle. *What happened to them?*

"Skinned alive," he heard someone behind him say, and the sounds of somebody else retching. He thought it was Mat, but it was all far away from him, inside the void. But that nauseous flickering was in there, too. He thought he might throw up himself.

"Cut them down," Ingtar said harshly. He hesitated a moment, then added, "Bury them. We cannot be sure they were Darkfriends. They could have been taken prisoner. They could have been. Let them know the last embrace of the mother, at least." Men rode forward gingerly with knives;

even for battle-hardened Shienarans it was no easy task, cutting down the flayed corpses of men they knew.

"Are you all right, Rand?" Ingtar said. "I am not used to this either."

"I . . . am all right, Ingtar." Rand let the void vanish. He felt less sick without it; his stomach still curdled, but it was better. Ingtar nodded and turned his horse so he could watch the men working.

The burial was simple. Two holes dug in the ground, and the bodies laid in as the rest of the Shienarans watched in silence. The grave diggers began shoveling earth into the graves with no more ado.

Rand was shocked, but Loial explained softly. "Shienarans believe we all came from earth, and must return to earth. They never use coffins or shrouds, and the bodies are never clothed. The earth must hold the body. The last embrace of the mother, they call it. And there are never any words except 'The Light shine on you, and the Creator shelter you. The last embrace of the mother welcome you home.'" Loial sighed and shook his huge head. "I do not think anyone will say them this time. No matter what Ingtar says, Rand, there cannot be much doubt that Changu and Nidao slew the guards at the Dog Gate and let the Darkfriends into the keep. It had to be they who were responsible for all of it."

"Then who shot the arrow at—at the Amyrlin?" Rand swallowed. *Who shot at me?* Loial said nothing.

Uno arrived with the rest of the men and the packhorses as the last earth was being shoveled onto the graves. Someone told him what they had found, and the one-eyed man spat. "Goat-kissing Trollocs do that along the Blight, sometimes. When they want to shake your bloody nerve, or flaming warn you not to follow. Burn me if it works here, either."

Before they rode away, Ingtar paused on his horse beside the unmarked graves, two mounds of bare earth that looked too small to hold men. After a moment he said, "The Light shine on you, and the Creator shelter you. The last embrace of the mother welcome you home." When he raised his head, he looked at each man in turn. There was no expression on any face, least of all on Ingtar's. "They saved Lord Agelmar at Tarwin's Gap," he said. Several of the lancers nodded. Ingtar turned his horse. "Which way, Hurin?"

"South, my Lord."

"Take the trail! We hunt!"

The forest soon gave way to gently rolling flatland, sometimes crossed by a shallow stream that had dug itself a high-banked channel, with never more than a low rise or a squat hill that barely deserved the name. Perfect country for the horses. Ingtar took advantage of it, setting a steady, ground-covering pace. Occasionally Rand saw what might have been a farmhouse in the distance, and once what he thought was a village, with smoke rising from chimneys a few miles off and something flashing white in the sun, but the land near them stayed empty of human life, long swathes of grass dotted with brush and occasional trees, with now and again a small thicket, never more than a hundred paces across.

Ingtar put out scouts, two men riding ahead, in sight only when they topped an occasional rise. He had a silver whistle hanging around his neck to call them back if Hurin said the trail had veered, but it did not. South. Always south.

"We will reach the field of Talidar in three or four days at this rate," Ingtar said as they rode. "Artur Hawkwing's greatest single victory, when the Halfmen led the Trollocs out of the Blight against him. Six days and nights, it lasted, and when it was done, the Trollocs fled back into the Blight and never dared challenge him again. He raised a monument there to his victory, a spire a hundred spans high. He would not let them put his own name on it, but rather the names of every man who fell, and a golden sun at the top, symbol that there the Light had triumphed over the Shadow."

"I would like to see that," Loial said. "I have never heard of this monument."

Ingtar was silent for a moment, and when he spoke his voice was quiet. "It is not there any longer, Builder. When Hawkwing died, the ones who fought over his empire could not bear to leave a monument to a victory of his, even if it did not mention his name. There's nothing left but the mound where it stood. In three or four days we can see that, at least." His tone did not allow much conversation afterwards.

With the sun hanging golden overhead, they passed a structure, square and made of plastered brick, less than a mile from their path. It was not tall, no more than two stories still standing anywhere he saw, but it covered a good hide of ground. An air of long abandonment hung about it, roofs gone except for a few stretches of dark tile clinging to bits of rafter, most of the once-white plaster fallen to bare the dark, weathered brick beneath, walls fallen to show courtyards and decaying chambers inside. Brush, and even trees, grew in the cracks of what had once been courtyards.

"A manor house," Ingtar explained. The little humor he had regained seemed to fade as he looked at the structure. "When Harad Dakar still stood, I expect the manorman farmed this land for a league around. Orchards, maybe. The Hardani loved their orchards."

"Harad Dakar?" Rand said, and Ingtar snorted.

"Does no one learn history any longer? Harad Dakar, the capital city of Hardan, which nation this once was that we are riding across."

"I've seen an old map," Rand replied in a tight voice. "I know about the nations that aren't there anymore. Maredo, and Goaban, and Carralain. But there wasn't any Hardan on it."

"There were once others that are gone now, too," Loial said. "Mar Haddon, which is now Haddon Mirk, and Almoth. Kintara. The War of the Hundred Years cut Artur Hawkwing's empire into many nations, large and small. The small were gobbled up by the large, or else united, like Altara and Murandy. Forced together would be a better word than united, I suppose."

"So what happened to them?" Mat demanded. Rand had not noticed Perrin and Mat ride up to join them. They had been at the rear, as far from Rand al'Thor as they could get, the last he had seen.

"They could not hold together," the Ogier replied. "Crops failed, or trade failed. People failed. Something failed in each case, and the nation dwindled. Often neighboring countries absorbed the land, when the nations were gone, but they never lasted, those annexations. In time, the land truly was abandoned. Some villages hang on here and there, but mostly they have all gone to wilderness. It is nearly three hundred years since Harad Dakar was finally abandoned, but even before that it was a shell, with a king who could not control what happened inside the city walls. Harad Dakar itself is completely gone now, I understand. All the towns and cities of Hardan are gone, the stone carted away by farmers and villagers for their own use. Most of the farms and villages made with it are gone, too. So I read, and I've seen nothing to change it."

"It was quite a quarry, Harad Dakar, for almost a hundred years," Ingtar said bitterly. "The people left, finally, and then the city was hauled away, stone by stone. All faded away, and what has not gone is fading. Everything, everywhere, fading. There is hardly a nation that truly controls the land it claims on a map, and there is hardly a land that claims today on a map what it did even a hundred years ago. When the War of the Hundred Years ended, a man rode from one nation into another without end from the Blight to the Sea of Storms. Now we can ride through wilderness claimed by no nation for almost the whole of the land. We in the Borderlands have our battle with the Blight to keep us strong, and whole. Perhaps they did not have what they needed to keep them strong. You say they failed, Builder? Yes, they failed, and what nation standing whole today will fail tomorrow? We are being swept away, humankind. Swept away like flotsam on a flood. How long until there is nothing left but the Borderlands? How long before we, too, go under, and there is nothing left but Trollocs and Myrddraal all the way to the Sea of Storms?"

There was a shocked silence. Not even Mat broke it. Ingtar rode lost in his own dark thoughts.

After a time the scouts came galloping back, straight in the saddles, lances erect against the sky. "A village ahead, my Lord. We were not seen, but it lies directly in our line of march."

Ingtar shook himself out of his brown study, but did not speak until they had reached the crest of a low ridge looking down on the village, and then it was only to command a halt while he dug a looking glass from his saddlebags and raised it to peer at the village.

Rand studied the village with interest. It was as big as Emond's Field, though that was not very big compared to some of the towns he had seen since leaving the Two Rivers, much less the cities. The houses were all low and plastered with white clay, and they appeared to have grass growing on sloping roofs. A dozen windmills, scattered through the village, turned lazily, their long, cloth-covered arms flashing white in the sun. A low wall encircled the village, grassy dirt and chest high, and outside that was a wide ditch with sharpened stakes thick in the bottom. There was no gate in the one opening he could see in the wall, but he supposed it could be blocked easily enough with a cart or wagon. He could not see any people.

"Not even a dog in sight," Ingtar said, returning the looking glass to his saddlebags. "Are you sure they did not see you?" he asked the scouts.

"Not unless they have the Dark One's own luck, my Lord," one of the men replied. "We never crested the rise. We didn't see anyone moving then either, my Lord."

Ingtar nodded. "The trail, Hurin?"

Hurin drew a deep breath. "Toward the village, my Lord. Straight to it, as near as I can tell from here."

"Watch sharp," Ingtar commanded, gathering his reins. "And do not believe that they're friendly just because they smile. If there is anyone there." He led them down toward the village at a slow walk, and reached up to loosen his sword in its scabbard.

Rand heard the sounds of others behind him doing the same. After a moment, he eased his, too. Trying to stay alive was not the same as trying to be a hero, he decided.

"You think these people would help Darkfriends?" Perrin asked Ingtar. The Shienaran was slow in answering.

"They have no great love for Shienarans," he said finally. "They think we should protect them. Us, or the Cairhienin. Cairhien did claim this land, once the last King of Hardan died. All the way to the Erinin, they claimed it. They could not hold it, though. They gave up the claim nearly a hundred years ago. The few people who still live here don't have to worry about Trollocs this far south, but there are plenty of human brigands. That's why they have the wall, and the ditch. All their villages do. Their fields will be hidden in hollows around here, but no one will live outside the wall. They would swear fealty to any king who would give them his protection, but we have all we can do against the Trollocs. They do not love us for it, though." As they reached the opening in the low wall, he added again, "Watch sharp!"

All the streets led toward a village square, but there was no one in the streets, no one peering from a window. Not even a dog moved, not so much as a chicken. Nothing living. Open doors swung, creaking in the wind, counterpoint to the rhythmic squeak of the windmills. The horses' hooves sounded loud on the packed dirt of the street.

"Like at the ferry," Hurin muttered, "but different." He rode hunched in his saddle, head down as if he were trying to hide behind his own shoulders. "Violence done, but . . . I don't know. It was bad here. It smells bad."

"Uno," Ingtar said, "take one file and search the houses. If you find anyone, bring them to me in the square. Do not frighten them this time, though. I want answers, not people running for their lives." He led the other soldiers toward the center of the village as Uno got his ten dismounted.

Rand hesitated, looking around. The creaking doors, the squealing windmills, the horses' hooves, all made too much noise, as if there were not another sound in the world. He scanned the houses. The curtains in an open window beat against the outside of the house. They all seemed lifeless. With a sigh he got down and walked to the nearest house, then stopped, staring at the door.

*It's just a door. What are you afraid of?* He wished he did not feel as if there was something waiting on the other side. He pushed it open.

Inside was a tidy room. Or had been. The table was set for a meal, ladder-back chairs gathered around, some plates already served. A few flies buzzed above bowls of turnips and peas, and more crawled on a cold roast sitting in its own congealed grease. There was a slice half carved from the roast, the fork still standing stuck in the meat and the carving knife lying partway in the platter as if dropped. Rand stepped inside.

Blink.

A smiling, bald-headed man in rough clothes laid a slice of meat on a plate held by a woman with a worn face. She was smiling, too, though. She added peas and turnips to the plate and passed it to one of the children lining the table. There were half a dozen children, boys and girls, from nearly grown down to barely tall enough to look over the table. The woman said something, and the girl taking the plate from her laughed. The man started to cut another slice.

Suddenly another girl screamed, pointing at the door to the street. The man dropped the carving knife and whirled, then he screamed, too, face tight with horror, and snatched up a child. The woman grabbed another, and motioned desperately to the others, her mouth working frantically, silently. They all scrabbled toward a door in the back of the room.

That door burst open, and—

Blink.

Rand could not move. The flies buzzing over the table sounded louder. His breath made a cloud in front of his mouth.

Blink.

A smiling, bald-headed man in rough clothes laid a slice of meat on a plate held by a woman with a worn face. She was smiling, too, though. She added peas and turnips to the plate and passed it to one of the children lining the table. There were half a dozen children, boys and girls, from nearly grown down to barely tall enough to look over the table. The woman said something, and the girl taking the plate from her laughed. The man started to cut another slice.

Suddenly another girl screamed, pointing at the door to the street. The man dropped the carving knife and whirled, then he screamed, too, face tight with horror, and snatched up a child. The woman grabbed another, and motioned desperately to the others, her mouth working frantically, silently. They all scrabbled toward the door in the back of the room.

That door burst open, and—

Blink.

Rand struggled, but his muscles seemed frozen. The room was colder; he wanted to shiver, but he could not move even that much. Flies crawled all over the table. He groped for the void. The sour light was there, but he did not care. He had to—

Blink.

A smiling, bald-headed man in rough clothes laid a slice of meat on a plate held by a woman with a worn face. She was smiling, too, though. She added peas and turnips to the plate and passed it to one of the children lining the table. There were half a dozen children, boys and girls, from nearly grown down to barely tall enough to look over the table. The woman said something, and the girl taking the plate from her laughed. The man started to cut another slice.

Suddenly another girl screamed, pointing at the door to the street. The man dropped the carving knife and whirled, then he screamed, too, face tight with horror, and snatched up a child. The woman grabbed another, and motioned desperately to the others, her mouth working frantically, silently. They all scrabbled toward a door in the back of the room.

That door burst open, and—

Blink.

The room was freezing. *So cold.* Flies blackened the table; the walls were a shifting mass of flies, the floor, the ceiling, all black with them. They crawled on Rand, covering him, crawled over his face, his eyes, into his nose, his mouth. *Light, help me. Cold.* The flies buzzed like thunder. *Cold.* It penetrated the void, mocking the emptiness, encasing him in ice. Desperately he reached for the flickering light. His stomach twisted, but the light was warm. Warm. Hot. He was hot.

Suddenly he was tearing at . . . something. He did not know what, or how. Cobwebs made of steel. Moonbeams carved from stone. They crumbled at his touch, but he knew he had not touched anything. They shriveled and melted with the heat that surged through him, heat like a forge fire, heat like the world burning, heat like—

It was gone. Panting, he looked around with wide eyes. A few flies lay on the half-carved roast, in the platter. Dead flies. *Six flies. Only six.* There were more in the bowls, half a dozen tiny black specks among the cold vegetables. All dead. He staggered out into the street.

Mat was just coming out of a house across the street, shaking his head. "Nobody there," he told Perrin, still on his horse. "It looks like they just got up in the middle of supper and walked away."

A shout came from the square.

"They've found something," Perrin said, digging his heels into his horse's flanks. Mat scrambled into his saddle and galloped after him.

Rand mounted Red more slowly; the stallion shied as if feeling his unease. He glanced at the houses as he rode slowly toward the square, but he could not make himself look at them for long. *Mat went in one, and nothing happened to him.* He resolved not to set foot inside another house in that village no matter what. Booting Red, he quickened his pace.

Everyone was standing like statues in front of a large building with wide double doors. Rand did not think it could be an inn; there was no sign, for one thing. Perhaps a village meeting place. He joined the silent circle, and stared along with the rest.

There was a man spread-eagled across the doors with thick spikes through wrists and shoulders. More spikes had been driven into his eyes to hold his head up. Dark, dried blood made fans down his cheeks. Scuff marks on the wood behind his boots showed that he had been alive when it was done. When it began, anyway.

Rand's breath caught. Not a man. Those black clothes, blacker than black, had never been worn by any human. The wind flapped an end of the cloak caught behind the body—which it did not always, he knew too well; the wind did not always touch those clothes—but there had never been any eyes in that pale, bloodless face.

"Myrddraal," he breathed, and it was as if his speaking released all the others. They began to move again, and breathe.

"Who," Mat began, and had to stop to swallow. "Who could do this to a Fade?" His voice squeaked at the end.

"I don't know," Ingtar said. "I do not know." He looked around, examining faces, or perhaps counting to be sure everyone was there. "And I do not think we will learn anything here. We ride. Mount! Hurin, find the trail out of this place."

"Yes, my Lord. Yes. With pleasure. That way, my Lord. They're still heading south."

They rode away leaving the dead Myrddraal where it hung, the wind stirring its black cloak. Hurin was first beyond the wall, not waiting on Ingtar for a change, but Rand came close behind him.

# CHAPTER 11

## *Glimmers of the Pattern*

For once, Ingtar called a halt to the day's march with the sun still golden above the horizon. The toughened Shienarans were feeling the effects of what they had seen in the village. Ingtar had not stopped so early before, and the campsite he chose had the look of a place that could be defended. It was a deep hollow, almost round, and big enough to hold all the men and horses comfortably. A sparse thicket of scrub oak and leatherleaf covered the outer slopes. The rim itself stood more than high enough to hide anyone in the campsite even without the trees. The height nearly passed for a hill, in that country.

"All I'm bloody saying," he heard Uno tell Ragan as they dismounted, "is that I bloody saw her, burn you. Just before we found the goat-kissing Halfman. The same flaming woman as at the flaming ferry. She was there, and then she bloody wasn't. You say what you bloody want to, but you watch how you flaming say it, or I'll bloody skin you myself, and burn the goat-kissing hide, you sheep-gutted milk-drinker."

Rand paused with one foot on the ground and the other still in the stirrup. *The same woman? But there wasn't any woman at the ferry, just some curtains blowing in the wind. And she couldn't have gotten to that village ahead of us if there had been.* The village. . . .

He shied away from the thought. Even more than the Fade nailed to the door, he wanted to forget that room, and the flies, and the people who were there and not there. The Halfman had been real—everybody had seen that—but the room. . . . *Maybe I'm finally going mad.* He wished Moiraine was there to talk to. *Wishing for an Aes Sedai. You* are *a fool. You're well out of that, now stay out. But am I out? What happened there?*

"Packhorses and supplies in the middle," Ingtar commanded as the lancers went about setting up camp. "Rub the horses down, then saddle them again in case we must move quickly. Every man sleeps by his mount, and there'll be no fires tonight. Watch changes every two hours. Uno, I want scouts out, as far as they can ride and return before dark. I want to know what is out there."

*He's feeling it,* Rand thought. *It isn't just some Darkfriends and a few Trollocs and maybe a Fade anymore.* Just some Darkfriends and a few Trollocs, and maybe a Fade! Even a few days before there would not have been any "just" about it. Even in the Borderlands, even with the Blight less than a day's ride, Darkfriends and Trollocs and Myrddraal had been bad enough for a nightmare, then. Before he had seen a Myrddraal nailed to a door. *What in the Light could have done* that*? What* not *in the Light?* Before he had walked into a room where a family had had their supper and their laughter cut off. *I must have imagined it. I must have.* Even in his own head he did not sound very convincing. He had not imagined the wind on the tower top, or the Amyrlin saying—

"Rand?" He jumped as Ingtar spoke at his shoulder. "Are you going to stay all night with one foot in the stirrup?"

Rand put his other foot on the ground. "Ingtar, what happened back at that village?"

"Trollocs took them. The same as the people at the ferry. That is what happened. The Fade. . . ." Ingtar shrugged and stared down at a flat, canvas-wrapped bundle, large and square, in his arms; he stared at it as if he saw hidden secrets he would rather not know. "The Trollocs took them for food. They do it in villages and farms near the Blight, too, sometimes, if a raid gets past the border towers in the night. Sometimes we get the people back, and sometimes not. Sometimes we get them back and almost wish we hadn't. Trollocs don't always kill before they start butchering. And Halfmen like to have their . . . fun. That's worse than what the Trollocs do." His voice was as steady as if he were talking of every day, and perhaps he was, for a Shienaran soldier.

Rand took a deep breath to steady his stomach. "The Fade back there didn't have any fun, Ingtar. What could nail a Myrddraal to a door, alive?"

Ingtar hesitated, shaking his head, then pushed the big bundle at Rand. "Here. Moiraine Sedai told me to give you this at the first camp south of the Erinin. I don't know what is in it, but she said you would need it. She said to tell you to take care of it; your life may depend on it."

Rand took it reluctantly; his skin prickled at the touch of the canvas. There was something soft inside. Cloth, maybe. He held it gingerly. *He doesn't want to think about the Myrddraal either. What happened in that room?* He realized suddenly that for him, the Fade, or even that room, was preferable to thinking about what Moiraine might have sent him.

"I was told to tell you at the same time that if anything happens to me, the lances will follow you."

"Me!" Rand gasped, forgetting the bundle and everything else. Ingtar met his incredulous stare with a calm nod. "That's crazy! I've never led anything but a flock of sheep, Ingtar. They would not follow me anyway. Besides, Moiraine can't tell you who your second is. It's Uno."

"Uno and I were called to Lord Agelmar the morning we left. Moiraine Sedai was there, but it was Lord Agelmar who told me. You are second, Rand."

"But why, Ingtar? Why?" Moiraine's hand was bright and clear in it, hers and the Amyrlin's, pushing him along the path they had chosen, but he had to ask.

The Shienaran looked as if he did not understand it either, but he was a soldier, used to odd commands in the endless war along the Blight. "I heard rumors from the women's apartments that you were really a. . . ." He spread gauntleted hands. "No matter. I know you deny it. Just as you deny the look of your own face. Moiraine Sedai says you're a shepherd, but I never saw a shepherd with a heron-mark blade. No matter. I'll not claim I would have chosen you myself, but I think you have it in you to do what is needed. You will do your duty, if it comes to it."

Rand wanted to say it was no duty of his, but instead he said, "Uno knows about this. Who else, Ingtar?"

"All the lances. When we Shienarans ride, every man knows who is next in line if the man in command falls. A chain unbroken right down to the last man left, even if he's nothing but a horseholder. That way, you see, even if he *is* the last man, he is not just a straggler running and trying to stay alive. He has the command, and duty calls him to do what must be done. If I go to the last embrace of the mother, the duty is yours. You will find the Horn, and you will take it where it belongs. You will." There was a peculiar emphasis in Ingtar's last words.

The bundle in Rand's arms seemed to weigh ten stone. *Light, she could be a hundred leagues off, and she still reaches out and tugs the leash. This way, Rand. That way. You're the Dragon Reborn, Rand.* "I don't want the duty,

Ingtar. I will not take it. Light, I'm just a shepherd! Why won't anybody believe that?"

"You will do your duty, Rand. When the man at the top of the chain fails, everything below him falls apart. Too much is falling apart. Too much already. Peace favor your sword, Rand al'Thor."

"Ingtar, I—" But Ingtar was walking away, calling to see if Uno had the scouts out yet.

Rand stared at the bundle in his arms and licked his lips. He was afraid he knew what was in it. He wanted to look, yet he wanted to throw it in a fire without opening it; he thought he might, if he could be sure it would burn without anyone seeing what was inside, if he could be sure what was inside would burn at all. But he could not look there, where other eyes than his might see.

He glanced around the camp. The Shienarans were unloading the pack animals, some already handing out a cold supper of dried meat and flatbread. Mat and Perrin tended their horses, and Loial sat on a stone reading a book, with his long-stemmed pipe clenched between his teeth and a wisp of smoke curling above his head. Gripping the bundle as if afraid he might drop it, Rand sneaked into the trees.

He knelt in a small clearing sheltered by thick-foliaged branches and set the bundle on the ground. For a time he just stared at it. *She wouldn't have. She couldn't.* A small voice answered, *Oh, yes, she could. She could and would.* Finally he set about untying the small knots in the cords that bound it. Neat knots, tied with a precision that spoke loudly of Moiraine's own hand; no servant had done this for her. She would not have dared let any servant see.

When he had the last cord unfastened, he opened out what was folded inside with hands that felt numb, then stared at it, his mouth full of dust. It was all of one piece, neither woven, nor dyed, nor painted. A banner, white as snow, big enough to be seen the length of a field of battle. And across it marched a rippling figure like a serpent scaled in gold and crimson, but a serpent with four scaled legs, each tipped with five golden claws, a serpent with eyes like the sun and a golden lion's mane. He had seen it once before, and Moiraine had told him what it was. The banner of Lews Therin Telamon, Lews Therin Kinslayer, in the War of the Shadow. The banner of the Dragon.

"Look at that! Look what he's got, now!" Mat burst into the clearing. Perrin came after him more slowly. "First fancy coats," Mat snarled, "and now a banner! We'll hear no end of lording it now, with—" Mat got close enough to see the banner clearly, and his jaw dropped. "Light!" He stumbled back a step. "Burn me!" He had been there, too, when Moiraine named the banner. So had Perrin.

Anger boiled up in Rand, anger at Moiraine and the Amyrlin Seat, pushing him, pulling him. He snatched up the banner in both hands and shook it at Mat, words boiling out uncontrollably. "That's right! The Dragon's banner!" Mat took another step back. "Moiraine wants me to be a puppet on Tar Valon strings, a false Dragon for the Aes Sedai. She's going to push it down my throat whatever I want. But—I—will—not—be—used!"

Mat had backed up against a tree trunk. "A false Dragon?" He swallowed. "You? That . . . that's crazy."

Perrin had not retreated. He squatted down with his thick arms on his knees and studied Rand with those bright golden eyes. In the evening shadows they seemed to shine. "If the Aes Sedai want you for a false Dragon. . . ." He paused, frowning, thinking things through. Finally, he said quietly, "Rand, can you channel?" Mat gave a strangled gasp.

Rand let the banner drop; he hesitated only a moment before nodding wearily. "I did not ask for it. I don't want it. But. . . . But I do not think I know how to stop it." The room with the flies came back unbidden to his mind. "I don't think they'll let me stop."

"Burn me!" Mat breathed. "Blood and bloody ashes! They'll kill us, you know. All of us. Perrin and me as well as you. If Ingtar and the others find out, they will cut our bloody throats for Darkfriends. Light, they'll probably think we were part of stealing the Horn, and killing those people in Fal Dara."

"Shut up, Mat," Perrin said calmly.

"Don't tell me to shut up. If Ingtar doesn't kill us, Rand will go mad and do it for him. Burn me! Burn me!" Mat slid down the tree to sit on the ground. "Why didn't they gentle you? If the Aes Sedai know, why didn't they gentle you? I never heard of them letting a man who can wield the Power just walk away."

"They don't all know," Rand sighed. "The Amyrlin—"

"The Amyrlin Seat! *She* knows? Light, no wonder she looked at me so strange."

"—and Moiraine told me I'm the Dragon Reborn, and then they said I could go wherever I wanted. Don't you see, Mat? They are trying to use me."

"Doesn't change you being able to channel," Mat muttered. "If I were you, I'd be halfway to the Aryth Ocean by now. And I would not stop until I found someplace where there were no Aes Sedai, and never likely to be any. And no people. I mean . . . well. . . ."

"Shut up, Mat," Perrin said. "Why *are* you here, Rand? The longer you stay around people, the more likely it is somebody will find out and send for Aes Sedai. Aes Sedai who *won't* tell you to go on about your business." He paused, scratching his head over that. "And Mat's right about Ingtar. I don't doubt he would name you Darkfriend and kill you. Kill all of us, maybe. He seems to like you, but he'd still do it, I think. A false Dragon? So would the others. Masema wouldn't need that much excuse, for you. So why aren't you gone?"

Rand shrugged. "I was going, but first the Amyrlin came, and then the Horn was stolen, and the dagger, and Moiraine said Mat was dying, and. . . . Light, I thought I could stay with you until we found the dagger, at least; I thought I could help with that. Maybe I was wrong."

"You came because of the dagger?" Mat said quietly. He rubbed his nose and grimaced. "I never thought of that. I never thought you wanted to. . . . Aaaah! Are you feeling all right? I mean, you aren't going mad already, are you?"

Rand dug a pebble out of the ground and threw it at him.

"Ouch!" Mat rubbed his arm. "I was just asking. I mean, all those fancy clothes, and all that talk about being a lord. Well, that isn't exactly right in the head."

"I was trying to get rid of you, fool! I was afraid I'd go mad and hurt you." His eyes dropped to the banner, and his voice lowered. "I will, eventually, if I don't stop it. Light, I don't know how to stop it."

"That is what I'm afraid of," Mat said, standing. "No offense, Rand, but I think I will just sleep as far away from you as I can, if you don't mind. That's if you are staying. I heard about a fellow who could channel, once. A merchant's guard told me. Before the Red Ajah found him, he woke one morning, and his whole village was smashed flat. All the houses, all the people, everything but the bed he was sleeping in, like a mountain had rolled over them."

Perrin said, "In that case, Mat, you should sleep cheek by jowl with him."

"I may be a fool, but I intend to be a live fool." Mat hesitated, looking sideways at Rand. "Look, I know you came along to help me, and I am grateful. I really am. But you just are not the same anymore. You understand that, don't you?" He waited as if he expected an answer. None came. Finally he vanished into the trees, back toward the camp.

"What about you?" Rand asked.

Perrin shook his head, shaggy curls swinging. "I don't know, Rand. You are the same, but then again, you aren't. A man channeling; my mother used to frighten me with that, when I was little. I just do not know." He stretched out his hand and touched a corner of the banner. "I think I would burn this, or bury it, if I were you. Then I'd run so far, so fast, no Aes Sedai would ever find me. Mat was right about that." He stood up, squinting at the western sky, beginning to turn red with the sinking sun. "Time to get back to the camp. You think on what I said, Rand. I'd run. But maybe you can't run. Think of that, too." His yellow eyes seemed to look inward, and he sounded tired. "Sometimes you can't run." Then he was gone, too.

Rand knelt there, staring at the banner spread out on the ground. "Well, sometimes you *can* run," he muttered. "Only, maybe she gave me this to make me run. Maybe she has something waiting for me, if I run. I won't do what she wants. I won't. I'll bury it right here. But she said my life may depend on it, and Aes Sedai never lie so you can see it. . . ." Suddenly his shoulders shook with silent laughter. "Now I'm talking to myself. Maybe I *am* going mad already."

When he returned to the camp, he carried the banner wrapped in the canvas once more, tied with knots less neat than Moiraine's had been.

The light had begun to fail and the shadow of the rim covered half the hollow. The soldiers were settling in, all with their horses by their sides, lances propped to hand. Mat and Perrin were bedding down alongside their horses. Rand gave them a sad look, then fetched Red, standing where he had been left with his reins dangling, and went to the other side of the hollow, where Hurin had joined Loial. The Ogier had given over reading and was examining the half-buried stone on which he had been sitting, tracing something on the stone with the long stem of his pipe.

Hurin stood and gave Rand something just short of a bow. "Hope you don't mind me making my bed here, Lord—uh—Rand. I was just listening to the Builder here."

"There you are, Rand," Loial said. "You know, I think this stone was worked once. See, it's weathered, but it looks as if it was a column of some kind. And there are markings, also. I can't quite make them out, but they look familiar, somehow."

"Maybe you'll be able to see them better in the morning," Rand said. He pulled the saddlebags from Red. "I'll be glad of your company, Hurin." *I'm glad of anybody's company who isn't afraid of me. How much longer can I have it, though?*

He shifted everything into one side of the saddlebags—spare shirts and breeches and woolen stockings, sewing kit, tinder box, tin plate and cup, a greenwood box with knife and fork and spoon, a packet of dried meat and flatbread for emergency rations, and all the other traveler's necessaries—then stuffed the canvas-wrapped banner into the empty pocket. It bulged, the straps barely reaching the buckles, but then, the other side bulged now, too. It would do.

Loial and Hurin seemed to sense his mood, leaving him in silence while he stripped saddle and bridle from Red, rubbed the big bay down with tufts of grass torn from the ground, then resaddled him. Rand refused their offer of food; he did not think he could have stomached the best meal he had ever seen just then. All three of them made their beds there beside the stone, a simple matter of a blanket folded for a pillow and cloak to cover.

The camp was silent now, but Rand lay awake past the fall of full dark. His mind darted back and forth. The banner. *What is she trying to make me do?* The village. *What could kill a Fade like that?* Worst of all, the house in the village. *Did it really happen? Am I going mad already? Do I run, or do I stay? I have to stay. I have to help Mat find the dagger.*

An exhausted sleep finally came, and with sleep, unbidden, the void surrounded him, flickering with an uneasy glow that disturbed his dreams.

Padan Fain stared northward out into the night, past the only fire in his camp, smiling a fixed smile that never touched his eyes. He still thought of himself as Padan Fain—Padan Fain was the core of him—but he had been changed, and he knew it. He knew many things, now, more than any of his old masters could suspect. He had been a Darkfriend long years before Ba'alzamon summoned him and set him on the track of the three young men from Emond's Field, distilling what he knew of them, distilling him, and feeding the essence back so that he could *feel* them, *smell* where they had been, follow wherever they ran. Especially the one. A part of him still cringed, remembering what Ba'alzamon had done to him, but it was a small part, hidden, suppressed. He was changed. Following the three had led him into Shadar Logoth. He had not wanted to go, but he had had to obey. Then. And in Shadar Logoth. . . .

Fain drew a deep breath and fingered the ruby-hilted dagger at his belt. That had come from Shadar Logoth, too. It was the only weapon he carried, the only one he needed; it felt like a part of him. He was whole within himself, now. That was all that mattered.

He cast a glance to either side of his fire. The twelve Darkfriends who were left, their once-fine clothes now rumpled and dirty, huddled in the darkness to one side, staring not at the fire, but at him. On the other squatted his Trollocs, twenty in number, the all-too-human eyes in those animal-twisted men's faces following his every move like mice watching a cat.

It had been a struggle at first, waking each morning to find himself not completely whole, to find the Myrddraal back in command, raging and demanding they go north, to the Blight, to Shayol Ghul. But bit by bit those mornings of weakness grew shorter, until. . . . He remembered the feel of the hammer in his hand, driving the spikes in, and he smiled; this time it did touch his eyes, with the joy of sweet memory.

Weeping from the dark caught his ear, and his smile faded. *I should never have let the Trollocs take so many.* An entire village to slow them down. If those few houses at the ferry had not been deserted, perhaps. . . . But Trollocs were greedy by nature, and in the euphoria of watching the Myrddraal die, he had not paid attention as he should.

He glanced at the Trollocs. Any one of them was nearly twice as tall as he, strong enough to break him to flinders with one hand, yet they edged back, still crouching. "Kill them. All. You may feed, but then make a pile of everything that remains—for our friends to find. Put the heads on top. Neatly, now." He laughed, and cut it off short. "Go!"

The Trollocs scrambled away, drawing scythe-like swords and raising spiked axes. In moments shrieks and bellows rose from where the villagers were bound. Pleas for mercy and children's screams were cut off by solid thuds and unpleasant squishing noises, like melons being broken.

Fain turned his back on the cacophony to look at his Darkfriends. They were his, too, body and soul. Such souls as they had left. Every one of them was mired as deeply as he had been, before he found his way out. Every one with nowhere to go except to follow him. Their eyes clung to him, fearful, pleading. "You think they will grow hungry again before we find another village or a farm? They may. You think I will be letting them have some more of you? Well, perhaps one or two. There aren't any more horses to spare."

"The others were only commoners," one woman managed in an unsteady voice. Dirt streaked her face above a finely cut dress that marked her as a merchant, and wealthy. Smears stained the good gray cloth, and a long tear marred her skirt. "They were peasants. We have served—*I* have served—"

Fain cut her off, his easy tone making his words all the harder. "What are you, to me? Less than peasants. Herd cattle for the Trollocs, perhaps? If you want to live, cattle, you must be useful."

The woman's face broke. She sobbed, and suddenly all the rest were babbling, telling him how useful they were, men and women who had had influence and position before they were called to fulfill their oaths at Fal Dara. They spilled out the names of important, powerful people whom they knew in the Borderlands, in Cairhien, and other lands. They babbled of the knowledge they alone had of this land or that, of political situations, alliances, intrigues, all the things they could tell him if he let them serve him. The noise of them blended with the sounds of the Trollocs' slaughter and fit right in.

Fain ignored all of it—he had no fear of turning his back on them, not since they had seen the Fade dealt with—and went to his prize. Kneeling, he ran his hands over the ornate, golden chest, feeling the power locked inside. He had to have a Trolloc carry it—he did not trust the humans enough to load it on a horse and packsaddle; some dreams of power might be strong enough to overcome even fear of him, but Trollocs never dreamed of anything except killing—and he had not yet puzzled out how to open it. But that would come. Everything would come. Everything.

Unsheathing the dagger, he laid it atop the chest before settling himself down beside the fire. That blade was a better guard than Trolloc or human. They had all seen what happened when he used it, once; none would come within a span of that bared blade without his command, and then reluctantly.

Lying there in his blankets, he stared northward. He could not feel al'Thor, now; the distance between them was too great. Or perhaps al'Thor was doing his vanishing trick. Sometimes, in the keep, the boy had suddenly vanished from Fain's senses. He did not know how, but always al'Thor came back, just as suddenly as he had gone. He would come back this time, too.

"This time you come to me, Rand al'Thor. Before, I followed you like a dog driven on the trail, but now you follow me." His laughter was a cackle that even he knew was mad, but he did not care. Madness was a part of him, too. "Come to me, al'Thor. The dance is not even begun yet. We'll dance on Toman Head, and I'll be free of you. I'll see you dead at last."

# CHAPTER
# 12

## *Woven in the Pattern*

Egwene hurried after Nynaeve toward the knot of Aes Sedai around
the Amyrlin Seat's horse-borne palanquin, her desire to know what
had caused the turmoil in Fal Dara keep outweighing even her
worry over Rand. He was beyond her reach, for the moment. Bela, her
shaggy mare, was with the Aes Sedai's horses, and Nynaeve's mount, too.

The Warders, hands on sword hilts and eyes searching everywhere, made
a steel circle around the Aes Sedai and the palanquin. They were an island
of relative calm in the courtyard, where Shienaran soldiers still ran amid
the keep's horrified inhabitants. Egwene pushed in beside Nynaeve—the
two of them all but ignored after a single sharp glance from the Warders;
all knew they would be leaving with the Amyrlin—and caught enough in
the crowd's murmurs to learn of an arrow that had flashed seemingly from
nowhere and a bowman yet uncaught.

Egwene stopped, wide-eyed, too shocked even to think that she was
surrounded by Aes Sedai. An attempt on the life of the Amyrlin Seat. It
went beyond thinking of.

The Amyrlin sat in her palanquin with the curtains drawn back, the
bloodstained rip in her sleeve drawing all eyes, and faced down Lord
Agelmar. "You will find the bowman or you will not, my son. Either way,

my business in Tar Valon is as urgent as that of Ingtar on his quest. I leave now."

"But, Mother," Agelmar protested, "this attempt on your life changes everything. We still do not know who sent the man, or why. An hour more, and I will have the bowman and the answers for you."

The Amyrlin barked a laugh with no amusement in it. "You'll need slyer bait or finer nets to catch this fish, my son. By the time you have the man, it will be too late in the day for leaving. There are too many who would cheer to see me dead for me to worry overmuch about this one. You may send me news of what you find, if you find anything at all." Her eyes traveled around the towers overlooking the courtyard, and the ramparts and archers' balconies, still jammed with people, though silent now. The arrow had to have come from one of those places. "I think this bowman is already fled from Fal Dara."

"But, Mother—"

The woman in the palanquin cut him off with a sharp gesture of finality. Not even the Lord of Fal Dara could press the Amyrlin Seat too far. Her eyes came to rest on Egwene and Nynaeve, piercing eyes that seemed to Egwene to be seeing everything about herself that she wanted to keep secret. Egwene took a step back, then caught herself and dropped a curtsy, wondering if that were proper; no one had ever explained to her the protocol of meeting the Amyrlin Seat. Nynaeve kept her back straight and returned the Amyrlin's stare, but she fumbled for Egwene's hand and gripped as hard as Egwene did.

"So these are your two, Moiraine," the Amyrlin said. Moiraine gave the barest nod, and the other Aes Sedai turned to stare at the two women from Emond's Field. Egwene swallowed. They all looked as if they *knew* things, things other people did not, and it was no help at all to know that they truly did. "Yes, I sense a fine spark in each of them. But what will kindle from it? That's the question, isn't it?"

Egwene's mouth felt dry as dust. She had seen Master Padwhin, the carpenter back home, look at his tools much the same way as the Amyrlin was looking at the two of them. This one for this purpose, that one for that.

The Amyrlin said abruptly, "It is time we were gone. To horse. Lord Agelmar and I can say what needs be said without you all gawking like novices on a freeday. To horse!"

At her command the Warders scattered to their mounts, still wary, and the Aes Sedai, all but Leane, glided away from the palanquin to their own horses. As Egwene and Nynaeve turned to obey, a servant appeared at Lord

Agelmar's shoulder with a silver chalice. Agelmar took it with a dissatisfied twist to his mouth.

"With this cup from my hand, Mother, take my wish that you fare well on this day, and every. . . ."

Whatever else they said was lost to Egwene as she scrambled onto Bela. By the time she had given the shaggy mare a pat, and arranged her skirts, the palanquin was already moving toward the open gates, its horses stepping without rein or lead. Leane rode beside the palanquin, her staff propped at her stirrup. Egwene and Nynaeve brought their horses along behind with the rest of the Aes Sedai.

Roars and cheers from the crowds lining the town streets greeted the procession, all but drowning the thunder of the drummers and the blare of the trumpeters. Warders led the column, with the banner bearing the White Flame waving in ripples, and rode guard around the Aes Sedai, keeping the mass of people back; archers and pikemen, the Flame blazoned on their chests, followed behind in precise ranks. The trumpets fell silent as the column wound its way out of the town and turned southward, yet the sounds of cheering from within the town followed still. Egwene glanced back often, until trees and hills hid Fal Dara's walls and towers.

Nynaeve, riding alongside, shook her head. "Rand will be all right. He has Lord Ingtar and twenty lances with him. In any case, there is nothing you can do about it. Nothing either of us can do." She glanced toward Moiraine; the Aes Sedai's trim white mare and Lan's tall black stallion made an odd pair off to one side by themselves. "Not yet."

The column angled westward as it traveled, and it did not cover the ground quickly. Even footmen in half armor could not move fast through the Shienaran hills, not and maintain the pace for long. Still, they pushed as hard as they could.

Camps came late each night, the Amyrlin allowing no stop until barely enough light remained to pitch the tents, flattened white domes just tall enough to stand in. Each pair of Aes Sedai from the same Ajah had one, while the Amyrlin and the Keeper had tents to themselves. Moiraine shared the tent of her two sisters of the Blue. The soldiers slept on the ground in their own encampment, and the Warders wrapped themselves in their cloaks near the tents of the Aes Sedai to whom they were bonded. The tent shared by the Red sisters looked oddly lonely without any Warders, while that of the Greens seemed almost festive, the two Aes Sedai often sitting outside long past dark to talk with the four Warders they had brought between them.

Lan came once to the tent Egwene shared with Nynaeve, taking the

Wisdom into the night a little distance away. Egwene peered around the tent flap to watch. She could not hear what they said, except that Nynaeve eventually erupted in anger and came stalking back to wrap herself in her blankets and refuse to talk at all. Egwene thought her cheeks were wet, though she hid her face with a corner of her blanket. Lan stood watching the tent from the darkness for a long time before he went away. After that he did not come again.

Moiraine did not come near them, giving them only a nod in passing. She seemed to spend her waking hours speaking with the other Aes Sedai, all but the Red sisters, drawing them aside one by one as they rode. The Amyrlin allowed few stops for rest, and those short.

"Maybe she doesn't have time for us anymore," Egwene observed sadly. Moiraine was the one Aes Sedai she knew. Perhaps—though she did not like to admit it—the only one she was sure she could trust. "She found us, and we are on our way to Tar Valon. I suppose she has other things to concern her, now."

Nynaeve snorted softly. "I'll believe she is done with us when she's dead—or we are. She is sly, that one."

Other Aes Sedai came to their tent. Egwene almost jumped out of her skin that first night out of Fal Dara, when the tent flap was pushed aside and a plump, square-faced Aes Sedai, with graying hair and a vaguely distracted look in her dark eyes, ducked into their tent. She glanced at the lantern hanging at the highest point of the tent, and the flame rose a little higher. Egwene thought she felt something, thought she almost saw some-thing about the Aes Sedai when the flame grew brighter. Moiraine had told her that one day—when she had more training—she would be able to *see* when another woman channeled, and to tell a woman who could channel even if she did nothing.

"I am Verin Mathwin," the woman said with a smile. "And you are Egwene al'Vere and Nynaeve al'Maera. From the Two Rivers, which was once Manetheren. Strong blood, that. It sings."

Egwene exchanged glances with Nynaeve as they got to their feet.

"Is this a summons to the Amyrlin Seat?" Egwene asked.

Verin laughed. The Aes Sedai had a smudge of ink on her nose. "Oh, my, no. The Amyrlin has more important things to deal with than two young women who are not even novices yet. Although, you never can tell. You both have considerable potential, especially you, Nynaeve. One day. . . ." She paused, rubbing a finger thoughtfully right atop the ink smudge. "But this is not one day. I am here to give you a lesson, Egwene. You have been poking in ahead of yourself, I fear."

Nervously, Egwene looked at Nynaeve. "What have I done? Nothing that I'm aware of."

"Oh, nothing wrong. Not exactly. Somewhat dangerous, perhaps, but not exactly wrong." Verin lowered herself to the canvas floor, folding her legs under her. "Sit, both of you. Sit. I don't mean to crane my neck." She shifted around until she had a comfortable position. "Sit."

Egwene settled cross-legged across from the Aes Sedai and did her best not to look at Nynaeve. *No need to look guilty until I know if I am. And maybe not then.* "What is it I've done that's dangerous but not exactly wrong?"

"Why, you've been channeling the Power, child."

Egwene could only gape. Nynaeve burst out, "That is ridiculous. Why are we going to Tar Valon, if not for that?"

"Moiraine has . . . I mean, Moiraine Sedai has been giving me lessons," Egwene managed.

Verin held up her hands for quiet, and they fell silent. She might seem vague, but she was Aes Sedai, after all. "Child, do you think Aes Sedai immediately teach every girl who says she wants to be one of us how to channel? Well, I suppose you are not exactly every girl, but just the same. . . ." She shook her head gravely.

"Then why did she?" Nynaeve demanded. There had been no lessons for her, and Egwene was still not sure if it rankled Nynaeve or not.

"Because Egwene had already channeled," Verin said patiently.

"So. . . . So have I." Nynaeve did not sound happy about it.

"Your circumstances are different, child. That you are still alive shows you weathered the various crises, and did it on your own. I think you know how lucky you are. Of every four women forced to do what you did, only one survives. Of course, wilders—" Verin grimaced. "Forgive me, but I am afraid that *is* what we in the White Tower often call women who, without any training, have managed some rough control—random, and barely enough to be called control, usually, like you, but still control of a sort. Wilders have difficulties, it is true. Almost always they have built up walls to keep themselves from knowing what it was they were doing, and those walls interfere with conscious control. The longer those walls have to build, the harder it is to tear them down, but if they can be demolished— well, some of the most adept sisters ever have been wilders."

Nynaeve shifted irritably, and looked at the entrance as if thinking of leaving.

"I don't see what any of that has to do with me," Egwene said.

Verin blinked at her, almost as if wondering where she had come from. "With you? Why, nothing. Your problem is quite different. Most girls who want to become Aes Sedai—even most girls with the seed inside them, like you—are afraid of it, too. Even after they reach the Tower, even after they've learned what to do and how, for months they need to be led, step by step, by a sister, or by one of the Accepted. But not you. From what Moiraine tells me, you leaped into it as soon as you knew you could, fumbling your way through the dark with never a thought of whether there was a bottomless pit under your next step. Oh, there have been others like you; you are not unique. Moiraine was one herself. Once she knew what you had done, there was nothing for it but for her to begin teaching you. Did Moiraine never explain any of this to you?"

"Never." Egwene wished her voice was not so breathless. "She had . . . other matters to deal with." Nynaeve snorted softly.

"Well, Moiraine has never believed in telling anyone anything they did not need to know. Knowing serves no real purpose, but then, neither does not knowing. Myself, I always prefer knowing to not."

"Is there one? A pit, I mean?"

"Obviously not so far," Verin said, tilting her head. "But the next step?" She shrugged. "You see, child, the more you *try* to touch the True Source, the more you *try* to channel the One Power, the easier it becomes to actually do it. Yes, in the beginning, you stretch out to the Source and more often than not it is like grasping at air. Or you actually touch *saidar,* but even when you feel the One Power flowing through you, you find you can do nothing with it. Or you do something, and it isn't what you intended at all. That is the danger. Usually, with guidance and training— and the girl's own fear slowing her down—the ability to touch the Source and the ability to channel the Power come together with the ability to control what she is doing. But you began trying to channel without anyone there to teach you any control at all of what you do. I know you don't think you're very far along, and you are not, but you are like someone who has taught herself to run up hills—sometimes, at least—without ever learning how to run down the other side, or to walk. Sooner or later you are going to fall, if you don't learn the rest of it. Now, I am not talking about anything like what happens when one of those poor men begins channeling—you will not go mad; you won't die, not with sisters to teach and guide you—but what might you do entirely by accident, never meaning to?" For an instant the vagueness had dropped from Verin's eyes. For an instant, it seemed, the Aes Sedai's gaze had flicked from Egwene to Nynaeve as sharply as the Amyrlin's had. "Your innate abilities are strong, child, and they will grow stronger. You must learn to control them before you harm yourself, or someone else, or a great many people. That is what Moiraine was trying to teach you. That is what I will try to help you with tonight, and what a sister will help you with every night until we put you into Sheriam's most capable hands. She is Mistress of Novices."

Egwene thought, *Can she know about Rand? It isn't possible. She'd never have let him leave Fal Dara if she even suspected.* But she was sure she had not imagined what she saw. "Thank you, Verin Sedai. I will try."

Nynaeve rose smoothly to her feet. "I will go sit by the fire and leave you two alone."

"You should stay," Verin said. "You could profit by it. From what Moiraine has told me, it should take only a little training for you to be raised to the Accepted."

Nynaeve hesitated only a moment before shaking her head firmly. "I thank you for the offer, but I can wait until we reach Tar Valon. Egwene, if you need me, I will be——"

"By any gauge," Verin cut in, "you are a woman grown, Nynaeve. Usually, the younger a novice, the better she does. Not with the training necessarily, but because a novice is expected to do as she is told, when she is told and without question. It is really only of use once the actual training has reached a certain point—a hesitation in the wrong place then, or a doubt of what you have been told to do, can have tragic consequences—but it is better to follow the discipline all the time. The Accepted, on the other hand, are expected to question things, as it is felt they know enough to know what questions to ask and when. Which do you think you would prefer?"

Nynaeve's hands tightened on her skirt, and she looked at the tent flap again, frowning. Finally she gave a short nod and settled back down on the floor. "I suppose I might as well," she said.

"Good," Verin said. "Now. You already know this part, Egwene, but for Nynaeve's sake I will take you through it step by step. In time, it will become second nature—you will do it all faster than you can think of it— but now it is best to go slowly. Close your eyes, please. It goes better in the beginning if you have no distractions at all." Egwene closed her eyes. There was a pause. "Nynaeve," Verin said, "please close your eyes. It will really go better." Another pause. "Thank you, child. Now, you must empty yourself. Empty your thoughts. There is only one thing in your mind. The bud of a flower. Only that. Only the bud. You can see it in every detail. You can smell it. You can feel it. Every vein of every leaf, every curve of every petal. You can feel the sap pulsing. Feel it. Know it. Be it. You and the bud are the same. You are one. You are the bud."

Her voice droned on hypnotically, but Egwene no longer really heard; she had done this exercise before, with Moiraine. It was slow, but Moiraine had said it would come more quickly with practice. Inside herself, she was a rosebud, red petals curled tightly. Yet suddenly there was something else. Light. Light pressing on the petals. Slowly the petals unfolded, turning toward the light, absorbing the light. The rose and the light were one. Egwene and the light were one. She could feel the merest trickle of it seeping through her. She stretched for more, strained for more. . . .

In an instant it was all gone, rose and light. Moiraine had also said it could not be forced. With a sigh, she opened her eyes. Nynaeve had a grim look on her face. Verin was as calm as ever.

"You cannot *make* it happen," the Aes Sedai was saying. "You must *let* it happen. You must surrender to the Power before you can control it."

"This is complete foolishness," Nynaeve muttered. "I don't feel like a flower. If anything, I feel like a blackthorn bush. I think I will wait by the fire after all."

"As you wish," Verin said. "Did I mention that novices do chores? They wash dishes, scrub floors, do laundry, serve at table, all sorts of things. I myself think the servants do a better job of it by far, but it is generally felt that such labor builds character. Oh, you are staying? Good. Well, child, remember that even a blackthorn bush has flowers sometimes, beautiful and white among the thorns. We will try it one at a time. Now, from the beginning, Egwene. Close your eyes."

Several times before Verin left, Egwene felt the flow of the Power through her, but it was never very strong, and the most she managed with it was to produce a stir in the air that made the tent flap stir slightly. She was sure a sneeze could have done as much. She had done better with Moiraine; sometimes, at least. She wished it was Moiraine doing the teaching.

Nynaeve never even felt a glimmer, or so she said. By the end her eyes were set and her mouth so tight that Egwene was afraid she was about to begin berating Verin as if the Aes Sedai were a village woman intruding on her privacy. But Verin simply told her to close her eyes once again, this time without Egwene.

Egwene was sitting, watching the other two between her yawns. The night had grown late, well past the time she would usually be asleep. Nynaeve wore a face like week-old death, her eyes clamped shut as if she never meant to open them and her hands white-knuckled fists in her lap. Egwene hoped the Wisdom's temper did not break loose, not after she had held it this long.

"Feel the flow through you," Verin was saying. Her voice did not change, but suddenly there was a gleam in her eyes. "Feel the flow. Flow of the Power. Flow like a breeze, a gentle stirring in the air." Egwene sat up straight. This was how Verin had guided her each time she had actually had the Power flowing through her. "A soft breeze, the slightest movement of air. Soft."

Abruptly the stacked blankets burst into flame like fatwood.

Nynaeve opened her eyes with a yell. Egwene was not sure if she screamed or not. All Egwene knew was that she was on her feet, trying to kick the burning blankets outside before they set the tent on fire. Before she managed a second kick, the flames vanished, leaving wispy smoke rising from a charred mass and the smell of burned wool.

"Well," Verin said. "Well. I did not expect to have to douse a fire. Don't faint on me, child. It's all right now. I took care of it."

"I—I was angry." Nynaeve spoke through trembling lips in a bloodless face. "I heard you talking about a breeze, telling me what to do, and fire just popped into my head. I—I didn't mean to burn anything. It was just a small fire, in—in my head." She shuddered.

"I suppose it was a small fire, at that." Verin barked a laugh that was gone with another look at Nynaeve's face. "Are you all right, child? If you feel ill, I can. . . ." Nynaeve shook her head, and Verin nodded. "Rest is what you need. Both of you. I've worked you too hard. You must rest. The Amyrlin will have us all up and away before first light." Standing, she toed the charred blankets. "I will have some more blankets brought to you. I hope this shows both of you how important control is. You must learn to do what you mean to do, and nothing more. Aside from harming someone else, if you draw more of the Power than you can safely handle—and you cannot handle much, yet; but it will grow—if you draw too much, you can destroy yourself. You can die. Or you can burn yourself out, destroy what ability you have." As if she had not told them they were walking a knife edge, she added a cheerful "Sleep well." With that, she was gone.

Egwene put her arms around Nynaeve and hugged her tight. "It is all right, Nynaeve. There is no need to be frightened. Once you learn to control—"

Nynaeve gave a croaking laugh. "I am not frightened." She glanced sideways at the smoking blankets and twitched her eyes away. "It takes more than a little fire to frighten me." But she did not look at the blankets again, even when a Warder came to take them away and leave new.

Verin did not come again, as she had said she would not. Indeed, as they journeyed on, south and west, day by day, as fast as the footmen could move, Verin paid the two women from Emond's Field no more mind than Moiraine did, than did any of the Aes Sedai. They were not precisely unfriendly, the Aes Sedai, but rather distant and aloof, as if preoccupied. Their coolness heightened Egwene's unease, and brought back all the tales she had heard as a child.

Her mother had always told her the tales about Aes Sedai were a lot of fool men's nonsense, but neither her mother nor any other woman in Emond's Field had ever met an Aes Sedai before Moiraine came there. She herself had spent a good deal of time with Moiraine, and Moiraine was proof to her that not all Aes Sedai were like the tales. Cold manipulators and merciless destroyers. Breakers of the World. She knew now that *those,* at least—the Breakers of the World—had been male Aes Sedai, when there were such, in the Age of Legends, but it did not help a great deal. Not *all* Aes Sedai were like the tales, but how many, and which?

The Aes Sedai who came to the tent each night were so mixed that they did not help at all in clearing her thoughts. Alviarin was as cool and businesslike as a merchant come to buy wool and tabac, surprised that Nynaeve was part of the lesson but accepting, sharp in her criticisms but always ready to try again. Alanna Mosvani laughed and spent as much time talking about the world, and men, as she did teaching. Alanna showed too much interest in Rand and Perrin and Mat for Egwene's comfort, though. Especially Rand. Worst of all was Liandrin, the only one who wore her shawl; the others had all packed them away before leaving Fal Dara. Liandrin sat fingering her red fringe and taught little, and reluctantly at that. She questioned Egwene and Nynaeve as if they had been accused of a crime, and her questions were all about the three boys. She kept it up until Nynaeve threw her out—Egwene was not sure why Nynaeve did so—and then she left with a warning.

"Watch yourselves, my daughters. You are in your village no longer. Now you dabble your toes where there are things to bite you."

Finally the column reached the village of Medo, on the banks of the Mora, which ran along the border between Shienar and Arafel and so into the River Erinin.

Egwene was sure it was the Aes Sedai's questions about Rand that had made her start dreaming of him, that and worrying about him, about whether he and the others had had to follow the Horn of Valere into the Blight. The dreams were always bad, but at first they were just the ordinary sort of nightmare. By the night they reached Medo, the dreams had changed, though.

"Pardon, Aes Sedai," Egwene asked diffidently, "but have you seen Moiraine Sedai?" The slender Aes Sedai waved her away and hurried on down the crowded, torch-lit village street, calling for someone to be careful with her horse. The woman was of the Yellow Ajah, though not wearing her shawl now; Egwene knew no more of her than that, not even her name.

Medo was a small village—though Egwene was shocked to realize that what she now thought of as a "small village" was as big as Emond's

Field—and it was overwhelmed now with many more outsiders than there were inhabitants. Horses and people filled the narrow streets, jostling to the docks past villagers who knelt whenever an unseeing Aes Sedai sped by. Harsh torchlight lit everything. The two docks jutted out into the River Mora like stone fingers, and each hosted a pair of small, two-masted ships. There, horses were being hoisted on board by booms and cables and canvas cradles under their bellies. More of the ships—high-sided and stout, with lanterns topping their masts—crowded the moon-streaked river, already loaded or waiting their turn. Rowboats ferried out archers and pikemen, the raised pikes making the boats look like gigantic pricklebacks swimming on the surface.

On the left-hand dock Egwene found Anaiya, watching the loading and chivying those who were not moving fast enough. Though she had never said more than two words to Egwene, Anaiya seemed different from the others, more like a woman from home. Egwene could picture her baking in her kitchen; she could not see any of the others so. "Anaiya Sedai, have you seen Moiraine Sedai? I need to talk to her."

The Aes Sedai looked around with an absent frown. "What? Oh, it's you, child. Moiraine is gone. And your friend, Nynaeve, is already out on the *River Queen*. I had to bundle her onto a boat myself, shouting that she would not go without you. Light, what a scramble! You should be aboard, yourself. Find a boat going out to the *River Queen*. You two will be traveling with the Amyrlin Seat, so mind yourself once you're on board. No scenes or tantrums."

"Which ship is Moiraine Sedai's?"

"Moiraine isn't on a ship, girl. She's gone, two days gone, and the Amyrlin is in a taking over it." Anaiya grimaced and shook her head, though most of her attention was still on the workers. "First Moiraine vanishes with Lan, then Liandrin right on Moiraine's heels, and then Verin, none of them with so much as a word for anyone. Verin did not even take her Warder; Tomas is chewing nails with worry over her." The Aes Sedai glanced at the sky. The waxing moon shone without the hindrance of clouds. "We will have to call the wind again, and the Amyrlin will not be pleased with that, either. She says she wants us on our way to Tar Valon within an hour, and she will brook no delays. I would not want to be Moiraine, or Liandrin, or Verin, when she sees them next. They'll wish they were novices again. Why, child, what's the matter?"

Egwene drew a deep breath. *Moiraine gone? She can't be! I have to tell somebody, somebody who won't laugh at me.* She imagined Anaiya back in Emond's Field, listening to her daughter's problems; the woman fit the picture. "Anaiya Sedai, Rand is in trouble."

Anaiya gave her a considering look. "That tall boy from your village? Missing him already, are you? Well, I shouldn't be surprised if he *is* in trouble. Young men his age usually are. Though it was the other one— Mat?—who had the look of trouble. Very well, child. I don't mean to mock you or make light. What kind of trouble, and how do you know? He and Lord Ingtar must have the Horn and be back in Fal Dara by now. Or else they've had to follow it into the Blight, and there's nothing to do about that."

"I—I don't think they're in the Blight, or back in Fal Dara. I had a dream." She said it half defiantly. It sounded silly when she said it, but it had seemed so real. A nightmare for true, but real. First there had been a man with a mask over his face, and fire in place of his eyes. Despite the mask, she had thought he was surprised to see her. His look had frightened her till she thought her bones would break from shivering, but suddenly he vanished, and she saw Rand sleeping on the ground, wrapped in a cloak. A woman had been standing over him, looking down. Her face was in shadow, but her eyes seemed to shine like the moon, and Egwene had known she was evil. Then there was a flash of light, and they were gone. Both of them. And behind it all, almost like another thing altogether, was the feel of danger, as if a trap was just beginning to snap shut on an unsuspecting lamb, a trap with many jaws. As though time had slowed, and she could watch the iron jaws creep closer together. The dream had not faded with waking, the way dreams did. And the danger felt so strong she still wanted to look over her shoulder—only somehow she knew that it was aimed at Rand, not at her.

She wondered if the woman had been Moiraine, and upbraided herself for the thought. Liandrin fit that part better. Or perhaps Alanna; she had been interested in Rand, too.

She could not bring herself to tell Anaiya. Formally, she said, "Anaiya Sedai, I know it sounds foolish, but he is in danger. Great danger. I know it. I could feel it. I still can."

Anaiya wore a thoughtful look. "Well, now," she said softly, "that's a possibility I'll wager no one has considered. You may be a Dreamer. It is a small chance, child, but. . . . We haven't had one of those in—oh—four or five hundred years. And Dreaming is close linked to Foretelling. If you really can Dream, it may be that you can Foretell, as well. *That* would be a finger in the Reds' eye. Of course, it could be just an ordinary nightmare, brought on by a late night, and cold food, and us traveling so hard since we left Fal Dara. And you missing your young man. Much more likely. Yes, yes, child, I know. You are worried about him. Did your dream indicate what kind of danger?"

Egwene shook her head. "He just vanished, and I felt danger. And evil. I felt it even before he vanished." She shivered and rubbed her hands together. "I can still feel it."

"Well, we will talk about it more on the *River Queen*. If you *are* a Dreamer, I will see you have the training Moiraine should be here to. . . . You there!" the Aes Sedai barked suddenly, and Egwene jumped. A tall man, who had just sat down on a cask of wine, jumped, too. Several others quickened their step. "That's for loading aboard, not resting on! We will talk on the boat, child. No, you fool! You can't carry it by yourself! Do you want to hurt yourself?" Anaiya went striding off down the dock, giving the unfortunate villagers a rougher side of her tongue than Egwene would have suspected she had.

Egwene peered into the dark, toward the south. He was out there, somewhere. Not in Fal Dara, not in the Blight. She was sure of it. *Hold on, you wool-headed idiot. If you get yourself killed before I can get you out of this, I will skin you alive.* It did not occur to her to ask how she was going to get him out of anything, going to Tar Valon as she was.

Snugging her cloak around her, she set out to find a boat to the *River Queen.*

# CHAPTER 13

## *From Stone to Stone*

The light of the rising sun woke Rand, and he wondered if he were dreaming. He sat up slowly, staring. Everything had changed, or almost everything. The sun and the sky were as he expected to see, if pallid and all but cloudless. Loial and Hurin still lay on either side of him, wrapped in their cloaks asleep, and their horses still stood hobbled a pace away, but everyone else was gone. Soldiers, horses, his friends, everyone and everything gone.

The hollow itself had changed, too, and they were in the middle of it now, no longer on the edge. At Rand's head rose a gray stone cylinder, every bit of three spans high and a full pace thick, covered with hundreds, perhaps thousands, of deeply incised diagrams and markings in some language he did not recognize. White stone paved the bottom of the hollow, as level as a floor, polished so smooth it almost glistened. Broad, high steps rose to the rim in concentric rings of different colored stone. And about the rim, the trees stood blackened and twisted as if a firestorm had roared through them. Everything seemed paler than it should be, just like the sun, more subdued, as if seen through mist. Only there was no mist. Just the three of them and the horses appeared truly solid. But when he touched the stone under him, it *felt* solid enough.

He reached out and shook Loial and Hurin. "Wake up! Wake up and tell me I'm dreaming. Please wake up!"

"Is it morning already?" Loial began, sitting up, then his mouth fell open, and his big, round eyes grew wider and wider.

Hurin woke with a start, then leaped to his feet, jumping like a flea on a hot rock to look this way, then that. "Where are we? What's happened? Where is everybody? Where are we, Lord Rand?" He sank to his knees, wringing his hands, but his eyes still darted. "What's happened?"

"I don't know," Rand said slowly. "I was hoping it was a dream, but. . . . Maybe it is a dream." He had had experience of dreams that were not dreams, experience he wanted neither to repeat nor to remember. He stood up carefully. Everything stayed as it was.

"I do not think so," Loial said. He was studying the column, and he did not appear happy. His long eyebrows sagged across his cheeks, and his tufted ears seemed to have wilted. "I think this is the same stone we went to sleep beside last night. I think I know what it is, now." For once, he sounded miserable about knowing.

"That's. . . ." *No.* That being the same stone was no more crazy than what he could see around him, Mat and Perrin and the Shienarans gone, and everything changed. *I thought I'd escaped, but it's started again, and there's no such thing as crazy anymore. Unless I am.* He looked at Loial and Hurin. They were not acting as if he were mad; they saw it, too. Something about the steps caught his eye, the different colors, seven rising from blue to red. "One for each Ajah," he said.

"No, Lord Rand," Hurin moaned. "No. Aes Sedai would not do this to us. They wouldn't! I walk in the Light."

"We all do, Hurin," Rand said. "The Aes Sedai won't hurt you." *Unless you get in the way.* Could this be Moiraine's doing somehow? "Loial, you said you know what the stone is. What is it?"

"I said I think I know, Rand. There was a piece of an old book, just a few pages, but one of them had a drawing of this stone, this Stone"—there was a distinct difference in the way he said it that marked importance—"or one very like it. And underneath, it said, 'From Stone to Stone run the lines of "if," between the worlds that might be.'"

"What does that mean, Loial? It doesn't make any sense."

The Ogier shook his massive head sadly. "It was only a few pages. Part of it said Aes Sedai in the Age of Legends, some of those who could Travel, the most powerful of them, could use these Stones. It did not say how, but I think, from what I could puzzle out, that perhaps those Aes Sedai used the Stones somehow to journey to those worlds." He glanced up at the seared trees and pulled his eyes down again quickly, as he did not want to think about what lay beyond the rim. "Yet even if Aes Sedai can use them, or could, we had no Aes Sedai with us to channel the Power, so I don't see how it can be."

Rand's skin prickled. *Aes Sedai used them. In the Age of Legends, when there were male Aes Sedai.* He had a vague memory of the void closing round him as he fell asleep, filled with that uneasy glow. And he remembered the room in the village, and the light he had reached for to escape. *If that was the male half of True Source. . . . No, it can't be. But what if it is? Light, I was wondering whether to run or not, and all the time it's right inside my head. Maybe I brought us here.* He did not want to think about it. "Worlds that might be? I don't understand, Loial."

The Ogier shrugged massively, and uneasily. "Neither do I, Rand. Most of it sounded like this. 'If a woman go left, or right, does Time's flow divide? Does the Wheel then weave two Patterns? A thousand, for each of her turnings? As many as the stars? Is one real, the others merely shadows and reflections?' You see, it was not very clear. Mainly questions, most of which seemed to contradict each other. And there just wasn't much of it." He went back to staring at the column, but he looked as if he wished it would go away. "There are supposed to be a good many of these Stones, scattered all over the world, or there were, once, but I never heard of anyone finding one. I never heard of anyone finding anything like this at all."

"My Lord Rand?" Now on his feet, Hurin seemed calmer, but he clutched his coat at the waist with both hands, his face urgent. "My Lord Rand, you'll get us back, won't you? Back where we belong? I've a wife, my Lord, and children. Melia'd take it bad enough, me dying, but if she doesn't even have my body to give to the mother's embrace, she'll grieve to the end of her days. You understand, my Lord. I can't leave her not knowing. You'll get us back. And if I die, if you can't take her my body, you'll let her know, so she has that, at least." He was no longer questioning at the end. A note of confidence had crept into his voice.

Rand opened his mouth to say again he was not a lord, then shut it without speaking. That was hardly important enough to mention, now. *You got him into this.* He wanted to deny it, but he knew what he was, knew he could channel, even if it always seemed to happen all by itself. Loial said Aes Sedai used the Stones, and that meant the One Power. What Loial said he knew, you could be sure of—the Ogier never claimed to know if he did not—and there was no one else nearby who could wield the Power. *You got him into it, you have to get him out. You have to try.*

"I wil! do my best, Hurin." And because Hurin was Shienaran, he added, "By my House and honor. A shepherd's House and a shepherd's honor, but I'll make them do as well as a lord's."

Hurin loosed his hold on his coat. The confidence reached his eyes, too. He bowed deeply. "Honor to serve, my Lord."

Guilt rippled through Rand. *He thinks you'll see him home, now, because Shienaran lords always keep their word. What are you going to do, Lord Rand?* "None of that, Hurin. There'll be no bowing. I'm not—" Suddenly he knew he could not tell the man again that he was not a lord. All that was holding the sniffer together was his belief in a lord, and he could not take that away, not now. Not here. "No bowing," he finished awkwardly.

"As you say, Lord Rand." Hurin's grin was almost as wide as when Rand first met him.

Rand cleared his throat. "Yes. Well, that's what I say."

They were both watching him, Loial curious, Hurin confident, both waiting to see what he would do. *I brought them here. I must have. So I have to get them back. And that means. . . .*

Drawing a deep breath, he walked across the white paving stones to the symbol-covered cylinder. Small lines of some language he did not know surrounded each symbol, odd letters that flowed in curves and spirals, suddenly turned to jagged hooks and angles, then flowed on. At least it was not Trolloc script. Reluctantly, he put his hands on the column. It looked like any dry, polished stone, but it felt curiously slick, like oiled metal.

He closed his eyes and formed the flame. The void came slowly, hesitantly. He knew his own fear was holding it back, fear of what he was trying. As fast as he fed fear into the flame, more came. *I can't do it. Channel the Power. I don't want to. Light, there has to be another way.* Grimly he forced the thoughts to stillness. He could feel sweat beading on his face. Determinedly he kept on, pushing his fears into the consuming flame, making it grow, and grow. And the void was there.

The core of him floated in emptiness. He could see the light—*saidin*— even with his eyes closed, feel the warmth of it, surrounding him, surrounding everything, suffusing everything. It wavered like a candle flame seen through oiled paper. Rancid oil. Stinking oil.

He reached for it—he was not sure *how* he reached, but it was something, a movement, a stretching toward the light, toward *saidin*—and caught nothing, as if running his hands through water. It felt like a slimy pond, scum floating atop clean water below, but he could not scoop up any of the water. Time and again it trickled through his fingers, not even droplets of the water remaining, only the slick scum, making his skin crawl.

Desperately, he tried to form an image of the hollow as it had been, with

Ingtar and the lances sleeping by their horses, with Mat and Perrin, and the Stone lying buried except for one end. Outside the void he formed it, clinging to the shell of emptiness that enclosed him. He tried to link the image with the light, tried to force them together. The hollow as it had been, and he and Loial and Hurin there together. His head hurt. Together, with Mat and Perrin and the Shienarans. Burning, in his head. Together!

The void shattered into a thousand razor shards, slicing his mind.

Shuddering, he staggered back, wide-eyed. His hands hurt from pressing the Stone, and his arms and shoulders quivered with aching; his stomach lurched from the feel of filth covering him, and his head. . . . He tried to steady his breathing. That had never happened before. When the void went, it went like a pricked bubble, just gone, in a twinkling. Never broken like glass. His head felt numb, as if the thousand slashes had happened so quickly the pain had not yet come. But every cut had felt as real as if done with a knife. He touched his temple, and was surprised not to see blood on his fingers.

Hurin still stood there watching him, still confident. If anything, the sniffer seemed more sure by the minute. Lord Rand was doing something. That was what lords were for. They protected the land and the people with their bodies and their lives, and when something was wrong, they set it aright and saw fairness and justice done. As long as Rand was doing something, anything, Hurin would have confidence that it would all come right in the end. That was what lords did.

Loial had a different look, a slightly puzzled frown, but his eyes were on Rand, too. Rand wondered what he was thinking.

"It was worth a try," he told them. The rancid oil feel, inside his head—*Light, it's inside me! I don't want it inside me!*—was fading slowly, but he still thought he might vomit. "I will try again, in a few minutes."

He hoped he sounded confident. He had no idea how the Stones worked, if what he was doing had any chance of success. *Maybe there are rules for working them. Maybe you have to do something special. Light, maybe you can't use the same Stone twice, or. . . .* He cut off that line of thought. There was no good in thinking like that. He had it to do. Looking at Loial and Hurin, he thought he knew what Lan had meant about duty pressing down like a mountain.

"My Lord, I think. . . ." Hurin let his words trail off, looking abashed for a moment. "My Lord, maybe, if we find the Darkfriends, we can make one of them tell us how to get back."

"I would ask a Darkfriend or the Dark One himself if I thought I'd get a true answer back," Rand said. "But we are all there is. Just us three." *Just me. I'm the one who has to do it.*

"We could follow their trail, my Lord. If we catch them. . . ."

Rand stared at the sniffer. "You can still smell them?"

"I can, my Lord." Hurin frowned. "It's faint, pale-like, like everything else here, but I can smell the trail. Right up there." He pointed to the rim of the hollow. "I don't understand it, my Lord, but— Last night, I could have sworn the trail went right on by the hollow back—back where we were. Well, it's in the same place now, only here, and fainter, like I said. Not old, not faint like that, but. . . . I don't know, Lord Rand, except that it's there."

Rand considered. If Fain and the Darkfriends were here—wherever here was—they might know how to get back. They had to, if they had reached here in the first place. And they had the Horn, and the dagger. Mat had to have that dagger. For that if for nothing else, he had to find them. What finally decided him, he was ashamed to realize, was that he was afraid to try again. Afraid to try channeling the Power. He was less afraid of confronting Darkfriends and Trollocs with only Hurin and Loial than he was of that.

"Then we will go after the Darkfriends." He tried to sound sure, the way Lan would, or Ingtar. "The Horn must be recovered. If we can't puzzle out a way to take it from them, at least we will know where they are when we find Ingtar again." *If only they don't ask how we're going to find him again.* "Hurin, make sure it really is the trail we're after."

The sniffer leaped into his saddle, eager to be doing something himself, perhaps eager to be away from the hollow, and scrambled his horse up the broad, colored steps. The animal's hooves rang loudly on the stone, but they made not a mark.

Rand stowed Red's hobbles in his saddlebags—the banner was still there; he would not have minded if that had been left behind—then gathered his bow and quiver and climbed to the stallion's back. The bundle of Thom Merrilin's cloak made a mound behind his saddle.

Loial led his big mount over to him; with the Ogier standing on the ground, Loial's head came almost to Rand's shoulder, and him in his saddle. Loial still looked puzzled.

"You think we should stay here?" Rand said. "Try again to use the Stone? If the Darkfriends are here, in place, we have to find them. We can't leave the Horn of Valere in Darkfriend hands; you heard the Amyrlin. And we have to get that dagger back. Mat will die without it."

Loial nodded. "Yes, Rand, we do. But, Rand, the Stones. . . ."

"We will find another. You said they were scattered all over, and if they're all like this—all this stonework around them—it should not be too hard to find one."

"Rand, that fragment said the Stones came from an older Age than the Age of Legends, and even the Aes Sedai then did not understand them, though they used them, some of the truly powerful did. They used them with the One Power, Rand. How did you think to use this Stone to take us back? Or any other Stone we find?"

For a moment Rand could only stare at the Ogier, thinking faster than he ever had in his life. "If they are older than the Age of Legends, maybe the people who built them didn't use the Power. There must be another way. The Darkfriends got here, and they certainly couldn't use the Power. Whatever this other way is, I will find it out. I will get us back, Loial." He looked at the tall stone column with its odd markings, and felt a prickle of fear. *Light, if only I* don't *have to use the Power to do it.* "I will, Loial, I promise. One way or another."

The Ogier gave a doubtful nod. He swung up onto his huge horse and followed Rand up the steps to join Hurin among the blackened trees.

The land stretched out, low and rolling, sparsely forested here and there with grassland between, crossed by more than one stream. In the middle distance Rand thought he could see another burned patch. It was all pale, the colors washed. There was no sign of anything made by men except the stone circle behind them. The sky was empty, no chimney smoke, no birds, only a few clouds and the pale yellow sun.

Worst of all, though, the land seemed to twist the eye. What was close at hand looked all right, and what was seen straight ahead in the distance. But whenever Rand turned his head, things that appeared distant when seen from the corner of his eye seemed to rush toward him, to be nearer when he stared straight at them. It made for dizziness; even the horses whickered nervously and rolled their eyes. He tried moving his head slowly; the apparent movement of things that should have been fixed was still there, but it seemed to help a little.

"Did your piece of a book say anything about this?" Rand asked.

Loial shook his head, then swallowed hard as if he wished he had kept it still. "Nothing."

"I suppose there's nothing to do for it. Which way, Hurin?"

"South, Lord Rand." The sniffer kept his eyes on the ground.

"South, then." *There has to be a way back besides using the Power.* Rand heeled Red's flanks. He tried to make his voice lighthearted, as if he saw no difficulty at all in what they were about. "What was it Ingtar said? Three or four days to that monument to Artur Hawkwing? I wonder if that exists here, too, the way the Stones do. If this is a world that *could* be, maybe it's still standing. Wouldn't that be something to see, Loial?"

They rode south.

# CHAPTER 14

## *Wolfbrother*

"**G**one?" Ingtar demanded of the air. "And my guards saw nothing. Nothing! They cannot just be gone!"

Listening, Perrin hunched his shoulders and looked at Mat, who stood a little way off frowning and muttering to himself. Arguing with himself was how Perrin saw it. The sun was peeking over the horizon, past time for them to have been riding. Shadows lay long across the hollow, stretched out and thinned, but still like the trees that made them. The packhorses, loaded and on their lead line, stamped impatiently, but everyone stood by his mount and waited.

Uno came striding up. "Not a goat-kissing track, my Lord." He sounded offended; failure touched on his skill. "Burn me, not so much as a flaming hoof scrape. They just bloody vanished."

"Three men and three horses do not just vanish," Ingtar growled. "Go over the ground again, Uno. If anyone can find where they went, it's you."

"Maybe they just ran away," Mat said. Uno stopped and glared at him. *Like he'd cursed an Aes Sedai,* Perrin thought wonderingly.

"Why would they run away?" Ingtar's voice was dangerously soft. "Rand, the Builder, my sniffer—my sniffer!—why would any of them run, much less all three?"

Mat shrugged. "I don't know. Rand was. . . ." Perrin wanted to throw something at him, hit him, anything to stop him, but Ingtar and Uno were watching. He felt a flood of relief when Mat hesitated, then spread his hands and muttered, "I don't know why. I just thought maybe they had."

Ingtar grimaced. "Ran away," he growled as if he did not believe it for an instant. "The Builder can go as he will, but Hurin would not run away. And neither would Rand al'Thor. He would not; he knows his duty, now. Go on, Uno. Search the ground again." Uno gave a half bow and hurried away, sword hilt bobbing over his shoulder. Ingtar grumbled, "Why would Hurin leave like that, in the middle of the night, without a word? He knows what we're about. How am I to track this Shadow-spawned filth without him? I would give a thousand gold crowns for a pack of trail hounds. If I did not know better, I would say the Darkfriends managed this so they can slip east or west without me knowing. Peace, I don't know if I *do* know better." He stumped off after Uno.

Perrin shifted uneasily. The Darkfriends were doubtless getting further away with every minute. Getting further away, and with them the Horn of Valere—and the dagger from Shadar Logoth. He did not think that Rand, whatever he had become, whatever had happened to him, would abandon that chase. *But where* did *he go, and why?* Loial might go with Rand for friendship—but why Hurin?

"Maybe he did run away," he muttered, then looked around. No one appeared to have heard; even Mat was not paying him any mind. He scrubbed a hand through his hair. If Aes Sedai had been after him to be a false Dragon, he would have run, too. But worrying about Rand was doing nothing to help track the Darkfriends.

There was a way, perhaps, if he was willing to take it. He did not want to take it. He had been running away from it, but perhaps, now, he could no longer run. *Serves me right for what I told Rand. I wish I could* run. Even knowing what he could do to help—what he had to do—he hesitated.

No one was looking at him. No one would know what they were seeing even if they did look. Finally, reluctantly, he closed his eyes and let himself drift, let his thoughts drift, out, away from him.

He had tried denying it from the first, long before his eyes began to change from dark brown to burnished golden yellow. At that first meeting, that first instant of recognition, he had refused to believe, and he had run from the recognition ever since. He still wanted to run.

His thoughts drifted, feeling for what must be out there, what was always out there in country where men were few or far between, feeling for his brothers. He did not like to think of them that way, but they were.

In the beginning he had been afraid that what he did had some taint of the Dark One, or of the One Power—equally bad for a man who wanted nothing more than to be a blacksmith and live his life in the Light, and in peace. From that time, he knew something of how Rand felt, afraid of himself, feeling unclean. He was still not past that entirely. This thing he did was older than humans using the One Power, though, something from the birth of Time. Not the Power, Moiraine had told him. Something long vanished, now come again. Egwene knew, too, though he wished she did not. He wished no one did. He hoped she had not told anyone.

Contact. He felt them, felt other minds. Felt his brothers, the wolves.

Their thoughts came to him as a whirlpool blend of images and emotions. At first he had not been able to make out anything except the raw emotion, but now his mind put words to them. *Wolfbrother. Surprise. Two-legs that talks.* A faded image, dim with time, old beyond old, of men running with wolves, two packs hunting together. *We have heard this comes again. You are Long Tooth?*

It was a faint picture of a man dressed in clothes made of hides, with a long knife in his hand, but overlaid on the image, more central, was a shaggy wolf with one tooth longer than the rest, a steel tooth gleaming in the sunlight as the wolf led the pack in a desperate charge through deep snow toward the deer that would mean life instead of slow death by starvation, and the deer thrashing to run in powder to their bellies, and the sun glinting on the white until it hurt the eyes, and the wind howling down the passes, swirling the fine snow like mist, and. . . . Wolves' names were always complex images.

Perrin recognized the man. Elyas Machera, who had first introduced him to wolves. Sometimes he wished he had never met Elyas.

*No,* he thought, and tried to picture himself in his mind.

*Yes. We have heard of you.*

It was not the image he had made, a young man with heavy shoulders and shaggy, brown curls, a young man with an axe at his belt, who others thought moved and thought slowly. That man was there, somewhere in the mind picture that came from the wolves, but stronger by far was a massive, wild bull with curved horns of shining metal, running through the night with the speed and exuberance of youth, curly-haired coat gleaming in the moonlight, flinging himself in among Whitecloaks on their horses, with the air crisp and cold and dark, and blood so red on the horns, and. . . .

*Young Bull.*

For a moment Perrin lost the contact in his shock. He had not dreamed they had given him a name. He wished he could not remember how he had earned it. He touched the axe at his belt, with its gleaming, half-moon blade. *Light help me, I killed two men. They would have killed me even quicker, and Egwene, but. . . .*

Pushing all that aside—it was done and behind him; he had no wish to remember any of it—he gave the wolves the smell of Rand, of Loial and Hurin, and asked if they had scented the three. It was one of the things that had come to him with the change in his eyes; he could identify people by their smell even when he could not see them. He could see more sharply, too, see in anything but pitch-darkness. He was always careful to light lamps or candles, now, sometimes before anyone else thought they were needed.

From the wolves came a view of men on horses approaching the hollow in late day. That was the last they had seen or smelled of Rand or the other two.

Perrin hesitated. The next step would be useless unless he told Ingtar. *And Mat will die if we don't find that dagger. Burn you, Rand, why did you take the sniffer?*

The one time he had gone to the dungeon, with Egwene, the smell of Fain had made his hair stand on end; not even Trollocs smelled so foul. He had wanted to rip through the bars of the cell and tear the man apart, and finding that inside himself had frightened him more than Fain did. To mask Fain's smell in his own mind, he added the scent of Trollocs before he howled aloud.

From the distance came the cries of a wolfpack, and in the hollow horses stamped and whickered fearfully. Some of the soldiers fingered their long-bladed lances and eyed the rim of the hollow uneasily. Inside Perrin's head, it was much worse. He felt the rage of the wolves, the hate. There were only two things wolves hated. All else they merely endured, but fire and Trollocs they hated, and they would go through fire to kill Trollocs.

Even more than the Trollocs, Fain's scent had put them into a frenzy, as if they smelled something that made Trollocs seem natural and right.

*Where?*

The sky rolled in his head; the land spun. East and west, wolves did not know. They knew the movements of sun and moon, the shift of seasons, the contours of the land. Perrin puzzled it out. South. And something more. An eagerness to kill the Trollocs. The wolves would let Young Bull share in the killing. He could bring the two-legs with their hard skins if he wanted, but Young Bull, and Smoke, and Two Deer, and Winter Dawn, and all the rest of the pack would hunt down the Twisted Ones who had dared come into their land. The inedible flesh and bitter blood would burn the tongue, but they must be killed. Kill them. Kill the Twisted Ones.

Their fury infected him. His lips peeled back in a snarl, and he took a step, to join them, run with them in the hunt, in the killing.

With an effort he broke the contact except for a thin sense that the wolves were there. He could have pointed to them across the intervening distance. He felt cold inside. *I'm a man, not a wolf. Light help me, I am a man!*

"Are you well, Perrin?" Mat said, moving closer. He sounded the way he always did, flippant—and bitter under it, too, of late—but he looked worried. "That is all I need. Rand run off, and then you get sick. I don't know where I'll find a Wisdom to look after you out here. I think I have some willowbark in my saddlebags. I can make you some willowbark tea, if Ingtar lets us stay that long. Serve you right if I make it too strong."

"I . . . I'm all right, Mat." Shaking off his friend, he went to find Ingtar. The Shienaran lord was scanning the ground on the rim with Uno, and Ragan, and Masema. The others frowned at him as he drew Ingtar aside. He made sure Uno and the rest were too far away to hear before he spoke. "I don't know where Rand or the others went, Ingtar, but Padan Fain and the Trollocs—and I guess the rest of the Darkfriends—are still heading south."

"How do you know this?" Ingtar said.

Perrin drew a deep breath. "Wolves told me." He waited, for what he was not sure. Laughter, scorn, an accusation of being a Darkfriend, of being mad. Deliberately, he tucked his thumbs behind his belt, away from the axe. *I will not kill. Not again. If he tries to kill me for a Darkfriend, I'll run, but I won't kill anybody else.*

"I have heard of things like this," Ingtar said slowly, after a moment. "Rumors. There was a Warder, a man called Elyas Machera, who some said could talk to wolves. He disappeared years ago." He seemed to catch something in Perrin's eyes. "You know him?"

"I know him," Perrin said flatly. "He's the one. . . . I don't want to talk about it. I didn't ask for it." *That's what Rand said. Light, I wish I were home working Master Luhhan's forge.*

"These wolves," Ingtar said, "they will track the Darkfriends and Trollocs for us?" Perrin nodded. "Good. I will have the Horn, whatever it takes." The Shienaran glanced around at Uno and the others still searching for tracks. "Better not to tell anyone else, though. Wolves are considered good luck in the Borderlands. Trollocs fear them. But still, better to keep this between us for the time. Some of them might not understand."

"I would as soon nobody else ever found out," Perrin said.

"I will tell them you think you have Hurin's talent. They know about that; they're easy with it. Some of them saw you wrinkling your nose back in that village, and at the ferry. I've heard jokes about your delicate nose. Yes. You keep us on the trail today, Uno will see enough of their tracks to confirm it *is* the trail, and before nightfall every last man will be sure you are a sniffer. I *will* have the Horn." He glanced at the sky, and raised his voice. "Daylight is wasting! To horse!"

To Perrin's surprise, the Shienarans seemed to accept Ingtar's story. A few of them looked skeptical—Masema went so far as to spit—but Uno nodded thoughtfully, and that was enough for most. Mat was the hardest to convince.

"A sniffer! You? You're going to track murderers by smell? Perrin, you are as crazy as Rand. I am the only sane one left from Emond's Field, with Egwene and Nynaeve trotting off to Tar Valon to become—" He cut himself short with an uneasy glance for the Shienarans.

Perrin took Hurin's place beside Ingtar as the small column rode south. Mat kept up a string of disparaging remarks, until Uno found the first tracks left by Trollocs and by men on horses, but Perrin paid him little mind. It was all he could do to keep the wolves from dashing on ahead to kill the Trollocs. The wolves cared only about killing the Twisted Ones; to them, Darkfriends were no different from any other two-legs. Perrin could almost see the Darkfriends scattering in a dozen directions while the wolves slew Trollocs, running away with the Horn of Valere. Running away with the dagger. And once the Trollocs were dead, he did not think he could interest the wolves in tracking the humans even if he had any idea which of them to track. He had a running argument with them, and sweat covered his forehead long before he got the first flash of images that turned his stomach.

He drew rein, stopping his horse dead. The others did the same, looking at him, waiting. He stared straight ahead and cursed softly, bitterly.

Wolves would kill men, but men were not a preferred prey. Wolves remembered the old hunting together, for one thing, and two-legs tasted bad, for another. Wolves were more particular about their food than he would have believed. They would not eat carrion, unless they were starving, and few would kill more than they could eat. What Perrin felt from the wolves could best be described as disgust. And there were the images. He could see them much more clearly than he wished. Bodies, men and women and children, heaped and tumbled about. Blood-soaked earth churned by hooves and frenzied attempts to escape. Torn flesh. Heads severed. Vultures flapping, their white wings stained red; bloody, featherless heads tearing and gorging. He broke loose before his stomach emptied itself.

Above some trees in the far distance he could just make out black specks whirling low, dropping then rising again. Vultures fighting over their meal.

"There's something bad up there." He swallowed, meeting Ingtar's gaze.

How could he fit telling them into the story of being a sniffer? *I don't want to get close enough to look at that. But they'll want to investigate once they can see the vultures. I have to tell them enough so they'll circle around.* "The people from that village. . . . I think the Trollocs killed them."

Uno began cursing quietly, and some of the other Shienarans muttered to themselves. None of them seemed to take his announcement as odd, though. Lord Ingtar said he was a sniffer, and sniffers could smell killing.

"And there is someone following us," Ingtar said.

Mat turned his horse eagerly. "Maybe it's Rand. I knew he wouldn't run out on me."

Thin, scattered puffs of dust rose to the north; a horse was running across patches where the grass grew thin. The Shienarans spread out, lances ready, watching in all directions. It was no place to be casual about a stranger.

A speck appeared—a horse and rider; a woman, to Perrin's eyes, long before anyone else could discern the rider—and quickly drew closer. She slowed to a trot as she came up on them, fanning herself with one hand. A plump, graying woman, with her cloak tied behind her saddle, who blinked at them all vaguely.

"That's one of the Aes Sedai," Mat said disappointedly. "I recognize her. Verin."

"Verin Sedai," Ingtar said sharply, then bowed to her from his saddle.

"Moiraine Sedai sent me, Lord Ingtar," Verin announced with a satisfied smile. "She thought you might need me. Such a gallop I've had. I thought I might not catch you short of Cairhien. You saw that village, of course? Oh, that was very nasty, wasn't it? And that Myrddraal. There were ravens and crows all over the rooftops, but never a one went near it, dead as it was. I had to wave away the Dark One's own weight in flies, though, before I could make out what it was. A shame I did not have time to take it down. I've never had a chance to study a—" Suddenly her eyes narrowed, and the absent manner vanished like smoke. "Where is Rand al'Thor?"

Ingtar grimaced. "Gone, Verin Sedai. Vanished last night, without a trace. Him, the Ogier, and Hurin, one of my men."

"The Ogier, Lord Ingtar? And your sniffer went with him? What would those two have in common with . . . ?" Ingtar gaped at her, and she snorted. "Did you think you could keep something like that secret?" She snorted again. "Sniffers. Vanished, you say?"

"Yes, Verin Sedai." Ingtar sounded unsettled. It was never easy discovering Aes Sedai knew the secrets you were trying to keep from them; Perrin hoped Moiraine had not told anyone about him. "But I have—I have a new sniffer." The Shienaran Lord gestured to Perrin. "This man seems to have

the ability, also. I will find the Horn of Valere, as I swore to, have no fear.
Your company will be welcome, Aes Sedai, if you wish to ride with us." To
Perrin's surprise, he did not sound as if he entirely meant it.

Verin glanced at Perrin, and he shifted uneasily. "A new sniffer, just
when you lose your old one. How . . . providential. You found no tracks?
No, of course not. You said no trace. Odd. Last night." She twisted in her
saddle, looking back north, and for a moment Perrin almost thought she
was going to ride back the way she had come.

Ingtar frowned at her. "You think their disappearance has something to
do with the Horn, Aes Sedai?"

Verin settled back. "The Horn? No. No, I . . . think not. But it is odd.
Very odd. I do not like odd things until I can understand them."

"I can have two men escort you back to where they disappeared, Verin
Sedai. They will have no trouble taking you right to it."

"No. If you say they vanished without a trace. . . ." For a long moment
she studied Ingtar, her face unreadable. "I will ride with you. Perhaps we
will find them again, or they will find us. Talk to me as we ride, Lord
Ingtar. Tell me everything you can about the young man. Everything he
did, everything he said."

They started off in a jingle of harness and armor, Verin riding close
beside Ingtar and questioning him closely, but too low to be overheard.
She gave Perrin a look when he tried to maintain his place, and he fell
back.

"It's Rand she's after," Mat murmured, "not the Horn."

Perrin nodded. *Wherever you've gotten to, Rand, stay there. It's safer than
here.*

# CHAPTER 15

## *Kinslayer*

The way the strangely faded distant hills seemed to slide toward Rand when he looked straight at them made his head spin, unless he wrapped himself in the void. Sometimes the emptiness crept up on him unawares, but he avoided it like death. Better to be dizzy than share the void with that uneasy light. Better by far to stare at the faded land. Still, he tried not to look at anything too far away unless it lay right ahead of them.

Hurin wore a fixed look as he concentrated on sniffing the trail, as if he were trying to ignore the land the trail crossed. When the sniffer did notice what lay around them, he would give a start and wipe his hands on his coat, then push his nose forward like a hound, eyes glazing, excluding everything else. Loial rode slumped in his saddle and frowned as he glanced around, ears twitching uneasily, muttering to himself.

Again they crossed land blackened and burned, even the soil crunching under the horses' hooves as if it had been seared. The burned swathes, sometimes a mile wide, sometimes only a few hundred paces, all ran east and west as straight as an arrow's flight. Twice Rand saw the end of a burn, once as they rode over it, once as they passed nearby; they tapered to points at the ends. At least, the ends he saw were so, but he suspected they were all the same.

Once he had watched Whatley Eldin decorate a cart for Sunday, back home in Emond's Field, What painting the scenes in bright colors, and the intricate scrollwork that surrounded them. For the borders, What let the point of his brush touch the cart, making a thin line that grew thicker as he pressed harder, then thinner again as he eased up. That was how the land looked, as if someone had streaked it with a monstrous brush of fire.

Nothing grew where the burns were, though some burns, at least, had the feel of a thing long done. Not so much as a hint of char remained in the air there, not a whiff even when he leaned down to break off a black twig and smell it. Old, yet nothing had come in to reclaim the land. Black gave way to green, and green to black, along knife-edge lines.

In its own way, the rest of the land lay as dead as the burns, though grass covered the ground and leaves covered the trees. Everything had that faded look, like clothes too often washed and too long left in the sun. There were no birds or animals, not that Rand saw or heard. No hawk wheeling in the sky, no bark of a hunting fox, no bird singing. Nothing rustled in the grass or lit on a tree branch. No bees, or butterflies. Several times they crossed streams, the water shallow, though often it had dug itself a deep gulley with steep banks the horses had to scramble down and climb on the other side. The water ran clear except for the mud the horses' hooves stirred, but never a minnow or tadpole wriggled out of the roiling, not even a waterspider dancing across the surface, or a hovering lacewing.

The water was drinkable, which was just as well, since their waterbottles could not last forever. Rand tasted it first, and made Loial and Hurin wait to see if anything happened to him before he let them drink. He had gotten them into this; it was his responsibility. The water was cool and wet, but that was the best that could be said for it. It tasted flat, as if it had been boiled. Loial made a face, and the horses did not like it either, shaking their heads and drinking reluctantly.

There was one sign of life; at least, Rand thought it must be so. Twice he saw a wispy streak crawling across the sky like a line drawn with cloud. The lines were too straight to be natural, it seemed, but he could not imagine what might make them. He did not mention the lines to the others. Perhaps they did not see, Hurin intent on the trail as he was and Loial drawn in on himself. They said nothing of the lines, at any rate.

When they had ridden half the morning, Loial abruptly swung down from his huge horse without a word and strode to a stand of giantsbroom, their trunks splitting into many thick branches, stiff and straight, not a pace above the ground. At the top, all split again, into the leafy brush that gave them their name.

Rand pulled Red up and started to ask what he was doing, but something about the Ogier's manner, as if he himself were uncertain, kept Rand silent. After staring at the tree, Loial put his hands on a trunk and began to sing in a deep, soft rumble.

Rand had heard Ogier treesong, once, when Loial had sung to a dying tree and brought it back to life, and he had heard of sung wood, objects wrought from trees by the treesong. The Talent was fading, Loial said; he was one of the few who had the ability, now; that was what made sung wood even more sought after and treasured. When he had heard Loial sing before, it had been as if the earth itself sang, but now the Ogier murmured his song almost diffidently, and the land echoed it in a whisper.

It seemed pure song, music without words, at least none that Rand could make out; if there were words, they faded into the music just as water pours into a stream. Hurin gasped and stared.

Rand was not sure what it was Loial did, or how; soft as the song was, it caught him up hypnotically, filling his mind almost the way the void did. Loial ran his big hands along the trunk, singing, caressing with his voice as well as his fingers. The trunk now seemed smoother, somehow, as if his stroking were shaping it. Rand blinked. He was sure the piece Loial worked on had had branches at its top just like the others, but now it stopped in a rounded end right above the Ogier's head. Rand opened his mouth, but the song quieted him. It seemed so familiar, that song, as if he should know it.

Abruptly Loial's voice rose to a climax—almost a hymn of thanks, it sounded—and ended, fading as a breeze fades.

"Burn me," Hurin breathed. He looked stunned. "Burn me, I never heard anything like. . . . Burn me."

In his hands Loial held a staff as tall as he was and as thick as Rand's forearm, smooth and polished. Where the trunk had been on the giants-broom was a small stem of new growth.

Rand took a deep breath. *Always something new, always something I didn't expect, and sometimes it isn't horrible.*

He watched Loial mount, resting the staff across his saddle in front of him, and wondered why the Ogier wanted a staff at all, since they were riding. Then he saw the thick rod, not as big as it was, but in relation to the Ogier, saw the way Loial handled it. "A quarterstaff," he said, surprised. "I didn't know Ogier carried weapons, Loial."

"Usually we do not," the Ogier replied almost curtly. "Usually. The price has always been too high." He hefted the huge quarterstaff and wrinkled his broad nose with distaste. "Elder Haman would surely say I am putting a long handle on my axe, but I am not just being hasty or rash, Rand. This place. . . ." He shivered, and his ears twitched.

"We'll find our way back soon," Rand said, trying to sound confident.

Loial spoke as if he had not heard. "Everything is . . . linked, Rand. Whether it lives or not, whether it thinks or not, everything that *is,* fits together. The tree does not think, but it is part of the whole, and the whole has a—a feeling. I can't explain any more than I can explain what being happy is, but. . . . Rand, this land was glad for a weapon to be made. Glad!"

"The Light shine on us," Hurin murmured nervously, "and the Creator's hand shelter us. Though we go to the last embrace of the mother, the Light illumine our way." He kept repeating the catechism as if it had a charm to protect him.

Rand resisted the impulse to look around. He definitely did not look up. All it would take to break them all was another of those smoky lines across the sky right at that moment. "There's nothing here to hurt us," he said firmly. "And we'll keep a good watch and make sure nothing does."

He wanted to laugh at himself, sounding so certain. He was not certain about anything. But watching the others—Loial with his tufted ears drooping, and Hurin trying not to look at anything—he knew one of them had to seem to be sure, at least, or fear and uncertainty would break them all apart. *The Wheel weaves as the Wheel wills.* He squeezed that thought out. *Nothing to do with the Wheel. Nothing to with* ta'veren, *or Aes Sedai, or the Dragon. It's just the way it is, that's all.*

"Loial, are you done here?" The Ogier nodded, regretfully rubbing the quarterstaff. Rand turned to Hurin. "Do you still have the trail?"

"I do, Lord Rand. I do that."

"Then let's keep on with it. Once we find Fain and the Darkfriends, why, we'll go home heroes, with the dagger for Mat, and the Horn of Valere. Lead out, Hurin." *Heroes? I'll settle for all of us getting out of here alive.*

"I do not like this place," the Ogier announced flatly. He held the quarterstaff as if he expected to have to use it soon.

"As well we don't mean to stay here, then, isn't it?" Rand said. Hurin barked a laugh as if he had made a joke, but Loial gave him a level look.

"As well we don't, Rand."

Yet as they rode on southward, he could see that his casual assumption that they would get home had picked them both up a little. Hurin sat a bit straighter in his saddle, and Loial's ears did not seem so wilted. It was no time or place to let them know he shared their fear, so he kept it to himself, and fought it by himself.

Hurin kept his humor through the morning, murmuring, "As well we don't mean to stay," then chuckling, until Rand felt like telling him to be quiet. Toward midday, the sniffer did fall silent, though, shaking his head and frowning, and Rand found he wished the man was still repeating his words and laughing.

"Is there something wrong with the trail, Hurin?" he asked.

The sniffer shrugged, looking troubled. "Yes, Lord Rand, and then again no, as you might say."

"It must be one or the other. Have you lost the trail? No shame if you have. You said it was weak to start. If we can't find the Darkfriends, we will find another Stone and get back that way." *Light, anything but that.* Rand kept his face smooth. "If Darkfriends can come here and leave, so can we."

"Oh, I haven't lost it, Lord Rand. I can still pick out the stink of them. It isn't that. It's just. . . . It's. . . ." With a grimace, Hurin burst out, "It's like I'm remembering it, Lord Rand, instead of smelling it. But I'm not. There's dozens of trails crossing it all the time, dozens and dozens, and all sorts of smells of violence, some of them fresh, almost, only washed out like everything else. This morning, right after we left the hollow, I could have sworn there were hundreds slaughtered right under my feet, just minutes before, but there weren't any bodies, and not a mark on the grass but our own hoofprints. A thing like that couldn't happen without the ground being torn up and bloodied, but there wasn't a mark. It's all like that, my Lord. But I am following the trail. I am. This place just has me all on edge. That's it. That must be it."

Rand glanced at Loial—the Ogier did come up with the oddest knowledge, at times—but he looked as puzzled as Hurin. Rand made his voice more confident than he felt. "I know you are doing your best, Hurin. We are all of us on edge. Just follow as best you can, and we'll find them."

"As you say, Lord Rand." Hurin booted his horse forward. "As you say."

But by nightfall, there was still no sign of the Darkfriends, and Hurin said the trail was fainter still. The sniffer kept muttering to himself about "remembering."

There had been no sign. Really no sign. Rand was not as good a tracker as Uno, but any boy in the Two Rivers was expected to track well enough to find a lost sheep, or a rabbit for dinner. He had seen nothing. It was as if no living thing had ever disturbed the land before they came. There should have been something if the Darkfriends were ahead of them. But Hurin kept following the trail he said he smelled.

As the sun touched the horizon they made camp in a stand of trees untouched by the burn, eating from their saddlebags. Flatbread and dried meat washed down with flat-tasting water; hardly a filling meal, tough and far from tasty. Rand thought they might have enough for a week. After

that. . . . Hurin ate slowly, determinedly, but Loial gulped his down with
a grimace and settled back with his pipe, the big quarterstaff close at hand.
Rand kept their fire small and well hidden in the trees. Fain and his
Darkfriends and Trollocs might be close enough to see a fire, for all of
Hurin's worries about the oddness of their trail.

It seemed odd to him that he had begun to think of them as Fain's
Darkfriends, Fain's Trollocs. Fain was just a madman. *Then why did they
rescue him?* Fain had been part of the Dark One's scheme to find him.
Perhaps it had something to do with that. *Then why is he running instead of
chasing me? And what killed that Fade? What happened in that room full of flies?
And those eyes, watching me in Fal Dara. And that wind, catching me like a
beetle in pine sap. No. No, Ba'alzamon has to be dead.* The Aes Sedai did not
believe it. Moiraine did not believe it, nor the Amyrlin. Stubbornly, he
refused to think about it any longer. All he had to think about now was
finding that dagger for Mat. Finding Fain, and the Horn.

*It's never over, al'Thor.*

The voice was like a thin breeze whispering in the back of his head, a
thin, icy murmur working its way into the crevices of his mind. He almost
sought the void to escape it, but remembering what waited for him there,
he pushed down the desire.

In the half dark of twilight, he worked the forms with his sword, the
way Lan had taught, though without the void. Parting the Silk. Hummingbird Kisses the Honeyrose. Heron Wading in the Rushes, for balance.
Losing himself in the swift, sure movements, forgetting for a time where
he was, he worked until sweat covered him. Yet when he was done, it all
came back; nothing was changed. The weather was not cold, but he shivered and pulled his cloak around him as he hunched by the fire. The others
caught his mood, and they finished eating quickly and in silence. No one
complained when he kicked dirt over the last fitful flames.

Rand took the first watch himself, walking the edges of the copse with
his bow, sometimes easing his sword in its scabbard. The chill moon was
almost full, standing high in the blackness, and the night was as silent as
the day had been, as empty. Empty was the right word. The land was as
empty as a dusty milk crock. It was hard to believe there was anyone in the
whole world, in this world, except for the three of them, hard to believe
even the Darkfriends were there, somewhere ahead.

To keep himself company, he unwrapped Thom Merrilin's cloak, exposing the harp and flute in their hard leather cases atop the many-colored
patches. He took the gold-and-silver flute from its case, remembering the
gleeman teaching him as he fingered it, and played a few notes of "The
Wind That Shakes the Willow," softly so as not to wake the others. Even

soft, the sad sound was too loud in that place, too real. With a sigh he replaced the flute and did up the bundle again.

He held the watch long into the night, letting the others sleep. He did not know how late it was when he suddenly realized a fog had risen. Close to the ground it lay, thick, making Hurin and Loial indistinct mounds seeming to hump out of clouds. Thinner higher up, it still shrouded the land around them, hiding everything except the nearest trees. The moon seemed viewed through watered silk. Anything at all could come right up to them unseen. He touched his sword.

"Swords do no good against me, Lews Therin. You should know that."

The fog swirled around Rand's feet as he spun, the sword coming into his hands, heron-mark blade upright before him. The void leaped up inside him; for the first time, he barely noticed the tainted light of *saidin*.

A shadowy figure drew nearer through the mist, walking with a tall staff. Behind it, as if the shadow's shadow were vast, the fog darkened till it was blacker than night. Rand's skin crawled. Closer the figure came, until it resolved into the shape of a man, clothed and gloved in black, with a black silk mask covering his face, and the shadow came with it. His staff was black, too, as if the wood had been charred, yet smooth and shining like water by moonlight. For an instant the eyeholes of the mask glowed, as if fires stood behind them rather than eyes, but Rand did not need that to know who it was.

"Ba'alzamon," he breathed. "This is a dream. It has to be. I fell asleep, and—"

Ba'alzamon laughed like the roar of an open furnace. "You always try to deny what is, Lews Therin. If I stretch out my hand, I can touch you, Kinslayer. I can always touch you. Always and everywhere."

"I am not the Dragon! My name is Rand al'—!" Rand clamped his teeth shut to stop himself.

"Oh, I know the name you use now, Lews Therin. I know every name you have used through Age after Age, long before you were even the Kinslayer." Ba'alzamon's voice began to rise in intensity; sometimes the fires of his eyes flared so high that Rand could see them through the openings in the silk mask, see them like endless seas of flame. "I know you, know your blood and your line back to the first spark of life that ever was, back to the First Moment. You can never hide from me. Never! We are tied together as surely as two sides of the same coin. Ordinary men may hide in the sweep of the Pattern, but *ta'veren* stand out like beacon fires on a hill, and you, *you* stand out as if ten thousand shining arrows stood in the sky to point you out! You are mine, and ever in reach of my hand!"

"Father of Lies!" Rand managed. Despite the void, his tongue wanted to cleave to the roof of his mouth. *Light, please let it be a dream.* The thought skittered outside the emptiness. *Even one of those dreams that isn't a dream. He can't really be standing in front of me. The Dark One is sealed in Shayol Ghul, sealed by the Creator at the moment of Creation.* . . . . He knew too much of the truth for it to help. "You're well named! If you could just take me, why haven't you? Because you cannot. I walk in the Light, and you cannot touch me!"

Ba'alzamon leaned on his staff and looked at Rand a moment, then moved to stand over Loial and Hurin, peering down at them. The vast shadow moved with him. He did not disturb the fog, Rand saw—he moved, the staff swung with his steps, but the gray mist did not swirl and eddy around his feet as it did around Rand's. That gave him heart. Perhaps Ba'alzamon really was *not* there. Perhaps it *was* a dream.

"You find odd followers," Ba'alzamon mused. "You always did. These two. The girl who tries to watch over you. A poor guardian and weak, Kinslayer. If she had a lifetime to grow, she would never grow strong enough for you to hide behind."

*Girl? Who? Moiraine is surely not a girl.* "I don't know what you are talking about, Father of Lies. You lie, and lie, and even when you tell the truth, you twist it to a lie."

"Do I, Lews Therin? You know what you are, who you are. I have told you. And so have those women of Tar Valon." Rand shifted, and Ba'alzamon gave a laugh, like a small thunderclap. "They think themselves safe in their White Tower, but my followers number even some of their own. The Aes Sedai called Moiraine told you who you are, did she not? Did she lie? Or is she one of mine? The White Tower means to use you like a hound on a leash. Do I lie? Do I lie when I say you seek the Horn of Valere?" He laughed again; calm of the void or no, it was all Rand could do not to cover his ears. "Sometimes old enemies fight so long that they become allies and never realize it. They think they strike at you, but they have become so closely linked it is as if you guided the blow yourself."

"You don't guide me," Rand said. "I deny you."

"I have a thousand strings tied to you, Kinslayer, each one finer than silk and stronger than steel. Time has tied a thousand cords between us. The battle we two have fought—do you remember any part of that? Do you have any glimmering that we have fought before, battles without number back to the beginning of Time? I know much that you do not! That battle will soon end. The Last Battle is coming. The last, Lews Therin. Do you really think you can avoid it? You poor, shivering worm. You will serve me or die! And this time the cycle will not begin anew with your death. The grave belongs to the Great Lord of the Dark. This time if you die, you will be destroyed utterly. This time the Wheel will be broken whatever you do, and the world remade to a new mold. Serve me! Serve Shai'tan, or be destroyed forever!"

With the utterance of that name, the air seemed to thicken. The darkness behind Ba'alzamon swelled and grew, threatening to swallow everything. Rand felt it engulfing him, colder than ice and hotter than coals both at the same time, blacker than death, sucking him into the depths of it, overwhelming the world.

He gripped his sword hilt till his knuckles hurt. "I deny you, and I deny your power. I walk in the Light. The Light preserves us, and we shelter in the palm of the Creator's hand." He blinked. Ba'alzamon still stood there, and the great darkness still hung behind him, but it was as if all the rest had been illusion.

"Do you want to see my face?" It was a whisper.

Rand swallowed. "No."

"You should." A gloved hand went to the black mask.

"No!"

The mask came away. It was a man's face, horribly burned. Yet between the black-edged, red crevices crossing those features, the skin looked healthy and smooth. Dark eyes looked at Rand; cruel lips smiled with a flash of white teeth. "Look at me, Kinslayer, and see the hundredth part of your own fate." For a moment eyes and mouth became doorways into endless caverns of fire. "This is what the Power unchecked can do, even to me. But I heal, Lews Therin. I know the paths to greater power. It will burn you like a moth flying into a furnace."

"I will not touch it!" Rand felt the void around him, felt *saidin.* "I won't."

"You cannot stop yourself."

"Leave—me—ALONE!"

"Power." Ba'alzamon's voice became soft, insinuating. "You can have power again, Lews Therin. You are linked to it now, this moment. I know it. I can see it. Feel it, Lews Therin. Feel the glow inside you. Feel the power that could be yours. All you must do is reach out for it. But the Shadow is there between you and it. Madness and death. You need not die, Lews Therin, not ever again."

"No," Rand said, but the voice went on, burrowing into him.

"I can teach you to control that power so that it does not destroy you. No one else lives who can teach you that. The Great Lord of the Dark can shelter you from the madness. The power can be yours, and you can live forever. Forever! All you must do in return is serve. Only serve. Simple words—I am yours, Great Lord—and power will be yours. Power beyond anything those women of Tar Valon dream of, and life eternal, if you will only offer yourself up and serve."

Rand licked his lips. *Not to go mad. Not to die.* "Never! I walk in the Light," he grated hoarsely, "and you can never touch me!"

"Touch you, Lews Therin? Touch you? I can consume you! Taste it and know, as I knew!"

Those dark eyes became fire again, and that mouth, flame that blossomed and grew until it seemed brighter than a summer sun. Grew, and suddenly Rand's sword glowed as if just drawn from the forge. He cried out as the hilt burned his hands, screamed and dropped the sword. And the fog caught fire, fire that leaped, fire that burned everything.

Yelling, Rand beat at his clothes as they smoked and charred and fell in ashes, beat with hands that blackened and shriveled as naked flesh cracked and peeled away in the flames. He screamed. Pain beat at the void inside him, and he tried to crawl deeper into the emptiness. The glow was there, the tainted light just out of sight. Half mad, no longer caring what it was, he reached for *saidin,* tried to wrap it around him, tried to hide in it from the burning and the pain.

As suddenly as the fire began, it was gone. Rand stared wonderingly at his hand sticking out of the red sleeve of his coat. There was not so much as a singe on the wool. *I imagined it all.* Frantically, he looked around. Ba'alzamon was gone. Hurin shifted in his sleep; the sniffer and Loial were still only two mounds sticking up out of the low fog. *I did imagine it.*

Before relief had a chance to grow, pain stabbed his right hand, and he turned it up to look. There across the palm was branded a heron. The heron from the hilt of his sword, angry and red, as neatly done as though drawn with an artist's skill.

Fumbling a kerchief from his coat pocket, he wrapped it around his hand. The hand throbbed, now. The void would help with that—he was *aware* of pain in the void, but he did not *feel* it—but he put the thought out of his head. Twice now, unknowing—and once on purpose; he could not forget that—he had tried to channel the One Power while he was in the void. It was with that that Ba'alzamon wanted to tempt him. It was that that Moiraine and the Amyrlin Seat wanted him to do. He would not.

# CHAPTER 16

## In the Mirror of Darkness

"You should not have done it, Lord Rand," Hurin said when Rand woke the others just at daybreak. The sun yet hid below the horizon, but there was light enough to see. The fog had melted away while dark still held, fading reluctantly. "If you use yourself up to spare us, my Lord, who will see to getting us home?"

"I needed to think," Rand said. Nothing showed the fog had ever been, or Ba'alzamon. He fingered the kerchief wrapped around his right hand. There was that to prove Ba'alzamon had been there. He wanted to be away from this place. "Time to be in the saddle if we are going to catch Fain's Darkfriends. Past time. We can eat flatbread while we ride."

Loial paused in the act of stretching, his arms reaching as high as Hurin could have standing on Rand's shoulders. "Your hand, Rand. What happened?"

"I hurt it. It's nothing."

"I have a salve in my saddlebags—"

"It is nothing!" Rand knew he sounded harsh, but one look at the brand would surely bring questions he did not want to answer. "Time's wasting. Let us be on our way." He set about saddling Red, awkwardly because of his injured hand, and Hurin jumped to his own horse.

"No need to be so touchy," Loial muttered.

A track, Rand decided as they set out, would be something natural in that world. There were too many unnatural things there. Even a single hoofprint would be welcome. Fain and the Darkfriends and the Trollocs had to leave some mark. He concentrated on the ground they passed over, trying to make out any trace that could have been made by another living thing.

There was nothing, not a turned stone, not a disturbed clod of earth. Once he looked at the ground behind them, just to reassure himself that the land did take hoofprints; scraped turf and bent grass marked their passage plainly, yet ahead the ground was undisturbed. But Hurin insisted he could smell the trail, faint and thin, but still heading south.

Once again the sniffer put all his attentions on the trail he followed, like a hound tracking deer, and once again Loial rode lost in his own thoughts, muttering to himself and rubbing the huge quarterstaff held across his saddle in front of him.

They had not been riding more than an hour when Rand saw the spire ahead. He was so busy watching for tracks that the tapering column already stood thick and tall above the trees in the middle distance when he first noticed it. "I wonder what that is." It lay directly in their path.

"I don't know what it can be, Rand," Loial said.

"If this—if this was our own world, Lord Rand. . . ." Hurin shifted uncomfortably in his saddle. "Well, that monument Lord Ingtar was talking about—the one to Artur Hawking's victory over the Trollocs—it was a great spire. But it was torn down a thousand years ago. There's nothing left but a big mound, like a hill. I saw it, when I went to Cairhien for Lord Agelmar."

"According to Ingtar," Loial said, "that is still three or four days ahead of us. If it is here at all. I don't know why it should be. I don't think there are any people here at all."

The sniffer put his eyes back on the ground. "That's just it, isn't it, Builder? No people, but there it is ahead of us. Maybe we ought to keep clear of it, my Lord Rand. No telling what it is, or who's there, in a place like this."

Rand drummed his fingers on the high pommel of his saddle for a moment, thinking. "We have to stick as close to the trail as we can," he said finally. "We don't seem to be getting any closer to Fain as it is, and I don't want to lose more time, if we can avoid it. If we see any people, or anything out of the ordinary, then we'll circle around until we pick it up again. But until then, we keep on."

"As you say, my Lord." The sniffer sounded odd, and he gave Rand a quick, sidelong look. "As you say."

Rand frowned for a moment before he understood, and then it was his turn to sigh. Lords did not explain to those who followed them, only to other lords. *I didn't ask him to take me for a bloody lord. But he did,* a small voice seemed to answer him, *and you let him. You made the choice; now the duty is yours.*

"Take the trail, Hurin," Rand said.

With a flash of relieved grin, the sniffer heeled his horse onward.

The weak sun climbed as they rode, and by the time it was overhead, they were only a mile or so from the spire. They had reached one of the streams, in a gully a pace deep, and the intervening trees were sparse. Rand could see the mound it was built on, like a round, flat-topped hill. The gray spire itself rose at least a hundred spans, and he could just make out now that the top was carved in the likeness of a bird with outstretched wings.

"A hawk," Rand said. "It *is* Hawkwing's monument. It must be. There were people here, whether there are now or not. They just built it in another place here, and never tore it down. Think of it, Hurin. When we get back, you'll be able to tell them what the monument really looked like. There will only be three of us in the whole world who have ever seen it."

Hurin nodded. "Yes, my Lord. My children would like to hear that tale, their father seeing Hawkwing's spire."

"Rand," Loial began worriedly.

"We can gallop the distance," Rand said. "Come on. A gallop will do us good. This place may be dead, but we're alive."

"Rand," Loial said, "I don't think that is a—"

Not waiting to hear, Rand dug his boots into Red's flanks, and the stallion sprang forward. He splashed across the shallow ribbon of water in two strides, then scrabbled up the far side. Hurin launched his horse right behind him. Rand heard Loial calling behind them, but he laughed, waved for the Ogier to follow, and galloped on. If he kept his eyes on one spot, the land did not seem to slip and slide so badly, and the wind felt good on his face.

The mound covered a good two hides, but the grassy slope rose at an easy slant. The gray spire reared into the sky, squared and broad enough despite its height to seem massive, almost squat. Rand's laughter died, and he pulled Red up, his face grim.

"Is that Hawkwing's monument, Lord Rand?" Hurin asked uneasily. "It doesn't look right, somehow."

Rand recognized the harsh, angular script that covered the face of the monument, and he recognized some of the symbols chiseled on the breadth, chiseled as tall as a man. The horned skull of the Da'vol Trollocs.

The iron fist of the Dhai'mon. The trident of the Ka'bol, and the whirl-wind of the Ahf'frait. There was a hawk, too, carved near the bottom. With a wingspan of ten paces, it lay on its back, pierced by a lightning bolt, and ravens pecked at its eyes. The huge wings atop the spire seemed to block the sun.

He heard Loial galloping up behind him.

"I tried to tell you, Rand," Loial said. "It is a raven, not a hawk. I could see it clearly." Hurin turned his horse, refusing even to look at the spire any longer.

"But how?" Rand said. "Artur Hawkwing won a victory over the Trollocs here. Ingtar said so."

"Not here," Loial said slowly. "Obviously not here. 'From Stone to Stone run the lines of if, between the worlds that might be.' I've been thinking on it, and I believe I know what the 'the worlds that might be' are. Maybe I do. Worlds our world might have been if things had happened differently. Maybe that's why it is all so . . . washed-out looking. Because it's an 'if,' a 'maybe.' Just a shadow of the real world. In this world, I think, the Trollocs won. Maybe that's why we have not seen any villages or people."

Rand's skin crawled. Where Trollocs won, they did not leave humans alive except for food. If they had won across an entire world. . . . "If the Trollocs had won, they would be everywhere. We'd have seen a thousand of them by now. We'd be dead since yesterday."

"I do not know, Rand. Perhaps, after they killed the people, they killed one another. Trollocs live to kill. That is all they do; that is all they are. I just don't know."

"Lord Rand," Hurin said abruptly, "something moved down there."

Rand whirled his horse, ready to see charging Trollocs, but Hurin was pointing back the way they had come, at nothing. "What did you see, Hurin? Where?"

The sniffer let his arm drop. "Right at the edge of that clump of trees there, about a mile. I thought it was . . . a woman . . . and something else I couldn't make out, but. . . ." He shivered. "It's so hard to make out things that aren't under your nose. Aaah, this place has my guts all awhirl. I'm likely imagining things, my Lord. This is a place for queer fancies." His shoulders hunched as if he felt the spire pressing on them. "No doubt it was just the wind, my Lord."

Loial said, "There's something else to consider, I'm afraid." He sounded troubled again. He pointed southward. "What do you see off there?"

Rand squinted against the way things far off seemed to slide toward him. "Land like what we've been crossing. Trees. Then some hills, and mountains. Nothing else. What do you want me to see?"

"The mountains," Loial sighed. The tufts on his ears drooped, and the ends of his eyebrows were down on his cheeks. "That has to be Kinslayer's Dagger, Rand. There aren't any other mountains they could be, unless this world is completely different from ours. But Kinslayer's Dagger lies more than a hundred leagues south of the Erinin. A good bit more. Distances are hard to judge in this place, but. . . . I think we will reach them before dark." He did not have to say any more. They could not have covered over a hundred leagues in less than three days.

Without thinking, Rand muttered, "Maybe this place is like the Ways." He heard Hurin moan, and instantly regretted not keeping a rein on his tongue.

It was not a pleasant thought. Enter a Waygate—they could be found just outside Ogier *stedding,* and in Ogier groves—enter and walk for a day, and you could leave by another Waygate a hundred leagues from where you started. The Ways were dark, now, and foul, and to travel them meant to risk death or madness. Even Fades feared to travel the Ways.

"If it is, Rand," Loial said slowly, "can a misstep kill us here, too? Are there things we have not yet seen that can do worse than kill us?" Hurin moaned again.

They had been drinking the water, riding along as if they had not a concern in the world. Unconcern would kill quickly in the Ways. Rand swallowed, hoping his stomach would settle.

"It is too late for worrying about what is past," he said. "From here on, though, we will watch our step." He glanced at Hurin. The sniffer's head had sunk between his shoulders, and his eyes darted as if he wondered what would leap at him, and from where. The man had run down murderers, but this was more than he had ever bargained for. "Hold on to yourself, Hurin. We are not dead, yet, and we won't be. We will just have to be careful from here on. That's all."

It was at that moment they heard the scream, thin with distance.

"A woman!" Hurin said. Even this much that was normal seemed to rouse him a little. "I knew I saw—"

Another scream came, more desperate than the first.

"Not unless she can fly," Rand said. "She's south of us." He kicked Red to a dead run in two strides.

"Be careful you said!" Loial shouted after him. "Light, Rand, remember! Be careful!"

Rand lay low on Red's back, letting the stallion run. The screams drew him on. It was easy to say be careful, but there was terror in that woman's voice. She did not sound as if she had time for him to be careful. On the edge of another stream, in a sheer-banked channel deeper than most, he drew rein; Red skidded in a shower of stones and dirt. The screams were coming. . . . *There!*

He took it all in at a glance. Perhaps two hundred paces away, the woman stood beside her horse in the stream, both of them backed against the far bank. With a broken length of branch, she was fending off a snarling . . . something. Rand swallowed, stunned for a moment. If a frog were as big as a bear, or if a bear had a frog's gray-green hide, it might look like that. A big bear.

Not letting himself think about the creature, he leaped to the ground, unlimbering his bow. If he took the time to ride closer, it might be too late. The woman was barely keeping the . . . thing . . . at the edge of the branch. It was a fair distance—he kept blinking as he tried to judge it; the distance seemed to change by spans every time the thing moved—yet a big target. His bandaged hand made drawing awkward, but he had an arrow loosed almost before his feet were set.

The shaft sank into the leathery hide for half its length, and the creature spun to face Rand. Rand took a step back despite the distance. That huge, wedge-shaped head had never been on any animal he could imagine, nor that wide, horny-lipped beak of a mouth, hooked for ripping flesh. And it had three eyes, small, and fierce, and ringed by hard-looking ridges. Gathering itself, the thing bounded toward him down the stream in great, splashing leaps. To Rand's eye, some of the leaps seemed to cover twice as much distance as others, though he was sure they were all the same.

"An eye," the woman called. She sounded surprisingly calm, considering her screams. "You must hit an eye to kill it."

He drew the fletching of another arrow back to his ear. Reluctantly, he sought the void; he did not want to, but it was for this that Tam had taught him, and he knew he could never make the shot without it. *My father,* he thought with a sense of loss, and emptiness filled him. The quavering light of *saidin* was there, but he shut it away. He was one with the bow, with the arrow, with the monstrous shape leaping toward him. One with the tiny eye. He did not even feel the arrow leave the bowstring.

The creature rose in another bound, and at the peak, the arrow struck its central eye. The thing landed, fountaining another huge splash of water and mud. Ripples spread out from it, but it did not move.

"Well shot, and bravely," the woman called. She was on her horse, riding to meet him. Rand felt vaguely surprised that she had not run once the thing's attention was diverted. She rode past the bulk, still surrounded by the ripples of its dying, without even a downward glance, scrambled her horse up the bank and dismounted. "Few men would stand to face the charge of a *grolm,* my Lord."

She was all in white, her dress divided for riding and belted in silver, and her boots, peeking out from under her hems, were tooled in silver, too. Even her saddle was white, and silver-mounted. Her snowy mare, with its arched neck and dainty step, was almost as tall as Rand's bay. But it was the woman herself—she was perhaps Nynaeve's age, he thought—who held his eyes. She was tall, for one thing; a hand taller and she could almost look him in the eyes. For another, she was beautiful, ivory-pale skin contrasting sharply with long, night-dark hair and black eyes. He had seen beautiful women. Moiraine was beautiful, if cool, and so was Nynaeve, when her temper did not get the better of her. Egwene, and Elayne, the Daughter-Heir of Andor, were each enough to take a man's breath. But this woman. . . . His tongue stuck to the roof of his mouth; he felt his heart start beating again.

"Your retainers, my Lord?"

Startled, he looked around. Hurin and Loial had joined them. Hurin was staring the way Rand knew he had been, and even the Ogier seemed fascinated. "My friends," he said. "Loial, and Hurin. My name is Rand. Rand al'Thor."

"I have never thought of it before," Loial said abruptly, sounding as if he were talking to himself, "but if there is such a thing as perfect human beauty, in face and form, then you—"

"Loial!" Rand shouted. The Ogier's ears stiffened in embarrassment. Rand's own ears were red; Loial's words had been too close to what he himself was thinking.

The woman laughed musically, but the next instant she was all regal formality, like a queen on her throne. "I am called Selene," she said. "You have risked your life, and saved mine. I am yours, Lord Rand al'Thor." And, to Rand's horror, she knelt before him.

Not looking at Hurin or Loial, he hastily pulled her to her feet. "A man who will not die to save a woman is no man." Immediately he disgraced himself by blushing. It was a Shienaran saying, and he knew it sounded pompous before it was out of his mouth, but her manner had infected him, and he could not stop it. "I mean. . . . That is, it was. . . ." *Fool, you can't tell a woman saving her life was nothing.* "It was my honor." That sounded vaguely Shienaran and formal. He hoped it would do; his mind was as blank of anything else to say as if he were still in the void.

Suddenly he became conscious of her eyes on him. Her expression had not changed, but her dark eyes made him feel as if he were naked. Unbidden, the thought came of Selene with no clothes. His face went red again. "Aaah! Ah, where are you from, Selene? We have not seen another human being since we came here. Is your town nearby?" She looked at him thoughtfully, and he stepped back. Her look made him too aware of how close to her he was.

"I'm not from this world, my Lord," she said. "There are no people here. Nothing living except the *grolm* and a few other creatures like them. I am from Cairhien. And as to how I came here, I don't know, exactly. I was out riding, and I stopped to nap, and when I woke, my horse and I were here. I can only hope, my Lord, that you can save me again, and help me go home."

"Selene, I am not a . . . that is, please call me Rand." His ears felt hot again. *Light, it won't hurt anything if she thinks I'm a lord. Burn me, it won't hurt anything.*

"If you wish it . . . Rand." Her smile made his throat tighten. "You will help me?"

"Of course, I will." *Burn me, but she's beautiful. And looking at me like I'm a hero in a story.* He shook his head to clear it of foolishness. "But first we have to find the men we are following. I'll try to keep you out of danger, but we must find them. Coming with us will be better than staying here alone."

For a moment she was silent, her face blank and smooth; Rand had no idea what she was thinking, except that she seemed to be studying him anew. "A man of duty," she said finally. A small smile touched her lips. "I like that. Yes. Who are these miscreants you follow?"

"Darkfriends and Trollocs, my Lady," Hurin burst out. He made an awkward bow to her from his saddle. "They did murder in Fal Dara keep and stole the Horn of Valere, my Lady, but Lord Rand will fetch it back."

Rand stared at the sniffer ruefully; Hurin gave a weak grin. *So much for secrecy.* It did not matter here, he supposed, but once back in their world. . . . "Selene, you must not say anything of the Horn to anyone. If it gets out, we'll have a hundred people on our heels trying to get the Horn for themselves."

"No, it would never do," Selene said, "for *that* to fall into the wrong hands. The Horn of Valere. I could not tell you how often I've dreamed of touching it, holding it in my hands. You must promise me, when you have it, you will let me touch it."

"Before I can do that, we have to find it. We had better be on our way." Rand offered his hand to help her mount; Hurin scrambled down to hold her stirrup. "Whatever that thing was I killed—a *grolm?*—there may be more of them around." Her hand was firm—there was surprising strength in her grip—and her skin was. . . . Silk? Something softer, smoother. Rand shivered.

"There always are," Selene said. The tall white mare frisked and bared her teeth once at Red, yet Selene's touch on the reins quieted her.

Rand slung his bow across his back and climbed onto Red. *Light, how could anyone's skin be so soft?* "Hurin, where's the trail? Hurin? Hurin!"

The sniffer gave a start, and left off staring at Selene. "Yes, Lord Rand. Ah . . . the trail. South, my Lord. Still south."

"Then let's ride." Rand gave an uneasy look at the gray-green bulk of the *grolm* lying in the stream. It had been better believing they were the only living things in that world. "Take the trail, Hurin."

Selene rode alongside Rand at first, talking of this and that, asking him questions and calling him lord. Half a dozen times he started to tell her he was no lord, only a shepherd, and every time, looking at her, he could not get the words out. A lady like her would not talk the same way with a shepherd, he was sure, even one who had saved her life.

"You will be a great man when you've found the Horn of Valere," she told him. "A man for the legends. The man who sounds the Horn will make his own legends."

"I don't want to sound it, and I don't want to be part of any legend." He did not know if she was wearing perfume, but there seemed to be a scent to her, something that filled his head with her. Spices, sharp and sweet, tickling his nose, making him swallow.

"Every man wants to be great. You could be the greatest man in all the Ages."

It sounded too close to what Moiraine had said. The Dragon Reborn would certainly stand out through the Ages. "Not me," he said fervently. "I'm just"—he thought of her scorn if he told her now that he was only a shepherd after letting her believe he was a lord, and changed what he had been going to say—"just trying to find it. And to help a friend."

She was silent a moment, then said, "You've hurt your hand."

"It is nothing." He started to put his injured hand inside his coat—it throbbed from holding the reins—but she reached out and took it.

He was so surprised he let her, and then there was nothing to do except either jerk away rudely or else let her unwrap the kerchief. Her touch felt cool and sure. His palm was angrily red and puffy, but the heron still stood out, plainly and clearly.

She touched the brand with a finger, but made no comment on it, not even to ask how he had come by it. "This could stiffen your hand if it's untended. I have an ointment that should help." From a pocket inside her cloak she produced a small stone vial, unstopped it, and began gently rubbing a white salve on the burn as they rode.

The ointment felt cold at first, then seemed to melt away warmly into his flesh. And it worked as well as Nynaeve's ointments sometimes did. He stared in amazement as the redness faded and the swelling went down under her stroking fingers.

"Some men," she said, not raising her eyes from his hand, "choose to seek greatness, while others are forced to it. It is always better to choose than to be forced. A man who's forced is never completely his own master. He must dance on the strings of those who forced him."

Rand pulled his hand free. The brand looked a week old or more, all but healed. "What do you mean?" he demanded.

She smiled at him, and he felt ashamed of his outburst. "Why, the Horn, of course," she said calmly, putting away her salve. Her mare, stepping along beside Red, was tall enough that her eyes were only a little below Rand's. "If you find the Horn of Valere, there will be no avoiding greatness. But will it be forced on you, or will you take it? That's the question."

He flexed his hand. She sounded so much like Moiraine. "Are you Aes Sedai?"

Selene's eyebrows lifted; her dark eyes glittered at him, but her voice was soft. "Aes Sedai? I? No."

"I didn't mean to offend you. I'm sorry."

"Offend me? I am not offended, but I'm no Aes Sedai." Her lip curled in a sneer; even that was beautiful. "They cower in what they think is safety when they could do so much. They serve when they could rule, let men fight wars when they could bring order to the world. No, never call me Aes Sedai." She smiled and laid her hand on his arm to show she was not angry—her touch made him swallow—but he was relieved when she let the mare drop back beside Loial. Hurin bobbed his head at her like an old family retainer.

Rand was relieved, but he missed her presence, too. She was only two spans away—he twisted in his saddle to stare at her, riding by Loial's side; the Ogier was bent half double in his saddle so he could talk with her— but that was not the same as being right there beside him, close enough for him to smell her heady scent, close enough to touch. He settled back angrily. It was not that he wanted to touch her, exactly—he reminded himself that he loved Egwene; he felt guilty at the need for reminding— but she was beautiful, and she thought he was a lord, and she said he could be a great man. He argued sourly with himself inside his head. *Moiraine says you can be great, too; the Dragon Reborn. Selene is not Aes Sedai. That's right; she's a Cairhienin noblewoman, and you're a shepherd. She doesn't know that. How long do you let her believe a lie? It's only till we get out of this place. If we get out. If.* On that note, his thoughts subsided to sullen silence.

He tried to keep a watch on the country through which they rode—if Selene said there were more of those things . . . those *grolm* . . . about, he believed her, and Hurin was too intent on smelling the trail to notice anything else; Loial was too wrapped up in his talk with Selene to see anything until it bit him on the heel—but it was hard to watch. Turning his head too quickly made his eyes water; a hill or a stand of trees could seem a mile off when seen from one angle and only a few hundred spans when seen from another.

The mountains were growing closer, of that much he was sure. Kinslayer's Dagger, looming against the sky now, a sawtooth expanse of snow-capped peaks. The land around them already rose in foothills heralding the coming of the mountains. They would reach the edge of the mountains proper well before dark, perhaps in only another hour or so. *More than a hundred leagues in less than three days. Worse than that. We spent most of a day south of the Erinin in the real world. Over a hundred leagues in less than two days, here.*

"She says you were right about this place, Rand."

Rand gave a start before he realized Loial had ridden up beside him. He looked for Selene and found her riding with Hurin; the sniffer was grinning and ducking his head and all but knuckling his forehead at everything she said. Rand glanced sideways at the Ogier. "I'm surprised you could let her go, the way you two had your heads together. What do you mean, I was right?"

"She is a fascinating woman, isn't she? Some of the Elders don't know as much as she does about history—especially the Age of Legends—and about—oh, yes. She says you were right about the Ways, Rand. The Aes Sedai, some of them, studied worlds like this, and that study was the basis of how they grew the Ways. She says there are worlds where it is time rather than distance that changes. Spend a day in one of those, and you might come back to find a year has passed in the real world, or twenty. Or it could be the other way round. Those worlds—this one, all the others— are reflections of the real world, she says. This one seems pale to us because it is a weak reflection, a world that had little chance of ever being. Others are almost as likely as ours. Those are as solid as our world, and have people. The same people, she says, Rand. Imagine it! You could go to one of them and meet yourself. The Pattern has infinite variation, she says, and every variation that can be, will be."

Rand shook his head, then wished he had not as the landscape flickered back and forth and his stomach lurched. He took a deep breath. "How does she know all that? You know about more things than anybody I ever met before, Loial, and all you knew about this world amounted to no more than a rumor."

"She's Cairhienin, Rand. The Royal Library in Cairhien is one of the greatest in the world, perhaps the greatest outside Tar Valon. The Aiel spared it deliberately, you know, when they burned Cairhien. They will not destroy a book. Did you know that they—"

"I don't care about Aielmen," Rand said hotly. "If Selene knows so much, I hope she read how to get us home from here. I wish Selene—"

"You wish Selene what?" The woman laughed as she joined them.

Rand stared at her as if she had been gone months; that was how he felt. "I wish Selene would come ride with me some more," he said. Loial chuckled, and Rand felt his face burn.

Selene smiled, and looked at Loial. "You will excuse us, *alantin*."

The Ogier bowed in his saddle and let his big horse fall back, the tufts on his ears drooping with reluctance.

For a time Rand rode in silence, enjoying Selene's presence. Now and again he looked at her out of the corner of his eye. He wished he could get his feelings about her straight. Could she be an Aes Sedai, despite her denial? Someone sent by Moiraine to push him along whatever path he was meant to follow in the Aes Sedai's plans? Moiraine could not have known he would be taken to this strange world, and no Aes Sedai would have tried to fend off that beast with a stick when she could strike it dead or send it running with the Power. Well. Since she took him for a lord and no one in Cairhien knew different, he might keep on letting her think it. She was surely the most beautiful woman he had ever seen, intelligent and learned, and she thought he was brave; what more could a man ask from a wife? *That's crazy, too. I'd marry Egwene if I could marry anyone, but I can't ask a woman to marry a man who's going to go mad, maybe hurt her.* But Selene was so beautiful.

She was studying his sword, he saw. He readied the words in his head. No, he was not a blademaster, but his father had given him the sword. *Tam. Light, why couldn't you really be my father?* He squashed the thought ruthlessly.

"That was a magnificent shot," Selene said.

"No, I'm not a—" Rand began, then blinked. "A shot?"

"Yes. A tiny target, that eye, moving, at a hundred paces. You've a wonderful hand with that bow."

Rand shifted awkwardly. "Ah . . . thank you. It's a trick my father taught me." He told her about the void, about how Tam had taught him how to use it with the bow. He even found himself telling her about Lan and his sword lessons.

"The Oneness," she said, sounding satisfied. She saw his questioning look and added, "That is what it is called . . . in some places. The Oneness. To learn the full use of it, it is best to wrap it around you continuously, to dwell in it at all times, or so I've heard."

He did not even have to think about what lay waiting for him in the void to know his answer to that, but what he said was, "I'll think about it."

"Wear this void of yours all the time, Rand al'Thor, and you'll learn uses for it you never suspected."

"I said I will think about it." She opened her mouth again, but he cut her off. "You know all these things. About the void—the Oneness, you call it. About this world. Loial reads books all the time; he's read more books than I've ever seen, and he's never seen anything but a fragment about the Stones."

Selene drew herself up straight in her saddle. Suddenly she reminded him of Moiraine, and of Queen Morgase, when they were angry.

"There was a book written about these worlds," she said tightly. "*Mirrors of the Wheel*. You see, the *alantin* has not seen *all* the books that are."

"What is this *alantin* you call him? I've never heard—"

"The Portal Stone beside which I woke is up there," Selene said, pointing into the mountains, off to the east of their path. Rand found himself wishing for her warmth again, and her smiles. "If you take me to it, you can return me to my home, as you promised. We can reach it in an hour."

Rand barely looked where she pointed. Using the Stone—Portal Stone, she called it—meant wielding the Power, if he were to take her back to the real world. "Hurin, how is the trail?"

"Fainter than ever, Lord Rand, but still there." The sniffer spared a quick grin and bob of his head for Selene. "I think it's starting to angle off to the west. There's some easier passes there, toward the tip of the Dagger, as I recall from when I went to Cairhien that time."

Rand sighed. *Fain, or one of his Darkfriends, has to know another way to use the Stones. A Darkfriend couldn't use the Power.* "I have to follow the Horn, Selene."

"How do you know your precious Horn is even in this world? Come with me, Rand. You'll find your legend, I promise you. Come with me."

"You can use the Stone, this Portal Stone, yourself," he said angrily. Before the words were out of his mouth he wanted them back. *Why does she have to keep talking about legends?* Stubbornly, he forced himself to go on. "The Portal Stone didn't bring you here by itself. You did it, Selene. If you made the Stone bring you here, you can make it take you back. I'll take you to it, but then I must go on after the Horn."

"I know nothing about using the Portal Stones, Rand. If I did anything, I don't know what it was."

Rand studied her. She sat her saddle, straight-backed and tall, just as regally as before, but somehow softer, too. Proud, yet vulnerable, and needing him. He had put Nynaeve's age to her—a handful of years older than himself—but he had been wrong, he realized. She was more his own age, and beautiful, and she needed him. The thought, just the thought, of the void flickered through his head, and of the light. *Saidin.* To use the Portal Stone, he must dip himself back into that taint.

"Stay with me, Selene," he said. "We'll find the Horn, and Mat's dagger, and we'll find a way back. I promise you. Just stay with me."

"You always. . . ." Selene drew a deep breath as if to calm herself. "You always are so stubborn. Well, I can admire stubbornness in a man. There is little to a man who's too easily biddable."

Rand colored; it was too much like the things Egwene sometimes said, and they had all but been promised in marriage since they were children. From Selene, the words, and the direct look that went with them, were a shock. He turned to tell Hurin to press on with the trail.

From behind them came a distant, coughing grunt. Before Rand could whirl Red to look, another bark sounded, and three more on its heels. At first he could make out nothing as the landscape seemed to waver in his eyes, but then he saw them through the widespread stands of trees, just topping a hill. Five shapes, it seemed, only half a mile distant, a bare thousand paces at most, and coming in thirty-foot bounds.

*"Grolm,"* Selene said calmly. "A small pack, but they have our scent, it seems."

# CHAPTER
# 17

## *Choices*

"We'll run for it," Rand said. "Hurin, can you gallop and still follow the trail?"

"Yes, Lord Rand."

"Then push on. We will—"

"It won't do any good," Selene said. Her white mare was the only one of their mounts not dancing at the gruff barks coming from the *grolm*. "They don't give up, not ever. Once they have your scent, *grolm* keep coming, day and night, until they run you down. You must kill them all, or find a way to go elsewhere. Rand, the Portal Stone can take us elsewhere."

"No! We *can* kill them. I can. I already killed one. There are only five. If I can just find. . . ." He cast around for the spot he needed, and found it. "Follow me!" Digging his heels in, he set Red to a gallop, confident before he heard their hooves that the others would come.

The place he had chosen was a low, round hill, bare of trees. Nothing could come close without him seeing. He swung down from his saddle and unlimbered his longbow. Loial and Hurin joined him on the ground, the Ogier hefting his huge quarterstaff, the sniffer with his short sword in his fist. Neither quarterstaff nor sword would be of much use if the *grolm* closed with them. *I won't let them get close.*

"This risk is not necessary," Selene said. She barely looked toward the *grolm,* bending from her saddle to concentrate on Rand. "We can easily reach the Portal Stone ahead of them."

"I will stop them." Hastily Rand counted the arrows remaining in his quiver. Eighteen, each as long as his arm, ten of them with points like chisels, designed to drive through Trolloc armor. They would do as well for *grolm* as for Trollocs. He stuck four of those upright in the ground in front of him; a fifth he nocked to the bow. "Loial, Hurin, you can do no good down here. Mount and be ready to take Selene to the Stone if any get through." He wondered whether he could kill one of the things with his sword, if it came to that. *You* are *mad! Even the Power is not as bad as this.*

Loial said something, but he did not hear; he was already seeking the void, as much to escape his own thoughts as for need. *You know what's waiting. But this way I don't have to touch it.* The glow was there, the light just out of sight. It seemed to flow toward him, but the emptiness was all. Thoughts darted across the surface of the void, visible in that tainted light. *Saidin. The Power. Madness. Death.* Extraneous thoughts. He was one with the bow, with the arrow, with the things topping the next rise.

The *grolm* came on, overreaching one another in their leaps, five great, leathery shapes, triple-eyed, with horny maws gaping. Their grunting calls rebounded from the void, barely heard.

Rand was not aware of raising his bow, or drawing the fletching against his cheek, to his ear. He was one with the beasts, one with the center eye of the first. Then the arrow was gone. The first *grolm* died; one of its companions leaped on it as it fell, beak of a mouth ripping gobbets of flesh. It snarled at the others, and they circled wide. But they came on, and as if compelled, it abandoned its meal and leaped after them, its horny maw already bloody.

Rand worked smoothly, unconsciously, nock and release. Nock and release.

The fifth arrow left his bow, and he lowered it, still deep in the void, as the fourth *grolm* fell like a huge puppet with its strings cut. Though the final arrow still flew, somehow he knew there was no need for another shot. The last beast collapsed as if its bones had melted, a feathered shaft jutting from its center eye. Always the center eye.

"Magnificent, Lord Rand," Hurin said. "I . . . I've never seen shooting like that."

The void held Rand. The light called to him, and he . . . reached . . . toward it. It surrounded him, filled him.

"Lord Rand?" Hurin touched his arm, and Rand gave a start, the emptiness filling up with what was around him. "Are you all right, my Lord?"

Rand brushed his forehead with fingertips. It was dry; he felt as if it should have been covered with sweat. "I. . . . I'm fine, Hurin."

"It grows easier each time you do it, I've heard," Selene said. "The more you live in the Oneness, the easier."

Rand glanced at her. "Well, I won't need it again, not for a while." *What happened? I wanted to. . . .* He still wanted to, he realized with horror. He *wanted* to go back into the void, wanted to feel that light filling him again. It had seemed as if he were truly alive then, sickliness and all, and now was only an imitation. No, worse. He had been almost alive, knowing what "alive" would be like. All he had to do was reach out to *saidin. . . .*

"Not again," he muttered. He gazed off at the dead *grolm,* five monstrous shapes lying on the ground. Not dangerous anymore. "Now we can be on our—"

A coughing bark, all too familiar, sounded beyond the dead *grolm,* beyond the next hill, and others answered it. Still more came, from the east, from the west.

Rand half raised his bow.

"How many arrows do you have left?" Selene demanded. "Can you kill twenty *grolm?* Thirty? A hundred? We *must* go to the Portal Stone."

"She is right, Rand," Loial said slowly. "You do not have any choice now." Hurin was watching Rand anxiously. The *grolm* called, a score of barks overlapping.

"The Stone," Rand agreed reluctantly. Angrily he threw himself back into his saddle, slung the bow on his back. "Lead us to this Stone, Selene."

With a nod she turned her mare and heeled it to a trot. Rand and the others followed, they eagerly, he holding back. The barks of *grolm* pursued them, hundreds it seemed. It sounded as if the *grolm* were ranged in a semicircle around them, closing in from every direction but the front.

Swiftly and surely Selene led them through the hills. The land rose in the beginning of mountains, slopes steepening so the horses scrambled over washed-out–looking rocky outcrops and the sparse, faded-looking brush that clung to them. The way became harder, the land slanting more and more upward.

*We're not going to make it,* Rand thought, the fifth time Red slipped and slid backwards in a shower of stone. Loial threw his quarterstaff aside; it would be of no use against *grolm,* and it only slowed him. The Ogier had given up riding; he used one hand to haul himself up, and pulled his tall horse behind him with the other. The hairy-fetlocked animal made heavy going, but easier than with Loial on its back. *Grolm* barked behind them, closer now.

Then Selene drew rein and pointed to a hollow nestled below them in the granite. It was all there, the seven wide, colored stairs around a pale floor, and the tall stone column in the middle.

She dismounted and led her mare into the hollow, down the stairs to the column. It loomed over her. She turned to look back up at Rand and the others. The *grolm* gave their grunting barks, scores of them, loud. Near. "They will be on us soon," she said. "You must use the Stone, Rand. Or else find a way to kill all the *grolm*."

With a sigh, Rand got down from his saddle and led Red into the hollow. Loial and Hurin followed hastily. He stared at the symbol-covered column, the Portal Stone, uneasily. *She must be able to channel, even if she doesn't know it, or it couldn't have brought her here. The Power doesn't harm women.* "If this brought you here," he began, but she interrupted him.

"I know what it is," she said firmly, "but I do not know how to use it. You must do what must be done." She traced one symbol, a little larger than the others, with a finger. A triangle standing on its point inside a circle. "This stands for the true world, our world. I believe it will help if you hold it in your mind while you. . . ." She spread her hands as if unsure exactly what it was he was supposed to do.

"Uh . . . my Lord?" Hurin said diffidently. "There isn't much time." He glanced over his shoulder at the rim of the hollow. The barking was louder. "Those things will be here in minutes, now." Loial nodded.

Drawing a deep breath, Rand put his hand on the symbol Selene had pointed out. He looked at her to see if he was doing it right, but she merely watched, not even the slightest frown of worry wrinkling her pale forehead. *She's confident you can save her. You have to.* The scent of her filled his nostrils.

"Uh . . . my Lord?"

Rand swallowed, and sought the void. It came easily, springing up around him without effort. Emptiness. Emptiness except for the light, wavering in a way that turned his stomach. Emptiness except for *saidin*. But even the queasiness was distant. He was one with the Portal Stone. The column felt smooth and slightly oily under his hand, but the triangle-and-circle seemed warm against the brand on his palm. *Have to get them to safety. Have to get them home.* The light drifted toward him, it seemed, surrounded him, and he . . . embraced . . . it.

Light filled him. Heat filled him. He could see the Stone, see the others watching him—Loial and Hurin anxiously, Selene showing no doubt that he could save her—but they might as well not have been there. The light was all. The heat and the light, suffusing his limbs like water sinking into dry sand, filling him. The symbol burned against his flesh. He tried to suck it all in, all the heat, all the light. All. The symbol. . . .

Suddenly, as if the sun had gone out for the blink of an eye, the world flickered. And again. The symbol was a live coal under his hand; he drank in the light. The world flickered. Flickered. It made him sick, that light; it was water to a man dying of thirst. Flicker. He sucked at it. It made him want to vomit; he wanted it all. Flicker. The triangle-and-circle seared him; he could feel it charring his hand. Flicker. He wanted it all! He screamed, howling with pain, howling with wanting.

Flicker . . . flicker . . . flickerflickerflicker. . . .

Hands pulled at him; he was only vaguely aware of them. He staggered back; the void was slipping away, the light, and the sickness that twisted at him. The light. He watched it go regretfully. *Light, that's crazy to want it. But I was so full of it! I was so.* . . . Dazed, he stared at Selene. It was she who held his shoulders, stared wonderingly into his eyes. He raised his hand in front of his face. The heron brand was there, but nothing else. No triangle-and-circle burned into his flesh.

"Remarkable," Selene said slowly. She glanced at Loial and Hurin. The Ogier looked stunned, his eyes as big as plates; the sniffer was squatting with one hand on the ground, as if unsure he could support himself else. "All of us here, and all of our horses. And you do not even know what you did. Remarkable."

"Are we. . . ?" Rand began hoarsely, and had to stop to swallow.

"Look around you," Selene said. "You've brought us home." She gave a sudden laugh. "You brought all of us home."

For the first time Rand became aware of his surroundings again. The hollow surrounded them without any stairs, through here and there lay a suspiciously smooth piece of stone, colored red, or blue. The column lay against the mountainside, half buried in the loose rock of a fall. The symbols were unclear, here; wind and water had worked long on them. And everything looked real. The colors were solid, the granite a strong gray, the brush green and brown. After that other place, it seemed almost too vivid.

"Home," Rand breathed, and then he was laughing, too. "We're home." Loial's laughter sounded like a bull bellowing. Hurin danced a caper.

"You did it," Selene said, leaning closer, until her face filled Rand's eyes. "I knew that you could."

Rand's laughter died. "I—I suppose I did." He glanced at the fallen Portal Stone and managed a weak laugh. "I wish I knew what it was I did, though."

Selene looked deep into his eyes. "Perhaps one day you will know," she said softly. "You are surely destined for great things."

Her eyes seemed as dark and deep as night, as soft as velvet. Her mouth. . . . *If I kissed her.* . . . He blinked and stepped back hurriedly, clearing his throat. "Selene, please don't tell anyone about this. About the Portal Stone, and me. I don't understand it, and neither will anybody else. You know how people are about things they don't understand."

Her face wore no expression at all. Suddenly he wished very much that Mat and Perrin were there. Perrin knew how to talk to girls, and Mat could lie with a straight face. He could manage neither very well.

Suddenly Selene smiled, and dropped a half-mocking curtsy. "I will keep your secret, my Lord Rand al'Thor."

Rand glanced at her, and cleared his throat again. *Is she angry with me? She'd certainly be angry if I had tried to kiss her. I think.* He wished she would not look at him as she was, as if she knew what he was thinking. "Hurin, is there any chance the Darkfriends used this Stone before us?"

The sniffer shook his head ruefully. "They were angling to the west of here, Lord Rand. Unless these Portal Stone things are more common than I've seen, I'd say they're still in that other world. But it wouldn't take me an hour to check it. The land's the same here as there. I could find the place here where I lost the trail there, if you see what I mean, and see if they've already gone by."

Rand glanced at the sky. The sun—a wonderfully strong sun, not pale at all—sat low to the west, stretching their shadows out across the hollow. Another hour would bring full twilight. "In the morning," he said. "But I fear we've lost them." *We can't lose that dagger! We can't!* "Selene, if that's the case, in the morning we will take you on to your home. Is it in the city of Cairhien itself, or. . . ?"

"You may not have lost the Horn of Valere yet," Selene said slowly. "As you know, I do know a *few* things about those worlds."

"*Mirrors of the Wheel*," Loial said.

She gave him a look, then nodded. "Yes. Exactly. Those worlds truly are mirrors in a way, especially the ones where there are no people. Some of them reflect only great events in the true world, but some have a shadow of that reflection even before the event occurs. The passage of the Horn of Valere would certainly be a great event. Reflections of what will be are fainter than reflections of what is or what was, just as Hurin says the trail he followed was faint."

Hurin blinked incredulously. "You mean to say, my Lady, I've been smelling where those Darkfriends are *going* to be? The Light help me, I wouldn't like that. It's bad enough smelling where violence *has* been, without smelling where it *will* be, too. There can't be many spots where there won't be *some* kind of violence, *some* time. It would drive me crazy, like as not. That place we just left nearly did. I could smell it all the time, there, killing and hurting, and the vilest evil you could think of. I could even smell it on us. On all of us. Even on you, my Lady, if you'll forgive me for saying so. It was just that place, twisting me the way it twisted your eye." He gave himself a shake. "I'm glad we're out of there. I can't get it out of my nostrils yet, all the way."

Rand rubbed absently at the brand on his palm. "What do you think, Loial? Could we really be ahead of Fain's Darkfriends?"

The Ogier shrugged, frowning. "I don't know, Rand. I don't know anything about any of this. I think we are back in our world. I think we are in Kinslayer's Dagger. Beyond that. . . ." He shrugged again.

"We should be seeing you home, Selene," Rand said. "Your people will be worried about you."

"A few days will see if I'm right," she said impatiently. "Hurin can find where he left the trail; he said so. We can watch over it. The Horn of Valere cannot be much longer reaching here. The Horn of Valere, Rand. Think of it. The man who sounds the Horn will live in legend forever."

"I don't want anything to do with legends," he said sharply. *But if the Darkfriends get by you. . . . What if Ingtar lost them? Then the Darkfriends have the Horn of Valere forever, and Mat dies.* "All right, a few days. At the worst, we will probably meet Ingtar and the others. I can't imagine they've stopped or turned back just because we . . . went away."

"A wise decision, Rand," Selene said, "and well thought out." She touched his arm and smiled, and he found himself again thinking of kissing her.

"Uh . . . we need to be closer to where they'll come. If they do come. Hurin, can you find us a camp before dark, somewhere we can watch the place where you lost the trail?" He glanced at the Portal Stone and thought about sleeping near it, thought of the way the void had crept up on him in sleep the last time, and the light in the void. "Somewhere well away from here."

"Leave it in my hands, Lord Rand." The sniffer scrambled to his saddle. "I vow, I'll never sleep again without first I see what kind of stone there is nearby."

As Rand rode Red up out of the hollow, he found himself watching Selene more than he did Hurin. She seemed so cool and self-possessed, no older than he, yet queenly, but when she smiled at him, as she did just then. . . . *Egwene wouldn't have said I was wise. Egwene would have called me a woolhead.* Irritably, he heeled Red's flanks.

# CHAPTER 18

## *To the White Tower*

Egwene balanced on the heeling deck as the *River Queen* sped down the wide Erinin under cloud-dark skies, sails full-bellied, White Flame banner whipping furiously at the mainmast. The wind had risen as soon as the last of them was aboard the ships, back in Medo, and it had not failed or flagged for an instant since, day or night. The river had begun to race in flood, as it still did, slapping the ships about while it drove them onward. Wind and river had not slowed, and neither had the ships, all clustered together. The *River Queen* led, only right for the vessel that carried the Amyrlin Seat.

The helmsman held his tiller grimly, feet planted and spread, and sailors padded barefoot at their work, intent on what they did; when they glanced at the sky or the river, they tore their eyes away with low mutters. A village was just fading from view behind, and a boy raced along the bank; he had kept up with the ships for a short distance, but now they were leaving him behind. When he vanished, Egwene made her way below.

In the small cabin they shared, Nynaeve glared up at her from her narrow bed. "They say we'll reach Tar Valon today. The Light help me, but I'll be glad to put foot on land again even if it is in Tar Valon." The ship lurched with wind and current, and Nynaeve swallowed. "I'll never step on a boat again," she said breathlessly.

Egwene shook the river spray out of her cloak and hung it on a peg by the door. It was not a big cabin—there were no big cabins on the ship, it seemed, not even the one the Amyrlin had taken over from the captain, though that was larger than the rest. With its two beds built into the walls, shelves beneath them and cabinets above, everything lay close to hand.

Except for keeping her balance, the movements of the ship did not bother her the way they did Nynaeve; she had given up offering Nynaeve food after the third time the Wisdom threw the bowl at her. "I'm worried about Rand," she said.

"I'm worried about all of them," Nynaeve replied dully. After a moment, she said, "Another dream last night? The way you've been staring at nothing since you got up. . . ."

Egwene nodded. She had never been very good at keeping things from Nynaeve, and she had not tried with the dreams. Nynaeve had tried to dose her at first, until she heard one of the Aes Sedai was interested; then she began to believe. "It was like the others. Different, but the same. Rand is in some kind of danger. I know it. And it is getting worse. He's done something, or he's going to do something, that puts him in. . . ." She dropped down on her bed and leaned toward the other woman. "I just wish I could make some sense of it."

"Channeling?" Nynaeve said softly.

Despite herself, Egwene looked around to see if anyone was there to hear. They were alone, with the door closed, but still she spoke just as softly. "I don't know. Maybe." There was no telling what Aes Sedai could do—she had seen enough already to make her believe every story of their powers—and she would not risk eavesdropping. *I won't risk Rand. If I did right, I'd tell them, but Moiraine knows, and she hasn't said anything. And it's Rand! I can't.* "I don't know what to do."

"Has Anaiya said anything more about these dreams?" Nynaeve seemed to make it a point never to add the honorific Sedai, even when the two of them were alone. Most of the Aes Sedai appeared not to care, but the habit had earned a few strange looks, and some hard ones; she was going to train in the White Tower, after all.

"'The Wheel weaves as the Wheel wills,'" Egwene quoted Anaiya. "'The boy is far away, child, and there's nothing we can do until we know more. I will see to testing you myself once we reach the White Tower, child.' Aaagh! She *knows* there is something in these dreams. I can tell she does. I like the woman, Nynaeve; I do. But she won't *tell* me what I want to know. And I can't tell her everything. Maybe if I could. . . ."

"The man in the mask again?"

Egwene nodded. Somehow, she was sure it was better not to tell Anaiya about him. She could not imagine why, but she was sure. Three times the man whose eyes were fire had been in her dreams each time when she dreamed a dream that convinced her Rand was in danger. He always wore a mask across his face; sometimes she could see his eyes, and sometimes she could only see fire where they should be. "He laughed at me. It was so . . . contemptuous. As though I were a puppy he was going to have to push out of his way with his foot. It frightens me. He frightens me."

"Are you sure it has anything to do with the other dreams, with Rand? Sometimes a dream is just a dream."

Egwene threw up her hands. "And sometimes, Nynaeve, you sound just like Anaiya Sedai!" She put a special emphasis on the title, and was pleased to see Nynaeve grimace.

"If I ever get out of this bed, Egwene—"

A knock at the door cut off whatever Nynaeve had been going to say. Before Egwene could speak or move, the Amyrlin herself came in and shut the door behind her. She was alone, for a wonder; she seldom left her cabin, and then always with Leane at her side, and maybe another of the Aes Sedai.

Egwene sprang to her feet. The room was a little crowded, with three of them in it.

"Both of you feeling well?" the Amyrlin said cheerily. She tilted her head at Nynaeve. "Eating well, too, I trust? In good temper?"

Nynaeve struggled to a sitting position, with her back against the wall. "My temper is just fine, thank you."

"We are honored, Mother," Egwene began, but the Amyrlin waved her to silence.

"It's good to be on the water again, but it grows boring as a mill pond after a while with nothing to do." The ship heeled, and she shifted her balance without seeming to notice. "I will give you your lesson today." She folded herself onto the end of Egwene's bed, feet tucked under her. "Sit, child."

Egwene sat, but Nynaeve began trying to push herself to her feet. "I think I will go on deck."

"I said, sit!" The Amyrlin's voice cracked like a whip, but Nynaeve kept rising, wavering. She still had both hands on the bed, but she was almost upright. Egwene held herself ready to catch her when she fell.

Closing her eyes, Nynaeve slowly lowered herself back to the bed. "Perhaps I will stay. It is no doubt windy up there."

The Amyrlin barked a laugh. "They told me you had a temper in you like a fisher-bird with a bone in its throat. Some of them, child, say you'd do well for some time as a novice, no matter how old you are. I say, if you have the ability I hear of, you deserve to be one of the Accepted." She gave another laugh. "I always believe in giving people what they deserve. Yes. I suspect you will learn a great deal once you reach the White Tower."

"I'd rather one of the Warders taught me how to use a sword," Nynaeve growled. She swallowed convulsively, and opened her eyes. "There is someone I'd like to use it on." Egwene looked at her sharply; did Nynaeve mean the Amyrlin—which was stupid, and dangerous besides—or Lan? She snapped at Egwene every time Lan was mentioned.

"A sword?" the Amyrlin said. "I never thought swords were much use— even if you have the skill, child, there are always men who have as much, and a deal more strength—but if you want a sword. . . ." She held up her hand—Egwene gasped, and even Nynaeve's eyes bulged—and there was a sword in it. With blade and hilt of an odd bluish white, it looked some-how . . . cold. "Made from the air, child, with Air. It's as good as most steel blades, better than most, but still not much use." The sword became a paring knife. There was no shrinking; it just was one thing, then the other. "This, now, is useful." The paring knife turned to mist, and the mist faded away. The Amyrlin put her empty hand back in her lap. "But either takes more effort than it is worth. Better, easier, simply to carry a good knife with you. You have to learn when to use your ability, as well as how, and when it's better to do things the way any other woman would. Let a blacksmith make knives for gutting fish. Use the One Power too often and too freely, and you can come to like it too much. That way lies danger. You begin to want more of it, and sooner or later you run the risk of drawing more than you've learned to handle. And that can burn you out like a guttered candle, or—"

"If I must learn all this," Nynaeve broke in stiffly, "I would as soon learn something useful. All this—this . . . 'Make the air stir, Nynaeve. Light the candle, Nynaeve. Now put it out. Light it again.' Paah!"

Egwene closed her eyes for a moment. *Please, Nynaeve. Please keep a check on your temper.* She bit her lip to keep from saying it out loud.

The Amyrlin was silent for a moment. "Useful," she said at last. "Something useful. You wanted a sword. Suppose a man came at me with a sword. What would I do? Something useful, you can be sure. This, I think."

For an instant, Egwene thought she saw a glow around the woman at the other end of her bed. Then the air seemed to thicken; nothing changed that Egwene could see, but she could surely feel it. She tried to lift her arm; it did not budge any more than if she were buried to her neck in thick jelly. Nothing could move except her head.

"Release me!" Nynaeve grated. Her eyes glared, and her head jerked from side to side, but the rest of her sat as rigidly as a statue. Egwene realized that she was not the only one held. "Let me go!"

"Useful, wouldn't you say? And it is nothing but Air." The Amyrlin spoke in a conversational tone, as if they were all chatting over tea. "Big man, with his muscles and his sword, and the sword does him as much good as the hair on his chest."

"Let me go, I say!"

"And if I don't like where he is, why, I can pick him up." Nynaeve squawked furiously as she slowly rose, still in a sitting position, until her head almost touched the ceiling. The Amyrlin smiled. "I've often wished I could use this to fly. The records say Aes Sedai *could* fly, in the Age of Legends, but they aren't clear on how, exactly. Not this way, though. It doesn't work like that. You might reach out with your hands and pick up a chest that weighs as much as you do; you look strong. But take hold of yourself however you will, you cannot pick yourself up."

Nynaeve's head jerked furiously, but not another muscle of her twitched. "The Light burn you, let me go!"

Egwene swallowed hard and hoped she was not also to be lifted.

"So," the Amyrlin continued, "big, hairy man, and so forth. He can do nothing to me, while I can do anything at all to him. Why, if I had a mind to"—she leaned forward, her eyes intent on Nynaeve; suddenly her smile did not seem very friendly—"I could turn him upside down and paddle his bottom. Just like—" Suddenly the Amyrlin flew backwards so hard her head rebounded from the wall, and there she stayed, as if something were pressing against her.

Egwene stared, her mouth dry. *This isn't happening. It isn't.*

"They were right," the Amyrlin said. Her voice sounded strained, as though she found it hard to breathe. "They said you learned quickly. And they said it took your temper burning to get to the heart of what you can do." She took a struggling breath. "Shall we release each other together, child?"

Nynaeve, floating in the air with her eyes ablaze, said, "You let me go right now, or I'll—" Abruptly a look of amazement came over her face, a look of loss. Her mouth worked slently.

The Amyrlin sat up, working her shoulders. "You don't know everything yet, do you, child? Not the hundredth part of everything. You did not suspect I could cut you off from the True Source. You can still feel it there, but you can't touch it any more than a fish can touch the moon. When you learn enough to be raised to full sisterhood, no one woman will be able to do that to you. The stronger you become, the more Aes Sedai it will take to shield you against your will. Do you think, now, you want to learn?" Nynaeve pressed her mouth shut in a thin line and stared her in the eye grimly. The Amyrlin sighed. "If you had a hair less potential than you do, child, I would send you to the Mistress of Novices and tell her to keep you the rest of your life. But you will get what you deserve."

Nynaeve's eyes widened, and she had just time to start a yell before she dropped, hitting her bed with a loud thud. Egwene winced; the mattresses were thin, and the wood beneath hard. Nynaeve's face stayed frozen as she shifted the way she sat, just a fraction.

"And now," the Amyrlin said firmly, "unless you would like further demonstration, we will get on with your lesson. Continue your lesson, we might say."

"Mother?" Egwene said faintly. She still could not twitch below her chin.

The Amyrlin looked at her questioningly, then smiled. "Oh. I am sorry, child. Your friend was occupying my attention, I'm afraid." Suddenly Egwene could move again; she raised her arms, just to convince herself that she could. "Are you both ready to learn?"

"Yes, Mother," Egwene said quickly.

The Amyrlin raised an eyebrow at Nynaeve.

After a moment, Nynaeve said in a tight voice, "Yes, Mother."

Egwene heaved a sigh of relief.

"Good. Now, then. Empty your thoughts of everything but a flower bud."

Egwene was sweating by the time the Amyrlin left. She had thought some of the other Aes Sedai had been hard teachers, but that smiling, plain-faced woman coaxed out every last drop of effort, drew it out, and when there was nothing left, she seemed to reach into you and pulled it out. It had gone well, though. As the door closed behind the Amyrlin, Egwene raised one hand; a tiny flame sprang to life, balanced a hairbreadth above the tip of her forefinger, then danced from fingertip to fingertip. She was not supposed to do this without a teacher—one of the Accepted, at the very least—to watch over her, but she was too excited at her progress to pay any mind to that.

Nynaeve bounded to her feet and threw her pillow at the closing door. "That—that vile, contemptible, miserable—hag! The Light burn her! I'd like to feed *her* to the fish. I'd like to dose her with things that would turn her green for the rest of her life! I don't care if she's old enough to be my mother, if I had her in Emond's Field, she wouldn't sit down comfortably for. . . ." Her teeth ground so loudly that Egwene jumped.

Letting the flame die, Egwene put her eyes firmly on her lap. She wished she could think of a way to sneak out of the room without catching Nynaeve's eye.

The lesson had not gone well for Nynaeve, because she had held her temper on a tight lead until the Amyrlin was gone. She never could do very much unless she was angry, and then it all burst out of her. After failure upon failure, the Amyrlin had done everything she could to rouse her again. Egwene wished Nynaeve could forget she had been there to see or hear any of it.

Nynaeve stalked stiffly to her bed and stood staring at the wall behind it, her fist clenched at her side. Egwene looked longingly at the door.

"It was not your fault," Nynaeve said, and Egwene gave a start. "Nynaeve, I—"

Nynaeve turned to look down at her. "It was not your fault," she repeated, sounding unconvinced. "But if you ever breathe one word, I'll— I'll. . . ."

"Not a word," Egwene said quickly. "I don't even remember anything to breathe a word about."

Nynaeve stared at her a moment longer, then nodded. Abruptly she grimaced. "Light, I did not think *anything* tasted worse than raw sheeps-tongue root. I'll remember that, the next time you act the goose, so watch yourself."

Egwene winced. That had been the first thing the Amyrlin had done trying to rouse Nynaeve's anger. A dark glob of something that glistened like grease and smelled vile had suddenly appeared and, while the Amyrlin held Nynaeve with the Power, had been forced into the Wisdom's mouth. The Amyrlin had even held her nose to make her swallow. And Nynaeve remembered things, if she had seen them done once. Egwene did not think there was any way of stopping her if she took it into her mind to do it; for all her own success in making a flame dance, *she* could never have held the Amyrlin against a wall. "At least being on the ship isn't making you sick anymore."

Nynaeve grunted, then gave a short, sharp laugh. "I'm too angry to be sick." With another mirthless laugh, she shook her head. "I'm too misera-ble to be sick. Light, I feel as if I've been dragged through a knothole backwards. If that is what novice training is like, you will have incentive to learn quickly."

Egwene scowled at her knees. Compared to Nynaeve, the Amyrlin had only coaxed her, smiled at her successes, sympathized with her failures, then coaxed again. But all the Aes Sedai had said things would be different in the White Tower; harder, though they would not say how. If she had to go through what Nynaeve had, day after day, she did not think she could stand it.

Something changed in the motion of the ship. The rocking eased, and feet thumped on the deck above their heads. A man shouted something Egwene could not quite make out.

She looked up at Nynaeve. "Do you think. . . . Tar Valon?"

"There is only one way to find out," Nynaeve replied, and determinedly took her cloak from its peg.

When they reached the deck, sailors were running everywhere, heaving at lines, shortening sail, readying long sweeps. The wind had died to a breeze, and the clouds were scattering, now.

Egwene rushed to the rail. "It is! It is Tar Valon!" Nynaeve joined her with an expressionless face.

The island was so big it looked more as if the river split in two than contained a bit of land. Bridges that seemed to be made of lace arched from either bank to the island, crossing marshy ground as well as the river. The walls of the city, the Shining Walls of Tar Valon, glistened white as the sun broke through the clouds. And on the west bank, its broken top leaking a thin wisp of smoke, Dragonmount reared black against the sky, one mountain standing among flat lands and rolling hills. Dragonmount, where the Dragon had died. Dragonmount, made by the Dragon's dying.

Egwene wished she did not think of Rand when she looked at the mountain. *A man channeling. Light, help him.*

The *River Queen* passed through a wide opening in a tall, circular wall that thrust out into the river. Inside, one long wharf surrounded a round harbor. Sailors furled the last sails and used sweeps alone to move the ship stern-first to its docking. Around the long wharf, the other ships that had come downriver were now being snugged into their berths among the ships already there. The White Flame banner set workers scurrying along the already busy wharf.

The Amyrlin came on deck before the shore lines were tied off, but dockworkers ran a gangplank aboard as soon as she appeared. Leane walked at her side, flame-tipped staff in hand, and the other Aes Sedai on the ship followed them ashore. None of them so much as glanced at Egwene or Nynaeve. On the wharf a delegation greeted the Amyrlin—shawled Aes Sedai, bowing formally, kissing the Amyrlin's ring. The wharf bustled, between ships unloading and the Amyrlin Seat arriving; soldiers formed up on disembarking, men set booms for cargo; trumpet flourishes rang from the walls, competing with cheers from the onlookers.

Nynaeve gave a loud sniff. "It seems they've forgotten us. Come along. We'll see to ourselves."

Egwene was reluctant to leave her first sight of Tar Valon, but she followed Nynaeve below to gather their things. When they came back topside, bundles in their arms, soldiers and trumpets were gone—and Aes Sedai, too. Men were swinging back hatches along the deck and lowering cables into the holds.

On the deck, Nynaeve caught a dockman's arm, a burly fellow in a coarse brown shirt with no sleeves. "Our horses," she began.

"I'm busy," he growled, pulling free. "Horses'll all be took to the White Tower." He looked them up and down. "If you've business with the Tower, best you take yourselves on. Aes Sedai don't hold with newlings being tardy." Another man, wrestling with a bale being swung out of the hold on a cable, shouted to him, and he left the women without a backwards glance.

Egwene exchanged looks with Nynaeve. It seemed they really were on their own.

Nynaeve stalked off the ship with grim determination on her face, but Egwene made her way dejectedly down the gangplank and through the tarry smell that hung over the wharf. *All that talk about wanting us here, and now they don't seem to care.*

Broad stairs led up from the dock to a wide arch of dark redstone. On reaching it, Egwene and Nynaeve stopped to stare.

Every building seemed a palace, though most of those close to the arch seemed to contain inns or shops, from the signs over the doors. Fanciful stonework was everywhere, and the lines of one structure seemed designed to complement and set off the next, leading the eye along as if everything were part of one vast design. Some structures did not look like buildings at all, but like gigantic waves breaking, or huge shells, or fanciful, wind-sculpted cliffs. Right in front of the arch lay a broad square, with a fountain and trees, and Egwene could see another square further on. Above everything rose the towers, tall and graceful, some with sweeping bridges between them, high in the sky. And over all rose one tower, higher and wider than all the rest, as white as the Shining Walls themselves.

"Fair takes the breath at first sight," said a woman's voice behind them. "At tenth sight, for that. And at hundredth."

Egwene turned. The woman was Aes Sedai; Egwene was sure of it, though she wore no shawl. No one else had that ageless look; and she held herself with an assurance, a confidence that seemed to confirm it. A glance at her hand showed the golden ring, the serpent biting its own tail. The Aes Sedai was a little plump, with a warm smile, and one of the oddest-appearing women Egwene had ever seen. Her plumpness could not hide high cheekbones, her eyes had a tilt to them and were the clearest, palest green, and her hair was almost the color of fire. Egwene barely stopped herself from goggling at that hair, those slightly slanted eyes.

"Ogier built, of course," the Aes Sedai went on, "and their best work ever, some say. One of the first cities built after the Breaking. There weren't half a thousand people here altogether then—no more than twenty sisters—but they built for what would be needed."

"It is a lovely city," Nynaeve said. "We are supposed to go to the White Tower. We came here for training, but no one seems to care if we go or stay."

"They care," the woman said, smiling. "I came here to meet you, but I was delayed speaking with the Amyrlin. I am Sheriam, the Mistress of Novices."

"I am not to be a novice," Nynaeve said in a firm voice, but a little too quickly. "The Amyrlin herself said I was to be one of the Accepted."

"So I was told." Sheriam sounded amused. "I have never heard of it being done so before, but they say you are . . . exceptional. Remember, though, even one of the Accepted can be called to my study. It requires more breaking of the rules than for a novice, but it has been known to happen." She turned to Egwene as if she had not seen Nynaeve frown. "And you are our new novice. It is always good to see a novice come. We have too few, these days. You will make forty. Only forty. And no more than eight or nine of those will be raised to the Accepted. Though I don't think you will have to worry about that too much, if you work hard and apply yourself. The work is hard, and even for one with the potential they tell me you have, it will not be made any easier. If you cannot stick to it, no matter how hard it is, or if you will break under the strain, better we find it out now, and let you go on your way, than wait until you are a full sister and others are depending on you. An Aes Sedai's life is not easy. Here, we will prepare you for it, if you have in you what is required."

Egwene swallowed. *Break under the strain?* "I will try, Sheriam Sedai," she said faintly. *And I will not break.*

Nynaeve looked at her worriedly. "Sheriam. . . ." She stopped and took a deep breath. "Sheriam Sedai"—she seemed to force the honorific out— "does it have to be so hard on her? Flesh and blood can only take so much. I know . . . something . . . of what novices must go through. Surely there's no need to try to break her just to find out how strong she is."

"You mean what the Amyrlin did to you today?" Nynaeve's back stiffened; Sheriam looked as though she were trying to keep amusement from her face. "I told you I spoke with the Amyrlin. Rest your worries for your friend. Novice training is hard, but not that hard. That is for the first few weeks of being one of the Accepted." Nynaeve's mouth fell open; Egwene thought the Wisdom's eyes were going to come right out of her head. "To catch the few who might have slipped through novice training when they should not have. We cannot risk having one of our number—a full Aes Sedai—who will break under the stress of the world outside." The Aes Sedai gathered them both up, an arm around the shoulders of each. Nynaeve hardly seemed to realize where she was going. "Come," Sheriam said, "I will see you settled in your rooms. The White Tower awaits."

# CHAPTER 19

## Beneath the Dagger

Night on the edge of Kinslayer's Dagger was cold, as nights in the mountains are always cold. The wind whipped down from the high peaks carrying the iciness of the snowcaps. Rand shifted on the hard ground, tugging at his cloak and blanket, and only half asleep. His hand went to his sword, lying beside him. *One more day,* he thought drowsily. *Just one more, and then we go. If no one comes tomorrow, Ingtar or Darkfriends one, I'll take Selene to Cairhien.*

He had told himself that before. Every day they had been there on the mountainside, watching the place where Hurin said the trail had been, in that other world—where Selene said the Darkfriends would surely appear in this world—he told himself it was time to leave. And Selene talked of the Horn of Valere, and touched his arm, and looked into his eyes, and before he knew it he had agreed to yet another day before they went on.

He shrugged against the chill of the wind, thinking of Selene touching his arm and looking into his eyes. *If Egwene saw that, she'd shear me for a sheep, and Selene, too. Egwene could already be in Tar Valon by now, learning to be an Aes Sedai. The next time she sees me, she'll probably try to gentle me.*

As he shifted over, his hand slid past the sword and touched the bundle holding Thom Merrilin's harp and flute. Unconsciously, his fingers tightened on the gleeman's cloak. *I was happy then, I think, even running for my life. Playing the flute for my supper. I was too ignorant to know what was going on. There's no turning back.*

Shivering, he opened his eyes. The only light came from the waning moon, not far past full and low in the sky. A fire would give them away to those for whom they watched. Loial muttered in his sleep, a low rumble. One of the horses stamped a hoof. Hurin had the first watch, from a stone outcrop a little way up the mountain; he would be coming to wake Rand for his turn, soon.

Rand rolled over . . . and stopped. In the moonlight he could see the shape of Selene, bending over his saddlebags, her hands on the buckles. Her white dress gathered the faint light. "Do you need something?"

She gave a jump, and stared toward him. "You—you startled me."

He rolled to his feet, shedding the blanket and wrapping the cloak around himself, and went to her. He was sure he had left the saddlebags right by his side when he lay down; he always kept them close. He took them from her. All the buckles were fastened, even those on the side that held the damning banner. *How can my life depend on keeping it? If anybody sees it and knows what it is, I'll die for having it.* He peered at her suspiciously.

Selene stayed where she was, looking up at him. The moon glistened in her dark eyes. "It came to me," she said, "that I've been wearing this dress too long. I could brush it, at least, if I had something else to wear while I did. One of your shirts, perhaps."

Rand nodded, feeling a sudden relief. Her dress looked as clean to him as when he first saw her, but he knew that if a spot appeared on Egwene's dress, nothing would do but that she cleaned it immediately. "Of course." He opened the capacious pocket into which he had stuffed everything except the banner and pulled out one of the white silk shirts.

"Thank you." Her hands went behind her back. To the buttons, he realized.

Eyes wide, he spun away from her.

"If you could help me with these, it would be much easier."

Rand cleared his throat. "It would not be proper. It isn't as if we were promised, or. . . ." *Stop thinking about that! You can never marry anyone.* "It just wouldn't be proper."

Her soft laugh sent a shiver down his back, as if she had run a finger along his spine. He tried not to listen to the rustlings behind him. He said, "Ah . . . tomorrow . . . tomorrow, we'll leave for Cairhien."

"And what of the Horn of Valere?"

"Maybe we were wrong. Maybe they are not coming here at all. Hurin says there are a number of passes through Kinslayer's Dagger. If they went only a little further west, they do not have to come into the mountains at all."

"But the trail we followed came here. They will come here. The Horn will come here. You may turn around, now."

"You say that, but we don't know. . . ." He turned, and the words died in his mouth. Her dress lay across her arm, and she wore his shirt, hanging in baggy folds on her. It was a long-tailed shirt, made for his height, but she was tall for a woman. The bottom of it came little more than halfway down her thighs. It was not as if he had never seen a girl's legs before; girls in the Two Rivers always tied up their skirts to go wading in Waterwood ponds. But they stopped doing it well before they were old enough to braid their hair, and this was in the dark, besides. The moonlight seemed to make her skin glow.

"What is it you don't know, Rand?"

The sound of her voice unfroze his joints. With a loud cough, he whirled to face the other way. "Ah . . . I think . . . ah . . . I . . . ah. . . ."

"Think of the glory, Rand." Her hand touched his back, and he almost shamed himself with a squeak. "Think of the glory that will come to the one who finds the Horn of Valere. How proud I'll be to stand beside him who holds the Horn. You have no idea the heights we will scale together, you and I. With the Horn of Valere in your hand, you can be a king. You can be another Artur Hawkwing. You. . . ."

"Lord Rand!" Hurin panted into the campsite. "My Lord, they. . . ." He skidded to a halt, suddenly making a gurgling sound. His eyes dropped to the ground, and he stood wringing his hands. "Forgive me, my Lady. I didn't mean to. . . . I. . . . Forgive me."

Loial sat up, his blanket and cloak falling away. "What's happening? Is it my turn to watch already?" He looked toward Rand and Selene, and even in the moonlight the widening of his eyes was plain.

Rand heard Selene sigh behind him. He stepped away from her, still not looking at her. *Her legs are so white, so smooth.* "What is it, Hurin?" He made his voice more moderate; was he angry with Hurin, himself, or Selene? *No reason to be angry with her.* "Did you see something, Hurin?"

The sniffer spoke without raising his eyes. "A fire, my Lord, down in the hills. I didn't see it at first. They made it small, and hid it, but they hid it from somebody following them, not somebody ahead, and up above. Two miles, Lord Rand. Less than three, for sure."

"Fain," Rand said. "Ingtar would not be afraid of anyone following him. It must be Fain." Suddenly he did not know what to do, now. They had been waiting for Fain, but now that the man was only a mile or so away, he was uncertain. "In the morning. . . . In the morning, we will follow. When Ingtar and the others catch up, we'll be able to point right to them."

"So," Selene said. "You will let this Ingtar take the Horn of Valere. And the glory."

"I don't want. . . ." Without thinking, he turned, and there she was, legs pale in the moonlight, and as unconcerned that they were bare as if she were alone. *As if we were alone,* the thought came. *She wants the man who finds the Horn.* "Three of us cannot take it away from them. Ingtar has twenty lances with him."

"You don't know you cannot take it. How many followers does this man have? You don't know that, either." Her voice was calm, but intent. "You don't even know if these men camped down there do have the Horn. The only way is to go down yourself and see. Take the *alantin;* his kind have sharp eyes, even by moonlight. And he has the strength to carry the Horn in its chest, if you make the right decision."

*She's right. You do not know for sure if it's Fain.* A fine thing it would be to have Hurin casting about for a trail that was not there, all of them out in the open if the real Darkfriends did finally come. "I will go alone," he said. "Hurin and Loial will stand guard for you."

Laughing, Selene came to him so gracefully it almost seemed she danced. Moonshadows veiled her face in mystery as she looked up at him, and mystery made her even more beautiful. "I am capable of guarding myself, until you return to protect me. Take the *alantin.*"

"She is right, Rand," Loial said, rising. "I can see better by moonlight than you. With my eyes, we may not need to go as close as you would alone."

"Very well." Rand strode over to his sword and buckled it at his waist. Bow and quiver he left where they lay; a bow was not of much use in the dark, and he intended to look, not fight. "Hurin, show me this fire."

The sniffer led him scrambling up the slope to the outcrop, like a huge stone thumb thrust out of the mountain. The fire was only a speck—he missed it the first time Hurin pointed. Whoever had made it did not mean for it to be seen. He fixed it in his head.

By the time they returned to the camp, Loial had saddled Red and his own horse. As Rand climbed to the bay's back, Selene caught his hand. "Remember the glory," she said softly. "Remember." The shirt seemed to fit her better than he recalled, molding itself to her form.

He drew a deep breath and took his hand back. "Guard her with your life, Hurin. Loial?" He heeled Red's flanks gently. The Ogier's big mount plodded along behind.

They did not try to move quickly. Night shrouded the mountainside, and moon-cast shadows made footing uncertain. Rand could not see the fire any longer—no doubt it was better hidden from eyes on the same level— but he had its location in his mind. For someone who had learned to hunt in the tangle of the Westwood, in the Two Rivers, finding the fire would be no great difficulty. *And what then?* Selene's face loomed before him. *How proud I'll be to stand beside him who holds the Horn.*

"Loial," he said suddenly, trying to clear his thoughts, "what's this *alantin* she calls you?"

"It's the Old Tongue, Rand." The Ogier's horse picked its way uncertainly, but he guided it almost as surely as if it were daylight. "It means Brother, and is short for *tia avende alantin*. Brother to the Trees. Treebrother. It is very formal, but then, I've heard the Cairhienin are formal. The noble Houses are, at least. The common people I saw there were not very formal at all."

Rand frowned. A shepherd would not be very acceptable to a formal Cairhienin noble House. *Light, Mat's right about you. You're crazy, and with a big head to boot. But if I could marry. . . .*

He wished he could stop thinking, and before he realized it, the void had formed within him, making thoughts distant things, as if part of someone else. *Saidin* shone at him, beckoned to him. He gritted his teeth and ignored it; it was like ignoring a burning coal inside his head, but at least he could hold it at bay. Barely. He almost left the void, but the Darkfriends were out there in the night, and closer, now. And the Trollocs. He needed the emptiness, needed even the uneasy calm of the void. *I don't have to touch it. I don't.*

After a time, he reined in Red. They stood at the base of a hill, the wide-scattered trees on its slopes black in the night. "I think we must be close by now," he said softly. "Best we go the rest of the way on foot." He slid from the saddle and tied the bay's reins to a branch.

"Are you all right?" Loial whispered, climbing down. "You sound odd."

"I'm fine." His voice sounded tight, he realized. Stretched. *Saidin* called to him. *No!* "Be careful. I can't be sure exactly how far it is, but that fire should be somewhere just ahead of us. On the hilltop, I think." The Ogier nodded.

Slowly Rand stole from tree to tree, placing each foot carefully, holding his sword tight so it did not clatter against a tree trunk. He was grateful for the lack of undergrowth. Loial followed like a big shadow; Rand could not see much more of him than that. Everything was moonshadows and darkness.

Suddenly some trick of the moonlight resolved the shadows ahead of him, and he froze, touching the rough bole of a leatherleaf. Dim mounds on the ground became men wrapped in blankets, and apart from them a group of larger mounds. Sleeping Trollocs. They had doused the fire. One moonbeam, moving through the branches, caught a shine of gold and silver on the ground, halfway between the two groups. The moonlight seemed to brighten; for an instant he could see clearly. The shape of a sleeping man lay close by to the gleam, but that was not what held his eye. *The chest. The Horn.* And something atop it, a point of red flashing in the moonbeam. *The dagger! Why would Fain put. . . ?*

Loial's huge hand settled over Rand's mouth, and a good part of his face besides. He twisted to look at the Ogier. Loial pointed off to his right, slowly, as if motion might attract attention.

At first Rand could not see anything, then a shadow moved, not ten paces away. A tall, bulky shadow, and snouted. Rand's breath caught. A Trolloc. It lifted its snout as if sniffing. Some of them hunted by scent.

For an instant the void wavered. Someone stirred in the Darkfriend camp, and the Trolloc turned to peer that way.

Rand froze, letting the calm of emptiness envelope him. His hand was on his sword, but he did not think of it. The void was all. Whatever happened, happened. He watched the Trolloc without blinking.

A moment longer the snouted shadow watched the Darkfriend camp, then, as if satisfied, folded itself down beside a tree. Almost immediately a low sound, like coarse cloth ripping, drifted from it.

Loial put his mouth close to Rand's ear. "It's asleep," he whispered incredulously.

Rand nodded. Tam had told him Trollocs were lazy, apt to give up any task but killing unless fear kept them to it. He turned back to the camp.

All was still and quiet there again. The moonbeam no longer shone on the chest, but he knew now which shadow it was. He could see it in his mind, floating beyond the void, glittering golden, chased with silver, in the glow of *saidin*. The Horn of Valere and the dagger Mat needed, both almost within reach of his hand. Selene's face drifted with the chest. They could follow Fain's party in the morning, and wait until Ingtar joined them. If Ingtar did come, if he still followed the trail without his sniffer. No, there would never be a better chance. All within reach of his hand. Selene was waiting on the mountain.

Motioning for Loial to follow, Rand dropped to his belly and crawled toward the chest. He heard the Ogier's muffled gasp, but his eyes were fixed on that one shadowed mound ahead.

Darkfriends and Trollocs lay to left and right of him, but once he had seen Tam stalk close enough to a deer to put his hand on its flank before the animal bounded off; he had tried to learn from Tam. *Madness!* The thought flew by dimly, almost out of reach. *This is madness! You—are—going—mad!* Dim thoughts; someone else's thoughts.

Slowly, silently, he slithered to that one special shadow, and put out a hand. Ornate traceries worked in gold met his touch. It *was* the chest that held the Horn of Valere. His hand touched something else, on the lid. The dagger, bare-bladed. In the dark, his eyes widened. Remembering what it had done to Mat, he jerked back, the void shifting with his agitation.

The man sleeping nearby—no more than two paces from the chest; no one else lay so close by spans—groaned in his sleep and thrashed at his blankets. Rand allowed the void to sweep thought and fear away. Murmuring uneasily in his sleep, the man stilled.

Rand let his hand go back to the dagger, not quite touching it. It had not harmed Mat in the beginning. Not much, at least; not quickly. In one swift motion he lifted the dagger, stuck it behind his belt, and pulled his hand away, as if it might help to minimize the time it touched his bare skin. Perhaps it would, and Mat would die without the dagger. He could feel it there, almost a weight pulling him down, pressing against him. But in the void sensation was as distant as thought, and the feel of the dagger faded quickly to something he was used to.

He wasted only a moment more staring at the shadow-wrapped chest—the Horn had to be inside, but he did not know how to open it and he could not lift it by himself—then he looked around for Loial. He found the Ogier crouched not far behind him, massive head swiveling as he peered back and forth from sleeping human Darkfriends to sleeping Trollocs. Even in the night it was plain Loial's eyes were as wide as they could go; they looked as big as saucers in the light of the moon. Rand reached out and took Loial's hand.

The Ogier gave a start and gasped. Rand put a finger across his lips, set Loial's hand on the chest, and mimed lifting. For a time—it seemed forever, in the night, with Darkfriends and Trollocs all around; it could not have been more than heartbeats—Loial stared. Then, slowly, he put his arms around the golden chest and stood. He made it seem effortless.

Ever so carefully, even more carefully than he had come in, Rand began to walk out of the camp, behind Loial and the chest. Both hands on his sword, he watched the sleeping Darkfriends, the still shapes of the Trollocs. All those shadowed figures began to be swallowed deeper in the darkness as they drew away. *Almost free. We've done it!*

The man who had been sleeping near the chest suddenly sat up with a strangled yell, then leaped to his feet. "It's gone! Wake, you filth! It's gooonnne!" Fain's voice; even in the void Rand recognized it. The others scrambled erect, Darkfriends and Trollocs, calling to know what was happening, growling and snarling. Fain's voice rose to a howl. "I know it is you, al'Thor! You're hiding from me, but I know you are out there! Find him! Find him! Al'Thoooor!" Men and Trollocs scattered in every direction.

Wrapped in emptiness, Rand kept moving. Almost forgotten in entering the camp, *saidin* pulsed at him.

"He cannot see us," Loial whispered low. "Once we reach the horses—"

A Trolloc leaped out of the dark at them, cruel eagle's beak in a man's face where mouth and nose should have been, scythe-like sword already whistling through the air.

Rand moved without thought. He was one with the blade. Cat Dances on the Wall. The Trolloc screamed as it fell, screamed again as it died.

"Run, Loial!" Rand commanded. *Saidin* called to him. "Run!"

He was dimly aware of Loial lumbering to an awkward gallop, but another Trolloc loomed from the night, boar-snouted and tusked, spiked axe raised. Smoothly Rand glided between Trolloc and Ogier; Loial must get the Horn away. Head and shoulders taller than Rand, half again as wide, the Trolloc came at him with a silent snarl. The Courtier Taps His Fan. No scream, this time. He walked backwards after Loial, watching the night. *Saidin* sang to him, such a sweet song. *The Power could burn them all, burn Fain and all the rest to cinders. No!*

Two more Trollocs, wolf and ram, gleaming teeth and curling horns. Lizard in the Thornbush. He rose smoothly from one knee as the second toppled, horns almost brushing his shoulder. The song of *saidin* caressed him with seduction, pulled him with a thousand silken strings. *Burn them all with the Power. No. No! Better dead than that. If I were dead, it would be done with.*

A knot of Trollocs came into sight, hunting uncertainly. Three of them, four. Suddenly one pointed to Rand and raised a howl the rest answered as they charged.

"Let it be done with!" Rand shouted, and leaped to meet them.

For an instant surprise slowed them, then they came on with guttural cries, gleeful, bloodthirsty, swords and axes raised. He danced among them to the song of *saidin*. Hummingbird Kisses the Honeyrose. So cunning that song, filling him. Cat on Hot Sand. The sword seemed alive in his hands as it had never been before, and he fought as if a heron-mark blade could keep *saidin* from him. The Heron Spreads Its Wings.

Rand stared at the motionless shapes on the ground around him. "Better to be dead," he murmured. He raised his eyes, back up the hill toward where the camp lay. Fain was there, and Darkfriends, and more Trollocs.

Too many to fight. Too many to face and live. He took a step that way. Another.

"Rand, come on!" Loial's urgent, whispered call drifted through the emptiness to him. "For life and the Light, Rand, come on!"

Carefully, Rand bent to wipe his blade on a Trolloc's coat. Then, as formally as if Lan were watching him train, he sheathed it.

"Rand!"

As though he knew of no urgency, Rand joined Loial by the horses. The Ogier was tying the golden chest atop his saddle with straps from his saddlebags. His cloak was stuffed underneath to help balance the chest on the rounded saddle seat.

*Saidin* sang no more. It was there, that stomach-turning glow, but it held back as if he truly had fought it off. Wonderingly, he let the void vanish. "I think I am going mad," he said. Suddenly realizing where they were, he peered back the way they had come. Shouts and howls came from half a dozen different directions; signs of search, but none of pursuit. Yet. He swung up onto Red's back.

"Sometimes I do not understand half of what you say," Loial said. "If you must go mad, could it at least wait until we are back with the Lady Selene and Hurin?"

"How are you going to ride with that in your saddle?"

"I will run!" The Ogier suited his words by breaking into a quick trot, pulling his horse behind him by the reins. Rand followed.

The pace Loial set was as fast as a horse could trot. Rand was sure the Ogier could not keep it for long, but Loial's feet did not flag. Rand decided that his boast of once outrunning a horse might really be true. Now and again Loial looked behind them as he ran, but the shouts of Darkfriends and howls of Trollocs faded with distance.

Even when the ground began to slope upwards more sharply, Loial's pace barely slowed, and he trotted into their campsite on the mountainside with only a little hard breathing.

"You have it." Selene's voice was exultant as her gaze rested on the ornately worked chest on Loial's saddle. She was wearing her own dress again; it looked as white as new snow to Rand. "I knew you would make the right choice. May I . . . have a look at it?"

"Did any of them follow, my Lord?" Hurin asked anxiously. He stared at the chest with awe, but his eyes slid off into the night, down the mountain. "If they followed, we'll have to move quick."

"I do not think they did. Go to the outcrop and see if you can see anything." Rand climbed down from his saddle as Hurin hurried up the

mountain. "Selene, I don't know how to open the chest. Loial, do you?"
The Ogier shook his head.

"Let me try. . . ." Even for a woman of Selene's height, Loial's saddle
was high above the ground. She reached up to touch the finely wrought
patterns on the chest, ran her hands across them, pressed. There was a
click, and she pushed the lid up, let it fall open.

As she stretched on tiptoe to put a hand inside, Rand reached over her
shoulder and lifted out the Horn of Valere. He had seen it once before, but
never touched it. Though beautifully made, it did not look a thing of great
age, or power. A curled golden horn, gleaming in the faint light, with
inlaid silver script flowing around the mouth of the bell. He touched the
strange letters with a finger. They seemed to catch the moon.

*"Tia mi aven Moridin isainde vadin,"* Selene said. "'The grave is no bar to
my call.' You *will* be greater than Artur Hawkwing ever was."

"I am taking it to Shienar, to Lord Agelmar." *It should go to Tar Valon,*
he thought, *but I'm done with Aes Sedai. Let Agelmar or Ingtar take it to them.*
He set the Horn back in the chest; it cast back the moonlight, pulled the
eye.

"That is madness," Selene said.

Rand flinched at the word. "Mad or not, it is what I'm doing. I told
you, Selene, I want no part of greatness. Back there, I thought I did. For a
while, I thought I wanted things. . . ." *Light, she's so beautiful. Egwene.
Selene. I'm not worthy of either of them.* "Something seemed to take hold of
me." Saidin *came for me, but I fought it off with a sword. Or is that mad, too?*
He breathed deeply. "Shienar is where the Horn of Valere belongs. Or if
not there, Lord Agelmar will know what to do with it."

Hurin appeared from up the mountain. "The fire's there again, Lord
Rand, and bigger than ever. And I thought I heard shouting. It was all
down in the hills. I don't think they've come upon the mountain, yet."

"You misunderstand me, Rand," Selene said. "You cannot go back,
now. You are committed. Those Friends of the Dark will not simply go
away because you've taken the Horn from them. Far from it. Unless you
know some way to kill them all, they will be hunting you now as you
hunted them before."

"No!" Loial and Hurin looked surprised at Rand's vehemence. He softened his tone. "I don't know any way to kill them all. They can live forever
for all of me."

Selene's long hair shifted in waves as she shook her head. "Then you
cannot go back, only onward. You can reach the safety of Cairhien's walls
long before you could return to Shienar. Does the thought of a few more
days in my company seem so onerous?"

Rand stared at the chest. Selene's company was far from burdensome, but near her he could not help thinking things he should not. Still, trying to ride back north meant risking Fain and his followers. She was right in that. Fain would never give up. Ingtar would not give up, either. If Ingtar came on southward, and Rand knew of no reason for him to turn aside, he would arrive at Cairhien, soon or late.

"Cairhien," he agreed. "You will have to show me where you live, Selene. I've never been to Cairhien." He reached to close the chest.

"You took something else from the Friends of the Dark?" Selene said. "You spoke earlier of a dagger."

*How could I forget?* He left the chest as it was and pulled the dagger from his belt. The bare blade curved like a horn, and the quillons were golden serpents. Set in the hilt, a ruby as big as his thumbnail winked like an evil eye in the moonlight. Ornate as it was, tainted as he knew it was, it felt no different from any other knife.

"Be careful," Selene said. "Do not cut yourself."

Rand felt a shiver inside. If simply carrying it was dangerous, he did not want to know what a cut from it would do. "This is from Shadar Logoth," he told the others. "It will twist whoever carries it for long, taint them to the bone the way Shadar Logoth is tainted. Without Aes Sedai Healing, that taint will kill, eventually."

"So that is what ails Mat," Loial said softly. "I never suspected." Hurin stared at the dagger in Rand's hand and wiped his own hands on the front of his coat. The sniffer did not look happy.

"None of us must handle it any more than is necessary," Rand went on. "I will find some way to carry it—"

"It is dangerous." Selene frowned at the blade as if the snakes were real, and poisonous. "Throw it away. Leave it, or bury it if you wish to keep it from other hands, but be rid of it."

"Mat needs it," Rand said firmly.

"It is too dangerous. You said so yourself."

"He needs it. The Am . . . the Aes Sedai said he would die without it to use in Healing him." *They still have a string on him, but this blade will cut it. Until I'm rid of it, and the Horn, they have a string on me, but I'll not dance however much they pull.*

He set the dagger in the chest, inside the curl of the Horn—there was just room for it—and pulled the lid down. It locked with a sharp snap. "That should shield us from it." He hoped it would. Lan said the time to sound most sure was when you were least certain.

"The chest will surely shield us," Selene said in a tight voice. "And now I mean to finish what is left of my night's sleep."

Rand shook his head. "We are too close. Fain seems able to find me, sometimes."

"Seek the Oneness if you are afraid," Selene said.

"I want to be as far from those Darkfriends come morning as we can be. I will saddle your mare."

"Stubborn!" She sounded angry, and when he looked at her, her mouth curved in a smile that never came close to her dark eyes. "A stubborn man is best, once. . . ." Her voice trailed off, and that worried him. Women often seemed to leave things unsaid, and in his limited experience it was what they did not say that proved the most trouble. She watched in silence as he slung her saddle onto the white mare's back and bent to fashion the girths.

"Gather them all in!" Fain snarled. The goat-snouted Trolloc backed away from him. The fire, piled high with wood now, lit the hilltop with flickering shadows. His human followers huddled near the blaze, fearful to be out in the dark with the rest of the Trollocs. "Gather them, every one that still lives, and if any think to run, let them know they'll get what that one got." He gestured to the first Trolloc that had brought him word al'Thor was not to be found. It still snapped at ground muddied with its own blood, hooves scraping trenches as they jerked. "Go," Fain whispered, and the goat-snouted Trolloc ran into the night.

Fain glanced contemptuously at the other humans—*They'll have their uses still*—then turned to stare into the night, toward Kinslayer's Dagger. Al'Thor was up there, somewhere, in the mountains. With the Horn. His teeth grated audibly at the thought. He did not know where, exactly, but something pulled him toward the mountains. Toward al'Thor. That much of the Dark One's . . . gift . . . remained to him. He had hardly thought of it, had tried not to think of it, until suddenly, after the Horn was gone—*Gone!*—al'Thor was there, drawing him as meat draws a starving dog.

"I am a dog no longer. A dog no longer!" He heard the others shifting uneasily around the fire, but he ignored them. "You will pay for what was done to me, al'Thor! The world will pay!" He cackled at the night with mad laughter. "The world will pay!"

# CHAPTER 20

## *Saidin*

Rand kept them moving through the night, allowing only a brief stop at dawn, to rest the horses. And to allow Loial rest. With the Horn of Valere in its gold-and-silver chest occupying his saddle, the Ogier walked or trotted ahead of his big horse, never complaining, never slowing them. Sometime during the night they had crossed the border of Cairhien.

"I want to see it again," Selene said as they halted. She dismounted and strode to Loial's horse. Their shadows, long and thin, pointed west from the sun just peeking over the horizon. "Bring it down for me, *alantin.*" Loial began to undo the straps. "The Horn of Valere."

"No," Rand said, climbing down from Red's back. "Loial, no." The Ogier looked from Rand to Selene, his ears twitching doubtfully, but he took his hands away.

"I want to see the Horn," Selene demanded. Rand was sure she was no older than he, but at that moment she suddenly seemed as old and as cold as the mountains, and more regal than Queen Morgase at her haughtiest.

"I think we should keep the dagger shielded," Rand said. "For all I know, looking at it may be as bad as touching it. Let it stay where it is until I can put it in Mat's hands. He—he can take it to the Aes Sedai." *And what price will they demand for that Healing? But he hasn't any choice. He* felt a little guilty over feeling relief that he, at least, was through with Aes Sedai. *I am done with them. One way or another.*

"The dagger! All you seem to care about is that dagger. I told you to be rid of it. The Horn of Valere, Rand."

"No."

She came to him, a sway in her walk that made him feel as if he had something caught in his throat. "All I want is to see it in the light of day. I won't even touch it. You hold it. It would be something for me to remember, you holding the Horn of Valere in your hands." She took his hands as she said it; her touch made his skin tingle and his mouth go dry.

Something to remember—when she had gone. . . . He could close the dagger up again as soon as the Horn was out of the chest. It would be something to hold the Horn in his hands where he could see it in the light.

He wished he knew more of the Prophecies of the Dragon. The one time he heard a merchant's guard telling a part of it, back in Emond's Field, Nynaeve had broken a broom across the man's shoulders. None of the little he had heard mentioned the Horn of Valere.

*Aes Sedai trying to make me do what they want.* Selene was still gazing intently into his eyes, her face so young and beautiful that he wanted to kiss her despite what he was thinking. He had never seen an Aes Sedai act the way she did, and she looked young, not ageless. *A girl my age couldn't be Aes Sedai. But. . . .*

"Selene," he said softly, "*are* you an Aes Sedai?"

"Aes Sedai," she almost spat, flinging his hands away. "Aes Sedai! Always you hurl that at me!" She took a deep breath and smoothed her dress, as if gathering herself. "I am what and who I am. And I am no Aes Sedai!" And she wrapped herself in a silent coldness that made even the morning sun seem chill.

Loial and Hurin bore it all with as good a grace as they could manage, trying to make conversation and hiding their embarrassment when she froze them with a look. They rode on.

By the time they made camp that night beside a mountain stream that provided fish for their supper, Selene seemed to have regained some of her temper, chatting with the Ogier about books, speaking kindly to Hurin.

She barely spoke to Rand, though, unless he spoke first, either that evening or the following day as they rode through mountains that reared on either side of them like huge, jagged gray walls, ever climbing. But whenever he looked at her, she was watching him and smiling. Sometimes it was the sort of smile that made him smile back, sometimes the sort that made him clear his throat and blush at his own thoughts, and sometimes the mysterious, knowing smile that Egwene sometimes wore. It was a kind of smile that always put his back up—but at least it was a smile.

*She* can't *be Aes Sedai.*

The way began to slope downwards, and with the promise of twilight in the air, Kinslayer's Dagger at last gave way to hills, rolling and round, with more brush than trees, more thickets than forest. There was no road, just a dirt track, such as might be used by a few carts now and again. Fields carved some of the hills into terraces, fields full of crops but empty of people at this hour. None of the scattered farm buildings lay close enough to the path they rode for Rand to make out more than that they were all made of stone.

When he saw the village ahead, lights already twinkled in a few windows against the coming of night.

"We'll sleep in beds tonight," he said.

"That I will enjoy, Lord Rand." Hurin laughed. Loial nodded agreement.

"A village inn," Selene sniffed. "Dirty, no doubt, and full of unwashed men swilling ale. Why can't we sleep under the stars again? I find I enjoy sleeping under the stars."

"You would not enjoy it if Fain caught up with us while we slept," Rand said, "him and those Trollocs. He's coming after me, Selene. After the Horn, too, but it is me he can find. Why do you think I've kept such a close watch these past nights?"

"If Fain catches us, you will deal with him." Her voice was coolly confident. "And there could be Darkfriends in the village, too."

"But even if they knew who we are, they can't do much with the rest of the villagers around. Not unless you think everyone in the village is a Darkfriend."

"And if they discover you carry the Horn? Whether you want greatness or not, even farmers dream of it."

"She is right, Rand," Loial said. "I fear even farmers might want to take it."

"Unroll your blanket, Loial, and throw it over the chest. Keep it covered." Loial complied, and Rand nodded. It was obvious there was a box or chest beneath the Ogier's striped blanket, but nothing suggested it was more than a travel chest. "My Lady's chest of clothes," Rand said with a grin and a bow.

Selene met his sally with silence and an unreadable look. After a moment, they started on again.

Almost immediately, off to Rand's left, a glitter from the setting sun reflected from something on the ground. Something large. Something very large, by the light it threw up. Curious, he turned his horse that way.

"My Lord?" Hurin said. "The village?"

"I just want to see this first," Rand said. *It's brighter than sunlight on water. What can it be?*

His eyes on the reflection, he was surprised when Red suddenly stopped. On the point of urging the bay on, he realized that they stood on the edge of a clay precipice, above a huge excavation. Most of the hill had been dug away to a depth of easily a hundred paces. Certainly more than one hill had vanished, and maybe some farmers' fields, for the hole was at least ten times as wide as it was deep. The far side appeared to have been packed hard to a ramp. There were men on the bottom, a dozen of them, getting a fire started; down there, night was already descending. Here and there among them armor turned the light, and swords swung at their sides. He hardly glanced at them.

Out of the clay at the bottom of the pit slanted a gigantic stone hand holding a crystal sphere, and it was this that shone with the last sunlight. Rand gaped at the size of it, a smooth ball—he was sure not so much as a scratch marred its surface—at least twenty paces through.

Some distance away from the hand, a stone face in proportion had been uncovered. A bearded man's face, it thrust out of the soil with the dignity of vast years; the broad features seemed to hold wisdom and knowledge.

Unsummoned, the void formed, whole and complete in an instant, *saidin* glowing, beckoning. So intent was he on the face and the hand that he did not even realize what had happened. He had once heard a ship captain speak of a giant hand holding a huge crystal sphere; Bayle Domon had claimed it stuck out of a hill on the island of Tremalking.

"This is dangerous," Selene said. "Come away, Rand."

"I believe I can find a way down there," he said absently. *Saidin* sang to him. The huge ball seemed to glow white with the light of the sinking sun. It seemed to him that in the depths of the crystal, light swirled and danced in time to the song of *saidin*. He wondered why the men below did not appear to notice.

Selene rode close and took hold of his arm. "Please, Rand, you must come away." He looked at her hand, puzzled, then followed her arm up to her face. She seemed genuinely worried, perhaps even afraid. "If this bank doesn't give way beneath our horses and break our necks with the fall, those men are guards, and no one puts guards on something they wish every passerby to examine. What good will it do you to avoid Fain, if some lord's guards arrest you? Come away."

Suddenly—a drifting, distant thought—he realized that the void surrounded him. *Saidin* sang, and the sphere pulsed—even without looking, he could *feel* it—and the thought came that if he sang the song *saidin* sang, that huge stone face would open its mouth and sing with him. With him and with *saidin*. All one.

"Please, Rand," Selene said. "I will go to the village with you. I won't mention the Horn again. Only come away!"

He released the void . . . and it did not go. *Saidin* crooned, and the light in the sphere beat like a heart. Like his heart. Loial, Hurin, Selene, they all stared at him, but they seemed oblivious to the glorious blaze from the crystal. He tried to push the void away. It held like granite; he floated in an emptiness as hard as stone. The song of *saidin,* the song of the sphere, he could feel them quivering along his bones. Grimly, he refused to give in, reached deep inside himself . . . *I will not.* . . .

"Rand." He did not know whose voice it was.

. . . reached for the core of who he was, the core of what he was . . . *. . . will not . . .*

"Rand." The song filled him, filled the emptiness.

. . . touched stone, hot from a pitiless sun, cold from a merciless night. . . .

*. . . not . . .*

Light filled him, blinded him.

"Till shade is gone," he mumbled, "till water is gone . . ."

Power filled him. He was one with the sphere.

". . . into the Shadow with teeth bared . . ."

The power was his. The Power was his.

". . . to spit in Sightblinder's eye . . ."

Power to Break the World.

". . . on the last day!" It came out as a shout, and the void was gone. Red shied at his cry; clay crumbled under the stallion's hoof, spilling into the pit. The big bay went to his knees. Rand leaned forward, gathering the reins, and Red scrambled to safety, away from the edge.

They were all staring at him, he saw. Selene, Loial, Hurin, all of them. "What happened?" *The void.* . . . He touched his forehead. The void had not gone when he released it, and the glow of *saidin* had grown stronger, and. . . . He could not remember anything more. *Saidin.* He felt cold. "Did I . . . do something?" He frowned, trying to remember. "Did I say something?"

"You just sat there stiff as a statue," Loial said, "mumbling to yourself no matter what anyone said. I couldn't make out what you were saying, not until you shouted 'day!' loud enough to wake the dead and nearly put your horse over the edge. Are you ill? You're acting more and more oddly every day."

"I'm not sick," Rand said harshly, then softened it. "I am all right, Loial." Selene watched him warily.

From the pit came the sound of men calling, the words indistinguishable.

"Lord Rand," Hurin said, "I think those guards have finally noticed us. If they know a way up this side, they could be here any minute."

"Yes," Selene said. "Let us leave here quickly."

Rand glanced at the excavation, then away again, quickly. The great crystal held nothing except reflected light from the evening sun, but he did not want to look at it. He could almost remember . . . *something* about the sphere. "I don't see any reason to wait for them. We didn't do anything. Let's find an inn." He turned Red toward the village, and they soon left pit and shouting guards behind.

As many villages did, Tremonsien covered the top of a hill, but like the farms they had passed, this hill had been sculpted into terraces with stone retaining walls. Square stone houses sat on precise plots of land, with exact gardens behind, along a few straight streets that crossed each other at right angles. The necessity of a curve to streets going around the hill seemed begrudged.

Yet the people seemed open and friendly enough, pausing to nod to each other as they hurried about their last chores before nightfall. They were a short folk—none taller than Rand's shoulder, and few as tall as Hurin—with dark eyes and pale, narrow faces, and dressed in dark clothes except for a few who wore slashes of color across the chest. Smells of cooking—oddly spiced, to Rand's nose—filled the air, though a handful of good-wives still hung over their doors to talk; the doors were split, so the top could stand open while the bottom was closed. The people eyed the new-comers curiously, with no sign of hostility. A few stared a moment longer at Loial, an Ogier walking alongside a horse as big as a Dhurran stallion, but never more than a moment longer.

The inn, at the very top of the hill, was stone like every other building in the town, and plainly marked by a painted sign hanging over the wide doors. The Nine Rings. Rand swung down with a smile and tied Red to one of the hitching posts out front. "The Nine Rings" had been one of his favorite adventure stories when he was a boy; he supposed it still was.

Selene still seemed uneasy when he helped her dismount. "Are you all right?" he asked. "I didn't frighten you back there, did I? Red would never fall over a cliff with me." He wondered what had really happened.

"You terrified me," she said in a tight voice, "and I do not frighten easily. You could have killed yourself, killed. . . ." She smoothed her dress. "Ride with me. Tonight. Now. Bring the Horn, and I will stay by your side forever. Think of it. Me by your side, and the Horn of Valere in your hands. And that will only be the beginning, I promise. What more could you ask for?"

Rand shook his head. "I can't, Selene. The Horn. . . ." He looked around. A man looked out his window across the way, then twitched the curtains closed; evening darkened the street, and there was no one else in sight now except Loial and Hurin. "The Horn is not mine. I told you that." She turned her back on him, her white cloak walling him off as effectively as bricks.

# CHAPTER 21

## *The Nine Rings*

Rand expected the common room to be empty, since it was nearly suppertime, but half a dozen men crowded one table, dicing among their jacks of ale, and another sat by himself over a meal. Though the dicers carried no weapons in sight and wore no armor, only plain coats and breeches of dark blue, something about the way they held themselves told Rand they were soldiers. His eyes went to the solitary man. An officer, with the tops of his high boots turned down, and his sword propped against the table beside his chair. A single slash of red and one of yellow crossed the chest of the officer's blue coat from shoulder to shoulder, and the front of his head was shaved, though his black hair hung long in the back. The soldiers' hair was clipped short, as if it all had been cut under the same bowl. All seven turned to look as Rand and the others came in.

The innkeeper was a lean woman with a long nose and graying hair, but her wrinkles seemed part of her ready smile more than anything else. She came bustling up, wiping her hands on a spotless white apron. "Good even to you"—her quick eyes took in Rand's gold-embroidered red coat, and Selene's fine white dress—"my Lord, my Lady. I am Maglin Madwen, my Lord. Be welcome to The Nine Rings. And an Ogier. Not many of your kind come this way, friend Ogier. Would you be up from Stedding Tsofu, then?"

Loial managed an awkward half bow under the weight of the chest. "No, good innkeeper. I come the other way, from the Borderlands."

"From the Borderlands, you say. Well. And you, my Lord? Forgive me for asking, but you've not the look of the Borderlands, if you don't mind my saying it."

"I'm from the Two Rivers, Mistress Madwen, in Andor." He glanced at Selene—she did not seem to admit he existed; her level look barely admitted that the room existed, or anyone in it. "The Lady Selene is from Cairhien, from the capital, and I am from Andor."

"As you say, my Lord." Mistress Madwen's glance flickered to Rand's sword; the bronze herons were plain on scabbard and hilt. She frowned slightly, but her face was clear again in a blink. "You'll be wanting a meal for yourself and your beautiful Lady, and your followers. And rooms, I expect. I'll have your horses seen to. I've a good table for you, right this way, and pork with yellow peppers on the fire. Would you be hunting the Horn of Valere, then, my Lord, you and your Lady?"

In the act of following her, Rand almost stumbled. "No! Why would you think we were?"

"No offense, my Lord. We've had two through here already, all polished to look like heroes—not to suggest anything of the kind about you, my Lord—in the last month. Not many strangers come here, except traders up from the capital to buy oats and barley. I'd not suppose the Hunt has left Illian, yet, but maybe some don't think they really need the blessing, and they'll get a jump on the others by missing it."

"We are not hunting the Horn, mistress." Rand did not glance at the bundle in Loial's arms; the blanket with its colorful stripes hung bunched over the Ogier's thick arms and disguised the chest well. "We surely are not. We are on our way to the capital."

"As you say, my Lord. Forgive me for asking, but is your Lady well?"

Selene looked at her, and spoke for the first time. "I am quite well." Her voice left a chill in the air that stifled talk for a moment.

"You're not Cairhienin, Mistress Madwen," Hurin said suddenly. Burdened down with their saddlebags and Rand's bundle, he looked like a walking baggage cart. "Pardon, but you don't sound it."

Mistress Madwen's eyebrows rose, and she shot a glance at Rand, then grinned. "I should have known you'd let your man speak freely, but I've grown used to—" Her glance darted toward the officer, who had gone back to his own meal. "Light, no, I'm not Cairhienin, but for my sins, I married one. Twenty-three years I lived with him, and when he died on me—the Light shine on him—I was all ready to go back to Lugard, but he had the last laugh, he did. He left me the inn, and his brother the money, when I was sure it would be the other way round. Tricksome and scheming, Barin was, like every man I've ever known, Cairhienin most of all. Will you be seated, my Lord? My Lady?"

The innkeeper gave a surprised blink when Hurin sat at table with them—an Ogier, it seemed, was one thing, but Hurin was clearly a servant in her eyes. With another quick look at Rand, she bustled off to the kitchens, and soon serving girls came with their meal, giggling and staring at the lord and the lady, and the Ogier, till Mistress Madwen chased them back to their work.

At first, Rand stared at his food doubtfully. The pork was cut in small bits, mixed with long strips of yellow peppers, and peas, and a number of vegetables and things he did not recognize, all in some sort of clear, thick sauce. It smelled sweet and sharp, both at the same time. Selene only picked at hers, but Loial was eating with a will.

Hurin grinned at Rand over his fork. "They spice their food oddly, Cairhienin do, Lord Rand, but for all that, it's not bad."

"It won't bite you, Rand," Loial added.

Rand took a hesitant mouthful, and almost gasped. It tasted just as it smelled, sweet and sharp together, the pork crisp on the outside and tender inside, a dozen different flavors, spices, all blending and contrasting. It tasted like nothing he had ever put in his mouth before. It tasted wonderful. He cleaned his plate, and when Mistress Madwen returned with the serving girls to clear away, he nearly asked for more the way Loial did. Selene's was still half full, but she motioned curtly for one of the girls to take it.

"A pleasure, friend Ogier." The innkeeper smiled. "It takes a lot to fill up one of you. Catrine, bring another helping, and be quick." One of the girls darted away. Mistress Madwen turned her smile on Rand. "My Lord, I had a man here who played the bittern, but he married a girl off one of the farms, and she has him strumming reins behind a plow, now. I couldn't help noticing what looks like a flute case sticking out of your man's bundle. Since my musician's gone, would you let your man favor us with a little music?"

Hurin looked embarrassed.

"He doesn't play," Rand explained. "I do."

The woman blinked. It appeared lords did not play the flute, at least not in Cairhien. "I withdraw the request, my Lord. Light's own truth, I meant no offense, I assure you. I'd never ask one such as yourself to be playing in a common room."

Rand hesitated only a moment. It had been too long since he had practiced the flute rather than the sword, and the coins in his pouch would not last forever. Once he was rid of his fancy clothes—once he turned the Horn over to Ingtar and the dagger over to Mat—he would need the flute to earn his supper again while he searched for somewhere safe from Aes Sedai. *And safe from myself? Something* did *happen back there. What?*

"I don't mind," he said. "Hurin, hand me the case. Just slide it out." There was no need to show a gleeman's cloak; enough unspoken questions shone in Mistress Madwen's dark eyes as it was.

Worked gold chased with silver, the instrument looked the sort a lord might play, if lords anywhere played the flute. The heron branded on his right palm did not interfere with his fingering. Selene's salves had worked so well he hardly thought of the brand unless he saw it. Yet it was in his thoughts now, and unconsciously he began to play "Heron on the Wing."

Hurin bobbed his head to the tune, and Loial beat time on the table with a thick finger. Selene looked at Rand as if wondering what he was— *I'm not a lord, my Lady. I'm a shepherd, and I play the flute in common rooms*— but the soldiers turned from their talk to listen, and the officer closed the wooden cover of the book he had begun reading. Selene's steady gaze struck a stubborn spark inside Rand. Determinedly he avoided any song that might fit in a palace, or a lord's manor. He played "Only One Bucket of Water" and "The Old Two Rivers Leaf," "Old Jak's Up a Tree" and "Goodman Priket's Pipe."

With the last, the six soldiers began to sing in raucous tones, though not the words Rand knew.

"We rode down to River Iralell
just to see the Taren come.
We stood along the riverbank
with the rising of the sun.
Their horses blacked the summer plain,
their banners blacked the sky.
But we stood our ground on the banks of River Iralell.
Oh, we stood our ground.
Yes, we stood our ground.
Stood our ground along the river in the morning."

It was not the first time that Rand had discovered a tune had different words and different names in different lands, sometimes even in villages in the same land. He played along with them until they let the words die away, slapping each other's shoulders and making rude comments on one another's singing.

When Rand lowered the flute, the officer rose and made a sharp gesture. The soldiers fell silent in mid-laugh, scraped back their chairs to bow to the officer with hand on breast—and to Rand—and left without a backwards look.

The officer came to Rand's table and bowed, hand to heart; the shaven front of his head looked as if he had dusted it with white powder. "Grace favor you, my Lord. I trust they did not bother you, singing as they did. They are a common sort, but they meant no insult, I assure you. I am Aldrin Caldevwin, my Lord. Captain in His Majesty's Service, the Light illumine him." His eyes slid over Rand's sword; Rand had the feeling Caldevwin had noticed the herons as soon as he came in.

"They didn't insult me." The officer's accent reminded him of Moiraine's, precise and every word pronounced to its full. *Did she really let me go? I wonder if she's following me. Or waiting for me.* "Sit down, Captain. Please." Caldevwin drew a chair from another table. "Tell me, Captain, if you don't mind. Have you seen any other strangers recently? A lady, short and slender, and a fighting man with blue eyes. He's tall, and sometimes he wears his sword on his back."

"I have seen no strangers at all," he said, lowering himself stiffly to his seat. "Saving yourself and your Lady, my Lord. Few of the nobility ever come here." His eyes flicked toward Loial with a minute frown; Hurin he ignored for a servant.

"It was only a thought."

"Under the Light, my Lord, I mean no disrespect, but may I hear your name? We have so few strangers here that I find I wish to know every one."

Rand gave it—he claimed no title, but the officer seemed not to notice—and said as he had to the innkeeper, "From the Two Rivers, in Andor."

"A wondrous place I have heard, Lord Rand—I may call you so?—and fine men, the Andormen. No Cairhienin has ever worn a blademaster's sword so young as you. I met some Andormen, once, the Captain-General of the Queen's Guards among them. I do not remember his name; an embarrassment. Perhaps you could favor me with it?"

Rand was conscious of the serving girls in the background, beginning to clean and sweep. Caldevwin seemed only to be making conversation, but there was a probing quality to his look. "Gareth Bryne."

"Of course. Young, to hold so much responsibility."

Rand kept his voice level. "Gareth Bryne has enough gray in his hair to be your father, Captain."

"Forgive me, my Lord Rand. I meant to say that he came to it young." Caldevwin turned to Selene, and for a moment he only stared. He shook himself, finally, as if coming out of a trance. "Forgive me for looking at you so, my Lady, and forgive me for speaking so, but Grace has surely favored you. Will you give me a name to put to such beauty?"

Just as Selene opened her mouth, one of the serving girls let out a cry and dropped a lamp she was taking down from a shelf. Oil splattered, and caught in a pool of flame on the floor. Rand leaped to his feet along with the others at the table, but before any of them could move, Mistress Madwen appeared, and she and the girl smothered the flames with their aprons.

"I have told you to be careful, Catrine," the innkeeper said, shaking her now-smutty apron under the girl's nose. "You'll be burning the inn down, and yourself in it."

The girl seemed on the point of tears. "I *was* being careful, Mistress, but I had such a twinge in my arm."

Mistress Madwen threw up her hands. "You always have some excuse, and you still break more dishes than all the rest. Ah, it's all right. Clean it up, and don't burn yourself." The innkeeper turned to Rand and the others, all still standing around the table. "I hope none of you take this amiss. The girl really won't burn down the inn. She's hard on the dishes when she starts mooning over some young fellow, but she's never mishandled a lamp before."

"I would like to be shown to my room. I do not feel well after all." Selene spoke in careful tones, as though uncertain of her stomach, but despite that she looked and sounded as cool and calm as ever. "The journey, and the fire."

The innkeeper clucked like a mother hen. "Of course, my Lady. I have a fine room for you and your Lord. Shall I fetch Mother Caredwain? She has a fine hand with soothing herbs."

Selene's voice sharpened. "No. And I wish a room by myself."

Mistress Madwen glanced at Rand, but the next moment she was bowing Selene solicitously toward the stairs. "As you wish, my Lady. Lidan, fetch the Lady's things like a good girl, now." One of the serving girls ran to take Selene's saddlebags from Hurin, and the women disappeared upstairs, Selene stiff-backed and silent.

Caldevwin stared after them until they were gone, then shook himself again. He waited until Rand had seated himself before taking his chair again. "Forgive me, my Lord Rand, for staring so at your Lady, but Grace has surely favored you in her. I mean no insult."

"None taken," Rand said. He wondered if every man felt the way he did when they looked at Selene. "As I was riding to the village, Captain, I saw a huge sphere. Crystal, it seemed. What is it?"

The Cairhienin's eyes sharpened. "It is part of the statue, my Lord Rand," he said slowly. His gaze flickered toward Loial; for an instant he seemed to be considering something new.

"Statue? I saw a hand, and a face, too. It must be huge."

"It is, my Lord Rand. And old." Caldevwin paused. "From the Age of Legends, so I am told."

Rand felt a chill. The Age of Legends, when use of the One Power was everywhere, if the stories could be believed. *What happened there? I know there was something.*

"The Age of Legends," Loial said. "Yes, it must be. No one has done work so vast since. A great piece of work to dig that up, Captain." Hurin sat silently, as if he not only was not listening, but was not there at all.

Caldevwin nodded reluctantly. "I have five hundred laborers in camp beyond the diggings, and even so it will be past summer's end before we have it clear. They are men from the Foregate. Half my work is to keep them digging, and the other half to keep them out of this village. Foregaters have a fondness for drinking and carousing, you understand, and these people lead quiet lives." His tone said his sympathies were all with the villagers.

Rand nodded. He had no interest in Foregaters, whoever they were. "What will you do with it?" The captain hesitated, but Rand only looked back at him until he spoke.

"Galldrian himself has ordered that it be taken to the capital."

Loial blinked. "A very great piece of work, that. I am not sure how something that big could be moved so far."

"His Majesty has ordered it," Caldevwin said sharply. "It will be set up outside the city, a monument to the greatness of Cairhien and of House Riatin. Ogier are not the only ones who know how to move stone." Loial looked abashed, and the captain visibly calmed himself. "Your pardon, friend Ogier. I spoke in haste, and rudely." He still sounded a little gruff. "Will you be staying in Tremonsien long, my Lord Rand?"

"We leave in the morning," Rand said. "We are going to Cairhien."

"As it happens, I am sending some of my men back to the city tomorrow. I must rotate them; they grow stale after too long watching men swing picks and shovels. You will not mind if they ride in your company?" He put it as a question, but as if acceptance were a foregone conclusion. Mistress Madwen appeared on the stairs, and he rose. "If you will excuse me, my Lord Rand, I must be up early. Until the morning, then. Grace favor you." He bowed to Rand, nodded to Loial, and left.

As the doors closed behind the Cairhienin, the innkeeper came to the table.

"I have your Lady settled, my Lord. And I've good rooms prepared for you and your man, and you, friend Ogier." She paused, studying Rand. "Forgive me if I overstep myself, my Lord, but I think I can speak freely to a lord who lets his man speak up. If I'm wrong . . . well, I mean no insult. For twenty-three years Barin Madwen and I were arguing when we weren't kissing, so to speak. That's by way of saying I have some experience. Right now, you're thinking your Lady never wants to see you again, but it's my way of thinking that if you tap on her door tonight, she'll be taking you in. Smile and say it was your fault, whether it was or not."

Rand cleared his throat and hoped his face was not turning red. *Light, Egwene would kill me if she knew I'd even thought of it. And Selene would kill me if I did it. Or would she?* That did make his cheeks burn. "I . . . thank you for your suggestion, Mistress Madwen. The rooms. . . ." He avoided looking at the blanket-covered chest by Loial's chair; they did not dare leave it without someone awake and guarding it. "We three will all sleep in the same room."

The innkeeper looked startled, but she recovered quickly. "As you wish, my Lord. This way, if you please."

Rand followed her up the stairs. Loial carried the chest under its blanket—the stairs groaned under the weight of him and the chest together, but the innkeeper seemed to think it was just an Ogier's bulk—and Hurin still carried all the saddlebags and the bundled cloak with the harp and flute.

Mistress Madwen had a third bed brought in and hastily assembled and made up. One of the beds already there stretched nearly from wall to wall in length, and had obviously been meant for Loial from the start. There was barely room to walk between the beds. As soon as the innkeeper was gone, Rand turned to the others. Loial had pushed the still-covered chest under his bed and was trying the mattress. Hurin was setting out the saddlebags.

"Do either of you know why that captain was so suspicious of us? He was, I'm sure of it." He shook his head. "I almost think he thought we might steal that statue, the way he was talking."

"*Daes Dae'mar,* Lord Rand," Hurin said. "The Great Game. The Game of Houses, some call it. This Caldevwin thinks you must be doing something to your advantage or you wouldn't be here. And whatever you're doing might be to his disadvantage, so he has to be careful."

Rand shook his head. "'The Great Game'? What game?"

"It isn't a game at all, Rand," Loial said from his bed. He had pulled a book from his pocket, but it lay unopened on his chest. "I don't know much about it—Ogier don't do such things—but I have heard of it. The nobles and the noble Houses maneuver for advantage. They do things they think will help them, or hurt an enemy, or both. Usually, it's all done in secrecy, or if not, they try to make it seem as if they're doing something other than what they are." He gave one tufted ear a puzzled scratch. "Even knowing what it is, I don't understand it. Elder Haman always said it would take a greater mind than his to understand the things humans do, and I don't know many as intelligent as Elder Haman. You humans are odd."

Hurin gave the Ogier a slanted look, but he said, "He has the right of *Daes Dae'mar*, Lord Rand. Cairhienin play it more than most, though all southerners do."

"These soldiers in the morning," Rand said. "Are they part of Caldevwin playing this Great Game? We can't afford to get mixed in anything like that." There was no need to mention the Horn. They were all too aware of its presence.

Loial shook his head. "I don't know, Rand. He's human, so it could mean anything."

"Hurin?"

"I don't know, either." Hurin sounded as worried as the Ogier looked. "He could be doing just what he said, or. . . . That's the way of the Game of Houses. You never know. I spent most of my time in Cairhien in the Foregate, Lord Rand, and I don't know much about Cairhienin nobles, but—well, *Daes Dae'mar* can be dangerous anywhere, but especially in Cairhien, I've heard." He brightened suddenly. "The Lady Selene, Lord Rand. She'll know better than me or the Builder. You can ask her in the morning."

But in the morning, Selene was gone. When Rand went down to the common room, Mistress Madwen handed him a sealed parchment. "If you'll forgive me, my Lord, you should have listened to me. You should have tapped on your Lady's door."

Rand waited until she went away before he broke the white wax seal. The wax had been impressed with a crescent moon and stars.

*I must leave you for a time. There are too many people here, and I do not like Caldevwin. I will await you in Cairhien. Never think that I am too far from you. You will be in my thoughts always, as I know that I am in yours.*

It was not signed, but that elegant, flowing script had the look of Selene.

He folded it carefully and put it in his pocket before going outside, where Hurin had the horses waiting.

Captain Caldevwin was there, too, with another, younger officer and fifty mounted soldiers crowding the street. The two officers were bare-headed, but wore steel-backed gauntlets, and gold-worked breastplates strapped over their blue coats. A short staff was fastened to the harness on each officer's back, bearing a small, stiff blue banner above his head. Caldevwin's banner bore a single white star, while the younger man's was crossed by two white bars. They were a sharp contrast to the soldiers in their plain armor and helmets that looked like bells with metal cut away to expose their faces.

Caldevwin bowed as Rand came out of the inn. "Good morning to you, my Lord Rand. This is Elricain Tavolin, who will command your escort, if I may call it that." The other officer bowed; his head was shaved as Caldevwin's was. He did not speak.

"An escort will be welcome, Captain," Rand said, managing to sound at ease. Fain would not try anything against fifty soldiers, but Rand wished he could be certain they were only an escort.

The captain eyed Loial, on his way to his horse with the blanket-covered chest. "A heavy burden, Ogier."

Loial almost missed a step. "I never like to be far from my books, Captain." His wide mouth flashed teeth in a self-conscious grin, and he hurried to strap the chest onto his saddle.

Caldevwin looked around, frowning. "Your Lady is not down yet. And her fine animal is not here."

"She left already," Rand told him. "She had to go on to Cairhien quickly, during the night."

Caldevwin's eyebrows lifted. "During the night? But my men. . . . Forgive me, my Lord Rand." He drew the younger officer aside, whispering furiously.

"He had the inn watched, Lord Rand," Hurin whispered. "The Lady Selene must have gotten past them unseen somehow."

Rand climbed to Red's saddle with a grimace. If there had been any chance Caldevwin did not suspect them of something, it seemed Selene had finished it. "Too many people, she says," he muttered. "There'll be more people by far in Cairhien."

"You said something, my Lord?"

Rand looked up as Tavolin joined him, mounted on a tall, dust-colored gelding. Hurin was in his saddle, too, and Loial stood beside his big horse's head. The soldiers were formed up in ranks. Caldevwin was nowhere to be seen.

"Nothing is happening the way I expect," Rand said.

Tavolin gave him a brief smile, hardly more than a twitch of his lips. "Shall we ride, my Lord?"

The strange procession headed for the hard-packed road that led to the city of Cairhien.

# CHAPTER 22

## Watchers

"Nothing is happening as I expect," Moiraine muttered, not expecting an answer from Lan.

The long, polished table before her was littered with books and papers, scrolls and manuscripts, many of them dusty from long storage and tattered with age, some only fragments. The room seemed almost made of books and manuscripts, filling shelves except where there were doors or windows or the fireplace. The chairs were high-backed and well padded, but half of them, and most of the small tables, held books, and some had books and scrolls tucked under them. Only the clutter in front of Moiraine was hers, though.

She rose and moved to the window, peered into the night toward the lights of the village, not far off. No danger of pursuit here. No one would expect her to come here. *Clear my head, and begin again,* she thought. *That is all there is to do.*

None of the villagers had any suspicion that the two elderly sisters living in this snug house were Aes Sedai. One did not suspect such things in a small place like Tifan's Well, a farming community deep in the grassy plains of Arafel. The villagers came to the sisters for advice on their problems and cures for their ills, and valued them as women blessed by the Light, but no more. Adeleas and Vandene had gone into voluntary retreat together so long ago that few even in the White Tower remembered they still lived.

With the one equally aged Warder who remained to them, they lived quietly, still intending to write the history of the world since the Breaking, and as much as they could include of before. One day. In the meantime, there was so much information to gather, so many puzzles to solve. Their house was the perfect place for Moiraine to find the information she needed. Except that it was not there.

Movement caught her eye, and she turned. Lan was lounging against the yellow brick fireplace, as imperturbable as a boulder. "Do you remember the first time we met, Lan?"

She was watching for some sign, or she would not have seen the quick twitch of his eyebrow. It was not often she caught him by surprise. This was a subject neither of them ever mentioned; nearly twenty years ago she had told him—with all the stiff pride of one still young enough to be called young, she recalled—that she would never speak of it again and expected the same silence of him.

"I remember," was all he said.

"And still no apology, I suppose? You threw me into a pond." She did not smile, though she could feel amusement at it, now. "Every stitch I had was soaked, and in what you Bordermen call new spring. I nearly froze."

"I recall I built a fire, too, and hung blankets so you could warm yourself in privacy." He poked at the burning logs and returned the firetool to its hook. Even summer nights were cool in the Borderlands. "I also recall that while I slept that night, you dumped half the pond on me. It would have saved a great deal of shivering on both our parts if you had simply told me you were Aes Sedai rather than demonstrating it. Rather than trying to separate me from my sword. Not a good way to introduce yourself to a Borderman, even for a young woman."

"I *was* young, and alone, and you were as large then as you are now, and your fierceness more open. I did not want you to know I was Aes Sedai. It seemed to me at the time you might answer my questions more freely if you did not know." She fell silent for a moment, thinking of the years since that meeting. It had been good to find a companion to join her in her quest. "In the weeks that followed, did you suspect that I would ask you to bond to me? I decided you were the one in the first day."

"I never guessed," he said dryly. "I was too busy wondering if I could escort you to Chachin and keep a whole skin. A different surprise you had for me every night. The ants I recall in particular. I don't think I had one good night's sleep that whole ride."

She permitted herself a small smile, remembering. "I was young," she repeated. "And does your bond chafe after all these years? You are not a man to wear a leash easily, even so light a one as mine." It was a stinging comment; she meant it to be so.

"No." His voice was cool, but he took up the firetool again and gave the blaze a fierce poking it did not need. Sparks cascaded up the chimney. "I chose freely, knowing what it entailed." The iron rod clattered back onto its hook, and he made a formal bow. "Honor to serve, Moiraine Aes Sedai. It has been and will be so, always."

Moiraine sniffed. "Your humility, Lan Gaidin, has always been more arrogance than most kings could manage with their armies at their backs. From the first day I met you, it has been so."

"Why all this talk of days past, Moiraine?"

For the hundredth time—or so it seemed to her—she considered the words to use. "Before we left Tar Valon I made arrangements, should anything happen to me, for your bond to pass to another." He stared at her, silent. "When you feel my death, you will find yourself compelled to seek her out immediately. I do not want you to be surprised by it."

"Compelled," he breathed softly, angrily. "Never once have you used my bond to compel me. I thought you more than disapproved of that."

"Had I left this thing undone, you would be free of the bond at my death, and not even my strongest command to you would hold. I will not allow you to die in a useless attempt to avenge me. And I will not allow you to return to your equally useless private war in the Blight. The war we fight is the same war, if you could only see it so, and I will see that you fight it to some purpose. Neither vengeance nor an unburied death in the Blight will do."

"And do you foresee your death coming soon?" His voice was quiet, his face expressionless, both like stone in a dead winter blizzard. It was a manner she had seen in him many times, usually when he was on the point of violence. "Have you planned something, without me, that will see you dead?"

"I am suddenly glad there is no pond in this room," she murmured, then raised her hands when he stiffened, offended at her light tone. "I see my death in every day, as you do. How could I not, with the task we have followed these years? Now, with everything coming to a head, I must see it as even more possible."

For a moment he studied his hands, large and square. "I had never thought," he said slowly, "that I might not be the first of us to die. Somehow, even at the worst, it always seemed. . . ." Abruptly he scrubbed his hands against each other. "If there is a chance I might be given like a pet lapdog, I would at least like to know to whom I am being given."

"I have never seen you as a pet," Moiraine said sharply, "and neither does Myrelle."

"Myrelle." He grimaced. "Yes, she would have to be Green, or else some slip of a girl just raised to full sisterhood."

"If Myrelle can keep her three Gaidin in line, perhaps she has a chance to manage you. Though she would like to keep you, I know, she has promised to pass your bond to another when she finds one who suits you better."

"So. Not a pet but a parcel. Myrelle is to be a—a caretaker! Moiraine, not even the Greens treat their Warders so. No Aes Sedai has passed her Warder's bond to another in four hundred years, but you intend to do it to me not once, but twice!"

"It is done, and I will not undo it."

"The Light blind me, if I am to be passed from hand to hand, do you at least have some idea in whose hand I will end?"

"What I do is for your own good, and perhaps it may be for another's, as well. It may be that Myrelle will find a slip of a girl just raised to sisterhood—was that not what you said?—who needs a Warder hardened in battle and wise in the ways of the world, a slip of a girl who may need someone who will throw her into a pond. You have much to offer, Lan, and to see it wasted in an unmarked grave, or left to the ravens, when it could go to a woman who needs it would be worse than the sin of which the Whitecloaks prate. Yes, I think she will have need of you."

Lan's eyes widened slightly; for him it was the same as another man gasping in shocked surmise. She had seldom seen him so off balance. He opened his mouth twice before he spoke. "And who do you have in mind for this—"

She cut him off. "Are you sure the bond does not chafe, Lan Gaidin? Do you realize for the first time, only now, the strength of that bond, the depth of it? You could end with some budding White, all logic and no heart, or with a young Brown who sees you as nothing more than a pair of hands to carry her books and sketches. I can hand you where I will, like a parcel—or a lapdog—and you can do no more than go. Are you sure it does not chafe?"

"Is that what this has been for?" he grated. His eyes burned like blue fire, and his mouth twisted. Anger; for the first time ever that she had seen, open anger etched his face. "Has all this talk been a test—a test!—to see if you could make my bond rub? After all this time? From the day I pledged to you, I have ridden where you said ride, even when I thought it foolish, even when I had reason to ride another way. Never did you need my bond to force me. On your word I have watched you walk into danger and kept my hands at my sides when I wanted nothing more than to out sword and carve a path to safety for you. After this, you test me?"

"Not a test, Lan. I spoke plainly, not twisting, and I have done as I said. But at Fal Dara, I began to wonder if you were still wholly with me." A wariness entered his eyes. *Lan, forgive me. I would not have cracked the walls you hold so hard, but I must know.* "Why did you do as you did with Rand?" He blinked; it was obviously not what he expected. She knew what he had thought was coming, and she would not let up now that he was off balance. "You brought him to the Amyrlin speaking and acting as a Border lord and a soldier born. It fit, in a way, with what I planned for him, but you and I never spoke of teaching him any of that. Why, Lan?"

"It seemed . . . right. A young wolfhound must meet his first wolf someday, but if the wolf sees him as a puppy, if he acts the puppy, the wolf will surely kill him. The wolfhound must be a wolfhound in the wolf's eyes even more than in his own, if he is to survive."

"Is that how you see Aes Sedai? The Amyrlin? Me? Wolves out to pull down your young wolfhound?" Lan shook his head. "You know what he is, Lan. You know what he must become. Must. What I have worked for since the day you and I met, and before. Do you now doubt what I do?"

"No. No, but. . . ." He was recovering himself, building his walls again. But they were not rebuilt yet. "How many times have you said that *ta'veren* pull those around them like twigs in a whirlpool? Perhaps I was pulled, too. I only know that it felt right. Those farm folk needed someone on their side. Rand did, at least. Moiraine, I believe in what you do, even as now, when I know not half of it; believe as I believe in you. I have not asked to be released from my bond, nor will I. Whatever your plans for dying and seeing me safely—disposed of—I will take great pleasure in keeping you alive and seeing those plans, at least, go for nothing."

*"Ta'veren,"* Moiraine sighed. "Perhaps it was that. Rather than guiding a chip floating down a stream, I am trying to guide a log through rapids. Every time I push at it, it pushes at me, and the log grows larger the farther we go. Yet I must see it through to the end." She gave a little laugh. "I will not be unhappy, my old friend, if you manage to put those plans awry. Now, please leave me. I need to be alone to think." He hesitated only a moment before turning for the door. At the last moment, though, she could not let him go without one more question. "Do you ever dream of something different, Lan?"

"All men dream. But I know dreams for dreams. This"—he touched his sword hilt—"is reality." The walls were back, as high and hard as ever.

For a time after he left, Moiraine leaned back in her chair, looking into the fire. She thought of Nynaeve and cracks in a wall. Without trying, without thinking what she was doing, that young woman had put cracks in Lan's walls and seeded the cracks with creepers. Lan thought he was secure, imprisoned in his fortress by fate and his own wishes, but slowly, patiently, the creepers were tearing down the walls to bare the man within. Already he was sharing some of Nynaeve's loyalties; in the beginning he had been indifferent to the Emond's Field folk, except as people in whom Moiraine had some interest. Nynaeve had changed that as she had changed Lan.

To her surprise, Moiraine felt a flash of jealousy. She had never felt that before, certainly not for any of the women who had thrown their hearts at his feet, or those who had shared his bed. Indeed, she had never thought of him as an object of jealousy, had never thought so of any man. She was married to her battle, as he was married to his. But they had been companions in those battles for so long. He had ridden a horse to death, then run himself nearly to death, carrying her in his arms at the last, to Anaiya for Healing. She had tended his wounds more than once, keeping with her arts a life he had been ready to throw away to save hers. He had always said he was wedded with death. Now a new bride had captured his eyes, though he was blind to it. He thought he still stood strong behind his walls, but Nynaeve had laced bridal flowers in his hair. Would he still find himself able to court death so blithely? Moiraine wondered when he would ask her to release him from his bond. And what she would do when he did.

With a grimace, she got to her feet. There were more important matters. Far more important. Her eyes ran over the open books and papers crowding the room. So many hints, but no answers.

Vandene came in with a teapot and cups on a tray. She was slender and graceful, with a straight back, and the hair gathered neatly at the nape of her neck was almost white. The agelessness of her smooth face was that of long, long years. "I would have had Jaem bring this, and not disturb you myself, but he's out in the barn practicing with his sword." She made a clucking sound as she pushed a battered manuscript aside to set the tray on the table. "Lan being here has him remembering he's more than a gardener and handyman. Gaidin are so stiff-necked. I thought Lan would still be here; that's why I brought an extra cup. Have you found what you were seeking?"

"I am not even sure what it is I am seeking." Moiraine frowned, studying the other woman. Vandene was of the Green Ajah, not Brown like her sister, yet the two of them had studied so long together that she knew as much of history as Adeleas.

"Whatever it is, you don't even seem to know where to look." Vandene shifted some of the books and manuscripts on the table, shaking her head. "So many subjects. The Trolloc Wars. The Watchers Over the Waves. The legend of the Return. Two treatises on the Horn of Valere. Three on dark prophecy, and— Light, here's Santhra's book on the Forsaken. Nasty, that. As nasty as this on Shadar Logoth. And the Prophecies of the Dragon, in three translations *and* the original. Moiraine, whatever *are* you after? The Prophecies, I can understand—we hear some news here, remote as we are. We hear some of what's happening in Illian. There's even a rumor in the village that someone has already found the Horn." She gestured with a manuscript on the Horn, and coughed in the dust that rose from it. "I discount that, of course. There would be rumors. But what—? No. You said you wanted privacy, and I'll give it to you."

"Stop a moment," Moiraine said, halting the other Aes Sedai short of the door. "Perhaps you can answer some questions for me."

"I will try." Vandene smiled suddenly. "Adeleas claims I should have chosen Brown. Ask." She poured two cups of tea and handed one to Moiraine, then took a chair by the fire.

Steam curled over the cups while Moiraine chose her questions carefully. *To find the answers, and not reveal too much.* "The Horn of Valere is not mentioned in the Prophecies, but is it linked to the Dragon anywhere?"

"No. Except for the fact that the Horn must be found before Tarmon Gai'don and that the Dragon Reborn is supposed to fight the Last Battle, there is no link between them at all." The white-haired woman sipped her tea and waited.

"Does anything link the Dragon with Toman Head?"

Vandene hesitated. "Yes, and no. This is a bone between Adeleas and me." Her voice took on a lecturing tone, and for a time she did sound like a Brown. "There is a verse in the original that translates literally as 'Five ride forth, and four return. Above the watchers shall he proclaim himself, bannered cross the sky in fire. . . .' Well, it goes on. The point is, the word *ma'vron.* I say it should be translated not simply as 'watchers,' which is *a'vron. Ma'vron* has more importance to it. I say it means the Watchers Over the Waves, though they call themselves *Do Miere A'vron,* of course, not *Ma'vron.* Adeleas tells me I am quibbling. But I believe it means the Dragon Reborn will appear somewhere above Toman Head, in Arad Doman, or Saldaea. Adeleas may think I'm foolish, but I listen to every scrap I hear coming from Saldaea these days. Mazrim Taim can channel, so I hear, and our sisters haven't managed to corner him yet. If the Dragon is Reborn, and the Horn of Valere found, then the Last Battle is coming soon. We may never finish our history." She gave a shiver, then abruptly laughed. "Odd thing to worry about. I suppose I *am* becoming more a Brown. Horrible thing to contemplate. Ask your next question."

"I do not think you need worry about Taim," Moiraine said absently. It was a link with Toman Head, however small and tenuous. "He will be dealt with as Logain was. What of Shadar Logoth?"

"Shadar Logoth!" Vandene snorted. "In brief, the city was destroyed by its own hate, every living thing except Mordeth, the councilor who began it all, using the tactics of the Darkfriends against the Darkfriends, and he now lies trapped there waiting for a soul to steal. It is not safe to enter, and nothing in the city is safe to touch. But every novice close to being Accepted knows as much as that. In full, you will have to stay here a month and listen to Adeleas lecture—she has the true knowledge of it—but even I can tell you there's nothing of the Dragon in it. That place was dead a hundred years before Yurian Stonebow rose from the ashes of the Trolloc Wars, and he lies closest to it in history of all the false Dragons."

Moiraine raised a hand. "I did not speak clearly, and I do not speak of the Dragon, now, Reborn or false. Can you think of any reason why a Fade would take something that had come from Shadar Logoth?"

"Not if it knew the thing for what it was. The hate that killed Shadar Logoth was hate they thought to use *against* the Dark One; it would destroy Shadow spawn as surely as it would those who walk in the Light. They rightly fear Shadar Logoth as much as we."

"And what can you tell me of the Forsaken?"

"You do leap from subject to subject. I can tell you little more than you learned as a novice. No one knows much more of the Nameless than that. Do you expect me to ramble on with what we both learned as girls?"

For an instant, Moiraine was silent. She did not want to say too much, but Vandene and Adeleas had more knowledge at their fingertips than existed anywhere else but the White Tower, and more complications awaited her there than she cared to deal with now. She let the name slip between her lips as if it were escaping. "Lanfear."

"For once," the other woman sighed, "I know not a whit more than I did as a novice. The Daughter of the Night remains as much a mystery as if she truly had cloaked herself in darkness." She paused, peering into her cup, and when she looked up, her eyes were sharp on Moiraine's face. "Lanfear was linked to the Dragon, to Lews Therin Telamon. Moiraine, do you have some clue as to where the Dragon will be Reborn? Or was Reborn? Has he come already?"

"If I did," Moiraine replied levelly, "would I be here, instead of in the White Tower? The Amyrlin knows as much as I, that I swear. Have you received a summons from her?"

"No, and I suppose we would. When the time comes that we must face the Dragon Reborn, the Amyrlin will need every sister, every Accepted, every novice who can light a candle unguided." Vandene's voice lowered, musing. "With such power as he will wield, we must overwhelm him before he has a chance to use it against us, before he can go mad and destroy the world. Yet first we must let him face the Dark One." She laughed mirthlessly at the look on Moiraine's face. "I am not a Red. I've studied the Prophecies enough to know we dare not gentle him first. If we *can* gentle him. I know as well as you, as well as any sister who cares to find out, that the seals holding the Dark One in Shayol Ghul are weakening. The Illianers call the Great Hunt of the Horn. False Dragons abound. And two of them, Logain and now this fellow in Saldaea, able to channel. When was the last time the Reds found two men channeling in less than a year? When did they last find one in five years? Not in my lifetime, and I am a good deal older than you. The signs are everywhere. Tarmon Gai'don is coming. The Dark One will break free. And the Dragon will be Reborn." Her cup rattled as she set it down. "I suppose that is why I feared you might have seen some sign of him."

"He will come," Moiraine said smoothly, "and we will do what must be done."

"If I thought it would do any good, I'd pull Adeleas's nose out of her book and set off for the White Tower. But I find I am glad to be here where I am instead. Perhaps we will have time to finish our history."

"I hope that you will, Sister."

Vandene rose to her feet. "Well, I have tasks to be about before bed. If you have no more questions, I will leave you to your studies." But she paused and revealed that however long she had spent with books, she was still of the Green Ajah. "You should do something about Lan, Moiraine. The man is rumbling inside worse than Dragonmount. Sooner or later, he will erupt. I've known enough men to see when one is troubled with a woman. You two have been together a long time. Perhaps he has finally come to see you are a woman as well as Aes Sedai."

"Lan sees me as what I am, Vandene. Aes Sedai. And still as a friend, I hope."

"You Blues. Always so ready to save the world that you lose yourselves."

After the white-haired Aes Sedai left, Moiraine gathered her cloak and, muttering to herself, went into the garden. There was something in what Vandene had said that tugged at her mind, but she could not remember what it was. An answer, or a hint to an answer, for a question she had not asked—but she could not bring the question to mind, either.

The garden was small, like the house, but neat even in moonlight aided by the yellow glow from the cottage windows, with sandy walks between careful beds of flowers. She settled her cloak loosely on her shoulders against the soft coolness of the night. *What was the answer, and what was the question?*

Sand crunched behind her, and she turned, thinking it was Lan.

A shadow loomed dimly only a few paces from her, a shadow that appeared to be a too-tall man wrapped in his cloak. But the face caught the moon, gaunt-cheeked, pale, with black eyes too big above a puckered, red-lipped mouth. The cloak opened, unfolding into great wings like a bat's.

Knowing it was too late, she opened herself to *saidar,* but the Draghkar began to croon, and its soft hum filled her, fragmenting her will. *Saidar* slipped away. She felt only a vague sadness as she stepped toward the creature; the deep crooning that drew her closer suppressed feeling. White, white hands—like a man's hands, but tipped with claws—reached for her, and lips the color of blood curved in a travesty of a smile, baring sharp teeth, but dimly, so dimly, she knew it would not bite or tear. Fear the Draghkar's kiss. Once those lips touched her, she would be as good as dead, to be drained of soul, then of life. Whoever found her, even if they came as the Draghkar let her fall, would find a corpse without a mark and cold as if dead two days. And if they came before she was dead, what they found would be worse, and not really her at all any longer. The croon pulled her within reach of those pale hands, and the Draghkar's head bent slowly toward her.

She felt only the smallest surprise when a sword blade flashed over her shoulder to pierce the Draghkar's breast, and little more when a second crossed her other shoulder to strike beside the first.

Dazed, swaying, she watched as if from a great distance as the creature was pushed back, away from her. Lan came into her view, then Jaem, the gray-haired Warder's bony arms holding his blade as straight and true as the younger man's. The Draghkar's pale hands bloodied as they tore at the sharp steel, wings buffeting the two men with thunderclaps. Suddenly, wounded and bleeding, it began to croon again. To the Warders.

With an effort, Moiraine gathered herself; she felt almost as drained as if the thing had managed its kiss. *No time to be weak.* In an instant she opened herself to *saidar* and, as the Power filled her, steeled herself to touch the Shadow spawn directly. The two men were too close; anything else would harm them, as well. Even using the One Power, she knew she would feel soiled by the Draghkar.

But even as she began, Lan cried out, "Embrace death!" Jaem echoed him firmly. "Embrace death!" And the two men stepped within reach of the Draghkar's touch, drove home their blades to the hilt.

Throwing back its head, the Draghkar bellowed, a shriek that seemed to pierce Moiraine's head with needles. Even wrapped in *saidar* she could feel it. Like a tree falling, the Draghkar toppled, one wing knocking Jaem to his knees. Lan sagged as if exhausted.

Lanterns hurried from the house, borne by Vandene and Adeleas.

"What was that noise?" Adeleas demanded. She was almost a mirror image of her sister. "Has Jaem gone and. . . ." The lantern light fell on the Draghkar; her voice trailed off.

Vandene took Moiraine's hands. "It did not. . . ?" She left the question unfinished as, to Moiraine's eyes, a nimbus surrounded her. Feeling strength flowing into her from the other woman, Moiraine wished, not for the first time, that Aes Sedai could do as much for themselves as they could for others.

"It did not," she said gratefully. "See to the Gaidin."

Lan looked at her, mouth tight. "If you had not made me so angry I had to go work forms with Jaem, so angry I gave it up to come back to the house. . . ."

"But I did," she said. "The Pattern takes everything into the weaving." Jaem was muttering, but still allowing Vandene to see to his shoulder. He was all bone and tendon, yet looked as hard as old roots.

"How," Adeleas demanded, "could any creature of the Shadow come so close without us sensing it?"

"It was warded," Moiraine said.

"Impossible," Adeleas snapped. "Only a sister could—" She stopped, and Vandene turned from Jaem to look at Moiraine.

Moiraine said the words none of them wanted to hear. "The Black Ajah." Shouts drifted from the village. "Best you hide this"—she gestured to the Draghkar, sprawled across a flower bed—"quickly. They will be coming to ask if you need help, but seeing this will start talk you will not like."

"Yes, of course," Adeleas said. "Jaem, go and meet them. Tell them you don't know what made the noise, but all is well here. Slow them down." The gray-haired Warder hurried into the night toward the sound of approaching villagers. Adeleas turned to study the Draghkar as if it were a puzzling passage in one of her books. "Whether Aes Sedai are involved or not, whatever could have brought it here?" Vandene regarded Moiraine silently.

"I fear I must leave you," Moiraine said. "Lan, will you ready the horses?" As he left, she said, "I will leave letters with you to be sent on to the White Tower, if you will arrange it." Adeleas nodded absently, her attention still on the thing on the ground.

"And will you find your answers where you are going?" Vandene asked.

"I may already have found one I did not know I sought. I only hope I am not too late. I will need pen and parchment." She drew Vandene toward the house, leaving Adeleas to deal with the Draghkar.

# CHAPTER 23

## The Testing

Nynaeve warily eyed the huge chamber, far beneath the White Tower, and eyed Sheriam, at her side, just as warily. The Mistress of Novices seemed expectant, perhaps even a little impatient. In her few days in Tar Valon, Nynaeve had seen only serenity in the Aes Sedai, and a smiling acceptance of events coming in their own time.

The domed room had been carved out of the bedrock of the island; the light of lamps on tall stands reflected from pale, smooth stone walls. Centered under the dome was a thing made of three rounded, silver arches, each just tall enough to walk under, sitting on a thick silver ring with their ends touching each other. Arches and ring were all of one piece. She could not see what lay inside; there the light flickered oddly, and made her stomach flutter with it if she looked too long. Where arch touched ring, an Aes Sedai sat cross-legged on the bare stone of the floor, staring at the silvery construction. Another stood nearby, beside a plain table on which sat three large silver chalices. Each, Nynaeve knew—or at least, she had been told—was filled with clear water. All four Aes Sedai wore their shawls, as Sheriam did; blue-fringed for Sheriam, red for the swarthy woman by the table, green, white, and gray for the three around the arches. Nynaeve still wore one of the dresses she had been given in Fal Dara, pale green embroidered with small white flowers.

"First you leave me to stare at my thumbs from morning to night," Nynaeve muttered, "and now it's all in a rush."

"The hour waits on no woman," Sheriam replied. "The Wheel weaves as the Wheel wills, and *when* it wills. Patience is a virtue that must be learned, but we must all be ready for the change of an instant."

Nynaeve tried not to glare. The most irritating thing she had yet discovered about the flame-haired Aes Sedai was that she sometimes sounded as if she were quoting sayings even when she was not. "What is that thing?"

"A *ter'angreal*."

"Well, that tells me nothing. What does it do?"

"*Ter'angreal* do many things, child. Like *angreal* and *sa'angreal,* they are remnants of the Age of Legends that use the One Power, though they are not quite so rare as the other two. While some *ter'angreal* must be made to work by Aes Sedai, as this one must, others will do what they do simply with the presence of any woman who can channel. There are even supposed to be some that will function for anyone at all. Unlike *angreal* and *sa'angreal,* they were made to do specific things. One other we have in the Tower makes oaths binding. When you are raised to full sisterhood, you will take your final vows holding that *ter'angreal.* To speak no word that is not true. To make no weapon for one man to kill another. Never to use the One Power as a weapon except against Darkfriends or Shadow spawn, or in the last extreme of defending your own life, that of your Warder, or that of another sister."

Nynaeve shook her head. It sounded either like too much to swear or too little, and she said so.

"Once, Aes Sedai were not required to swear oaths. It was known what Aes Sedai were and what they stood for, and there was no need for more. Many of us wish it were so still. But the Wheel turns, and the times change. That we swear these oaths, that we are known to be bound, allows the nations to deal with us without fearing that we will throw up our own power, the One Power, against them. Between the Trolloc Wars and the War of the Hundred Years we made these choices, and because of them the White Tower still stands, and we can still do what we can against the Shadow." Sheriam drew a deep breath. "Light, child, I am trying to teach you what any other woman standing where you are would have learned over the course of years. It cannot be done. *Ter'angreal* are what must concern you, now. We don't know why they were made. We dare use only a handful of them, and the ways in which we do dare to use them may be nothing like the purposes the makers intended. Most, we have learned to our cost to

avoid. Over the years, no few Aes Sedai have been killed or had their Talent
burned out of them, learning that."

Nynaeve shivered. "And you want me to walk into this one?" The light
inside the arches flickered less, now, but she could see what lay in it no
better.

"We know what this one does. It will bring you face-to-face with your
greatest fears." Sheriam smiled pleasantly. "No one will ask you what you
have faced; you need tell no more than you wish. Every woman's fears are
her own property."

Vaguely, Nynaeve thought about her nervousness concerning spiders, especially in the dark, but she did not think that was what Sheriam meant.
"I just walk through one arch and out another? Three times through, and
it's done?"

The Aes Sedai adjusted her shawl with an irritated hitch of her shoulder.
"If you wish to boil it down that far, yes," she said dryly. "I told you on
the way here what you must know about the ceremony, as much as anyone
is allowed to know beforehand. If you were a novice come to this, you
would know it by heart, but don't worry about making mistakes. I will
remind you, if necessary. Are you sure you are ready to face it? If you want
to stop now, I can still write your name in the novice book."

"No!"

"Very well, then. Two things I will tell you now that no woman hears
until she is in this room. The first is this. Once you begin, you must
continue to the end. Refuse to go on, and no matter your potential, you
will be very kindly put out of the Tower with enough silver to support you
for a year, and you will never be allowed back." Nynaeve opened her
mouth to say she would not refuse, but Sheriam cut her off with a sharp
gesture. "Listen, and speak when you know what to say. Second. To seek,
to strive, is to know danger. You will know danger here. Some women
have entered, and never come out. When the *ter'angreal* was allowed to
grow quiet, they—were—not—there. And they were never seen again. If
you will survive, you must be steadfast. Falter, fail, and. . . ." Her silence
was more eloquent than any words. "This is your last chance, child. You
may turn back now, right now, and I will put your name in the novice
book, and you will have only one mark against you. Twice more you will
be allowed to come here, and only at the third refusal will you be put out
of the Tower. It is no shame to refuse. Many do. I myself could not do it,
my first time here. Now you may speak."

Nynaeve gave the silver arches a sidelong look. The light in them no
longer flickered; they were filled with a soft, white glow. To learn what she

wanted to learn, she needed the freedom of the Accepted to question, to study on her own, with no more guidance than she asked for. *I must make Moiraine pay for what she has done to us. I must.* "I am ready."

Sheriam started slowly into the chamber. Nynaeve went beside her.

As if that were a signal, the Red sister spoke in loud, formal tones. "Whom do you bring with you, Sister?" The three Aes Sedai around the *ter'angreal* continued their attentions to it.

"One who comes as a candidate for Acceptance, Sister," Sheriam replied just as formally.

"Is she ready?"

"She is ready to leave behind what she was, and, passing through her fears, gain Acceptance."

"Does she know her fears?"

"She has never faced them, but now is willing."

"Then let her face what she fears."

Sheriam stopped, two spans from the arches, and Nynaeve stopped with her. "Your dress," Sheriam whispered, not looking at her.

Nynaeve's cheeks colored at forgetting already what Sheriam had told her on the way down from her room. Hastily she removed her clothes, her shoes and stockings. For a moment she could almost forget the arches in folding her garments and putting them neatly to one side. She tucked Lan's ring carefully under her dress; she did not want anyone staring at that. Then she was done, and the *ter'angreal* was still there, still waiting.

The stone felt cold under her bare feet, and she broke out all over in goose bumps, but she stood straight and breathed slowly. She would not let any of them see she was afraid.

"The first time," Sheriam said, "is for what was. The way back will come but once. Be steadfast."

Nynaeve hesitated. Then she stepped forward, through the arch and into the glow. It surrounded her, as if the air itself were shining, as if she were drowning in light. The light was everywhere. The light was everything.

Nynaeve gave a start when she realized she was naked, then stared in amazement. A stone wall stood to either side of her, twice as tall as she was and smooth, as if carved. Her toes wriggled on dusty, uneven stone paving. The sky above seemed flat and leaden, for all the lack of clouds, and the sun hung overhead swollen and red. In both directions were openings in the wall, gateways marked by short, square columns. The walls narrowed her field of view, but the ground sloped down from where she stood, both in front and behind. Through the gateways she could see more thick walls, and passages between. She was in a gigantic maze.

*Where is this? How did I come here?* Like a different voice, another thought came. *The way out will come but once.*

She shook her head. "If there's only one way out, I'll not find it standing here." At least the air was warm and dry. "I hope I find some clothes before I find people," she muttered.

Dimly, she remembered playing mazes on paper as a child; there had been a trick to finding your way out, but she could not bring it to mind. Everything in the past seemed vague, as if it had happened to someone else. Trailing a hand along the wall, she started out, dust rising in puffs beneath her bare feet.

At the first opening in the wall, she found herself peering down another passage that seemed indistinguishable from the one she was in already. Taking a deep breath, she went on straight, through more passages that all looked exactly alike. Presently she came to something different. The way forked. She took the left turning, and eventually it forked again. Once more she went left. At the third fork, left brought her to a blank wall.

Grimly she walked back to the last fork and went right. This time it took four turnings right to bring her to a dead end. For a moment, she stood glaring at it. "How did I get here?" she demanded loudly. "Where is this place?" *The way out will come but once.*

Once more she turned back. She was sure there had to be a trick to the maze. At the last fork, she went left, then right at the next. Determined, she kept on. Left, then right. Straight until she came to a fork. Left, then right.

It seemed to her to be working. At least, she had gone past a dozen forkings this time without finding an end. She came to another.

Out of the corner of her eye, she caught a flicker of motion. When she turned to look, there was only the dusty passage between smooth stone walls. She started to take the left fork . . . and spun around at another glimpse of movement. There was nothing there, but this time she was sure. There had been someone behind her. Was someone. She broke into a nervous trot in the opposite direction.

Again and again, now, just at the edge of vision down this side passage or that, she saw something move, too quick to make out, gone before she could turn her head to see it plainly. She broke into a run. Few boys had been able to outrun her when she was a girl in the Two Rivers. *The Two Rivers? What is that?*

A man stepped out from an opening ahead of her. His dark clothes had a musty, half-rotted look, and he was old. Older than old. Skin like crazed parchment covered his skull too tightly, as if there were no flesh beneath.

Wispy tufts of brittle hair covered a scabbed scalp, and his eyes were so sunken they seemed to peer out of two caves.

She skidded to a stop, the uneven paving stones rough under her feet.

"I am Aginor," he said, smiling, "and I have come for you."

Her heart tried to leap out of her chest. One of the Forsaken. "No. No, it cannot be!"

"You are a pretty one, girl. I will enjoy you."

Suddenly Nynaeve remembered she wore not a stitch. With a yelp and a face red only partly from anger, she darted away down the nearest crossing passage. Cackling laughter pursued her, and the sound of a shuffling run that seemed to match her best speed, and breathy promises of what he would do when he caught her, promises that curdled her stomach even only half heard.

Desperately she searched for a way out, peering frantically as she ran with fists clenched. *The way out will come but once. Be steadfast.* There was nothing, only more of the endless maze. As hard as she could run, his filthy words came always right behind her. Slowly, fear turned completely to anger.

"Burn him!" she sobbed. "The Light burn him! He has no right!" Within her she felt a flowering, an opening up, an unfolding to light.

Teeth bared, she turned to face her pursuer just as Aginor appeared, laughing, in a lurching gallop.

"You have no right!" She flung her fist toward him, fingers opening as if she were throwing something. She was only half surprised to see a ball of fire leave her hand.

It exploded against Aginor's chest, knocking him to the ground. For only an instant he sprawled there, then rose, staggering. He seemed unaware of the smoldering front of his coat. "You dare? You dare!" He quivered, and spittle leaked down his chin.

Abruptly there were clouds in the sky, threatening billows of gray and black. Lightning leaped from the cloud, straight for Nynaeve's heart.

It seemed to her, just for a heartbeat, as if time had suddenly slowed, as though that heartbeat took forever. She felt the flow inside her—*saidar,* came a distant thought—felt the answering flow in the lightning. And she altered the direction of the flow. Time leaped forward.

With a crash, the bolt shattered stone above Aginor's head. The Forsaken's sunken eyes widened, and he tottered back. "You cannot! It cannot be!" He leaped away as lightning struck where he had stood, stone erupting in a fountain of shards.

Grimly Nynaeve started toward him. And Aginor fled.

*Saidar* was a torrent racing through her. She could feel the rocks around her, and the air, feel the tiny, flowing bits of the One Power that suffused them, and made them. And she could feel Aginor doing . . . something, as well. Dimly she felt it, and far distant, as if it were something she could never truly know, but around her she saw the effects and knew them for what they were.

The ground rumbled and heaved under her feet. Walls toppled in front of her, piles of stone to block her way. She scrambled over them, uncaring if sharp rock cut hands and feet, always keeping Aginor in sight. A wind rose, howling down the passages against her, raging till it flattened her cheeks and made her eyes water, trying to knock her down; she changed the flow, and Aginor tumbled along the passageway like an uprooted bush. She touched the flow in the ground, redirected it, and stone walls collapsed around Aginor, sealing him in. Lightning fell with her glare, striking around him, stone exploding ever closer and closer. She could feel him fighting to push it back at her, but foot by foot the dazzling bolts moved toward the Forsaken.

Something gleamed off to her right, something uncovered by the collapsing walls.

Nynaeve could feel Aginor weakening, feel his efforts to strike at her grow more feeble and more frantic. Yet somehow she knew he had not given up. If she let him go now, he would chase after her as strongly as before, convinced she was too weak to defeat him after all, too weak to stop him from doing with her as he wished.

A silver arch stood where stone had been, an arch filled with soft silver radiance. *The way back. . . .*

She knew when the Forsaken abandoned his attack, the moment when all his efforts were given over to staving her off. And his power was not enough, he could no longer deflect her blows. Now he had to fling himself away from the leaping gouts of stone thrown up by her lightning, the explosions flinging him down again.

*The way back will come but once. Be steadfast.*

The lightning no longer fell. Nynaeve turned from the scrabbling Aginor to look at the arch. She looked back at Aginor, just in time to see him crawl out of sight over the mounded stone and disappear. She hissed in frustration. Much of the maze still stood, and a hundred new places to hide in the rubble she and the Forsaken had made. It would take time to find him again, but she was sure if she did not find him first, he would find her. In his full strength, he would come on her when she least expected him.

*The way back will come but once.*

Frightened, she looked again and was relieved to see the arch still there. If she could find Aginor quickly. . . .

*Be steadfast.*

With a cry of thwarted anger, she climbed over the tumbled stone toward the arch. "Whoever's responsible for me being here," she muttered, "I'll make them wish they had gotten what Aginor got. I'll—" She stepped into the arch, and the light overwhelmed her.

"I'll—" Nynaeve stepped out of the arch and stopped to stare. It was all as she remembered—the silver *ter'angreal,* the Aes Sedai, the chamber—but remembering was like a blow, absent memories crashing back into her head. She had come out of the same arch by which she went in.

The Red sister raised one of the silver chalices high and poured a stream of cool, clear water over Nynaeve's head. "You are washed clean of what sin you may have done," the Aes Sedai intoned, "and of those done against you. You are washed clean of what crime you may have committed, and of those committed against you. You come to us washed clean and pure, in heart and soul."

Nynaeve shivered as the water ran down her body, dripping on the floor.

Sheriam took her arm with a relieved smile, but the Mistress of Novices' voice gave no hint of past worry. "You do well so far. Coming back is doing well. Remember what your purpose is, and you will continue to be well." The redhead began to lead her around the *ter'angreal* to another arch.

"It was so real," Nynaeve said in a whisper. She could remember everything, remember channeling the One Power as easily as lifting her hand. She could remember Aginor, and the things the Forsaken wanted to do to her. She shivered again. "Was it real?"

"No one knows," Sheriam replied. "It seems real in memory, and some have come out bearing the actual wounds of hurts taken inside. Others have been cut to the bone inside, and come back without a mark. It is all of it different every time for every woman who goes in. The ancients said there were many worlds. Perhaps this *ter'angreal* takes you to them. Yet if so, it does so under very stringent rules for something meant just to take you from one place to another. I believe it is not real. But remember, whether what happens is real or not, the *danger* is as real as a knife plunging into your heart."

"I channeled the Power. It was so easy."

Sheriam missed a step. "That isn't supposed to be possible. You should not even remember being able to channel." She studied Nynaeve. "And yet you are not harmed. I can still sense the ability in you, as strong as it ever was."

"You sound as if it were dangerous," Nynaeve said slowly, and Sheriam hesitated before answering.

"It isn't thought necessary to give a warning, since you shouldn't be able to remember it, but. . . . This *ter'angreal* was found during the Trolloc Wars. We have the records of its examination in the archives. The first sister to enter was warded as strongly as she could be, since no one knew what it would do. She kept her memories, and she channeled the One Power when she was threatened. And she came out with her abilities burned to nothing, unable to channel, unable even to sense the True Source. The second to go in was also warded, and she, too, was destroyed in the same way. The third went unprotected, remembered nothing once she was inside, and returned unharmed. That is one reason why we send you completely unprotected. Nynaeve, you must not channel inside the *ter'angreal* again. I know it is hard to remember anything, but try."

Nynaeve swallowed. She could remember everything, could remember not remembering. "I won't channel," she said. *If I can remember not to.* She wanted to laugh hysterically.

They had reached the next arch. The glow still filled them all. Sheriam gave Nynaeve a last warning look, and left her standing alone.

"The second time is for what is. The way back will come but once. Be steadfast."

Nynaeve stared at the shining silver arch. *What is in there this time?* The others were waiting, watching. She stepped firmly through into the light.

Nynaeve stared down at the plain brown dress she wore with surprise, then gave a start. Why was she staring at her own dress? *The way back will come but once.*

Looking around her, she smiled. She stood on the edge of the Green in Emond's Field, with thatch-roofed houses all around, and the Winespring Inn right in front of her. The Winespring itself rose in a gush from the stone outcrop thrusting up through the grass of the Green, and the Winespring Water rushed off east under the willows beside the inn. The streets were empty, but most people would be at their chores this time of the morning.

Looking at the inn, her smile faded. There was more than an air of neglect about it, whitewash faded, a shutter hanging loose, the rotted end of a rafter showing at a gap in the roof tiles. *What's gotten into Bran? Is he spending so much time being Mayor he's forgetting to take care of his inn?*

The inn door swung open, and Cenn Buie came out, stopping dead when he saw her. The old thatcher was as gnarled as an oak root, and the look he gave her was just as friendly. "So you've come back, have you? Well, you might as well be off again."

She frowned as he spat at her feet and hurried on past her; Cenn was never a pleasant man, but he was seldom openly rude. Never to her, at least. Never to her face. Following him with her eye, she saw signs of neglect all through the village, thatch that should have been mended, weeds filling yards. The door on Mistress al'Caar's house hung aslant on a broken hinge.

Shaking her head, Nynaeve pushed into the inn. *I'll have more than one word with Bran about this.*

The common room was empty except for a lone woman, her thick, graying braid pulled over her shoulder. She was wiping a table, but from the way she stared at the tabletop, Nynaeve did not think she was aware of what she was doing. The room seemed dusty.

"Marin?"

Marin al'Vere jumped, one hand clutching her throat, and stared. She looked years older than Nynaeve remembered. Worn. "Nynaeve? Nynaeve! Oh, it is you. Egwene? Have you brought Egwene back? Say you have."

"I. . . ." Nynaeve put a hand to her head. *Where is Egwene?* It seemed she *should* be able to remember. "No. No, I haven't brought her back." *The way back will come but once.*

Mistress al'Vere sagged into one of the straight-backed chairs. "I was so hoping. Ever since Bran died. . . ."

"Bran is dead?" Nynaeve could not imagine it; that broad, smiling man had always seemed as if he would go on forever. "I should have been here."

The other woman jumped to her feet and hurried to peer anxiously through a window at the Green and the village. "If Malena knows you're here, there will be trouble. I just know Cenn went scurrying off to find her. He's the Mayor, now."

"Cenn? How did even those wool-headed men choose Cenn?"

"It was Malena. She had the whole Women's Circle after their husbands for him." Marin pressed her face almost against the window, trying to look every way at once. "Silly men don't talk about whose name they're putting in the box beforehand; I suppose every man who voted for Cenn thought he was the only one whose wife had badgered him into it. Thought one vote would make no difference. Well, they learned better. We all did."

"Who is this Malena who has the Women's Circle doing her bidding? I've never heard of her."

"She's from Watch Hill. She's the Wis. . . ." Marin turned from the window wringing her hands. "Malena Aylar's the Wisdom, Nynaeve. When you didn't come back. . . . Light, I hope she doesn't find out you're here."

Nynaeve shook her head in wonder. "Marin, you're afraid of her. You are shaking. What kind of woman is she? Why did the Women's Circle ever choose someone like her?"

Mistress al'Vere gave a bitter laugh. "We must have been mad. Malena came down to see Mavra Mallen the day before Mavra had to go back to Deven Ride, and that night some children took sick, and Malena stayed to look after them, and then the sheep started dying, and Malena took care of that, too. It just seemed natural to choose her, but. . . . She's a bully, Nynaeve. She browbeats you into doing what she wants. She keeps at you, and keeps at you, until you're too tired to say no anymore. And worse. She knocked Alsbet Luhhan down."

A picture flashed in Nynaeve's head of Alsbet Luhhan and her husband, Haral, the blacksmith. She was nearly as tall as him, and stoutly built, though handsome. "Alsbet's almost as strong as Haral. I can't believe. . . ."

"Malena's not a big woman, but she's—she's fierce, Nynaeve. She beat Alsbet all around the Green with a stick, and none of us who saw had the nerve to try to stop it. When they found out, Bran and Haral said she had to go, even if they were interfering in Women's Circle business. I think some of the Circle might have listened, but Bran and Haral both took sick the same night, and died within a day of each other." Marin bit her lip and looked around the room as if she thought someone might be hiding there. Her voice lowered. "Malena mixed medicine for them. She said it was her duty even if they had spoken against her. I saw. . . . I saw gray fennel in what she took away with her."

Nynaeve gasped. "But. . . . Are you sure, Marin? Are you certain?" The other woman nodded, her face wrinkling on the point of tears. "Marin, if you even suspected this woman might have poisoned Bran, how could you not go to the Circle?"

"She said Bran and Haral didn't walk in the Light," Marin mumbled, "talking against the Wisdom the way they did. She said that was why they died; the Light abandoned them. She talks about sin all the time. She said Paet al'Caar sinned, talking against her after Bran and Haral died. All he said was she didn't have the way with Healing you did, but she drew the Dragon's Fang on his door, right out where everyone could see her with the charcoal in her hand. Both his boys were dead before the week was out— just dead when their mother went to wake them. Poor Nela. We found her wandering, laughing and crying all at the same time, screaming that Paet was the Dark One, and he'd killed her boys. Paet hung himself the next day." She shuddered, and her voice went so soft Nynaeve could barely hear it. "I have four daughters still living under my roof. Living, Nynaeve. Do you understand what I'm saying. They're still alive, and I want to keep them alive."

Nynaeve felt cold to her bones. "Marin, you can't allow this." *The way back will come but once. Be steadfast.* She pushed it away. "If the Women's Circle stands together, you can be rid of her."

"Stand together against Malena?" Marin's laugh was nearer a sob. "We're all afraid of her. But she's good with the children. There are always children sick these days, it seems, but Malena does the best she can. Almost no one ever died of sickness when you were Wisdom."

"Marin, listen to me. Don't you see why there are always children sick? If she can't make you afraid of her, she makes you think you need her for the children. She's doing it, Marin. Just as she did it to Bran."

"She couldn't," Marin breathed. "She wouldn't. Not the little ones."

"She is, Marin." *The way back—* Nynaeve suppressed the thought ruthlessly. "Is there anyone in the Circle who isn't afraid? Anyone who will listen?"

The other woman said, "No one who isn't afraid. But Corin Ayellin might listen. If she does, she might bring two or three more. Nynaeve, if enough of the Circle listens, will you be our Wisdom again? I think you may be the only one who won't back down to Malena, even if we all know. You don't know what she's like."

"I will." *The way back— No! These are my people!* "Get your cloak, and we'll go to Corin."

Marin was hesitant about leaving the inn, and once Nynaeve had her outside she slunk along from doorstep to doorstep, crouching and watching.

Before they were halfway to Corin Ayellin's house, Nynaeve saw a tall, scrawny woman striding down the other side of the Green toward the inn, slashing the heads off weeds with a thick willow switch. Bony as she was, she had a look of wiry strength, and a set, determined slash of a mouth. Cenn Buie scuttled along in her wake.

"Malena." Marin pulled Nynaeve into the space between two houses, and whispered as if afraid the woman might hear across the Green. "I knew Cenn would go to her."

Something made Nynaeve look over her shoulder. Behind her stood a silver arch, reaching from house to house, glowing whitely. *The way back will come but once. Be steadfast.*

Marin gave a soft scream. "She's seen us. Light help us, she's coming this way!"

The tall woman had turned across the Green, leaving Cenn standing uncertainly. There was no uncertainty on Malena's face. She walked slowly, as if there were no hope of escape, a cruel smile growing with every step.

Marin tugged at Nynaeve's sleeve. "We have to run. We have to hide. Nynaeve, come on. Cenn will have told her who you are. She hates anyone even to speak of you."

The silver arch pulled Nynaeve's eyes. *The way back. . . .* She shook her head, trying to remember. *It is not real.* She looked at Marin; stark terror twisted the woman's face. *You must be steadfast to survive.*

"Please, Nynaeve. She's seen me with you. She—has—seen—me! Please, Nynaeve!"

Malena came closer, implacable. *My people.* The arch shone. *The way back. It is not real.*

With a sob, Nynaeve tore her arm out of Marin's grasp and plunged toward the silvery glow.

Marin's shriek hounded her. "For the love of the Light, Nynaeve, help me! HELP ME!"

The glow enveloped her.

Staring, Nynaeve staggered out of the arch, barely aware of the chamber or the Aes Sedai. Marin's last cry still rang in her ears. She did not flinch when cold water was suddenly poured over her head.

"You are washed clean of false pride. You are washed clean of false ambition. You come to us washed clean, in heart and soul." As the Red Aes Sedai stepped back, Sheriam came to take Nynaeve's arm.

Nynaeve gave a start, then realized who it was. She seized the collar of Sheriam's dress in both hands. "Tell me it was not real. Tell me!"

"Bad?" Sheriam pried her hands loose as if she were used to this reaction. "It is always worse, and the third is the worst of all."

"I left my friend . . . I left my *people* . . . in the Pit of Doom to come back." *Please, Light, it was not real. I didn't really. . . . I have to make Moiraine pay. I have to!*

"There is always some reason not to return, something to prevent you, or distract you. This *ter'angreal* weaves traps for you from your own mind, weaves them tight and strong, harder than steel and more deadly than poison. That is why we use it as a test. You must want to be Aes Sedai more than anything else in the whole world, enough to face anything, fight free of anything, to achieve it. The White Tower cannot accept less. We demand it of you."

"You demand a great deal." Nynaeve stared at the third arch as the red-haired Aes Sedai took her toward it. *The third is the worst.* "I'm afraid," she whispered. *What could be worse than what I just did?*

"Good," Sheriam said. "You seek to be Aes Sedai, to channel the One Power. No one should approach that without fear and awe. Fear will keep you cautious; caution will keep you alive." She turned Nynaeve to face the arch, but she did not step back immediately. "No one will force you to enter a third time, child."

Nynaeve licked her lips. "If I refuse, you'll put me out of the Tower and never let me come back." Sheriam nodded. "And this is the worst." Sheriam nodded again. Nynaeve drew breath. "I am ready."

"The third time," Sheriam intoned formally, "is for what will be. The way back will come but once. Be steadfast."

Nynaeve threw herself at the arch in a run.

Laughing, she ran through swirling clouds of butterflies rising from wildflowers that covered the hilltop meadow with a knee-deep blanket of color. Her gray mare danced nervously, reins dangling, at the edge of the meadow, and Nynaeve stopped running so as not to frighten the animal more. Some of the butterflies settled on her dress, on flowers of embroidery and seed pearls, or flittered around the sapphires and moonstones in her hair, hanging loose about her shoulders.

Below the hill, the necklace of the Thousand Lakes spread through the city of Malkier, reflecting the cloud-brushing Seven Towers, with Golden Crane banners flying at their heights in the mists. The city had a thousand gardens, but she preferred this wild garden on the hilltop. *The way back will come but once. Be steadfast.*

The sound of hooves made her turn.

Al'Lan Mandragoran, King of Malkier, leaped from the back of his charger and strolled toward her through the butterflies, laughing. His face had the look of a hard man, but the smiles he wore for her softened the stony planes.

She gaped at him, taken by surprise when he gathered her into his arms and kissed her. For a moment she clung to him, lost, kissing him back. Her feet dangled a foot in the air, and she did not care.

Suddenly she pushed at him, pulled her face back. "No." She pushed harder. "Let me go. Put me down." Puzzled, he lowered her until her feet touched ground; she backed away from him. "Not this," she said. "I cannot face this. Anything but this." *Please, let me face Aginor again.* Memory swirled. *Aginor?* She did not know where that thought had come from. Memory lurched and tilted, shifting fragments like broken ice on a flooding river. She clawed for the pieces, clawed for something to hang on to.

"Are you well, my love?" Lan asked worriedly.

"Do not call me that! I am not your love! I cannot marry you!"

He startled her by throwing back his head and roaring with laughter. "Your implication that we are not married might upset our children, wife. And how are you not my love? I have no other, and will have no other."

"I must go back." Desperately she looked for the arch, found only meadow and sky. *Harder than steel and more deadly than poison. Lan. Lan's babies. Light, help me!* "I must go back now."

"Go back? Where? To Emond's Field? If you wish it. I'll send letters to Morgase, and command an escort."

"Alone," she muttered, still searching. *Where is it? I have to go.* "I won't be tangled up in this. I couldn't bear it. Not this. I have to go *now!*"

"Tangled up in what, Nynaeve? What is it you couldn't bear? No, Nynaeve. You can ride alone here if you wish it, but if the Queen of the Malkieri came to Andor without a proper escort, Morgase would be scandalized, if not offended. You don't want to offend her, do you? I thought you two were friends."

Nynaeve felt as if she had been hit in the head, blow after dazing blow. "Queen?" she said hesitantly. "We have babies?"

"Are you certain you're well? I think I had better take you to Sharina Sedai."

"No." She backed away from him again. "No Aes Sedai." *It isn't real. I won't be pulled into it this time. I won't!*

"Very well," he said slowly. "As my wife, how could you not be Queen? We are Malkieri here, not southlanders. You were crowned in the Seven Towers at the same time we exchanged rings." Unconsciously he moved his left hand; a plain gold band encircled his forefinger. She glanced at her own hand, at the ring she knew would be there; she clasped her other hand over it, but whether to deny its presence by hiding it or to hold it, she could not have said. "Do you remember, now?" he went on. He stretched out a hand as if to brush her cheek, and she went back another six steps. He sighed. "As you wish, my love. We have three children, though only one can properly be called a baby. Maric is almost to your shoulder and can't decide if he likes horses or books better. Elnore has already begun practicing how to turn boys' heads, when she is not pestering Sharina about when she'll be old enough to go to the White Tower."

"Elnore was my mother's name," she said softly.

"So you said when you chose it. Nynaeve——"

"No. I will not be pulled into it this time. Not this. I won't!" Beyond him, among the trees beside the meadow, she saw the silver arch. The trees had hidden it before. *The way back will come but once.* She turned toward it.

"I must go." He caught her hand, and it was as if her feet had become rooted in stone; she could not make herself pull away.

"I do not know what is troubling you, wife, but whatever it is, tell me and I will make it right. I know I am not the best of husbands. I was all hard edges when I found you, but you've smoothed some of them away, at least."

"You are the very best of husbands," she murmured. To her horror, she found herself remembering him as her husband, remembering laughter and tears, bitter arguments and sweet making up. They were dim memories, but she could feel them growing stronger, warmer. "I cannot." The arch stood there, only a few steps away. *The way back will come but once. Be steadfast.*

"I do not know what is happening, Nynaeve, but I feel as if I were losing you. I could not bear that." He put a hand in her hair; closing her eyes, she pressed her cheek against his fingers. "Stay with me, always."

"I want to stay," she said softly. "I want to stay with you." When she opened her eyes, the arch was gone . . . *come but once.* "No. No!"

Lan turned her to face him. "What troubles you? You must tell me if I'm to help."

"This is not real."

"Not real? Before I met you, I thought nothing except the sword was real. Look around you, Nynaeve. It *is* real. Whatever you want to be real, we can make real together, you and I."

Wonderingly, she did look around. The meadow was still there. The Seven Towers still stood over the Thousand Lakes. The arch was gone, but nothing else had changed. *I could stay here. With Lan. Nothing has changed.* Her thoughts turned. *Nothing has changed. Egwene is alone in the White Tower. Rand will channel the Power and go mad. And what of Mat and Perrin? Can they take back any shred of their lives? And Moiraine, who tore all our lives apart, still walks free.*

"I must go back," she whispered. Unable to bear the pain on his face, she pulled free of him. Deliberately she formed a flower bud in her mind, a white bud on a blackthorn branch. She made the thorns sharp and cruel, wishing they could pierce her flesh, feeling as if she already hung in the blackthorn's branches. Sheriam Sedai's voice danced just out of hearing, telling her it was dangerous to attempt to channel the Power. The bud opened, and *saidar* filled her with light.

"Nynaeve, tell me what is the matter."

Lan's voice slid across her concentration; she refused to let herself hear it. There had to be a way back still. Staring at where the silver arch had been, she tried to find some trace of it. There was nothing.

"Nynaeve . . ."

She tried to picture the arch in her mind, to shape it and form it to the last detail, curve of gleaming metal filled with a glow like snowy fire. It seemed to waver there, in front of her, first there between her and the trees, then not, then there.

". . . I love you . . ."

She drew at *saidar,* drinking in the flow of the One Power till she thought she would burst. The radiance filling her, shining around her, hurt her own eyes. The heat seemed to consume her. The flickering arch firmed, steadied, stood whole before her. Fire and pain seemed to fill her; her bones felt as if they were burning; her skull seemed a roaring furnace.

". . . with all my heart."

She ran toward the silver curve, not letting herself look back. She had been sure the bitterest thing she would ever hear was Marin al'Vere's cry for help as Nynaeve abandoned her, but that was honey beside the sound of Lan's anguished voice pursuing her. "Nynaeve, please don't leave me."

The white glow consumed her.

Naked, Nynaeve staggered through the arch and fell to her knees, slack-mouthed and sobbing, tears streaming down her cheeks. Sheriam knelt beside her. She glared at the red-haired Aes Sedai. "I hate you!" she managed fiercely, gulping. "I hate all Aes Sedai!"

Sheriam gave a small sigh, then pulled Nynaeve to her feet. "Child, almost every woman who does this says much the same thing. It is no small thing to be made to face your fears. What is this?" she said sharply, turning Nynaeve's palms up.

Nynaeve's hands quivered with a sudden pain she had not felt before. Driven through the palm of each hand, right in the center, was a long black thorn. Sheriam drew them out carefully; Nynaeve felt the cool Healing of the Aes Sedai's touch. When each thorn came free, it left only a small scar on front and back of the hand.

Sheriam frowned. "There shouldn't be any scarring. And how did you only get two, and both placed so precisely? If you tangled yourself in a blackthorn bush, you should be covered with scratches and thorns."

"I should," Nynaeve agreed bitterly. "Maybe I thought I had already paid enough."

"There is always a price," the Aes Sedai agreed. "Come, now. You have paid the first price. Take what you have paid for." She gave Nynaeve a slight push forward.

Nynaeve realized there were more Aes Sedai in the chamber. The Amyrlin in her striped stole was there, with a shawled sister from each

Ajah ranged to either side of her, all of them watching Nynaeve. Remembering Sheriam's instruction, Nynaeve tottered forward and knelt before
the Amyrlin. It was she who held the last chalice, and she tipped it slowly
over Nynaeve's head.

"You are washed clean of Nynaeve al'Maera from Emond's Field. You are
washed clean of all ties that bind you to the world. You come to us washed
clean, in heart and soul. You are Nynaeve al'Maera, Accepted of the White
Tower." Handing the chalice to one of the sisters, the Amyrlin drew
Nynaeve to her feet. "You are sealed to us, now."

The Amyrlin's eyes seemed to hold a dark glow. Nynaeve's shiver had
nothing to do with being naked and wet.

# CHAPTER
# 24

## New Friends and Old Enemies

Egwene followed the Accepted through the halls of the White Tower. Tapestries and paintings covered walls as white as the outside of the tower; patterned tiles made the floor. The Accepted's white dress was exactly like hers, except for seven narrow bands of color at hem and cuffs. Egwene frowned, looking at that dress. Since yesterday Nynaeve had worn an Accepted's dress, and she seemed to have no joy of it, nor of the golden ring, a serpent eating its own tail, that marked her level. The few times Egwene had been able to see the Wisdom, Nynaeve's eyes had seemed shadowed, as if she had seen things she wished with all her heart not to have seen.

"In here," the Accepted said curtly, gesturing to a door. Named Pedra, she was a short, wiry woman, a little older than Nynaeve, and with a briskness always in her voice. "You're given this time because it is your first day, but I'll expect you in the scullery when the gong sounds High, and not one moment later."

Egwene curtsied, then stuck out her tongue at the Accepted's retreating back. It might have been only the evening before that Sheriam had finally put her name in the novice book, but already she knew she did not like Pedra. She pushed open the door and went in.

The room was plain and small, with white walls, and there was a young woman, with reddish gold hair spilling around her shoulders, sitting on one of two hard benches. The floor was bare; novices did not get much use of rooms with carpets. Egwene thought the girl was about her own age, but there was a dignity and self-possession about her that made her seem older. The plainly cut novice dress appeared somehow more, on her. Elegant. That was it.

"My name is Elayne," she said. She tilted her head, studying Egwene. "And you are Egwene. From Emond's Field, in the Two Rivers." She said it as if it had some significance, but went right on anyway. "Someone who has been here a little while is always assigned to a new novice for a few days, to help her find her way. Sit, please."

Egwene took the other bench, facing Elayne. "I thought the Aes Sedai would teach me, now that I'm finally a novice. But all that's happened so far is that Pedra woke me a good two hours before first light and put me to sweeping the halls. She says I have to help wash dishes after dinner, too."

Elayne grimaced. "I hate washing dishes. I never had to—well, that doesn't matter. You will have training. From now on, you will be at training at this hour every day, as a matter of fact. From breakfast until High, then again from dinner to Trine. If you are especially quick or especially slow, they may take you from supper to Full, as well, but that is usually for more chores." Elayne's blue eyes took on a thoughtful expression. "You were born with it, weren't you?" Egwene nodded. "Yes, I thought I felt it. So was I, born with it. Do not be disappointed if you did not know. You will learn to feel the ability in other women. I had the advantage of growing up around an Aes Sedai."

Egwene wanted to ask about that—*Who grows up with Aes Sedai?*—but Elayne went on.

"And also do not be disappointed if it takes you some time before you can achieve anything. With the One Power, I mean. Even the simplest thing takes a little time. Patience is a virtue that must be learned." Her nose wrinkled. "Sheriam Sedai always says that, and she does her best to make us all learn it, too. Try to run when she says walk, and she'll have you in her study before you can blink."

"I've had a few lessons already," Egwene said, trying to sound modest. She opened herself to *saidar*—that part of it was easier now—and felt the warmth suffuse her body. She decided to try the biggest thing she knew how to do. She stretched out her hand, and a glowing sphere formed over it, pure light. It wavered—she still could not manage to hold it steady—but it was there.

Calmly, Elayne held out her hand, and a ball of light appeared above her palm. Hers flickered, too.

After a moment, a faint light glowed all around Elayne. Egwene gasped, and her ball vanished.

Elayne giggled suddenly, and her light went out, both the sphere and the light around her. "You saw it around me?" she said excitedly. "I saw it around you. Sheriam Sedai said I would, eventually. This was the first time. For you, too?"

Egwene nodded, laughing along with the other girl. "I like you, Elayne. I think we're going to be friends."

"I think so, too, Egwene. You are from the Two Rivers, from Emond's Field. Do you know a boy named Rand al'Thor?"

"I know him." Abruptly Egwene found herself remembering a tale Rand had told, a tale she had not believed, about falling off a wall into a garden and meeting. . . . "You're the Daughter-Heir of Andor," she gasped.

"Yes," Elayne said simply. "If Sheriam Sedai as much as heard I'd mentioned it, I think she would have me into her study before I finished talking."

"Everyone talks about being called to Sheriam's study. Even the Accepted. Does she scold so fiercely? She seems kindly to me."

Elayne hesitated, and when she spoke it was slowly, not meeting Egwene's eye. "She keeps a willow switch on her desk. She says if you can't learn to follow the rules in a civilized way, she will teach you another way. There are so many rules for novices, it is very hard not to break some of them," she finished.

"But that's—that's horrible! I'm not a child, and neither are you. I won't be treated as one."

"But we are children. The Aes Sedai, the full sisters, are the grown women. The Accepted are the young women, old enough to be trusted without someone looking over their shoulders every moment. And novices are the children, to be protected and cared for, guided in the way they should go, and punished when they do what they should not. That is the way Sheriam Sedai explains it. No one is going to punish you over your lessons, not unless you try something you've been told not to. It is hard not to try, sometimes; you will find you want to channel as much as you want to breathe. But if you break too many dishes because you are daydreaming when you should be washing, if you're disrespectful to an Accepted, or leave the Tower without permission, or speak to an Aes Sedai before she speaks to you, or. . . . The only thing to do is the best you can. There isn't anything else *to* do."

"It sounds almost as if they're trying to make us want to leave," Egwene protested.

"They aren't, but then again, they are. Egwene, there are only forty novices in the Tower. Only forty, and no more than seven or eight will become Accepted. That is not enough, Sheriam Sedai says. She says there are not enough Aes Sedai now to do what needs to be done. But the Tower will not . . . cannot . . . lower its standards. The Aes Sedai cannot take a woman as a sister if she does not have the ability, and the strength, and the desire. They can't give the ring and the shawl to one who cannot channel the Power well enough, or who will allow herself to be intimidated, or who will turn back when the road turns rough. Training and testing take care of the channeling, and for strength and desire. . . . Well, if you want to go, they will let you. Once you know enough that you won't die of ignorance."

"I suppose," Egwene said slowly, "Sheriam told us some of that. I never thought about there not being enough Aes Sedai, though."

"She has a theory. She says we have culled humankind. You know about culling? Cutting out of the herd those animals that have traits you don't like?" Egwene nodded impatiently; no one could grow up around sheep without knowing about culling the flock. "Sheriam Sedai says that with the Red Ajah hunting down men who could channel for three thousand years, we are culling the ability to channel out of us all. I would not mention this around any Reds, if I were you. Sheriam Sedai has been in more than one shouting match over it, and we are only novices."

"I won't."

Elayne paused, and then said, "Is Rand well?"

Egwene felt a sudden stab of jealousy—Elayne was very pretty—but over it came a stronger stab of fear. She went over the little she knew of Rand's one meeting with the Daughter-Heir, reassuring herself: Elayne could not possibly know that Rand could channel.

"Egwene?"

"He is as well as he can be." *I hope he is, the wool-headed idiot.* "He was riding with some Shienaran soldiers the last I saw him."

"Shienarans! He told me he was a shepherd." She shook her head. "I find myself thinking of him at the oddest times. Elaida thinks he is important in some way. She didn't come right out and say so, but she ordered a search for him, and she was in a fury when she learned he had left Caemlyn."

"Elaida?"

"Elaida Sedai. My mother's councilor. She is Red Ajah, but Mother seems to like her despite that."

Egwene's mouth felt dry. *Red Ajah, and interested in Rand.* "I—I don't know where he is, now. He left Shienar, and I don't think he was going back."

Elayne gave her a level look. "I would not tell Elaida where to find him if I knew, Egwene. He has done no wrong that I know, and I fear she wants to use him in some manner. Anyway, I've not seen her since the day we arrived, with Whitecloaks dogging our trail. They are still camped on the Dragonmount side." Abruptly she bounded to her feet. "Let us talk of happier things. There are two others here who know Rand, and I would like you to meet one of them." She took Egwene's hand and pulled her out of the room.

"Two girls? Rand seems to meet a lot of girls."

"Ummm?" Still drawing Egwene down the corridor, Elayne studied her. "Yes. Well. One of them is a lazy chit named Else Grinwell. I don't think she will be here long. She shirks her chores, and she is always sneaking off to watch the Warders practice their swords. She says Rand came to her father's farm, with a friend of his. Mat. It seems they put notions of the world beyond the next village into her head, and she ran away to come be an Aes Sedai."

"Men," Egwene muttered. "I dance a few dances with a nice boy, and Rand goes around looking like a dog with a sore tooth, but he—" She cut off as a man stepped into the hall ahead of them. Beside her, Elayne stopped, too, and her hand tightened on Egwene's.

There was nothing alarming about him, aside from the suddenness of his appearance. He was tall and handsome, short of middle years, with long, dark curling hair, but his shoulders sagged, and there was sadness in his eyes. He made no move toward Egwene and Elayne, only stood looking at them until one of the Accepted appeared at his shoulder.

"You should not be in here," she said to him, not unkindly.

"I wanted to walk." His voice was deep, and as sad as his eyes.

"You can walk out in the garden, where you are supposed to be. The sunshine will be good for you."

The man rumbled a bitter laugh. "With two or three of you watching my every move? You're just afraid I'll find a knife." At the look in the Accepted's eyes, he laughed again. "For myself, woman. For myself. Lead me to your garden, and your watching eyes."

The Accepted touched his arm lightly, and led him away.

"Logain," Elayne said when he was gone.

"The false Dragon!"

"He has been gentled, Egwene. He is no more dangerous than any other man, now. But I remember seeing him before, when it took six Aes Sedai to keep him from wielding the Power and destroying us all." She shivered.

Egwene did, too. That was what the Red Ajah would do to Rand.

"Do they always have to be gentled?" she asked. Elayne stared at her, mouth agape, and she quickly added, "It is just that I'd think the Aes Sedai would find some other way to deal with them. Anaiya and Moiraine both said the greatest feats of the Age of Legends required men and women working together with the Power. I just thought they'd try to find a way."

"Well, do not let any Red sister hear you thinking it aloud. Egwene, they did try. For three hundred years after the White Tower was built, they tried. They gave up because there was nothing to find. Come on. I want you to meet Min. Not in the garden where Logain is going, thank the Light."

The name sounded vaguely familiar to Egwene, and when she saw the young woman, she knew why. There was a narrow stream in the garden, with a low stone bridge over it, and Min sat cross-legged on the wall of the bridge. She wore a man's tight breeches and baggy shirt, and with her dark hair cut short she could almost pass for a boy, though an uncommonly pretty one. A gray coat lay beside her on the coping.

"I know you," Egwene said. "You worked at the inn in Baerlon." A light breeze riffled the water beneath the bridge, and graywings warbled in the trees of the garden.

Min smiled. "And you were one of those who brought the Darkfriends down on us to burn it down. No, don't worry. The messenger who came to fetch me brought enough gold that Master Fitch is building it back again twice as big. Good morning, Elayne. Not slaving over your lessons? Or over some pots?" It was said in a bantering tone, as between friends, as Elayne's answering grin proved.

"I see Sheriam has not yet managed to get you into a dress."

Min's laugh was wicked. "I'm no novice." She made her voice squeaky. "Yes, Aes Sedai. No, Aes Sedai. May I sweep another floor, Aes Sedai? I," she said, resuming her own low voice, "clothe myself the way I want." She turned to Egwene. "Is Rand well?"

Egwene's mouth tightened. *He should wear ram's horns like a Trolloc,* she thought angrily. "I was sorry when your inn caught fire, and I am glad Master Fitch was able to rebuild. Why have you come to Tar Valon? It's clear you do not mean to be an Aes Sedai." Min arched an eyebrow in what Egwene was sure was amusement.

"She likes him," Elayne explained.

"I know." Min glanced at Egwene, and for an instant Egwene thought she saw sadness—or regret?—in her eyes. "I am here," Min said carefully, "because I was sent for, and was given the choice between riding and coming tied in a sack."

"You always exaggerate it," Elayne said. "Sheriam Sedai saw the letter, and she says it was a request. Min sees things, Egwene. That's why she's here; so the Aes Sedai can study how she does it. It isn't the Power."

"Request," Min snorted. "When an Aes Sedai requests your presence, it's like a command from a queen with a hundred soldiers to back it up."

"Everybody sees things," Egwene said.

Elayne shook her head. "Not like Min. She sees—auras—around people. And images."

"Not all the time," Min put in. "Not around everybody."

"And she can read things about you from them, though I'm not sure she always tells the truth. She said I'd have to share my husband with two other women, and I'd never put up with that. She just laughs, and says it was never her idea of how to run things, either. But she said I would be a queen before she knew who I was; she said she saw a crown, and it was the Rose Crown of Andor."

Despite herself, Egwene asked, "What do you see when you look at me?"

Min glanced at her. "A white flame, and. . . . Oh, all sorts of things. I don't know what it means."

"She says that a great deal," Elayne said dryly. "One of the things she said she saw looking at me was a severed hand. Not mine, she says. She claims she does not know what it means, either."

"Because I don't," Min said. "I don't know what half of it means."

The crunch of boots on the walk brought them around to look at two young men with their shirts and coats across their arms, leaving sweaty chests bare, and scabbarded swords in their hands. Egwene found herself staring at the most handsome man she had ever seen. Tall and slim, but hard, he moved with a cat-like grace. She suddenly realized he was bowing over her hand—she had not even felt him take it in his—and fumbled in her mind for the name she had heard.

"Galad," she murmured. His dark eyes stared back into hers. He was older than she. Older than Rand. At the thought of Rand, she gave a start and came to herself.

"And I am Gawyn"—the other young man grinned—"since I don't think you heard the first time." Min was grinning, too, and only Elayne wore a frown.

Egwene abruptly remembered her hand, still held by Galad, and freed it.

"If your duties allow," Galad said, "I would like to see you again, Egwene. We could walk, or if you obtain permission to leave the Tower, we could picnic outside the city."

"That—that would be nice." She was uncomfortably aware of the others, Min and Gawyn still with their amused grins, Elayne still with her scowl.

She tried to settle herself, to think of Rand. *He's so . . . beautiful.* She gave a jump, half afraid she had spoken aloud.

"Until then." Finally taking his eyes from hers, Galad bowed to Elayne. "Sister." Lithe as a blade, he strolled on across the bridge.

"That one," Min murmured, peering after him, "will always do what is right. No matter who it hurts."

"Sister?" Egwene said. Elayne's scowl had lessened only slightly. "I thought he was your. . . . I mean, the way you're frowning. . . ." She had thought Elayne was jealous, and she still was not sure.

"I am not his sister," Elayne said firmly. "I refuse to be."

"Our father was his father," Gawyn said dryly. "You cannot deny that, unless you want to call Mother a liar, and that, I think, would take more nerve than we have between us."

For the first time Egwene realized that he had the same reddish gold hair as Elayne, though darkened and curled by sweat.

"Min is right," Elayne said. "Galad has not the smallest part of humanity in him. He takes right above mercy, or pity, or. . . . He is no more human than a Trolloc."

Gawyn's grin came back. "I do not know about that. Not from the way he was looking at Egwene, here." He caught her look, and his sister's, and held up his hands as if to fend them off with his sheathed sword. "Besides, he has the best hand with a sword I've ever seen. The Warders only need show him something once, and he's learned it. They sweat me nearly to death to learn half what Galad does without trying."

"And being good with a sword is enough?" Elayne sniffed. "Men! Egwene, as you may have guessed, this disgracefully unclothed lummox is my brother. Gawyn, Egwene knows Rand al'Thor. She is from the same village."

"Is she? Was he really born in the Two Rivers, Egwene?"

Egwene made herself nod calmly. *What does he know?* "Of course, he was. I grew up with him."

"Of course," Gawyn said slowly. "Such a strange fellow. A shepherd, he said, though he never looked or acted like any shepherd I ever saw. Strange. I have met all sorts of people, and they've met Rand al'Thor. Some do not even know his name, but the description could not be anyone else, and he's shifted every one of their lives. There was an old farmer who came to Caemlyn just to see Logain, when Logain was brought through on his way here; yet the farmer stayed to stand for Mother when the riots started. Because of a young man off to see the world, who made him think there was more to life than his farm. Rand al'Thor. You could almost think he was *ta'veren*. Elaida is certainly interested in him. I wonder if meeting him will shift our lives in the Pattern?"

Egwene looked at Elayne and Min. She was sure they could not have a clue that Rand really was *ta'veren*. She had never really thought about that part of it before; he was Rand, and he had been cursed with the ability to channel. But *ta'veren* did move people, whether they wanted to be moved or not. "I really do like you," she said abruptly, including both girls in her gesture. "I want to be your friend."

"And I want to be yours," Elayne said.

Impulsively, Egwene hugged her, and then Min jumped down, and the three of them stood there on the bridge hugging one another all together.

"We three *are* tied together," Min said, "and we cannot let any man get in the way of that. Not even him."

"Would one of you mind telling me what this is all about?" Gawyn inquired gently.

"You would not understand," his sister said, and the three girls all caught a fit of the giggles.

Gawyn scratched his head, then shook it. "Well, if it has anything to do with Rand al'Thor, be sure you don't let Elaida hear of it. She has been at me like a Whitecloak Questioner three times since we arrived. I do not think she means him any—" He gave a start; there was a woman crossing the garden, a woman in a red-fringed shawl. "'Name the Dark One,'" he quoted, "'and he appears.' I do not need another lecture about wearing my shirt when I'm out of the practice yards. Good morning to you all."

Elaida spared a glance for the departing Gawyn as she came up the bridge. She was a handsome woman rather than beautiful, Egwene thought, but that ageless look marked her as surely as her shawl; only the newest-made sisters lacked it. When her gaze swept over Egwene, pausing only a moment, Egwene suddenly saw a hardness in the Aes Sedai. She had always thought of Moiraine as strong, steel under silk, but Elaida dispensed with the silk.

"Elaida," Elayne said, "this is Egwene. She was born with the seed in her, too. And she has already had some lessons, so she is as far along as I am. Elaida?"

The Aes Sedai's face was blank and unreadable. "In Caemlyn, child, I am councilor to the Queen your mother, but this is the White Tower, and you, a novice." Min made as if to go, but Elaida stopped her with a sharp, "Stay, girl. I would speak with you."

"I've known you all my life, Elaida," Elayne said incredulously. "You watched me grow up, and made the gardens bloom in winter so I could play."

"Child, there you were the Daughter-Heir. Here you are a novice. You must learn that. You will be great one day, but you must learn!"

"Yes, Aes Sedai."

Egwene was astounded. If someone had snubbed her so before others, she would have been in a fury.

"Now, off with both of you." A gong began to toll, deep and sonorous, and Elaida tilted her head. The sun stood halfway to its pinnacle. "High," Elaida said. "You must hurry, if you do not want further admonishment. And Elayne? See the Mistress of Novices in her study after your chores. A novice does not speak to Aes Sedai unless bidden to. Run, both of you. You will be late. Run!"

They ran, holding their skirts up. Egwene looked at Elayne. Elayne had two spots of color in her cheeks and a determined look on her face.

"I will be Aes Sedai," Elayne said softly, but it sounded like a promise.

Behind them, Egwene heard the Aes Sedai begin, "I am given to understand, girl, that you were brought here by Moiraine Sedai."

She wanted to stay and listen, to hear if Elaida asked about Rand, but High rang through the White Tower, and she was summoned to chores. She ran as she had been commanded to run.

"I will be Aes Sedai," she growled. Elayne flashed a quick smile of understanding, and they ran faster.

Min's shirt clung to her when she finally left the bridge. Not sweat from the sun, but from the heat of Elaida's questions. She looked over her shoulder to make sure the Aes Sedai was not following her, but Elaida was nowhere in sight.

How did Elaida know that Moiraine had summoned her? Min had been sure that was a secret known only to her, Moiraine, and Sheriam. And all those questions about Rand. It had not been easy keeping a smooth face and a steady eye while telling an Aes Sedai to her face that she had never heard of him and knew nothing of him. *What does she want with him? Light, what does Moiraine want with him? What is he? Light, I don't want to fall in love with a man I've only met once, and a farmboy at that.*

"Moiraine, the Light blind you," she muttered, "whatever you brought me here for, come out from wherever you're hiding and tell me so I can go!"

The only answer was the sweet song of the graywings. With a grimace she went in search of a place to cool off.

# CHAPTER 25

## *Cairhien*

The city of Cairhien lay across hills against the River Alguenya, and Rand's first sight of it came from the hills to the north, by the light of the midday sun. Elricain Tavolin and the fifty Cairhienin soldiers still seemed like guards to him—the more since crossing the bridge at the Gaelin; they became more stiff the further south they rode— but Loial and Hurin did not appear to mind, so he tried not to. He studied the city, as large as any he had seen. Fat ships and broad barges filled the river, and tall granaries sprawled along the far bank, but Cairhien seemed to be laid out in a precise grid behind its high, gray walls. Those walls themselves made a perfect square, with one side hard along the river. In just as exact a pattern, towers rose within the walls, soaring as much as twenty times the height of the wall, yet even from the hills Rand could see that each one ended in a jagged top.

Outside the city walls, surrounding them from riverbank to riverbank, lay a warren of streets, crisscrossing at all angles and teeming with people. Foregate, Rand knew it was called, from Hurin; once there had been a market village for every city gate, but over the years they had all grown into one, a hodgepodge of streets and alleys growing up every which way.

As Rand and the others rode into those dirt streets, Tavolin put some of his soldiers to clearing a path through the throng, shouting and urging their horses forward as if to trample any who did not get out of the way quickly. People moved aside with no more than a glance, as if it were an everyday occurrence. Rand found himself smiling, though.

The Foregate people's clothes were shabby more often than not, yet much of it was colorful, and there was a raucous bustle of life to the place. Hawkers cried their wares, and shopkeepers called for people to examine the goods displayed on tables before their shops. Barbers, fruit-peddlers, knife-sharpeners, men and women offering a dozen services and a hundred things for sale, wandered through the crowds. Music drifted through the babble from more than one structure; at first Rand thought they were inns, but the signs out front all showed men playing flutes or harps, tumbling or juggling, and large as they were, they had no windows. Most of the buildings in Foregate seemed to be wood, however big they were, and a good many looked new, if poorly made. Rand gaped at several that stood seven stories or more; they swayed slightly, though the people hurrying in and out did not seem to notice.

"Peasants," Tavolin muttered, staring straight ahead in disgust. "Look at them, corrupted by outland ways. They should not be here."

"Where should they be?" Rand asked. The Cairhienin officer glared at him and spurred his horse forward, flogging at the crowd with his quirt.

Hurin touched Rand's arm. "It was the Aiel War, Lord Rand." He looked to make sure none of the soldiers were close enough to hear. "Many of the farmers were afraid to go back to their lands near the Spine of the World, and they all came here, near enough. That's why Galldrian has the river full of grain barges up from Andor and Tear. There's no crops coming from farms in the east because there aren't any farms anymore. Best not to mention it to a Cairhienin though, my Lord. They like to pretend the war never happened, or at least that they won it."

Despite Tavolin's quirt, they were forced to halt while a strange procession crossed their path. Half a dozen men, beating tambours and dancing, led the way for a string of huge puppets, each half again as tall as the men who worked them with long poles. Giant crowned figures of men and women in long, ornate robes bowed to the crowd amid the shapes of fanciful beasts. A lion with wings. A goat, walking on its hind legs, with two heads, both of which were apparently meant to be breathing fire, from the crimson streamers hanging from the two mouths. Something that seemed to be half cat and half eagle, and another with a bear's head on a man's body, which Rand took to be a Trolloc. The crowd cheered and laughed as they pranced by.

"Man who made that never saw a Trolloc," Hurin grumbled. "Head's too big, and it's too skinny. Likely didn't believe in them, either, my

Lord, any more than in those other things. The only monsters these Foregate folk believe in are Aiel."

"Are they having a festival?" Rand asked. He did not see any sign of it
other than the procession, but he thought that there must be a reason for
that. Tavolin ordered his soldiers forward again.

"No more than every day, Rand," Loial said. Walking alongside his
horse, the blanket-wrapped chest still strapped to his saddle, the Ogier
drew as many looks as the puppets had. Some even laughed and clapped as
they had for the puppets. "I fear Galldrian keeps his people quiet by entertaining them. He gives gleemen and musicians the King's Gift, a bounty
in silver, to perform here in the Foregate, and he sponsors horse races down
by the river every day. There are fireworks many nights, too." He sounded
disgusted. "Elder Haman says Galldrian is a disgrace." He blinked, realizing what he had said, and looked around hurriedly to see if any of the
soldiers had heard. None seemed to have.

"Fireworks," Hurin said, nodding. "The Illuminators have built a chapter house here, I've heard, the same as in Tanchico. I didn't half mind
seeing the fireworks, when I was here before."

Rand shook his head. He had never seen fireworks elaborate enough to
require even one Illuminator. He had heard they only left Tanchico to put
on displays for rulers. It was a strange place he was coming to.

At the tall, square archway of the city gate, Tavolin ordered a halt and
dismounted by a squat stone building just inside the walls. It had arrowslits instead of windows, and a heavy, iron-bound door.

"A moment, my Lord Rand," the officer said. Tossing his reins to one of
the soldiers, he disappeared inside.

With a wary look at the soldiers—they sat their horses rigidly in two
long files; Rand wondered what they would do if he and Loial and Hurin
tried to leave—he took the opportunity to study the city that lay before
him.

Cairhien proper was a sharp contrast to the chaotic bustle of the Foregate. Broad, paved streets, wide enough to make the people in them seem
fewer than they were, crossed each other at right angles. Just as in Tremonsien, the hills had been carved and terraced to straight lines. Closed sedan
chairs, some with small pennants bearing the sigil of a House, moved with
deliberateness, and carriages rolled down the streets slowly. People went
silently in dark clothes, with no bright colors except here and there slashes
across the breast of coat or dress. The more slashes, the more proudly the
wearer moved, but no one laughed, or even smiled. The buildings on their
terraces were all of stone, and the ornamentation was straight-lined and
sharp-angled. There were no hawkers or peddlers in the streets, and even

the shops seemed subdued, with only small signs and no wares displayed outside.

He could see the great towers more clearly, now. Scaffolds of lashed poles surrounded them, and workmen swarmed on the scaffolding, laying new stones to push the towers higher still.

"The Topless Towers of Cairhien," Loial murmured sadly. "Well, they were tall enough to warrant the name, once. When the Aiel took Cairhien, about the time you were born, the towers burned, and cracked, and fell. I don't see any Ogier among the stonemasons. No Ogier could like working here—the Cairhienin want what they want, without embellishment—but there were Ogier when I was here before."

Tavolin came out, trailing another officer and two clerks, one carrying a large, wood-bound ledger and the other a tray with writing implements. The front of the officer's head was shaven like Tavolin's, though advancing baldness seemed to have taken more hair than the razor. Both officers looked from the Rand to the chest hidden by Loial's striped blanket and back again. Neither asked what was under the blanket. Tavolin had looked at it often on the way from Tremonsien, but he had never asked, either. The balding man looked at Rand's sword, too, and pursed his lips for an instant.

Tavolin gave the other officer's name as Asan Sandair, and announced loudly, "Lord Rand of House al'Thor, in Andor, and his man, called Hurin, with Loial, an Ogier of Stedding Shangtai." The clerk with the ledger opened it across his two arms, and Sandair wrote the names in a round hand.

"You must return to this guardhouse by this same hour tomorrow, my Lord," Sandair said, leaving the sanding to the second clerk, "and give the name of the inn where you are staying."

Rand looked at the staid streets of Cairhien, then back at the liveliness of the Foregate. "Can you tell me the name of a good inn out there?" He nodded to the Foregate.

Hurin made a frantic *hsst* and leaned close. "It would not be proper, Lord Rand," he whispered. "If you stay in the Foregate, being a lord and all, they'll be sure you are up to something."

Rand could see the sniffer was right. Sandair's mouth had dropped open and Tavolin's brows had risen at his question, and they were both still watching him intently. He wanted to tell them he was not playing their Great Game, but instead he said, "We will take rooms in the city. We can go now?"

"Of course, my Lord Rand." Sandair made a bow. "But . . . the inn?"

"I will let you know when we find one." Rand turned Red, then paused.

Selene's note crackled in his pocket. "I need to find a young woman from Cairhien. The Lady Selene. She is my age, and beautiful. I don't know her House."

Sandair and Tavolin exchanged looks, then Sandair said, "I will make inquiries, my Lord. Perhaps I will be able to tell you something when you come tomorrow."

Rand nodded and led Loial and Hurin into the city. They attracted little notice, though there were few riders. Even Loial attracted almost none. The people seemed nearly ostentatious about minding their own business.

"Will they take it the wrong way," Rand asked Hurin, "my asking after Selene?"

"Who can say with Cairhienin, Lord Rand? They seem to think everything has to do with *Daes Dae'mar*."

Rand shrugged. He felt as if people were looking at him. He could not wait to get a good, plain coat again, and stop pretending to be what he was not.

Hurin knew several inns in the city, though his time in Cairhien had been spent mainly in the Foregate. The sniffer led them to one called The Defender of the Dragonwall, the sign bearing a crowned man with his foot on another man's chest and his sword at the man's throat. The fellow on his back had red hair.

A hostler came to take their horses, darting quick looks at Rand and at Loial when he thought he was not observed. Rand told himself to stop having fancies; not everyone in the city could be playing this Game of theirs. And if they were, he was no part of it.

The common room was neat, with the tables laid out as strictly as the city, and only a few people at them. They glanced up at the newcomers, then back to their wine immediately; Rand had the feeling they were still watching, though, and listening. A small fire burned in the big fireplace, though the day was warming.

The innkeeper was a plump, unctuous man with a single stripe of green across his dark gray coat. He gave a start at his first sight of them, and Rand was not surprised. Loial, with the chest in his arms under its striped blanket, had to duck his head to make it in through the door, Hurin was burdened with all their saddlebags and bundles, and his own red coat was a sharp contrast to the somber colors the people at the tables wore.

The innkeeper took in Rand's coat and his sword, and his oily smile came back. He bowed, washing his smooth hands. "Forgive me, my Lord. It was just that for a moment I took you for— Forgive me. My brain is not what it was. You wish rooms, my Lord?" He added another, lesser bow for Loial. "I am called Cuale, my Lord."

*He thought I was Aiel,* Rand thought sourly. He wanted to be gone from Cairhien. But it was the one place Ingtar might find them. And Selene had said she would wait for him in Cairhien.

It took a little time for their rooms to be readied, Cuale explaining with too many smiles and bows that it was necessary to move a bed for Loial. Rand wanted them all to share a room again, but between the innkeeper's scandalized looks and Hurin's insistence—"We have to show these Cairhienin we know what's right as well as they do, Lord Rand"—they ended with two, one for him alone, with a connecting door.

The rooms were much the same except that theirs had two beds, one sized for an Ogier, while his had only one bed, and that almost as big as the other two, with massive square posts that nearly reached the ceiling. His tall-backed, padded chair and the washstand were square and massive, too, and the wardrobe standing against his wall was carved in a heavy, rigid style that made the thing look ready enough to fall over on him. A pair of windows siding his bed looked out on the street, two floors below.

As soon as the innkeeper left, Rand opened the door and admitted Loial and Hurin into his room. "This place gnaws at me," he told them. "Everybody looks at you as if they think you're doing something. I'm going back to the Foregate, for an hour anyway. At least the people laugh, there. Which of you is willing to take the first watch on the Horn?"

"I will stay," Loial said quickly. "I'd like a chance to do a little reading. Just because I didn't see any Ogier does not mean there are no stonemasons down from Stedding Tsofu. It is not far from the city."

"I'd think you would want to meet them."

"Ah . . . no, Rand. They asked enough questions the last time about why I was outside alone as it was. If they've had word from Stedding Shangtai. . . . Well, I will just rest here and read, I think."

Rand shook his head. He often forgot that Loial had run away from home, in effect, to see the world. "What about you, Hurin? There's music in the Foregate, and people laughing. I'll wager no one is playing *Daes Dae'mar* there."

"I would not be so certain of that myself, Lord Rand. In any case, I thank you for the invitation, but I think not. There's so many fights—and killings, too—in Foregate, that it stinks, if you know what I mean. Not that they're likely to bother a lord, of course; the soldiers would be down on them if they did. But if it pleases you, I would like to have a drink in the common room."

"Hurin, you don't need my permission for anything. You know that."

"As you say, my Lord." The sniffer gave a suggestion of a bow.

Rand took a deep breath. If they did not leave Cairhien soon, Hurin would be bowing and scraping left and right. And if Mat and Perrin saw that, they would never let him forget it. "I hope nothing delays Ingtar. If he doesn't come quickly, we'll have to take the Horn back to Fal Dara ourselves." He touched Selene's note through his coat. "We will have to. Loial, I'll come back so you can see some of the city."

"I'd rather not risk it," Loial said.

Hurin accompanied Rand downstairs. As soon as they reached the common room, Cuale was bowing in front of Rand, pushing a tray at him. Three folded and sealed parchments lay on the tray. Rand took them, since that was what the innkeeper seemed to intend. They were a fine grade of parchment, soft and smooth to his touch. Expensive.

"What are these?" he asked.

Cuale bowed again. "Invitations, of course, my Lord. From three of the noble Houses." He bowed himself away.

"Who would send me invitations?" Rand turned them over in his hand. None of the men at the tables looked up, but he had the feeling they were watching just the same. He did not recognize the seals. None was the crescent moon and stars Selene had used. "Who would know I was here?"

"Everyone by now, Lord Rand," Hurin said quietly. He seemed to feel eyes watching, too. "The guards at the gate would not keep their mouths closed about an outland lord coming to Cairhien. The hostler, the innkeeper . . . everybody tells what they know where they think it will do them the most good, my Lord."

With a grimace, Rand took two steps and hurled the invitations into the fire. They caught immediately. "I am not playing *Daes Dae'mar*," he said, loudly enough for everyone to hear. Not even Cuale looked at him. "I've nothing to do with your Great Game. I am just here to wait for some friends."

Hurin caught his arm. "Please, Lord Rand." His voice was an urgent whisper. "Please don't do that again."

"Again? You really think I'll receive more?"

"I'm certain. Light, but you mind me of the time Teva got so mad at a hornet buzzing round his ears, he kicked the nest. You've likely just convinced everyone in the room you are in some deep part of the Game. It must be deep, as they'll see it, if you deny playing at all. *Every* lord and lady in Cairhien plays it." The sniffer glanced at the invitations, curling blackly in the fire, and winced. "And you have surely made enemies of three Houses. Not great Houses, or they'd not have moved so quickly, but still noble. You must answer any more invitations you receive, my Lord. Decline if you will—though they'll read things into whose invitations you do decline. And into whose you accept. Of course, if you decline them all, or accept them all—"

"I'll have no part of it," Rand said quietly. "We are leaving Cairhien as soon as we can." He thrust his fists into his coat pockets, and felt Selene's note crumple. Pulling it out, he smoothed it on his coat front. "As soon as we can," he muttered, putting it back in his pocket again. "Have your drink, Hurin."

He stalked out angrily, not sure whether he was angry with himself, or with Cairhien and its Great Game, or Selene for vanishing, or Moiraine. She had started it all, stealing his coats and giving him a lord's clothes instead. Even now that he called himself free of them, an Aes Sedai still managed to interfere in his life, and without even being there.

He went back through the same gate by which he had entered the city, since that was the way he knew. A man standing in front of the guardhouse took note of him—his bright coat marked him out, as well as his height among the Cairhienin—and hurried inside, but Rand did not notice. The laughter and music of the Foregate were pulling him on.

If his gold-embroidered red coat made him stand out inside the walls, it fit right into the Foregate. Many of the men milling through the crowded streets were dressed just as darkly as those in the city, but just as many wore coats of red, or blue, or green, or gold—some bright enough to be a Tinker's clothes—and even more of the women had embroidered dresses and colored scarves or shawls. Most of the finery was tattered and ill-fitting, as if made for someone else originally, but if some of those who wore it eyed his fine coat, none seemed to take it amiss.

Once he had to stop for another procession of giant puppets. While the drummers beat their tambours and capered, a pig-faced Trolloc with tusks fought a man in a crown. After a few desultory blows, the Trolloc collapsed to laughter and cheers from the onlookers.

Rand grunted. *They don't die so easily as that.*

He glanced into one of the large, windowless buildings, stopping to look through the door. To his surprise, it seemed to be one huge room, open to the sky in the middle and lined with balconies, with a large dais at one end. He had never seen or heard of anything like it. People jammed the balconies and the floor watching people perform on the dais. He peeked into others as he passed them, and saw jugglers, and musicians, any number of tumblers, and even a gleeman, with his cloak of patches, de-claiming a story from *The Great Hunt of the Horn* in sonorous-voice High Chant.

That made him think of Thom Merrilin, and he hurried on. Memories of

Thom were always sad. Thom had been a friend. A friend who had died for him. *While I ran away and let him die.*

In another of the big structures, a woman in voluminous white robes appeared to make things vanish from one basket and appear in another, then disappear from her hands in great puffs of smoke. The crowd watching her *oohed* and *aahed* loudly.

"Two coppers, my good Lord," a ratty little man in the doorway said. "Two coppers to see the Aes Sedai."

"I don't think so." Rand glanced back at the woman. A white dove had appeared in her hands. *Aes Sedai?* "No." He gave the ratty man a small bow and left.

He was making his way through the throng, wondering what to see next, when a deep voice, accompanied by the plucking of a harp, drifted out from a doorway with the sign of a juggler over it.

". . . cold blows the wind down Shara Pass; cold lies the grave unmarked. Yet every year at Sunday, upon those piled stones appears a single rose, one crystal teardrop like dew upon the petals, laid by the fair hand of Dunsinin, for she keeps fast to the bargain made by Rogosh Eagle-eye."

The voice drew Rand like a rope. He pushed through the doorway as applause rose within.

"Two coppers, my good Lord," said a rat-faced man who could have been twin to the other. "Two coppers to see—"

Rand dug out some coins and thrust them at the man. He walked on in a daze, staring at the man bowing on the dais to the clapping of his listeners, cradling his harp in one arm and with the other spreading his patch-covered cloak as if to trap all the sound they made. He was a tall man, lanky and not young, with long mustaches as white as the hair on his head. And when he straightened and saw Rand, the eyes that widened were sharp and blue.

"Thom." Rand's whisper was lost in the noise of the crowd.

Holding Rand's eye, Thom Merrilin nodded slightly toward a small door beside the dais. Then he was bowing again, smiling and basking in the applause.

Rand made his way to the door and through it. It was only a small hallway, with three steps leading up to the dais. In the other direction from the dais Rand could see a juggler practicing with colored balls, and six tumblers limbering themselves.

Thom appeared on the steps, limping as though his right leg did not bend as well as it had. He eyed the juggler and the tumblers, blew out his mustaches disdainfully, and turned to Rand. "All they want to hear is *The*

*Great Hunt of the Horn.* You would think, with the news from Haddon
Mirk and Saldaea, one of them would ask for *The Karaethon Cycle.* Well,
maybe not that, but I'd pay myself to tell something else." He looked
Rand up and down. "You look as if you're doing well, boy." He fingered
Rand's collar and pursed his lips. "Very well."

Rand could not help laughing. "I left Whitebridge sure you were dead.
Moiraine said you were still alive, but I. . . . Light, Thom, it's good to see
you again! I should have gone back to help you."

"Bigger fool if you had, boy. That Fade"—he looked around; there was
no one close enough to hear, but he lowered his voice anyway—"had no
interest in me. It left me a little present of a stiff leg and ran off after you
and Mat. All you could have done was die." He paused, looking
thoughtful. "Moiraine said I was still alive, did she? Is she with you,
then?"

Rand shook his head. To his surprise, Thom seemed disappointed.

"Too bad, in a way. She's a fine woman, even if she is. . . ." He left it
unsaid. "So it was Mat or Perrin she was after. I won't ask which. They
were good boys, and I don't want to know." Rand shifted uneasily, and
gave a start when Thom fixed him with a bony finger. "What I do want to
know is, do you still have my harp and flute? I want them back, boy.
What I have now are not fit for a pig to play."

"I have them, Thom. I'll bring them to you, I promise. I can't believe
you are alive. And I can't believe you aren't in Illian. The Great Hunt
setting out. The prize for the best telling of *The Great Hunt of the Horn.*
You were dying to go."

Thom snorted. "After Whitebridge? Likely I'd die if I did go. Even if I
could have reached the boat before it sailed, Domon and his whole crew
would be spreading the tale all over Illian about how I was being chased by
Trollocs. If they saw the Fade, or heard of it, before Domon cut his
lines. . . . Most Illianers think Trollocs and Fades are fables, but enough
others might want to know why a man was pursued by them to make Illian
somewhat more than uncomfortable."

"Thom, I have so much to tell you."

The gleeman cut him off. "Later, boy." He was exchanging glares down
the length of the hall with the narrow-faced man from the door. "If I don't
go back and tell another, he will no doubt send the juggler out, and that
lot will tear the hall down around our heads. You come to The Bunch of
Grapes, just beyond the Jangai Gate. I have a room there. Anyone can tell
you where to find it. I'll be there in another hour or so. One more tale will
have to satisfy them." He started back up the steps, flinging over his shoulder, "And bring my harp and my flute!"

# CHAPTER
## 26

*Discord*

Rand darted through the common room of The Defender of the
Dragonwall and hurried upstairs, grinning at the startled look the
innkeeper had given him. Rand wanted to grin at everything.
*Thom's alive!*

He flung open the door to his room and went straight to the wardrobe.
Loial and Hurin put their heads in from the other room, both in their
shirtsleeves and with pipes in their teeth trailing thin streams of smoke.

"Has something happened, Lord Rand?" Hurin asked anxiously.

Rand slung the bundle made from Thom's cloak on his shoulder. "The
best thing that could, next to Ingtar coming. Thom Merrilin's alive. And
he's here, in Cairhien."

"The gleeman you told me about?" Loial said. "That is wonderful,
Rand. I would like to meet him."

"Then come with me, if Hurin's willing to keep watch awhile."

"It would be a pleasure, Lord Rand." Hurin took the pipe out of his
mouth. "That lot in the common room kept trying to pump me—without
letting on what they were doing, of course—about who you are, my Lord,
and why we're in Cairhien. I told them we were waiting here to meet
friends, but being Cairhienin, they figured I was hiding something
deeper."

"Let them think what they want. Come on, Loial."

"I think not." The Ogier sighed. "I really would rather stay here." He raised a book with a thick finger marking his place. "I can meet Thom Merrilin some other time."

"Loial, you can't stay cooped up in here forever. We do not even know how long we'll be in Cairhien. Anyway, we didn't see any Ogier. And if we do, they would not be hunting for you, would they?"

"Not hunting, precisely, but. . . . Rand, I may have been too hasty in leaving Stedding Shangtai the way I did. When I do go home, I may be in a great deal of trouble." His ears wilted. "Even if I wait until I'm as old as Elder Haman. Perhaps I could find an abandoned *stedding* to stay in until then."

"If Elder Haman won't let you come back, you can live in Emond's Field. It's a pretty place." *A beautiful place.*

"I am sure it is, Rand, but that would never work. You see—"

"We will talk about it when it comes to that, Loial. Now you are coming to see Thom."

The Ogier stood half again as tall as Rand, but Rand pushed him into his long tunic and cloak and down the stairs. When they came pounding through the common room, Rand winked at the innkeeper, then laughed at his startled look. *Let him think I'm off to play his bloody Great Game. Let him think what he wants. Thom's alive.*

Once through the Jangai Gate, in the east wall of the city, everyone seemed to know The Bunch of Grapes. Rand and Loial quickly found themselves there, on a street that was quiet for the Foregate, with the sun halfway down the afternoon sky.

It was an old three-story structure, wooden and rickety, but the common room was clean and full of people. Some men were playing at dice in one corner, and some women at darts in another. Half had the look of Cairhienin, slight and pale, but Rand heard Andoran accents as well as others he did not know. All wore the clothes of the Foregate, though, a blend of the styles of half a dozen countries. A few looked around when he and Loial came in, but they all turned back to what they had been doing.

The innkeeper was a woman with hair as white as Thom's, and sharp eyes that studied Loial as well as Rand. She was not Cairhienin, by her dark skin and her speech. "Thom Merrilin? Aye, he has a room. Top of the stairs, first door on the right. Likely Dena will let you wait for him there"—she eyed Rand's red coat, with its herons on the high collar and golden brambles embroidered up the sleeves, and his sword—"my Lord."

The stairs creaked under Rand's boots, let alone Loial's. Rand was not sure if the building would stand up much longer. He found the door and knocked, wondering who Dena was.

"Come in," a woman's voice called. "I cannot open it for you."

Rand opened the door hesitantly and put his head in. A big, rumpled bed was shoved against one wall, and the rest of the room was all but taken up by a pair of wardrobes, several brass-bound trunks and chests, a table and two wooden chairs. The slender woman sitting cross-legged on the bed with her skirts tucked under her was keeping six colored balls spinning in a wheel between her hands.

"Whatever it is," she said, looking at her juggling, "leave it on the table. Thom will pay you when he comes back."

"Are you Dena?" Rand asked.

She snatched the balls out of the air and turned to regard him. She was only a handful of years older than he, pretty, with fair Cairhienin skin and dark hair hanging loose to her shoulders. "I do not know you. This is my room, mine and Thom Merrilin's."

"The innkeeper said you might let us wait here for Thom," Rand said. "If you're Dena?"

"Us?" Rand moved into the room so Loial could duck inside, and the young woman's eyebrows lifted. "So the Ogier have come back. I am Dena. What do you want?" She looked at Rand's coat so deliberately that the failure to add "my Lord" had to be purposeful, though her brows went up again at the herons on his scabbard and sword hilt.

Rand hefted the bundle he carried. "I've brought Thom back his harp and his flute. And I want to visit with him," he added quickly; she seemed on the point of telling him to leave them. "I haven't seen him in a long time."

She eyed the bundle. "Thom always moans about losing the best flute and the best harp he ever had. You would think he was a court-bard, the way he carries on. Very well. You can wait, but I must practice. Thom says he will let me perform in the halls next week." She rose gracefully and took one of the two chairs, motioning Loial to sit on the bed. "Zera would make Thom pay for six chairs if you broke one of these, friend Ogier."

Rand gave their names as he sat in the other chair—it creaked alarmingly under even his weight—and asked doubtfully, "Are you Thom's apprentice?"

Dena gave a small smile. "You might say that." She had resumed her juggling, and her eyes were on the whirling balls.

"I have never heard of a woman gleeman," Loial said.

"I will be the first." The one big circle became two smaller, overlapping circles. "I will see the whole world before I am done. Thom says once we have enough money, we will go down to Tear." She switched to juggling three balls in each hand. "And then maybe out to the Sea Folk's islands. The Atha'an Miere pay gleemen well."

Rand eyed the room, with all the chests and trunks. It did not look like the room of someone intending to move on soon. There was even a flower growing in a pot on the windowsill. His gaze fell on the single big bed, where Loial was sitting. *This is my room, mine and Thom Merrilin's.* Dena gave him a challenging look through the large wheel she had resumed. Rand's face reddened.

He cleared his throat. "Maybe we ought to wait downstairs," he began when the door opened and Thom came in with his cloak flapping around his ankles, patches fluttering. Cased flute and harp hung on his back; the cases were reddish wood, polished by handling.

Dena made the balls disappear inside her dress and ran to throw her arms around Thom's neck, standing atiptoe to do it. "I missed you," she said, and kissed him.

The kiss went on for some time, so long that Rand was beginning to wonder if he and Loial should leave, but Dena let her heels drop to the floor with a sigh.

"Do you know what that lack-wit Seaghan's done now, girl?" Thom said, looking down at her. "He's taken on a pack of louts who call themselves 'players.' They walk around pretending to *be* Rogosh Eagle-eye, and Blaes, and Gaidal Cain, and. . . . Aaagh! They hang a scrap of painted canvas behind them, supposed to make the audience believe these fools are in Matuchin Hall, or the high passes of the Mountains of Dhoom. *I* make the listener see every banner, smell every battle, feel every emotion. I make them believe *they* are Gaidal Cain. Seaghan will have his hall torn down around his ears if he puts this lot on to follow me."

"Thom, we have visitors. Loial, son of Arent son of Halan. Oh, and a boy who calls himself Rand al'Thor."

Thom looked over her head at Rand, frowning. "Leave us for a while, Dena. Here." He pressed some silver coins into her hand. "Your knives are ready. Why don't you go pay Ivon for them?" He brushed her smooth cheek with a gnarled knuckle. "Go on. I'll make it up to you."

She gave him a dark look, but she tossed her cloak around her shoulders, muttering, "Ivon better have the balance right."

"She'll be a bard one day," Thom said with a note of pride after she was gone. "She listens to a tale once—once only, mind!—and she has it right, not just the words, but every nuance, every rhythm. She has a fine hand on the harp, and she played the flute better the first time she picked it up than you ever did." He set the wooden instrument cases atop one of the larger trunks, then dropped into the chair she had abandoned. "When I passed through Caemlyn on the way here, Basel Gill told me you'd left in company with an Ogier. Among others." He bowed toward Loial, even managing a flourish of his cloak despite the fact that he was sitting on it. "I am pleased to meet you, Loial, son of Arent son of Halan."

"And I to meet you, Thom Merrilin." Loial stood to make his bow in return; when he straightened, his head almost brushed the ceiling, and he quickly sat down again. "The young woman said she wants to be a gleeman."

Thom's head shake was disparaging. "That's no life for a woman. Not much of a life for a man, for that. Wandering from town to town, village to village, wondering how they'll try to cheat you this time, half the time wondering where your next meal is coming from. No, I'll talk her around. She'll be Court-bard to a king or a queen before she's done. Aaaah! You didn't come here to talk about Dena. My instruments, boy. You've brought them?"

Rand pushed the bundle across the table. Thom undid it hurriedly—he blinked when he saw it was his old cloak, all covered with colorful patches like the one he wore—and opened the hard leather flute case, nodding at the sight of the gold-and-silver flute nestled inside.

"I earned my bed and meals with that after we parted," Rand said.

"I know," the gleeman replied dryly. "I stopped at some of the same inns, but I had to make do with juggling and a few simple stories since you had my— You didn't touch the harp?" He pulled open the other dark leather case and took out a gold-and-silver harp as ornate as the flute, cradling it in his hands like a baby. "Your clumsy sheepherder's fingers were never meant for the harp."

"I didn't touch it," Rand assured him.

Thom plucked two strings, wincing. "At least you could have kept it in tune," he muttered.

Rand leaned across the table toward him. "Thom, you wanted to go to Illian, to see the Great Hunt set out, and be one of the first to make new stories about it, but you couldn't. What would you say if I told you you could still be a part of it? A big part?"

Loial stirred uneasily. "Rand, are you sure. . . ?" Rand waved him to silence, his eyes on Thom.

Thom glanced at the Ogier and frowned. "That would depend on what part, and how. If you've reason to believe one of the Hunters is coming this way. . . . I suppose they could have left Illian already, but he'd be weeks reaching here if he rode straight on, and why would he? Is this one of the fellows who never went to Illian? He'll never make it into the stories without the blessing, whatever he does."

"It doesn't matter if the Hunt has left Illian or not." Rand heard Loial's breath catch. "Thom, we have the Horn of Valere."

For a moment there was dead silence. Thom broke it with a great guffaw of laughter. "You two have the Horn? A shepherd and a beardless Ogier have the Horn of. . . ." He doubled over, pounding his knee. "The Horn of Valere!"

"But we do have it," Loial said seriously.

Thom drew a deep breath. Small aftershocks of laughter still seemed to catch him unaware. "I don't know what you found, but I can take you to ten taverns where a fellow will tell you that he knows a man who knows the man who's already found the Horn, and he will tell you how it was found, too—as long as you buy his ale. I can take you to three men who will *sell* you the Horn, and swear their souls under the Light it's the real one and true. There is even a lord in the city has what he claims is the Horn locked up inside his manor. He says it's a treasure handed down in his House since the Breaking. I don't know if the Hunters will ever find the Horn, but they will hunt down ten thousand lies along the way."

"Moiraine says it's the Horn," Rand said.

Thom's mirth was cut short. "She does, does she? I thought you said she was not with you."

"She isn't, Thom. I have not seen her since I left Fal Dara, in Shienar, and for a month before that she said no more than two words together to me." He could not keep the bitterness out of his voice. *And when she did talk, I wished she'd kept on ignoring me. I'll never dance to her tune again, the Light burn her and every other Aes Sedai. No. Not Egwene. Not Nynaeve.* He was conscious of Thom watching him closely. "She isn't here, Thom. I do not know where she is, and I do not care."

"Well, at least you have sense enough to keep it secret. If you hadn't, it would be all over the Foregate by now, and half a Cairhien would be lying in wait to take it away. Half the world."

"Oh, we've kept it secret, Thom. And I have to bring it back to Fal Dara without Darkfriends or anyone else taking it away. That's story enough for you right there, isn't it? I could use a friend who knows the world. You've been everywhere; you know things I can't even imagine. Loial and Hurin know more than I do, but we're all three floundering in deep water."

"Hurin. . . ? No, don't tell me how. I do not want to know." The gleeman pushed back his chair and went to stare out of the window. "The Horn of Valere. That means the Last Battle is coming. Who will notice?

Did you see the people laughing in the streets out there? Let the grain barges stop a week, and they won't laugh. Galldrian will think they've all become Aiel. The nobles all play the Game of Houses, scheming to get close to the King, scheming to gain more power than the King, scheming to pull down Galldrian and *be* the next King. Or Queen. They will think Tarmon Gai'don is only a ploy in the Game." He turned away from the window. "I don't suppose you are talking about simply riding to Shienar and handing the Horn to—who?—the King? Why Shienar? The legends all tie the Horn to Illian."

Rand looked at Loial. The Ogier's ears were sagging. "Shienar, because I know who to give it to, there. And there are Trollocs and Darkfriends after us."

"Why does that not surprise me? No. I may be an old fool, but I will be an old fool in my own way. You take the glory, boy."

"Thom—"

"No!"

There was a silence, broken only by the creaking of the bed as Loial shifted. Finally, Rand said, "Loial, would you mind leaving Thom and me alone for a bit? Please?"

Loial looked surprised—the tufts on his ears went almost to points—but he nodded and rose. "That dice game in the common room looked interesting. Perhaps they will let me play." Thom eyed Rand suspiciously as the door closed behind the Ogier.

Rand hesitated. There were things he needed to know, things he was sure Thom knew—the gleeman had once seemed to know a great deal about a surprising number of things—but he was not sure how to ask. "Thom," he said at last, "are there any books that have *The Karaethon Cycle* in them?" Easier to call it that than the Prophecies of the Dragon.

"In the great libraries," Thom said slowly. "Any number of translations, and even in the Old Tongue, here and there." Rand started to ask if there was any way for him to find one, but the gleeman went on. "The Old Tongue has music in it, but too many even of the nobles are impatient with listening to it these days. Nobles are all expected to know the Old Tongue, but many only learn enough to impress people who don't. Translations don't have the same sound, unless they're in High Chant, and sometimes that changes meanings even more than most translations. There is one verse in the Cycle—it doesn't scan well, translated word for word, but there's no meaning lost—that goes like this.

"Twice and twice shall he be marked,
    twice to live, and twice to die.

Once the heron, to set his path.
Twice the heron, to name him true.
Once the Dragon, for remembrance lost.
Twice the Dragon, for the price he must pay."

He reached out and touched the herons embroidered on Rand's high collar.

For a moment, Rand could only gape at him, and when he could speak, his voice was unsteady. "The sword makes five. Hilt, scabbard, and blade." He turned his hand down on the table, hiding the brand on his palm. For the first time since Selene's salve had done its work, he could feel it. Not hurting, but he knew it was there.

"So they do." Thom barked a laugh. "There's another comes to mind.

"Twice dawns the day when his blood is shed.
Once for mourning, once for birth.
Red on black, the Dragon's blood stains the rock of Shayol Ghul.
In the Pit of Doom shall his blood free men from the Shadow."

Rand shook his head, denying, but Thom seemed not to notice. "I don't see how a day can dawn twice, but then a lot of it doesn't really make much sense. The Stone of Tear will never fall till Callandor is wielded by the Dragon Reborn, but the Sword That Cannot Be Touched lies in the Heart of the Stone, so how can he wield it first, eh? Well, be that as it may. I suspect Aes Sedai would want to make events fit the Prophecies as closely as they can. Dying somewhere in the Blasted Lands would be a high price to pay for going along with them."

It was an effort for Rand to make his voice calm, but he did it. "No Aes Sedai are using me for anything. I told you, the last I saw of Moiraine was in Shienar. She said I could go where I wanted, and I left."

"And there's no Aes Sedai with you now? None at all?"

"None."

Thom knuckled his dangling white mustaches. He seemed satisfied, and at the same time puzzled. "Then why ask about the Prophecies? Why send the Ogier out of the room?"

"I . . . didn't want to upset him. He's nervous enough about the Horn. That's what I wanted to ask. Is the Horn mentioned in the—the Prophecies?" He still could not make himself say it all the way out. "All these false Dragons, and now the Horn is found. Everybody thinks the Horn of Valere is supposed to summon dead heroes to fight the Dark One in the Last Battle, and the . . . the Dragon Reborn . . . is supposed to fight the Dark One in the Last Battle. It seemed natural enough to ask."

"I suppose it is. Not many know that about the Dragon Reborn fighting the Last Battle, or if they do, they think he'll fight alongside the Dark One. Not many read the Prophecies to find out. What was that you said about the Horn? 'Supposed to'?"

"I've learned a few things since we parted, Thom. They will come for whoever blows the Horn, even a Darkfriend."

Bushy eyebrows rose nearly to Thom's hairline. "Now that I didn't know. You have learned a few things."

"It doesn't mean I would let the White Tower use me for a false Dragon. I don't want anything to do with Aes Sedai, or false Dragons, or the Power, or. . . ." Rand bit his tongue. *Get mad and you start babbling. Fool!*

"For a time, boy, I thought you were the one Moiraine wanted, and I even thought I knew why. You know, no man chooses to channel the Power. It is something that happens to him, like a disease. You cannot blame a man for falling sick, even if it might kill you, too."

"Your nephew could channel, couldn't he? You told me that was why you helped us, because your nephew had had trouble with the White Tower and there was nobody to help him. There's only one kind of trouble men can have with Aes Sedai."

Thom studied the tabletop, pursing his lips. "I don't suppose there is any use in denying it. You understand, it is not the kind of thing a man talks about, having a male relative who could channel. Aaagh! The Red Ajah never gave Owyn a chance. They gentled him, and then he died. He just gave up wanting to live. . . ." He exhaled sadly.

Rand shivered. *Why didn't Moiraine do that to me?* "A chance, Thom? Do you mean there was some way he could have dealt with it? Not gone mad? Not died?"

"Owyn held it off almost three years. He never hurt anyone. He didn't use the Power unless he had to, and then only to help his village. He. . . ." Thom threw up his hands. "I suppose there was no choice. The people where he lived told me he was acting strange that whole last year. They did not much want to talk about it, and they nearly stoned me when they found out I was his uncle. I suppose he *was* going mad. But he was my blood, boy. I can't love the Aes Sedai for what they did to him, even if they had to. If Moiraine's let you go, then you are well out of it."

For a moment Rand was silent. *Fool! Of course there's no way to deal with it. You're going to go mad and die whatever you do. But Ba'alzamon said—* "No!" He colored under Thom's scrutiny. "I mean . . . I am out of it,

Thom. But I still have the Horn of Valere. Think of it, Thom. The Horn of Valere. Other gleemen might tell tales about it, but you could say you had it in your hands." He realized he sounded like Selene, but all that did was make him wonder where she was. "There's nobody I'd rather have with us than you, Thom."

Thom frowned as if considering it, but in the end he shook his head firmly. "Boy, I like you well enough, but you know as well as I do that I only helped before because there was an Aes Sedai mixed in it. Seaghan doesn't try to cheat me more than I expect, and with the King's Gift added in, I could never earn as much in the villages. To my very great surprise, Dena seems to love me, and—as much a surprise—I return the feeling. Now, why should I leave that to go be chased by Trollocs and Darkfriends? The Horn of Valere? Oh, it is a temptation, I'll admit, but no. No, I will not get mixed up in it again."

He leaned over to pick up one of the wooden instrument cases, long and narrow. When he opened it, a flute lay inside, plainly made but mounted with silver. He closed it again and slid it across the table. "You might need to earn your supper again someday, boy."

"I might at that," Rand said. "At least we can talk. I will be in—"

The gleeman was shaking his head. "A clean break is best, boy. If you're always coming around, even if you never mention it, I won't be able to get the Horn out of my head. And I won't be tangled in it. I won't."

After Rand left, Thom threw his cloak on the bed and sat with his elbows on the table. *The Horn of Valere. How did that farmboy find. . . .* He shut off that line of thought. Think about the Horn too long, and he would find himself running off with Rand to carry it to Shienar. *That would make a story, carrying the Horn of Valere to the Borderlands with Trollocs and Darkfriends pursuing.* Scowling, he reminded himself of Dena. Even if she had not loved him, talent such as hers was not to be found every day. And she did love, even if he could not begin to imagine why.

"Old fool," he muttered.

"Aye, an old fool," Zera said from the door. He gave a start; he had been so absorbed in his thoughts that he had not heard the door open. He had known Zera for years, off and on in his wanderings, and she always took full advantage of the friendship to speak her mind. "An old fool who's playing the Game of Houses again. Unless my ears are failing, that young lord has the sound of Andor on his tongue. He's no Cairhienin, that's for certain sure. *Daes Dae'mar* is dangerous enough without letting an outland lord mix you in his schemes."

Thom blinked, then considered the way Rand had looked. That coat had surely been fine enough for a lord. He was growing old, letting things like that slip by him. Ruefully, he realized he was considering whether to tell Zera the truth or let her continue thinking as she did. *All it takes is to think about the Great Game, and I start playing it.* "The boy is a shepherd, Zera, from the Two Rivers."

She laughed scornfully. "And I'm the Queen of Ghealdan. I tell you, the Game has grown dangerous in Cairhien the last few years. Nothing like what you knew in Caemlyn. There are murders done, now. You'll have your throat cut for you, if you don't watch out."

"I tell you, I am not in the Great Game any longer. That's all twenty years in the past, near enough."

"Aye." She did not sound as if she believed it. "But be that as it may, and young outland lords aside, you've begun performing at the lords' manors."

"They pay well."

"And they'll pull you into their plots as soon as they see how. They see a man, and think how to use him, as naturally as breathing. This young lord of yours won't help you; they will eat him alive."

He gave up on trying to convince her he was out of it. "Is that what you came up to say, Zera?"

"Aye. Forget playing the Great Game, Thom. Marry Dena. She'll take you, the more fool her, bony and white-haired as you are. Marry her, and forget this young lord and *Daes Dae'mar*."

"I thank you for the advice," he said dryly. *Marry her? Burden her with an old husband. She'll never be a bard with my past hanging around her neck.* "If you don't mind, Zera, I want to be alone for a while. I perform for Lady Arilyn and her guests tonight, and I need to prepare."

She gave him a snort and a shake of her head and banged the door shut behind her.

Thom drummed his fingers on the table. Coat or no coat, Rand was still only a shepherd. If he had been more, if he had been what Thom once suspected—a man who could channel—neither Moiraine nor any other Aes Sedai would ever have let him walk away ungentled. Horn or no Horn, the boy was only a shepherd.

"He is out of it," he said aloud, "and so am I."

# CHAPTER
## 27

### *The Shadow in the Night*

"I do not understand it," Loial said. "I was winning, most of the time. And then Dena came in and joined the game, and she won it all right back. Every toss. She called it a little lesson. What did she mean by that?"

Rand and the Ogier were making their way through the Foregate, The Bunch of Grapes behind them. The sun sat low in the west, a red ball half below the horizon, throwing long shadows behind them. The street was empty save for one of the big puppets, a goat-horned Trolloc with a sword at its belt, coming toward them with five men working the poles, but sounds of merriment drifted still from other parts of the Foregate, where the halls of entertainment and the taverns stood. Here, doors were already barred and windows shuttered.

Rand stopped fingering the wooden flute case and slung it on his back. *I suppose I couldn't expect him to throw over everything and come with me, but at least he could talk to me. Light, I wish Ingtar would show up.* He stuffed his hands in his pockets and felt Selene's note.

"You don't suppose she. . . ." Loial paused uncomfortably. "You don't suppose she cheated, do you? Everybody was grinning as if she were doing something clever."

Rand shrugged at his cloak. *I have to take the Horn and go. If we wait for*

*Ingtar, anything can happen. Fain will come sooner or later. I have to stay ahead of him.* The men with the puppet were almost to them.

"Rand," Loial said suddenly, "I don't think that's a—"

Abruptly the men let their poles clatter to the packed dirt street; instead of collapsing, the Trolloc leaped for Rand with outstretched hands.

There was no time to think. Instinct brought the sword out of its sheath in a flashing arc. The Moon Rises Over the Lakes. The Trolloc staggered back with a bubbling cry, snarling even as it fell.

For an instant everyone stood frozen. Then the men—the Darkfriends, they had to be—looked from the Trolloc lying in the street to Rand, with the sword in his hands and Loial at his side. They turned and ran.

Rand was staring at the Trolloc, too. The void had surrounded him before his hand touched hilt; *saidin* shone in his mind, beckoning, sickening. With an effort, he made the void vanish, and licked his lips. Without the emptiness, fear crawled on his skin.

"Loial, we have to get back to the inn. Hurin's alone, and they—" He grunted as he was lifted into the air by a thick arm long enough to pin both of his to his chest. A hairy hand grabbed his throat. He caught sight of a tusked snout just over his head. A rank smell filled his nose, equal parts sour sweat and pigsty.

As quickly as it had seized him, the hand at his throat was torn away. Stunned, Rand stared at it, at the thick Ogier fingers clutching the Trolloc's wrist.

"Hold on, Rand." Loial's voice sounded strained. The Ogier's other hand came around and took hold of the arm still holding Rand above the ground. "Hold on."

Rand was shaken from side to side as Ogier and Trolloc struggled. Abruptly he fell free. Staggering, he took two steps to get clear and turned back with sword raised.

Standing behind the boar-snouted Trolloc, Loial had it by wrist and forearm, holding its arms spread wide, breathing hard with the effort. The Trolloc snarled gutturally in the harsh Trolloc tongue, throwing its head back in efforts to catch Loial with a tusk. Their boots scuffled across the dirt of the street.

Rand tried to find a place to put his blade in the Trolloc without hurting Loial, but Ogier and Trolloc spun in their rough dance so much that he could find no opening.

With a grunt, the Trolloc pulled its left arm free, but before it could loose itself completely, Loial snapped his own arm around its neck, hugging the creature close. The Trolloc clawed at its sword; the scythe-like blade hung on the wrong side for left-handed use, but inch by inch the dark steel began sliding out of the scabbard. And still they thrashed about so that Rand could not strike without risking Loial.

*The Power.* That could do it. How, he did not know, but he knew nothing else to try. The Trolloc had its sword half unsheathed. When the curved blade was bare, it would kill Loial.

Reluctantly, Rand formed the void. *Saidin* shone at him, pulled at him. Dimly, he seemed to recall a time when it had sung to him, but now it only drew him, a flower's perfume drawing a bee, a midden's stench drawing a fly. He opened himself up, reached for it. There was nothing there. He could as well have been reaching for light in truth. The taint slid off onto him, soiling him, but there was no flow of light inside him. Driven by a distant desperation, he tried again and again. And again and again there was only the taint.

With a sudden heave, Loial threw the Trolloc aside, so hard that the thing cartwheeled against the side of a building. It struck, headfirst, with a loud crack, and slid down the wall to lie with its neck twisted at an impossible angle. Loial stood staring at it, his chest heaving.

Rand looked out of the emptiness for a moment before he realized what had happened. As soon as he did, though, he let void and tainted light go, and hurried to Loial's side.

"I never . . . killed before, Rand." Loial drew a shuddering breath.

"It would have killed you if you hadn't," Rand told him. Anxiously, he looked at the alleys and shuttered windows and barred doors. Where there were two Trollocs, there had to be more. "I'm sorry you had to do it, Loial, but it would have killed both of us, or worse."

"I know. But I cannot like it. Even a Trolloc." Pointing toward the setting sun, the Ogier seized Rand's arm. "There's another of them."

Against the sun, Rand could not make out details, but it appeared to be another group of men with a huge puppet, coming toward Loial and him. Except that now he knew what to look for, the "puppet" moved its legs too naturally, and the snouted head rose to sniff the air without anyone lifting a pole. He did not think the Trolloc and Darkfriends could see him among the evening shadows, or what lay in the street around him; they moved too slowly for that. Yet it was plain they were hunting, and coming closer.

"Fain knows I am out here somewhere," he said, hastily wiping his blade on a dead Trolloc's coat. "He's set them to find me. He is afraid of the Trollocs being seen, though, or he wouldn't have them disguised. If we can reach a street where there are people, we'll be safe. We have to get back to Hurin. If Fain finds him, alone with the Horn. . . ."

He pulled Loial along to the next corner and turned toward the nearest sounds of laughter and music, but long before they reached it, another group of men appeared ahead of them in the otherwise empty street with a puppet that was no puppet. Rand and Loial took the next turning. It led east.

Every time Rand tried to reach the music and laughter, there was a Trolloc in the way, often sniffing the air for a scent. Some Trollocs hunted by scent. Sometimes, here where there were no eyes to see, a Trolloc stalked alone. More than once he was sure it was one he had seen before. They were closing in, and making sure he and Loial did not leave the deserted streets with their shuttered windows. Slowly the two of them were forced east, away from the city and Hurin, away from other people, along narrow, slowly darkening streets that ran in all directions, uphill and down. Rand eyed the houses they passed, the tall buildings closed up tight for the night, with more than a little regret. Even if he pounded on a door until someone opened it, even if they took Loial and him in, none of the doors he saw would stop a Trolloc. All that would do would be to offer up more victims with Loial and himself.

"Rand," Loial said finally, "there is nowhere else to go."

They had reached the eastern edge of the Foregate; the tall buildings to either side of them were the last. Lights in windows on the upper stories mocked him, but the lower floors were all shut tight. Ahead lay the hills, cloaked in first twilight and bare of so much as a farmhouse. Not entirely empty, though. He could just make out pale walls surrounding one of the larger hills, perhaps a mile away, and buildings inside.

"Once they push us out there," Loial said, "they won't have to worry who sees them."

Rand gestured to the walls around the hill. "Those should stop a Trolloc. It must be a lord's manner. Maybe they'll let us in. An Ogier, and an outland lord? This coat has to be good for something sooner or later." He looked back down the street. No Trollocs in sight yet, but he drew Loial around the side of the building anyway.

"I think that is the Illuminators' chapter house, Rand. Illuminators guard their secrets tightly. I don't think they would let Galldrian himself inside there."

"What trouble have you gotten yourself into now?" said a familiar woman's voice. There was suddenly a spicy perfume in the air.

Rand stared: Selene stepped around the corner they had just rounded, her white dress bright in the dimness. "How did you get here? What are you doing here? You have to leave immediately. Run! There are Trollocs after us."

"So I saw." Her voice was dry, yet cool and composed. "I came to find you, and I find you allowing Trollocs to herd you like sheep. Can the man who possesses the Horn of Valere let himself be treated so?"

"I don't have it with me," he snapped, "and I don't know how it could help if I did. The dead heroes are not supposed to come back to save me from Trollocs. Selene, you have to get away. Now!" He peered around the corner.

Not more than a hundred paces away, a Trolloc was sticking its horned head cautiously into the street, smelling the night. A large shadow by its side had to be another Trolloc, and there were smaller shadows, too. Darkfriends.

"Too late," Rand muttered. He shifted the flute case to pull off his cloak and wrap it around her. It was long enough to hide her white dress entirely, and trail on the ground besides. "You'll have to hold that up to run," he told her. "Loial, if they won't let us in, we will have to find a way to sneak in."

"But, Rand—"

"Would you rather wait for the Trollocs?" He gave Loial a push to start him, and took Selene's hand to follow at a trot. "Find us a path that won't break our necks, Loial."

"You're letting yourself become flustered," Selene said. She seemed to have less trouble following Loial in the failing light than Rand did. "Seek the Oneness, and be calm. One who would be great must always be calm."

"The Trollocs might hear you," he told her. "I don't want greatness." He thought he heard an irritated grunt from her.

Stones sometimes turned underfoot, but the way across the hills was not hard despite the twilight shadows. Trees, and even brush, had long since been cleared from the hills for firewood. Nothing grew except knee-high grass that rustled softly around their legs. A night breeze came up softly. Rand worried that it might carry their scent to the Trollocs.

Loial stopped when they reached the wall; it stood twice as high as the Ogier, the stones covered with a whitish plaster. Rand peered back toward the Foregate. Bands of lighted windows reached out like spokes of a wheel from the city walls.

"Loial," he said softly, "can you see them? Are they following us?"

The Ogier looked in the direction of the Foregate, and nodded unhappily. "I only see some of the Trollocs, but they are coming this way. Running. Rand, I really don't think—"

Selene cut him off. "If he wants to go in, *alantin,* he needs a door. Such as that one." She pointed to a dark patch a little down the wall. Even with her telling him, Rand was not certain it *was* a door, but when she strode to it and pulled, it opened.

"Rand," Loial began.

Rand pushed him to the door. "Later, Loial. And softly. We're hiding, remember?" He got them inside and closed the door behind them. There were brackets for a bar, but no bar to be seen. It would not stop anyone, but maybe the Trollocs would hesitate to come inside the walls.

They were in an alleyway leading up the hill between two long, low windowless buildings. At first he thought they were stone, too, but then he realized the white plaster had been laid over wood. It was dark enough now for the moon reflecting from the walls to give a semblance of light.

"Better to be arrested by the Illuminators than taken by Trollocs," he murmured, starting up the hill.

"But that is what I was trying to tell you," Loial protested. "I've heard the Illuminators kill intruders. They keep their secrets hard and fast, Rand."

Rand stopped dead and stared back at the door. The Trollocs were still out there. At the worst, humans had to be better to deal with than Trollocs. He might be able to talk the Illuminators into letting them go; Trollocs did not listen before they killed. "I'm sorry I got you into this, Selene."

"Danger adds a certain something," she said softly. "And so far, you handle it well. Shall we see what we find?" She brushed past him up the alleyway. Rand followed, the spicy smell of her filling his nostrils.

Atop the hill, the alleyway opened onto a wide expanse of smoothly flattened clay, almost as pale as the plaster and nearly surrounded by more white, windowless buildings with the shadows of narrow alleys between, but to Rand's right stood one building with windows, light falling onto the pale clay. He pulled back into the shadows of the alley as a man and a woman appeared, walking slowly across the open space.

Their clothes were certainly not Cairhienin. The man wore breeches as baggy as his shirt sleeves, both in a soft yellow, with embroidery on the legs of his breeches and across the chest of his shirt. The woman's dress, worked elaborately across the breast, seemed a pale green, and her hair was done in a multitude of short braids.

"All is in readiness, you say?" the woman demanded. "You are certain, Tammuz? All?"

The man spread his hands. "Always you check behind me, Aludra. All is in readiness. The display, it could be given this very moment."

"The gates and doors, they are all barred? All of the. . . ?" Her voice faded as they moved on to the far end of the lighted building.

Rand studied the open area, recognizing almost nothing. In the middle of it, several dozen upright tubes, each nearly as tall as he and a foot or more across, sat on large wooden bases. From each tube, a dark, twisted cord ran across the ground and behind a low wall, perhaps three paces long, on the far side. All around the open space stood a welter of wooden racks with troughs and tubes and forked sticks and a score of other things.

All the fireworks he had ever seen could be held in one hand, and that was as much as he knew, except that they burst with a great roar, or whizzed along the ground in spirals of sparks, or sometimes shot into the air. They always came with warnings from the Illuminators that opening one could cause it to go off. In any case, fireworks were too expensive for the Village Council to have allowed anybody unskilled to open one. He could well remember the time when Mat had tried to do just that; it was nearly a week before anyone but Mat's own mother would speak to him. The only thing that Rand found familiar at all was the cords—the fuses. That, he knew, was where you set the fire.

With a glance back at the unbarred door, he motioned the others to follow and started around the tubes. If they were going to find a place to hide, he wanted to be as far from that door as he could.

It meant making their way between the racks, and Rand held his breath every time he brushed against one. The things in them shifted with the slightest touch, rattling. All of them seemed to be made of wood, without a piece of metal. He could imagine the racket if one were knocked over. He eyed the tall tubes warily, remembering the bang made by one the size of his finger. If those were fireworks, he did not want to be this close to them.

Loial muttered to himself continually, especially when he bumped one of the racks, then started back so fast that he bumped another. The Ogier crept along in a cloud of clatters and muttering.

Selene was no less unnerving. She strode as casually as if they were on a city street. She did not bump anything, did not make a sound, but she also made no effort to keep the cloak closed. The white of her dress seemed brighter than all the walls together. He peered at the lighted windows, waiting for someone to appear. All it would take was one; Selene could not fail to be seen, the alarm given.

The windows remained empty, though. Rand was just breathing a sigh of relief as they approached the low wall—and the alleys and buildings behind it—when Loial brushed against another rack, standing right beside the wall. It held ten soft-looking sticks, as long as Rand's arm, with thin streams of smoke rising from their tips. The rack made hardly a sound when it fell, the smoldering sticks sprawling across one of the fuses. With a crackling hiss, the fuse burst into flame, and the flame raced toward one of the tall tubes.

Rand goggled for an instant, then he tried to whisper a shout. "Behind the wall!"

Selene made an angry noise when he bore her to the ground behind the wall, but he did not care. He tried to spread himself over her protectively as Loial crowded beside them. Waiting for the tube to burst, he wondered if there would be anything left of the wall. There was a hollow thump that he felt through the ground as much as heard. Cautiously, he lifted himself off of Selene enough to peer around the edge of the wall. She fisted him in the ribs, hard, and wriggled out from under him with an oath in a language he did recognize, but he was beyond noticing.

A trickle of smoke was leaking from the top of one of the tubes. That was all. He shook his head wonderingly. *If that's all there is to it. . . .*

With a crash like thunder, a huge flower of red and white bloomed high in the now dark sky, then slowly began drifting away in sparkles.

As he goggled at it, the lighted building erupted with noise. Shouting men and women filled the windows, staring and pointing.

Rand longingly eyed the dark alleyway, only a dozen steps away. And the first step would be in full view of the people at the windows. Pounding feet poured from the building.

He pressed Loial and Selene back against the wall, hoping they looked like just another shadow. "Be still and be silent," he whispered. "It's our only hope."

"Sometimes," Selene said quietly, "if you are very still, no one can see you at all." She did not sound the least bit worried.

Boots thumped back and forth on the other side of the wall, and voices were raised in anger. Especially the one Rand recognized as Aludra.

"You great buffoon, Tammuz! You great pig, you! Your mother, she was a goat, Tammuz! One day you will kill us all."

"I am not to blame for this, Aludra," the man protested. "I have been sure to put everything where it belonged, and the punks, they were—"

"You will not speak to me, Tammuz! A great pig does not deserve to speak like a human!" Aludra's voice changed in answer to another man's question. "There is no time to prepare another. Galldrian, he must be satisfied with the rest for tonight. And one early. And you, Tammuz! You will set everything right, and tomorrow you will leave with the carts to buy the manure. Does anything else go wrong this night, I will not trust you again even with so much as the manure!"

Footsteps faded back toward the building to the accompaniment of Aludra's muttering. Tammuz remained, growling under his breath about the unfairness of it all.

Rand stopped breathing as the man came over to right the toppled stand. Pressed back in the shadows against the wall, he could see Tammuz's back and shoulder. All the man had to do was turn his head, and he could not miss seeing Rand and the others. Still complaining to himself, Tammuz arranged the smoldering sticks in the stand, then stalked off toward the building where everyone else had gone.

Letting his breath go, Rand took a quick look after the man, then pulled back into the shadows. A few people still stood at the windows. "We can't expect any more luck tonight," he whispered.

"It is said great men make their own luck," Selene said softly.

"Will you stop that," he told her wearily. He wished the smell of her did not fill his head so; it made it hard to think clearly. He could remember the feel of her body when he pushed her down—softness and firmness in a disturbing blend—and that did not help either.

"Rand?" Loial was peering around the end of the wall away from the lighted building. "I think we need some more luck, Rand."

Rand shifted to look over the Ogier's shoulder. Beyond open space, in the alleyway that led to the barless door, three Trollocs were peering cautiously out of the shadows toward the lighted windows. One woman was standing at a window; she did not seem to see the Trollocs.

"So," Selene said quietly. "It becomes a trap. These people may kill you if they take you. The Trollocs surely will. But perhaps you can slay the Trollocs too quickly for them to make any outcry. Perhaps you can stop the people from killing you to preserve their little secrets. You may not want greatness, but it will take a great man to do these things."

"You don't have to sound happy about it," Rand said. He tried to stop thinking about how she smelled, how she felt, and the void almost surrounded him. He shook it away. The Trollocs did not seem to have located them, yet. He settled back, staring at the nearest dark alleyway. Once they made a move toward it, the Trollocs would surely see, and so would the woman at the window. It would be a race as to whether Trollocs or Illuminators reached them first.

"Your greatness will make me happy." Despite the words, Selene sounded angry. "Perhaps I should leave you to find your own way for a time. If you'll not take greatness when it is in your grasp, perhaps you deserve to die."

Rand refused to look at her. "Loial, can you see if there's another door down that alley?"

The Ogier shook his head. "There is too much light here and too much dark there. If I were in the alley, yes."

Rand fingered the hilt of his sword. "Take Selene. As soon as you see a door—*if* you do—call out, and I'll follow. If there isn't a door at the end, you will have to lift her so she can reach the top of the wall and climb over."

"All right, Rand." Loial sounded worried. "But when we move, those Trollocs will come after us, no matter who is watching. Even if there is a door, they will be on our heels."

"You let me worry about the Trollocs." *Three of them. I might do it, with the void.* The thought of *saidin* decided him. Too many strange things had happened when he let the male half of the True Source come close. "I will follow as soon as I can. Go." He turned to peer around the wall at the Trollocs.

From the corner of his eye, he had an impression of Loial's bulk moving, of Selene's white dress, half covered by his cloak. One of the Trollocs beyond the tubes pointed to them excitedly, but still the three hesitated, glancing up at the window where the woman still watched. *Three of them. There has to be a way. Not the void. Not* saidin.

"There is a door!" came Loial's soft call. One of the Trollocs took a step out of the shadows, and the others followed, gathering themselves. As from a distance, Rand heard the woman at the window cry out, and Loial shouted something.

Without thinking, Rand was on his feet. He had to stop the Trollocs somehow, or they would run him down, and Loial and Selene. He snatched one of the smoldering sticks and hurled himself at the nearest tube. It tilted, started to fall over, and he caught the square wooden base; the tube pointed straight at the Trollocs. They slowed uncertainly—the woman at the window screamed—and Rand touched the smoking end of the stick to the fuse right where it joined the tube.

The hollow thump came immediately, and the thick wooden base slammed against him, knocking him down. A roar like a thunderclap broke the night and a blinding burst of light tore away the dark.

Blinking, Rand staggered his feet, coughing in thick, acrid smoke, ears ringing. He stared in amazement. Half the tubes and all of the racks lay on their sides, and one corner of the building beside which the Trollocs had stood was simply gone, flames licking at ends of planks and rafters. Of the Trollocs there was no sign.

Through the ringing in his ears, Rand heard shouts from the Illuminators in the building. He broke into a tottering run, lumbered into the alley. Halfway down it he stumbled over something and realized it was his cloak. He snatched it up without pausing. Behind him, the cries of the Illuminators filled the night.

Loial was bouncing impatiently on his feet beside the open door. And he was alone.

"Where is Selene?" Rand demanded.

"She went back, Rand. I tried to grab her, and she slipped right out of my hands."

Rand turned back toward the noise. Through the incessant sound in his ears, some of the shouts were barely distinguishable. There was light there, now, from the flames.

"The sand buckets! Fetch the sand buckets quickly!"

"This is disaster! Disaster!"

"Some of them went that way!"

Loial grabbed Rand's shoulder. "You cannot help her, Rand. Not by being taken yourself. We must go." Someone appeared at the end of the alley, a shadow outlined by the glow of flames behind, and pointed toward them. "Come on, Rand!"

Rand let himself be pulled out of the door into the darkness. The fire faded behind them until it was only a glow in the night, and the lights of the Foregate came closer. Rand almost wished more Trollocs would appear, something he could fight. But there was only the night breeze ruffling the grass.

"I tried to stop her," Loial said. There was a long silence. "We really couldn't have done anything. They would just have taken us, too."

Rand sighed. "I know, Loial. You did what you could." He walked backwards a few steps, staring at the glow. It seemed less; the Illuminators must be putting out the flames. "I have to help her somehow." *How?* Saidin? *The Power?* He shivered. "I have to."

They went through the Foregate by the lighted streets, wrapped in a silence that shut out the gaiety around them.

When they entered The Defender of the Dragonwall, the innkeeper held out his tray with a sealed parchment.

Rand took it, and stared at the white seal. A crescent moon and stars. "Who left this? When?"

"An old woman, my Lord. Not a quarter of an hour gone. A servant, though she did not say from what House." Cuale smiled as if inviting confidences.

"Thank you," Rand said, still staring at the seal. The innkeeper watched them go upstairs with a thoughtful look.

Hurin took his pipe out of his mouth when Rand and Loial entered the room. Hurin had his short sword and sword-breaker on the table, wiping them with an oily rag. "You were long with the gleeman, my Lord. Is he well?"

Rand gave a start. "What? Thom? Yes, he's. . . ." He broke open the seal with his thumb and read.

*When I think I know what you are going to do, you do something else. You are a dangerous man. Perhaps it will not be long before we are together again. Think of the Horn. Think of the glory. And think of me, for you are always mine.*

Again, it bore no signature but the flowing hand itself.

"Are all women crazy?" Rand demanded of the ceiling. Hurin shrugged. Rand threw himself into the other chair, the one sized for an Ogier; his feet dangled above the floor, but he did not care. He stared at the blanket-covered chest under the edge of Loial's bed. *Think of the glory.* "I wish Ingtar would come."

# CHAPTER 28

## A New Thread in the Pattern

Perrin watched the mountains of Kinslayer's Dagger uncomfortably as he rode. The way still slanted upwards, and looked as if it would climb forever, though he thought the crest of the pass must not be too much further. To one side of the trail, the land sloped sharply down to a shallow mountain stream, dashing itself to froth over sharp rocks; to the other side the mountains reared in a series of jagged cliffs, like frozen stone waterfalls. The trail itself ran through fields of boulders, some the size of a man's head, and some as big as a cart. It would take no great skill to hide in that.

The wolves said there were people in the mountains. Perrin wondered if they were some of Fain's Darkfriends. The wolves did not know, or care. They only knew the Twisted Ones were somewhere ahead. Still far ahead, though Ingtar had pressed the column hard. Perrin noticed that Uno was watching the mountains around them much the way he himself was.

Mat, his bow slung across his back, rode with seeming unconcern, juggling three colored balls, yet he looked paler than he had. Verin examined him two and three times a day now, frowning, and Perrin was sure she had even tried Healing at least once, but it made no difference Perrin could see. In any case, she seemed to be more absorbed in something about which she did not speak.

*Rand,* Perrin thought, looking at the Aes Sedai's back. She always rode at the head of the column with Ingtar, and she always wanted them to move even faster than the Shienaran lord would allow. *Somehow, she knows about Rand.* Images from the wolves flickered in his head—stone farmhouses and terraced villages, all beyond the mountain peaks; the wolves saw them no differently than they saw hills or meadows, except with a feeling that they were spoiled land. For a moment he found himself sharing that regret, remembering places the two-legs had long since abandoned, remembering the swift rush through the trees, and the ham-stringing snap of his jaws as the deer tried to flee, and. . . . With an effort he pushed the wolves out of his head. *These Aes Sedai are going to destroy all of us.*

Ingtar let his horse fall back beside Perrin's. Sometimes, to Perrin's eyes, the crescent crest on the Shienaran's helmet looked like a Trolloc's horns. Ingtar said softly, "Tell me again what the wolves said."

"I've told you ten times," Perrin muttered.

"Tell me again! Anything I may have missed, anything that will help me find the Horn. . . ." Ingtar drew a breath and let it out slowly. "I must find the Horn of Valere, Perrin. Tell me again."

There was no need for Perrin to order it in his mind, not after so many repetitions. He droned it out. "Someone—or something—attacked the Darkfriends in the night and killed those Trollocs we found." His stomach no longer lurched at that. Ravens and vultures were messy feeders. "The wolves call him—or it—Shadowkiller; I think it was a man, but they wouldn't go close enough to see clearly. They are not afraid of this Shadowkiller; awe is more like it. They say the Trollocs now follow Shadowkiller. And they say Fain is with them"—even after so long the remembered smell of Fain, the feel of the man, made his mouth twist—"so the rest of the Darkfriends must be, too."

"Shadowkiller," Ingtar murmured. "Something of the Dark One, like a Myrddraal? I have seen things in the Blight that might be called Shadow-killers, but. . . . Did they see nothing else?"

"They would not come close to him. It was not a Fade. I've told you, they will kill a Fade quicker than they will a Trolloc, even if they lose half the pack. Ingtar, the wolves who saw it passed this to others, then still others, before it reached me. I can only tell you what they passed on, and after so many tellings. . . ." He let the words die as Uno joined them.

"Aielman in the rocks," the one-eyed man said quietly.

"This far from the Waste?" Ingtar said incredulously. Uno somehow managed to look offended without changing his expression, and Ingtar added, "No, I don't doubt you. I am just surprised."

"He flaming wanted me to see him, or I likely wouldn't have." Uno

sounded disgusted at admitting it. "And his bloody face wasn't veiled, so
he's not out for killing. But when you see one bloody Aiel, there's always
more you don't." Suddenly his eye widened. "Burn me if it doesn't look
like he bloody wants more than to be seen." He pointed: a man had
stepped into the way ahead of them.

Instantly Masema's lance dropped to a couch, and he dug his heels into
his horse, leaping to a dead gallop in three strides. He was not the only
one; four steel points hurtled toward the man on the ground.

"Hold!" Ingtar shouted. "Hold, I said! I'll have the ears of any man who
doesn't stop where he stands!"

Masema pulled in his horse viciously, sawing the reins. The others also
stopped, in a cloud of dust not ten paces from the man, their lances still
held steady on the man's chest. He raised a hand to wave away the dust as
it drifted toward him; it was the first move he had made.

He was a tall man, with skin dark from the sun and red hair cut short
except for a tail in the back that hung to his shoulders. From his soft, laced
knee-high boots to the cloth wrapped loosely around his neck, his clothes
were all in shades of brown and gray that would blend into rock or earth.
The end of a short horn bow peeked over his shoulder, and a quiver bristled
with arrows at his belt at one side. A long knife hung at the other. In his
left hand he gripped a round hide buckler and three short spears, no more
than half as long as he was tall, with points fully as long as those of the
Shienaran lances.

"I have no pipers to play the tune," the man announced with a smile,
"but if you wish the dance. . . ." He did not change his stance, but Perrin
caught a sudden air of readiness. "My name is Urien, of the Two Spires
sept of the Reyn Aiel. I am a Red Shield. Remember me."

Ingtar dismounted and walked forward, removing his helmet. Perrin
hesitated only a moment before climbing down to join him. He could not
miss the chance to see an Aiel close up. Acting like a black-veiled Aiel. In
story after story Aiel were as deadly and dangerous as Trollocs—some even
said they were all Darkfriends—but Urien's smile somehow did not look
dangerous despite the fact that he seemed poised to leap. His eyes were
blue.

"He looks like Rand." Perrin looked around to see that Mat had joined
them, too. "Maybe Ingtar's right," Matt added quietly. "Maybe Rand is an
Aiel."

Perrin nodded. "But it doesn't change anything."

"No, it doesn't." Mat sounded as if he were talking about something
beside what Perrin meant.

"We are both far from our homes," Ingtar said to the Aiel, "and we, at least, have come for other things than fighting." Perrin revised his opinion of Urien's smile; the man actually looked disappointed.

"As you wish it, Shienaran." Urien turned to Verin, just getting down off her horse, and made an odd bow, digging the points of his spears into the ground and extending his right hand, palm up. His voice became respectful. "Wise One, my water is yours."

Verin handed her reins to one of the soldiers. She studied the Aiel as she came closer. "Why do you call me that? Do you take me for an Aiel?"

"No, Wise One. But you have the look of those who have made the journey to Rhuidean and survived. The years do not touch the Wise Ones in the same way as other women, or as they touch men."

An excited look appeared on the Aes Sedai's face, but Ingtar spoke impatiently. "We are following Darkfriends and Trollocs, Urien. Have you seen any sign of them?"

"Trollocs? Here?" Urien's eyes brightened. "It is one of the signs the prophecies speak of. When the Trollocs come out of the Blight again, we will leave the Three-fold Land and take back our places of old." There was muttering from the mounted Shienarans. Urien eyed them with a pride that made him seem to be looking down from a height.

"The Three-fold Land?" Mat said.

Perrin thought he looked still paler; not sick, exactly, but as if he had been out of the sun too long.

"You call it the Waste," Urien said. "To us it is the Three-fold Land. A shaping stone, to make us; a testing ground, to prove our worth; and a punishment for the sin."

"What sin?" Mat asked. Perrin caught his breath, waiting for the spears in Urien's hand to flash.

The Aiel shrugged. "So long ago it was, that none remember. Except the Wise Ones and the clan chiefs, and they will not speak of it. It must have been a very great sin if they cannot bring themselves to tell us, but the Creator punishes us well."

"Trollocs," Ingtar persisted. "Have you seen Trollocs?"

Urien shook his head. "I would have killed them if I had, but I have seen nothing but the rocks and the sky."

Ingtar shook his head, losing interest, but Verin spoke, sharp concentration in her voice. "This Rhuidean. What is it? Where is it? How are the girls chosen to go?"

Urien's face went flat, his eyes hooded. "I cannot speak of it, Wise One."

In spite of himself Perrin's hand gripped his axe. There was that in Urien's voice. Ingtar had also set himself, ready to reach for his sword, and there was a stir among the mounted men. But Verin stepped up to the Aiel, until she was almost touching his chest, and looked up into his face.

"I am not a Wise One as you know them, Urien," she said insistently. "I am Aes Sedai. Tell me what you can say of Rhuidean."

The man who had been ready to face twenty men now looked as if he wished for an escape from this one plump woman with graying hair. "I . . . can tell you only what is known to all. Rhuidean lies in the lands of the Jenn Aiel, the thirteenth clan. I cannot speak of them except to name them. None may go there save women who wish to become Wise Ones, or men who wish to be clan chiefs. Perhaps the Jenn Aiel choose among them; I do not know. Many go; few return, and those are marked as what they are— Wise Ones, or clan chiefs. No more can I say, Aes Sedai. No more."

Verin continued to look up at him, pursing her lips.

Urien looked at the sky as though he was trying to remember it. "Will you slay me now, Aes Sedai?"

She blinked. "What?"

"Will you slay me now? One of the old prophecies says that if ever we fail the Aes Sedai again, they will slay us. I know your power is greater than that of the Wise Ones." The Aiel laughed suddenly, mirthlessly. There was a wild light in his eyes. "Bring your lightnings, Aes Sedai. I will dance with them."

The Aiel thought he was going to die, and he was not afraid. Perrin realized his mouth was open and closed it with a snap.

"What would I not give," Verin murmured, gazing up at Urien, "to have you in the White Tower. Or just willing to talk. Oh, be still, man. I won't harm you. Unless you mean to harm me, with your talk of dancing."

Urien seemed astounded. He looked at the Shienarans, sitting their horses all around, as if he suspected some trick. "You are not a Maiden of the Spear," he said slowly. "How could I strike at a woman who has not wedded the spear? It is forbidden except to save life, and then I would take wounds to avoid it."

"Why are you here, so far from your own lands?" she asked. "Why did you come to us? You could have remained in the rocks, and we would never have known you were there." The Aiel hesitated, and she added, "Tell only what you are willing to say. I do not know what your Wise Ones do, but I'll not harm you, or try to force you."

"So the Wise Ones say," Urien said dryly, "yet even a clan chief must have a strong belly to avoid doing as they want." He seemed to be picking his words carefully. "I search for . . . someone. A man." His eye ran across Perrin, Mat, the Shienarans, dismissing them all. "He Who Comes With the Dawn. It is said there will be great signs and portents of his coming. I saw that you were from Shienar by your escort's armor, and you had the look of a Wise One, so I thought you might have word of great events, the events that might herald him."

"A man?" Verin's voice was soft, but her eyes were as sharp as daggers. "What are these signs?"

Urien shook his head. "It is said we will know them when we hear of them, as we will know him when we see him, for he will be marked. He will come from the west, beyond the Spine of the World, but be of our blood. He will go to Rhuidean, and lead us out of the Three-fold Land." He took a spear in his right hand. Leather and metal creaked as soldiers reached for their swords, and Perrin realized he had taken hold of his axe again, but Verin waved them all to stillness with an irritated look. In the dirt Urien scraped a circle with his spearpoint, then drew across it a sinuous line. "It is said that under this sign, he will conquer."

Ingtar frowned at the symbol, no recognition on his face, but Mat muttered something coarsely under his breath, and Perrin felt his mouth go dry. *The ancient symbol of the Aes Sedai.*

Verin scraped the marking away with her foot. "I cannot tell you where he is, Urien," she said, "and I have heard of no signs or portents to guide you to him."

"Then I will continue my search." It was not a question, yet Urien waited until she nodded before he eyed the Shienarans proudly, challengingly, then turned his back on them. He walked away smoothly, and vanished into the rocks without looking back.

Some of the soldiers began muttering. Uno said something about "crazy bloody Aiel," and Masema growled that they should have left the Aiel for the ravens.

"We have wasted valuable time," Ingtar announced loudly. "We will ride harder to make it up."

"Yes," Verin said, "we must ride harder."

Ingtar glanced at her, but the Aes Sedai was staring at the smudged ground, where her foot had obliterated the symbol. "Dismount," he ordered. "Armor on the packhorses. We're inside Cairhien, now. We do not want the Cairhienin thinking we have come to fight them. Be quick about it!"

Mat leaned close to Perrin. "Do you. . . ? Do you think he was talking about Rand? It's crazy, I know, but even Ingtar thinks he's Aiel."

"I don't know," Perrin said. "Everything has been crazy since we got mixed up with Aes Sedai."

Softly, as to herself, Verin spoke, still staring at the ground. "It must be a part, and yet how? Does the Wheel of Time weave threads into the

Pattern of which we know nothing? Or does the Dark One touch the Pattern again?"

Perrin felt a chill.

Verin looked up at the soldiers removing their armor. "Hurry!" she commanded with more snap than Ingtar and Uno combined. "We must hurry!"

# CHAPTER 29

## Seanchan

Geofram Bornhald ignored the smell of burning houses and the bodies that lay sprawled on the dirt of the street. Byar and a white-cloaked guard of a hundred rode into the village at his heels, half the men he had with him. His legion was too scattered for his liking, with Questioners having too many of the commands, but his orders had been explicit: Obey the Questioners.

There had been but slight resistance here; only half a dozen dwellings gave off columns of smoke. The inn was still standing, he saw, white-plastered stone like almost every structure on Almoth Plain.

Reining up before the inn, his eyes went past the prisoners his soldiers held near the village well to the long gibbet marring the village green. It was hastily made, only a long pole on uprights, but it held thirty bodies, their clothes ruffled by the breeze. There were small bodies hanging among their elders. Even Byar stared at that in disbelief.

"Muadh!" he roared. A grizzled man trotted away from those holding the prisoners. Muadh had fallen into the hands of Darkfriends, once; his scarred face took even the strongest aback. "Is this your work, Muadh, or the Seanchan?"

"Neither, my Lord Captain." Muadh's voice was a hoarse, whispered growl, another leaving of the Darkfriends. He said no more.

Bornhald frowned. "Surely that lot did not do it," he said, gesturing to
the prisoners. The Children did not look so neat as when he had brought
them across Tarabon, but they seemed ready to parade compared with the
rabble that crouched under their watchful eyes. Men in rags and bits of
armor, with sullen faces. Remnants of the army Tarabon had sent against
the invaders on Toman Head.

Muadh hesitated, then said carefully, "The villagers say they wore Taraboner cloaks, my Lord Captain. There was a big man among them, with
gray eyes and a long mustache, that sounds twin to Child Earwin, and a
young lad, trying to hide a pretty face behind a yellow beard, who fought
with his left hand. Sounds almost like Child Wuan, my Lord Captain."

"Questioners!" Bornhald spat. Earwin and Wuan were among those he
had had to hand over to the Questioners' command. He had seen Questioner tactics before, but this was the first time he had ever been faced with
children's bodies.

"If my Lord Captain says so." Muadh made it sound like fervent agreement.

"Cut them down," Bornhald said wearily. "Cut them down, and make
sure the villagers know there will be no more killing." *Unless some fool
decides to be brave because his woman is watching, and I have to make an example.*
He dismounted, eyeing the prisoners again, as Muadh hurried off calling
for ladders and knives. He had more to think about than Questioners'
overzealousness; he wished he could stop thinking about Questioners altogether.

"They do not put up much fight, my Lord Captain," Byar said, "either
these Taraboners or what is left of the Domani. They snap like cornered
rats, but run as soon as anything snaps back."

"Let us see how we do against the invaders, Byar, before we look down
on these men, yes?" The prisoners' faces bore a defeated look that had been
there before his men came. "Have Muadh pick one out for me." Muadh's
face was enough to soften most men's resolve by itself. "An officer, preferably. One who looks intelligent enough to tell what he has seen without
embroidery, but young enough not to have yet grown a full backbone. Tell
Muadh to be not too gentle about it, yes? Make the fellow believe that I
mean to see worse happen to him than he ever dreamed of, unless he con-
vinces me otherwise." He tossed his reins to one of the Children and strode
into the inn.

The innkeeper was there, for a wonder, an obsequious, sweating man,
his dirty shirt straining over his belly until the embroidered red scrollwork
seemed ready to pop off. Bornhald waved the man away; he was vaguely

aware of a woman and some children huddling in a doorway, until the fat innkeeper shepherded them out.

Bornhald pulled off his gauntlets and sat at one of the tables. He knew too little about the invaders, the strangers. That was what almost everyone called them, those who did not just babble about Artur Hawkwing. He knew they called themselves the Seanchan, and *Hailene*. He had enough of the Old Tongue to know the latter meant Those Who Come Before, or the Forerunners. They also called themselves *Rhyagelle*, Those Who Come Home, and spoke of *Corenne*, the Return. It was almost enough to make him believe the tales of Artur Hawkwing's armies come back. No one knew where the Seanchan had come from, other than that they had landed in ships. Bornhald's requests for information from the Sea Folk had been met with silence. Amador did not hold the Atha'an Miere in good favor, and the attitude was returned with interest. All he knew of the Seanchan he had heard from men like those outside. Broken, beaten rabble who spoke, wide-eyed and sweating, of men who came into battle riding monsters as often as horses, who fought with monsters by their sides, and brought Aes Sedai to rend the earth under their enemies' feet.

A sound of boots in the doorway made him put on a wolfish grin, but Byar was not accompanied by Muadh. The Child of the Light who stood beside him, back braced and helmet in the crook of his arm, was Jeral, who Bornhald expected to be a hundred miles away. Over his armor, the young man wore a cloak of Domani cut, trimmed with blue, not the white cloak of the Children.

"Muadh is talking to a young fellow now, my Lord Captain," Byar said. "Child Jeral has just ridden in with a message."

Bornhald waved for Jeral to begin.

The young man did not unbend. "The compliments of Jaichim Carridin," he started, looking straight ahead, "who guides the Hand of the Light in—"

"I have no need of the Questioner's compliments," Bornhald growled, and saw the young man's startled look. Jeral was young, yet. For that matter, Byar looked uncomfortable, as well. "You will give me his message, yes? Not word for word, unless I ask it. Simply tell me what he wants."

The Child, set to recite, swallowed before he began. "My Lord Captain, he—he says you are moving too many men too close to Toman Head. He says the Darkfriends on Almoth Plain must be rooted out, and you are—forgive me, Lord Captain—you are to turn back at once and ride toward the heart of the plain." He stood stiffly, waiting.

Bornhald studied him. The dust of the plain stained Jeral's face as well as his cloak and his boots. "Go and get yourself something to eat," Bornhald told him. "There should be wash water in one of these houses, if you wish it. Return to me in an hour. I will have messages for you to carry." He waved the young man out.

"The Questioners may be right, my Lord Captain," Byar said when Jeral was gone. "There are many villages scattered on the plain, and the Darkfriends—"

Bornhald's hand slapping the table cut him off. "What Darkfriends? I have seen nothing in any village he has ordered taken except farmers and craftsmen worried that we will burn their livelihoods, and a few old women who tend the sick." Byar's face was a study in lack of expression; he was always readier than Bornhald to see Darkfriends. "And children, Byar? Do children here become Darkfriends?"

"The sins of the mother are visited to the fifth generation," Byar quoted, "and the sins of the father to the tenth." But he looked uneasy. Even Byar had never killed a child.

"Has it never occurred to you, Byar, to wonder why Carridin has taken away our banners, and the cloaks of the men the Questioners lead? Even the Questioners themselves have put off the white. This suggests something, yes?"

"He must have his reasons, Lord Captain," Byar said slowly. "The Questioners always have reasons, even when they do not tell the rest of us."

Bornhald reminded himself that Byar was a good soldier. "Children to the north wear Taraboner cloaks, Byar, and those to the south Domani. I do not like what this suggests to me. There are Darkfriends here, but they are in Falme, not on the plain. When Jeral rides, he will not ride alone. Messages will go to every group of the Children I know how to find. I mean to take the legion onto Toman Head, Byar, and see what the true Darkfriends, these Seanchan, are up to."

Byar looked troubled, but before he could speak, Muadh appeared with one of the prisoners. The sweating young man in a battered, ornate breastplate shot frightened looks at Muadh's hideous face.

Bornhald drew his dagger and began trimming his nails. He had never understood why that made some men nervous, but he used it just the same. Even his grandfatherly smile made the prisoner's dirty face pale. "Now, young man, you will tell me everything you know about these strangers, yes? If you need to think on what to say, I will send you back out with Child Muadh to consider it."

The prisoner darted a wide-eyed look at Muadh. Then words began to pour out of him.

*    *    *

The long swells of the Aryth Ocean made *Spray* roll, but Domon's spread feet balanced him as he held the long tube of the looking glass to his eye and studied the large vessel that pursued them. Pursued, and was slowly overtaking. The wind where *Spray* ran was not the best or the strongest, but where the other ship smashed the swells into mountains of foam with its bluff bow, it could not have blown better. The coastline of Toman Head loomed to the east, dark cliffs and narrow strips of sand. He had not cared to take *Spray* too far out, and now he feared he might pay for it.

"Strangers, Captain?" Yarin had the sound of sweat in his voice. "Is it a strangers' ship?"

Domon lowered the looking glass, but his eye still seemed filled by that tall, square-looking ship with its odd ribbed sails. "Seanchan," he said, and heard Yarin groan. He drummed his thick fingers on the rail, then told the helmsman, "Take her closer in. That ship will no dare enter the shallow waters *Spray* can sail."

Yarin shouted commands, and crewmen ran to haul in booms as the helmsman put the tiller over, pointing the bow more toward the shoreline. *Spray* moved more slowly, heading so far into the wind, but Domon was sure he could reach shoal waters before the other vessel came up on him. *Did her holds be full, she could still take shallower water than ever that great hull can.*

His ship rode a little higher in the water than she had on sailing from Tanchico. A third of the cargo of fireworks he had taken on there was gone, sold in the fishing villages on Toman Head, but with the silver that flowed for the fireworks had come disturbing reports. The people spoke of visits from the tall, boxy ships of the invaders. When Seanchan ships anchored off the coast, the villagers who drew up to defend their homes were rent by lightning from the sky while small boats were still ferrying the invaders ashore, and the earth erupted in fire under their feet. Domon had thought he was hearing nonsense until he was shown the blackened ground, and he had seen it in too many villages to doubt any longer. Monsters fought beside the Seanchan soldiers, not that there was ever much resistance left, the villagers said, and some even claimed that the Seanchan themselves were monsters, with heads like huge insects.

In Tanchico, no one had even known what they called themselves, and the Taraboners spoke confidently of their soldiers driving the invaders into the sea. But in every coastal town, it was different. The Seanchan told astonished people they must swear again oaths they had forsaken, though never deigning to explain when they had forsaken them, or what the oaths meant. The young women were taken away one by one to be examined, and

some were carried aboard the ships and never seen again. A few older
women had also vanished, some of the Guides and Healers. New mayors
were chosen by the Seanchan, and new Councils, and any who protested the
disappearances of the women or having no voice in the choosing might be
hung, or burst suddenly into flame, or be brushed aside like yapping dogs.
There was no way of telling which it would be until it was too late.

And when the people had been thoroughly cowed, when they had been
made to kneel and swear, bewildered, to obey the Forerunners, await the
Return, and serve Those Who Come Home with their lives, the Seanchan
sailed away and usually never returned. Falme, it was said, was the only
town they held fast.

In some of the villages they had left, men and women crept back toward
their former lives, to the extent of talking about electing their Councils
again, but most eyed the sea nervously and made pale-cheeked protests that
they meant to hold to the oaths they had been made to swear even if they
did not understand them.

Domon had no intention of meeting any Seanchan, if he could avoid it.

He was raising the glass to see what he could make out on the nearing
Seanchan decks, when, with a roar, the surface of the sea broke into fountaining water and flame not a hundred paces from his larboard side. Before
he had even begun to gape, another column of flame split the sea on the
other side, and as he was spinning to stare at that, another burst up ahead.
The eruptions died as quickly as they were born, spray from them blown
across the deck. Where they had been, the sea bubbled and steamed as if
boiling.

"We . . . we'll reach shallow water before they can close with us," Yarin
said slowly. He seemed to be trying not to look at the water roiling under
clouds of mist.

Domon shook his head. "Whatever they did, they can shatter us, even
do I take her into the breakers." He shivered, thinking of the flame inside
the fountains of water, and his holds full of fireworks. "Fortune prick me,
we might no live to drown." He tugged at his beard and rubbed his bare
upper lip, reluctant to give the order—the vessel and what it contained
were all he had in the world—but finally he made himself speak. "Bring
her into the wind, Yarin, and down sail. Quickly, man, quickly! Before
they do think we still try to escape."

As crewmen ran to lower the triangular sails, Domon turned to watch
the Seanchan ship approach. *Spray* lost headway and pitched in the swells.
The other vessel stood taller above the water than Domon's ship, with
wooden towers at bow and stern. Men were in the rigging, raising those
strange sails, and armored figures stood atop the towers. A longboat was

put over the side, and sped toward *Spray* under ten oars. It carried armored shapes, and—Domon frowned in surprise—two women crouched in the stern. The longboat thumped against *Spray*'s hull.

The first to climb up was one of the armored men, and Domon saw immediately why some of the villagers claimed the Seanchan themselves were monsters. The helmet looked very much like some monstrous insect's head, with thin red plumes like feelers; the wearer seemed to be peering out through mandibles. It was painted and gilded to increase the effect, and the rest of the man's armor was also worked with paint and gold. Overlapping plates in black and red outlined with gold covered his chest and ran down the outsides of his arms and the fronts of his thighs. Even the steel backs of his gauntlets were red and gold. Where he did not wear metal, his clothes were dark leather. The two-handed sword on his back, with its curved blade, was scabbarded and hilted in black-and-red leather.

Then the armored figure removed his helmet, and Domon stared. He was a woman. Her dark hair was cut short, and her face was hard, but there was no mistaking it. He had never heard of such a thing, except among the Aiel, and Aiel were well known to be crazed. Just as disconcerting was the fact that her face did not look as different as he had expected of a Seanchan. Her eyes were blue, it was true, and her skin exceedingly fair, but he had seen both before. If this woman wore a dress, no one would look at her twice. He eyed her and revised his opinion, that cold stare and those hard cheeks would make her remarked anywhere.

The other soldiers followed the woman onto the deck. Domon was relieved to see, when some of them removed their strange helmets, that they, at least, were men; men with black eyes, or brown, who could have gone unnoticed in Tanchico or Illian. He had begun to have visions of armies of blue-eyed women with swords. *Aes Sedai with swords,* he thought, remembering the sea erupting.

The Seanchan woman surveyed the ship arrogantly, then picked Domon out as captain—it had to be him or Yarin, by their clothes; the way Yarin had his eyes closed and was muttering prayers under his breath pointed to Domon—and fixed him with a stare like a spike.

"Are there any women among your crew or passengers?" She spoke with a soft slurring that made her hard to understand, but there was a snap in her voice that said she was used to getting answers. "Speak up, man, if you are the captain. If not, wake that other fool and tell him to speak."

"I do be captain, my Lady," Domon said cautiously. He had no idea how to address her, and he did not want to put a foot wrong. "I have no passengers, and there be no women in my crew." He thought of the girls and women who had been carried off, and, not for the first time, wondered what these folk wanted with them.

The two women dressed as women were coming up from the longboat, one drawing the other—Domon blinked—by a leash of silvery metal as she climbed aboard. The leash went from a bracelet worn by the first woman to a collar around the neck of the second. He could not tell whether it was woven or jointed—it seemed somehow to be both—but it was clearly of a piece with both bracelet and collar. The first woman gathered the leash in coils as the other came onto the deck. The collared woman wore plain dark gray and stood with her hands folded and her eyes on the planks under her feet. The other had red panels bearing forked, silver lightning bolts on the breast of her blue dress and on the sides of her skirts, which ended short of the ankles of her boots. Domon eyed the women uneasily.

"Speak slowly, man," the blue-eyed woman demanded in her slurred speech. She came across the deck to confront him, staring up at him and in some way seeming taller and larger than he. "You are even harder to understand than the rest in this Light-forsaken land. And I make no claim to be of the Blood. Not yet. After *Corenne*. . . . I am Captain Egeanin."

Domon repeated himself, trying to speak slowly, and added, "I do be a peaceful trader, Captain. I mean no harm to you, and I have no part in your war." He could not help eyeing the two women connected by the leash again.

"A peaceful trader?" Egeanin mused. "In that case, you will be free to go once you have sworn fealty again." She noticed his glances and turned to smile at the women with the pride of ownership. "You admire my *damane*? She cost me dear, but she was worth every coin. Few but nobles own a *damane,* and most are property of the throne. She is strong, trader. She could have broken your ship to splinters, had I wished it so."

Domon stared at the women and the silver leash. He had connected the one wearing the lightning with the fiery fountains in the sea, and assumed she was an Aes Sedai. Egeanin had just set his head whirling. *No one could do that to. . . .* "She is Aes Sedai?" he said disbelievingly.

He never saw the casual backhand blow coming. He staggered as her steel-backed gauntlet split his lip.

"That name is never spoken," Egeanin said with a dangerous softness. "There are only the *damane,* the Leashed Ones, and now they serve in truth as well as name." Her eyes made ice seem warm.

Domon swallowed blood and kept his hand clenched at his sides. If he had had a sword to hand, he would not have led his crew to slaughter against a dozen armored soldiers, but it was an effort to make his voice humble. "I meant no disrespect, Captain. I know nothing of you or your ways. If I do offend, it is ignorance, no intention."

She looked at him, then said, "You are all ignorant, Captain, but you will pay the debt of your forefathers. This land was ours, and it will be ours again. With the Return, it will be ours again." Domon did not know what to say—*Surely she can no mean that nattering about Artur Hawkwing be true?*—so he kept his mouth shut. "You will sail your vessel to Falme"—he tried to protest, but her glare silenced him—"where you and your ship will be examined. If you are no more than a peaceful trader, as you claim, you will be allowed to go your way when you have sworn the oaths."

"Oaths, Captain? What oaths?"

"To obey, to await, and to serve. Your ancestors should have remembered."

She gathered her people—except for a single man in plain armor, which marked him of low rank as much as the depth of his bow to Captain Egeanin—and their longboat pulled away toward the larger ship. The remaining Seanchan gave no orders, only sat cross-legged on the deck and began sharpening his sword while the crew put sail on and got under way. He seemed to have no fear at being alone, and Domon would have personally thrown overboard any crewman who raised a hand to him, for as *Spray* made her way along the coast, the Seanchan ship followed, out in deeper water. There was a mile between the two vessels, but Domon knew there was no hope of escape, and he meant to deliver the man back to Captain Egeanin as safely as if he had been cradled in his mother's arms.

It was a long passage to Falme, and Domon finally persuaded the Seanchan to talk, a little. A dark-eyed man in his middle years, with an old scar above his eyes and another nicking his chin, his name was Caban, and he had nothing but contempt for anyone this side of the Aryth Ocean. That gave Domon a moment's pause. *Maybe they truly do be. . . . No, that do be madness.* Caban's speech had the same slur as Egeanin's, but where hers was silk sliding across iron, his was leather rasping on rock, and mostly he wanted to talk about battles, drinking, and women he had known. Half the time, Domon was not certain if he were speaking of here and now, or of wherever he had come from. The man was certainly not forthcoming about anything Domon wanted to know.

Once Domon asked about the *damane*. Caban reached up from where he sat in front of the helmsman and put the point of his sword to Domon's throat. "Watch what your tongue touches, or you will lose it. That's the business of the Blood, not your kind. Or mine." He grinned while he said it, and as soon as he was done, he went back to sliding a stone along his heavy, curved blade.

Domon touched the point of blood welling above his collar and resolved not to ask that again, at least.

The closer the two vessels came to Falme, the more of the tall, square-looking Seanchan ships they passed, some under sail, but more anchored. Every one was bluff-bowed and towered, as big as anything Domon had ever seen, even among the Sea Folk. A few local craft, he saw, with their sharp bows and slanted sails, darted across the green swells. The sight gave him confidence that Egeanin had spoken the truth about letting him go free.

When *Spray* came up on the headland where Falme stood, Domon gaped at the numbers of the Seanchan ships anchored off the harbor. He tried counting them and gave up at a hundred, less than halfway done. He had seen as many ships in one place before—in Illian, and Tear, and even Tanchico—but those vessels had included many smaller craft. Muttering glumly to himself, he took *Spray* into the harbor, shepherded by her great Seanchan watchdog.

Falme stood on a spit of land at the very tip of Toman Head, with nothing further west of it except the Aryth Ocean. High cliffs ran to the harbor mouth on both sides, and atop one of those, where every ship running into the harbor had to pass under them, stood the towers of the Watchers Over the Waves. A cage hung over the side of one of the towers, with a man sitting in it despondently, legs dangling through the bars.

"Who is that?" Domon asked.

Caban had finally given over sharpening his sword, after Domon had begun to wonder if he meant to shave with it. The Seanchan glanced up to where Domon pointed. "Oh. That is the First Watcher. Not the one who sat in the chair when we first came, of course. Every time he dies, they choose another, and we put him in the cage."

"But why?" Domon demanded.

Caban's grin showed too many teeth. "They watched for the wrong thing, and forgot when they should have been remembering."

Domon tore his eyes away from the Seanchan. *Spray* slid down the last real sea swell and into the quieter waters of the harbor. *I do be a trader, and it is none of my business.*

Falme rose from stone docks up the slopes of the hollow that made the harbor. Domon could not decide whether the dark stone houses made up a goodly sized town or a small city. Certainly he saw no building in it to rival the smallest palace in Illian.

He guided *Spray* to a place at one of the docks, and wondered, while the crew tied the ship fast, if the Seanchan might buy some of the fireworks in his hold. *None of my business.*

To his surprise, Egeanin had herself rowed to the dock with her *damane*. There was another woman wearing the bracelet this time, with the red panels and forked lightning on her dress, but the *damane* was the same sad-faced woman who never looked up unless the other spoke to her. Egeanin had Domon and his crew herded off the ship to sit on the dock under the eyes of a pair of her soldiers—she seemed to think no more were needed, and Domon was not about to argue with her—while others searched *Spray* under her direction. The *damane* was part of the search.

Down the dock, a thing appeared. Domon could think of no other way to describe it. A hulking creature with a leathery, gray-green hide and a beak of a mouth in a wedge-shaped head. And three eyes. It lumbered along beside a man whose armor bore three painted eyes, just like those of the creature. The local people, dockmen and sailors in roughly embroidered shirts and long vests to their knees, shied away as the pair passed, but no Seanchan gave them a second glance. The man with the beast seemed to be directing it with hand signals.

Man and creature turned in among the buildings, leaving Domon staring and his crew muttering to themselves. The two Seanchan guards sneered at them silently. *No my business,* Domon reminded himself. His business was his ship.

The air had a familiar smell of salt water and pitch. He shifted uneasily on the stone, hot from the sun, and wondered what the Seanchan were searching for. What the *damane* was searching for. Wondered what that thing had been. Gulls cried, wheeling above the harbor. He thought of the sounds a caged man might make. *It is no my business.*

Eventually Egeanin led the others back onto the dock. The Seanchan captain had something wrapped in a piece of yellow silk, Domon noted warily. Something small enough to carry in one hand, but which she held carefully in both.

He got to his feet—slowly, for the soldiers' sake, though their eyes held the same contempt Caban's did. "You see, Captain? I do be only a peaceful trader. Perhaps your people would care to buy some fireworks?"

"Perhaps, trader." There was an air of suppressed excitement about her that made him uneasy, and her next words increased the feeling. "You will come with me."

She told two soldiers to come along, and one of them gave Domon a push to get him started. It was not a rough shove; Domon had seen farmers push a cow in the same way to make it move. Setting his teeth, he followed Egeanin.

The cobblestone street climbed the slope, leaving the smell of the harbor behind. The slate-roofed houses grew larger and taller as the street climbed. Surprisingly for a town held by invaders, the streets held more local people than Seanchan soldiers, and now and again a curtained palanquin was borne past by bare-chested men. The Falmen seemed to be going about their business as if the Seanchan were not there. Or almost not there. When palanquin or soldier passed, both poor folk, with only a curling line or two worked on their dirty clothes, and the richer, with shirts, vests, and dresses covered from shoulder to waist in intricately embroidered patterns, bowed and remained bent until the Seanchan were gone. They did the same for Domon and his guard. Neither Egeanin nor her soldiers so much as glanced at them.

Domon realized with a sudden shock that some of the local people they passed wore daggers at their belts, and in a few cases swords. He was so surprised that he spoke without thinking. "Some of them be on your side?"

Egeanin frowned over her shoulder at him, obviously puzzled. Without slowing, she looked at the people and nodded to herself. "You mean the swords. They are our people, now, trader; they have sworn the oaths." She stopped abruptly, pointing at a tall, heavy-shouldered man with a heavily embroidered vest and a sword swinging on a plain leather baldric. "You."

The man halted in mid-step, one foot in the air and a frightened look suddenly on his face. It was a hard face, but he looked as if he wanted to run. Instead, he turned to her and bowed, hands on knees, eyes fixed on her boots. "How may this one serve the captain?" he asked in a tight voice.

"You are a merchant?" Egeanin said. "You have sworn the oaths?"

"Yes, Captain. Yes." He did not take his eyes from her feet.

"What do you tell the people when you take your wagons inland?"

"That they must obey the Forerunners, Captain, await the Return, and serve Those Who Come Home."

"And do you never think to use that sword against us?"

The man's hands went white-knuckled gripping his knees, and there was suddenly sweat in his voice. "I have sworn the oaths, Captain. I obey, await, and serve."

"You see?" Egeanin said, turning to Domon. "There is no reason to forbid them weapons. There must be trade, and merchants must protect themselves from bandits. We allow the people to come and go as they will, so long as they obey, await, and serve. Their forefathers broke their oaths, but these have learned better." She started back up the hill, and the soldiers pushed Domon after her.

He looked back at the merchant. The man stayed bent as he was till

Egeanin was ten paces up the street, then he straightened and hurried the other way, leaping down the sloping street.

Egeanin and his guards did not look around, either, when a mounted Seanchan troop passed them, climbing the street. The soldiers rode creatures that looked almost like cats the size of horses, but with lizards' scales rippling bronze beneath their saddles. Clawed feet grasped the cobblestones. A three-eyed head turned to regard Domon as the troop climbed by; aside from everything else, it seemed too—knowing—for Domon's peace of mind. He stumbled and almost fell. All along the street, the Falmen were pressing themselves back against the fronts of the buildings, some closing their eyes. The Seanchan paid them no heed.

Domon understood why the Seanchan could allow the people as much freedom as they did. He wondered if he would have had nerve enough to resist. *Damane.* Monsters. He wondered if there was anything to stop the Seanchan from marching all the way to the Spine of the World. *No my business,* he reminded himself roughly, and considered whether there was any way to avoid the Seanchan in his future trading.

They reached the top of the incline, where the town gave way to hills. There was no town wall. Ahead were the inns that served merchants who traded inland, and wagon yards and stables. Here, the houses would have made respectable manors for the minor lords in Illian. The largest of them had an honor guard of Seanchan soldiers out front, and a blue-edged banner bearing a golden, spread-winged hawk rippling above it. Egeanin surrendered her sword and dagger before taking Domon inside. Her two soldiers remained in the street. Domon began to sweat. He smelled a lord in this; it was never good to do business with a lord on the lord's own ground.

In the front hall Egeanin left Domon at the door and spoke to a servant. A local man, judging by the full sleeves of his shirt and the spirals embroidered across his chest; Domon believed he caught the words "High Lord." The servant hurried away, returning finally to lead them to what was surely the largest room in the house. Every stick of furniture had been cleared out of it, even the rugs, and the stone floor was polished to a bright gleam. Folding screens painted with strange birds hid walls and windows.

Egeanin stopped just inside the room. When Domon tried to ask where they were and why, she silenced him with a savage glare and a wordless growl. She did not move, but she seemed on the point of bouncing on her toes. She held whatever it was she had taken from his ship as if it were precious. He tried to imagine what it could be.

Suddenly a gong sounded softly, and the Seanchan woman dropped to her knees, setting the silk-wrapped something carefully beside her. At a look from her, Domon got down as well. Lords had strange ways, and he suspected Seanchan lords might have stranger ones than he knew.

Two men appeared in the doorway at the far end of the room. One had the left side of his scalp shaved, his remaining pale golden hair braided and hanging down over his ear to his shoulder. His deep yellow robe was just long enough to let the toes of yellow slippers peek out when he walked. The other wore a blue silk robe, brocaded with birds and long enough to trail nearly a span on the floor behind him. His head was shaved bald, and his fingernails were at least an inch long, those on the first two fingers of each hand lacquered blue. Domon's mouth dropped open.

"You are in the presence of the High Lord Turak," the yellow-haired man intoned, "who leads Those Who Come Before, and succors the Return."

Egeanin prostrated herself with her hands at her sides. Domon imitated her with alacrity. *Even the High Lords of Tear would no demand this,* he thought. Out of the corner of his eye, he saw Egeanin kissing the floor. With a grimace, he decided there was a limit to imitation. *They can no see whether I do or no anyway.*

Egeanin suddenly stood. He started to rise as well, and made it as far as one knee before a growl in her throat and a scandalized look on the face of the man with the braid put him back down, face to the floor and muttering under his breath. *I would no do this for the King of Illian and the Council of Nine together.*

"Your name is Egeanin?" It had to be the voice of the man in the blue robe. His slurring speech had a rhythm almost like singing.

"I was so named on my sword-day, High Lord," she replied humbly.

"This is a fine specimen, Egeanin. Quite rare. Do you wish a payment?"

"That the High Lord is pleased is payment enough. I live to serve, High Lord."

"I will mention your name to the Empress, Egeanin. After the Return, new names will be called to the Blood. Show yourself fit, and you may shed the name Egeanin for a higher."

"The High Lord honors me."

"Yes. You may leave me."

Domon could see nothing but her boots backing out of the room, pausing at intervals for bows. The door closed behind her. There was a long silence. He was watching sweat from his forehead drip onto the floor when Turak spoke again.

"You may rise, trader."

Domon got to his feet, and saw what Turak held in his long-nailed fingers. The *cuendillar* disk shaped into the ancient seal of the Aes Sedai.

Remembering Egeanin's reaction when he mentioned Aes Sedai, Domon began to sweat in earnest. There was no animosity in the High Lord's dark eyes, only a slight curiosity, but Domon did not trust lords.

"Do you know what this is, trader?"

"No, High Lord." Domon's reply was as steady as a rock; no trader lasted long who could not lie with a straight face and an easy voice.

"And yet you kept it in a secret place."

"I do collect old things, High Lord, from times past. There do be those who would steal such, did they lay easy to hand."

Turak regarded the black-and-white disk for a moment. "This is *cuendillar,* trader—do you know that name?—and older than you perhaps know. Come with me."

Domon followed the man cautiously, feeling a little more sure of himself. With any lord of the lands he knew, if guards were going to be summoned, they already would have been. But the little he had seen of Seanchan told him they did not do things as other men did. He schooled his face to stillness.

He was led into another room. He thought the furniture here had to have been brought by Turak. It seemed to be made of curves, with no straight lines at all, and the wood was polished to bring out strange graining. There was one chair, on a silk carpet woven in birds and flowers, and one large cabinet made in a circle. Folding screens made new walls.

The man with the braid opened the doors of the cabinet to reveal shelves holding an odd assortment of figurines, cups, bowls, vases, fifty different things, no two alike in size or shape. Domon's breath caught as Turak carefully set the disk beside its exact twin.

"*Cuendillar,*" Turak said. "That is what I collect, trader. Only the Empress herself has a finer collection."

Domon's eyes almost popped out of his head. If everything on those shelves was truly *cuendillar,* it was enough to buy a kingdom, or at the least to found a great House. Even a king might beggar himself to buy so much of it, if he even knew where to find so much. He put on a smile.

"High Lord, please accept this piece as a gift." He did not want to let it go, but that was better than angering this Seanchan. *Maybe the Darkfriends will chase him now.* "I do be but a simple trader. I want only to trade. Let me sail, and I do promise that—"

Turak's expression never changed, but the man with the braid cut Domon off with a snapped, "Unshaven dog! You speak of giving the High Lord what Captain Egeanin has already given. You bargain, as if the High Lord were a—a merchant! You will be flayed alive over nine days, dog, and—" The barest motion of Turak's finger silenced him.

"I cannot allow you to leave me, trader," the High Lord said. "In this shadowed land of oath-breakers, I find none who can converse with a man of sensibilities. But you are a collector. Perhaps your conversation will be interesting." He took the chair, lolling back in its curves to study Domon.

Domon put on what he hoped was an ingratiating smile. "High Lord, I do be a simple trader, a simple man. I do no have the way of talking with great Lords."

The man with the braid glared at him, but Turak seemed not to hear. From behind one of the screens, a slim, pretty young woman appeared on quick feet to kneel beside the High Lord, offering a lacquered tray bearing a single cup, thin and handleless, of some steaming black liquid. Her dark, round face was vaguely reminiscent of the Sea Folk. Turak took the cup carefully in his long-nailed fingers, never looking at the young woman, and inhaled the fumes. Domon took one look at the girl and pulled his eyes away with a strangled gasp; her white silk robe was embroidered with flowers, but so sheer he could see right through it, and there was nothing beneath but her own slimness.

"The aroma of *kaf*," Turak said, "is almost as enjoyable as the flavor. Now, trader. I have learned that *cuendillar* is even more rare here than in Seanchan. Tell me how a simple trader came to possess a piece." He sipped his *kaf* and waited.

Domon took a deep breath and set about trying to lie his way out of Falme.

# CHAPTER 30

## *Daes Dae'mar*

In the room shared by Hurin and Loial, Rand peered through the window at the ordered lines and terraces of Cairhien, the stone buildings and slate roofs. He could not see the Illuminators' chapter house; even if huge towers and great lords' houses had not been in the way, the city walls would have prevented it. The Illuminators were on everyone's tongues in the city, even now, days after the night when they had lofted only one nightflower into the sky, and that early. A dozen different versions of the scandal were being told, discounting minor variations, but none close to the truth.

Rand turned away. He hoped no one had been hurt in the fire, but the Illuminators had not so far admitted there had been a fire. They were a close-mouthed lot about what went on inside their chapter house.

"I will take the next watch," he told Hurin, "as soon as I come back."

"There is no need, my Lord." Hurin bowed as deeply as any Cairhienin. "I can keep watch. Truly, my Lord need not trouble himself."

Rand drew a deep breath and exchanged looks with Loial. The Ogier only shrugged. The sniffer was growing more formal every day they remained in Cairhien; the Ogier simply commented that humans often acted oddly.

"Hurin," Rand said, "you used to call me Lord Rand, and you used not to bow every time I looked at you." *I want him to unbend and call me Lord Rand again,* he thought with amazement. *Lord Rand! Light, we have to get out of here before I start* wanting *him to bow.* "Will you please sit down? You make me tired, looking at you."

Hurin stood with his back stiff, yet appeared ready to leap to perform any task Rand might request. He neither sat down nor relaxed now. "It wouldn't be proper, my Lord. We have to show these Cairhienin we know how to be every bit as proper as—"

"Will you stop saying that!" Rand shouted.

"As you wish, my Lord."

It was an effort for Rand not to sigh again. "Hurin, I'm sorry. I should not have shouted at you."

"It's your right, my Lord," Hurin said simply. "If I don't do the way you want, it's your right to shout."

Rand stepped toward the sniffer with the intention of grabbing the man's collar and shaking him.

A knock on the connecting door to Rand's room froze them all, but Rand was pleased to see that Hurin did not wait to ask permission before picking up his sword. The heron-mark blade was at Rand's waist; going out, he touched its hilt. He waited for Loial to seat himself on his long bed, arranging his legs and the tails of his coat to further obscure the blanket-covered chest under the bed, then yanked open the door.

The innkeeper stood there, rocking with eagerness and pushing his tray at Rand. Two sealed parchments lay on the tray. "Forgive me, my Lord," Cuale said breathlessly. "I could not wait until you came down, and then you were not in your own room, and—and. . . . Forgive me, but. . . ." He jiggled the tray.

Rand snatched the invitations—there had been so many—without looking at them, took the innkeeper's arm, and turned him toward the door to the hall. "Thank you, Master Cuale, for taking the trouble. If you'll leave us alone, now, please. . . ."

"But, my Lord," Cuale protested, "these are from—"

"Thank you." Rand pushed the man into the hall and pulled the door shut firmly. He tossed the parchments onto the table. "He hasn't done that before. Loial, do you think he was listening at the door before he knocked?"

"You are starting to think like these Cairhienin." The Ogier laughed, but his ears twitched thoughtfully and he added, "Still, he is Cairhienin, so he may well have been. I don't think we said anything he should not have heard."

Rand tried to remember. None of them had mentioned the Horn of

Valere, or Trollocs, or Darkfriends. When he found himself wondering what Cuale could make of what they actually had said, he gave himself a shake. "This place is getting to you, too," he muttered to himself.

"My Lord?" Hurin had picked up the sealed parchments and was gazing wide-eyed at the seals. "My Lord, these are from Lord Barthanes, High Seat of House Damodred, and from"—his voice dropped with awe—"the King."

Rand waved them away. "They still go in the fire like the rest. Unopened."

"But, my Lord!"

"Hurin," Rand said patiently, "you and Loial between you have explained this Great Game to me. If I go wherever it is they've invited me, the Cairhienin will read something into it and think I am part of somebody's plot. If I don't go, they'll read something into that. If I send back an answer, they will dig for meaning in it, and the same if I don't answer. And since half of Cairhien apparently spies on the other half, everybody knows what I do. I burned the first two, and I will burn these, just like all the others." One day there had been twelve in the pile he tossed into the common-room fireplace, seals unbroken. "Whatever they make of it, at least it's the same for everybody. I am not for anyone in Cairhien, and I am not against anyone."

"I have tried to tell you," Loial said, "I don't think it works that way. Whatever you do, Cairhienin will see some sort of plot in it. At least, that is what Elder Haman always said."

Hurin held the sealed invitations out to Rand as if offering gold. "My Lord, this one bears the personal seal of Galldrian. His personal seal, my Lord. And this one the personal seal of Lord Barthanes, who is next to the King himself in power. My Lord, burn these, and you make enemies as powerful as you can find. Burning them's worked so far because the other Houses are all waiting to see what you're up to, and thinking you must have powerful allies to risk insulting them. But Lord Barthanes—and the King! Insult them, and they'll act for sure."

Rand scrubbed his hands through his hair. "What if I refuse them both?"

"It won't work, my Lord. Every last House has sent you an invitation, now. If you decline these—well, for sure at least one of the other Houses will figure, if you're not allied with the King or Lord Barthanes, then they can answer your insult of burning their invitation. My Lord, I hear the Houses in Cairhien use killers, now. A knife in the street. An arrow from a rooftop. Poison slipped in your wine."

"You could accept them both," Loial suggested. "I know you don't want to, Rand, but it might even be fun. An evening at a lord's manor, or even at the Royal Palace. Rand, the Shienarans believed in you."

Rand grimaced. He knew it had been chance that the Shienarans thought he was a lord; a chance likeness of names, a rumor among the servants, and Moiraine and the Amyrlin stirring it all. But Selene had believed it, too. *Maybe she'll be at one of these.*

Hurin was shaking his head violently, though. "Builder, you don't know *Daes Dae'mar* as well as you think you do. Not the way they play it in Cairhien, not now. With most Houses, it wouldn't matter. Even when they're plotting against each other to the knife, they act like they aren't, out where everybody can see. But not these two. House Damodred held the throne until Laman lost it, and they want it back. The King would crush them, if they weren't nearly as powerful as he is. You can't find bitterer rivals than House Riatin and House Damodred. If my Lord accepts both, both Houses will know it as soon as he sends his answers, and they'll both think he's part of some plot by the other against them. They'll use the knife and the poison as quick as look at you."

"And I suppose," Rand growled, "if I only accept one, the other will think I'm allied with that House." Hurin nodded. "And they will probably try to kill me to stop whatever I'm involved in." Hurin nodded again. "Then do you have any suggestion as to how I avoid *any* of them wanting to see me dead?" Hurin shook his head. "I wish I'd never burned those first two."

"Yes, my Lord. But it wouldn't have made much difference, I'm guessing. Whoever you accepted or rejected, these Cairhienin would see something in it."

Rand held out his hand, and Hurin laid the two folded parchments in it. The one was sealed, not with the Tree and Crown of House Damodred, but with Barthanes's Charging Boar. The other bore Galldrian's Stag. Personal seals. Apparently he had managed to rouse interest in the highest quarters by doing nothing at all.

"These people are crazy," he said, trying to think of a way out of this.

"Yes, my Lord."

"I will let them see me in the common room with these," he said slowly. Whatever was seen in the common room at midday was known in ten Houses before nightfall, and in all of them by daybreak next. "I won't break the seals. That way, they will know I have not answered either one yet. As long as they are waiting to see which way I jump, maybe I can earn a few more days. Ingtar has to come soon. He has to."

"Now that is thinking like a Cairhienin, my Lord," Hurin said, grinning.

Rand gave him a sour look, then stuffed the parchments into his pocket on top of Selene's letters. "Let's go, Loial. Maybe Ingtar has arrived."

When he and Loial reached the common room, no man and woman in it looked at Rand. Cuale was polishing a silver tray as if his life depended on its gleam. The serving girls hurried between the tables as if Rand and the Ogier did not exist. Every last person at the tables stared into his or her mug as if the secrets of power lay in wine or ale. Not one of them said a word.

After a moment, he pulled the two invitations from his pocket and studied the seals, then stuck them back. Cuale gave a little jump as Rand started for the door. Before it closed behind him, he heard conversation spring up again.

Rand strode down the street so fast that Loial did not have to shorten his stride to stay beside him. "We have to find a way out of the city, Loial. This trick with the invitations can't work more than two or three days. If Ingtar doesn't come by then, we must leave anyway."

"Agreed," Loial said.

"But how?"

Loial began ticking off points on his thick fingers. "Fain is out there, or there would not have been Trollocs in the Foregate. If we ride out, they will be on us as soon as we are out of sight of the city. If we travel with a merchant train, they'll certainly attack it." No merchant would have more than five or six guards, and they would probably run as soon as they saw a Trolloc. "If only we knew how many Trollocs Fain has, and how many Darkfriends. You have cut his numbers down." He did not mention the Trolloc he had killed, but from his frown, his long eyebrows hanging down onto his cheeks, he was thinking of it.

"It doesn't matter how many he has," Rand said. "Ten are as bad as a hundred. If ten Trollocs attack us, I don't think we'll get away again." He avoided thinking of the way he might, just might, deal with ten Trollocs. It had not worked when he tried to help Loial, after all.

"I do not think we could, either. I don't think we have money to take passage very far, but even so, if we tried to reach the Foregate docks— well, Fain must have Darkfriends watching. If he thought we were taking ship, I don't believe he would care who saw the Trollocs. Even if we fought free of them somehow, we would have to explain ourselves to the city guards, and they would certainly not believe we cannot open the chest, so—"

"We are not letting any Cairhienin see that chest, Loial."

The Ogier nodded. "And the city docks are no good, either." The city docks were reserved for the grain barges and the pleasure craft of the lords and ladies. No one came to them without permission. One could look down on them from the wall, but it was a drop that would break even Loial's neck. Loial wiggled his thumb as if trying to think of a point for that, too. "I suppose it is too bad we cannot reach Stedding Tsofu. Trollocs would never come into a *stedding*. But I don't suppose they would let us get that far without attacking."

Rand did not answer. They had reached the big guardhouse just inside the gate by which they had first entered Cairhien. Outside, the Foregate teemed and milled, and a pair of guards kept watch on them. Rand thought a man, dressed in what had once been good Shienaran clothes, ducked back into the crowd at the sight of him, but he could not be sure. There were too many people in clothes from too many lands, all of them hurrying. He went up the steps into the guardhouse, past breastplated guards on either side of the door.

The large anteroom had hard wooden benches for people with business there, mainly folk waiting with a humble patience, wearing the plain, dark garments that marked the poorer commoners. There were a few Foregaters among them, picked out by shabbiness and bright colors, no doubt hoping for permission to seek work inside the walls.

Rand went straight to the long table in the back of the room. There was only one man seated behind it, not a soldier, with one green bar across his coat. A plump fellow whose skin looked too tight, he adjusted documents on the table and shifted the position of his inkwell twice before looking up at Rand and Loial with a false smile.

"How may I help you, my Lord?"

"The same way I hoped you could help me yesterday," Rand said with more patience than he felt, "and the day before, and the day before that. Has Lord Ingtar come?"

"Lord Ingtar, my Lord?"

Rand took a deep breath and let it out slowly. "Lord Ingtar of House Shinowa, from Shienar. The same man I have asked after every day I've come here."

"No one of that name has entered the city, my Lord."

"Are you certain? Don't you need to look at your lists, at least?"

"My Lord, the lists of foreigners who have come to Cairhien are exchanged among the guardhouses at sunrise and at sunset, and I examine them as soon as they come before me. No Shienaran lord has entered Cairhien in some time."

"And the Lady Selene? Before you ask again, I do not know her House. But I've given you her name, and I have described her to you three times. Isn't that enough?"

The man spread his hands. "I am sorry, my Lord. Not knowing her House makes it very difficult." He had a bland look on his face. Rand wondered whether he would tell even if he knew.

A movement at one of the doors behind the desk caught Rand's eye—a man starting to step into the anteroom, then turning away hurriedly. "Perhaps Captain Caldevwin can help me," Rand told the clerk.

"Captain Caldevwin, my Lord?"

"I just saw him behind you."

"I am sorry, my Lord. If there was a Captain Caldevwin in the guard-house, I would know."

Rand stared at him until Loial touched his shoulder. "Rand, I think we might as well go."

"Thank you for your help," Rand said in a tight voice. "I will return tomorrow."

"It is my pleasure to do what I may," the man said with his false smile.

Rand stalked out of the guardhouse so fast that Loial had to hurry to catch him up in the street. "He was lying, you know, Loial." He did not slow down, but rather hurried along as if he could burn away some of his frustration through physical exertion. "Caldevwin was there. He could be lying about all of it. Ingtar could already be here, looking for us. I'll bet he knows who Selene is, too."

"Perhaps, Rand. *Daes Dae'mar*—"

"Light, I'm tired of hearing about the Great Game. I don't want to play it. I do not want to be any part of it." Loial walked beside him, saying nothing. "I know," Rand said at last. "They think I'm a lord, and in Cairhien, even outland lords are part of the Game. I wish I'd never put on this coat." *Moiraine,* he thought bitterly. *She's still causing me trouble.* Almost immediately, though, if reluctantly, he admitted that she could hardly be blamed for this. There had always been some reason to pretend to be what he was not. First keeping Hurin's spirits up, and then trying to impress Selene. After Selene, there had not seemed to be any way out of it. His steps slowed until he came to a halt. "When Moiraine let me go, I thought things would be simple again. Even chasing after the Horn, even with—with everything, I thought it would be simple." *Even with saidin inside your head?* "Light, what I wouldn't give to have everything be simple again."

"*Ta'veren,*" Loial began.

"I do not want to hear about that, either." Rand started off again as fast as before. "All I want is to give the dagger to Mat, and the Horn to Ingtar." *Then what? Go mad? Die? If I die before I go mad, at least I won't hurt anybody else. But I don't want to die, either. Lan can talk about Sheathing the Sword, but I'm a shepherd, not a Warder.* "If I can just not touch it," he muttered, "maybe I can. . . . Owyn almost made it."

"What, Rand? I didn't hear that."

"It was nothing," Rand said wearily. "I wish Ingtar would get here. And Mat, and Perrin."

They walked along in silence for a time, with Rand lost in thought. Thom's nephew had lasted almost three years by channeling only when he thought he had to. If Owyn had managed to limit how often he channeled, it must be possible to not channel at all, no matter how seductive *saidin* was.

"Rand," Loial said, "there's a fire up ahead."

Rand got rid of his unwelcome thoughts and looked off into the city, frowning. A thick column of black smoke billowed up above the rooftops. He could not see what lay at the base of it, but it was too close to the inn.

"Darkfriends," he said, staring at the smoke. "Trollocs can't come inside the walls without being seen, but Darkfriends. . . . Hurin!" He broke into a run, Loial easily keeping pace beside him.

The closer they came, the more certain it was, until they rounded the last stone-terraced corner and there was The Defender of the Dragonwall, smoke pouring out of its upper windows and flames breaking through the roof. A crowd had gathered in front of the inn. Cuale, shouting and jumping about, was directing men carrying furnishings out into the street. A double line of men passed inside buckets filled with water from a well down the street and empty buckets back out. Most of the people only stood and watched; a new gout of flame burst through the slate roof, and they gave a loud *aaaah*.

Rand pushed through the crowd to the innkeeper. "Where is Hurin?"

"Careful with that table!" Cuale shouted. "Do not scrape it!" He looked at Rand and blinked. His face was smudged with smoke. "My Lord? Who? Your manservant? I do not remember seeing him, my Lord. No doubt he went out. Do not drop those candlesticks, fool! They are silver!" Cuale danced off to harangue the men lugging his belongings out of the inn.

"Hurin wouldn't have gone out," Loial said. "He would not have left the. . . ." He looked around and left it unsaid; some of the onlookers seemed to find an Ogier as interesting as the fire.

"I know," Rand said, and plunged into the inn.

The common room hardly seemed as if the building were on fire. The double line of men stretched up the stairs, passing their buckets, and others scrambled to carry out what furniture was left, but there was no more smoke down here than if something had been burning the kitchen. As Rand pressed upstairs, it began to thicken. Coughing, he ran up the steps.

The lines stopped short of the second landing, men halfway up the stairs hurling their water up into a smoke-filled hallway. Flames licking up the walls flickered red through the black smoke.

One of the men grabbed Rand's arm. "You cannot go up there, my Lord. It is all lost above here. Ogier, speak to him."

It was the first Rand realized that Loial had followed him. "Go back, Loial. I'll bring him out."

"You cannot carry Hurin and the chest both, Rand." The Ogier shrugged. "Besides, I won't leave my books to burn."

"Then keep low. Under the smoke." Rand dropped to his hands and knees on the stairs, and scrambled up the rest of the way. There was cleaner air down near the floor; still smoky enough to make him cough, but he could breathe it. Yet even the air seemed blistering hot. He could not get enough of it through his nose. He breathed through his mouth, and felt his tongue drying.

Some of the water the men threw landed on him, soaking him to the skin. The coolness was only a momentary relief; the heat came right back. He crawled on determinedly, aware of Loial behind him only from the Ogier's coughing.

One wall of the hallway was almost solid flame, and the floor near it had already begun to add thin tendrils to the cloud that hung over his head. He was glad he could not see what lay above the smoke. Ominous crackling told enough.

The door to Hurin's room had not caught yet, but it was hot enough that he had to try twice before he could manage to push it open. The first thing to meet his eye was Hurin, sprawled on the floor. Rand crawled to the sniffer and lifted him up. There was a lump on the side of his head the size of a plum.

Hurin opened unfocused eyes. "Lord Rand?" he murmured faintly. ". . . knock at the door . . . thought it was more invi. . . ." His eyes rolled back in his head. Rand felt for a heartbeat, and sagged with relief when he found it.

"Rand. . . ." Loial coughed. He was beside his bed, with the covers thrown up to reveal the bare boards underneath. The chest was gone.

Above the smoke, the ceiling creaked, and flaming pieces of wood fell to the floor.

Rand said, "Get your books. I will take Hurin. Hurry." He started to drape the limp sniffer over his shoulders, but Loial took Hurin from him.

"The books will have to burn, Rand. You can't carry him and crawl, and if you stand up, you will never reach the stairs." The Ogier pulled Hurin up onto his broad back, arms and legs hanging to either side. The ceiling gave a loud crack. "We must hurry, Rand."

"Go, Loial. Go, and I'll follow."

The Ogier crawled into the hall with his burden, and Rand started after him. Then he stopped, staring back at the connecting door to his room. The banner was still in there. The banner of the Dragon. *Let it burn,* he thought, and an answering thought came as if he had heard Moiraine say it. *Your life may depend on it. She's still trying to use me. Your life may depend on it. Aes Sedai never lie.*

With a groan, he rolled across the floor and kicked open the door to his room.

The other room was a mass of flame. The bed was a bonfire, red runners already crossed the floor. There would be no crawling across that. Getting to his feet, he ran crouching into the room, flinching from the heat, coughing, choking. Steam rose from his damp coat. One side of the wardrobe was already burning. He snatched open the door. His saddlebags lay inside, still protected from the fire, one side bulging with the banner of Lews Therin Telamon, the wooden flute case beside them. For an instant, he hesitated. *I could still let it burn.*

The ceiling above him groaned. He grabbed saddlebags and flute case and threw himself back through the door, landing on his knees as burning timbers crashed where he had stood. Dragging his burden, he crawled into the hall. The floor shook with more falling beams.

The men with the buckets were gone when he reached the stairs. He all but slid down the steps to the next landing, scrambled to his feet and ran through the now-empty building into the street. The onlookers stared at him, with his face blackened and his coat covered with smut, but he staggered to where Loial had propped Hurin against the wall of a house across the street. A woman from the crowd was wiping Hurin's face with a cloth, but his eyes were still closed, and his breath came in heaves.

"Is there a Wisdom nearby?" Rand demanded. "He needs help." The woman looked at him blankly, and he tried to remember the other names he had heard people call the women who would be Wisdoms in the Two Rivers. "A Wise Woman? A woman you call Mother somebody? A woman who knows herbs and healing?"

"I am a Reader, if that is what you mean," the woman said, "but all I know to do for this one is to make him comfortable. Something is broken inside his head, I fear."

"Rand! It *is* you!"

Rand stared. It was Mat, leading his horse through the crowd, with his bow strung across his back. A Mat whose face was pale and drawn, but still

Mat, and grinning, if weakly. And behind him came Perrin, his yellow eyes shining in the fire and earning as many looks as the blaze. And Ingtar, dismounting in a high-collared coat instead of armor, but still with his sword hilt sticking up over his shoulder.

Rand felt a shiver run through him. "It's too late," he told them. "You came too late." And he sat down in the street and began to laugh.

# CHAPTER
# 31

## *On the Scent*

Rand did not know Verin was there until the Aes Sedai took his face in her hands. For a moment he could see worry in her face, perhaps even fear, and then suddenly he felt as if he had been doused with cold water, not the wet but the tingle. He gave one abrupt shudder and stopped laughing; she left him to crouch over Hurin. The Reader watched her carefully. So did Rand. *What is she doing here? As if I didn't know.*

"Where did you go?" Mat demanded hoarsely. "You all just disappeared, and now you're in Cairhien ahead of us. Loial?" The Ogier shrugged uncertainly and eyed the crowd, his ears twitching. Half the people had turned from the fire to watch the newcomers. A few edged closer trying to listen.

Rand let Perrin give him a hand up. "How did you find the inn?" He glanced at Verin, kneeling with her hands on the sniffer's head. "Her?"

"In a way," Perrin said. "The guards at the gate wanted our names, and a fellow coming out of the guardhouse gave a jump when he heard Ingtar's name. He said he didn't know it, but he had a smile that shouted 'lie' a mile off."

"I think I know the man you mean," Rand said. "He smiles that way all the time."

"Verin showed him her ring," Mat put in, "and whispered in his ear."

He looked and sounded sick, his cheeks flushed and tight, but he managed a grin. Rand had never noticed his cheekbones before. "I couldn't hear what she said, but I didn't know whether his eyes were going to pop out of his head or he was going to swallow his tongue first. All of a sudden, he couldn't do enough for us. He told us you were waiting for us, and right where you were staying. Offered to guide us himself, but he really looked relieved when Verin told him no." He snorted. "Lord Rand of House al'Thor."

"It's too long a story to explain now," Rand said. "Where are Uno and the rest? We will need them."

"In the Foregate." Mat frowned at him, and went on slowly, "Uno said they'd rather stay there than inside the walls. From what I can see, I'd rather be with them. Rand, why will we need Uno? Have you found . . . *them?*"

It was the moment Rand realized suddenly he had been avoiding. He took a deep breath and looked his friend in the eye. "Mat, I had the dagger, and I lost it. The Darkfriends took it back." He heard gasps from the Cairhienin listening, but he did not care. They could play their Great Game if they wanted, but Ingtar had come, and he was finished with it at last. "They can't have gone far, though."

Ingtar had been silent, but now he stepped forward and gripped Rand's arm. "You had it? And the"—he looked around at the onlookers—"the other thing?"

"They took that back, too," Rand said quietly. Ingtar pounded a fist into his palm and turned away; some of the Cairhienin backed off from the look on his face.

Mat chewed his lip, then shook his head. "I didn't know it was found, so it isn't as if I had lost it again. It is just still lost." It was plain he was speaking of the dagger, not the Horn of Valere. "We'll find it again. We have two sniffers, now. Perrin is one, too. He followed the trail all the way to the Foregate, after you vanished with Hurin and Loial. I thought you might have just run off . . . well, you know what I mean. Where *did* you go? I still don't understand how you got so far ahead of us. That fellow said you have been here days."

Rand glanced at Perrin—*He's a sniffer?*—and found Perrin studying him in return. He thought Perrin muttered something. *Shadowkiller? I must have heard him wrong.* Perrin's yellow gaze held him for a moment, seeming to hold secrets about him. Telling himself he was having fancies—*I'm not mad. Not yet.*—he pulled his eyes away.

Verin was just helping a still-shaky Hurin to his feet. "I feel right as goose feathers," he was saying. "Still a little tired, but. . . ." He let the words trail off, seeming to see her for the first time, to realize what had happened for the first time.

"The tiredness will last a few hours," she told him. "The body must strain to heal itself quickly."

The Cairhienin Reader rose. "Aes Sedai?" she said softly. Verin inclined her head, and the Reader made a full curtsy.

As quiet as they had been, the words "Aes Sedai" ran through the crowd in tones ranging from awe to fear to outrage. Everyone was watching now—not even Cuale gave any attention to his own burning inn—and Raud thought a little caution might not be amiss after all.

"Do you have rooms yet?" he asked. "We need to talk, and we can't do it here."

"A good idea," Verin said. "I have stayed here before at The Great Tree. We will go there."

Loial went to fetch the horses—the inn roof had now fallen in completely, but the stables had not been touched—and soon they were making their way through the streets, all riding except for Loial, who claimed he had grown used to walking again. Perrin held the lead line to one of the packhorses they had brought south.

"Hurin," Rand said, "how soon can you be ready to follow their trail again? Can you follow it? The men who hit you and started the fire left a trail, didn't they?"

"I can follow it now, my Lord. And I could smell them in the street. It won't last long, though. There weren't any Trollocs, and they didn't kill anybody. Just men, my Lord. Darkfriends, I suppose, but you can't always be sure of that by smell. A day, maybe, before it fades."

"I don't think they can open the chest either, Rand," Loial said, "or they would just have taken the Horn. It would be much easier to take that if they could, rather than the whole chest."

Rand nodded. "They must have put it in a cart, or on a horse. Once they get it beyond the Foregate, they'll join the Trollocs again, for sure. You will be able to follow that trail, Hurin."

"I will, my Lord."

"Then you rest until you're fit," Rand told him. The sniffer looked steadier, but he rode slumped, and his face was weary. "At best, they will only be a few hours ahead of us. If we ride hard. . . ." Suddenly he noticed that the others were looking at him, Verin and Ingtar, Mat and Perrin. He realized what he had been doing, and his face colored. "I am sorry, Ingtar. It's just that I've become used to being in charge, I suppose. I'm not trying to take your place."

Ingtar nodded slowly. "Moiraine chose well when she made Lord

Agelmar name you my second. Perhaps it would have been better if the Amyrlin Seat had given you the charge." The Shienaran barked a laugh. "At least you have actually managed to touch the Horn."

After that they rode in silence.

The Great Tree could have been twin to The Defender of the Dragon-wall, a tall stone cube of a building with a common room paneled in dark wood and decorated with silver, a large, polished clock on the mantel over the fireplace. The innkeeper could have been Cuale's sister. Mistress Tiedra had the same slightly plump look and the same unctuous manner—and the same sharp eyes, the same air of listening to what was behind the words you spoke. But Tiedra knew Verin, and her welcoming smile for the Aes Sedai was warm; she never mentioned Aes Sedai aloud, but Rand was sure she knew.

Tiedra and a swarm of servants saw to their horses and settled them in their rooms. Rand's room was as fine as the one that had burned, but he was more interested in the big copper bathtub two serving men wrestled through the door, and the steaming buckets of water scullery maids brought up from the kitchen. One look in the mirror above the washstand showed him a face that looked as if he had rubbed it with charcoal, and his coat had black smears across the red wool.

He stripped off and climbed into the tub, but he thought as much as washed. Verin was there. One of three Aes Sedai that he could trust not to try to gentle him themselves, or turn him over to those who would. Or so it seemed, at least. One of three who wanted him to believe he was the Dragon Reborn, to use him as a false Dragon. *She's Moiraine's eyes watching me, Moiraine's hand trying to pull my strings. But I have cut the strings.*

His saddlebags had been brought up, and a bundle from the packhorse containing fresh clothes. He toweled off and opened the bundle—and sighed. He had forgotten that both the other coats he had were as ornate as the one he had tossed on the back of a chair for a maid to clean. After a moment, he chose the black coat, to suit his mood. Silver herons stood on the high collar, and silver rapids ran down his sleeves, water battered to froth against jagged rocks.

Transferring things from his old coat to his new, he found the parchments. Absently, he stuffed the invitations in his pocket as he studied Selene's two letters. He wondered how he could have been such a fool. She was the beautiful young daughter of a noble House. He was a shepherd whom Aes Sedai were trying to use, a man doomed to go mad if he did not die first. Yet he could still feel the pull of her just looking at her writing, could almost smell the perfume of her.

"I am a shepherd," he told the letters, "not a great man, and if I could marry anyone, it would be Egwene, but she wants to be Aes Sedai, and how can I marry any woman, love any woman, when I'll go mad and maybe kill her?"

Words could not lessen his memory of Selene's beauty, though, or the way she made his blood go warm just by looking at him. It almost seemed to him that she was in the room with him, that he could smell her perfume, so much so that he looked around, and laughed to find himself alone.

"Having fancies like I'm addled already," he muttered.

Abruptly he tipped back the mantle of the lamp on the bedside table, lit it, and thrust the letters into the flame. Outside the inn, the wind picked up to a roar, leaking in through the shutters and fanning the flames to engulf the parchment. Hurriedly he tossed the burning letters into the cold hearth just before the fire reached his fingers. He waited until the last blackened curl went out before he buckled on his sword and left the room.

Verin had taken a private dining room, where shelves along the dark walls held even more silver than those in the common room. Mat was juggling three boiled eggs and trying to appear nonchalant. Ingtar peered into the unlit fireplace, frowning. Loial had a few books from Fal Dara still in his pockets, and was reading one beside a lamp.

Perrin slouched at the table, studying his hands clasped on the tabletop. To his nose, the room smelled of beeswax used to polish the paneling. *It was him,* he thought. *Rand is the Shadowkiller. Light, what's happening to all of us?* His hands tightened into fists, large and square. *These hands were meant for a smith's hammer, not an axe.*

He glanced up as Rand entered. Perrin thought he looked determined, set on some course of action. The Aes Sedai motioned Rand to a high-backed armchair across from her.

"How is Hurin?" Rand asked her, arranging his sword so he could sit. "Resting?"

"He insisted on going out," Ingtar answered. "I told him to follow the trail only until he smelled Trollocs. We can follow it from there tomorrow. Or do you want to go after them tonight?"

"Ingtar," Rand said uneasily, "I really wasn't trying to take command. I just didn't think." Yet not as nervously as he would have once, Perrin thought. *Shadowkiller. We're all of us changing.*

Ingtar did not answer, but only kept staring into the fireplace.

"There are some things that interest me greatly, Rand," Verin said quietly. "One is how you vanished from Ingtar's camp without a trace.

Another is how you arrived in Cairhien a week before us. That clerk was very clear on that. You would have had to fly."

One of Mat's eggs hit the floor and cracked. He did not look at it, though. He was looking at Rand, and Ingtar had turned around. Loial pretended to be reading still, but he wore a worried look, and his ears were up in hairy points.

Perrin realized he was staring, too. "Well, he did not fly," he said. "I don't see any wings. Maybe he has more important things to tell us." Verin shifted her attention to him, just for a moment. He managed to meet her eyes, but he was the first to look away. *Aes Sedai. Light, why were we ever fools enough to follow an Aes Sedai?* Rand gave him a grateful look, too, and Perrin grinned at him. He was not the old Rand—he seemed to have grown into that fancy coat; it looked right on him, now—but he was still the boy Perrin had grown up with. *Shadowkiller. A man the wolves hold in awe. A man who can channel.*

"I don't mind," Rand said, and told his tale simply.

Perrin found himself gaping. Portal Stones. Other worlds, where the land seemed to shift. Hurin following the trail of where the Darkfriends *would* be. And a beautiful woman in distress, just like one in a gleeman's tale.

Mat gave a soft, wondering whistle. "And she brought you back? By one of these—these Stones?"

Rand hesitated for a second. "She must have," he said. "So you see, that's how we got so far ahead of you. When Fain came, Loial and I managed to steal back the Horn of Valere in the night, and we rode on to Cairhien because I didn't think we could make it past them once they were roused, and I knew Ingtar would keep coming south after them and reach Cairhien eventually."

*Shadowkiller.* Rand looked at him, eyes narrowing, and Perrin realized he had spoken the name aloud. Apparently not loud enough for anyone else to hear, though. No one else glanced at him. He found himself wanting to tell Rand about the wolves. *I know about you. It's only fair you know my secret, too.* But Verin was there. He could not say it in front of her.

"Interesting," the Aes Sedai said, a thoughtful expression on her face. "I would very much like to meet this girl. If she can use a Portal Stone. . . . Even that name is not very widely known." She gave herself a shake. "Well, that is for another time. A tall girl should not be difficult to find in the Cairhienin Houses. Aah, here is our meal."

Perrin smelled lamb even before Mistress Tiedra led in a procession bearing trays of food. His mouth watered more for that than for the peas and squash, the carrots and cabbage that came with it, or the hot crusty rolls. He still found vegetables tasty, but sometimes, of late, he dreamed of red meat. Not even cooked, usually. It was disconcerting to find himself thinking that the nicely pink slices of lamb that the innkeeper carved were too well done. He firmly took helpings of everything. And two of the lamb.

It was a quiet meal, with everyone concentrating on his own thoughts. Perrin found it painful to watch Mat eat. Mat's appetite was as healthy as ever, despite the feverish flush to his face, and the way he shoveled food into his mouth made it look like his last meal before dying. Perrin kept his eyes on his plate as much as possible, and wished they had never left Emond's Field.

After the maids cleared the table and left again, Verin insisted they remain together until Hurin returned. "He may bring word that will mean we must move at once."

Mat returned to his juggling, and Loial to his reading. Rand asked the innkeeper if there were any more books, and she brought him *The Travels of Jain Farstrider.* Perrin liked that one, too, with its stories of adventures among the Sea Folk and journeys to the lands beyond the Aiel Waste, where silk came from. He did not feel like reading, though, so he set up a stones board on the table with Ingtar. The Shienaran played with a slashing, daring style. Perrin had always played doggedly, giving ground reluctantly, but he found himself placing the stones with as much recklessness as Ingtar. Most of the games ended in a draw, but he managed to win as many as Ingtar did. The Shienaran was eyeing him with a new respect by early evening, when the sniffer returned.

Hurin's grin was at the same time triumphant and perplexed. "I found them, Lord Ingtar. Lord Rand. I tracked them to their lair."

"Lair?" Ingtar said sharply. "You mean they're hiding somewhere close by?"

"Aye, Lord Ingtar. The ones who took the Horn, I followed straight there, and there was Trolloc scent all around the place, though sneaking as if they didn't dare be seen, even there. And no wonder." The sniffer took a deep breath. "It's the great manor Lord Barthanes just finished building."

"Lord Barthanes!" Ingtar exclaimed. "But he . . . he's . . . he's. . . ."

"There are Darkfriends among the high as well as the low," Verin said smoothly. "The mighty give their souls to the Shadow as often as the weak." Ingtar scowled as if he did not want to think of that.

"There's guards," Hurin went on. "We'll not get in with twenty men, not and get out again. A hundred could do it, but two would be better. That's what I think, my Lord."

"What about the King?" Mat demanded. "If this Barthanes is a Darkfriend, the King will help us."

"I am quite sure," Verin said dryly, "that Galldrian Riatin would move against Barthanes Damodred on the *rumor* that Barthanes is a Darkfriend, and glad of the excuse. I am also quite sure Galldrian would never let the Horn of Valere out of his grasp once he had it. He would bring it out on feastdays to show the people and tell them how great and mighty Cairhien is, and no one would ever see it else."

Perrin blinked with shock. "But the Horn of Valere has to be there when the Last Battle is fought. He couldn't just keep it."

"I know little of Cairhienin," Ingtar told him, "but I've heard enough of Galldrian. He would feast us and thank us for the glory we had brought to Cairhien. He would stuff our pockets with gold and heap honors on our heads. And if we tried to leave with the Horn, he'd cut our honored heads off without pausing to take a breath."

Perrin ran a hand through his hair. The more he found out about kings, the less he liked them.

"What about the dagger?" Mat asked diffidently. "He wouldn't want that, would he?" Ingtar glared at him, and he shifted uncomfortably. "I know the Horn is important, but I'm not going to be fighting in the Last Battle. That dagger. . . ."

Verin rested her hands on the arms of her chair. "Galldrian shall not have it, either. What we need is some way inside Barthanes's manor house. If we can only find the Horn, we may also find a way to take it back. Yes, Mat, and the dagger. Once it is known that an Aes Sedai is in the city— well, I usually avoid these things, but if I let slip to Tiedra that I would like to see Barthanes's new manor, I should have an invitation in a day or two. It should not be difficult to bring at least some of the rest of you. What is it, Hurin?"

The sniffer had been rocking anxiously on his heels from the moment she mentioned an invitation. "Lord Rand already has one. From Lord Barthanes."

Perrin stared at Rand, and he was not the only one.

Rand pulled two sealed parchments from his coat pocket and handed them to the Aes Sedai without a word.

Ingtar came to look wonderingly over her shoulder at the seals. "Barthanes, and. . . . And Galldrian! Rand, how did you come by these? What have you been doing?"

"Nothing," Rand said. "I haven't done anything. They just sent them to me." Ingtar let out a long breath. Mat's mouth was hanging open. "Well,

they did just send them," Rand said quietly. There was a dignity to him
that Perrin did not remember; Rand was looking at the Aes Sedai and the
Shienaran lord as equals.

Perrin shook his head. *You are fitting that coat. We're all changing.*

"Lord Rand burned all the rest," Hurin said. "Every day they came, and
every day he burned them. Until these, of course. Every day from mightier
Houses." He sounded proud.

"The Wheel of Time weaves us all into the Pattern as it wills," Verin
said, looking at the parchments, "but sometimes it provides what we need
before we know we need it."

Casually she crumpled the King's invitation and tossed it into the fireplace, where it lay white on the cold logs. Breaking the other seal with her
thumb, she read. "Yes. Yes, this will do very well."

"How can I go?" Rand asked her. "They will know I'm no lord. I am a
shepherd, and a farmer." Ingtar looked skeptical. "I am, Ingtar. I told you
I am." Ingtar shrugged; he still did not look convinced. Hurin stared at
Rand with flat disbelief.

*Burn me,* Perrin thought, *if I didn't know him, I wouldn't believe it either.*
Mat was watching Rand with his head tilted, frowning as if looking at
something he had never seen before. *He sees it, too, now.* "You can do it,
Rand," Perrin said. "You can."

"It will help," Verin said, "if you don't tell everyone what you are not.
People see what they expect to see. Beyond that, look them in the eye and
speak firmly. The way you have been talking to me," she added dryly, and
Rand's cheeks colored, but he did not drop his eyes. "It doesn't matter
what you say. They will attribute anything out of place to your being an
outlander. It will also help if you remember the way you behaved before
the Amyrlin. If you are that arrogant, they will believe you are a lord if you
wear rags." Mat snickered.

Rand threw up his hands. "All right. I'll do it. But I still think they
will know five minutes after I open my mouth. When?"

"Barthanes has asked you for five different dates, and one is tomorrow
night."

"Tomorrow!" Ingtar exploded. "The Horn could be fifty miles downriver
by tomorrow night, or—"

Verin cut him off. "Uno and your soldiers can watch the manor. If they
try to take the Horn anywhere, we can easily follow, and perhaps retrieve it
more easily than from inside Barthanes's walls."

"Perhaps so," Ingtar agreed grudgingly. "I just do not like to wait, now
that the Horn is almost in my hands. I will have it. I must! I must!"

Hurin stared at him. "But, Lord Ingtar, that isn't the way. What happens, happens, and what is meant to be, will—" Ingtar's glare cut him off, though he still muttered under his breath, "It isn't the way, talking of 'must.'"

Ingtar turned back to Verin stiffly. "Verin Sedai, Cairhienin are very strict in their protocol. If Rand does not send a reply, Barthanes may be so insulted he will not let us in, even with that parchment in our hands. But if Rand does . . . well, Fain, at least, knows him. We could be warning them to set a trap."

"We will surprise them." Her brief smile was not pleasant. "But I think Barthanes will want to see Rand in any case. Darkfriend or not, I doubt he has given up plots against the throne. Rand, he says you took an interest in one of the King's projects, but he doesn't say what. What does he mean?"

"I don't know," Rand said slowly. "I haven't done anything at all since I arrived. Wait. Maybe he means the statue. We came through a village where they were digging up a huge statue. From the Age of Legends, they said. The King means to move it to Cairhien, though I don't know how he can move something that big. But all I did was ask what it was."

"We passed it in the day, and did not stop to ask questions." Verin let the invitation fall in her lap. "Not a wise thing for Galldrian to do, perhaps, unearthing that. Not that there is any real danger, but it is never wise for those who don't know what they are doing to meddle with things from the Age of Legends."

"What is it?" Rand asked.

"A *sa'angreal*." She sounded as if it were really not very important, but Perrin suddenly had the feeling the two of them had entered a private conversation, saying things no one else could hear. "One of a pair, the two largest ever made, that we know of. And an odd pair, as well. One, still buried on Tremalking, can only be used by a woman. This one can only be used by a man. They were made during the War of the Powers, to be a weapon, but if there is anything to be thankful for in the end of that Age or the Breaking of the World, it is that the end came before they could be used. Together, they might well be powerful enough to Break the World again, perhaps even worse than the first Breaking."

Perrin's hands tightened to knots. He avoided looking directly at Rand, but even from the corner of his eye he could see a whiteness around Rand's mouth. He thought Rand might be afraid, and he did not blame him a bit.

Ingtar looked shaken, as well he might. "That thing should be buried again, and as deeply as they can pile dirt and stone. What would have happened if Logain had found it? Or any wretched man who can channel, let alone one claiming he's the Dragon Reborn. Verin Sedai, you must warn Galldrian what he's doing."

"What? Oh, there is no need for that, I think. The two must be used in unison to handle enough of the One Power to Break the World—that was the way in the Age of Legends; a man and a woman working together were always ten times as strong as they were apart—and what Aes Sedai today would aid a man in channeling? One by itself is powerful enough, but I can think of few women strong enough to survive the flow through the one on Tremalking. The Amyrlin, of course. Moiraine, and Elaida. Perhaps one or two others. And three still in training. As for Logain, it would have taken all his strength simply to keep from being burned to a cinder, with nothing left for doing anything. No, Ingtar, I don't think you need worry. At least, not until the real Dragon Reborn proclaims himself, and then we will all have enough to worry about as it is. Let us worry now about what we shall do when we are inside Barthanes's manor."

She was talking to Rand. Perrin knew it, and from the queasy look in Mat's eye, he did, too. Even Loial shifted nervously in his chair. *Oh, Light, Rand,* Perrin thought. *Light, don't let her use you.*

Rand's hands were pressing the tabletop so hard that his knuckles were white, but his voice was steady. His eyes never left the Aes Sedai. "First we have to take back the Horn, and the dagger. And then it is done, Verin. Then it is done."

Watching Verin's smile, small and mysterious, Perrin felt a chill. He did not think Rand knew half what he thought he did. Not half.

# CHAPTER
## 32

### *Dangerous Words*

Lord Barthanes's manor crouched like a huge toad in the night, covering as much ground as a fortress, with all its walls and out-buildings. It was no fortress, though, with tall windows everywhere, and lights, and the sounds of music and laughter drifting out, yet Rand saw guards moving on the tower tops and along the roofwalks, and none of the windows were close to the ground. He got down from Red's back and smoothed his coat, adjusted his sword belt. The others dismounted around him, at the foot of broad, whitestone stairs leading up to the wide, heavily carved doors of the manor.

Ten Shienarans, under Uno, made an escort. The one-eyed man exchanged small nods with Ingtar before taking his men to join the other escorts, where ale had been provided and a whole ox was roasting on a spit by a big fire.

The other ten Shienarans had been left behind, along with Perrin. Every one of them had to be there for a purpose, Verin had said, and Perrin had no purpose to serve this night. An escort was necessary for dignity in Cairhienin eyes, but more than ten would seem suspicious. Rand was there because he had received the invitation. Ingtar had come to lend the prestige of his title, while Loial was there because Ogier were sought after in the upper reaches of the Cairhienin nobility. Hurin pretended to be Ingtar's bodyservant. His true purpose was to sniff out the Darkfriends and Trollocs if he could; the Horn of Valere should not be far from them. Mat, still grumbling about it, was pretending to be Rand's servant, since he could feel the dagger when it was close. If Hurin failed, perhaps he could find the Darkfriends.

When Rand had asked Verin why she was there, she had only smiled and said, "To keep the rest of you out of trouble."

As they mounted the stairs, Mat muttered, "I still don't see why I have to be a servant." He and Hurin followed behind the others. "Burn me, if Rand can be a lord, I can put on a fancy coat, too."

"A servant," Verin said without looking back at him, "can go many places another man cannot, and many nobles will not even see him. You and Hurin have your tasks."

"Be quiet now, Mat," Ingtar put in, "unless you want to give us away." They were approaching the doors, where half a dozen guards stood with the Tree and Crown of House Damodred on their chests, and an equal number of men in dark green livery with Tree and Crown on the sleeve.

Taking a deep breath, Rand proffered the invitation. "I am Lord Rand of House al'Thor," he said all in a rush, to get it over with. "And these are my guests. Verin Aes Sedai of the Brown Ajah. Lord Ingtar of House Shinowa, in Shienar. Loial, son of Arent son of Halan, from Stedding Shangtai." Loial had asked that his *stedding* be left out of it, but Verin insisted they needed every bit of formality they could offer.

The servant who had reached for the invitation with a perfunctory bow gave a little jerk at each additional name; his eyes popped at Verin's. In a strangled voice he said, "Be welcome in House Damodred, my lords. Be welcome, Aes Sedai. Be welcome, friend Ogier." He waved the other servants to open the doors wide, and bowed Rand and the others inside, where he hurriedly passed the invitation to another liveried man and whispered in his ear.

This man had the Tree and Crown large on the chest of his green coat. "Aes Sedai," he said, using his long staff to make a bow, almost bending his head to his knees, to each of them in turn. "My lords. Friend Ogier. I am called Ashin. Please to follow me."

The outer hall held only servants, but Ashin led them to a great room filled with nobles, with a juggler performing at one end and tumblers at the other. Voices and music coming from elsewhere said these were not the only guests, or the only entertainments. The nobles stood in twos, and threes and fours, sometimes men and women together, sometimes only one or the other, always with careful space between so no one could overhear what was said. The guests wore the dark Cairhienin colors, each with

bright stripes at least halfway down his or her chest, and some had them all
the way to their waists. The women had their hair piled high in elaborate
towers of curls, every one different, and their dark skirts were so wide they
would have had to turn sideways to pass through any doorway narrower
than those of the manor. None of the men had the shaved heads of soldiers—they all wore dark velvet hats over long hair, some shaped like
bells, others flat—and as with the women, lace ruffles like dark ivory almost hid their hands.

Ashin rapped his staff and announced them in a loud voice, Verin first.

They drew every eye. Verin wore her brown-fringed shawl, embroidered
in grape vines; the announcement of an Aes Sedai sent a murmur through
the lords and ladies, and made the juggler drop one of his hoops, though
no one was watching him any longer. Loial received almost as many looks,
even before Ashin spoke his name. Despite the silver embroidery on collar
and sleeves, the otherwise unrelieved black of Rand's coat made him seem
almost stark beside the Cairhienin, and his and Ingtar's swords drew many
glances. None of the lords appeared to be armed. Rand heard the words
"heron-mark blade" more than once. Some of the glances he was receiving
looked like frowns; he suspected they came from men he had insulted by
burning their invitations.

A slim, handsome man approached. He had long, graying hair, and
multihued stripes crossed the front of his deep gray coat from his neck
almost to the hem just above his knees. He was extremely tall for a
Cairhienin, no more than half a head shorter than Rand, and he had a way
of standing that made him seem even taller, with his chin up so he seemed
to be looking down at everyone else. His eyes were black pebbles. He
looked warily at Verin, though.

"Grace honors me with your presence, Aes Sedai." Barthanes
Damodred's voice was deep and sure. His gaze swept across the others. "I
did not expect so distinguished a company. Lord Ingtar. Friend Ogier."
His bow to each was little more than a nod of the head; Barthanes knew
exactly how powerful he was. "And you, my young Lord Rand. You excite
much comment in the city, and in the Houses. Perhaps we will have a
chance to talk this night." His tone said that he would not miss it if the
chance never came, that he had not been excited to any comment, but his
eyes slid a fraction before he caught them, to Ingtar and Loial, and to
Verin. "Be welcome." He let himself be drawn away by a handsome
woman who laid a beringed hand buried in lace on his arm, but his gaze
drifted back to Rand as he walked away.

The murmur of conversation picked up once more, and the juggler spun
his hoops again in a narrow loop that almost reached the worked plaster

ceiling, a good four spans up. The tumblers had never stopped; a woman leaped into the air from the cupped hands of one of her compatriots, her oiled skin shining in the light of a hundred lamps as she spun, and landed on her feet on the hands of a man who was already standing atop another's shoulders. He lifted her up on outstretched arms as the man below raised him in the same way, and she spread her arms as if for applause. None of the Cairhienin seemed to notice.

Verin and Ingtar drifted into the crowd. The Shienaran received a few wary looks; some looked at the Aes Sedai with wide eyes, others with the worried frowns of those finding a rabid wolf within arm's reach. The latter came from men more often than women, and some of the women spoke to her.

Rand realized that Mat and Hurin had already disappeared to the kitchens, where all the servants who had come with the guests would be gathering until sent for. He hoped they would not have trouble sneaking away.

Loial bent down to speak for his ear alone. "Rand, there is a Waygate nearby. I can feel it."

"You mean this was an Ogier grove?" Rand said softly, and Loial nodded.

"Stedding Tsofu had not been found again when it was planted, or the Ogier who helped build Al'cair'rahienallen would not have needed a grove to remind them of the *stedding*. This was all forest when I came through Cairhien before, and belonged to the King."

"Barthanes probably took it away in some plot." Rand looked around the room nervously. Everyone was still talking, but more than a few were watching the Ogier and him. He could not see Ingtar. Verin stood at the center of a knot of women. "I wish we could stay together."

"Verin says not, Rand. She says it would make them all suspicious and angry, thinking we were holding ourselves aloof. We have to allay suspicion until Mat and Hurin find whatever they find."

"I heard what she said as well as you, Loial. But I still say, if Barthanes is a Darkfriend, then he must know why we're here. Going off by ourselves is just asking to be knocked on the head."

"Verin says he won't do anything until he finds out whether he can make use of us. Just do what she told us, Rand. Aes Sedai know what they are about." Loial walked into the crowd, gathering a circle of lords and ladies before he had gone ten steps.

Others started toward Rand, now that he was alone, but he turned in the other direction and hurried away. *Aes Sedai may know what they're about, but I wish I did. I don't like this. Light, but I wish I knew if she was telling the*

*truth. Aes Sedai never lie, but the truth you hear may not be the truth you think
it is.*

He kept moving to avoid talking with the nobles. There were many
other rooms, all filled with lords and ladies, all with entertainers: three
different gleemen in their cloaks, more jugglers and tumblers, and musicians playing flutes, bitterns, dulcimers, and lutes, plus five different sizes
of fiddle, six kinds of horn, straight or curved or curled, and ten sizes of
drum from tambour to kettle. He gave some of the horn players a second
look, those with curled horns, but the instruments were all plain brass.

*They wouldn't have the Horn of Valere out here, fool,* he thought. *Not unless
Barthanes means to have dead heroes come as part of the entertainment.*

There was even a bard in silver-worked Taren boots and a yellow coat,
strolling through the rooms plucking his harp and sometimes stopping to
declaim in High Chant. He glared contemptuously at the gleemen and did
not linger in the rooms where they were, but Rand saw little difference
between him and them except for their clothes.

Suddenly Barthanes was walking by Rand's side. A liveried servant immediately offered his silver tray with a bow. Barthanes took a blown-glass
goblet of wine. Walking backwards ahead of them still bowing, the servant
held the tray toward Rand until Rand shook his head, then melted into the
crowd.

"You seem restless," Barthanes said, sipping.

"I like to walk." Rand wondered how to follow Verin's advice, and
remembering what she had said about his visit to the Amyrlin, he settled
into Cat Crosses the Courtyard. He knew no more arrogant way to walk
than that. Barthanes's mouth tightened, and Rand thought perhaps the
lord found it too arrogant, but Verin's advice was all he had to go by, so he
did not stop. To take some of the edge off, he said pleasantly, "This is a
fine party. You have many friends, and I've never seen so many entertainers."

"Many friends," Barthanes agreed. "You can tell Galldrian how many,
and who. Some of the names might surprise him."

"I have never met the King, Lord Barthanes, and I don't expect I ever
will."

"Of course. You just happened to be in that flyspeck village. You were
not checking on the progress of retrieving that statue. A great undertaking,
that."

"Yes." He had begun thinking of Verin again, wishing she had given
him some advice on how to talk with a man who assumed he was lying. He

added without thinking, "It's dangerous to meddle with things from the Age of Legends if you don't know what you are doing."

Barthanes peered into his wine, musing as if Rand had just said something profound. "Are you saying you do not support Galldrian in this?" he asked finally.

"I told you, I've never met the King."

"Yes, of course. I did not know Andormen played at the Great Game so well. We do not see many here in Cairhien."

Rand took a deep breath to stop from telling the man angrily that he was not playing their Game. "There are many grain barges from Andor in the river."

"Merchants and traders. Who notices such as they? As well notice the beetles on the leaves." Barthanes's voice carried equal contempt for both beetles and merchants, but once again he frowned as if Rand had hinted at something. "Not many men travel in company with Aes Sedai. You seem too young to be a Warder. I suppose Lord Ingtar is Verin Sedai's Warder?"

"We are who we said we are," Rand said, and grimaced. *Except me.*

Barthanes was studying Rand's face almost openly. "Young. Young to carry a heron-mark blade."

"I am less than a year old," Rand said automatically, and immediately wished he had it back. It sounded foolish, to his ear, but Verin had said act as he had with the Amyrlin Seat, and that was the answer Lan had given him. A Borderman considered the day he was given his sword to be his nameday.

"So. An Andorman, and yet Borderland-trained. Or is it Warder-trained?" Barthanes's eyes narrowed, studying Rand. "I understand Morgase has only one son. Named Gawyn, I have heard. You must be much like him in age."

"I have met him," Rand said cautiously.

"Those eyes. That hair. I have heard the Andoran royal line has almost Aiel coloring in their hair and eyes."

Rand stumbled, though the floor was smooth marble. "I'm not Aiel, Lord Barthanes, and I'm not of the royal line, either."

"As you say. You have given me much to think on. I believe we may find common ground when we talk again." Barthanes nodded and raised his glass in a small salute, then turned to speak to a gray-haired man with many stripes of color down his coat.

Rand shook his head and moved on, away from more conversation. It had been bad enough talking to one Cairhienin lord; he did not want to risk two. Barthanes appeared to find deep meanings in the most trivial comments. Rand realized he had just now learned enough of *Daes Dae'mar* to know he had no idea at all how it was played. *Mat, Hurin, find* something *fast, so we can get out of here. These people are crazy.*

And then he entered another room, and the gleeman at the end of it, strumming his harp and reciting a tale from *The Great Hunt of the Horn,* was Thom Merrilin. Rand stopped dead. Thom did not seem to see him, though the gleeman's gaze passed over him twice. It seemed that Thom had meant what he said. A clean break.

Rand turned to go, but a woman stepped smoothly in front of him and put a hand on his chest, the lace falling back from a soft wrist. Her head did not quite come to his shoulder, but her tall array of curls easily reached as high as his eyes. The high neck of her gown put lace ruffles under her chin, and stripes covered the front of her dark blue dress below her breasts. "I am Alaine Chuliandred, and you are the famous Rand al'Thor. In Barthanes's own manor, I suppose he has the right to speak to you first, but we are all fascinated by what we hear of you. I even hear that you play the flute. Can it be true?"

"I play the flute." *How did she. . . ? Caldevwin. Light, everybody does hear everything in Cairhien.* "If you will excuse——"

"I have heard that some outland lords play music, but I never believed it. I would like very much to hear you play. Perhaps you will talk with me, of this and that. Barthanes seemed to find your conversation fascinating. My husband spends his days sampling his own vineyards, and leaves me quite alone. He is never there to talk with me."

"You must miss him," Rand said, trying to edge around her and her wide skirts. She gave a tinkling laugh as if he had said the funniest thing in the world.

Another woman sidled in beside the first, and another hand was laid on his chest. She wore as many stripes as Alaine, and they were of an age, a good ten years older than he. "Do you think to keep him to yourself, Alaine?" The two women smiled at each other while their eyes threw daggers. The second turned her smile on Rand. "I am Belevaere Osiellin. Are all Andormen so tall? And so handsome?"

He cleared his throat. "Ah . . . some are as tall. Pardon me, but if you will——"

"I saw you talking with Barthanes. They say you know Galldrian, as well. You must come to see me, and talk. My husband is visiting our estates in the south."

"You have the sublety of a tavern wench," Alaine hissed at her, and immediately was smiling up at Rand. "She has no polish. No man could like a woman with a manner so rough. Bring your flute to my manor, and we will talk. Perhaps you will teach me to play?"

"What Alaine thinks of as subtlety," Belevaere said sweetly, "is but lack of courage. A man who wears a heron-mark sword must be brave. That truly is a heron-mark blade, is it not?"

Rand tried backing away from them. "If you will just excuse me, I—" They followed step for step until his back hit the wall; the width of their skirts together made another wall in front of him.

He jumped as a third woman crowded in beside the other two, her skirts joining theirs to the wall on that side. She was older than they, but just as pretty, with an amused smile that did not lessen the sharpness of her eyes. She wore half again as many stripes as Alaine and Belevaere; they made tiny curtsies and glared at her sullenly.

"Are these two spiders trying to toil you in their webs?" The older woman laughed. "Half the time they tangle themselves more firmly than anyone else. Come with me, my fine young Andoran, and I will tell you some of the troubles they would give you. For one thing, I have no husband to worry about. Husbands always make trouble."

Over Alaine's head he could see Thom, straightening from a bow to no applause or notice whatsoever. With a grimace the gleeman snatched a goblet from the tray of a startled servant.

"I see someone I must speak to," Rand told the women, and squeezed out of the box they had put him in just as the last woman reached for his arm. All three stared after him as he hurried to the gleeman.

Thom eyed him over the lip of the goblet, then took another long swallow.

"Thom, I know you said a clean break, but I had to get away from those women. All they wanted to talk about was their husbands being away, but they were already hinting at other things." Thom choked on his wine, and Rand slapped his back. "You drink too fast, and something always goes down the wrong way. Thom, they think I am plotting with Barthanes, or maybe Galldrian, and I don't think they will believe me when I say I'm not. I just needed an excuse to leave them."

Thom stroked his long mustaches with one knuckle and peered across the room at the three women. They were still standing together, watching Rand and him. "I recognize those three, boy. Breane Taborwin alone would give you an education such as every man should have at least once in his life, if he can live through it. Worried about their husbands. I like that, boy." Abruptly his eyes sharpened. "You told me you were clear of Aes Sedai. Half the talk here tonight is of the Andoran *lord* appearing with no warning, and an Aes Sedai at his side. Barthanes and Galldrian. You've let the White Tower put you in the cooking pot this time."

"She only came yesterday, Thom. And as soon as the Horn is safe, I'll be free of them again. I mean to see to it."

"You sound as if it isn't safe now," Thom said slowly. "You didn't sound that way before."

"Darkfriends stole it, Thom. They brought it here. Barthanes is one of them."

Thom seemed to study his wine, but his eyes darted to make sure no one was close enough to listen. More than the three women were watching them with sideways glances while pretending to talk among themselves, but every knot maintained its distance from every other. Still, Thom spoke softly. "A dangerous thing to say if it isn't true, and more dangerous if it is. An accusation like that, against the most powerful man in the kingdom. . . . You say he has the Horn? I suppose you're after my help again, now that you're tangled with the White Tower once more."

"No." He had decided Thom had been right, even if the gleeman did not know why. He could not involve anyone else in his troubles. "I just wanted to get away from those women."

The gleeman blew out his mustaches, taken aback. "Well. Yes. That is well. The last time I helped you, I got a limp out of it, and you seem to have let yourself be tied to Tar Valon strings again. You'll have to get yourself out of it this time." He sounded as if he were trying to convince himself.

"I will, Thom. I will." *Just as soon as the Horn is safe and Mat has that bloody dagger back. Mat, Hurin, where are you?*

As if the thought had been a summons, Hurin appeared in the room, eyes searching among the lords and ladies. They looked through him; servants did not exist unless needed. When he found Rand and Thom, he made his way between the small clusters of nobles and bowed to Rand. "My Lord, I was sent to tell you. Your manservant had a fall and twisted his knee. I don't know how bad, my Lord."

For a moment Rand stared before he understood. Conscious of all the eyes on him, he spoke loudly enough for the nobles closest to overhear. "Clumsy fool. What good is he to me if he can't walk? I suppose I'd better come see how badly he's hurt himself."

It seemed to be the right thing to say. Hurin sounded relieved when he bowed again and said, "As my Lord wishes. If my Lord will follow me?"

"You play very well at being a lord," Thom said softly. "But remember this. Cairhienin may play *Daes Dae'mar,* but it was the White Tower made the Great Game in the first place. Watch yourself, boy." With a glare at the nobles, he set his empty goblet on the tray of a passing servant and strolled away, plucking his harp. He began reciting *Goodwife Mili and the Silk Merchant.*

"Lead on, man," Rand told Hurin, feeling foolish. As he followed the sniffer out of the room, he could feel the eyes following him.

# CHAPTER 33

## *A Message From the Dark*

"Have you found it?" Rand asked as he followed Hurin down a cramped flight of stairs. The kitchens lay on the lower levels, and the servants who had come attending the guests had all been sent there. "Or is Mat really hurt?"

"Oh, Mat's fine, Lord Rand." The sniffer frowned. "At least, he sounds all right, and he grumbles like a hale man. I didn't mean to worry you, but I needed a reason for you to come below. I found the trail easy enough. The men who set fire to the inn all entered a walled garden behind the manor. Trollocs joined them, went in to the garden with them. Sometime yesterday, I think. Maybe even night before last." He hesitated. "Lord Rand, they didn't come out again. They must still be in there."

At the foot of the stairs the sounds of the servants enjoying themselves drifted down the hall, laughter and singing. Someone had a bittern, strumming a raucous tune to clapping and the thump of dancing. There was no worked plaster or fine tapestries here, only bare stone and plain wood. Light in the halls came from rush torches, smoking the ceiling and spread far enough apart that the light faded between them.

"I'm glad you are talking to me naturally again," Rand said. "The way you have been bowing and scraping, I was beginning to think you were more Cairhienin than the Cairhienin."

Hurin's face colored. "Well, as to that. . . ." He glanced down the hall toward the noise and looked as if he wanted to spit. "They all pretend to be so proper, but. . . . Lord Rand, every one of them says he's loyal to his master or mistress, but they all hint they're willing to sell what they know, or have heard. And when they have a few drinks in them, they'll tell you, all whispering in your ear, things about the lords and ladies they serve that'd fair make your hair stand on end. I know they're Cairhienin, but I never heard of such goings on."

"We will be out of here soon, Hurin." Rand hoped it was true. "Where is this garden?" Hurin turned down a side hall leading toward the back of the manor. "Did you bring Ingtar and the others down already?"

The sniffer shook his head. "Lord Ingtar had let himself be cornered by six or seven of those who call themselves ladies. I couldn't get close enough to speak to him. And Verin Sedai was with Barthanes. She gave me such a look when I came near, I never even tried to tell her."

They rounded another corner just then, and there were Loial and Mat, the Ogier standing a little stooped for the lower ceiling.

Loial's grin almost split his face. "There you are. Rand, I was never so glad to get away from anyone as from those people upstairs. They kept asking me if the Ogier were coming back, and if Galldrian had agreed to pay what was owed. It seems the reason all the Ogier stonemasons left is because Galldrian stopped paying them, except with promises. I kept telling them I didn't know anything about it, but half of them seemed to think that I was lying, and the other half that I was hinting at something."

"We'll be out of here soon," Rand assured him. "Mat, are you all right?" His friend's face looked more hollow-cheeked than he remembered, even back at the inn, and his cheekbones more prominent.

"I feel fine," Mat said grumpily, "but I certainly didn't have any trouble leaving the *other* servants. The ones who weren't asking if you starved me thought I was sick and didn't want to come too close."

"Have you sensed the dagger?" Rand asked.

Mat shook his head glumly. "The only thing I've sensed is that somebody's watching me, most of the time. These people are as bad as Fades for sneaking around. Burn me, I nearly jumped out of my skin when Hurin told me he'd located the Darkfriends' trail. Rand, I can't feel it at all, and I've been through this bloody building from rafters to basement."

"That does not mean it isn't here, Mat. I put it in the chest with the Horn, remember. Maybe that keeps you from feeling it. I don't think Fain knows how to open it, else he'd not have gone to the trouble of carrying the weight when he fled Fal Dara. Even that much gold isn't important beside the Horn of Valere. When we find the Horn, we will find the dagger. You'll see."

"As long as I don't have to pretend to be your servant anymore," Mat muttered. "As long as you don't go mad and. . . ." He let the words die with a twist of his mouth.

"Rand is not mad, Mat," Loial said. "The Cairhienin would never have let him in here if he were not a lord. They are the ones who are mad."

"I'm not mad," Rand said harshly. "Not yet. Hurin, show me this garden."

"This way, Lord Rand."

They went out into the night by a small door that Rand had to duck to get through; Loial was forced to bend over and hunch his shoulders. There was enough light in yellow pools from the windows above for Rand to make out brick walks between square flower beds. The shadows of stables and other outbuildings bulked in the darkness to either side. Occasional fragments of music drifted out, from the servants below or from those entertaining their masters above.

Hurin led them along the walks until even the dim glow failed and they made their way by moonlight alone, their boots crunching softly on the brick. Bushes that would have been bright with flowers by daylight now made strange humps in the dark. Rand fingered his sword and did not let his eyes stay on any one spot too long. A hundred Trollocs could be hiding around them unseen. He knew Hurin would have smelled Trollocs if they were there, but that did not help a great deal. If Barthanes was a Darkfriend, then at least some of his servants and guards had to be, too, and Hurin could not always smell a Darkfriend. Darkfriends leaping out of the night would not be much better than Trollocs.

"There, Lord Rand," Hurin whispered, pointing.

Ahead, stone walls not much higher than Loial's head enclosed a square perhaps fifty paces on a side. Rand could not be sure, in the shadows, but it looked as if the gardens stretched on beyond the walls. He wondered why Barthanes had built a walled enclosure in the middle of his garden. No roof showed above the wall. *Why would they go in there and stay?*

Loial bent to put his mouth close to Rand's ear. "I told you this was all an Ogier grove, once. Rand, the Waygate is within that wall. I can feel it."

Rand heard Mat sigh despairingly. "We can't give up, Mat," he said.

"I'm not giving up. I just have enough brains not to want to travel the Ways again."

"We may have to," Rand told him. "Go find Ingtar and Verin. Get them alone somehow—I don't care how—and tell them I think Fain has taken the Horn through a Waygate. Just don't let anyone else hear. And remember to limp; you are supposed to have had a fall." It was a wonder to him that even Fain would risk the Ways, but it seemed the only answer. *They wouldn't spend a day and a night just sitting in there, without a roof over their heads.*

Mat swept a low bow, and his voice was heavy with sarcasm. "At once, my Lord. As my Lord wishes. Shall I carry your banner, my Lord?" He started back for the manor, his grumbles fading away. "Now I have to limp. Next it'll be a broken neck, or. . . ."

"He's just worried about the dagger, Rand," Loial said.

"I know," Rand said. *But how long before he tells somebody what I am, not even meaning to?* He could not believe Mat would betray him on purpose; there was that much of their friendship left, at least. "Loial, boost me up where I can see over the wall."

"Rand, if the Darkfriends are still—"

"They aren't. Boost me up, Loial."

The three of them moved close to the wall, and Loial made a stirrup with his hands for Rand's foot. The Ogier straightened easily with the weight, lifting Rand's head just high enough to see over the top of the wall.

The thin, waning moon gave little light, and most of the area was in shadow, but there did not seem to be any flowers or shrubs inside the walled square. Only a lone bench of pale marble, placed as if one man might sit on it to stare at what stood in the middle of the space like a huge upright stone slab.

Rand caught the top of the wall and pulled himself up. Loial gave a low *hsst* and grabbed at his foot, but he jerked free and rolled over the wall, dropping inside. There was close-cropped grass under his feet; he thought vaguely that Barthanes must let sheep in, at least. Staring at the shadowed stone slab, the Waygate, he was startled to hear boots thump to the ground beside him.

Hurin climbed to his feet, dusting himself off. "You should be careful doing that, Lord Rand. Could be anybody hiding in here. Or anything." He peered into the darkness within the walls, feeling at his belt as if for the short sword and sword-breaker he had had to leave at the inn; servants did not go armed in Cairhien. "Jump in a hole without looking, and there'll be a snake in it every time."

"You would smell them," Rand said.

"Maybe." The sniffer inhaled deeply. "But I can only smell what they've done, not what they intend."

There was a scraping sound from over Rand's head, and then Loial was

letting himself down from the wall. The Ogier did not even have to
straighten his arms completely before his boots touched the ground.
"Rash," he muttered. "You humans are always so rash and hasty. And now
you have me doing it. Elder Haman would speak to me severely, and my
mother. . . ." The darkness hid his face, but Rand was sure his ears were
twitching vigorously. "Rand, if you don't start being a little careful, you
are going to get me in trouble."

Rand walked to the Waygate, walked all the way around it. Even close
up it looked like nothing more than a thick square of stone, taller than he
was. The back was smooth and cool to the touch—he only brushed his
hand against it quickly—but the front had been carved by an artist's
hands. Vines, leaves, and flowers covered it, each so finely done that in the
dim moonlight they seemed almost real. He felt the ground in front of it;
the grass had been scraped partly away in two arcs such as those gates
would make in opening.

"Is that a Waygate?" Hurin asked uncertainly. "I've heard tell of them,
of course, but. . . ." He sniffed the air. "The trail goes right to it and
stops, Lord Rand. How are we going to follow them, now? I've heard if
you go through a Waygate, you come out mad, if you come out at all."

"It can be done, Hurin. I've done it, and Loial, and Mat and Perrin."
Rand never took his eyes from the tangles of leaves on the stone. There was
one unlike any other carved there, he knew. The trefoil leaf of fabled
*Avendesora*, the Tree of Life. He put his hand on it. "I'll bet you can smell
their trail along the Ways. We can follow anywhere they can run." It
would not hurt to prove to himself that he could make himself step
through a Waygate. "I'll prove it to you." He heard Hurin groan. The leaf
was worked in the stone just as the others were, but it came away in his
hand. Loial groaned, too.

In an instant the illusion of living plants seemed suddenly real. Stone
leaves appeared to stir with a breeze, flowers appeared to have color even in
the dark. Down the center of the mass a line appeared, and the two halves
of the slab swung slowly toward Rand. He stepped back to let them open.
He did not find himself looking at the other side of the walled square, but
neither did he see the dull silver reflection he remembered. The space between the opening gates was a black so dark it seemed to make the night
around it lighter. The pitch-blackness oozed out between the still-moving
gates.

Rand leaped back with a shout, dropping the *Avendesora* leaf in his haste,
and Loial cried out, "*Machin Shin*. The Black Wind."

The sound of wind filled their ears; the grass stirred in ripples toward the
walls, and dirt swirled up, sucked into the air. And in the wind a thousand

insane voices seemed to cry, ten thousand, overlapping, drowning each other. Rand could make out some of them, though he tried not to.

*. . . blood so sweet, so sweet to drink the blood, the blood that drips, drips, drops so red; pretty eyes, fine eyes, I have no eyes, pluck the eyes from out of your head; grind your bones, split your bones inside your flesh, suck your marrow while you scream; scream, scream, singing screams, sing your screams. . . .* And worst of all, a whispering thread through all the rest. *Al'Thor. Al'Thor. Al'Thor.*

Rand found the void around him and embraced it, never minding the tantalizing, sickening glow of *saidin* just out of his sight. Greatest of all the dangers along the Ways was the Black Wind that took the souls of those it killed, and drove mad those it let live, but *Machin Shin* was a part of the Ways; it could not leave them. Only it was flowing into the night, and the Black Wind called his name.

The Waygate was not yet fully open. If they could only put the *Avendesora* leaf back. . . . He saw Loial scrambling on his hands and knees, fumbling and searching the grass in the darkness.

*Saidin* filled him. He felt as if his bones were vibrating, felt the red-hot, ice-cold flow of the One Power, felt truly alive as he never was without it, felt the oil-slick taint. . . . *No!* And silently he screamed back at himself from beyond the emptiness, *It's coming for you! It'll kill all of us!* He hurled it all at the black bulge, standing out a full span from the Waygate, now. He did not know what it was that he hurled, or how, but in the heart of that darkness bloomed a coruscating fountain of light.

The Black Wind shrieked, ten thousand wordless howls of agony. Slowly, giving way inch by reluctant inch, the bulge lessened; slowly the oozing reversed, back into the still-open Waygate.

The Power raced through Rand in a torrent. He could feel the link between himself and *saidin,* like a river in flood, between himself and the pure fire blazing in the heart of the Black Wind, a raging cataract. The heat inside him went to white-heat, and beyond, to a shimmer that would have melted stone and vaporized steel and made the air burst into flame. The cold grew till the breath in his lungs should have frozen solid and hard as metal. He could feel it overwhelming him, feel life eroding like a soft clay riverbank, feel what was him wearing away.

*Can't stop! If it gets out. . . . Have to kill it! I—can—not—stop!* Desperately he clung to fragments of himself. The One power roared through him; he rode it like a chip of wood in rapids. The void began to melt and flow; the emptiness steamed with freezing cold.

The motion of the Waygate halted, and reversed.

Rand stared, sure, in the dim thoughts floating outside the void, that he was only seeing what he wanted to see.

The gates drifted closer together, pushing back *Machin Shin* as if the Black Wind had solid substance. The inferno still roared in its breast.

With a vague, distant wondering, Rand saw Loial, still on hands and knees, backing away from the closing gates.

The gap narrowed, vanished. The leaves and vines merged into a solid wall, and were stone.

Rand felt the link between him and the fire snap, the flow of Power through him cease. A moment more, and it would have swept him away completely. Shaking, he dropped to his knees. It was still there inside. *Saidin.* No longer flowing, but there, in a pool. He was a pool of the One Power. He trembled with it. He could smell the grass, the dirt beneath, the stone of the walls. Even in the darkness he could see each blade of grass, separate and whole, all of them at once. He could feel each minute stirring of the air on his face. His tongue curdled with the taste of the taint; his stomach knotted and spasmed.

Frantically he clawed his way out of the void; still on his knees, not moving, he fought free. And then all that was left was the fading foulness on his tongue, and the cramping in his stomach, and the memory. *So— alive.*

"You saved us, Builder." Hurin had his back pressed against the wall, and his voice was hoarse. "That thing—that was the Black Wind?—it was worse than—was it going to hurl that fire at us? Lord Rand! Did it harm you? Did it touch you?" He came running as Rand got to his feet, helping him the last bit. Loial was getting up, too, dusting his hands and his knees.

"We'll never follow Fain through that." Rand touched Loial's arm. "Thank you. You *did* save us." *You saved me, at least. It was killing me. Killing me, and it felt—wonderful.* He swallowed; a faint trace of the taste still coated his mouth. "I want something to drink."

"I only found the leaf and put it back," Loial said, shrugging. "It seemed that if we could not get the Waygate closed, it would kill us. I am afraid I'm not a very good hero, Rand. I was so afraid I could hardly think."

"We were both afraid," Rand said. "We may be a poor pair of heroes, but we are what there is. It's a good thing Ingtar is with us."

"Lord Rand," Hurin said diffidently, "could we—leave, now?"

The sniffer made a fuss about Rand going over the wall first, with not knowing who was waiting outside, until Rand pointed out that he had the only weapon among them. Even then Hurin did not seem to like letting Loial lift Rand to catch the top of the wall and pull himself over.

Rand landed on his feet with a thud, listening and peering into the night. For a moment he thought he saw something move, heard a boot scrape on the brick walk, but neither was repeated, and he dismissed it as nervousness. He thought that he had a right to be nervous. He turned to help Hurin down.

"Lord Rand," the sniffer said as soon as his feet were solidly on the ground, "how are we going to follow them now? From what I've heard of those things, the whole lot of them could be halfway across the world by now, in any direction."

"Verin will know a way." Rand suddenly wanted to laugh; to find the Horn and the dagger—if they could be found, now—he had to go back to the Aes Sedai. They had let him loose, and now he had to go back. "I won't let Mat die without trying."

Loial joined them, and they went back toward the manor, to be met at the small door by Mat, who opened it just as Rand reached for the handle. "Verin says you're not to do anything. If Hurin's found where the Horn is kept, then she says that's all we can do, now. She says we'll leave as soon as you come back, and make a plan. And I say this is the last time I go running back and forth with messages. If you want to say something to somebody, you can talk to them yourself from now on." Mat peered past them into the darkness. "Is the Horn out there somewhere? In an outbuilding? Did you see the dagger?"

Rand turned him around and got him back inside. "It isn't in an outbuilding, Mat. I hope Verin has a good idea of what to do now; I don't have any."

Mat looked as if he wanted to ask questions, but he let himself be pushed along the dimly lit corridor. He even remembered to limp as they started upstairs.

When Rand and the others reentered the rooms filled with nobles, they received a number of looks. Rand wondered if they somehow knew something of what had happened outside, or if he should have sent Hurin and Mat to the front hall to wait, but then he realized the looks were no different from what they had been before, curious and calculating, wondering what the lord and the Ogier had been up to. Servants were invisible to these people. No one tried to approach them, since they were together. It seemed there were protocols to conspiracy in the Great Game; anyone might try to listen to a private conversation, but they would not intrude on it.

Verin and Ingtar were standing together, and thus also alone. Ingtar looked a little dazed. Verin gave Rand and the other three a brief glance, frowned at their expressions, then resettled her shawl and started for the entry hall.

As they reached it, Barthanes appeared as if someone had told him they were leaving. "You go so soon? Verin Sedai, can I not entreat you to stay longer?"

Verin shook her head. "We must go, Lord Barthanes. I've not been in Cairhien in some years. I was glad of your invitation to young Rand. It has been . . . interesting."

"Then Grace see you safely to your inn. The Great Tree, is it not? Perhaps you will favor me with your presence again? You would honor me, Verin Sedai, and you, Lord Rand, and you, Lord Ingtar, not to mention you, Loial, son of Arent son of Halan." His bow was a little deeper for the Aes Sedai than for the others, but still no more than a slight inclination.

Verin nodded in acknowledgment. "Perhaps. The Light illumine you, Lord Barthanes." She turned for the doors.

As Rand moved to follow the others, Barthanes caught his sleeve with two fingers, holding him back. Mat looked as if he might stay, too, until Hurin pulled him to join Verin and the rest.

"You wade even deeper in the Game than I thought," Barthanes said softly. "When I heard your name, I could not believe it, yet you came, and you fit the description, and. . . . I was given a message for you. I think I *will* deliver it after all."

Rand had felt a prickling along his backbone as Barthanes spoke, but at the last, he stared. "A message? From whom? Lady Selene?"

"A man. Not the sort for whom I would usually carry messages, but he has . . . certain . . . claims on me that I cannot ignore. He gave no name, but he was a Lugarder. Aaah! You know him."

"I know him." *Fain left a message?* Rand looked around the wide hall. Mat and Verin and the others were waiting by the doors. Liveried servants stood stiffly along the walls, ready to leap at a command yet appearing neither to hear nor see. The sounds of the gathering floated from deeper in the manor. It did not look like a place where Darkfriends might attack. "What message?"

"He says he will wait for you on Toman Head. He has what you seek, and if you want it, you must follow. If you refuse to follow him, he says he will hound your blood, and your people, and those you love until you will face him. It sounds mad, of course, a man like that saying he will hound a lord, and yet, there was something about him. I think he *is* mad—he even denied you are a lord, as any eye can plainly see—but there is still something. What is it he carries with him, with Trollocs to guard it? What is it you seek?" Barthanes seemed shocked at the directness of his own questions.

"The Light illumine you, Lord Barthanes." Rand managed a bow, but his legs wobbled as he joined Verin and the others. *He* wants *me to follow? And he'll hurt Emond's Field, Tam, if I don't.* He had no doubt Fain could do it, would do it. *At least Egwene is safe, in the White Tower.* He had sickening images of Trollocs descending in hordes on Emond's Field, of eyeless Fades stalking Egwene. *But how* can *I follow him? How?*

Then he was out in the night, mounting Red. Verin and Ingtar and the others were all already on their horses, and the escort of Shienarans was closing round them.

"What did you find?" Verin demanded. "Where does he keep it?" Hurin cleared his throat loudly, and Loial shifted in his high saddle. The Aes Sedai peered at them.

"Fain has taken the Horn to Toman Head through a Waygate," Rand said dully. "By this time, he's probably already waiting there for me."

"We will speak of this later," Verin said, so firmly that no one spoke at all on the ride back to the city, to The Great Tree.

Uno left them there, after a quiet word from Ingtar, taking the soldiers back to their inn in the Foregate. Hurin took one look at Verin's set face by the light of the common room, muttered something about ale, and scurried to a table in a corner, alone. The Aes Sedai brushed aside the innkeeper's solicitous hopes that she had enjoyed herself, and silently led Rand and the rest to the private dining room.

Perrin looked up from *The Travels of Jain Farstrider* when they walked in, and frowned when he saw their faces. "It didn't go well, did it?" he said, closing the leatherbound book. Lamps and beeswax candles around the room gave a good light; Mistress Tiedra charged heavily, but she did not stint.

Verin carefully folded her shawl and laid it across the back of a chair. "Tell me again. The Darkfriends took the Horn through a *Waygate?* At Barthanes's manor?"

"The ground under the manor used to be an Ogier grove," Loial explained. "When we built. . . ." His voice trailed off and his ears wilted under her look.

"Hurin followed them right to it." Rand wearily threw himself into a chair. *I have to follow more than ever, now. But how?* "I opened it to show him he could still follow the trail wherever they went, and the Black Wind was there. It tried to reach us, but Loial managed to close the gates before it could come all the way out." He colored a little at that, but Loial *had* closed the gates, and for all he knew *Machin Shin* might have made it out without that. "It was standing guard."

"The Black Wind," Mat breathed, frozen halfway into a chair. Perrin

was staring at Rand, too. So were Verin and Ingtar. Mat dropped into the
chair with a thump.

"You must be mistaken," Verin said at last. "*Machin Shin* could not be
used as a guard. No one can constrain the Black Wind to do anything."

"It's a creature of the Dark One," Mat said numbly. "They're
Darkfriends. Maybe they knew how to ask it for help, or make it help."

"No one knows exactly what *Machin Shin* is," Verin said, "unless, perhaps, it is the essence of madness and cruelty. It cannot be reasoned with,
Mat, or bargained with, or talked to. It cannot even be forced, not by any
Aes Sedai living today, and perhaps not by any who ever lived. Do you
really think Padan Fain could do what ten Aes Sedai could not?" Mat shook
his head.

There was an air of despair in the room, of hope and purpose lost. The
goal they had sought had vanished, and even Verin's face wore a floundering expression.

"I'd never have thought Fain had the courage for the Ways." Ingtar
sounded almost mild, but suddenly he banged his fist against the wall. "I
do not care how, or even if, *Machin Shin* works on Fain's behalf. They have
taken the Horn of Valere into the Ways, Aes Sedai. By now they could be
in the Blight, or halfway to Tear or Tanchico, or the other side of the Aiel
Waste. The Horn is lost. I am lost." His hands dropped to his sides, and
his shoulders slumped. "I am lost."

"Fain is taking it to Toman Head," Rand said, and was immediately the
object of all eyes again.

Verin studied him narrowly. "You said that before. How do you know?"

"He left a message with Barthanes," Rand said.

"A trick," Ingtar sneered. "He'd not tell us where to follow."

"I don't know what the rest of you are going to do," Rand said, "but I
am going to Toman Head. I have to. I leave at first light."

"But, Rand," Loial said, "it will take us months to reach Toman Head.
What makes you think Fain will wait there for us?"

"He will wait." *But how long before he decides I'm not coming? Why did he set
that guard if he wants me to follow?* "Loial, I mean to ride as hard as I can,
and if I ride Red to death, I'll buy another horse, or steal another, if I have
to. Are you sure you want to come?"

"I've stayed with you this long, Rand. Why would I stop now?" Loial
pulled out his pipe and pouch and began thumbing tabac into the big
bowl. "You see, I like you. I would like you even if you weren't *ta'veren*.
Maybe I like you despite it. You do seem to get me neck-deep in hot
water. In any case, I am going with you." He sucked on the pipestem to
test the draw, then took a splinter from the stone jar on the mantel and

thrust it into a candle flame for a light. "And I don't think you can really stop me."

"Well, I'm going," Mat said. "Fain still has that dagger, so I'm going. But all that servant business ended tonight."

Perrin sighed, an introspective look in his yellow eyes. "I suppose I'll come along, too." After a moment, he grinned. "Somebody has to keep Mat out of trouble."

"Not even a clever trick," Ingtar muttered. "Somehow, I'll get Barthanes alone, and I will learn the truth. I mean to have the Horn of Valere, not chase Jak o' the Wisps."

"It may not be a trick," Verin said carefully, seeming to study the floor under her toes. "There were certain things left in the dungeons at Fal Dara, writings that indicated a connection between what happened that night and"—she gave Rand a quick glance under lowered brows—"Toman Head. I still do not understand them completely, but I believe we must go to Toman Head. And I believe we will find the Horn there."

"Even if they are going to Toman Head," Ingtar said, "by the time we reach it, Fain or one of the other Darkfriends could have blown the Horn a hundred times, and the heroes returned from the grave will ride for the Shadow."

"Fain could have blown the Horn a hundred times since leaving Fal Dara," Verin told him. "And I think he would have, if he could open the chest. What we must worry about is that he might find someone who does know how to open it. We must follow him along the Ways."

Perrin's head came up sharply, and Mat shifted in his chair. Loial gave a low moan.

"Even if we could somehow sneak past Barthanes's guards," Rand said, "I think we'll find *Machin Shin* still there. We cannot use the Ways."

"How many of us could sneak onto Barthanes's grounds?" Verin said dismissively. "There are other Waygates. Stedding Tsofu lies not far from the city, south and east. It is a young *stedding*, rediscovered only perhaps six hundred years ago, but the Ogier Elders were still growing the Ways, then. Stedding Tsofu will have a Waygate. It is there and we will ride at first light."

Loial made a slightly louder sound, and Rand was not sure whether it referred to the Waygate or the *stedding*.

Ingtar still did not seem convinced, but Verin was as smooth and as implacable as snow sliding down a mountainside. "You will have your soldiers ready to ride, Ingtar. Send Hurin to tell Uno before he goes to bed. I think we should all go to bed as soon as possible. These Darkfriends have gained at least a day on us already, and I mean to make up as much of it as

I can tomorrow." So firm was the plump Aes Sedai's manner that she was already herding Ingtar to the door before she finished speaking.

Rand followed the others out, but at the door he stopped beside the Aes Sedai and watched Mat heading down the candle-lit hall. "Why does he look like that?" he asked her. "I thought you Healed him, enough to give him some time, anyway."

She waited until Mat and the others had turned up the stairs before speaking. "Apparently, it did not work so well as we believed. The sickness takes an interesting course in him. His strength remains; he will keep that to the end, I think. But his body wastes away. Another few weeks, at most, I would say. You see, there is reason for haste."

"I do not need another spur, Aes Sedai," Rand said, making the title sound hard. *Mat. The Horn. Fain's threat. Light, Egwene! Burn me, I don't need another spur.*

"And what of you, Rand al'Thor? Do you feel well? Do you fight it still, or have you yet surrendered to the Wheel?"

"I ride with you to find the Horn," he told her. "Beyond that, there is nothing between me and any Aes Sedai. Do you understand me? Nothing!"

She did not speak, and he walked away from her, but when he turned to take the stairs she was still watching him, dark eyes sharp and considering.

# CHAPTER
# 34

## *The Wheel Weaves*

The first light of morning already pearled the sky by the time Thom Merrilin found himself trudging back to The Bunch of Grapes. Even where the halls and taverns lay thickest, there was a brief time when the Foregate lay quiet, gathering its breath. In his present mood, Thom would not have noticed if the empty street had been on fire.

Some of Barthanes's guests had insisted on keeping him long after most had gone, long after Barthanes had taken himself to bed. It had been his own fault for leaving *The Great Hunt of the Horn,* changing to the sort of tales he told and songs he sang in the villages, "Mara and the Three Foolish Kings" and *How Susa Tamed Jain Farstrider* and stories of Anla the Wise Councilor. He had meant the choices to be a private comment on their stupidity, never dreaming any of them might listen, much less be intrigued. Intrigued in a way. They had demanded more of the same, but they had laughed in the wrong places, at the wrong things. They had laughed at him, too, apparently thinking he would not notice, or else that a full purse stuffed in his pocket would heal any wounds. He had almost thrown it away twice already.

The heavy purse burning his pocket and pride was not the only reason for his mood, nor even the nobles' contempt. They had asked questions about Rand, not even bothering to be subtle with a mere gleeman. Why was Rand in Cairhien? Why had an Andoran lord taken him, a gleeman, aside? Too many questions. He was not sure his answers had been clever enough. His reflexes for the Great Game were rusty.

Before turning toward The Bunch of Grapes, he had gone to The Great Tree; it was not difficult to find where someone was staying in Cairhien, if you pressed a palm or two with silver. He was still not sure what he had intended to say. Rand was gone with his friends, and the Aes Sedai. It left a feeling of something not done. *The boy's on his own, now. Burn me, I'm out of it!*

He strode through the common room, empty as it seldom was, and took the steps two at a time. At least, he tried to; his right leg did not bend well, and he nearly fell. Muttering to himself, he climbed the rest of the way at a slower pace, and opened the door to his room softly, so as not to wake Dena.

Despite himself, he smiled when he saw her lying on the bed with her face turned to the wall, still in her dress. *Fell asleep waiting for me. Fool girl.* But it was a kindly thought; he was not sure there was anything she would do that he would not forgive or excuse. Deciding on the spur of the moment that tonight was the night he'd let her perform for the first time, he lowered his harp case to the floor and put a hand on her shoulder, to wake her and tell her.

She rolled limply onto her back, staring up at him, glazed eyes open wide above the gash across her throat. The side of the bed that had been hidden by her body was dark and sodden.

Thom's stomach heaved; if his throat had not been so tight he could not breathe, he would have vomited, or screamed, or both.

He had only the creaking of wardrobe doors for warning. He spun, knives coming out of his sleeves and leaving his hands in the same motion. The first blade took the throat of a fat, balding man with a dagger in his hand; the man stumbled back, blood bubbling around his clutching fingers as he tried to cry out.

Spinning on his bad leg threw Thom's other blade off, though; the knife stuck in the right shoulder of a heavily muscled man with scars on his face, who was climbing out of the other wardrobe. The big man's knife dropped from a hand that suddenly would not do what he wanted, and he lumbered for the door.

Before he could take a second step, Thom produced another knife and slashed him across the back of his leg. The big man yelled and stumbled, and Thom seized a handful of greasy hair, slamming his face against the wall beside the door; the man screamed again as the knife hilt sticking out of his shoulder hit the door.

Thom thrust the blade in his hand to within an inch of the man's dark eye. The scars on the big man's face gave him a hard look, but he stared at the point without blinking and did not move a muscle. The fat man, lying half in the wardrobe, kicked a last kick and was still.

"Before I kill you," Thom said, "tell me. Why?" His voice was quiet, numb; he felt numb inside.

"The Great Game," the man said quickly. His accent was of the streets, and his clothes as well, but they were a shade too fine, too unworn; he had more coin to spend than any Foregater should. "Nothing against you personal, you see? It is just the Game."

"The Game? I'm not mixed up in *Daes Dae'mar*! Who would want to kill me for the Great Game?" The man hesitated. Thom moved his blade closer. If the fellow blinked, his eyelashes would brush the point. "Who?"

"Barthanes," came the hoarse answer. "Lord Barthanes. We would not have killed you. Barthanes wants information. We just wanted to find out what you know. There can be gold in it for you. A nice, fat golden crown for what you know. Maybe two."

"Liar! I was in Barthanes's manor last night, as close to him as I am to you. If he wanted anything of me, I'd never have left alive."

"I tell you, we have been looking for you, or anyone who knows about this Andoran lord, for days. I never heard your name until last night, downstairs. Lord Barthanes is generous. It could be five crowns."

The man tried to pull his head away from the knife in Thom's hand, and Thom pushed him harder against the wall. "What Andoran lord?" But he knew. The Light help him, he knew.

"Rand. Of House al'Thor. Tall. Young. A blademaster, or at least he wears the sword. I know he came to see you. Him and an Ogier, and you talked. Tell me what you know. I might even throw in a crown or two, myself."

"You fool," Thom breathed. *Dena died for this? Oh, Light, she's dead.* He felt as if he wanted to cry. "The boy's a shepherd." *A shepherd in a fancy coat, with Aes Sedai around him like bees around honeyroses.* "Just a shepherd." He tightened his grip in the man's hair.

"Wait! Wait! You can make more than any five crowns, or even ten. A hundred, more like. Every House wants to know about this Rand al'Thor. Two or three have approached me. With what you know, and my knowing who wants to know it, we could both fill our pockets. And there has been a woman, a lady, I have seen more than once while asking after him. If we can find out who she is . . . why, we could sell that, too."

"You've made one real mistake in it all," Thom said.

"Mistake?" The man's far hand was beginning to slide down toward his belt. No doubt he had another dagger there. Thom ignored it.

"You should never have touched the girl."

The man's hand darted for his belt, then he gave one convulsive start as Thom's knife went home.

Thom let him fall over away from the door and stood a moment before bending tiredly to tug his blades free. The door banged open, and he whirled with a snarl on his face.

Zera jerked back, a hand to her throat, staring at him. "That fool Ella just told me," she said unsteadily, "that two of Barthanes's men were asking after you last night, and with what I've heard this morning. . . . I thought you said you didn't play in the Game anymore."

"They found me," he said wearily.

Her eyes dropped from his face and widened as they took in the bodies of the two men. Hastily she stepped into the room, shutting the door behind her. "This is bad, Thom. You'll have to leave Cairhien." Her gaze fell on the bed, and her breath caught. "Oh, no. Oh, no. Oh, Thom, I'm so sorry."

"I cannot leave yet, Zera." He hesitated, then tenderly drew a blanket over Dena, covering her face. "I have another man to kill, first."

The innkeeper gave herself a shake and pulled her eyes away from the bed. Her voice was more than a little breathy. "If you mean Barthanes, you're too late. Everybody's talking about it already. He is dead. His servants found him this morning, torn to pieces in his bedchamber. The only way they knew it was him was his head stuck on a spike over the fireplace." She laid a hand on his arm. "Thom, you can't hide that you were there last night, not from anybody who wants to know. Add these two in, and there's nobody in Cairhien who won't believe you were involved." There was a slight questioning note in her last words, as if she, too, were wondering.

"It doesn't matter, I suppose," he said dully. He could not stop looking down at the blanket-covered shape on the bed. "Perhaps I will go back to Andor. To Caemlyn."

She took his shoulders, turning him away from the bed. "You men," she sighed, "always thinking with either your muscles or your hearts, and never your heads. Caemlyn is as bad as Cairhien, for you. Either place, you'll end up dead, or in prison. Do you think she'd want that? If you want to honor her memory, stay alive."

"Will you take care of. . . ." He could not say it. *Growing old,* he thought. *Going soft.* He pulled the heavy purse from his pocket and folded her hands around it. "This should take care of . . . everything. And help when they start asking questions about me, too."

"I will see to everything," she said gently. "You must go, Thom. Now."

He nodded reluctantly, and slowly began stuffing a few things in a set of saddlebags. While he worked, Zera got her first close look at the fat man sprawled partway in the wardrobe, and she gave a loud gasp. He looked at her inquiringly; as long as he had known her, she had never been one to go faint over blood.

"These aren't Barthanes's men, Thom. At least, that one isn't." She nodded toward the fat man. "It's the worst kept secret in Cairhien that he works for House Riatin. For Galldrian."

"Galldrian," he said flatly. *What has that bloody shepherd gotten me into? What have the Aes Sedai gotten us both into? But it was Galldrian's men murdered her.*

There must have been something of his thoughts on his face. Zera said sharply, "Dena wants you alive, you fool! You try to kill the King, and you'll be dead before you get within a hundred spans of him, if you come that close!"

A roar came from the city walls, as if half of Cairhien were shouting. Frowning, Thom peered from his window. Beyond the top of the gray walls above the rooftops of the Foregate, a thick column of smoke was rising into the sky. Far beyond the walls. Beside the first black pillar, a few gray tendrils quickly grew into another, and more wisps appeared further on. He estimated the distance and took a deep breath.

"Perhaps you had better think about leaving, too. It looks as if someone is firing the granaries."

"I have lived through riots before. Go now, Thom." With a last look at Dena's shrouded form, he gathered his things, but as he started to leave, Zera spoke again. "You have a dangerous look in your eyes, Thom Merrilin. Imagine Dena sitting here, alive and hale. Think what she would say. Would she let you go off and get yourself killed to no purpose?"

"I'm only an old gleeman," he said from the door. *And Rand al'Thor is only a shepherd, but we both do what we must.* "Who could I possibly be dangerous to?"

As he pulled the door to, hiding her, hiding Dena, a mirthless, wolfish grin came onto his face. His leg hurt, but he barely felt it as he hurried purposefully down the stairs and out of the inn.

Padan Fain reined in his horse atop a hill above Falme, in one of the few sparse thickets remaining on the hills outside the town. The packhorse bearing his precious burden bumped his leg, and he kicked it in the ribs

without looking; the animal snorted and jerked back to the end of the lead
he had tied to his saddle. The woman had not wanted to give up her horse,
no more than any of the Darkfriends who had followed him had wanted to
be left alone in the hills with the Trollocs, without Fain's protecting presence. He had solved both problems easily. Meat in a Trolloc cookpot had
no need of a horse. The woman's companions had been shaken by the
journey along the Ways, to a Waygate outside a long-abandoned *stedding* on
Toman Head, and watching the Trollocs prepare their dinner had made the
surviving Darkfriends extremely biddable.

From the edge of the trees, Fain studied the unwalled town and sneered.
One short merchant train was rumbling in among the stables and horse lots
and wagon yards that bordered the town, while another rumbled out, raising little dust from dirt packed by many years of such traffic. The men
driving the wagons and the few riding beside them were all local men by
their clothing, yet the mounted men, at least, had swords on baldrics, and
even a few spears and bows. The soldiers he saw, and there were few, did
not seem to be watching the armed men they had supposedly conquered.

He had learned something of these people, these Seanchan, in his day
and a night on Toman Head. At least, as much as the defeated folk knew.
It was never hard to find someone alone, and they always answered questions properly put. Men gathered more information on the invaders, as if
they actually believed they would eventually do something with what they
knew, but they sometimes tried to hold back. Women, by and large,
seemed interested in going on with their lives whoever their rulers were,
yet they noted details men did not, and they talked more quickly once they
stopped screaming. Children talked the quickest of all, but they seldom
said much that was worthwhile.

He had discarded three quarters of what he had heard as nonsense and
rumors growing into fables, but he took some of those conclusions back,
now. Anyone at all could enter Falme, it appeared. With a start, he saw
the truth of a little more "nonsense" as twenty soldiers rode out of the
town. He could not make out their mounts clearly, but they were certainly
not horses. They ran with a fluid grace, and their dark skins seemed to have
a glint in the morning sun, as of scales. He craned his neck to watch them
disappear inland, then booted his horse toward the town.

The local folk among the stables and parked wagons and fenced horse
lots gave him no more than a glance or two. He had no interest in them,
either; he rode on into the town, onto its cobblestone streets sloping down
to the harbor. He could see the harbor clearly, and the large, oddly shaped
Seanchan ships anchored there. No one bothered him as he searched streets
that were neither crowded nor empty. There were more Seanchan soldiers

here. The people hurried about their business with eyes down, bowing whenever soldiers passed, but the Seanchan paid them no mind. It all seemed peaceful on the surface, despite the armored Seanchan in the streets and the ships in the harbor, but Fain could sense the tension underneath. He always did well where men were tense and afraid.

He came to a large house with more than a dozen soldiers standing guard before it. Fain stopped and dismounted. Except for one obvious officer, most wore armor of unrelieved black, and their helmets made him think of locusts' heads. Two leathery-skinned beasts with three eyes and horny beaks instead of mouths flanked the front door, squatting like crouching frogs; the soldier standing by each of the creatures had three eyes painted on the breast of his armor. Fain eyed the blue-bordered banner flapping above the roof, the spread-winged hawk clutching lightning bolts, and chortled inside himself.

Women went in and out of a house across the street, women linked by silver leashes, but he ignored them. He knew about *damane* from the villagers. They might be of some use later, but not now.

The soldiers were looking at him, especially the officer, whose armor was all gold and red and green.

Forcing an ingratiating smile onto his face, Fain made himself bow deeply. "My lords, I have something here that will interest your Great Lord. I assure you, he will want to see it, and me, personally." He gestured to the squarish shape on his packhorse, still wrapped in the huge, striped blanket in which his people had found it.

The officer stared him up and down. "You sound a foreigner to this land. Have you taken the oaths?"

"I obey, await, and will serve," Fain replied smoothly. Everyone he had questioned spoke of the oaths, though none had understood what they meant. If these people wanted oaths, he was prepared to swear anything. He had long since lost count of the oaths he had taken.

The officer motioned two of his men to see what was under the blanket. Surprised grunts at the weight as they lifted it down from the packsaddle turned to gasps when they stripped the blanket away. The officer stared with no expression on his face at the silver-worked golden chest resting on the cobblestones, then looked at Fain. "A gift fit for the Empress herself. You will come with me."

One of the soldiers searched Fain roughly, but he endured it in silence, noting that the officer and the two soldiers who took up the chest surrendered their swords and daggers before going inside. Anything he could learn of these people, however small, might help, though he was confident of his plan already. He was always confident, but never more than where lords feared an assassin's knife from their own followers.

As they went through the door, the officer frowned at him, and for a moment Fain wondered why. *Of course. The beasts.* Whatever they were, they were certainly no worse than Trollocs, nothing at all beside a Myrddraal, and he had not given them a second look. It was too late to pretend to be afraid of them now. But the Seanchan said nothing, only led him deeper into the house.

And so Fain found himself on his face, in a room bare of furnishings except for folding screens that hid its walls, while the officer told the High Lord Turak of him and his offering. Servants brought a table on which to set the chest so the High Lord would have no need to stoop; all Fain saw of them were scurrying slippers. He bided his time impatiently. Eventually there would come a time when he was not the one to bow.

Then the soldiers were dismissed, and Fain told to rise. He did so slowly, studying both the High Lord, with his shaven head and his long fingernails and his blue silk robe brocaded with blossoms, and the man who stood beside him with the unshaven half of his pale hair in a long braid. Fain was sure the fellow in green was only a servant, however great, but servants could be useful, especially if they stood high in their master's sight.

"A marvelous gift." Turak's eyes lifted from the chest to Fain. A scent of roses wafted from the High Lord. "Yet the question asks itself; how did one like you come by a chest many lesser lords could not afford? Are you a thief?"

Fain tugged at his worn, none-too-clean coat. "It is sometimes necessary for a man to appear less than he is, High Lord. My present shabbiness allowed me to bring this to you unmolested. This chest is old, High Lord—as old as the Age of Legends—and within it lies a treasure such as few eyes have ever seen. Soon—very soon, High Lord—I will be able to open it, and give you that which will enable you to take this land as far as you wish, to the Spine of the World, the Aiel Waste, the lands beyond. Nothing will stand against you, High Lord, once I—" He cut off as Turak began running his long-nailed fingers over the chest.

"I have seen chests such as this, chests from the Age of Legends," the High Lord said, "though none so fine. They are meant to be opened only by those who know the pattern, but I—ah!" He pressed among the ornate whorls and bosses, there was a sharp click, and he lifted back the lid. A flicker of what might have been disappointment passed across his face.

Fain bit the inside of his mouth till blood came to keep from snarling. It lessened his bargaining position that he was not the one who had opened the chest. Still, all the rest could go as he had planned if he could only make himself be patient. But he had been patient so long.

"These are treasure from the Age of Legends?" Turak said, lifting out the curled Horn in one hand and the curved dagger with the ruby in its golden hilt in the other. Fain clutched his hands in fists at his sides so he would not grab the dagger. "The Age of Legends," Turak repeated softly, tracing the silver script inlaid around the golden bell of the Horn with the tip of the dagger's blade. His brows rose in startlement, the first open expression Fain had seen from him, but in the next instant Turak's face was as smooth as ever. "Do you have any idea what this is?"

"The Horn of Valere, High Lord," Fain said smoothly, pleased to see the mouth of the man with the braid drop open. Turak only nodded as if to himself.

The High Lord turned away. Fain blinked and opened his mouth, then, at a sharp gesture from the yellow-haired man, followed without speaking.

It was another room with all the original furnishings gone, replaced by folding screens and a single chair facing a tall round cabinet. Still holding the Horn and the dagger, Turak looked at the cabinet, then away. He said nothing, but the other Seanchan snapped quick orders, and in moments men in plain woolen robes appeared through a door behind the screens bearing another small table. A young woman with hair so pale it was almost white came behind them, her arms full of small stands of polished wood in various sizes and shapes. Her garment was white silk, and so thin that Fain could see her body clearly through it, but he had eyes only for the dagger. The Horn was a means to an end, but the dagger was a part of him.

Turak briefly touched one of the wooden stands the girl held, and she placed it on the center of the table. The men turned the chair to face it under the direction of the man with the braid. The lower servants' hair hung to their shoulders. They scurried out with bows that almost put their heads on their knees.

Placing the Horn on the stand so that it stood upright, Turak laid the dagger on the table in front of it and went to sit in the chair.

Fain could stand it no longer. He reached for the dagger.

The yellow-haired man caught his wrist in a crushing grip. "Unshaven dog! Know that the hand that touches the property of the High Lord unbidden is cut off."

"It is mine," Fain growled. *Patience! So long.*

Turak, lounging back in the chair, lifted one blue-lacquered fingernail, and Fain was pulled out of the way so the High Lord could view the Horn unobstructed.

"Yours?" Turak said. "Inside a chest you could not open? If you interest me sufficiently, I may give you the dagger. Even if it is from the Age of Legends, I have no interest in such as that. Before all else, you will answer me a question. Why have you brought the Horn of Valere to me?"

Fain eyed the dagger longingly a moment more, then jerked his wrist free and rubbed it as he bowed. "That you may sound it, High Lord. Then you may take all of this land, if you wish. All of the world. You may break the White Tower and grind the Aes Sedai to dust, for even their powers cannot stop heroes come back from the dead."

"*I* am to sound it." Turak's tone was flat. "And break the White Tower. Again, why? You claim to obey, await, and serve, but this is a land of oath-breakers. Why do you give your land to me? Do you have some private quarrel with these . . . women?"

Fain tried to make his voice convincing. *Patient, like a worm boring from within.* "High Lord, my family has passed down a tradition, generation upon generation. We served the High King, Artur Paendrag Tanreall, and when he was murdered by the witches of Tar Valon, we did not abandon our oaths. When others warred and tore apart what Artur Hawkwing had made, we held to our swearing, and suffered for it, but held to it still. This is our tradition, High Lord, handed father to son, and mother to daughter, down all the years since the High King was murdered. That we await the return of the armies Artur Hawkwing sent across the Aryth Ocean, that we await the return of Artur Hawkwing's blood to destroy the White Tower and take back what was the High King's. And when the Hawkwing's blood returns, we will serve and advise, as we did for the High King. High Lord, except for its border, the banner that flies over this roof is the banner of Luthair, the son Artur Paendrag Tanreall sent with his armies across the ocean." Fain dropped to his knees, giving a good imitation of being overwhelmed. "High Lord, I wish only to serve and advise the blood of the High King."

Turak was silent so long that Fain began to wonder if he needed further convincing; he was ready with more, as much as was required. Finally, though, the High Lord spoke. "You seem to know what none, neither the high nor the low, has spoken since sighting this land. The people here speak it as one rumor among ten, but you know. I can see it in your eyes, hear it in your voice. I could almost think you were sent to entangle me in a trap. But who, possessing the Horn of Valere, would use it so? None of those of the Blood who came with the *Hailene* could have had the Horn, for the legend says it was hidden in this land. And surely any lord of this land would use it against me rather than put it in my hands. How did you come to possess the Horn of Valere? Do you claim to be a hero, as in the legend? Have you done valorous deeds?"

"I am no hero, High Lord." Fain ventured a self-deprecating smile, but Turak's face did not alter, and he let it go. "The Horn was found by an ancestor of mine during the turmoil after the High King's death. He knew how to open the chest, but that secret died with him in the War of the Hundred Years, that rent Artur Hawkwing's empire, so that all we who followed him knew was that the Horn lay within and we must keep it safe until the High King's blood returned."

"Almost could I believe you."

"Believe, High Lord. Once you sound the Horn—"

"Do not ruin what convincing you have managed to do. I shall not sound the Horn of Valere. When I return to Seanchan, I shall present it to the Empress as the chiefest of my trophies. Perhaps the Empress will sound it herself."

"But, High Lord," Fain protested, "you must—" He found himself lying on his side, his head ringing. Only when his eyes cleared did he see the man with the pale braid rubbing his knuckles and realize what had happened.

"Some words," the fellow said softly, "are never used to the High Lord."

Fain decided how the man was going to die.

Turak looked from Fain to the Horn as placidly as if he had seen nothing. "Perhaps I will give you to the Empress along with the Horn of Valere. She might find you amusing, a man who claims his family held true where all others broke their oaths or forgot them."

Fain hid his sudden elation in the act of climbing back to his feet. He had not even known of the existence of an Empress until Turak mentioned her, but access to a ruler again . . . that opened new paths, new plans. Access to a ruler with the might of the Seanchan beneath her and the Horn of Valere in her hands. Much better than making this Turak a Great King. He could wait for some parts of his plan. *Softly. Mustn't let him know how much you want it. After so long, a little more patience will not hurt.* "As the High Lord wishes," he said, trying to sound like a man who only wanted to serve.

"You seem almost eager," Turak said, and Fain barely suppressed a wince. "I will tell you why I will not sound the Horn of Valere, or even keep it, and perhaps that will cure your eagerness. I do not wish a gift of mine to offend the Empress by his actions; if your eagerness cannot be cured, it will never be satisfied, for you will never leave these shores. Do you know that whoever blows the Horn of Valere is linked to it thereafter?

That so long as he or she lives, it is no more than a horn to any other?" He did not sound as if he expected answers, and in any case, he did not pause for them. "I stand twelfth in line of succession to the Crystal Throne. If I kept the Horn of Valere, all between myself and the throne would think I meant to be first hereafter, and while the Empress, of course, wishes that we contend with one another so that the strongest and most cunning will follow her, she currently favors her second daughter, and she would not look well on any threat to Tuon. If I sounded it, even if I then laid this land at her feet, and every woman in the White Tower leashed, the Empress, may she live forever, would surely believe I meant to be more than merely her heir."

Fain stopped himself short of suggesting how possible that would be with the aid of the Horn. Something in the High Lord's voice suggested— as hard as Fain found it to believe—that he actually meant his wish for her to live forever. *I must be patient. A worm in the root.*

"The Empress's Listeners may be anywhere," Turak continued. "They may be anyone. Huan was born and raised in the House of Aladon, and his family for eleven generations before him, yet even he could be a Listener." The man with the braid half made a protesting gesture, before jerking himself back to stillness. "Even a high lord or a high lady can find their deepest secrets known to Listeners, can wake to find themselves already handed over to the Seekers for Truth. Truth is always difficult to find, but the Seekers spare no pain in their search, and they will search as long as they think there is need. They make great efforts not to allow a high lord or high lady to die in their care, of course, for no man's hand may slay one in whose veins flows the blood of Artur Hawkwing. If the Empress must order such a death, the unfortunate one is placed alive in a silken bag, and that bag hung over the side of the Tower of the Ravens and left there until it rots away. No such care would be taken for one such as you. At the Court of the Nine Moons, in Seandar, one such as you could be given to the Seekers for a shift of your eye, for a misspoken word, for a whim. Are you still eager?"

Fain managed a tremble in his knees. "I wish only to serve and advise, High Lord. I know much that may be useful." This court of Seandar sounded a place where his plans and skills would find fertile soil.

"Until I sail back to Seanchan, you will amuse me with your tales of your family and its tradition. It is a relief to find a second man in this Light-forsaken land who can amuse me, even if you both tell lies, as I suspect. You may leave me." No other word was spoken, but the girl with the nearly white hair and the almost-transparent robe appeared on quick feet to kneel with downcast head beside the High Lord, offering a single steaming cup on a lacquered tray.

"High Lord," Fain said. The man with the braid, Huan, took hold of his arm, but he pulled loose. Huan's mouth tightened angrily as Fain made his deepest bow yet. *I will kill him slowly, yes.* "High Lord, there are those who follow me. They mean to take the Horn of Valere. Darkfriends and worse, High Lord, and they cannot be more than a day or two behind me."

Turak took a sip of black liquid from the thin cup balanced on long-nailed fingertips. "Few Darkfriends remain in Seanchan. Those who survive the Seekers for Truth meet the axe of the headsman. It might be amusing to meet a Darkfriend."

"High Lord, they are dangerous. They have Trollocs with them. They are led by one who calls himself Rand al'Thor. A young man, but vile in the Shadow beyond belief, with a lying, devious tongue. In many places he has claimed to be many things, but always the Trollocs come when he is there, High Lord. Always the Trollocs come . . . and kill."

"Trollocs," Turak mused. "There were no Trollocs in Seanchan. But the Armies of the Night had other allies. Other things. I have often wondered if a *grolm* could kill a Trolloc. I will have watch kept for your Trollocs and your Darkfriends, if they are not another lie. This land wearies me with boredom." He sighed and inhaled the fumes from his cup.

Fain let the grimacing Huan pull him out of the room, hardly even listening to the snarled lecture on what would happen if he ever again failed to leave Lord Turak's presence when given permission to do so. He barely noticed when he was pushed into the street with a coin and instructions to return on the morrow. Rand al'Thor was his, now. *I will see him dead at last. And then the world will pay for what was done to me.*

Giggling under his breath, he led his horses down into the town in search of an inn.

# CHAPTER 35

## Stedding Tsofu

The river hills on which the city of Cairhien stood gave way to flatter lands and forests when Rand and the others had ridden half a day, the Shienarans still with their armor on the packhorses. There were no roads where they went, only a scattering of cart tracks, and few farms or villages. Verin pressed for speed, and Ingtar—grumbling constantly that they were letting themselves be tricked, that Fain would never have told them where he was really going, yet grumbling at the same time about riding in the opposite direction from Toman Head, as if part of him believed and Toman Head were not months away except by the way they took—Ingtar obliged her. The Gray Owl banner flew on the wind of their passage.

Rand rode with grim determination, avoiding conversation with Verin. He had this thing to do—this duty, Ingtar would have called it—and then he could be free of Aes Sedai once and for all. Perrin seemed to share something of his mood, staring straight ahead at nothing as they rode. When they finally stopped for the night at the edge of a forest, with full dark almost on them, Perrin asked Loial questions about the *stedding*. Trollocs would not enter a *stedding;* would wolves? Loial replied shortly that it was only creatures of the Shadow that were reluctant to enter *stedding*. And Aes Sedai, of course, since they could not touch the True Source inside a *stedding,* or channel the One Power. The Ogier himself appeared the most reluctant of all to go to Stedding Tsofu. Mat was the only one who seemed eager, almost desperately so. His skin looked as if he had not seen the sun in a year, and his cheeks had begun to go hollow, though he said he felt ready to run a footrace. Verin put her hands on him for Healing before he rolled into his blankets, and again before they mounted their horses in the morning, but it made no difference in how he looked. Even Hurin frowned when he looked at Mat.

The sun stood high on the second day when Verin suddenly sat up straight in her saddle and looked around. Beside her, Ingtar gave a start.

Rand could not see anything different about the forest now surrounding them. The undergrowth was not too thick; they had found an easy way under the canopy of oak and hickory, blackgum and beech, pierced here and there by a tall pine or leatherleaf, or the white slash of a paperbark. But as he followed them, he suddenly felt a chill pass through him, as though he had leaped into a Waterwood pond in winter. It flashed through him and was gone, leaving behind a feeling of refreshment. And there was a dull and distant sense of loss, too, though he could not imagine of what.

Every rider, as he reached that point, gave a jerk or made some exclamation. Hurin's mouth dropped open, and Uno whispered, "Bloody, flaming. . . ." Then he shook his head as if he could not think of anything else to say. There was a look of recognition in Perrin's yellow eyes.

Loial took a deep, slow breath and let it out. "It feels . . . good . . . to be back in a *stedding.*"

Frowning, Rand looked around. He had expected a *stedding* to be somehow different, but except for that one chill, the forest was the same as what they had been riding through all day. There was the sudden sense of being rested, of course. Then an Ogier stepped out from behind an oak.

She was shorter than Loial—which meant she stood head and shoulders taller than Rand—but with the same broad nose and big eyes, the same wide mouth and tufted ears. Her eyebrows were not so long as Loial's, though, and her features seemed delicate beside his, the tufts on her ears finer. She wore a long green dress and a green cloak embroidered with flowers, and carried a bunch of silverbell blossoms as if she had been gathering them. She looked at them calmly, waiting.

Loial scrambled down from his tall horse and bowed hastily. Rand and the others did the same, if not so quickly as Loial; even Verin inclined her head. Loial gave their names formally, but he did not mention the name of his *stedding.*

For a moment the Ogier girl—Rand was sure she was no older than Loial—studied them, then smiled. "Be welcome to Stedding Tsofu." Her voice was a lighter version of Loial's, too; the softer rumble of a smaller bumblebee. "I am Erith, daughter of Iva daughter of Alar. Be welcome. We have had so few human visitors since the stonemasons left Cairhien, and now so many at once. Why, we even had some of the Traveling People, though, of course, they left when the. . . . Oh, I talk too much. I will take you to the Elders. Only. . . ." She searched among them for the one in charge, and settled finally on Verin. "Aes Sedai, you have so many men with you, and armed. Could you please leave some of them Outside? Forgive me, but it is always unsettling to have very many armed humans in the *stedding* at once."

"Of course, Erith," Verin said. "Ingtar, will you see to it?"

Ingtar gave orders to Uno, and so it was that he and Hurin were the only Shienarans to follow Erith deeper into the *stedding*.

Leading his horse like the others, Rand looked up as Loial came closer, with many glances at Erith up ahead with Verin and Ingtar. Hurin walked midway between, staring around in amazement, though Rand was not sure at what exactly. Loial bent to speak quietly. "Is she not beautiful, Rand? And her voice sings."

Mat snickered, but when Loial looked at him questioningly, he said, "Very pretty, Loial. A little tall for my taste, you understand, but very pretty, I'm sure."

Loial frowned uncertainly, but nodded. "Yes, she is." His expression lightened. "It does feel good to be back in a *stedding*. Not that the Longing was taking me, you understand."

"The Longing?" Perrin said. "I do not understand, Loial."

"We Ogier are bound to the *stedding*, Perrin. It is said that before the Breaking of the World, we could go where we wished for as long as we wished, like you humans, but that changed with the Breaking. Ogier were scattered like every other people, and they could not find any of the *stedding* again. Everything was moved, everything changed. Mountains, rivers, even the seas."

"Everybody knows about the Breaking," Mat said impatiently. "What does it have to do with this—this Longing?"

"It was during the Exile, while we wandered lost, that the Longing first came on us. The desire to know the *stedding* once more, to know our homes again. Many died of it." Loial shook his head sadly. "More died than lived. When we finally began to find the *stedding* again, one at a time, in the years of the Covenant of the Ten Nations, it seemed we had defeated the Longing at last, but it had changed us, put seeds in us. Now, if an Ogier is Outside too long, the Longing comes again; he begins to weaken, and he dies if he does not return."

"Do you need to stay here awhile?" Rand asked anxiously. "There's no need to kill yourself to go with us."

"I will know it when it comes." Loial laughed. "It will be long before it is strong enough to cause harm to me. Why, Dalar spent ten years among the Sea Folk without ever seeing a *stedding,* and she came safely home."

An Ogier woman appeared out of the trees, pausing a moment to speak with Erith and Verin. She looked Ingtar up and down and seemed to dismiss him, which made him blink. Her eyes swept across Loial, flicked over Hurin and the Emond's Fielders, before she went off into the forest again; Loial seemed to be trying to hide behind his horse. "Besides," he said, peering cautiously across his saddle after her, "it is a dull life in the *stedding* compared to traveling with three *ta'veren.*"

"If you are going to start that again," Mat muttered, and Loial spoke up quickly. "Three friends, then. You are my friends, I hope."

"I am," Rand said simply, and Perrin nodded.

Mat laughed. "How could I not be friends with somebody who dices so badly?" He threw up his hands when Rand and Perrin looked at him. "Oh, all right. I like you, Loial. You're my friend. Just don't go on about. . . . Aaah! Sometimes you're as bad to be around as Rand." His voice sank to a mutter. "At least we're safe here in a *stedding.*"

Rand grimaced. He knew what Mat meant. *Here in a* stedding, *where I can't channel.*

Perrin punched Mat's shoulder, but looked sorry that he had when Mat grimaced at him with that gaunt face.

It was the music Rand became aware of first, unseen flutes and fiddles in a jolly tune that floated through the trees, and deep voices singing and laughing.

> "Clear the field, smooth it low.
> Let no weed or stubble stand.
> Here we labor, here we toil,
> here the towering trees will grow."

Almost at the same moment he realized that the huge shape he was seeing through the trees was itself a tree, with a ridged, buttressed trunk that must have been twenty paces thick. Gaping, he followed it up with his eyes, up through the forest canopy, to branches spreading like the top of a gigantic mushroom a good hundred paces above the ground. And beyond it were taller still.

"Burn me," Mat breathed. "You could build ten houses from just one of those. Fifty houses."

"Cut down a Great Tree?" Loial sounded scandalized, and more than a little angry. His ears were stiff and still, his long eyebrows down on his cheeks. "We never cut down one of the Great Trees, not unless it dies, and they almost never do. Few survived the Breaking, but some of the largest were seedlings during the Age of Legends."

"I'm sorry," Mat said. "I was just saying how big they are. I won't hurt your trees." Loial nodded, seeming mollified.

More Ogier appeared now, walking among the trees. Most seemed intent on whatever they were about; though all looked at the newcomers, and even gave a friendly nod or a small bow, none stopped or spoke. They had a curious way of moving, in some manner blending a careful deliberateness with an almost childlike carefree joyfulness. They knew and liked who and what they were and where they were, and they seemed at peace with themselves and everything around them. Rand found himself envying them.

Few of the Ogier men were any taller than Loial, but it was easy to pick out the older men; one and all they wore mustaches as long as their dangling eyebrows and narrow beards under their chins. All of the younger were smooth-shaven, like Loial. Many of the men were in their shirtsleeves, and carried shovels and mattocks or saws and buckets of pitch; the others wore plain coats that buttoned to the neck and flared about their knees like kilts. The women seemed to favor embroidered flowers, and many wore flowers in their hair, too. The embroidery was limited to the cloaks of the younger women; the older women's dresses were embroidered, as well, and some women with gray hair had flowers and vines from neck to hem. A handful of the Ogier, women and girls for the most part, did seem to take special notice of Loial; he walked staring straight ahead, ears twitching more wildly the further they went.

Rand was startled to see an Ogier apparently walking up out of the ground, out of one of the grassy, wildflower-covered mounds that lay scattered all among the trees here. Then he saw windows in the mounds, and an Ogier woman standing at one apparently rolling a piecrust, and realized he was looking at Ogier houses. The window frames were stone, but they not only seemed natural formations, they appeared to have been sculpted by wind and water over generations.

The Great Trees, with their massive trunks and spreading roots as thick as horses, needed a great deal of room between them, but several grew right in the town. Dirt ramps took the paths over the roots. In fact, aside from the pathways, the only way to tell town from forest at a glance was a large open space in the center of the town, around what could only be the stump of one of the Great Trees. Nearly a hundred paces across, its surface was polished as smooth as any floor, and there were steps built up to it at several places. Rand was imagining how tall that tree had been when Erith spoke loudly enough for them all to hear.

"Here come our other guests."

Three human women came walking around the side of the huge stump. The youngest was carrying a wooden bowl.

"Aiel," Ingtar said. "Maidens of the Spear. As well I *did* leave Masema with the others." Yet he stepped away from Verin and Erith, and reached over his shoulder to loosen his sword in its scabbard.

Rand studied the Aiel with an uneasy curiosity. They were what too many people had tired to tell him he was. Two of the women were mature, the other little more than a girl, but all three were tall for women. Their short-cut hair ranged from a reddish brown to almost golden, with a narrow, shoulder-length tail left long at the back. They wore loose breeches tucked into soft boots, and all their clothes were some shade of brown or gray or green; he thought the garments would fade into rock or woods almost as well as a Warder's cloak. Short bows poked over their shoulders, quivers and long knives hung at their belts, and each carried a small, round shield of hide and a cluster of spears with short shafts and long points. Even the youngest moved with a grace that suggested she knew how to use the weapons she carried.

Abruptly the women became aware of the other humans; they seemed as startled at being startled as they did at the sight of Rand and the others, but they moved like lightning. The youngest one shouted, "Shienarans!" and turned to set the bowl carefully behind her. The other two quickly lifted brown cloths from around their shoulders, wrapping them around their heads instead. The older women were raising black veils across their faces, hiding everything but their eyes, and the youngest straightened to imitate them. Crouching low, they advanced at a deliberate pace, shields held forward with their clusters of spears, except for the one each woman held ready in her other hand.

Ingtar's sword came out of its sheath. "Stand clear, Aes Sedai. Erith, stand clear." Hurin snatched out his sword-breaker, wavered between cudgel and sword for his other hand; after another glance at the Aiel's spears, he chose the sword.

"You must not," the Ogier girl protested. Wringing her hands, she turned from Ingtar to the Aiel and back. "You must not."

Rand realized the heron-mark blade was in his hands. Perrin had his axe half out of the loop at his belt and was hesitating, shaking his head.

"Are you two crazy?" Mat demanded. His bow still slanted across his back. "I don't care if they are Aiel, they're women."

"Stop this!" Verin demanded. "Stop this immediately!" The Aiel never broke stride, and the Aes Sedai clenched her fists in frustration.

Mat moved back to put a foot in his stirrup. "I'm leaving," he announced. "You hear me? I'm not staying to let them stick those things in me, and I am not going to shoot a woman!"

"The Pact!" Loial was shouting. "Remember the Pact!" It had no more effect than the continued pleas from Verin and Erith.

Rand noticed that both the Aes Sedai and the Ogier girl were keeping well out of the Aiel's way. He wondered if Mat had the right idea. He was not sure he could hurt a woman even if she *was* trying to kill him. What decided him was the thought that even if he did manage to reach Red's saddle, the Aiel were now no more than thirty paces away. He suspected those short spears could be thrown that far. As the women came closer, still crouching, spears ready, he stopped worrying about not hurting them and began worrying about how to stop them from hurting him.

Nervously, he sought the void, and it came. And the distant thought floated outside it that it was only the void. The glow of *saidar* was not there. The emptiness was more empty than he ever remembered, vaster, like a hunger great enough to consume him. A hunger for more; there was *supposed* to be something more.

Abruptly an Ogier strode in between the two groups, his narrow beard quivering. "What is the meaning of this? Put up your weapons." He sounded scandalized. "For you"—his glare took in Ingtar and Hurin, Rand and Perrin, and did not spare Mat for all his empty hands—"there is some excuse, but for you—" He rounded on the Aiel women, who had stopped their advance. "Have you forgotten the Pact?"

The women uncovered their heads and faces so hastily that it seemed they were trying to pretend they had never been covered. The girl's face was bright red, and the other women looked abashed. One of the older women, the one with the reddish hair, said, "Forgive us, Treebrother. We remember the Pact, and we would not have bared steel, but we are in the land of the Treekillers, where every hand is against us, and we saw armed men." Her eyes were gray, Rand saw, like his own.

"You are in a *stedding,* Rhian," the Ogier said gently. "Everyone is safe in the *stedding,* little sister. There is no fighting here, and no hand raised against another." She nodded, ashamed, and the Ogier looked at Ingtar and the others.

Ingtar sheathed his sword, and Rand did the same, though not so quickly as Hurin, who looked almost as embarrassed as the Aiel. Perrin had never gotten his axe all the way out. As he took hand from hilt, Rand let the void go, too, and shivered. The void went, but it left behind a slowly fading echo of the emptiness all through him, and a desire for something to fill it.

The Ogier turned to Verin and bowed. "Aes Sedai, I am Juin, son of Lacel son of Laud. I have come to take you to the Elders. They would know why an Aes Sedai comes among us, with armed men and one of our own youths." Loial hunched his shoulders as if trying to disappear.

Verin gave the Aiel a regretful look, as if she wanted to talk with them, then motioned Juin to lead, and he took her away without another word or even the first look at Loial.

For a few moments, Rand and the others stood facing the three Aiel women uneasily. At least, Rand knew he was uneasy. Ingtar seemed steady as a stone, with no more expression than one. The Aiel might have unveiled their faces, but they still had spears in their hands, and they studied the four men as though trying to see inside them. Rand in particular received increasingly angry looks. He heard the youngest woman mutter, "He is wearing a sword," in tones of mingled horror and contempt. Then the three were leaving, stopping to retrieve the wooden bowl and looking over their shoulders at Rand and the others until they vanished among the trees.

"Maidens of the Spear," Ingtar muttered. "I never thought they'd stop once they veiled their faces. Certainly not for a few words." He looked at Rand and his two friends. "You should see a charge by Red Shields, or Stone Soldiers. As easy to stop as an avalanche."

"They would not break the Pact once it was recalled to them," Erith said, smiling. "They came for sung wood." A note of pride entered her voice. "We have two Treesingers in Stedding Tsofu. They are rare, now. I have heard that Stedding Shangtai has a young Treesinger who is very talented, but we have two." Loial blushed, but she did not appear to notice. "If you will come with me, I will show you where you may wait until the Elders have spoken."

As they followed her, Perrin murmured, "Sung wood, my left foot. Those Aiel are searching for He Who Comes With the Dawn."

And Mat added dryly, "They're looking for you, Rand."

"For me! That is crazy. What makes you think—"

He cut off as Erith showed them down the steps of a wildflower-covered house apparently set aside for human guests. The rooms were twenty paces from stone wall to stone wall, with painted ceilings a good two spans above the floor, but the Ogier had done their best making something that would be comfortable for humans. Even so, the furniture was a little too large for comfort, the chairs tall enough to lift a man's heels off the floor, the table higher than Rand's waist. Hurin, at least, could have walked erect into the stone fireplace, which seemed to have been worn by water rather than made by hands. Erith eyed Loial doubtfully, but he waved away her concern and pulled one of the chairs into the corner least easily seen from the door.

As soon as the Ogier girl left, Rand got Mat and Perrin over to one side. "What do you mean they're looking for me? Why? For what reason? They looked right at me, and went away."

"They looked at you," Mat said with a grin, "like you hadn't bathed in a month, and had doused yourself with sheepdip besides." His grin faded. "But they could be looking for you. We met another Aiel."

Rand listened in growing amazement to their tale of the meeting in Kinslayer's Dagger. Mat told most of it, with Perrin putting in a correcting word now and again when he embellished too much. Mat made a great show of how dangerous the Aielman had been, and how close the meeting had come to a fight.

"And since you're the only Aiel we know," he finished, "well, it could be you. Ingtar says Aiel never live outside the Waste, so you must be the only one."

"I don't think that's funny, Mat," Rand growled. "I am not an Aiel." *The Amyrlin said you are. Ingtar thinks you are. Tam said. . . . He was sick, fevered.* They had severed the roots he had thought he had, the Aes Sedai and Tam between them, though Tam had been too sick to know what he was saying. They had cut him loose to tumble before the wind, then offered him something new to hold on to. False Dragon. Aiel. He could not claim those for roots. He would not. "Maybe I don't belong to anyone. But the Two Rivers is the only home I know."

"I didn't mean anything," Mat protested. "It's just. . . . Burn me, Ingtar says you are. Masema says you are. Urien could have been your cousin, and if Rhian put on a dress and said she was your aunt, you'd believe it yourself. Oh, all right. Don't look at me like that, Perrin. If he wants to say he isn't, all right. What difference does it make, anyway?" Perrin shook his head.

Ogier girls brought water and towels for washing faces and hands, and cheese and fruit and wine, with pewter goblets a little too large to be comfortable in the hand. Other Ogier women came, too, their dresses all embroidered. One by one they appeared, a dozen of them all told, to ask if the humans were comfortable, if they needed anything. Each turned her attentions to Loial just before she left. He gave his answers respectfully but in as few words as Rand had ever heard him use, standing with an Ogier-sized, wood-bound book clutched to his chest like a shield, and when they went, he huddled in his chair with the book held up in front of his face. The books in the house were one thing not sized for humans.

"Just smell this air, Lord Rand," Hurin said, filling his lungs with a smile. His feet dangled from one of the chairs at the table; he swung them like a boy. "I never thought most places smelled bad, but this. . . . Lord Rand, I don't think there's *ever* been any killing here. Not even any hurting, except by accident."

"The *stedding* are supposed to be safe for everyone," Rand said. He was watching Loial. "That's what the stories say, anyway." He swallowed a last bit of white cheese and went over to the Ogier. Mat followed with a goblet in his hand. "What's the matter, Loial?" Rand said. "You've been as nervous as a cat in a dogyard ever since we came here."

"It is nothing," Loial said, giving the door an uneasy glance from the corner of his eye.

"Are you afraid they'll find out you left Stedding Shangtai without permission from your Elders?"

Loial looked around wildly, the tufts on his ears vibrating. "Don't say that," he hissed. "Not where anyone can hear. If they found out. . . ." With a heavy sigh, he slumped back, looking from Rand to Mat. "I don't know how humans do it, but among Ogier. . . . If a girl sees a boy she likes, she goes to her mother. Or sometimes the mother sees someone she thinks is suitable. In any case, if they agree, the girl's mother goes to the boy's mother, and the next thing the boy knows, his marriage is all arranged."

"Doesn't the boy have any say in it?" Mat asked incredulously.

"None. The women always say we would spend our lives married to the trees if it was left to us." Loial shifted, grimacing. "Half of our marriages take place between *stedding;* groups of young Ogier visit from *stedding* to *stedding* so they can see, and be seen. If they discover I'm Outside without permission, the Elders will almost certainly decide I need a wife to settle me down. Before I know it, they'll have sent a message to Stedding Shangtai, to my mother, and she will come here and have me married before she washes off the dust of her journey. She's always said I am too hasty and need a wife. I think she was looking when I left. Whatever wife she chooses for me . . . well, any wife at all won't let me go back Outside until I have gray in my beard. Wives always say no man should be allowed Outside until he's settled enough to control his temper."

Mat gave a guffaw loud enough to draw every head, but at Loial's frantic gesture he spoke softly. "Among us, men do the choosing, and no wife can stop a man doing what he wants."

Rand frowned, remembering how Egwene had begun following him around when they were both little. It was then that Mistress al'Vere had begun taking a special interest in him, more than in any of the other boys.

Later, some girls would dance with him on feastdays and some would not, and those who would were always Egwene's friends, while those who would not were girls Egwene did not like. He also seemed to remember Mistress al'Vere taking Tam aside—*And she was muttering about Tam not having a wife for her to talk to!*—and after that, Tam and everyone else had acted as if he and Egwene were promised, even though they had not knelt before the Women's Circle to say the words. He had never thought about it this way before; things between Egwene and him had always just seemed to be the way they were, and that was that.

"I think we do it the same way," he muttered, and when Mat laughed, he added, "Do you remember your father ever doing anything your mother really didn't want him to?" Mat opened his mouth with a grin, then frowned thoughtfully and closed it again.

Juin came down the steps from outside. "If you please, will all of you come with me? The Elders would see you." He did not look at Loial, but Loial still almost dropped the book.

"If the Elders try to make you stay," Rand said, "we'll say we need you to go with us."

"I'll bet it isn't about you at all," Mat said. "I'll bet they are just going to say we can use the Waygate." He shook himself, and his voice fell even lower. "We really have to do it, don't we." It was not a question.

"Stay and get married, or travel the Ways." Loial grimaced ruefully. "Life is very unsettling with *ta'veren* for friends."

# CHAPTER 36

## Among the Elders

As Juin took them through the Ogier town, Rand saw that Loial was growing more and more anxious. Loial's ears were as stiff as his back; his eyes grew bigger every time he saw another Ogier looking at him, especially the women and girls, and a large number of them did seem to take notice of him. He looked as if he expected his own execution.

The bearded Ogier gestured to wide steps leading down into a grassy mound that was bigger by far than any other; it was a hill, for all practical purposes, almost at the base of one of the Great Trees.

"Why don't you wait out here, Loial?" Rand said.

"The Elders—" Juin began.

"—Probably just want to see the rest of us," Rand finished for him.

"Why don't they leave him alone," Mat put in.

Loial nodded vigorously. "Yes. Yes, I think. . . ." A number of Ogier women were watching him, from white-haired grandmothers to daughters Erith's age, a knot of them talking among themselves but with all eyes on him. His ears jerked, but he looked at the broad door to which the stone steps led down, and nodded again. "Yes, I will sit out here, and I'll read. That is it. I will read." Fumbling in his coat pocket, he produced a book. He settled himself on the mound beside the steps, the book small in his hands, and fixed his eyes on the pages. "I will just sit here and read until you come out." His ears twitched as if he could feel the women's eyes.

Juin shook his head, then shrugged and motioned to the steps again. "If you please. The Elders are waiting."

The huge, windowless room inside the mound was scaled for Ogier, with a thick-beamed ceiling more than four spans up; it could have fit in any palace, for size at least. The seven Ogier seated on the dais directly in front of the door made it shrink a little by their size, but Rand still felt as if he were in a cavern. The somber floorstones were smooth, if large and irregular in shape, but the gray walls could have been the rough side of a cliff. The ceiling beams, rough-hewn as they were, looked like great roots.

Except for a high-backed chair where Verin sat facing the dais, the only furnishings were the heavy, vine-carved chairs of the Elders. The Ogier woman in the middle of the dais sat in a chair raised a little higher than those of the others, three bearded men to her left in long, flaring coats, three women to her right in dresses like her own, embroidered in vines and flowers from neckline to hem. All had aged faces and pure white hair, even to the tufts on their ears, and an air of massive dignity.

Hurin gaped at them openly, and Rand felt like staring himself. Not even Verin had the appearance of wisdom that was in the Elders' huge eyes, nor Morgase in her crown their authority, nor Moiraine their calm serenity. Ingtar was the first to bow, as formally as Rand had ever seen from him, while the others still stood rooted.

"I am Alar," the Ogier woman on the highest chair said when they had finally taken their places beside Verin, "Eldest of the Elders of Stedding Tsofu. Verin has told us that you have need to use the Waygate here. To recover the Horn of Valere from Darkfriends is a great need, indeed, but we have allowed none to travel the Ways in more than one hundred years. Neither us, nor the Elders of any other *stedding*."

"I will find the Horn," Ingtar said angrily. "I must. If you will not permit us to use the Waygate. . . ." He fell silent as Verin looked at him, but the scowl remained on his face.

Alar smiled. "Be not so hasty, Shienaran. You humans never take time for thought. Only decisions reached in calm can be sure." Her smile faded to seriousness, but her voice kept its own measured calm. "The dangers of the Ways are not to be faced with a sword in your hand, not charging Aiel or ravening Trollocs. I must tell you that to enter the Ways is to risk not only death and madness, but perhaps your very souls."

"We have seen *Machin Shin*," Rand said, and Mat and Perrin agreed. They could not manage to sound eager to do it again.

"I will follow the Horn to Shayol Ghul itself, if need be," Ingtar said firmly. Hurin only nodded as if including himself in Ingtar's words.

"Bring Trayal," Alar commanded, and Juin, who had remained by the door, bowed and left. "It is not enough," she told Verin, "to hear what can happen. You must see it, know it in your heart."

There was an uncomfortable silence until Juin returned, and it became more uncomfortable still as two Ogier women followed him, guiding a dark-bearded Ogier of middle years, who shambled between them as if he did not quite know how his legs worked. His face sagged, without any expression at all, and his big eyes were vacant and unblinking, not staring, not looking, not even seeming to see. One of the women gently wiped drool from the corner of his mouth. They took his arms to stop him; his foot went forward, hesitated, then fell back with a thump. He seemed as content to stand as to walk, or at least as uncaring.

"Trayal was one of the last among us to go along the Ways," Alar said softly. "He came out as you see him. Will you touch him, Verin?"

Verin gave her a long look, then rose and strode to Trayal. He did not move as she laid her hands on his wide chest, not even a flicker of an eye to acknowledge her touch. With a sharp hiss, she jerked back, staring up at him, then whirled to face the Elders. "He is . . . empty. This body lives, but there is nothing inside it. Nothing." Every Elder wore a look of unbearable sadness.

"Nothing," one of the Elders to Alar's right said softly. Her eyes seemed to hold all the pain Trayal's no longer could. "No mind. No soul. Nothing of Trayal remains but his body."

"He was a fine Treesinger," one of the men sighed.

Alar motioned, and the two women turned Trayal to lead him out; they had to move him before he began to walk.

"We know the risks," Verin said. "But whatever the risks, we must follow the Horn of Valere."

The Eldest nodded. "The Horn of Valere. I do not know whether it is worse news that it is in Darkfriend hands, or that it has been found at all." She looked down the row of Elders; each nodded in turn, one of the men tugging his beard doubtfully first. "Very well. Verin tells me time is urgent. I will show you to the Waygate myself." Rand was feeling half relieved and half afraid, when she added, "You have with you a young Ogier. Loial, son of Arent son of Halan, from Stedding Shangtai. He is far from his home."

"We need him," Rand said quickly. His words slowed under surprised stares from the Elders and Verin, but he went on stubbornly. "We need him to go with us, and he wants to."

"Loial's a friend," Perrin said, at the same time that Mat said, "He doesn't get in the way, and he carries his own weight." Neither of them appeared comfortable at having the Elders' focus shift to them, but they did not back down.

"Is there some reason he cannot come with us?" Ingtar asked. "As Mat says, he has held his own. I don't know that we need him, but if he wants to come, why—?"

"We do need him," Verin broke in smoothly. "Few any longer know the Ways, but Loial has studied them. He can decipher the Guidings."

Alar eyed them each in turn, then settled to a study of Rand. She looked as if she knew things; all the Elders did, but she most of all. "Verin says you are *ta'veren*," she said at last, "and I can feel it in you. That I can do so means that you must be very strongly *ta'veren* indeed, for such Talents ever run weakly in us, if at all. Have you drawn Loial, son of Arent son of Halan, into *ta'maral'ailen*, the Web the Pattern weaves around you?"

"I. . . . I just want to find the Horn and. . . ." Rand let the rest of it die. Alar had not mentioned Mat's dagger. He did not know whether Verin had told the Elders, or held it back for some reason. "He is my friend, Eldest."

"Your friend," Alar said. "He is young by our way of thinking. You are young, too, but *ta'veren*. You will look after him, and when the weaving is done, you will see that he comes safely home to Stedding Shangtai."

"I will," he told her. It had the feeling of a commitment, the swearing of an oath.

"Then we will go to the Waygate."

Outside, Loial scrambled to his feet when they appeared, Alar and Verin leading. Ingtar sent Hurin off at a run to fetch Uno and the other soldiers. Loial eyed the Eldest warily, then fell in with Rand at the rear of the procession. The Ogier women who had been watching him were all gone. "Did the Elders say anything about me? Did she. . . ?" He peered at Alar's broad back as she ordered Juin to have their horses brought. She started off with Verin while Juin was still bowing himself away, bending her head to talk quietly.

"She told Rand to take care of you," Mat told Loial solemnly as they followed, "and see you got home safely as a babe. I don't see why you can't stay here and get married."

"She said you could come with us." Rand glared at Mat, which made Mat chortle under his breath. It sounded odd, coming from that drawn face. Loial was twirling the stem of a trueheart blossom between his fingers. "Did you go picking flowers?" Rand asked.

"Erith gave it to me." Loial watched the yellow petals spin. "She really is very pretty, even if Mat does not see it."

"Does that mean you don't want to go with us after all?"

Loial gave a start. "What? Oh, no. I mean, yes. I do want to go. She only gave me a flower. Just a flower." He took a book out of his pocket, though, and pressed the blossom under the front cover. As he returned the book, he murmured to himself, barely loud enough for Rand to hear, "And she said I was handsome, too." Mat let out a wheeze and doubled over, staggering along clutching his sides, and Loial's cheeks colored. "Well . . . she said it. I didn't."

Perrin rapped Mat smartly on the top of his head with his knuckles. "Nobody ever said Mat was handsome. He's just jealous."

"That's not true," Mat said, straightening abruptly. "Neysa Ayellin thinks I'm handsome. She's told me so more than once."

"Is Neysa pretty?" Loial asked.

"She has a face like a goat," Perrin said blandly. Mat choked, trying to get his protests out.

Rand grinned in spite of himself. Neysa Ayellin was almost as pretty as Egwene. And this was almost like old times, almost like being back home, bantering back and forth, and nothing more important in the world than a laugh and twitting the other fellow.

As they made their way through the town, Ogier greeted the Eldest, bowing or curtsying, eyeing the human visitors with interest. Alar's set face kept anyone from stopping to speak, though. The only thing that indicated when they left the town was the absence of the mounds; there were still Ogier about, examining trees, or sometimes working with pitch and saw or axe where there were dead limbs or where a tree needed more sunlight. They handled the tasks tenderly.

Juin joined them, leading their horses, and Hurin came riding with Uno and the other soldiers, and the packhorses, just before Alar pointed and said, "It is over there." The banter died.

Rand felt a momentary surprise. The Waygate had to be Outside the *stedding*—the Ways had been begun with the One Power; they could not have been made inside—but there was nothing to indicate they had crossed the boundary. Then he realized there was a difference; the sense of something lost that he had felt since entering the *stedding* was gone. That gave him another sort of chill. *Saidin* was there again. Waiting.

Alar led them past a tall oak, and there in a small clearing stood the big slab of the Waygate, the front of it delicately worked in tightly woven vines and leaves from a hundred different plants. Around the edge of the clearing the Ogier had built a low stone coping that seemed as if it had grown there, suggesting a circle of roots. The look of it made Rand uncomfortable. It took him a moment to realize that the roots suggested were those of bramble and briar, burningleaf and itch oak. Not the sort of plants into which anyone would want to stumble.

The Eldest stopped short of the coping. "The wall is meant to warn away any who comes here. Not that many of us do. I myself will not cross it. But you may." Juin did not go as close as she did; he kept rubbing his hands on the front of his coat, and would not look at the Waygate.

"Thank you," Verin told her. "The need is great, or I would not have asked it."

Rand tensed as the Aes Sedai stepped over the coping and approached the Waygate. Loial took a deep breath and muttered to himself. Uno and the rest of the soldiers shifted in their saddles and loosened swords in their scabbards. There was nothing along the Ways against which a sword would be any use, but it was something to convince themselves they were ready. Only Ingtar and the Aes Sedai seemed calm; even Alar gripped her skirt with both hands.

Verin plucked the *Avendesora* leaf, and Rand leaned forward intently. He knew an urge to assume the void, to be where he could reach *saidin* if he needed to.

The greenery carved across the Waygate stirred in an unfelt breeze, leaves fluttering as a gap opened down the center of the mass and the two halves began to swing open.

Rand stared at the first crack. There was no dull, silvery reflection behind it, only blackness blacker than pitch. "Close it!" he shouted. "The Black Wind! Close it!"

Verin took one startled look and thrust the three-pointed leaf back in among all the varied leaves already there; it stayed when she took her hand away and backed toward the coping. As soon as the *Avendesora* leaf was back in its place, the Waygate immediately began to close. The crack disappeared, vines and leaves merging, hiding the blackness of *Machin Shin,* and the Waygate was only stone again, if stone carved in a nearer semblance of life than seemed possible.

Alar let out a shuddering breath. "*Machin Shin.* So close."

"It didn't try to come out," Rand said. Juin made a strangled sound.

"I have told you," Verin said, "the Black Wind is a creature of the Ways. It cannot leave them." She sounded calm, but she still wiped her hands on her skirt. Rand opened his mouth, then gave it up. "And yet," she went on, "I wonder at it being here. First in Cairhien, now here. I wonder." She gave Rand a sidelong glance that made him jump. The look was so quick that he did not think anyone else noticed it, but to Rand it seemed to connect him with the Black Wind.

"I have never heard of this," Alar said slowly, *"Machin Shin* waiting when a Waygate was opened. It always roamed the Ways. But it has been long, and perhaps the Black Wind hungers, and hopes to catch some unwary one entering a gate. Verin, assuredly you cannot use this Waygate. And however great your need, I cannot say I am sorry. The Ways belong to the Shadow, now."

Rand frowned at the Waygate. *Could it be following me?* There were too many questions. Had Fain somehow ordered the Black Wind? Verin said it could not be done. And why would Fain demand that he follow, then try to stop him? He only knew that he believed the message. He had to go to Toman Head. If they found the Horn of Valere and Mat's dagger under a bush tomorrow, he still had to go.

Verin stood with eyes unfocused in thought. Mat was sitting on the coping with his head in his hands, and Perrin watched him worriedly. Loial seemed relieved that they could not use the Waygate, and ashamed at being relieved.

"We are done for here," Ingtar announced. "Verin Sedai, I followed you here against my better judgment, but I can no longer follow. I mean to return to Cairhien. Barthanes can tell me where the Darkfriends went, and somehow I will make him do it."

"Fain went to Toman Head," Rand said wearily. "And where he went, that's where the Horn is, and the dagger."

"I suppose. . . ." Perrin shrugged reluctantly. "I suppose we could try another Waygate. At another *stedding?"*

Loial stroked his chin and spoke quickly, as if to make up for his relief at the failure here. "Stedding Cantoine lies just above the River Iralell, and Stedding Taijing is east of it in the Spine of the World. But the Waygate in Caemlyn, where the grove was, is closer, and the gate in the grove at Tar Valon is closest of all."

"Whichever Waygate we try to use," Verin said absently, "I fear we will find *Machin Shin* waiting." Alar looked at her questioningly, but the Aes Sedai said no more that anyone could hear. She muttered to herself instead, shaking her head as if arguing with herself.

"What we need," Hurin said diffidently, "is one of those Portal Stones." He looked to Alar, then Verin, and when neither told him to stop, he went on, sounding increasingly confident. "The Lady Selene said those old Aes Sedai had studied those worlds, and that was how they knew how to make the Ways. And that place we were . . . well, it only took us two days—less—to travel a hundred leagues. If we could use a Portal Stone to go to that world, or one like it, why, it'd take no more than a week or two to reach the Aryth Ocean, and we could come back right on Toman Head. Maybe it isn't so quick as the Ways, but it's a long sight quicker than riding off west. What do you say, Lord Ingtar? Lord Rand?"

Verin answered him. "What you suggest might be possible, sniffer, but as well hope to open this Waygate again and find *Machin Shin* gone as hope to find a Portal Stone. I know none closer than the Aiel Waste. Though we could go back into Kinslayer's Dagger, if you, or Rand, or Loial think you could find that Stone again."

Rand looked at Mat. His friend had lifted his head hopefully at this talk of the Stones. A few weeks, Verin had said. If they simply rode west, Mat would never live to see Toman Head.

"I can find it," Rand said reluctantly. He felt ashamed. *Mat's going to die, Darkfriends have the Horn of Valere, Fain will hurt Emond's Field if you don't follow him, and you're afraid to channel the Power. Once to go and once to come back. Twice more won't drive you mad.* What really made him afraid, though, was the eagerness that leaped inside him at the thought of channeling again, of feeling the Power fill him, of feeling truly alive.

"I do not understand this," Alar said slowly. "The Portal Stones have not been used since the Age of Legends. I did not think there was anyone who still knew how to use them."

"The Brown Ajah knows many things," Verin said dryly, "and I know how the Stones may be used."

The Eldest nodded. "Truly there are wonders in the White Tower of which we do not dream. But if you can use a Portal Stone, there is no need for you to ride to Kinslayer's Dagger. There is a Stone not far from where we stand."

"The Wheel weaves as the Wheel wills, and the Pattern provides what is needful." The absent look dropped from Verin's face altogether. "Take us to it," she said briskly. "We have lost more than enough time already."

# CHAPTER 37

## *What Might Be*

Alar led them away from the Waygate at a dignified pace, though Juin seemed more than anxious to leave the Waygate behind. Mat, at least, looked ahead eagerly, and Hurin seemed confident, while Loial appeared concerned more that Alar might change her mind about his going than about anything else. Rand did not hurry as he pulled Red along by the reins. He did not think Verin meant to use the Stone herself.

The gray stone column stood upright near a beech almost a hundred feet tall and four paces thick; Rand would have thought it a big tree before he saw the Great Trees. There was no warning coping here, only a few wildflowers pushing through the leafy mulch of the forest floor. The Portal Stone itself was weathered, but the symbols covering it were still clear enough to make out.

The mounted Shienaran soldiers spread out in a loose circle around the Stone and those afoot.

"We stood it upright," Alar said, "when we found it many years ago, but we did not move it. It . . . seemed to . . . resist being moved." She went right up to it, and laid a big hand on the Stone. "I have always thought of it as a symbol of what has been lost, what has been forgotten. In the Age of Legends, it could be studied and somewhat understood. To us, it is only stone."

"More than that, I hope." Verin's voice grew brisker. "Eldest, I thank you for your help. Forgive us for our lack of ceremony in leaving you, but the Wheel waits for no woman. At least we will no longer disturb the peace of your *stedding*."

"We called the stonemasons back from Cairhien," Alar said, "but we still hear what happens in the world Outside. False Dragons. The Great Hunt of the Horn. We hear, and it passes us by. I do not think Tarmon Gai'don will pass us by, or leave us in peace. Fare you well, Verin Sedai. All of you, fare well, and may you shelter in the palm of the Creator's hand. Juin." She paused only for a glance at Loial and a last admonitory look at Rand, and then the Ogier were gone among the trees.

There was a creaking of saddles as the soldiers shifted. Ingtar looked around the circle they made. "Is this necessary, Verin Sedai? Even if it can be done. . . . We do not even know if the Darkfriends really have taken the Horn to Toman Head. I still believe I can make Barthanes—"

"If we cannot be sure," Verin said mildly, cutting him off, "then Toman Head is as good a place to look as any other. More than once I've heard you say you would ride to Shayol Ghul if need be to recover the Horn. Do you hold back now, at this?" She gestured to the Stone under the smooth-barked tree.

Ingtar's back stiffened. "I hold back at nothing. Take us to Toman Head or take us to Shayol Ghul. If the Horn of Valere lies at the end, I will follow you."

"That is well, Ingtar. Now, Rand, you have been transported by a Portal Stone more recently than I. Come." She motioned to him, and he led Red over to her at the Stone.

"You've used a Portal Stone?" He glanced over his shoulder to make sure no one else was close enough to hear. "Then you don't mean for me to." He gave a relieved shrug.

Verin looked at him blandly. "I have never used a Stone; that is why your use is more recent than mine. I am well aware of my limits. I would be destroyed before I came close to channeling enough Power to work a Portal Stone. But I know a little of them. Enough to help you, a bit."

"But I don't know *anything*." He led his horse around the Stone, looking it up and down. "The one thing I remember is the symbol for our world. Selene showed me, but I don't see it here."

"Of course not. Not on a Stone *in* our world; the symbols are aids in getting *to* a world." She shook her head. "What would I not give to talk with this girl of yours? Or better, to put my hands on her book. It is generally thought that no copy of *Mirrors of the Wheel* survived the Breaking whole. Serafelle always tells me there are more books that we believe lost than I could credit waiting to be found. Well, no use in worrying over what I don't know. I do know some things. The symbols on the top half of the Stone stand for worlds. Not all the Worlds That Might Be, of course. Apparently, not every Stone connects to every world, and the Aes Sedai of the Age of Legends believed that there were possible worlds no Stones at all touched. Do you see nothing that sparks a memory?"

"Nothing." If he found the right symbol, he could use it to find Fain and the Horn, to save Mat, to stop Fain hurting Emond's Field. If he found the symbol, he would have to touch *saidin*. He wanted to save Mat and stop Fain, but the did not want to touch *saidin*. He was afraid to channel, and he hungered for it like a starving man for food. "I don't remember anything."

Verin sighed. "The symbols at the bottom indicate Stones at other places. If you know the trick of it, you could take us, not to this same Stone in another world, but to one of those others there, or even to one of them here. It was something akin to Traveling, I think, but just as no one remembers how to Travel, no one remembers the trick. Without that knowledge, trying it might easily destroy us all." She pointed to two parallel wavy lines crossed by an odd squiggle, carved low on the column. "That indicates a Stone on Toman Head. It is one of three Stones for which I know the symbol; the only one of those three I've visited. And what I learned—after nearly being caught by the snows in the Mountains of Mist and freezing my way across Almoth Plain—was absolutely nothing. Do you play at dice, or cards, Rand al'Thor?"

"Mat's the gambler. Why?"

"Yes. Well, we'll leave him out of this, I think. These other symbols are also known to me."

With one finger she outlined a rectangle containing eight carvings that were much alike, a circle and an arrow, but in half the arrow was contained inside the circle, while in the others the point pierced the circle through. The arrows pointed left, right, up and down, and surrounding each circle was a different line of what Rand was sure was script, though in no language he knew, all curving lines that suddenly became jagged hooks, then flowed on again.

"At least," Verin went on, "I know this much about them. Each stands for a world, the study of which led eventually to the making of the Ways. These are not all of the worlds studied, but the only ones for which I know the symbols. This is where gambling comes in. I don't know what any of these worlds is like. It is believed there are worlds where a year is only a

day here, and others where a day is a year here. There are supposed to be
worlds where the very air would kill us at a breath, and worlds that barely
have enough reality to hold together. I would not speculate on what might
happen if we found ourselves in one of those. You must choose. As my
father would have said, it's time to roll the dice."

Rand stared, shaking his head. "I could kill all of us, whatever I
choose."

"Are you not willing to take that risk? For the Horn of Valere? For
Mat?"

"Why are you so willing to take it? I don't even know if I can do it.
It—it doesn't work every time I try." He knew no one had come any
closer, but he looked anyway. All of them waited in a loose circle around
the Stone, watching, but not close enough to eavesdrop. "Sometimes *saidin*
is just there. I can feel it, but it might as well be on the moon as far as
touching it. And even if it does work, what if I take us someplace we can't
breathe? What good will that do Mat? Or the Horn?"

"You are the Dragon Reborn," she said quietly. "Oh, you can die, but I
don't think the Pattern will let you die until it is done with you. Then
again, the Shadow lies on the Pattern, now, and who can say how that
affects the weaving? All you can do is follow your destiny."

"I am Rand al'Thor," he growled. "I am not the Dragon Reborn. I
won't be a false Dragon."

"You are what you are. Will you choose, or will you stand here until
your friend dies?"

Rand heard his teeth grinding and forced himself to unclench his jaw.
The symbols could all have been exactly alike, for all they meant to him.
The script could as well have been a chicken's scratchings. At last he settled on one, with an arrow pointing left because it pointed toward Toman
Head, an arrow that pierced the circle because it had broken free, as he
wanted to. He wanted to laugh. Such small things on which to gamble all
their lives.

"Come closer," Verin ordered the others. "It will be best if you are
near." They obeyed, with only a little hesitation. "It is time to begin," she
said as they gathered round.

She threw back her cloak and put her hands on the column, but Rand
saw her watching him from the corner of her eye. He was aware of nervous
coughing and throat-clearing from the men around the Stone, a curse from
Uno at someone hanging back, a weak joke from Mat, a loud gulp from
Loial. He took the void.

It was so easy, now. The flame consumed fear and passion and was gone
almost before he thought to form it. Gone, leaving only emptiness, and

shining *saidin,* sickening, tantalizing, stomach-turning, seductive. He . . . reached for it . . . and it filled him, made him alive. He did not move a muscle, but he felt as if he were quivering with the rush of the One Power into him. The symbol formed itself, an arrow piercing a circle, floating just beyond the void, as hard as the stuff it was carved on. He let the One Power flow through him to the symbol.

The symbol shimmered, flickered.

"Something is happening," Verin said. "Something . . ."

The world flickered.

The iron lock spun across the farmhouse floor, and Rand dropped the hot teakettle as a huge figure with ram's horns on its head loomed in the doorway with the darkness of Winternight behind it.

"Run!" Tam shouted. His sword flashed, and the Trolloc toppled, but it grappled with Tam as it fell, pulling him down.

More crowded in at the door, black-mailed shapes with human faces distorted with muzzles and beaks and horns, oddly curved swords stabbing at Tam as he tried to struggle to his feet, spiked axes swinging, red blood on steel.

"Father!" Rand screamed. Clawing his belt knife from its sheath, he threw himself over the table to help his father, and screamed again as the first sword ran through his chest.

Blood bubbled up into his mouth, and a voice whispered inside his head, *I have won again, Lews Therin.*

*Flicker.*

Rand struggled to hold the symbol, dimly aware of Verin's voice. ". . . is not . . ."

The Power flooded.

*Flicker.*

Rand was happy after he married Egwene, and tried to not let the moods take him, the times when he thought there should have been something more, something different. News of the world outside came into the Two Rivers with peddlers, and merchants come to buy wool and tabac, always news of fresh troubles, of wars and false Dragons everywhere. There was a year when neither merchants nor peddlers came, and when they returned the next they brought word that Artur Hawkwing's armies had come back, or their descendants, at least. The old nations were broken, it was said, and the world's new masters, who used chained Aes Sedai in their battles, had torn down the White Tower and salted the ground where Tar Valon had stood. There were no more Aes Sedai.

It all made little difference in the Two Rivers. Crops still had to be planted, sheep sheared, lambs tended. Tam had grandsons and grand-daughters to dandle on his knee before he was laid to rest beside his wife, and the old farmhouse grew new rooms. Egwene became Wisdom, and most thought she was even better than the old Wisdom, Nynaeve al'Maera, had been. It was as well she was, for her cures that worked so miraculously on others were only just able to keep Rand alive from the sickness that constantly seemed to threaten him. His moods grew worse, blacker, and he raged that this was not what was meant to be. Egwene grew frightened when the moods were on him, for strange things sometimes happened when he was at his bleakest—lightning storms she had not heard listening to the wind, wildfires in the forest—but she loved him and cared for him and kept him sane, though some muttered that Rand al'Thor was crazy and dangerous.

When she died, he sat alone for long hours by her grave, tears soaking his gray-flecked beard. His sickness came back, and he wasted; he lost the last two fingers on his right hand and one on his left, his ears looked like scars, and men muttered that he smelled of decay. His blackness deepened.

Yet when the dire news came, none refused to accept him at their side. Trollocs and Fades and things undreamed of had burst out of the Blight, and the world's new masters were being thrown back, for all the powers they wielded. So Rand took up the bow he had just fingers enough left to shoot and limped with those who marched north to the River Taren, men from every village, farm, and corner of the Two Rivers, with their bows, and axes, and boarspears, and swords that had lain rusting in attics. Rand wore a sword, too, with a heron on the blade, that he had found after Tam died, though he knew nothing of how to use it. Women came, too, shouldering what weapons they could find, marching alongside the men. Some laughed, saying that they had the strange feeling they had done this before.

And at the Taren the people of the Two Rivers met the invaders, endless ranks of Trollocs led by nightmare Fades beneath a dead black banner that seemed to eat the light. Rand saw that banner and thought the madness had taken him again, for it seemed that this was what he had been born for, to fight that banner. He sent every arrow at it, straight as his skill and the void would serve, never worrying about the Trollocs forcing their way across the river, or the men and women dying to either side of him. It was one of those Trollocs that ran him through, before it loped howling for blood deeper into the Two Rivers. And as he lay on the bank of the Taren,

watching the sky seem to grow dark at noon, breath coming ever slower, he heard a voice say, *I have won again, Lews Therin.*
*Flicker.*

The arrow-and-circle contorted into parallel wavy lines, and he fought it back again.
Verin's voice. ". . . right. Something . . ."
The Power raged.
*Flicker.*

Tam tried to console Rand when Egwene took sick and died just a week before their wedding. Nynaeve tried, too, but she was shaken herself, since for all her skill she had no idea what it was that had killed the girl. Rand had sat outside Egwene's house while she died, and there seemed to be nowhere in Emond's Field he could go that he did not still hear her screaming. He knew he could not stay. Tam gave him a sword with a heron-mark blade, and though he explained little of how a shepherd in the Two Rivers had come by such a thing, he taught Rand how to use it. On the day Rand left, Tam gave him a letter he said might get Rand taken into the army of Illian, and hugged him, and said, "I've never had another son, or wanted another. Come back with a wife like I did, if you can, boy, but come back in any case."

Rand had his money stolen in Baerlon, though, and his letter of introduction, and almost his sword, and he met a woman called Min who told him such crazy things about himself that he finally left the city to get away from her. Eventually his wanderings brought him to Caemlyn, and there his skill with the sword earned him a place in the Queen's Guards. Sometimes he found himself looking at the Daughter-Heir, Elayne, and at such times he was filled with odd thoughts that this was not the way things were supposed to be, that there should be something more to his life. Elayne did not look at him, of course; she married a Taren prince, though she did not seem happy in it. Rand was just a soldier, once a shepherd from a small village so far toward the western border that only lines on a map any longer truly connected it to Andor. Besides, he had a dark reputation, as a man of violent moods.

Some said he was mad, and in ordinary times perhaps not even his skill with the sword would have kept him in the Guard, but these were not ordinary times. False Dragons sprang up like weeds. Every time one was taken down, two more proclaimed themselves, or three, till every nation was torn by war. And Rand's star rose, for he had learned the secret of his

madness, a secret he knew he had to keep and did. He could channel.
There were always places, times, in a battle when a little channeling, not
big enough to be noticed in the confusion, could make luck. Sometimes it
worked, this channeling, and sometimes not, but it worked often enough.
He knew he was mad, and did not care. A wasting sickness came on him,
and he did not care about that, either, and neither did anyone else, for
word had come that Artur Hawkwing's armies had returned to reclaim the
land.

Rand led a thousand men when the Queen's Guards crossed the Mountains of Mist—he never thought of turning aside to visit the Two Rivers;
he seldom thought of the Two Rivers at all, anymore—and he commanded
the Guard when the shattered remnants retreated back across the mountains. The length of Andor he fought and fell back, amid hordes of fleeing
refugees, until at last he came to Caemlyn. Many of the people of Caemlyn
had fled already, and many counseled the army to retreat further, but
Elayne was Queen, now, and vowed she would not leave Caemlyn. She
would not look at his ruined face, scarred by his sickness, but he could not
leave her, and so what was left of the Queen's Guards prepared to defend
the Queen while her people ran.

The Power came to him during the battle for Caemlyn, and he hurled
lightning and fire among the invaders, and split the earth under their feet,
yet the feeling came again, too, that he had been born for something else.
For all he did, there were too many of the enemy to stop, and they also had
those who could channel. At last, a lightning bolt hurled Rand from the
Palace wall, broken, bleeding, and burned, and as his last breath rattled in
his throat, he heard a voice whisper, *I have won again, Lews Therin.*

*Flicker.*

Rand struggled to hold the void as it quivered under the hammer blows
of the world flickering, to hold the one symbol as a thousand of them
darted along the surface of the void. He struggled to hold on to any one
symbol.

". . . is wrong!" Verin screamed.

The Power was everything.

*Flicker. Flicker. Flicker. Flicker. Flicker. Flicker.*

He was a soldier. He was a shepherd. He was a beggar, and a king. He
was farmer, gleeman, sailor, carpenter. He was born, lived, and died an
Aiel. He died mad, he died rotting, he died of sickness, accident, age. He
was executed, and multitudes cheered his death. He proclaimed himself the
Dragon Reborn and flung his banner across the sky; he ran from the Power

and hid; he lived and died never knowing. He held off the madness and the sickness for years; he succumbed between two winters. Sometimes Moiraine came and took him away from the Two Rivers, alone or with those of his friends who had survived Winternight; sometimes she did not. Sometimes other Aes Sedai came for him. Sometimes the Red Ajah. Egwene married him; Egwene, stern-faced in the stole of the Amyrlin Seat, led the Aes Sedai who gentled him; Egwene, with tears in her eyes, plunged a dagger into his heart, and he thanked her as he died. He loved other women, married other women. Elayne, and Min, and a fair-haired farmer's daughter met on the road to Caemlyn, and women he had never seen before he lived those lives. A hundred lives. More. So many he could not count them. And at the end of every life, as he lay dying, as he drew his final breath, a voice whispered in his ear. *I have won again, Lews Therin.*

*Flicker flicker flicker flicker flicker flicker flicker flicker flicker flicker flicker flicker flicker flicker flicker flicker flicker flicker flicker flicker flicker flicker flicker flicker flicker flicker.*

The void vanished, contact with *saidin* fled, and Rand fell with a thud that would have knocked the breath out of him if he had not already been half numb. He felt rough stone under his cheek, and his hands. It was cold.

He was aware of Verin, struggling from her back to hands and knees. He heard someone vomit roughly, and raised his head. Uno was kneeling on the ground, scrubbing the back of his hand across his mouth. Everyone was down, and the horses stood stiff-legged and quivering, eyes wild and rolling. Ingtar had his sword out, gripping the hilt so hard the blade shook, staring at nothing. Loial sat sprawled, wide-eyed and stunned. Mat was huddled in a ball with his arms wrapped around his head, and Perrin had his fingers dug into his face as if he wanted to rip away whatever he had seen, or perhaps rip out the eyes that had seen it. None of the soldiers were any better. Masema wept openly, tears streaming down his face, and Hurin was looking around as if for a place to run.

"What. . . ?" Rand stopped to swallow. He was lying on rough, weathered stone half buried in the dirt. "What happened?"

"A surge of the One Power." The Aes Sedai tottered to her feet and pulled her cloak tight with a shiver. "It was as if we were being forced . . . pushed. . . . It seemed to come out of nowhere. You must learn to control it. You must! That much of the Power could burn you to a cinder."

"Verin, I. . . . I lived. . . . I was. . . ." He realized the stone under him was rounded. The Portal Stone. Hastily, shakily, he pushed himself to his feet. "Verin, I lived and died, I don't know how many times. Every time it was different, but it was me. It was me."

"The Lines that join the Worlds That Might Be, laid by those who knew the Numbers of Chaos." Verin shuddered; she seemed to be talking to herself. "I've never heard it, but there is no reason we would not be born in those worlds, yet the lives we lived would be different lives. Of course. Different lives for the different ways things might have happened."

"Is that what happened? I . . . we . . . saw how our lives could have been?" *I have won again, Lews Therin. No! I am Rand al'Thor!*

Verin gave herself a shake and looked at him. "Does it surprise you that your life might go differently if you made different choices, or different things happened to you? Though I never thought I— Well. The important thing is, we are here. Though not as we hoped."

"Where is here?" he demanded. The woods of Stedding Tsofu were gone, replaced by rolling land. There seemed to be forest not far to the west, and a few hills. It had been high in the day when they gathered around the Stone in the *stedding* but here the sun stood low toward afternoon in a gray sky. The handful of trees nearby were bare branched, or else held a few leaves bright with color. A cold wind gusted from the east, sending leaves scurrying across the ground.

"Toman Head," Verin said. "This is the Stone I visited. You should not have tried to bring us directly here. I don't know what went wrong—I don't suppose I ever will—but from the trees, I would say it is well into late autumn. Rand, we haven't gained any time by it. We've lost time. I would say we have easily spent four months in coming here."

"But I didn't—"

"You must let me guide you in these things. I cannot teach you, it's true, but perhaps I can at least keep you from killing yourself—and the rest of us—by overreaching. Even if you do not kill yourself, if the Dragon Reborn burns himself out like a guttering candle, who will face the Dark One then?" She did not wait for him to renew his protests, but went to Ingtar instead.

The Shienaran gave a start when she touched his arm, and looked at her with frantic eyes. "I walk in the Light," he said hoarsely. "I will find the Horn of Valere and pull down Shayol Ghul's power. I will!"

"Of course you will," she said soothingly. She took his face in her hands, and he drew a sudden breath, abruptly recovering from whatever had held him. Except that memory still lay in his eyes. "There," she said. "That will do for you. I will see how I can help the rest. We may still recover the Horn, but our path has not grown smoother."

As she started around among the others, stopping briefly by each, Rand went to his friends. When he tried to straighten Mat, Mat jerked and stared at him, then grabbed Rand's coat with both hands. "Rand, I'd never tell anyone about—about you. I wouldn't betray you. You have to believe that!" He looked worse than ever, but Rand thought it was mostly fright.

"I do," Rand said. He wondered what lives Mat had lived, and what he had done. *He must have told someone, or he wouldn't be so anxious about it.* He could not hold it against him. Those had been other Mats, not this one. Besides, after some of the alternatives he had seen for himself. . . . "I believe you. Perrin?"

The curly-haired youth dropped his hands from his face with a sigh. Red marks scored his forehead and cheeks where his nails had dug in. His yellow eyes hid his thoughts. "We don't have many choices really, do we, Rand? Whatever happens, whatever we do, some things are almost always the same." He let out another long breath. "Where are we? Is this one of those worlds you and Hurin were talking about?"

"It's Toman Head," Rand told him. "In our world. Or so Verin says. And it is autumn."

Mat looked worried. "How could—? No, I don't want to know how it happened. But how are we going to find Fain and the dagger now? He could be anywhere by this time."

"He's here," Rand assured him. He hoped he was right. Fain had had time to take ship for anyplace he wanted to go. Time to ride to Emond's Field. Or Tar Valon. *Please, Light, he didn't get tired of waiting. If he's hurt Egwene, or anybody in Emond's Field, I'll. . . . Light burn me, I tried to come in time.*

"The larger towns on Toman Head are all west of here," Verin announced loudly enough for all to hear. Everyone was on their feet again, except for Rand and his two friends; she came and put her hands on Mat as she spoke. "Not that there are many villages large enough to call towns. If we are to find any trace of the Darkfriends, to the west is the place to begin. And I think we should not waste the daylight sitting here."

When Mat blinked and stood up—he still looked ill, but he moved spryly—she put her hands on Perrin. Rand backed away when she reached for him.

"Don't be foolish," she told him.

"I don't want your help," he said quietly. "Or any Aes Sedai help."

Her lips twitched. "As you wish."

They mounted immediately and rode west, leaving the Portal Stone behind. No one protested, Rand least of all. *Light, let me not be too late.*

# CHAPTER 38

## *Practice*

Sitting cross-legged on her bed in her white dress, Egwene made three tiny balls of light weave patterns above her hands. She was not supposed to do this without at least one the Accepted to supervise, but Nynaeve, glaring and striding up and down in front of the small fireplace, did after all wear the Serpent ring given to the Accepted, and her white dress had the colored rings encircling the hem, even if she was not allowed to try to teach anyone yet. And Egwene had found over these last thirteen weeks that she could not resist. She knew how easy it was to touch *saidar* now. She could always feel it there, waiting for her, like the smell of perfume or the feel of silk, drawing her, drawing her. And once she did touch it, she could rarely stop from channeling, or at least trying to. She failed almost as often as she succeeded, but that was only another spur to keep on.

It often frightened her. How much she wanted to channel frightened her, and how drab and dreary she felt when she was not channeling, compared to when she was. She wanted to drink it all in, despite the cautions about burning herself out, and that wanting frightened her most of all. Sometimes she wished she had never come to Tar Valon. But the fright could not make her stop for long, any more than the fear of being caught by an Aes Sedai or by any of the Accepted beside Nynaeve.

It was safe enough here, though, in her own room. Min was there, sitting on the three-legged stool watching her, but she knew Min well enough now to know Min would never report her. She thought she was lucky to have made two good friends since coming to Tar Valon.

It was a little, windowless room, as all novices' rooms were. Three short paces took Nynaeve from wall to white-plastered wall; Nynaeve's own room was much larger, but since she had made no friends among the other Accepted, she came to Egwene's room when she needed someone to talk to, even as now when she did not talk at all. The tiny fire on the narrow hearth handily kept the first chill of approaching autumn at bay, though Egwene was sure it would not serve so well when winter came. A small table for study completed the furnishings, and her belongings hung neatly on a row of pegs on the wall or sat on the short shelf above the table. Novices were usually kept too busy to spend time in their rooms, but today was a freeday, only the third since she and Nynaeve had come to the White Tower.

"Else was making calf's eyes at Galad today while he was working with the Warders," Min said, rocking the stool on two legs.

The small balls faltered for an instant above Egwene's hands. "She can look at whoever she wants," Egwene said casually. "I can't imagine why I would be interested."

"No reason, I suppose. He is awfully handsome, if you don't mind him being so rigid. Very nice to look at, especially with his shirt off."

The balls spun furiously. "I certainly have no desire to look at Galad, with or without his shirt."

"I shouldn't tease you," Min said contritely. "I'm sorry for that. But you do like to look at him—don't grimace at me like that—and so does nearly every woman in the White Tower who isn't a Red. I've seen Aes Sedai down at the practice yards when he's working forms, especially Greens. Checking on their Warders, they say, but I don't see so many when Galad isn't there. Even the cooks and maids come out to watch him."

The balls stopped dead, and for a moment Egwene stared at them. They vanished. Suddenly she giggled. "He *is* good-looking, isn't he? Even when he walks he looks as if he's dancing." The color in her cheeks deepened. "I know I shouldn't stare at him, but I can't help myself."

"I can't either," Min said, "and I can see what he is like."

"But if he is good—?"

"Egwene, Galad is so good he'd make you tear your hair out. He'd hurt a person because he had to serve a greater good. He wouldn't even notice who was hurt, because he'd be so intent on the other, but if he did, he would expect them to understand and think it was all well and right."

"I suppose you know," Egwene said. She had seen Min's ability to look

at people and read all sorts of things about them; Min did not tell everything she saw, and she did not always see anything, but there had been
enough for Egwene to believe. She glanced at Nynaeve—the other woman
was still pacing, muttering to herself—then reached for *saidar* again and
resumed her juggling in a desultory fashion.

Min shrugged. "I guess I might as well tell you. He didn't even notice
what Else was doing. He asked her if she knew whether you might be
walking the South Garden after supper, since today is a freeday. I felt sorry
for her."

"Poor Else," Egwene murmured, and the balls of light became more
lively above her hands. Min laughed.

The door banged open, caught by the wind. Egwene gave a yelp and let
the balls vanish before she saw it was only Elayne.

The golden-haired Daughter-Heir of Andor pushed the door shut and
hung up her cloak on a peg. "I just heard," she said. "The rumors are true.
King Galldrian is dead. That makes it a war of succession."

Min snorted. "Civil war. War of succession. A lot of silly names for the
same thing. Do you mind if we don't talk about it? That's all we hear. War
in Cairhien. War on Toman Head. They may have caught the false Dragon
in Saldaea, but there's still war in Tear. Most of it is rumors, anyway.
Yesterday, I heard one of the cooks saying she'd heard Artur Hawkwing
was marching on Tanchico. Artur Hawkwing!"

"I thought you did not want to talk about it," Egwene said.

"I saw Logain," Elayne said. "He was sitting on a bench in the Inner
Court, crying. He ran when he saw me. I cannot help feeling sorry for
him."

"Better he cries than the rest of us, Elayne," Min said.

"I know what he is," Elayne said calmly. "Or rather, what he was. He
isn't anymore, and I can feel sorry for him."

Egwene slumped back against the wall. *Rand.* Logain always made her
think of Rand. She had not dreamed about him in months, now, not the
kind of dreams she had had on the *River Queen.* Anaiya still made her write
down everything she dreamed, and the Aes Sedai checked them for signs,
or connections to events, but there was never anything about Rand except
dreams that, Anaiya said, meant she missed him. Oddly, she felt almost as
if he were not there any longer, as if he had ceased to exist, along with her
dreams, a few weeks after reaching the White Tower. *And I sit thinking
about how nicely Galad walks,* she thought bitterly. *Rand has to be all right. If
he'd been caught and gentled, I'd have heard something.*

That sent a chill through her, as it never failed to do, the thought of
Rand being gentled, Rand weeping and wanting to die as Logain did.

Elayne sat down beside her on the bed, tucking her feet up under her. "If you are mooning over Galad, Egwene, you will have no sympathy from me. I'll have Nynaeve dose you with one of those horrible concoctions she's always talking about." She frowned at Nynaeve, who had taken no notice of her entrance. "What is the matter with her? Don't tell me she has started sighing after Galad, too!"

"I wouldn't bother her." Min leaned toward the two of them and lowered her voice. "That skinny Accepted Irella told her she was as clumsy as a cow and had half the Talents, and Nynaeve clouted her ear." Elayne winced. "Exactly," Min murmured. "They had her up to Sheriam's study before you could blink, and she hasn't been fit to live with since."

Apparently Min had not dropped her voice enough, for there was a growl from Nynaeve. Suddenly the door whipped open once more, and a gale howled into the room. It did not ruffle the blankets on Egwene's bed, but Min and the stool toppled, to roll against the wall. Immediately the wind died, and Nynaeve stood with a stricken look on her face.

Egwene hurried to the door and peeked out. The noonday sun was burning off the last reminders of last night's rainstorm. The still-damp balcony around the Novices' Court was empty, the long row of doors to novices' rooms all shut. The novices who had taken advantage of the freeday to enjoy themselves in the gardens were no doubt catching up on their sleep. No one could have seen. She closed the door and took her place beside Elayne again as Nynaeve helped Min to her feet.

"I'm sorry, Min," Nynaeve said in a tight voice. "Sometimes my temper. . . . I can't ask you to forgive me, not for this." She took a deep breath. "If you want to report me to Sheriam, I will understand. I deserve it."

Egwene wished she had not heard that admission; Nynaeve could grow prickly over such things. Searching for something on which to focus, something Nynaeve could believe she had had her attention on, she found herself touching *saidar* once more, and began juggling the balls of light again. Elayne quickly joined her; Egwene saw the glow form around the Daughter-Heir even before three tiny balls appeared above her hands. They began to pass the little glowing spheres back and forth in increasingly intricate patterns. Sometimes one winked out as one girl or the other failed to maintain it as it came to her, then winked back a little altered in color or size.

The One Power filled Egwene with life. She smelled the faint rose aroma of soap from Elayne's morning bath. She could feel the rough plaster of the walls, the smooth stones of the floor, as well as she could the bed where she sat. She could hear Min and Nynaeve breathe, much less their quiet words.

"If it comes to forgiving," Min said, "maybe you should forgive me.

You have a temper, and I have a big mouth. I will forgive you if you forgive me." With murmurs of "forgiven" that sounded meant on both sides, the two women hugged. "But if you do it again," Min said with a laugh, "I might clout *your* ear."

"Next time," Nynaeve replied, "I will throw something at you." She was laughing, too, but her laughter ceased abruptly as her eye fell on Egwene and Elayne. "You two stop that, or there *will* be someone going to the Mistress of Novices. Two someones."

"Nynaeve, you wouldn't!" Egwene protested. When she saw the look in Nynaeve's eyes, though, she hastily severed all contact with *saidar*. "Very well. I believe you. There's no need to prove it."

"We have to practice," Elayne said. "They ask more and more of us. If we did not practice on our own, we would never keep up." Her face showed calm composure, but she had let go of *saidar* as hastily as Egwene herself had.

"And what happens when you draw too much," Nynaeve asked, "and there's no one there to stop you? I wish you were more afraid. I am. Don't you think I know what it is like for you? It's always there, and you want to fill yourself with it. Sometimes it is all I can do to make myself stop; I want all of it. I know it would burn me to a crisp, and I want it anyway." She shivered. "I just wish you were more afraid."

"I am afraid," Egwene said with a sigh. "I'm terrified. But it doesn't seem to help. What about you, Elayne?"

"The only thing that terrifies me," Elayne said airily, "is washing dishes. It seems as if I have to wash dishes every day." Egwene threw her pillow at her. Elayne pulled it off her head and threw it back, but then her shoulders slumped. "Oh, very well. I am so scared I don't know why my teeth are not chattering. Elaida told me I'd be so frightened that I would want to run away with the Traveling People, but I did not understand. A man who drove oxen as hard as they drive us would be shunned. I am tired all the time. I wake up tired and go to bed exhausted, and sometimes I'm so afraid that I will slip and channel more of the Power than I can handle that I. . . ." Peering into her lap, she let the words trail off.

Egwene knew what she had not spoken. Their rooms lay right next to each other, and as in many of the novice rooms, a small hole had long ago been bored through the wall between, too small to be seen unless you knew where to look, but useful for talk after the lamps were extinguished, when the girls could not leave their rooms. Egwene had heard Elayne crying herself to sleep more than once, and she had no doubt that Elayne had heard her own crying.

"The Traveling People are tempting," Nynaeve agreed, "but wherever

you go, it will not change what you can do. You cannot run from *saidar*."
She did not sound as if she liked what she was saying.

"What do you see, Min?" Elayne said. "Are we all going to be powerful
Aes Sedai, or will we spend the rest of our lives washing dishes as novices,
or. . . ." She shrugged uncomfortably as if she did not want to voice the
third alternative that came to mind. Sent home. Put out of the Tower. Two
novices had been put out since Egwene came, and everyone spoke of them
in whispers, as if they were dead.

Min shifted on her stool. "I don't like reading friends," she muttered.
"Friendship gets in the way of the reading. It makes me try to put the best
face on what I see. That's why I don't do it for you three anymore. Anyway, nothing has changed about you that I can. . . ." She squinted at
them, and suddenly frowned. "That's new," she breathed.

"What?" Nynaeve asked sharply.

Min hesitated before answering. "Danger. You are all in some kind of
danger. Or you will be, very soon. I can't make it out, but it is danger."

"You see," Nynaeve said to the two girls sitting on the bed. "You must
take care. We all must. You must both promise not to channel again without someone to guide you."

"I don't want to talk about it anymore," Egwene said.

Elayne nodded eagerly. "Yes. Let's talk about something else. Min, if
you put on a dress, I'll wager Gawyn would ask you to go walking with
him. You know he's been looking at you, but I think the breeches and the
man's coat put him off."

"I dress the way I like, and I won't change for a lord, even if he is your
brother." Min spoke absently, still squinting at them and frowning; it was
a conversation they had had before. "Sometimes it is useful to pass as a
boy."

"No one who looks twice believes you are a boy." Elayne smiled.

Egwene was uncomfortable. Elayne was forcing a semblance of gaiety,
Min was hardly paying attention, and Nynaeve looked as if she wanted to
warn them again.

When the door swung open once more, Egwene bounded to her feet to
close it, grateful for something to do besides watch the others pretend.
Before she reached it, though, a dark-eyed Aes Sedai with her blond hair
done in a multitude of braids stepped into the room. Egwene blinked in
surprise, as much at it being any Aes Sedai as at Liandrin. She had not
heard that Liandrin had returned to the White Tower, but beyond that,
novices were sent for if an Aes Sedai wanted them; it could mean no good,
a sister coming herself.

The room was crowded with five women in it. Liandrin paused to adjust her red-fringed shawl, eyeing them. Min did not move, but Elayne rose, and the three standing curtsied, though Nynaeve barely flexed her knee. Egwene did not think Nynaeve would ever grow used to having others in authority over her.

Liandrin's eyes settled on Nynaeve. "And why are you here, in the novices' quarters, child?" Her tone was ice.

"I am visiting with friends," Nynaeve said in a tight voice. After a moment she added a belated, "Liandrin Sedai."

"The Accepted, they can have no friends among the novices. This you should have learned by this time, child. But it is as well that I find you here. You and you"—her finger stabbed at Elayne and Min—"will go."

"I will return later." Min rose casually, making a great show of being in no hurry to obey, and strolled by Liandrin with a grin, of which Liandrin took no notice at all. Elayne gave Egwene and Nynaeve a worried look before she dropped a curtsy and left.

After Elayne closed the door behind her, Liandrin stood studying Egwene and Nynaeve. Egwene began to fidget under the scrutiny, but Nynaeve held herself straight, with only a little heightening of her color.

"You two are from the same village as the boys who traveled with Moiraine. Is it not so?" Liandrin said suddenly.

"Do you have some word of Rand?" Egwene asked eagerly. Liandrin arched an eyebrow at her. "Forgive me, Aes Sedai. I forget myself."

"Have you word of them?" Nynaeve said, just short of a demand. The Accepted had no rule about not speaking to an Aes Sedai until spoken to.

"You have concern for them. That is good. They are in danger, and you might be able to help them."

"How do you know they're in trouble?" There was no doubt about the demand in Nynaeve's voice this time.

Liandrin's rosebud mouth tightened, but her tone did not change. "Though you are not aware of it, Moiraine has sent letters to the White Tower concerning you. Moiraine Sedai, she worries about you, and about your young . . . friends. These boys, they are in danger. Do you wish to help them, or leave them to their fate?"

"Yes," Egwene said, at the same time that Nynaeve said, "What kind of trouble? Why do *you* care about helping them?" Nynaeve glanced at the red fringe on Liandrin's shawl. "And I thought you didn't like Moiraine."

"Do not presume too much, child," Liandrin said sharply. "To be Accepted is not to be a sister. Accepted and novices alike listen when a sister speaks, and do as they are told." She drew a breath and went on; her tone was coldy serene again, but angry white spots marred her cheeks. "Someday, I am sure, you will serve a cause, and you will learn then that to serve

it you must work even with those whom you dislike. I tell you I have
worked with many with whom I would not share a room if it were left to
me alone. Would you not work alongside the one you hated worst, if it
would save your friends?"

Nynaeve nodded reluctantly. "But you still haven't told us what kind of
danger they're in. Liandrin Sedai."

"The danger comes from Shayol Ghul. They are hunted, as I understand
they once before were. If you will come with me, some dangers, at least,
may be eliminated. Do not ask how, for I cannot tell you, but I tell you
flatly it is so."

"We will come, Liandrin Sedai," Egwene said.

"Come where?" Nynaeve said. Egwene shot her an exasperated look.

"Toman Head."

Egwene's mouth fell open, and Nynaeve muttered, "There's a war on
Toman Head. Does this danger have something to do with Artur Hawkwing's armies?"

"You believe rumors, child? But even if they were true, is that enough
to stop you? I thought you called these men friends." A twist to Liandrin's
words said she would never do the same.

"We will come," Egwene said. Nynaeve opened her mouth again, but
Egwene went right on. "We will go, Nynaeve. If Rand needs our help—
and Mat, and Perrin—we have to give it."

"I know that," Nynaeve said, "but what I want to know is, why us?
What can we do that Moiraine—or you, Liandrin—cannot?"

The white grew in Liandrin's cheeks—Egwene realized Nynaeve had forgotten the honorific in addressing her—but what she said was, "You two
come from their village. In some way I do not entirely understand, you are
connected to them. Beyond that, I cannot say. And no more of your foolish
questions will I answer. Will you come with me for their sake?" She paused
for their assent; a visible tension left her when they nodded. "Good. You
will meet me at the northernmost edge of the Ogier grove one hour before
sunset with your horses and whatever you will need for the journey. Tell no
one of this."

"We are not supposed to leave the Tower grounds without permission,"
Nynaeve said slowly.

"You have my permission. Tell no one. No one at all. The Black Ajah
walks the halls of the White Tower."

Egwene gasped, and heard an echoed gasp from Nynaeve, but Nynaeve
recovered quickly. "I thought all Aes Sedai denied the existence of—of
that."

Liandrin's mouth tightened into a sneer. "Many do, but Tarmon Gai'don

approaches, and the time leaves when denials can be made. The Black
Ajah, it is the opposite of everything for which the Tower stands, but it
exists, child. It is everywhere, any woman could belong to it, and it serves
the Dark One. If your friends are pursued by the Shadow, do you think the
Black Ajah will leave you alive and free to help them? Tell no one—no
one!—or you may not live to reach Toman Head. One hour before sunset.
Do not fail me." With that, she was gone, the door closing firmly behind
her.

Egwene collapsed onto her bed with her hands on her knees. "Nynaeve,
she's Red Ajah. She can't know about Rand. If she did. . . ."

"She cannot know," Nynaeve agreed. "I wish I knew why a Red wanted
to help. Or why she's willing to work with Moiraine. I'd have sworn neither of them would give the other water if she were dying of thirst."

"You think she's lying?"

"She is Aes Sedai," Nynaeve said dryly. "I'll wager my best silver pin
against a blueberry that every word she said was true. But I wonder if we
heard what we thought we did."

"The Black Ajah." Egwene shivered. "There was no mistaking what she
said about that, the Light help us."

"No mistaking," Nynaeve said. "And she's forestalled us asking anyone
for advice, because after that, who can we trust? The Light help us indeed."

Min and Elayne came bustling in, slamming the door behind them.
"Are you really going?" Min asked, and Elayne gestured toward the tiny
hole in the wall above Egwene's bed, saying, "We listened from my room.
We heard everything."

Egwene exchanged glances with Nynaeve, wondering how much they
had overheard, and saw the same concern on Nynaeve's face. *If they manage
to cipher out about Rand. . . .*

"You have to keep this to yourselves," Nynaeve cautioned them. "I suppose Liandrin has arranged permission from Sheriam for us to go, but even
if she hasn't, even if they start searching the Tower from top to bottom for
us tomorrow, you mustn't say a word."

"Keep it to myself?" Min said. "No fear on that. I'm going with you.
All I do all day is try to explain to one Brown sister or another something I
don't understand myself. I can't even go for a walk without the Amyrlin
herself popping out and asking me to read whoever we see. When that
woman asks you to do something, there doesn't seem to be any way out of
it. I must have read half the White Tower for her, but she always wants
another demonstration. All I needed was an excuse to leave, and this is it."
Her face wore a look of determination that allowed no argument.

Egwene wondered why Min was so determined to go with them rather than simply leaving on her own, but before she had time to do more than wonder, Elayne said, "I am going, too."

"Elayne," Nynaeve said gently, "Egwene and I are the boys' kith from Emond's Field. You are the Daughter-Heir of Andor. If you disappear from the White Tower, why, it—it could start a war."

"Mother wouldn't start a war with Tar Valon if they dried and salted me, which they may be trying to do. If you three can go off and have an adventure, you needn't think I am going to stay here and wash dishes, and scrub floors, and have some Accepted berating me because I didn't make the fire the exact shade of blue she wanted. Gawyn will die from envy when he finds out." Elayne grinned and reached over to tug playfully at Egwene's hair. "Besides, if you leave Rand lying about loose, I might have a chance to pick him up."

"I don't think either of us is going to have him," Egwene said sadly.

"Then we'll find whoever he does choose and make her life miserable. But he couldn't be fool enough to choose someone else when he could have one of us. Oh, please smile, Egwene. I know he's yours. I just feel"—she hesitated, searching for the word—"free. I've never had an adventure. I'll bet we won't either of us cry ourselves to sleep on an adventure. And if we do, we will make sure the gleemen leave that part out."

"This is foolishness," Nynaeve said. "We are going to Toman Head. You've heard the news, and the rumors. It will be dangerous. You must stay here."

"I heard what Liandrin Sedai said about the—the Black Ajah, too." Elayne's voice dropped almost to a whisper at that name. "How safe will I be here, if *they* are here? If Mother even suspected the Black Ajah really existed, she would pitch me into the middle of a battle to get me away from them."

"But, Elayne—"

"There is only one way for you to stop me coming. That is to tell the Mistress of Novices. We will make a pretty picture, all three of us lined up in her study. All four of us. I don't think Min would escape from something like this. So since you are not going to tell Sheriam Sedai, I am coming, too."

Nynaeve threw up her hands. "Perhaps you can say something to convince her," she told Min.

Min had been leaning against the door, squinting at Elayne, and now she shook her head. "I think she has to come as much as the rest of you. The rest of us. I can see the danger around all of you more clearly, now.

Not clearly enough to make it out, but I think it has something to do with you deciding to go. That's why it is clearer; because it is more certain."

"That's no reason for her to come," Nynaeve said, but Min shook her head again.

"She is linked to—to those boys as much as you, or Egwene, or me. She's part of it, Nynaeve, whatever it is. Part of the Pattern, I suppose an Aes Sedai would say."

Elayne seemed taken aback, and interested, too. "I am? What part, Min?"

"I can't see it clearly." Min looked at the floor. "Sometimes I wish I couldn't read people at all. Most people aren't satisfied with what I see anyway."

"If we are all going," Nynaeve said, "then we had best be about making plans." However much she might argue beforehand, once a course of action had been decided, Nynaeve always went right to the practicalities: what they had to take with them, and how cold it would be by the time they reached Toman Head, and how they could get their horses from the stables without being stopped.

Listening to her, Egwene could not help wondering what the danger was that Min saw for them, and what danger threatened Rand. She knew of only one danger that could threaten him, and it made her cold to think of it. *Hold on, Rand. Hold on, you wool-headed idiot. I'll help you somehow.*

# CHAPTER
## 39

## *Flight From the White Tower*

Egwene and Elayne inclined their heads briefly to each group of women they passed as they made their way through the Tower. It was a good thing there were so many women from outside in the Tower today, Egwene thought, too many for each to have an Aes Sedai or an Accepted for escort. Alone or in small groups, garbed richly or poorly, in dress from half a dozen different lands, some still dusty from their journey to Tar Valon, they kept to themselves and waited their turn to ask their questions of the Aes Sedai, or present their petitions. Some women—ladies or merchants or merchants' wives—had female servants with them. Even a few men had come with petitions, standing by themselves, looking unsure about being in the White Tower, and eyeing everyone else uneasily.

In the lead, Nynaeve kept her eyes purposefully ahead, her cloak swirling behind her, walking as if she knew where they were going—which she did, as long as no one stopped them—and had a perfect right to go there—which was a different matter altogether, of course. Dressed now in the clothes they had brought to Tar Valon, they certainly did not look like residents of the Tower. Each had chosen her best dress that had a skirt divided for riding, and cloaks of fine wool rich with embroidery. As long as they kept away from all who might recognize them—they had already dodged several who knew their faces—Egwene thought they might make it.

"This would do better for a turn in some lord's park than a ride to Toman Head," Nynaeve had said dryly as Egwene helped her with the buttons of a gray silk with thread-of-gold work and pearled flowers across the bosom and down the sleeves, "but it may allow us to leave unnoticed."

Now Egwene shifted her cloak and smoothed her own gold-embroidered, green silk dress and glanced at Elayne, in blue slashed with cream, hoping Nynaeve had been right. So far, everyone had taken them for petitioners, nobles, or at least women of wealth, but it seemed that they should stand out. She was surprised to realize why; she felt uncomfortable in the fine dress after wearing a novice's plain white for the past few months.

A little cluster of village women in stout, dark woolens dropped curtsies as they passed. Egwene glanced back at Min as soon as they were beyond. Min had kept her breeches and baggy man's shirt under a boy's brown cloak and coat, with an old, wide-brimmed hat pulled down over her short hair. "One of us has to be the servant," she had said, laughing. "Women dressed the way you are always have at least one. You'll wish you had my breeches if we have to run." She was burdened with four sets of saddlebags bulging with warm clothes, for it would surely be winter before they returned. There were also packets of food pilfered from the kitchens, enough to last until they could buy more.

"Are you sure I can't carry some of those, Min?" Egwene asked softly.

"They're just awkward," Min said with a grin, "not heavy." She seemed to think it was all a game, or else was pretending to think so. "And people would be sure to wonder why a fine lady such as yourself was carrying her own saddlebags. You can carry yours—and mine, too, if you want—once we—" Her grin vanished, and she whispered fiercely, "Aes Sedai!"

Egwene whipped her eyes forward. An Aes Sedai with long, smooth black hair and aged-ivory skin was coming toward them down the corridor, listening to a woman wearing rough farm clothes and a patched cloak. The Aes Sedai had not seen them yet, but Egwene recognized her; Takima, of the Brown Ajah, who taught the history of the White Tower and Aes Sedai, and who could recognize one of her pupils at a hundred paces.

Nynaeve turned down a side hall without breaking stride, but there one of the Accepted, a lanky woman with a permanent frown, hurried past them hauling a red-faced novice by the ear.

Egwene had to swallow before she could speak. "That was Irella, and Else. Did they notice us?" She could not make herself look back to see.

"No," Min said after a moment. "All they saw was our clothes." Egwene let out a long, relieved breath, and heard one from Nynaeve, too.

"My heart may burst before we reach the stables," Elayne murmured. "Is this what an adventure is like all the time, Egwene? Your heart in your mouth, and your stomach in your feet?"

"I suppose it is," Egwene said slowly. She found it hard to think that there had been a time when she had been eager to have an adventure, to do something dangerous and exciting like the people in stories. Now she thought the exciting part was what you remembered when you looked back, and the stories left out a good deal of unpleasantness. She told Elayne as much.

"Still," the Daughter-Heir said firmly, "I have never had any real excitement before, and never likely to as long as Mother has any say in it, which she will until I take the throne myself."

"You two be quiet," Nynaeve said. They were alone in the hall for a change, with no one in sight in either direction. She pointed to a narrow flight of stairs going down. "That should be what we want. If I haven't gotten turned around completely, with all the twists and turns we've made."

She took the stairs as if she were certain anyway, and the others followed. Surely enough, the small door at the bottom let out into the dusty yard of the South Stable, where novices' horses were kept, for those who had them, until they had need of mounts again, which was generally not until they became Accepted or were sent home. The gleaming bulk of the Tower itself rose behind them; the Tower grounds spread over a good many hides of land, with its own walls higher than some city walls.

Nynaeve strode into the stable as if she owned it. It had a clean smell of hay and horse, and two long rows of stalls ran back into shadows barred with light from the vents above. For a wonder, shaggy Bela and Nynaeve's gray mare stood in stalls near the doors. Bela put her nose over the stall door and whickered softly to Egwene. There was only one groom in evidence, a pleasant-looking fellow with gray in his beard, chewing a straw.

"We will have our horses saddled," Nynaeve told him in her most commanding tone. "Those two. Min, find your horse and Elayne's." Min dropped the saddlebags and drew Elayne deeper into the stables.

The stableman frowned after them and slowly took the straw from his mouth. "There must be some mistake, my Lady. Those animals—"

"—are ours," Nynaeve said firmly, folding her arms so that the Serpent ring was obvious. "You will saddle them now."

Egwene held her breath; it was a last-ditch plan, that Nynaeve would try to pass as an Aes Sedai if they had difficulties with anyone who might actually accept her as one. No Aes Sedai or Accepted would, of course, and probably not even a novice, but a stableman. . . .

The man blinked at Nynaeve's ring, then at her. "I was told two," he said at last, sounding unimpressed. "One of the Accepted and a novice. Wasn't nothing said about four of you."

Egwene felt like laughing. Of course Liandrin would not have believed them able to get their horses by themselves.

Nynaeve looked disappointed, and her voice sharpened. "You trot those horses out and saddle them, or you'll have need of Liandrin's Healing, if she will give it to you."

The groom mouthed Liandrin's name, but one look at Nynaeve's face and he saw to the horses with no more than a mutter or two, not loud enough for any but himself to hear. Min and Elayne came back with their own mounts just as he finished tightening the second girth. Min's was a tall dust-colored gelding, Elayne's a bay mare with an arched neck.

When they were mounted, Nynaeve addressed herself to the stableman again. "No doubt you were told to keep this quiet, and that hasn't changed whether we are two or two hundred. If you think it has, think about what Liandrin will do if you talk what you were told to keep quiet."

As they were riding out, Elayne tossed him a coin and murmured, "For your trouble, goodman. You have done well." Outside, she caught Egwene's eye and smiled. "Mother says a stick and honey always work better than a stick alone."

"I hope we don't need either with the guards," Egwene said. "I hope Liandrin spoke to them, too."

At Tarlomen's Gate, though, piercing the tall south wall of the Tower grounds, there was no telling if anyone had spoken to the guards or not. They waved the four women through with no more than a glance and a cursory bow. Guards were meant to keep out those who were dangerous; apparently these had no orders about keeping anyone in.

A cool river breeze gave them an excuse to pull up the hoods of their cloaks as they rode slowly through the streets of the city. The ring of their horses' hooves on the paving stones was lost in the murmur of the crowds filling the streets and the music that came from some of the buildings they passed. People dressed in garments from every land, from the dark and somber mode of Cairhien to the bright, brilliant colors of the Traveling People, and every style in between, split around the horsewomen like a river around a rock, but they still could not move at more than a slow walk.

Egwene gave no attention to the fabulous towers with their sky-borne bridges or the buildings that looked more like breaking waves, or wind-sculpted cliffs, or fanciful shells, than anything made from stone. Aes Sedai often went into the city, and in that crowd they could come face-to-face with one before they knew it. After a time she realized the other women were keeping as close a watch as she, but she still felt more than a glimmer of relief when the Ogier grove came into view.

The Great Trees were now visible beyond the rooftops, their spreading tops a hundred spans and more in the air. Towering oaks and elms, leather-leafs and firs, were dwarfed beneath them. A wall of sorts encompassed the grove, which was a good two miles across, but it was only an endless series of spiraling stone arches, each five spans high and twice as wide. By the outer side of the wall, carriages, carts, and people bustled along a street, while inside lay a wilderness of sorts. The grove had neither the tame look of a park nor the complete haphazardness of the forest depths. Rather, it seemed to be the ideal of nature, as if this were the perfect woods, the most beautiful forest that could be. Some of the leaves had already begun to turn, and even the small swathes of orange and yellow and red among the green seemed to Egwene to be exactly the way autumn foliage should look.

A few people strolled just inside the open arches, and no one looked twice when the four women rode in under the trees. The city was quickly lost to view, even the sounds of it softened, then blocked, by the grove. In the space of ten strides they seemed to be miles from the nearest town.

"The north edge of the grove, she said," Nynaeve muttered, peering around. "There isn't any point of it further north than—" She cut off as two horses burst from a copse of black elder, a dark, glossy mare with a rider and a lightly laden packhorse.

The dark mare reared, pawing the air, as Liandrin reined her harshly. The Aes Sedai's face wore fury like a mask. "I told you not to tell anyone of this! Not anyone!" Egwene noticed pole-lanterns on the packhorse, and thought it odd.

"These are friends," Nynaeve began, her back stiffening, but Elayne broke in on her.

"Forgive us, Liandrin Sedai. They did not tell us; we overheard. We did not mean to listen to anything we should not have, but we did overhear. And we want to help Rand al'Thor, too. And the other boys, of course," she added quickly.

Liandrin peered at Elayne and Min. The late afternoon sunlight, slanting through the branches, shadowed their faces beneath the hoods of their cloaks. "So," she said finally, still watching those two. "I had made arrangements for you to be taken care of, but as you are here, you are here. Four can make this journey as well as two."

"Taken care of, Liandrin Sedai?" Elayne said. "I do not understand."

"Child, you and that other are known as friends of these two. Do you not think there are those who would question you when they are found to be gone? Do you believe the Black Ajah would be gentle with you just because you are heir to a throne? Had you remained in the White Tower, you might not have lived the night." That silenced them all for a moment, but Liandrin wheeled her horse and called, "Follow me!"

The Aes Sedai led them deeper into the grove, until they came to a tall fence of stout ironwork topped with a hedge of razor-sharp spikes. Curving slightly, as if it enclosed a large area, the fence ran out of sight among the trees to left and right. There was a gate in the fence, secured with a big lock. Liandrin unfastened this with a large key she produced from her cloak, motioned them through, then relocked it behind them and rode on ahead immediately. A squirrel chittered at them from a branch overhead, and from somewhere came the sharp drumming of a woodpecker.

"Where are we going?" Nynaeve demanded. Liandrin did not answer, and Nynaeve looked angrily at the others. "Why are we just riding deeper into these woods? We have to cross a bridge, or else take ship, if we're going to leave Tar Valon, and there isn't any bridge or ship in—"

"There is this," Liandrin announced. "The fence, it keeps away those who might harm themselves, but we have a need this day." What she gestured to was a tall, thick slab of what seemed to be stone, standing on edge, one side carved intricately in vines and leaves.

Egwene's throat tightened; suddenly she knew why Liandrin had brought lanterns, and she did not like what she knew. She heard Nynaeve whisper, "A Waygate." They both remembered the Ways all too well.

"We did it once," she told herself as much as Nynaeve. "We can do it again." *If Rand and the others need us, we have to help them. That's all there is to it.*

"Is that really. . . ?" Min began in a choked voice and could not finish.

"A Waygate," Elayne breathed. "I did not think the Ways could be used any longer. At least, I did not think their use was allowed."

Liandrin had already dismounted and plucked the trefoil *Avendesora* leaf out of the carving; like two huge doors woven of living vines, the gates were swinging open, revealing what appeared to be a dull, silvery mirror that gave their reflections back dimly.

"You do not have to come," Liandrin said. "You can wait here for me, safely enclosed by the fence until I come for you. Or perhaps the Black Ajah will find you before anyone else." Her smile was not pleasant. Behind her, the Waygate came open to its fullest and stopped.

"I did not say I wouldn't come," Elayne said, but she gave the shadowed woods a lingering look.

"If we are going to do this," Min said hoarsely, "then let's do it." She was staring at the Waygate, and Egwene thought she heard her mutter, "The Light burn you, Rand al'Thor."

"I must go last," Liandrin said. "All of you, in. I will follow." She was eyeing the woods now, too, as if she thought someone might be following them. "Quickly! Quickly!"

Egwene did not know what Liandrin expected to see, but if anyone at all came they would probably stop them from using the Waygate. *Rand, you wool-headed idiot,* she thought, *why can't you just once get yourself into some kind of trouble that doesn't force me to act like the heroine in a story?*

She dug her heels into Bela's flanks, and the shaggy mare, restive from too much time in a stable, leaped forward.

"Slowly!" Nynaeve shouted, but it was too late.

Egwene and Bela surged toward their own dull reflections; two shaggy horses touched noses, appeared to flow into each other. Then Egwene was merging into her own image with an icy shock. Time seemed to stretch out, as if the cold crept over her by the width of one hair at a time, and every hair took minutes.

Suddenly Bela was stumbling in pitch-blackness, moving so fast the mare almost pitched over on her head. She caught herself and stood trembling as Egwene dismounted hurriedly, feeling the mare's legs in the dark to see if she had been hurt. She was almost glad of the dark, to hide her crimson face. She knew that time as well as distance were different the other side of a Waygate; she had moved before thinking.

There was only the blackness around her in every direction, except for the rectangle of the open Waygate, like a window of smoked glass when seen from this side. It let no light in—the black seemed to press right up against it—but through it Egwene could see the others, moving by the slowest increments, like figures in a nightmare. Nynaeve was insisting on handing around the pole-lanterns and lighting them; Liandrin was acceding with a bad grace, apparently insisting on speed.

When Nynaeve came though the Waygate—leading her gray mare slowly, ever so slowly—Egwene almost ran to hug her, and at least half of her feeling was for the lantern Nynaeve carried. The lantern made a smaller pool of light than it should have—the darkness pressed against the light, trying to force it back into the lantern—but Egwene had begun to feel that darkness pressing against her, as if it had weight. Instead, she contented herself with saying, "Bela's all right, and I did not break my neck the way I deserved to."

Once there had been light along the Ways, before the taint on the Power with which they had first been made, the taint of the Dark One on *saidin,* had begun to corrupt them.

Nynaeve thrust the pole of the lantern into her hands and turned to pull another from under her saddle girth. "As long as you know you deserved to," she murmured, "then you didn't deserve to." Suddenly she chuckled. "Sometimes I think it was sayings like that more than anything else that created the title of Wisdom. Well, here's another. You break your neck, and I'll see it mended just so I can break it again."

It was said lightly, and Egwene found herself laughing, too—until she recalled where she was. Nynaeve's amusement did not last long either.

Min and Elayne came though the Waygate hesitantly, leading their horses and carrying lanterns, obviously expecting to find monsters waiting at the least. They looked relieved, at first, to find nothing but darkness, but the oppressiveness of it soon had them shifting nervously from foot to foot. Liandrin replaced the *Avendesora* leaf and rode through the closing Waygate leading the packhorse.

Liandrin did not wait for the gate to finish closing, but tossed the lead line of the packhorse to Min without a word and started along a white line, dimly made out by the light of her lantern, leading into the Ways. The floor seemed to be stone, eaten and pitted by acid. Egwene scrambled hurriedly onto Bela's back, but she was no quicker to follow the Aes Sedai than anyone else. There seemed to be nothing in the world except the rough floor under the horses' hooves.

Straight as an arrow the white line led through the dark to a large stone slab covered with Ogier script inlaid in silver. The same pocking that marked the floor also broke the script in places.

"A Guiding," Elayne murmured, twisting in her saddle to look around uneasily. "Elaida taught me a little about the Ways. She would not say much. Not enough," she added glumly. "Or maybe too much."

Calmly Liandrin compared the Guiding with a parchment, then stuffed it back into a pocket of her cloak before Egwene could get a look.

Their lanterns' light stopped abruptly rather than fading out at the edges, but it was enough for Egwene to see a thick stone balustrade, eaten away in places, as the Aes Sedai led them away from the Guiding. An Island, Elayne called it; the darkness made judging the Island's size difficult, but Egwene thought it might be a hundred paces across.

Stone bridges and ramps pierced the balustrade, each with a stone post beside it marked with a single line in Ogier script. The bridges seemed to arch out into nothing. The ramps led up or down. It was impossible to see more than the beginning of any of them, as they rode past.

Pausing only to eye the stone posts, Liandrin took a ramp that led down, and quickly there was nothing but the ramp and the darkness. A dampening silence hung over everything; Egwene had the feeling that even the clatter of the horses' hooves on the rough stone did not travel very far beyond the light.

Down and down the ramp ran, curving back on itself, until it reached another Island, with its broken balustrade between bridges and ramps, its Guiding that Liandrin compared with her parchment. The Island seemed like solid stone, just as the first one had. Egwene wished she was not sure that the first Island was directly over their heads.

Nynaeve spoke up suddenly, voicing Egwene's thoughts. Her voice sounded steady, but she paused to swallow in the middle of it.

"It—it might be," Elayne said faintly. Her eyes rolled upwards, and quickly dropped again. "Elaida says the rules of nature do not hold in the Ways. At least, not the way they do outside."

"Light!" Min muttered, then raised her voice. "How long do you mean us to stay in here?"

The Aes Sedai's honey-colored braids swung as she turned to regard them. "Until I take you out," she said flatly. "The more you bother me, the longer that will be." She bent back to studying the parchment and the Guiding.

Egwene and the others fell silent.

Liandrin pushed on from Guiding to Guiding, by ramps and bridges that seemed to run unsupported through the endless dark. The Aes Sedai paid very little heed to the rest of them, and Egwene found herself wondering whether Liandrin would turn back to search if one of them fell behind. The others perhaps had the same thought, for they all rode bunched tightly on the dark mare's heels.

Egwene was surprised to realize that she still felt the attraction of *saidar,* both the presence of the female half of the True Source and the desire to touch it, to channel its flow. Somehow, she had thought the Shadow's taint on the Ways would hide it from her. She could sense that taint, after a fashion. It was faint and had nothing to do with *saidar,* but she was sure that reaching for the True Source here would be like baring her arm to foul, greasy smoke in order to reach a clean cup. Whatever she did would be tainted. For the first time in weeks she had no trouble at all in resisting the attraction of *saidar.*

It was well into what would have been night in the world outside the Ways when, on an Island, Liandrin abruptly dismounted and announced that they would halt for supper and sleep, and that there was food on the packhorse.

"Parcel it out," she said, not bothering to assign the task. "It will take us the better part of two days to reach Toman Head. I would not have you arrive hungry if you were too foolish to bring food yourselves." Briskly she unsaddled and hobbled her mare, but then she sat down on her saddle and waited for one of them to bring her something to eat.

Elayne took Liandrin her flatbread and cheese. The Aes Sedai made it obvious that she did not want their company, so the rest of them ate their bread and cheese a little apart from her, sitting on their saddles drawn close together. The darkness beyond their lanterns made a poor sauce.

After a time, Egwene said, "Liandrin Sedai, what if we encounter the Black Wind?" Min mouthed the word questioningly, but Elayne gave a squeak. "Moiraine Sedai said it could not be killed, or even hurt very much, and I can feel the taint on this place waiting to twist anything we do with the Power."

"You will not so much as think of the Source unless I tell you to," Liandrin said sharply. "Why, if one such as you tried to channel here, in the Ways, you might well go as mad as a man. You have not the training to deal with the taint of those men who made this. If the Black Wind appears, I will deal with it." She pursed her lips, studying a lump of white cheese. "Moiraine does not know so much as she thinks." She popped the cheese into her mouth with a smile.

"I do not like her," Egwene muttered, low enough to make sure the Aes Sedai could not hear.

"If Moiraine can work with her," Nynaeve said quietly, "so can we. Not that I like Moiraine any better than I do Liandrin, but if they're meddling with Rand and the others again. . . ." She fell silent, hitching her cloak up. The darkness was not cold, but it seemed as if it should be.

"What is this Black Wind?" Min asked. When Elayne had explained, with a great deal of what Elaida had said and what her mother had said, Min sighed. "The Pattern has a great deal to answer for. I don't know that any man is worth this."

"You did not have to come," Egwene reminded her. "You could have gone at any time. No one would have tried to stop you leaving the Tower."

"Oh, I could have wandered off," Min said wryly. "As easily as you, or Elayne. The Pattern doesn't much care what we want. Egwene, what if, after all you are going through for him, Rand doesn't marry you? What if he marries some woman you've never seen before, or Elayne, or me? What then?"

Elayne chortled. "Mother would never approve."

Egwene was silent for a time. Rand might not live to marry anyone. And if he did. . . . She could not imagine Rand hurting anyone. *Not even after he's gone mad?* There had to be some way to stop that, some way to change it; Aes Sedai knew so much, could do so much. *If they could stop it, why don't they?* The only answer was because they could not, and that was not the one she wanted.

She tried to put lightness in her voice. "I don't suppose I *will* marry him. Aes Sedai seldom do marry, you know. But I would not set my heart on him if were you. Or you, Elayne. I do not think. . . ." Her voice caught, and she coughed to cover it. "I do not think he will ever marry. But if he does, I wish well to whoever ends up with him, even one of you." She thought she sounded as if she meant it. "He is stubborn as a mule, and wrongheaded to a fault, but he *is* gentle." Her voice shook, but she managed to turn the quaver into a laugh.

"However much you say you do not care," Elayne said, "I think you'd approve less than Mother would. He *is* interesting, Egwene. More interesting than any man I've ever met, even if he is a shepherd. If you are silly enough to throw him away, you will have only yourself to blame if I decide to face down you and Mother both. It would not be the first time the Prince of Andor had no title before he wed. But you won't be that silly, so don't try to pretend you will. No doubt you will choose the Green Ajah, and make him one of your Warders. The only Greens I know with only one Warder are married to them."

Egwene made herself go along with it, saying if she did become a Green she would have ten Warders.

Min watched her, frowning, and Nynaeve watched Min thoughtfully. They all fell silent by the time they changed into more suitable clothes for traveling, from their saddlebags. It was not easy, keeping spirits up in that place.

Sleep came slowly to Egwene, fitfully, and it was filled with bad dreams. She did not dream of Rand, but of the man whose eyes were fire. His face was not masked this time, and it was horrible with almost healed burns. He only looked at her and laughed, but that was worse than the dreams that followed, the dreams of being lost in the Ways forever, the ones where the Black Wind was chasing her. She was grateful when the toe of Liandrin's riding boot dug into her ribs to waken her; she felt as if she had not slept at all.

Liandrin pushed them hard through the next day, or what passed for day, with only their lanterns for a sun, not letting them stop for sleep until they were swaying in their saddles. Stone made a hard bed, but Liandrin roused them ruthlessly after a few hours, hardly waiting for them to mount before riding on. Ramps and bridges, Islands and Guidings. Egwene saw so many of them in that pitch-dark that she lost count. She had long since lost any count of hours or of days. Liandrin allowed only brief halts to eat

and rest the horses, and the darkness weighed down on their shoulders.
They slumped in their saddles like sacks of grain, except for Liandrin. The
Aes Sedai seemed unaffected by tiredness, or the dark. She was as fresh as
she had been back in the White Tower, and as cold. She would not let
anyone glimpse the parchment she compared to the Guidings, stuffing it
away with a curt, "It is nothing you would understand," when Nynaeve
asked.

And then, while Egwene blinked wearily, Liandrin was riding away from
a Guiding, not toward another bridge or ramp, but down a pitted white
line that led off into the darkness. Egwene stared at her friends, and then
they all hurried to follow. Ahead, by the light of her lantern, the Aes Sedai
was already removing the *Avendesora* leaf from the carvings on a Waygate.

"We are here," Liandrin said, smiling. "I have brought you at last to
where you must go."

# CHAPTER 40

## *Damane*

Egwene dismounted as the Waygate opened, and when Liandrin motioned them through, she led the shaggy mare carefully out. Even so, she and Bela both stumbled in brush flattened by the opening Waygate as they suddenly seemed to be moving even more slowly. A screen of dense shrubs had surrounded and hidden the Waygate. There were only a few trees close by, and a morning breeze ruffled foliage with a little more color than the leaves had had in Tar Valon.

Watching her friends emerge after her, she had been standing there a good minute before she became aware that others were already there, just out of sight on the other side of the gates. When she did notice them she stared uncertainly; they were as odd a group as she had ever seen, and she had heard too many rumors of the war on Toman Head.

Armored men, at least fifty of them, with overlapping steel plates down their chests and dull black helmets shaped like insects' heads, sat their saddles or stood beside their horses, staring at her and the emerging women, staring at the Waygate, muttering among themselves. The only bareheaded man among them, a tall, dark-faced, hook-nosed fellow standing with a gilded-and-painted helmet on his hip, looked astonished at what he was seeing. There were women with the soldiers, too. Two wore plain, dark gray dresses and wide silver collars, and stood staring intently

at those coming out of the Waygate, each with another woman close behind her as if ready to speak into her ear. Two other women, standing a
little apart, wore wide, divided skirts that came well short of their ankles,
and panels embroidered with forked lightning bolts on their bosoms and
skirts. Oddest of all was the last woman, reclining on a palanquin borne by
eight muscular, bare-chested men in baggy black trousers. The sides of her
scalp were shaved so that only a wide crest of black hair remained to fall
down her back. A long, cream-colored robe worked in flowers and birds on
blue ovals was carefully arranged to show her skirts of pleated white, and
her fingernails were a good inch long, the first two on each hand lacquered
blue.

"Liandrin Sedai," Egwene asked uneasily, "do you know who these people are?" Her friends fingered their reins as if wondering whether to mount
and run, but Liandrin replaced the *Avendesora* leaf and stepped forward
confidently as the Waygate began to close.

"The High Lady Suroth?" Liandrin said, making it halfway between a
question and statement.

The women on the palanquin nodded fractionally. "You are Liandrin."
Her speech was slurred, and it took Egwene a moment to understand. "Aes
Sedai," Suroth added with a twist to her lips, and a murmur rose among
the soldiers. "We must be done here quickly, Liandrin. There are patrols,
and it would not do to be found. You would enjoy the attentions of the
Seekers for Truth no more than I. I mean to be back in Falme before Turak
knows I am gone."

"What are you talking about?" Nynaeve demanded. "What is she talking about, Liandrin?"

Liandrin laid a hand on Nynaeve's shoulder and one on Egwene's. "These
are the two of whom you were told. And there is another." She nodded
toward Elayne. "She is the Daughter-Heir of Andor."

The two women with the lightning on their dresses were approaching
the party in front of the Waygate—they carried coils of some silvery metal
in their hands, Egwene noticed—and the bareheaded soldier came with
them. He did not put a hand near the sword hilt sticking up above his
shoulder, and he wore a casual smile, but Egwene still watched him narrowly. Liandrin gave no sign of agitation; otherwise Egwene would have
jumped onto Bela right then.

"Liandrin Sedai," she said urgently, "who are these people? Are they
here to help Rand and the others, too?"

The hook-nosed man suddenly seized Min and Elayne by the scruffs of
their necks, and in the next instant everything seemed to happen at once.
The man yelled a curse, and a woman screamed, or perhaps more than one

woman; Egwene could not be sure. Abruptly the breeze was a gale that whipped away Liandrin's angry shout in clouds of dirt and leaves and made the trees bend and groan. Horses reared and whinnied shrilly. And one of the women reached out and fastened something around Egwene's neck.

Cloak flapping like a sail, Egwene braced against the wind and tugged at what felt like a collar of smooth metal. It would not budge; under her frantic fingers, it felt all of one piece, though she knew it had to have some kind of clasp. The silvery coils the woman had carried now trailed over Egwene's shoulder, their other end joining a bright bracelet on the woman's left wrist. Balling her fist tightly, Egwene hit the woman as hard as she could, right in her eye—and staggered and fell to her knees herself, head ringing. It felt as if a large man had struck her in the face.

When she could see straight once more, the wind had died. A number of horses wandered loose, Bela and Elayne's mare among them, and some of the soldiers were cursing and picking themselves up off the ground. Liandrin was calmly brushing dust and leaves from her dress. Min knelt, supporting herself with her hands, groggily trying to rise further. The hook-nosed man stood over her, his hand dripping blood. Min's knife lay just out of her reach, the blade stained red along one side. Nynaeve and Elayne were nowhere to be seen, and Nynaeve's mare was gone, too. So were some of the soldiers, and one of the pairs of women. The other two were still there, and Egwene could see now that they were linked by a silver cord just like the one that still joined her to the woman standing over her.

That woman was rubbing her cheek as she squatted beside Egwene; there was a bruise already coming up around her left eye. With long, dark hair and big brown eyes, she was pretty, and perhaps as much as ten years older than Nynaeve. "Your first lesson," she said emphatically. There was no animosity in her voice, but what almost sounded like friendliness. "I will not punish you further this time, since I should have been on guard with a newly caught *damane*. Know this. You are a *damane*, a Leashed One, and I am a *sul'dam*, a Holder of the Leash. When *damane* and *sul'dam* are joined, whatever hurt the *sul'dam* feels, the *damane* feels twice over. Even to death. So you must remember that you may never strike at a *sul'dam* in any way, and you must protect your *sul'dam* even more than yourself. I am Renna. How are you called?"

"I am not . . . what you said," Egwene muttered. She pulled at the collar again; it gave no more than before. She thought of knocking the woman down and trying to pry the bracelet from her wrist, but rejected it. Even if the soldiers did not try to stop her—and so far they seemed to be ignoring her and Renna altogether—she had the sinking feeling the woman was telling the truth. Touching her left eye brought a wince; it did not feel puffy, so perhaps she was not actually growing a bruise to match Renna's, but it still hurt. Her left eye, and Renna's left eye. She raised her voice. "Liandrin Sedai? Why are you letting them do this?" Liandrin dusted her hands together, never looking in her direction.

"The very first thing you must learn," Renna said, "is to do exactly as you are told, and without delay."

Egwene gasped. Suddenly her skin burned and prickled as if she had rolled in stinging nettles, from the soles of her feet to her scalp. She tossed her head as the burning sensation increased.

"Many *sul'dam*," Renna went on in that almost friendly tone, "do not believe *damane* should be allowed names, or at least only names they are given. But I am the one who took you, so I will be in charge of your training, and I will allow you to keep your own name. If you do not displease me too far. I am mildly upset with you now. Do you really wish to keep on until I am angry?"

Quivering, Egwene gritted her teeth. Her nails dug into her palms with the effort of not scratching wildly. *Idiot! It's only your name.* "Egwene," she managed to get out. "I am Egwene al'Vere." Instantly the burning itch was gone. She let out a long, unsteady breath.

"Egwene," Renna said. "That is a good name." And to Egwene's horror, Renna patted her on the head as she would a dog.

That, she realized, was what she had detected in the woman's voice—a certain good will for a dog in training, not quite the friendliness one might have toward another human being.

Renna chuckled. "Now you are even angrier. If you intend to strike at me again, remember to make it a small blow, for you will feel it twice as hard as I. Do not attempt to channel; that you will never do without my express command."

Egwene's eye throbbed. She pushed herself to her feet and tried to ignore Renna, as much as it was possible to ignore someone who held a leash fastened to a collar around your neck. Her cheeks burned when the other woman chuckled again. She wanted to go to Min, but the amount of leash Renna had let out would not reach that far. She called softly, "Min, are you all right?"

Sitting slowly back on her heels, Min nodded, then put a hand to her head as if she wished she had not moved it.

Jagged lightning crackled across the clear sky, then struck among the trees some distance off. Egwene jumped, and suddenly smiled. Nynaeve was still free, and Elayne. If anyone could free her and Min, Nynaeve could. Her smile faded into a glare for Liandrin. For whatever the reason

the Aes Sedai had betrayed them, there would be a reckoning. *Someday.*
*Somehow.* The glare did no good; Liandrin did not look away from the
palanquin.

The bare-chested men knelt, lowering the palanquin to the ground, and
Suroth stepped down, carefully arranging her robe, then picked her way to
Liandrin on soft-slippered feet. The two women were much of a size.
Brown eyes stared levelly into black.

"You were to bring me two," Suroth said. "Instead, I have only one,
while two run loose, one of them more powerful by far than I had been led
to believe. She will attract every patrol of ours within two leagues."

"I brought you three," Liandrin said calmly. "If you cannot manage to
hold them, perhaps our master should find another among you to serve
him. You take fright at trifles. If patrols come, kill them."

Lightning flashed again in the near distance, and moments later something roared like thunder not far from where it struck; a cloud of dust rose
into the air. Neither Liandrin nor Suroth took any notice.

"I could still return to Falme with two new *damane,*" Suroth said. "It
grieves me to allow an . . . Aes Sedai"—she twisted the words like a
curse—"to walk free."

Liandrin's face did not change, but Egwene saw a nimbus abruptly glow
around her.

"Beware, High Lady," Renna called. "She stands ready!"

There was a stir among the soldiers, a reaching for swords and lances,
but Suroth only steepled her hands, smiling at Liandrin over her long nails.
"You will make no move against me, Liandrin. Our master would disap-
prove, as I am surely needed here more than you, and you fear him more
than you fear being made *damane.*"

Liandrin smiled, though white spots marked her cheeks with anger.
"And you, Suroth, fear him more than you fear me burning you to a cinder
where you stand."

"Just so. We both fear him. Yet even our master's needs will change
with time. All *marath'damane* will be leashed eventually. Perhaps I will be
the one who places the collar around your lovely throat."

"As you say, Suroth. Our master's needs will change. I will remind you
of it on the day when you kneel to me."

A tall leatherleaf perhaps a mile away suddenly became a roaring torch.

"This grows tiresome," Suroth said. "Elbar, recall them." The hook-
nosed man produced a horn no bigger than his fist; it made a hoarse,
piercing cry.

"You must find the woman Nynaeve," Liandrin said sharply. "Elayne is of no importance, but both the woman and this girl here must be taken with you on your ships when you sail."

"I know very well what has been commanded, *marath'damane,* though I would give much to know why."

"However much you were told, child," Liandrin sneered, "that is how much you are allowed to know. Remember that you serve and obey. These two must be removed to the other side of the Aryth Ocean and kept there."

Suroth sniffed. "I will not remain here to find this Nynaeve. My usefulness to our master will be at an end if Turak hands me over to the Seekers for Truth." Liandrin opened her mouth angrily, but Suroth refused to allow her a word. "The woman will not remain free for long. Neither of them will. When we sail again, we will take with us every woman on this miserable spit of land who can channel even slightly, leashed and collared. If you wish to remain and search for her, do so. Patrols will be here soon, thinking to engage the rabble that still hides in the countryside. Some patrols take *damane* with them, and they will not care what master you serve. Should you survive the encounter, the leash and collar will teach you a new life, and I do not believe our master will trouble to deliver one foolish enough to let herself be taken."

"If either is allowed to remain here," Liandrin said tightly, "our master will trouble himself with you, Suroth. Take them both, or pay the price." She strode to the Waygate, clutching the reins of her mare. Soon it was closing behind her.

The soldiers who had gone after Nynaeve and Elayne came galloping back with the two women linked by leash, collar, and bracelet, the *damane* and the *sul'dam* riding side by side. Three men led horses with bodies across the saddles. Egwene felt a surge of hope when she realized the bodies all wore armor. They had not caught Nynaeve or Elayne, either one.

Min started to rise to her feet, but the hook-nosed man planted a boot between her shoulder blades and drove her to the ground. Gasping for breath, she twitched there weakly. "I beg permission to speak, High Lady," he said. Suroth made a small motion with her hand, and he went on. "This peasant cut me, High Lady. If the High Lady has no use for her. . . ?" Suroth motioned slightly again, already turning away, and he reached over his shoulder for the hilt of his sword.

"No!" Egwene shouted. She heard Renna curse softly, and suddenly the burning itch covered her skin again, worse than before, but she did not stop. "Please! High Lady, please! She is my friend!" Pain such as she had never known wracked her through the burning. Every muscle knotted and cramped; she pitched on her face in the dirt, mewling, but she could still see Elbar's heavy, curved blade come free of its sheath, see him raise it with both hands. "Please! Oh, Min!"

Abruptly, the pain was gone as if it had never been; only the memory remained. Suroth's blue velvet slippers, dirt-stained now, appeared in front of her face, but it was at Elbar that she stared. He stood there with his sword over his head and all his weight on the foot on Min's back . . . and he did not move.

"This peasant is your friend?" Suroth said.

Egwene started to rise, but at a surprised arching of Suroth's eyebrow, she remained lying where she was and only raised her head. She had to save Min. *If it means groveling.* . . . She parted her lips and hoped her gritted teeth would pass for a smile. "Yes, High Lady."

"And if I spare her, if I allow her to visit you occasionally, you will work hard and learn as you are taught?"

"I will, High Lady." She would have promised much more to keep that sword from splitting Min's skull. *I'll even keep it,* she thought sourly, *as long as I have to.*

"Put the girl on her horse, Elbar," Suroth said. "Tie her on, if she cannot sit her saddle. If this *damane* proves a disappointment, perhaps then I will let you have the head of the girl." She was already moving toward her palanquin.

Renna pulled Egwene roughly to her feet and pushed her toward Bela, but Egwene had eyes only for Min. Elbar was no gentler with Min than Renna with her, but she thought Min was all right. At least Min shrugged off Elbar's attempt to tie her across her saddle and climbed onto her gelding with only a little help.

The odd party started off, westward, with Suroth leading and Elbar slightly to the rear of her palanquin, but close enough to heed any summons immediately. Renna and Egwene rode at the back with Min, and the other *sul'dam* and *damane,* behind the soldiers. The woman who had apparently meant to collar Nynaeve fondled the coiled silver leash she still carried and looked angry. Sparse forest covered the rolling land, and the smoke of the burning leatherleaf was soon only a smudge in the sky behind them.

"You were honored," Renna said after a time, "having the High Lady speak to you. Another time, I would let you wear a ribbon to mark the honor. But since you brought her attention on yourself. . . ."

Egwene cried out as a switch seemed to lash across her back, then another across her leg, her arm. From every direction they seemed to come; she knew there was nothing to block, but she could not help throwing her arms about as if to stop the blows. She bit her lip to stifle her moans, but tears still rolled down her cheeks. Bela whinnied and danced, but Renna's grip on the silver leash kept her from carrying Egwene away. None of the soldiers even looked back.

"What are you doing to her?" Min shouted. "Egwene? Stop it!"

"You live on sufferance . . . Min, is it?" Renna said mildly. "Let this be a lesson for you as well. So long as you try to interfere, it will not stop."

Min raised a fist, then let it fall. "I won't interfere. Only, please, stop it. Egwene, I'm sorry."

The unseen blows went on for a few moments more, as if to show Min her intervention had done nothing, then ceased, but Egwene could not stop shuddering. The pain did not go away this time. She pushed back the sleeve of her dress, thinking to see weals; her skin was unmarked, but the feel of them was still there. She swallowed. "It was not your fault, Min." Bela tossed her head, eyes rolling, and Egwene patted the mare's shaggy neck. "It wasn't yours, either."

"It was your fault, Egwene," Renna said. She sounded so patient, dealing so kindly with someone who was too dense to see the right, that Egwene wanted to scream. "When a *damane* is punished, it is always her fault, even if she does not know why. A *damane* must anticipate what her *sul'dam* wants. But this time, you do know why. *Damane* are like furniture, or tools, always there ready to be used, but never pushing themselves forward for attention. Especially not for the attention of one of the Blood."

Egwene bit her lip until she tasted blood. *This is a nightmare. It can't be real. Why did Liandrin do this? Why is this happening?* "May . . . may I ask a question?"

"Of me, you may." Renna smiled. "Many *sul'dam* will wear your bracelet over the years—there are always many more *sul'dam* than *damane*—and some would have your hide in strips if you took your eyes off the floor or opened your mouth without permission, but I see no reason not to let you speak, so long as you are careful in what you say." One of the other *sul'dam* snorted loudly; she was linked to a pretty, dark-haired woman in her middle years who kept her eyes on her hands.

"Liandrin"—Egwene would not give her the honorific, not ever again—"and the High Lady spoke of a master they both serve." The thought came into her head of a man with almost healed burns marring his face, and eyes and mouth that sometimes turned to fire, but even if he was only a figure in her dreams that seemed too horrible to contemplate. "Who is he? What does he want with me and—and Min?" She knew it was silly to avoid naming Nynaeve—she did not think any of these people would forget her just because her name was not mentioned, especially the blue-eyed *sul'dam* stroking her empty leash—but it was the only way she could think of fighting back at the moment.

"The affairs of the Blood," Renna said, "are not for me to take notice of, and certainly not for you. The High Lady will tell me what she wishes me to know, and I will tell you what I wish you to know. Anything else that you hear or see must be to you as if it never was said, as if it never happened. This way lies safety, most especially for a *damane*. *Damane* are too valuable to be killed out of hand, but you might find yourself not only soundly punished, but absent a tongue to speak or hands to write. *Damane* can do what they must without these things."

Egwene shivered, though the air was not very cold. Pulling her cloak up onto her shoulders, her hand brushed the leash, and she jerked at it fitfully. "This is a horrible thing. How can you do this to anyone? What diseased mind ever thought of it?"

The blue-eyed *sul'dam* with the empty leash growled, "This one could do without her tongue already, Renna."

Renna only smiled patiently. "How is it horrible? Could we allow anyone to run loose who can do what a *damane* can? Sometimes men are born who would be *marath'damane* if they were women—it is so here also, I have heard—and they must be killed, of course, but the women do not go mad. Better for them to become *damane* than make trouble contending for power. As for the mind that first thought of the *a'dam*, it was the mind of a woman who called herself Aes Sedai."

Egwene knew incredulity must be painting her face, because Renna laughed openly. "When Luthair Paendrag Mondwin, son of the Hawkwing, first faced the Armies of the Night, he found many among them who called themselves Aes Sedai. They contended for power among themselves and used the One Power on the field of battle. One such, a woman named Deain, who thought she could do better serving the Emperor—he was not Emperor then, of course—since he had no Aes Sedai in his armies, came to him with a device she had made, the first *a'dam*, fastened to the neck of one of her sisters. Though that woman did not want to serve Luthair, the *a'dam* required her to serve. Deain made more *a'dam*, the first *sul'dam* were found, and women captured who called themselves Aes Sedai discovered that they were in fact only *marath'damane*, Those Who Must Be Leashed. It is said that when she herself was leashed, Deain's screams shook the Towers of Midnight, but of course she, too, was a *marath'damane*, and *marath'damane* cannot be allowed to run free. Perhaps you will be one of those who has the ability to make *a'dam*. If so, you will be pampered, you may rest assured."

Egwene looked yearningly at the countryside through which they rode. The land was beginning to rise in low hills, and the thin forest had dwindled to scattered thickets, but she was sure she could lose herself in them. "Am I supposed to look forward to being pampered like a pet dog?" she said bitterly. "A lifetime of being chained to men and women who think I am some kind of animal?"

"Not men." Renna chuckled. "All *sul'dam* are women. If a man put on this bracelet, most of the time it would be no different than if it were hanging on a peg on the wall."

"And sometimes," the blue-eyed *sul'dam* put in harshly, "you and he would both die screaming." The woman had sharp features and a tight, thin-lipped mouth, and Egwene realized that anger was apparently her permanent expression. "From time to time the Empress plays with lords by linking them to a *damane*. It makes the lords sweat and entertains the Court of the Nine Moons. The lord never knows until it is done whether he will live or die, and neither does the *damane*." Her laugh was vicious.

"Only the Empress can afford to waste *damane* in such a way, Alwhin," Renna snapped, "and I do not mean to train this *damane* only to have her thrown away."

"I have not seen any training at all so far, Renna. Only a great deal of chatter, as if you and this *damane* were girlhood friends."

"Perhaps it is time to see what she can do," Renna said, studying Egwene. "Do you have enough control yet to channel at that distance?" She pointed to a tall oak standing alone on a hilltop.

Egwene frowned at the tree, perhaps half a mile from the line followed by the soldiers and Suroth's palanquin. She had never tried anything much beyond arm's reach, but she thought it might be possible. "I don't know," she said.

"Try," Renna told her. "Feel the tree. Feel the sap in the tree. I want you to make it all not only hot, but so hot that every drop of sap in every branch flashes to steam in an instant. Do it."

Egwene was shocked to discover an urge to do as Renna commanded. She had not channeled, or even touched *saidar,* in two days; the desire to fill herself with the One Power made her shiver. "I"—in half a heartbeat she discarded "will not"; the weals that were not there still burned too sharply for her to be quite that foolish—"cannot," she finished instead. "It is too far, and I've never done anything like that before."

One of the *sul'dam* laughed raucously, and Alwhin said, "She never even tried."

Renna shook her head almost sadly. "When one has been a *sul'dam* long enough," she told Egwene, "one learns to tell many things about *damane* even without the bracelet, but with the bracelet one can always tell whether a *damane* has tried to channel. You must never lie to me, or to any *sul'dam,* not even by a hair."

Suddenly the invisible switches were back, striking at her everywhere. Yelling, she tried to hit Renna, but the *sul'dam* casually knocked her fist away, and Egwene felt as if Renna had hit her arm with a stick. She dug her heels into Bela's flanks, but the *sul'dam*'s grip on the leash nearly pulled her out of her saddle. Frantically she reached for *saidar,* meaning to hurt Renna enough to make her stop, just the kind of hurt she herself had been given. The *sul'dam* shook her head wryly; Egwene howled as her own skin was suddenly scalded. Not until she fled from *saidar* completely did the burn begin to fade, and the unseen blows never ceased or slowed. She tried to shout that she would try, if only Renna would stop, but all she could manage was to scream and writhe.

Dimly, she was aware of Min shouting angrily and trying to ride to her side, of Alwhin tearing Min's reins from her hands, of another *sul'dam* speaking sharply to her *damane,* who looked at Min. And then Min was yelling, too, arms flapping as if trying to ward off blows or beat away stinging insects. In her own pain, Min's seemed distant.

Their cries together were enough to make some of the soldiers twist in their saddles. After one look, they laughed and turned back. How *sul'dam* dealt with *damane* was no affair of theirs.

To Egwene it seemed to go on forever, but at last there was an end. She lay sprawled weakly across the cantle of her saddle, cheeks wet with tears, sobbing into Bela's mane. The mare whickered uneasily.

"It is good that you have spirit," Renna said calmly. "The best *damane* are those who have spirit to be shaped and molded."

Egwene squeezed her eyes shut. She wished she could close her ears, too, to shut out Renna's voice. *I have to get away. I have to, but how? Nynaeve, help me. Light, somebody help me.*

"You will be one of the best," Renna said in tones of satisfaction. Her hand stroked Egwene's hair, a mistress soothing her dog.

Nynaeve leaned out of her saddle to peer around the screen of prickly leafed shrubs. Scattered trees met her eyes, some with leaves turning color. The expanses of grass and brush between seemed empty. Nothing moved that she could see except the thinning column of smoke, wavering in a breeze, from the leatherleaf.

That had been her work, the leatherleaf, and once the lightning called from a clear sky, and a few other things she had not thought to try until those two women tried them on her. She thought they must work together in some way, though she could not understand their relation to each other, apparently leashed as they were. One wore a collar, but the other was chained as surely as she. What Nynaeve was sure of was that one or both were Aes Sedai. She had never had a clear enough sight of them to see the glow of channeling, but it had to be.

*I'll certainly take pleasure in telling Sheriam about them,* she thought dryly. *Aes Sedai don't use the Power as a weapon, do they?*

She certainly had. She had at least knocked the two women down with that lightning strike, and she had seen one of the soldiers, or his body rather, burn from the ball of fire she made and hurled at them. But she had not seen any of the strangers at all in some time now.

Sweat beaded on her forehead, and it was not all from exertion. Her contact with *saidar* was gone, and she could not bring it back. In that first fury of knowing that Liandrin had betrayed them, *saidar* had been there almost before she knew it, the One Power flooding her. It had seemed she could do anything. And as long as they had chased her, rage at being hunted like an animal had fueled her. Now the chase had vanished. The longer she had gone without seeing an enemy at whom she could strike, the more she had begun to worry that they might be sneaking up on her somehow, and the more she had had time to worry about what was happening to Egwene, and Elayne, and Min. Now she was forced to admit that what she felt most was fear. Fear for them, fear for herself. It was anger she needed.

Something stirred behind a tree.

Her breath caught, and she fumbled for *saidar,* but all the exercises Sheriam and the others had taught her, all the blossoms unfolding in her mind, all the imagined streams that she held like riverbanks, did no good. She could feel it, sense the Source, but she could not touch it.

Elayne stepped from behind the tree in a wary crouch, and Nynaeve sagged with relief. The Daughter-Heir's dress was dirty and torn, her golden hair was a tangle of snarls and leaves, and her searching eyes were as wide as those of a frightened fawn, but she held her short-bladed dagger in a steady hand. Nynaeve picked up her reins and rode into the open.

Elayne gave a convulsive jump, then her hand went to her throat and she drew a deep breath. Nynaeve dismounted, and the two women hugged, taking comfort in having found each other.

"For a moment," Elayne said as they finally stepped apart, "I thought you were. . . . Do you know where they are? There were two men following me. Another few minutes and they would have caught me, but a horn sounded and they turned their horses and galloped off. They could see me, Nynaeve, and they just left."

"I heard it, too, and I haven't seen any of them since. Have you seen Egwene, or Min?"

Elayne shook her head, slumping to sit on the ground. "Not since. . . . That man hit Min, knocked her down. And one of those women was trying to put something around Egwene's neck. I saw that much before I ran. I don't think they got away, Nynaeve. I should have done something. Min cut the hand that was holding me, and Egwene. . . . I just ran, Nynaeve. I realized I was free, and I ran. Mother had better marry Gareth Bryne and have another daughter as soon as she can. I am not fit to take the throne."

"Don't be a goose," Nynaeve said sharply. "Remember, I have a packet of sheepstongue root among my herbs." Elayne had her head in her hands; the gibe did not even produce a murmur. "Listen to me, girl. Did you see me stay to fight twenty or thirty armed men, not to mention the Aes Sedai? If you had waited, the most likely thing by far is that you would be a prisoner, too. If they didn't just kill you. They seemed to be interested in Egwene and me for some reason. They might not have cared whether you remained alive or not." *Why* are *they interested in Egwene and me? Why us in particular? Why did Liandrin do this? Why?* She had no more answers now than she had had the first time she asked herself these questions.

"If I had died trying to help them—" Elayne began.

"—you'd be dead. And little good you'd be then, to yourself or them. Now get on your feet and brush off your dress." Nynaeve rummaged in her saddlebags for a hairbrush. "And fix your hair."

Elayne got up slowly, and took the brush with a small laugh. "You sound like Lini, my old nurse." She began to run the brush through her hair, wincing as tangles pulled. "But how are we going to help them, Nynaeve? You may be as strong as a full sister when you are angry, but they have women who can channel, too. I cannot think they're Aes Sedai, but they might as well be. We do not even know in which direction they took them."

"West," Nynaeve said. "That creature Suroth mentioned Falme, and that's as far west on Toman Head as you can go. We will go to Falme. I hope Liandrin is there. I will make her curse the day her mother laid eyes on her father. But first I think we had better find some clothes of the country. I've seen Taraboner and Domani women in the Tower, and what they wear is nothing like what we have on. We would stand out in Falme as strangers."

"I would not mind a Domani dress—though Mother would surely have a fit if she ever found out I'd worn one, and Lini would never let me hear the end of it—but even if we find a village, can we afford new dresses? I have no idea how much money you have, but I have only ten gold marks and

perhaps twice that in silver. That will keep us two or three weeks, but I
don't know what we will do after that."

"A few months as a novice in Tar Valon," Nynaeve said, laughing, "has
not stopped you thinking like the heir to a throne. I don't have a tenth
what you do, but altogether it will keep us two or three months, in comfort. Longer, if we are careful. I have no intention of buying us dresses, and
they won't be new in any case. My gray silk dress will do us some good,
with all those pearls and that gold thread. If I can't find a woman who will
trade us each two or three sturdy changes for that, I will give you this ring,
and I will be the novice." She swung up into her saddle and reached a hand
down to pull Elayne up behind her.

"What are we going to do when we reach Falme?" Elayne asked as she
settled on the mare's rump.

"I won't know that until we are there." Nynaeve paused, letting the
horse stand. "Are you sure you want to do this? It will be dangerous."

"More dangerous than it is for Egwene and Min? They would come after
us if our circumstances were reversed; I know they would. Are we going to
stay here all day?" Elayne dug her heels in, and the mare started off.

Nynaeve turned the horse until the sun, still short of its noonday crest,
shone at their backs. "We are going to have to be cautious. The Aes Sedai
we know can recognize a woman who can channel just by being within
arm's length of her. These Aes Sedai may be able to pick us out of a crowd
if they are looking for us, and we had better assume they are." *They were
certainly looking for Egwene and me. But why?*

"Yes, cautious. You were right before, too. We will not do them any
good letting ourselves be caught as well." Elayne was silent for a moment.
"Do you think it was all lies, Nynaeve? What Liandrin told us about Rand
being in danger? And the others? Aes Sedai do not lie."

It was Nynaeve's turn to be silent, remembering Sheriam telling her of
the oaths a woman took on being raised to full sisterhood, oaths spoken
inside a *ter'angreal* that bound her to keep them. *To speak no word that is not
true.* That was one, but everyone knew that the truth an Aes Sedai said
might not be the truth you thought you heard. "I expect Rand is warming
his feet in front of Lord Agelmar's fire in Fal Dara this minute," she said. *I
can't worry about him, now. I have to think about Egwene and Min.*

"I suppose he is," Elayne said with a sigh. She shifted behind the saddle.
"If it is very far to Falme, Nynaeve, I expect to ride in the saddle half the
time. This is not a very comfortable seat. We will never reach Falme at all
if you let this horse set her own pace the whole way."

Nynaeve booted the mare to a quick trot, and Elayne yelped and caught at her cloak. Nynaeve told herself that she would take a turn riding behind and not complain if Elayne put the horse to a gallop, but for the most part she ignored the gasps of the woman bouncing behind her. She was too busy hoping that by the time they reached Falme, she could stop being afraid and start being angry.

The breeze freshened, cool and brisk with a hint of cold yet to come.

# CHAPTER
# 41

## Disagreements

Thunder rumbled across the slate-dark afternoon sky. Rand pulled the hood of his cloak further up, hoping to keep at least some of the cold rain off. Red stepped through muddy puddles doggedly. The hood hung sodden around Rand's head, as the rest of the cloak did around his shoulders, and his fine black coat was just as wet, and as cold. The temperature would not have far to drop before snow or sleet came down instead of rain. Snow would fall soon, again; the people in the village they had passed through said two snows had already come this year. Shivering, Rand almost wished it was snowing. Then, at least, he would not be soaked to the skin.

The column plodded along, keeping a wary eye on the rolling country. Ingtar's Gray Owl hung heavily even when the wind gusted. Hurin sometimes pulled his cowl back to sniff the air; he said neither rain nor cold had any effect on a trail, certainly not on the kind of trail he was seeking, but so far the sniffer had found nothing. Behind him, Rand heard Uno mutter a curse. Loial kept checking his saddlebags; he did not seem to mind getting wet himself, but he worried continually about his books. Everyone was miserable except for Verin, who appeared too lost in thought to even notice that her hood had slid back, exposing her face to the rain.

"Can't you do something about this?" Rand demanded of her. A small

voice in the back of his head told him he could do it himself. All he need
do was embrace *saidin*. So sweet, the call of *saidin*. To be filled with the
One Power, to be one with the storm. Turn the skies to sunlight, or ride
the storm as it raged, whip it to fury and scour Toman Head clean from the
sea to the plain. Embrace *saidin*. He suppressed the longing ruthlessly.

The Aes Sedai gave a start. "What? Oh. I suppose. A little. I couldn't
stop a storm this big, not by myself—it covers too much area—but I could
lessen it some. Where we are, at least." She wiped rain from her face,
seemed to realize for the first time that her hood had slipped, and pulled it
back up absently.

"Then why don't you?" Mat said. The shivering face peering out from
under his hood looked at death's door, but his voice was vigorous.

"Because if I used that much of the One Power, any Aes Sedai closer
than ten miles would know someone had channeled. We don't want to
bring these Seanchan down on us with some of their *damane*." Her mouth
tightened angrily.

They had learned a little of the invaders in that village, called Atuan's
Mill, though most of what they had heard hatched more questions than it
answered. The people had babbled one moment and clamped their mouths
shut the next, trembling and looking over their shoulders. They all shook
with fear that the Seanchan would return with their monsters and their
*damane*. That women who should have been Aes Sedai were instead leashed
like animals frightened the villagers even more than the strange creatures
the Seanchan commanded, things the folk of Atuan's Mill could only describe in whispers as coming from nightmares. And worst of all, the exam-
ples the Seanchan had made before leaving still chilled the people to their
marrow. They had buried their dead, but they feared to clean away the
large charred patch in the village square. None of them would say what had
happened there, but Hurin had vomited as soon as they entered the village,
and he would not go near the blackened ground.

Atuan's Mill had been half deserted. Some had fled to Falme, thinking
the Seanchan would not be so harsh in a town they held fast, and others
had gone east. More had said they were thinking of it. There was fighting
on Almoth Plain, Taraboners battling Domani it was said, but such houses
and barns as were burned there were kindled by torches in the hands of
men. Even a war was easier to face than what the Seanchan had done, what
they might do.

"Why did Fain bring the Horn here?" Perrin muttered. The question
had been asked by each of them at one time or another, and no one had an
answer. "There's war, and these Seanchan, and their monsters. Why here?"

Ingtar turned in his saddle to look back at them. His face appeared almost as haggard as Mat's. "There are always men who see chances for their own advantage in the confusion of war. Fain is one like that. No doubt he thinks to steal the Horn again, from the Dark One this time, and use it for his own profit."

"The Father of Lies never lays simple plans," Verin said. "It may be that he wants Fain to bring the Horn here for some reason known only in Shayol Ghul."

"Monsters," Mat snorted. His cheeks were sunken, now, his eyes hollow. That he *sounded* healthy only made it worse. "They saw some Trollocs, or a Fade, if you ask me. Well, why not? If the Seanchan have Aes Sedai fighting for them, why not Fades and Trollocs?" He caught Verin staring at him and flinched. "Well, they are, on leashes or not. They can channel, and that makes them Aes Sedai." He glanced at Rand and gave a ragged laugh. "That makes you Aes Sedai, the Light help us all."

Masema came galloping from ahead, through the mud and the steady rain. "There is another village ahead, my Lord," he said as he pulled in beside Ingtar. His eyes only swept past Rand, but they tightened, and he did not look at Rand again. "It's empty, my Lord. No villagers, no Seanchan, nobody at all. The houses all look sound, though, except for two or three that . . . well, they aren't there anymore, my Lord."

Ingtar raised his hand and signaled for a trot.

The village Masema had found covered the slopes of a hill, with a paved square at the top around a circle of stone walls. The houses were of stone, all flat-roofed and few more than a single story. Three that had been larger, along one side of the square, were only heaps of blackened rubble; shattered chunks of stone and roof beams lay scattered across the square. A few shutters banged when the wind gusted.

Ingtar dismounted in front of the only large building still standing. The creaking sign above its door bore a woman juggling stars, but no name; rain came off the corners in two steady drizzles. Verin hurried inside while Ingtar spoke. "Uno, search every house. If there is anyone left, perhaps they can tell us what happened here, and maybe a little more about these Seanchan. And if there's any food, bring that, too. And blankets." Uno nodded and began telling off men. Ingtar turned to Hurin. "What do you smell? Did Fain come through here?"

Hurin, rubbing his nose, shook his head. "Not him, my Lord, and not the Trollocs, neither. Whoever did that left a stench, though." He pointed to the wreckage that had been houses. "It was killing, my Lord. There were people in there."

"Seanchan," Ingtar growled. "Let's get inside. Ragan, find some sort of stable for the horses."

Verin already had fires going in both of the big fireplaces, at either end of the common room, and was warming her hands at one, her sodden cloak spread out on one of the tables dotting the tiled floor. She had found a few candles, too, now burning on a table stuck in their own tallow. Emptiness and quiet, except for the occasional grumble of thunder, added to the flickering shadows to give the place a cavernous feel. Rand tossed his equally wet cloak and coat on a table and joined her. Only Loial seemed more interested in checking his books than in warming himself.

"We will never find the Horn of Valere this way," Ingtar said. "Three days since we . . . since we arrived here"—he shuddered and scrubbed a hand through his hair; Rand wondered what the Shienaran had seen in his other lives—"another two, at least, to Falme, and we have not found so much as a hair of Fain or Darkfriends. There are scores of villages along the coast. He could have gone to any of them and taken ship anywhere by now. If he was ever here."

"He is here," Verin said calmly, "and he went to Falme."

"And he's still here," Rand said. *Waiting for me. Please, Light, he's still waiting.*

"Hurin still hasn't caught a whiff of him," Ingtar said. The sniffer shrugged as if he felt himself at fault for the failure. "Why would he choose Falme? If those villagers are to be believed, Falme is held by these Seanchan. I would give my best hound to know who they are, and where they came from."

"Who they are is not important to us." Verin knelt and unfastened her saddlebags, pulling out dry clothes. "At least we have rooms in which to change our clothes, though it will do us little good unless the weather changes. Ingtar, it may well be that what the villagers told us is right, that they are the descendants of Artur Hawkwing's armies come back. What matters is that Padan Fain has gone to Falme. The writings in the dungeon at Fal Dara—"

"—never mentioned Fain. Forgive me, Aes Sedai, but that could have been a trick as easily as dark prophecy. I can't believe even Trollocs would be stupid enough to tell us everything they were going to do before they did it."

She twisted to look up at him. "And what do you mean to do, if you will not take my advice?"

"I mean to have the Horn of Valere," Ingtar said firmly. "Forgive me, but I have to trust my own senses before some words scrawled by a Trolloc . . ."

"A Myrddraal, surely," Verin murmured, but he did not even pause.

". . . or a Darkfriend seeming to betray himself out of his own mouth. I mean to quarter the ground until Hurin smells a trail or we find Fain in the flesh. I must have the Horn, Verin Sedai. I must!"

"That isn't the way," Hurin said softly. "Not 'must.' What happens, happens." No one paid him any mind.

"We all must," Verin murmured, peering into her saddlebags, "yet some things may be even more important than that."

She did not say more, but Rand grimaced. He longed to get away from her and her prods and hints. *I am not the Dragon Reborn. Light, but I wish I could just get away from Aes Sedai completely.* "Ingtar, I think I'm riding on to Falme. Fain is there—I'm sure he is—and if I don't come soon, he—he will do something to hurt Emond's Field." He had not mentioned that part before.

They all stared at him, Mat and Perrin frowning, worried but considering; Verin as if she had just seen a new piece added to a puzzle. Loial looked astonished, and Hurin seemed confused. Ingtar was openly disbelieving.

"Why would he do that?" the Shienaran said.

"I don't know," Rand lied, "but that was part of the message he left with Barthanes."

"And did Barthanes say Fain was going to Falme?" Ingtar demanded. "No. It wouldn't matter if he had." He gave a bitter laugh. "Darkfriends lie as naturally as they breathe."

"Rand," Mat said, "if I knew how to stop Fain from hurting Emond's Field, I would. If I was sure he was going to. But I need that dagger, Rand, and Hurin has the best chance of finding it."

"I will go wherever you go, Rand," Loial said. He had finished making sure the books were dry and was taking off his sodden coat. "But I don't see where a few more days will change anything one way or another, now. Try being a little less hasty for once."

"It doesn't matter to me whether we go to Falme now, later, or never," Perrin said with a shrug, "but if Fain really is threatening Emond's Field . . . well, Mat's right. Hurin is the best way to find him."

"I can find him, Lord Rand," Hurin put in. "Let me get one sniff of him, and I'll take you right to him. There's never anything else left a trail like his."

"You must make your own choice, Rand," Verin said carefully, "but remember that Falme is held by invaders about whom we still know next to nothing. If you go to Falme alone, you may find yourself a prisoner, or worse, and that will serve nothing. I am sure whatever choice you make will be the right one."

"*Ta'veren,*" Loial rumbled.

Rand threw up his hands.

Uno came in from the square, shaking rain off his cloak. "Not a flaming soul to be found, my Lord. Looks to me like they ran like striped pigs. Livestock's all gone, and there isn't a bloody cart or wagon left, either. Half the houses are stripped to the flaming floors. I'll wager my next month's pay you could follow them by the bloody furniture they tossed on the side of the road when they realized it was only weighing down their flaming wagons."

"What about clothes?" Ingtar asked.

Uno blinked his one eye in surprise. "Just a few bits and pieces, my Lord. Mainly what they didn't think was bloody worth taking with them."

"They will have to do. Hurin, I mean to dress you and a few more as local people, as many as we can manage, so you won't stand out. I want you to swing wide, north and south, until you cross the trail." More soldiers were coming in, and they all gathered around Ingtar and Hurin to listen.

Rand leaned his hands on the mantel over the fireplace and stared into the flames. They made him think of Ba'alzamon's eyes. "There isn't much time," he said. "I feel . . . something . . . pulling me to Falme, and there isn't much time." He saw Verin watching him, and added harshly, "Not that. It's Fain I have to find. It has nothing to do with . . . that."

Verin nodded. "The Wheel weaves as the Wheel wills, and we are all woven into the Pattern. Fain has been here weeks before us, perhaps months. A few more days will make little difference in whatever is going to happen."

"I'm going to get some sleep," he muttered, picking up his saddlebags. "They can't have carried off all the beds."

Upstairs, he did find beds, but only a few still had mattresses, and those so lumpy he thought it might be more comfortable to sleep on the floor. Finally he chose a bed where the mattress simply sagged in the middle. There was nothing else in the room except one wooden chair and a table with a rickety leg.

He took off his wet things, putting on a dry shirt and breeches before lying down, since there were no sheets or blankets, and propped his sword beside the head of the bed. Wryly, he thought that the only thing dry he had for a coverlet was the Dragon's banner; he left it safely buckled inside the saddlebags.

Rain drummed on the roof, and thunder growled overhead, and now and again a lightning flash lit the windows. Shivering, he rolled this way and that on the mattress, seeking some comfortable way to lie, wondering if the

banner would not do for a blanket after all, wondering if he should ride on
to Falme.

He rolled to his other side, and Ba'alzamon was standing beside the chair
with the pure white length of the Dragon's banner in his hands. The room
seemed darker there, as if Ba'alzamon stood on the edge of a cloud of oily
black smoke. Nearly healed burns crisscrossed his face, and as Rand looked,
his pitch-dark eyes vanished for an instant, replaced by endless caverns of
fire. Rand's saddlebags lay by his feet, buckles undone, flap thrown back
where the banner had been hidden.

"The time comes closer, Lews Therin. A thousand threads draw tight,
and soon you will be tied and trapped, set to a course you cannot change.
Madness. Death. Before you die, will you once more kill everything you
love?"

Rand glanced at the door, but he made no move except to sit up on the
side of the bed. What good to try running from the Dark One? His throat
felt like sand. "I am not the Dragon, Father of Lies!" he said hoarsely.

The darkness behind Ba'alzamon roiled, and furnaces roared as Ba'alzamon laughed. "You honor me. And belittle yourself. I know you too
well. I have faced you a thousand times. A thousand times a thousand. I
know you to your miserable soul, Lews Therin Kinslayer." He laughed
again; Rand put a hand in front of his face against the heat of that fiery
mouth.

"What do you want? I will not serve you. I will not do anything that
you want. I'll die first!"

"You *will* die, worm! How many times have you died across the span of
the Ages, fool, and how much has death availed you? The grave is cold and
lonely, save for the worms. The grave is mine. This time there will be no
rebirth for you. This time the Wheel of Time will be broken and the world
remade in the image of the Shadow. This time your death will be forever!
Which will you choose? Death everlasting? Or life eternal—and power!"

Rand hardly realized that he was on his feet. The void had surrounded
him, *saidin* was there, and the One Power flowed into him. That fact
almost cracked the emptiness. Was this real? Was it a dream? Could he
channel in a dream? But the torrent rushing into him swept away his
doubts. He hurled it at Ba'alzamon, hurled the pure One Power, the force
that turned the Wheel of Time, a force that could make seas burn and eat
mountains.

Ba'alzamon took half a step back, holding the banner clutched before
him. Flames leaped in his wide eyes and mouth, and the darkness seemed
to cloak him in shadow. In the Shadow. The Power sank into that black
mist and vanished, soaked up like water on parched sand.

Rand drew on *saidin,* pulled for more, and still more. His flesh seemed so cold it must shatter at a touch; it burned as if it must boil away. His bones felt on the point of crisping to cold crystal ash. He did not care; it was like drinking life itself.

"Fool!" Ba'alzamon roared. "You will destroy yourself!"

*Mat.* The thought floated somewhere beyond the consuming flood. *The dagger. The Horn. Fain. Emond's Field. I can't die yet.*

He was not sure how he did it, but suddenly the Power was gone, and *saidin,* and the void. Shuddering uncontrollably, he fell to his knees beside the bed, arms wrapped around himself in a vain effort to stop their twitching.

"That is better, Lews Therin." Ba'alzamon tossed the banner to the floor and put his hands on the chair back; wisps of smoke rose from between his fingers. The shadow no longer encompassed him. "There is your banner, Kinslayer. Much good will it do you. A thousand strings laid over a thousand years have drawn you here. Ten thousand woven throughout the Ages tie you like a sheep for slaughter. The Wheel itself holds you prisoner to your fate Age after Age. But I can set you free. You cowering cur, I alone in the entire world can teach you how to wield the Power. I alone can stop it killing you before you have a chance to go mad. I alone can stop the madness. You have served me before. Serve me again, Lews Therin, or be destroyed forever!"

"My name," Rand forced between chattering teeth, "is Rand al'Thor." His shivering forced him to squeeze his eyes shut, and when he opened them again, he was alone.

Ba'alzamon was gone. The shadow was gone. His saddlebags stood against the chair with the buckles done up and one side bulging with the bulk of the Dragon's banner, just as he had left it. But on the chair back, tendrils of smoke still rose from the charred impressions of fingers.

# CHAPTER
## 42

*Falme*

Nynaeve pressed Elayne back into the narrow alleyway between a cloth merchant's shop and a potter's works as the pair of women linked by a silvery leash passed by, heading down the cobblestone street toward Falme harbor. They did not dare allow that pair to come too close. The people in the street made way for those two even more quickly than they did for Seanchan soldiers, or the occasional noble's palanquin, thickly curtained now that the days were cold. Even the street artists did not offer to draw them in chalks or pencils, although they pestered everyone else. Nynaeve's mouth tightened as her eyes followed the *sul'dam* and the *damane* through the crowd. Even after weeks in the town, the sight sickened her. Perhaps it sickened her more, now. She could not imagine doing that to any woman, not even Moiraine or Liandrin.

*Well, maybe Liandrin,* she admitted sourly. Sometimes, at night, in the small, smelly room the two of them had rented above a fishmonger, she thought of what she would like to do to Liandrin when she got her hands on her. Liandrin even more than Suroth. More than once she had been shocked at her own cruelty, even while she was delighted at her inventiveness.

Still trying to keep the pair in sight, her eyes fell on a bony man, well down the street, before the shifting throng hid him again. She had only a

flash of a big nose in a narrow face. He wore a rich bronze velvet robe of
Seanchan cut over his clothes, but she thought that he was no Seanchan,
though the servant following him was, and a servant of high degree, with
one temple shaved. The local people had not taken to Seanchan fashions,
particularly that one. *That looked like Padan Fain,* she thought incredulously. *It couldn't be. Not here.*

"Nynaeve," Elayne said softly, "could we move on, now? That fellow
selling apples is looking at his table as if he's thinking he had more a few
moments ago, and I would not want him wondering what I have in my
pockets."

They both wore long coats made of sheepskin, with the fleece turned in
and bright red spirals embroidered across the breast. It was country garb,
but it passed well enough in Falme, where many people had come in from
the farms and villages. Among so many strangers the two of them had been
able to sink in unnoticed. Nynaeve had combed out her braid, and her gold
ring, the serpent eating its own tail, now nestled under her dress beside
Lan's heavy ring on the leather cord around her neck.

The large pockets of Elayne's coat bulged suspiciously.

"You stole those apples?" Nynaeve hissed quietly, pulling Elayne out
into the crowded street. "Elayne, we don't have to steal. Not yet, anyway."

"No? How much money do we have left? You have been 'not hungry'
very often at mealtimes the last few days."

"Well, I am not hungry," Nynaeve snapped, trying to ignore the hollow
in her middle. Everything cost considerably more than she had expected;
she had heard local people complaining about how prices had risen since
the Seanchan came. "Give me one of those." The apple Elayne dug out of
her pocket was small and hard, but it crunched with a delicious sweetness
when Nynaeve bit into it. She licked the juice from her lips. "How did you
manage to—" She jerked Elayne to a halt and peered into her face. "Did
you. . . ? Did you. . . ?" She could not think of a way to say it with so
many streaming by, but Elayne understood.

"Only a little. I made that stack of old melons with the soft spots fall,
and when he started putting them back. . . ." She did not even have the
grace, as Nynaeve saw it, to blush or look embarrassed. Unconcernedly
eating one of the apples, she shrugged. "There is no need to frown at me
like that. I looked carefully to make sure there was no *damane* close." She
sniffed. "If I were being held prisoner, I would not help my captors find
other women to enslave. Although, the way these Falmen behave, you
would think they were lifelong servants of those who should be their enemies to the death." She looked around, openly contemptuous, at the people hurrying by; it was possible to follow the path of any Seanchan, even

common soldiers and even at a distance, by the ripples of bowing. "They should resist. They should fight back."

"How? Against . . . that."

They had to step to the side of the street along with everyone else as a Seanchan patrol neared, climbing from the direction of the harbor. Nynaeve managed the bow, hands on knees, with face schooled to a perfect smoothness; Elayne was slower, and made her bow with a distasteful twist of her mouth.

There were twenty armored men and women in the patrol, riding horses, for which Nynaeve was grateful. She could not become used to seeing people riding things that looked like bronze-scaled, tailless cats, and a rider on one of the flying beasts was always enough to make her feel dizzy; she was glad there were so few of them. Still, two leashed creatures trotted along with the patrol, like wingless birds with coarse leather skin, and sharp beaks higher above the cobblestones than the helmeted heads of the soldier. Their long, sinewy legs looked as if they could run faster than any horse.

She straightened slowly after the Seanchan were gone. Some of those who had bowed for the patrol came close to running; no one was comfortable at the sight of the Seanchan's beasts except the Seanchan themselves. "Elayne," she said softly as they resumed their climb, "if we are caught, I swear that before they kill us, or do whatever they do, I will beg them on bended knees to let me stripe you from top to bottom with the stoutest switch I can find! If you still can't learn to be careful, maybe it's time to think about sending you back to Tar Valon, or home to Caemlyn, or anywhere but here."

"I am careful. At least I looked to be sure there was no *damane* close by. What about you? I have seen you channel with one in plain sight."

"I made sure they weren't looking at me," Nynaeve muttered. She had had to ball up all her anger at women being chained like animals to manage it. "And I only did it once. And it was only a trickle."

"A trickle? We had to spend three days hiding in our room breathing fish while they searched the town for whoever had done it. Do you call that being careful?"

"I had to know if there was a way to unfasten those collars." She thought there was. She would have to test one more collar at least before she was certain, and she was not looking forward to it. She had thought, like Elayne, that the *damane* must all be prisoners eager to escape, but it had been the woman in the collar who raised the cry.

A man pushing a barrow that bumped over the cobblestones passed by them, crying his services to sharpen scissors and knives. "They should resist, somehow," Elayne growled. "They act as if they do not see anything that happens around them if there's a Seanchan in it."

Nynaeve only sighed. It did not help that she thought Elayne was at least partly right. At first she had thought some of the Falmen submission, at least, must be a pose, but she had found no evidence of any resistance at all. She had looked at first, hoping to find help in freeing Egwene and Min, but everyone took fright at the merest hint that they might oppose the Seanchan, and she stopped asking before she drew the wrong sort of attention. In truth, she could not imagine how the people *could* fight. *Monsters and Aes Sedai. How can you fight monsters and Aes Sedai?*

Ahead stood five tall stone houses, among the largest in the town, all together making up a block. One street short of them, Nynaeve found an alleyway beside a tailor shop, where they could keep an eye on some of the tall houses' entrances, at least. It was not possible to see every door at once—she did not want to risk letting Elayne go off on her own to watch more—but it was not wise to go any closer. Above the rooftops, on the next street, the golden hawk banner of the High Lord Turak flapped in the wind.

Only women went in or out of those houses, and most of those were *sul'dam,* alone or with *damane* in tow. The buildings had been taken over by the Seanchan to house the *damane.* Egwene had to be in there, and likely Min; they had found no sign of Min so far, though it was possible she was as hidden by the crowds as they. Nynaeve had heard many tales of women and girls being seized on the streets or brought in from the villages; they all went into those houses, and if they were seen again, they wore a collar.

Settling herself on a crate beside Elayne, she dug into the other woman's coat for a handful of the small apples. There were fewer local folk in the streets here. Everyone knew what the houses were, and everyone avoided them, just as they avoided the stables where the Seanchan kept their beasts. It was not difficult to keep an eye on the doors through spaces between the passersby. Just two women stopping for a bite; just two more people who could not afford to eat at an inn. Nothing to attract more than a passing glance.

Eating mechanically, Nynaeve tried once more to plan. Being able to open the collar—if she really could—did no good at all unless she could reach Egwene. The apples did not taste so sweet anymore.

From the narrow window of her tiny room under the eaves, one of a number roughly walled together from whatever had been there before, Egwene could see the garden where *damane* were being walked by their *sul'dam.* It had been several gardens before the Seanchan knocked down the walls that separated them and took the big houses to keep their *damane*. The trees were all but leafless, but the *damane* were still taken out for air, whether they wanted it or not. Egwene watched the garden because Renna was down there, talking with another *sul'dam,* and as long as she could see Renna, then Renna was not going to enter and surprise her.

Some other *sul'dam* might come—there were many more *sul'dam* than *damane,* and every *sul'dam* wanted her turn wearing a bracelet; they called it being complete—but Renna still had charge of her training, and it was Renna who wore her bracelet four times out of five. If anyone came, they would find no impediment to entering. There were no locks on the doors of *damane*'s rooms. Egwene's room held only a hard, narrow bed, a washstand with a chipped pitcher and bowl, one chair and a small table, but it had no room for more. *Damane* had no need of comfort, or privacy, or possessions. *Damane* were possessions. Min had a room just like this, in another house, but Min could come and go as she would, or almost as she would. Seanchan were great ones for rules; they had more, for everyone, than the White Tower did for novices.

Egwene stood far back from the window. She did not want any of the women below to look up and see the glow that she knew surrounded her as she channeled the One Power, probing delicately at the collar around her neck, searching futilely; she could not even tell whether the band was woven or made of links—sometimes it seemed one, sometimes the other— but it seemed all of a piece all the time. It was only a tiny trickle of the Power, the merest drip that she could imagine, but it still beaded sweat on her face and made her stomach clench. That was one of the properties of the *a'dam;* if a *damane* tried to channel without a *sul'dam* wearing her bracelet, she felt sick, and the more of the Power she channeled, the sicker she became. Lighting a candle beyond the reach of her arm would have made Egwene vomit. Once Renna had ordered her to juggle her tiny balls of light with the bracelet lying on the table. Remembering still made her shudder.

Now, the silver leash snaked across the bare floor and up the unpainted wooden wall to where the bracelet hung on a peg. The sight of it hanging there made her jaws clench with fury. A dog leashed so carelessly could have run away. If a *damane* moved her bracelet as much as a foot from where it had last been touched by a *sul'dam.* . . . Renna had made her do that, too—had made her carry her own bracelet across the room. Or try to. She was sure it had only been minutes before the *sul'dam* snapped the bracelet firmly on her own wrist, but to Egwene the screaming and the cramps that had had her writhing on the floor had seemed to go on for hours.

Someone tapped at the door, and Egwene jumped, before she realized it could not be a *sul'dam*. None of them would knock first. She let *saidar* go, anyway; she was beginning to feel decidedly ill. "Min?"

"Here I am for my weekly visit," Min announced as she slipped inside and shut the door. Her cheeriness sounded a little forced, but she always did what she could to keep Egwene's spirits up. "How do you like it?" She spun in a little circle, showing off her dark green wool dress of Seanchan cut. A heavy, matching cloak hung over her arm. There was even a green ribbon catching up her dark hair, though her hair was hardly long enough for it. Her knife was still in its sheath at her waist, though. Egwene had been surprised when Min first showed up wearing it, but it seemed the Seanchan trusted everyone. Until they broke a rule.

"It's pretty," Egwene said cautiously. "But, why?"

"I haven't gone over to the enemy, if that is what you are thinking. It was this, or else find someplace to stay out in the town, and maybe not be able to visit you again." She started to straddle the chair as she would have in breeches, gave a wry shake of her head, and turned it around to sit. "'Everyone has a place in the Pattern,'" she mimicked, "'and the place of everyone must be readily apparent.' That old hag Mulaen apparently got tired of not knowing what my place was on sight and decided I ranked with the serving girls. She gave me the choice. You should see some of the things Seanchan serving girls wear, the ones who serve the lords. It might be fun, but not unless I was betrothed, or, better yet, married. Well, there's no going back. Not yet, anyway. Mulaen burned my coat and breeches." Grimacing to show what she thought of that, she picked up a rock from a small pile on the table and bounced it from hand to hand. "It isn't so bad," she said with a laugh, "except that it has been so long since I wore skirts that I keep tripping over them."

Egwene had had to watch her clothes being burned, too, including that lovely green silk. It had made her glad she had not brought more of the clothes the Lady Amalisa had given her, though she might never see any of them, or the White Tower, again. What she had on now was the same dark gray all *damane* wore. Damane *have no possessions,* it had been explained to her. *The dress a* damane *wears, the food she eats, the bed she sleeps in, are all gifts from her* sul'dam. *If a* sul'dam *chooses that a* damane *sleep on the floor instead of in a bed, or in a stall in a stable, it is purely the choice of the* sul'dam. Mulaen, who had charge of the *damane* quarters, had a droning nasal voice, but she was sharp with any *damane* who did not remember every word of her boring lectures.

"I don't think there will be any going back for me ever," Egwene said, sighing, sinking down on her bed. She gestured to the rocks on the table.

"Renna gave me a test, yesterday. I picked out the piece of iron ore, and the copper ore, blindfolded, every time she mixed them up. She left them all here to remind me of my success. She seemed to think it was some kind of reward to be reminded."

"It doesn't seem any worse than the rest—not nearly as bad as making things explode like fireworks—but couldn't you have lied? Told her you didn't know which was which?"

"You still do not know what this is like." Egwene tugged at the collar; pulling did no more good than channeling had. "When Renna is wearing that bracelet, she knows what I am doing with the Power, and what I am not. Sometimes she even seems to know when she isn't wearing it; she says *sul'dam* develop—an affinity, she calls it—after a while." She sighed. "No one even thought to test me on this earlier. Earth is one of the Five Powers that was strongest in men. When I picked out those rocks, she took me outside the town, and I was able to point right to an abandoned iron mine. It was all overgrown, and there wasn't any opening to be seen at all, but once I knew how, I could feel the iron ore still in the ground. There hasn't been enough to make it worth working in a hundred years, but I knew it was there. I couldn't lie to her, Min. She knew I had sensed the mine as soon as I did. She was so excited, she promised me a pudding with my supper." She felt her cheeks growing hot, in anger and embarrassment. "Apparently," she said bitterly, "I am now too valuable to be wasted making things explode. Any *damane* can do that; only a handful can find ores in the ground. Light, I hate making things explode, but I wish that was all I could do."

The color in her cheeks deepened. She did hate it, making trees tear themselves to splinters and the earth erupt; that was meant for battle, for killing, and she wanted no part of it. Yet anything the Seanchan let her do was another chance to touch *saidar,* to feel the Power flowing through her. She hated the things Renna and the other *sul'dam* made her do, but she was sure that she could handle much more of the Power now than she could before leaving Tar Valon. She certainly knew she could do things with it that no sister in the Tower had ever thought of doing; they never thought of tearing the earth apart to kill men.

"Perhaps you won't have to worry about any of it much longer," Min said, grinning. "I've found us a ship, Egwene. The captain has been held here by the Seanchan, and he is about ready to sail with or without permission."

"If he will take you, Min, go with him," Egwene said wearily. "I told you I'm valuable, now. Renna says in a few days they're sending a ship back to Seanchan. Just to take me."

Min's grin vanished, and they stared at each other. Suddenly Min hurled her rock at the pile on the table, scattering them. "There has to be a way out of here. There has to be a way to take that bloody thing off your neck!"

Egwene leaned her head back against the wall. "You know the Seanchan have collected every woman they've been able to find who can channel even a speck. They come from all over, not just from here in Falme, but from the fishing villages, and from farming towns inland. Taraboner and Domani women, passengers off ships they've stopped. There are two Aes Sedai among them."

"Aes Sedai!" Min exclaimed. By habit she looked around to make sure no Seanchan had overheard her saying that name. "Egwene, if there are Aes Sedai here, they can help us. Let me talk to them, and—"

"They can't even help themselves, Min. I only talked to one—her name is Ryma; the *sul'dam* don't call her that, but that's her name; she wanted to make sure I knew it—and she told me there is another. She told me in between bouts of tears. She's Aes Sedai, and she was crying, Min! She has a collar on her neck, they make her answer to Pura, and she can't do anything more about it than I can. They captured her when Falme fell. She was crying because she's beginning to stop fighting against it, because she cannot take being punished anymore. She was crying because she wants to take her own life, and she cannot even do that without permission. Light, I know how she feels!"

Min shifted uneasily, smoothing her dress with suddenly nervous hands. "Egwene, you don't want to. . . . Egwene, you must not think of harming yourself. I will get you out somehow. I will!"

"I am not going to kill myself," Egwene said dryly. "Even if I could. Let me have your knife. Come on. I won't hurt myself. Just hand it to me."

Min hesitated before slowly taking her knife from its sheath at her waist. She held it out warily, obviously ready to leap if Egwene tried anything.

Egwene took a deep breath and reached for the hilt. A soft quiver ran through the muscles of her arm. As her hand came within a foot of the knife, a cramp suddenly contorted her fingers. Eyes fixed, she tried to force her hand closer. The cramp seized her whole arm, knotting muscles to her shoulder. With a groan, she sank back, rubbing her arm and concentrating her thoughts on *not* touching the knife. Slowly, the pain began to lessen.

Min stared at her incredulously. "What. . . ? I don't understand."

"*Damane* are not allowed to touch a weapon of any kind." She worked her arm, feeling the tightness go. "Even our meat is cut for us. I don't want to hurt myself, but I could not if I did want to. No *damane* is ever left

alone where she might jump from a height—that window is nailed shut—
or throw herself in a river."

"Well, that's a good thing. I mean. . . . Oh, I don't know what I mean.
If you could jump in a river, you might escape."

Egwene went on dully, as if the other woman had not spoken. "They are
training me, Min. The *sul'dam* and the *a'dam* are training me. I cannot
touch anything I even think of as a weapon. A few weeks ago I considered
hitting Renna over the head with that pitcher, and I could not pour wash
water for three days. Once I'd thought of it that way, I not only had to
stop thinking about hitting her with it, I had to convince myself I would
never, under any circumstances, hit her with it before I could touch it
again. She knew what had happened, told me what I had to do, and would
not let me wash anywhere except with that pitcher and bowl. You are lucky
it happened between your visiting days. Renna made sure I spent those
days sweating from the time I woke to the time I fell asleep, exhausted. I
am trying to fight them, but they are training me as surely as they're
training Pura." She clapped a hand to her mouth, moaning through her
teeth. "Her name is Ryma. I have to remember *her* name, not the name
they've put on her. She is Ryma, and she's Yellow Ajah, and she has fought
them as long and as hard as she could. It is no fault of hers that she hasn't
the strength left to fight any longer. I wish I knew who the other sister is
that Ryma mentioned. I wish I knew her name. Remember both of us,
Min. Ryma, of the Yellow Ajah, and Egwene al'Vere. Not Egwene the
*damane;* Egwene al'Vere of Emond's Field. Will you do that?"

"Stop it!" Min snapped. "You stop it right this instant! If you get
shipped off to Seanchan, I'll be right there with you. But I don't think you
will. You know I've read you, Egwene. I don't understand most of it—I
almost never do—but I see things I am sure link you to Rand, and Perrin,
and Mat, and—yes, even Galad, the Light help you for a fool. How can
any of that happen if the Seanchan take you off across the ocean?"

"Maybe they're going to conquer the whole world, Min. If they conquer
the world, there's no reason Rand and Galad and the rest could not end up
in Seanchan."

"You ninny-headed goose!"

"I am being practical," Egwene said sharply. "I don't intend to stop
fighting, not as long as I can breathe, but I don't see any hope that I'll ever
have the *a'dam* off me, either. Just as I don't see any hope that anyone is
going to stop the Seanchan. Min, if this ship captain will take you, go with
him. At least then one of us will be free."

The door swung open, and Renna stepped in.

Egwene jumped to her feet and bowed sharply, as did Min. The tiny room was crowded for bowing, but Seanchan insisted on protocol before comfort.

"Your visiting day, is it?" Renna said. "I had forgotten. Well, there is training to be done even on visiting days."

Egwene watched sharply as the *sul'dam* took down the bracelet, opened it, and fastened it again around her wrist. She could not see how it was done. If she could have probed with the One Power, she would have, but Renna would have known that immediately. As the bracelet closed around Renna's wrist a look came onto the *sul'dam*'s face that made Egwene's heart sink.

"You have been channeling." Renna's voice was deceptively mild; there was a spark of anger in her eyes. "You know that is forbidden except when we are complete." Egwene wet her lips. "Perhaps I have been too lenient with you. Perhaps you believe that because you are valuable now, you will be allowed license. I think I made a mistake letting you keep your old name. I had a kitten called Tuli when I was a child. From now on, your name is Tuli. You will go now, Min. Your visiting day with Tuli is ended."

Min hesitated only long enough for one anguished look at Egwene before leaving. Nothing Min could say or do would do anything except make matters worse, but Egwene could not help looking longingly at the door as it closed behind her friend.

Renna took the chair, frowning at Egwene. "I must punish you severely for this. We will both be called to the Court of the Nine Moons—you for what you can do; I as your *sul'dam* and trainer—and I will not allow you to disgrace me in the eyes of the Empress. I will stop when you tell me how much you love being *damane* and how obedient you will be after this. And, Tuli. Make me believe every word."

# CHAPTER 43

## A Plan

Outside in the low-ceilinged hallway, Min dug her nails into her palms at the first piercing cry from the room. She took a step toward the door before she could stop herself, and when she did stop, tears sprang up in her eyes. *Light help me, all I can do is make it worse. Egwene, I'm sorry. I'm sorry.*

Feeling worse than useless, she picked up her skirts and ran, and Egwene's screams pursued her. She could not make herself stay, and leaving made her feel a coward. Half blind with weeping, she found herself in the street before she knew it. She had intended to go back to her room, but now she could not do it. She could not stand the thought that Egwene was being hurt while she sat warm and safe under the next roof. Scrubbing the tears from her eyes, she swept her cloak around her shoulders and started down the street. Every time she cleared her eyes, new tears began trickling along her cheeks. She was not accustomed to weeping openly, but then she was not accustomed to feeling so helpless, so useless. She did not know where she was going, only that it had to be as far as she could reach from Egwene's cries.

"Min!"

The low-pitched shout brought her up short. At first, she could not make out who had called. Relatively few people walked the street this close to where the *damane* were housed. Aside from a lone man trying to interest two Seanchan soldiers in buying the picture he would draw of them with his colored chalks, everyone local tried to step along quickly without actually appearing to run. A pair of *sul'dam* strolled by, *damane* trailing behind with eyes down; the Seanchan women were talking about how many more *marath'damane* they expected to find before they sailed. Min's eyes passed right over the two women in long fleece coats, then swung back in wonder as they came toward her. "Nynaeve? Elayne?"

"None other." Nynaeve's smile was strained; both women had tight eyes, as if they fought worried frowns. Min thought she had never seen anything as wonderful as the sight of them. "That color becomes you," Nynaeve continued. "You should have taken up dresses long since. Though I've thought of breeches myself since I saw them on you." Her voice sharpened as she drew close enough to see Min's face. "What is the matter?"

"You've been crying," Elayne said. "Has something happened to Egwene?"

Min gave a start and looked back over her shoulder. A *sul'dam* and *damane* came down the steps she had used and turned the other way, toward the stables and horse yards. Another woman with the lightning panels on her dress stood at the top of the stairs talking with someone still inside. Min grabbed her friends by the arms and hurried them down the street toward the harbor. "It's dangerous for you two here. Light, it's dangerous for you to be in Falme. There are *damane* everywhere, and if they find you. . . . You do know what *damane* are? Oh, you don't know how good it is to see you both."

"I imagine about as half as good as it is to see you," Nynaeve said. "Do you know where Egwene is? Is she in one of those buildings? Is she all right?"

Min hesitated a fraction before saying, "She's as well as can be expected." Min could see it all too well, if she told them what was happening to Egwene right that moment. Nynaeve was as likely as not to go storming back in an attempt to stop it. *Light, let it be over by now. Light, make her bend her stubborn neck just once before they almost break it first.* "I don't know how to get her out, though. I found a ship captain who I think will take us if we can reach his ship with her—he won't help unless we make it that far, and I cannot say I blame him—but I have no idea how to do even that much."

"A ship," Nynaeve said thoughtfully. "I had meant to simply ride east, but I must say I've worried about it. As nearly as I can make out, we would have to be almost off Toman Head before we were clear of Seanchan patrols completely, and then there's supposed to be fighting of some sort on Almoth Plain. I never thought of a ship. We have horses, and we do not have money for passage. How much does this man want?"

Min shrugged. "I never got that far. We don't have any money, either. I thought I could put off paying until after we sail. Afterwards . . . well, I don't think he'll put into any port where there are Seanchan. Wherever he threw us off, it would have to be better than here. The problem is convincing him to sail at all. He wants to, but they patrol off the harbor, too, and there is no way of telling if there's a *damane* on one of their ships until it's too late. 'Give me a *damane* of my own on my deck,' he says, 'and I will sail this instant.' Then he starts talking about drafts and shoals and lee shores. I don't understand any of that, but as long as I smile and nod every now and then, he keeps talking, and I think if I can keep him talking long enough, he'll talk himself into sailing." She drew a shuddering breath; her eyes started stinging again. "Only, I don't think there's time to let him talk himself into it anymore. Nynaeve, they're going to send Egwene back to Seanchan, and soon."

Elayne gasped. "But, why?"

"She is able to find ore," Min said miserably. "A few days, she says, and I don't know if a few days is enough for this man to convince himself to sail. Even if it is, how do we take that Shadow-spawned collar off her? How do we get her out of the house?"

"I wish Rand were here." Elayne sighed, and when they both looked at her, she blushed and quickly added, "Well, he does have a sword. I wish we had somebody with a sword. Ten of them. A hundred."

"It isn't swords or brawn we need now," Nynaeve said, "but brains. Men usually think with the hair on their chests." She touched her chest absently, as if feeling something through her coat. "Most of them do."

"We would need an army," Min said. "A large army. The Seanchan were outnumbered when they faced the Taraboners, and the Domani, and they won every battle easily, from what I hear." She hurriedly pulled Nynaeve and Elayne to the opposite side of the street as a *damane* and *sul'dam* climbed past them on the other side. She was relieved there was no need for urging; the other two watched the linked women go as warily as she. "Since we don't have an army, the three of us will have to do it. I hope one of you can think of something I haven't; I've wracked my brains, and I always stumble when it comes to the *a'dam,* the leash and collar. *Sul'dam* don't like anyone watching too closely when they open them. I think I can get you inside, if that will help. One of you, anyway. They think of me as a servant, but servants may have visitors, as long as they keep to the servants' quarters."

Nynaeve wore a thoughtful frown, but her face cleared almost immediately, taking on a purposeful look. "Don't you worry, Min. I have a few ideas. I have not spent my time here idly. You take me to this man. If he is any harder to handle than the Village Council with their backs up, I will eat this coat."

Elayne nodded, grinning, and Min felt the first real hope she had had since arriving in Falme. For an instant Min found herself reading the auras of the other two women. There was danger, but that was to be expected—and new things, too, among the images she had seen before; it was like that, sometimes. A man's ring of heavy gold floated above Nynaeve's head, and above Elayne's, a red-hot iron and an axe. They meant trouble, she was sure, but it seemed distant, somewhere in the future. Only for a moment did the reading last, and then all she saw was Elayne and Nynaeve, watching her expectantly.

"It's down near the harbor," she said.

The sloping street became more crowded the further down they went. Street peddlers rubbed elbows with merchants who had brought wagons in from the inland villages and would not go out again until winter had come and gone, hawkers with their trays called to the passersby, Falmen in embroidered cloaks brushed past farm families in heavy fleece coats. Many people had fled here from villages further from the coast. Min saw no point to it—they had leaped from the possibility of a visit from the Seanchan to the certainty of Seanchan all around them—but she had heard what the Seanchan did when they first came to a village, and she could not blame the villagers too much for fearing another appearance. Everyone bowed when Seanchan walked past or a curtained palanquin was carried by up the steep street.

Min was glad to see Nynaeve and Elayne knew about the bowing. Barechested bearers paid no more mind to the people who bent themselves than did arrogant, armored soldiers, but failure to bow would surely catch their eyes.

They talked a little as they moved down the street, and she was surprised at first to learn they had been in the town only a few days less than Egwene and herself. After a moment, though, she decided it was no wonder they had not met earlier, not with the crowds in the streets. She had been reluctant to spend time further from Egwene than was necessary; there was always the fear that she would go for her allowed visit and find Egwene gone. *And now she will be. Unless Nynaeve can think of something.*

The smell of salt and pitch grew heavy in the air, and gulls cried, wheeling overhead. Sailors appeared in the throng, many still barefoot despite the cold.

The inn had been hastily renamed The Three Plum Blossoms, but part of the word "Watcher" still showed through the slapdash paint work on the sign. Despite the crowds outside, the common room was little more than half full; prices were too high for many people to afford time sitting over ale. Roaring fires on hearths at either end of the room warmed it, and the fat innkeeper was in his shirtsleeves. He eyed the three women, frowning, and Min thought it was her Seanchan dress that stopped him from telling them to leave. Nynaeve and Elayne, in their farm women's coats, certainly did not look as if they had money to spend.

The man she was looking for was alone at a table in a corner, in his accustomed place, muttering into his wine. "Do you have time to talk, Captain Domon?" she said.

He looked up, brushing a hand across his beard when he saw she was not alone. She still thought his bare upper lip looked odd with the beard. "So you do bring friends to drink up my coin, do you? Well, that Seanchan lord bought my cargo, so coin I have. Sit." Elayne jumped as he suddenly bellowed, "Innkeeper! Mulled wine here!"

"It's all right," Min told her, taking a place on the end of one of the benches at the table. "He only looks and sounds like a bear." Elayne sat down on the other end, looking doubtful.

"A bear, do I be?" Domon laughed. "Maybe I do. But what of you, girl? Have you given over thought of leaving? That dress do look Seanchan to me."

"Never!" Min said fiercely, but the appearance of a serving girl with the steaming, spiced wine made her fall silent.

Domon was just as wary. He waited until the girl had gone with his coins before saying, "Fortune prick me, girl, I mean no offense. Most people only want to go on with their lives, whether their lords be Seanchan or any other."

Nynaeve leaned her forearms on the table. "We also want to go on with our lives, Captain, but without any Seanchan. I understand you intend to sail soon."

"I would sail today, if I could," Domon said glumly. "Every two or three days that Turak do send for me to tell him tales of the old things I have seen. Do I look a gleeman to you? I did think I could spin a tale or two and be on my way, but now I think when I no entertain him any longer, it be an even wager whether he do let me go or have my head cut off. The man do look soft, but he be as hard as iron, and as coldhearted."

"Can your ship avoid the Seanchan?" Nynaeve asked.

"Fortune prick me, could I make it out of the harbor without a *damane* rips *Spray* to splinters, I can. If I do no let a Seanchan ship with a *damane* come too close once I do make the sea. There be shoal waters all along this coast, and *Spray* do have a shallow draft. I can take her into waters those lumbering Seanchan hulks can no risk. They must be wary of the winds close inshore this time of year, and once I do have *Spray*—"

Nynaeve cut him off. "Then we will take passage with you, Captain. There will be four of us, and I will expect you to be ready to sail as soon as we are aboard."

Domon scrubbed a finger across his upper lip and peered into his wine. "Well, as to that, there still do be the matter of getting out of the harbor, you see. These *damane*—"

"What if I tell you you will sail with something better than *damane?*" Nynaeve said softly. Min's eyes widened as she realized what Nynaeve intended.

Almost under her breath, Elayne murmured, "And you tell me to be careful."

Domon had eyes only for Nynaeve, and they were wary eyes. "What do you mean?" he whispered.

Nynaeve opened her coat to fumble at the back of her neck, finally pulling out a leather cord that had been tucked inside her dress. Two gold rings hung on the cord. Min gasped when she saw one—it was the heavy man's ring she had seen when she read Nynaeve in the street—but she knew it was the other, slighter and made for a woman's slender finger, that made Domon's eyes bulge. A serpent biting its own tail.

"You know what this means," Nynaeve said, starting to slip the Serpent ring from the cord, but Domon closed his hand over it.

"Put it away." His eyes darted uneasily; no one was looking at them that Min could see, but he looked as if he thought everyone was staring. "That ring do be dangerous. If it be seen. . . ."

"As long as you know what it means," Nynaeve said with a calm that made Min envious. She pulled the cord from Domon's hand and retied it around her neck.

"I know," he said hoarsely. "I do know what it means. Maybe there do be a chance if you. . . . Four, you say? This girl who do like to listen to my tongue wag, she do be one of the four, I take it. And you, and. . . ." He frowned at Elayne. "Surely this child is no—no one like you."

Elayne straightened angrily, but Nynaeve put a hand on her arm and smiled soothingly at Domon. "She travels with me, Captain. You might be surprised by what we can do even before we earn the right to a ring. When we sail, you will have three on your ship who can fight *damane* if need be."

"Three," he breathed. "There do be a chance. Maybe. . . ." His face brightened for a moment, but as he looked at them, it grew serious again. "I should take you to *Spray* right now and cast off, but Fortune prick me if

I can no tell you what you face here if you stay, and maybe even if you go with me. Listen to me, and mark what I do say." He took another cautious look around, and still lowered his voice and chose his words carefully. "I did see a—a woman who wore a ring like that taken by the Seanchan. A pretty, slender little woman she was, with a big War—a big man with her who did look as if he did know how to use his sword. One of them must have been careless, for the Seanchan did have an ambush laid for them. The big man put six, seven soldiers on the ground before he did die himself. The—the woman. . . . Six *damane* they did put around her, stepping out of the alleys of a sudden. I did think she would . . . do something—you know what I mean—but. . . . I know nothing of these things. One moment she did look as if she would destroy them all, then a look of horror did come on her face, and she did scream."

"They cut her off from the True Source." Elayne's face was white.

"No matter," Nynaeve said calmly. "We will not allow the same to be done to us."

"Aye, mayhap it will be as you say. But I will remember it until I die. Ryma, help me. That is what she did scream. And one of the *damane* did fall down crying, and they did put one of those collars on the neck of the . . . woman, and I . . . I did run." He shrugged, and rubbed his nose, and peered into his wine. "I have seen three women taken, and I have no stomach for it. I would leave my aged grandmother standing on the dock to sail from here, but I did have to tell you."

"Egwene said they have two prisoners," Min said slowly. "Ryma, a Yellow, and she didn't know who the other is." Nynaeve gave her a sharp look, and she fell silent, blushing. From the look on Domon's face, it had not furthered their cause any to tell him the Seanchan held two Aes Sedai, not just one.

Yet abruptly he stared at Nynaeve and took a long gulp of wine. "Do that be why you are here? To free . . . those two? You did say there would be three of you."

"You know what you need to know," Nynaeve told him briskly. "You must be ready to sail on the instant anytime in the next two or three days. Will you do it, or will you remain here to see if they will cut off your head after all? There are other ships, Captain, and I mean to have passage assured on one of them today."

Min held her breath; under the table, her fingers were knotted.

Finally, Domon nodded. "I will be ready."

When they returned to the street, Min was surprised to see Nynaeve sag against the front of the inn as soon as the door closed. "Are you ill, Nynaeve?" she asked anxiously.

Nynaeve drew a long breath and stood up straight, tugging at her coat. "With some people," she said, "you have to be certain. If you show them one glimmer of doubt, they'll sweep you off in some direction you don't want to go. Light, but I was afraid he was going to say no. Come, we have plans yet to make. There are still one or two small problems to work out."

"I hope you don't mind fish, Min," Elayne said.

*One or two small problems?* Min thought as she followed them. She hoped very much that Nynaeve was not just being certain again.

# CHAPTER 44

## *Five Will Ride Forth*

Perrin eyed the villagers warily, self-consciously hitching at a too-short cloak, embroidered on the chest and with some holes in it not even patched, but none of them gave him a second glance despite his strange mix of clothes and the axe on his hip. Hurin had a coat with blue spirals across the chest under his cloak, and Mat wore a pair of baggy trousers that made bunches where they were stuffed into his boots. That had been all they had been able to find that would fit back in the abandoned village. Perrin wondered if this one would be abandoned soon. Half the stone houses were empty, and in front of the inn, up the dirt street from them, three ox carts, loaded too heavily in great mounds and everything covered with roped canvas, stood with families gathered around them.

As he watched them, huddling together and saying their goodbyes to those who were staying, at least for the time being, Perrin decided it was not lack of interest in strangers on the villagers' part; they were carefully avoiding looking at him and the others. These people had learned not to show curiosity about strangers, even strangers who were obviously not Seanchan. Strangers might be dangerous these days on Toman Head. They had encountered the same studious indifference in other villages. There were more towns here within a few leagues of the coast, every one holding itself independent. At any rate, they had until the Seanchan came.

"I say it's time to go get the horses," Mat said, "before they decide to start asking questions. There has to be a first time for it."

Hurin was staring at a big, blackened circle of ground that marred the brown grass of the village green. It had a weathered look, but no one had done anything to erase it. "Maybe six or eight months ago," he muttered, "and it still stinks. The whole Village Council and their families. Why would they do a thing like that?"

"Who knows why they do anything?" Mat muttered. "Seanchan don't seem to need a reason for killing people. None I can figure out, anyway."

Perrin tried not to look at the charred patch. "Hurin, are you sure about Fain? Hurin?" It had been hard to make the sniffer look at anything else since they entered the village. "Hurin!"

"What? Oh. Fain. Yes." Hurin's nostrils flared, and right away he wrinkled his nose. "There's no mistaking that, even old as it is. Makes a Myrddraal smell like roses. He passed through here all right, but I think he was alone. No Trollocs, anyway, and if he had any Darkfriends with him, they hadn't been up to much lately."

There was some sort of agitation up by the inn, people shouting and pointing. Not at Perrin and the other two, but at something Perrin could not see in the low hills east of the village.

"Can we get the horses now?" Mat said. "That could be Seanchan."

Perrin nodded, and they broke into a run for where they had tied their horses behind an abandoned house. As Mat and Hurin disappeared around the corner of the house, Perrin looked back toward the inn and stopped in astonishment. The Children of the Light were riding into town, a long column of them.

He leaped after the others. "Whitecloaks!"

They wasted only an instant staring at him in disbelief before they were scrambling into their saddles. Keeping houses between them and the main street of the village, the three galloped out of the village westward, watching over their shoulders for pursuit. Ingtar had told them to avoid anything that might slow them down, and Whitecloaks asking questions would certainly do that, even if they could manage answers that satisfied. Perrin kept an even closer watch than the other two; he had his own reasons for not wanting to meet Whitecloaks. *The axe in my hands. Light, what I wouldn't give to change that.*

The lightly wooded hills soon hid the village, and Perrin began to think maybe there was nothing chasing them after all. He reined in and motioned the other two to stop. When they did, eyeing him questioningly, he listened. His ears were sharper than they once had been, but he heard no sounds of hoofbeats.

Reluctantly, he reached out with his mind in search of wolves. Almost immediately he found them, a small pack lying up for the day in the hills above the village they had just left. There were moments of astonishment so strong he almost thought it was his own; these wolves had heard rumors, but they had not really believed there were two-legs who could talk to their kind. He sweated through the minutes it took to get past introducing himself—he gave the image of Young Bull in spite of himself, and added his own smell, according to the custom among wolves; wolves were great ones for formalities on first meetings—but finally he managed to get his question through. They really had no interest in any two-legs who could not talk to them, but at last they glided down to take a look, unseen by the dull eyes of the two-legs.

After a time, images came back to him, what the wolves saw. White-cloaked men on horses crowding around the village, riding among the houses, riding around it, but none leaving. Especially not westward. The wolves said all they smelled moving west was himself and two other two-legs with three of the hard-footed tall ones.

Perrin let go the contact with the wolves gratefully. He was aware of Hurin and Mat looking at him.

"They aren't following," he said.

"How can you be sure?" Mat demanded.

"I am!" he snapped, then more softly, "I just am."

Mat opened his mouth and closed it again, and finally said, "Well, if they aren't coming after us, I say we go back to Ingtar and get on Fain's trail. That dagger isn't coming any closer just standing here."

"We can't pick it up again this close to that village," Hurin said. "Not without risking running into Whitecloaks. I don't think Lord Ingtar would appreciate that, and not Verin Sedai, neither."

Perrin nodded. "We'll follow it on a few miles, anyway. But keep a close lookout. We can't be too far from Falme, now. It won't do any good to avoid the Whitecloaks and ride right into a Seanchan patrol."

As they started out again, he could not help wondering what White-cloaks were doing there.


Geofram Bornhald peered down the village street, sitting his saddle while the legion spread through the small town and surrounded it. There had been something about the heavy-shouldered man who had dashed out of sight, something that tickled his memory. *Yes, of course. The lad who claimed to be a blacksmith. What was his name?*

Byar pulled up in front of him, hand on heart. "The village is secured, my Lord Captain."

Villagers in heavy sheepskin coats milled uneasily as white-cloaked soldiers herded them together near the overloaded carts in front of the inn. Crying children clung to their mothers' skirts, but no one looked defiant. Dull eyes stared out of the adult faces, waiting passively for whatever was going to happen. For that much, Bornhald was grateful. He had no real desire to make an example of any of these people, and no wish at all to waste time.

Dismounting, he tossed his reins to one of the Children. "See that the men are fed, Byar. Put the prisoners in the inn with as much food and water as they can carry, then nail all the doors and shutters closed. Make them think I am leaving some men to stand guard, yes?"

Byar touched his heart again and wheeled his horse to shout orders. The herding began anew, into the flat-roofed inn, while other Children ransacked houses searching for hammers and nails.

Watching the sullen faces that filed past him, Bornhald thought it should be two or three days before any of them found enough courage to break out of the inn and find there were no guards. Two or three days was all he needed, but he did not intend to risk alerting the Seanchan to his presence now.

Leaving enough men behind to make the Questioners believe his entire legion was still scattered across Almoth Plain, he had brought more than a thousand of the Children nearly the length of Toman Head without giving alarm, so far as he knew. Three skirmishes with Seanchan patrols had ended quickly. The Seanchan had grown used to facing already defeated rabble; the Children of the Light had been a deadly surprise. Yet the Seanchan knew how to fight like the Dark One's hordes, and he could not help remembering the one skirmish that had cost him better than fifty men. He was still not sure which of the two arrow-riddled women he had stared at afterwards had been the Aes Sedai.

"Byar!" One of Bornhald's men handed him water in a pottery cup from one of the carts; it was icy in his throat.

The gaunt-faced man swung down from his saddle. "Yes, my Lord Captain?"

"When I engage the enemy, Byar," Bornhald said slowly, "you will not take part. You will watch from a distance, and you will carry word to my son of what happens."

"But my Lord Captain——!"

"That is my order, Child Byar!" he snapped. "You will obey, yes?"

Byar's back stiffened, and he stared straight ahead. "As you command, my Lord Captain."

Bornhald studied him for a moment. The man would do as he was told, but it would be better to give him another reason than letting Dain know how his father had died. It was not as if he did not have knowledge that was urgently needed in Amador. Since that skirmish with the Aes Sedai—— *Was it one of them, or both? Thirty Seanchan soldiers, good fighters, and two women cost me twice the casualties they did.*——since then, he no longer expected to live to leave Toman Head. In the small chance the Seanchan did not see to it, very likely the Questioners would.

"When you have found my son——he should be with Lord Captain Eamon Valda near Tar Valon——and told him, you will ride to Amador, and report to the Lord Captain Commander. To Pedron Niall personally, Child Byar. You will tell him what we have learned of the Seanchan; I will write it out for you. Be sure he understands that we can no longer count on the Tar Valon witches being content with manipulating events from the shadows. If they fight openly for the Seanchan, we will surely face them elsewhere." He hesitated. That last was the most important of all. They had to know under the Dome of Truth that for all their vaunted oaths, Aes Sedai would march into battle. It gave him a sinking feeling, a world where Aes Sedai wielded the Power in battle; he was not sure that he would regret leaving it. But there was one more message he wanted carried to Amador. "And, Byar . . . tell Pedron Niall how we were used by the Questioners."

"As you command, my Lord Captain," Byar said, but Bornhald sighed at the expression on his face. The man did not understand. To Byar, orders were to be obeyed whether they came from the Lord Captain or the Questioners, whatever they were.

"I will write that out for you to hand to Pedron Niall as well," he said. He was not sure how much good it would do in any case. A thought came to him, and he frowned at the inn, where some of his men were loudly hammering nails through shutters and doors. "Perrin," he muttered. "That was his name. Perrin, from the Two Rivers."

"The Darkfriend, my Lord Captain?"

"Perhaps, Byar." He was not entirely certain, himself, but surely a man who seemed to have wolves fight for him could be nothing else. Certainly, this Perrin had killed two of the Children. "I thought I saw him when we rode in, but I do not remember anyone among the prisoners who looked like a blacksmith."

"Their blacksmith left a month ago, my Lord Captain. Some of them were complaining that they'd have been gone before we came if they had not had to mend their cartwheels themselves. Do you believe it was the man Perrin, my Lord Captain?"

"Whoever it was, he is not accounted for, no? And he may carry word of us to the Seanchan."

"A Darkfriend would surely do so, my Lord Captain."

Bornhald gulped the last of the water and tossed the cup aside. "There will be no meal for the men here, Byar. I will not let these Seanchan catch me napping, whether it is Perrin of the Two Rivers or someone else who warns them. Mount the legion, Child Byar!"

Far above their heads, a huge, winged shape circled, unnoticed.

In the clearing amid the hilltop thicket where they had made their camp, Rand worked the forms with his sword. He wanted to keep from thinking. He had had his chances to search with Hurin for Fain's trail; they all had, in twos and threes so they would not attract attention, and they had all found nothing so far. Now they waited for Mat and Perrin to come back with the sniffer; they should have been back hours ago.

Loial was reading, of course, and there was no telling if his ear-twitching was over his book or the scouting party's lateness, but Uno and most of the Shienaran soldiers sat tensely, oiling their swords, or kept watch through the trees as if they expected Seanchan to appear any moment. Only Verin appeared unconcerned. The Aes Sedai sat on a log beside their small fire, murmuring to herself and writing in the dirt with a long stick; every so often she would shake her head and scrub it all out with her foot and start over again. All the horses were saddled and ready to go, the Shienarans' animals each tied to a lance driven into the ground.

"Heron Wading in the Rushes," Ingtar said. He sat with his back against a tree, sliding a sharpening stone along his sword and watching Rand. "You should not be bothering with that one. It leaves you completely open."

For an instant Rand balanced on the ball of one foot, sword held reversed in both hands over his head, then shifted smoothly to the other foot. "Lan says it's good for developing balance." It was not easy keeping his balance. In the void it often seemed he could maintain his equilibrium atop a rolling boulder, but he did not dare assume the void. He wanted to too much to trust himself.

"What you practice too often, you use without thinking. You will put your sword in the other man with that, if you're quick, but not before he has his through your ribs. You are practically inviting him. I don't think I could see a man face me so open and not put my sword in him, even knowing he might strike home at me if I did."

"It's only for balance, Ingtar." Rand wavered on one foot, and had to put the other down to keep from falling. He slammed the blade into its scabbard and picked up the gray cloak that had been his disguise. It was moth-eaten, and ragged around the bottom, but lined with thick fleece, and the wind was picking up, cold and out of the west. "I wish they'd come back."

As if his wish had been a signal, Uno spoke up with quiet urgency. "Bloody horsemen coming, my Lord." Scabbards rattled as men who did not already have their blades out bared them. Some leaped into their saddles, snatching up lances.

The tension faded as Hurin led the others into the clearing at a trot, and came again as he spoke. "We found the trail, Lord Ingtar."

"We followed it almost to Falme," Mat said as he dismounted. A flush in his pale cheeks seemed a mocking of health; the skin was tight over his skull. The Shienarans gathered around, as excited as he was. "It's just Fain, but there isn't anywhere else he could be going. He must have the dagger."

"We found Whitecloaks, too," Perrin said, swinging down from his saddle. "Hundreds of them."

"Whitecloaks?" Ingtar exclaimed, frowning. "Here? Well, if they do not trouble us, we will not trouble them. Perhaps if the Seanchan are occupied with them, it will help us reach the Horn." His eyes fell on Verin, still seated by the fire. "I suppose you will tell me I should have listened to you, Aes Sedai. The man did go to Falme."

"The Wheel weaves as the Wheel wills," Verin said placidly. "With *ta'veren*, what happens is what was meant to happen. It may be the Pattern demanded these extra days. The Pattern puts everything in its place precisely, and when we try to alter it, especially if *ta'veren* are involved, the weaving changes to put us back into the Pattern as we were meant to be." There was an uneasy silence that she did not seem to notice; she sketched on idly with the stick. "Now, however, I think perhaps we should make plans. The Pattern has brought us to Falme at last. The Horn of Valere has been taken to Falme."

Ingtar squatted across the fire from her. "When enough people say the same thing, I tend to believe it, and the local people say the Seanchan do not seem to care who comes or goes in Falme. I will take Hurin and a few others into the town. Once he follows Fain's trail to the Horn . . . well, then we shall see what we shall see."

With her foot, Verin scrubbed out a wheel she had drawn in the dirt. In its place she drew two short lines that touched at one end. "Ingtar and

Hurin. And Mat, as he can sense the dagger if he comes close enough. You do want to go, don't you, Mat?"

Mat appeared torn, but he gave a jerky nod. "I have to, don't I? I have to find that dagger."

A third line made a bird track. Verin looked sideways at Rand.

"I'll go," he said. "That is why I came." An odd light appeared in the Aes Sedai's eyes, a knowing glimmer that made him uneasy. "To help Mat find the dagger," he said sharply, "and Ingtar find the Horn." *And Fain,* he added to himself. *I have to find Fain if it isn't already too late.*

Verin scratched a fourth line, turning the bird track to a lopsided star. "And who else?" she said softly. She held the stick poised.

"Me," Perrin said, a hair before Loial chimed in with, "I think I would like to go, too," and Uno and the other Shienarans all began clamoring to join.

"Perrin spoke first," Verin said, as if that settled it. She added a fifth line and drew a circle around all five. The hair on Rand's neck stirred; it was the same wheel she had rubbed out in the first place. "Five ride forth," she murmured.

"I really would like to see Falme," Loial said. "I've never seen the Aryth Ocean. Besides, I can carry the chest, if the Horn is still in it."

"You'd better include me at least, my Lord," Uno said. "You and Lord Rand will need another sword at your backs if those bloody Seanchan try to stop you." The rest of the soldiers rumbled the same sentiment.

"Do not be silly," Verin said sharply. Her stare silenced them all. "All of you cannot go. No matter how uncaring the Seanchan are about strangers, they will surely take notice of twenty soldiers, and you look like nothing else even without armor. And one or two of you will make no difference. Five is few enough to enter without attracting attention, and it is fitting that three of them should be the three *ta'veren* among us. No, Loial, you must stay behind, too. There are no Ogier on Toman Head. You would attract as many eyes as all the rest put together."

"What about you?" Rand asked.

Verin shook her head. "You forget the *damane.*" Her mouth twisted around the word in distaste. "The only way I could help you would be if I channeled the Power, and that would be no help at all if I brought those down on you. Even if they were not close enough to see, one might well feel a woman—or a man, for that matter—channeling, if care was not taken to keep the Power channeled small." She did not look at Rand; to him, she seemed ostentatious in not doing so, and Mat and Perrin were suddenly intent on their own feet.

"A man," Ingtar snorted. "Verin Sedai, why add problems? We have enough already without supposing men channeling. But it would be well if you were there. If we have need of you—"

"No, you five must go alone." Her foot scrubbed across the wheel drawn in the dirt, partially obliterating it. She studied each of them in turn, intent and frowning. "Five will ride forth."

For a moment it seemed that Ingtar would ask again, but meeting her level gaze, he shrugged and turned to Hurin. "How long to reach Falme?"

The sniffer scratched his head. "If we left now and rode through the night, we could be there by sunrise tomorrow morning."

"Then that is what we will do. I'll waste no more time. All of you saddle your horses. Uno, I want you to bring the others along behind us, but keep out of sight, and do not let anyone. . . ."

Rand peered at the sketched wheel as Ingtar went on with his instructions. It was a broken wheel, now, with only four spokes. For some reason that made him shiver. He realized Verin was watching him, dark eyes bright and intent like a bird's. It took an effort to pull his gaze away and begin getting his things together.

*You're letting fancies take you*, he told himself irritably. *She can't do anything if she isn't there.*

# CHAPTER
# 45

*Blademaster*

The rising sun pushed its crimson edge above the horizon and sent long shadows down the cobblestone streets of Falme toward the harbor. A sea breeze bent the smoke of breakfast cook fires inland from the chimneys. Only the early risers were already out of doors, their breath making steam in the morning cold. Compared to the crowds that would fill the streets in another hour, the town seemed nearly empty.

Sitting on an upended barrel in front of a still-closed ironmonger's shop, Nynaeve warmed her hands under her arms and surveyed her army. Min sat on a doorstep across the way, swathed in her Seanchan cloak and eating a wrinkled plum, and Elayne in her fleece coat huddled at the edge of an alley just down the street from her. A large sack, pilfered from the docks, lay neatly folded beside Min. *My army,* Nynaeve thought grimly. *But there isn't anybody else.*

She caught sight of a *sul'dam* and a *damane* climbing the street, a yellow-haired woman wearing the bracelet and a dark woman the collar, both yawning sleepily. The few Falmen sharing the street with them averted their eyes and gave them a wide berth. As far as she could see down toward the harbor, there was not another Seanchan. She did not turn her head the other way. Instead, she stretched and shrugged as if working cold shoulders before settling back as she had been.

Min tossed her half-eaten plum aside, glanced casually up the street, and leaned back on the doorpost. The way was clear there, too, or she would have put her hands on her knees. Min had started rubbing her hands nervously, and Nynaeve realized that Elayne was now bouncing eagerly on her toes.

*If they give us away, I'll thump both their heads.* But she knew if they were discovered, it would be the Seanchan who would say what happened to all three of them. She was all too aware that she had no real notion of whether what she planned would work or not. It could easily be her own failure that would give them away. Once again she resolved that if anything went wrong, she would somehow pull attention to herself while Min and Elayne escaped. She had told them to run if anything went wrong, and let them think she would run, too. What she would do then, she did not know. *Except I won't let them take me alive. Please, Light, not that.*

*Sul'dam* and *damane* came up the street until they were bracketed by the three waiting women. A dozen Falmen walked wide of the linked pair.

Nynaeve gathered all of her anger. Leashed Ones and Leash Holders. They had put their filthy collar on Egwene's neck, and they would put it on hers, and Elayne's, if they could. She had made Min tell her how *sul'dam* enforced their will. She was sure Min had kept some back, the worst, but what she told was enough to heat Nynaeve to white-hot fury. In an instant a white blossom on a black, thorny branch had opened to light, to *saidar,* and the One Power filled her. She knew there was a glow around her, for those who could see it. The pale-skinned *sul'dam* gave a start, and the dark *damane*'s mouth fell open, but Nynaeve gave them no chance. It was only a trickle of the Power that she channeled, but she cracked it, a whip snapping a dust mote out of the air.

The silver collar sprang open and clattered to the cobblestones. Nynaeve heaved a sigh of relief even as she leaped to her feet.

The *sul'dam* stared at the fallen collar as if at a poisonous snake. The *damane* put a shaking hand to her throat, but before the woman in the lightning-marked dress had time to move, the *damane* turned and punched her in the face; the *sul'dam*'s knees buckled, and she almost fell.

"Good for you!" Elayne shouted. She was already running forward, too, and so was Min.

Before any of them reached the two women, the *damane* took one startled look around, then ran as hard as she could.

"We won't hurt you!" Elayne called after her. "We are friends!"

"Be quiet!" Nynaeve hissed. She produced a handful of rags from her pocket and ruthlessly stuffed them into the gaping mouth of the still-staggering *sul'dam*. Min hastily shook out the sack in a cloud of dust and plunged it over the *sul'dam*'s head, shrouding the woman to the waist. "We are already attracting too much attention."

It was true, and yet not entirely true. The four of them stood in a rapidly emptying street, but the people who had decided to be elsewhere were avoiding looking at them. Nynaeve had been counting on that—people doing their best to ignore anything that had to do with Seanchan—to gain them a few moments. They would talk eventually, but in whispers; it might take hours for the Seanchan to learn anything had happened.

The hooded woman began to struggle, making rag-muffled shouts from the sack, but Nynaeve and Min threw their arms around her and wrestled her toward a nearby alley. The leash and collar trailed across the cobblestones behind them, clinking.

"Pick it up," Nynaeve snapped at Elayne. "It won't bite you!"

Elayne took a deep breath, then gathered the silver metal gingerly, as if she feared it very well might. Nynaeve felt some sympathy, but not much; everything rested on each of them doing as they had planned.

The *sul'dam* kicked and tried to throw herself free, but between them, Nynaeve and Min forced her along, down the alley into another, slightly wider passage behind houses, to yet another alley and at last into a rough wooden shed that had apparently once housed two horses, by the stalls. Few could afford to keep horses since the Seanchan came, and in a day of Nynaeve's watching, no one had gone near it. The interior had a musty dustiness that spoke of abandonment. As soon as they were inside, Elayne dropped the silver leash and wiped her hands on some straw.

Nynaeve channeled another trickle, and the bracelet fell to the dirt floor. The *sul'dam* squalled and hurled herself about.

"Ready?" Nynaeve asked. The other two nodded, and they yanked the sacking off their prisoner.

The *sul'dam* wheezed, blue eyes teary from dust, but her red face was red as much from anger as from the sack. She darted for the door, but they caught her in the first step. She was not weak, yet they were three, and when they were done the *sul'dam* was stripped to her shift and lying in one of the stalls, bound hand and foot with stout cord, with another piece of cord to keep her from forcing the gag out.

Soothing a puffy lip, Min eyed the lightning-paneled dress and soft boots they had laid out. "It might fit you, Nynaeve. It won't fit Elayne or me." Elayne was picking straw out of her hair.

"I can see that. You were never a choice anyway, not really. They know you too well." Nynaeve hurriedly removed her own clothes. She tossed them aside and donned the *sul'dam*'s dress. Min helped with the buttons.

Nynaeve wiggled her toes in the boots; they were a little tight. The dress was tight, too, across the bosom, and loose elsewhere. The hem hung almost to the ground, lower than *sul'dam* wore them, but the fit would have been even worse on any of the others. Snatching up the bracelet, she took a deep breath and closed it around her left wrist. The ends merged, and it seemed solid. It did not feel like anything except a bracelet. She had been afraid that it would.

"Get the dress, Elayne." They had dyed a pair of dresses—one of hers and one of Elayne's—to the gray *damane* were, or as close as they could manage, and hidden them here. Elayne did not move except to stare at the open collar and lick her lips. "Elayne, you have to wear it. Too many of them have seen Min for her to do it. I would have worn it, if this dress had fit you instead." She thought she would have gone mad if she had had to wear the collar; that was why she could not make her voice sharp with Elayne now.

"I know." Elayne sighed. "I just wish I knew more of what it does to you." She drew her red-gold hair out of the way. "Min, help me, please." Min began undoing the buttons down the back of her dress.

Nynaeve managed to pick up the silver collar without flinching. "There is one way to find out." With only a moment of hesitation, she bent and snapped it around the neck of the *sul'dam. She deserves it if anyone does,* she told herself firmly. "She might be able to tell us something useful, any-way." The blue-eyed woman glanced at the leash trailing from her neck to Nynaeve's wrist, then glared up at her contemptuously.

"It doesn't work that way," Min said, but Nynaeve barely heard.

She was . . . aware . . . of the other woman, aware of what she was feeling, cord digging into her ankles and into her wrists behind her back, the rank fish taste of the rags in her mouth, straw pricking her through the thin cloth of her shift. It was not as if she, Nynaeve, felt these things, but in her head was a lump of sensations that she knew belonged to the *sul'dam.*

She swallowed, trying to ignore them—they would not go away—and addressed the bound woman. "I won't hurt you if you answer my questions truthfully. We aren't Seanchan. But if you lie to me. . . ." She lifted the leash threateningly.

The woman's shoulders shook, and her mouth curled around the gag in a sneer. It took Nynaeve a moment to realize the *sul'dam* was laughing.

Her mouth tightened, but then a thought came to her. That bundle of sensation inside her head seemed to be everything physical that the other woman felt. Experimentally, she tried adding to it.

Eyes suddenly bulging out of her head, the *sul'dam* gave a cry that the gag only partially stopped. Fanning her hands behind her as if trying to ward off something, she humped through the straw in a vain effort to escape.

Nynaeve gaped, and hastily rid herself of the extra feelings she had added. The *sul'dam* sagged, weeping.

"What. . . . What did you . . . do to her?" Elayne asked faintly. Min only stared, her mouth hanging open.

Nynaeve answered gruffly. "The same thing Sheriam did to you when you threw a cup at Marith." *Light, but this is a filthy thing.*

Elayne gulped loudly. "Oh."

"But an *a'dam* isn't supposed to work that way," Min said. "They always claimed it won't work on any woman who cannot channel."

"I do not care how it is supposed to work, so long as it does." Nynaeve seized the silver metal leash right where it joined the collar, and pulled the woman up enough to look her in the eyes. Frightened eyes, she saw. "You listen to me, and listen well. I want answers, and if I don't get them, I'll make you think I have had the hide off you." Stark terror rolled across the woman's face, and Nynaeve's stomach heaved as she suddenly realized the *sul'dam* had taken her literally. *If she thinks I can, it's because she knows. That is what these leashes are for.* She took firm hold of herself to stop from clawing the bracelet off her wrist. Instead, she hardened her face. "Are you ready to answer me? Or do you need more convincing?"

The frantic head-shaking was answer enough. When Nynaeve removed the gag, the woman only paused to swallow once before babbling, "I will not report you. I swear it. Only take this from my neck. I have gold. Take it. I swear, I will never tell anyone."

"Be quiet," Nynaeve snapped, and the woman shut her mouth immediately. "What is your name?"

"Seta. Please. I will answer you, but please take—it—off! If anyone sees it on me. . . ." Seta's eyes rolled down to stare at the leash, then squeezed shut. "Please?" she whispered.

Nynaeve realized something. She could never make Elayne wear that collar.

"Best we get on with it," Elayne said firmly. She was down to her shift, too, now. "Give me a moment to put this other dress on, and—"

"Put your own clothes back on," Nynaeve said.

"Someone has to pretend to be a *damane,*" Elayne said, "or we will never reach Egwene. That dress fits you, and it cannot be Min. That leaves me."

"I said put your clothes on. We have somebody to be our Leashed One." Nynaeve tugged at the leash that held Seta, and the *sul'dam* gasped.

"No! No, please! If anyone sees me—" She cut off at Nynaeve's cold stare.

"As far as I am concerned, you are worse than a murderer, worse than a Darkfriend. I can't think of anything worse than you. The fact that I have to wear this thing on my wrist, to be the same as you for even an hour, sickens me. So if you think there is anything I'll balk at doing to you, think again. You don't want to be seen? Good. Neither do we. No one really looks at a *damane,* though. As long as you keep your head down the way a Leashed One is supposed to, no one will even notice you. But you had better do the best you can to make sure the rest of us aren't noticed, either. If we are, you surely will be seen, and if that is not enough to hold you, I promise you I'll make you curse the first kiss your mother ever gave your father. Do we understand each other?"

"Yes," Seta said faintly. "I swear it."

Nynaeve had to remove the bracelet in order for them to slide Elayne's gray-dyed dress down the leash and over Seta's head. It did not fit the woman well, being loose at the bosom and tight across the hips, but Nynaeve's would have been as bad, and too short besides. Nynaeve hoped people really did not look at *damane.* She put the bracelet back on reluctantly.

Elayne gathered up Nynaeve's clothes, wrapped the other dyed dress around them, and made a bundle, a bundle for a woman in farm clothes to be carrying as she followed a *sul'dam* and a *damane.* "Gawyn will eat his heart out when he hears about this," she said, and laughed. It sounded forced.

Nynaeve looked at her closely, then at Min. It was time for the dangerous part. "Are you ready?"

Elayne's smile faded. "I am ready."

"Ready," Min said curtly.

"Where are you . . . we . . . going?" Seta said, quickly adding, "If I may ask?"

"Into the lions' den," Elayne told her.

"To dance with the Dark One," Min said.

Nynaeve sighed and shook her head. "What they are trying to say is, we are going where all the *damane* are kept, and we intend to free one of them."

Seta was still gaping in astonishment when they hustled her out of the shed.

Bayle Domon watched the rising sun from the deck of his ship. The docks were already beginning to bustle, though the streets leading up from the harbor stood largely empty. A gull perched on a piling stared at him; gulls had pitiless eyes.

"Are you sure about this, Captain?" Yarin asked. "If the Seanchan wonder what we're all doing aboard—"

"You just make certain there do be an axe near every mooring line," Domon said curtly. "And, Yarin? Do any man try to cut a line before those women are aboard, I will split his skull."

"What if they don't come, Captain? What if it's Seanchan soldiers instead?"

"Settle your bowels, man! If soldiers come, I will make a run for the harbor mouth, and the Light have mercy on us all. But until soldiers do come, I mean to wait for those women. Now go look as if you are no doing anything."

Domon turned back to peering up into the town, toward where the *damane* were held. His fingers drummed a nervous tattoo on the railing.

The breeze from the sea brought the smell of breakfast cook fires to Rand's nose, and tried to flap at his moth-eaten cloak, but he held it closed with one hand as Red neared the town. There had not been a coat to fit him in the clothes they had found, and he thought it best to keep the fine silver embroidery on his sleeves and the herons on his collar hidden. The Seanchan attitude toward conquered people carrying weapons might not extend to those with heron-mark swords, either.

The first shadows of morning stretched out ahead of him. He could just see Hurin riding in among the wagon yards and horse lots. Only one or two men moved among the lines of merchant wagons, and they wore the long aprons of wheelwrights or blacksmiths. Ingtar, the first in, was already out of sight. Perrin and Mat followed behind Rand at spaced intervals. He did not look back to check on them. There was not supposed to be anything to connect them; five men coming into Falme at an early hour, but not together.

The horse lots surrounded him, horses already crowding the fences, waiting to be fed. Hurin put his head out from between two stables, their doors still closed and barred, saw Rand and motioned to him before ducking back. Rand turned the bay stallion that way.

Hurin stood holding his horse by the reins. He had on one of the long vests instead of his coat, and despite the heavy cloak that hid his short sword and sword-breaker, he shivered with the cold. "Lord Ingtar's back there," he said, nodding down the narrow passage. "He says we'll leave the horses here and go the rest of the way on foot." As Rand dismounted, the sniffer added, "Fain went right down that street, Lord Rand. I can almost smell it from here."

Rand led Red down the way to where Ingtar had already tied his own horse behind the stable. The Shienaran did not look very much a lord in a dirty fleece coat with holes worn through the leather in several places, and his sword looked odd belted over it. His eyes had a feverish intensity.

Tying Red alongside Ingtar's stallion, Rand hesitated over his saddlebags. He had not been able to leave the banner behind. He did not think any of the soldiers would have gone into the bags, but he could not say the same for Verin, nor predict what she would do if she found the banner. Still, it made him uneasy to have it with him. He decided to leave the saddlebags tied behind his saddle.

Mat joined them, and a few moments later Hurin came with Perrin. Mat wore baggy trousers stuffed into the tops of his boots, and Perrin his too-short cloak. Rand thought they all looked like villainous beggars, but they had all passed largely unnoticed in the villages.

"Now," Ingtar said. "Let us see what we see."

They strolled out to the dirt street as if they had no particular destination in mind, talking among themselves, and ambled past the wagon yards onto sloping cobblestone streets. Rand was not sure what he himself said, much less anyone else. Ingtar's plan had been for them to look like any other group of men walking together, but there were all too few people out-of-doors. Five men made a crowd on those cold morning streets.

They walked in a bunch, but it was Hurin who led them, sniffing the air and turning up this street and down that. The rest turned when he did, as if that was what they had intended all along. "He's crisscrossed this town," Hurin muttered, grimacing. "His smell is everywhere, and it stinks so, it's hard to tell old from new. At least I know he's still here. Some of it cannot be older than a day or two, I'm sure. I am sure," he added less doubtfully.

A few more people began to appear, here a fruit peddler setting his wares on tables, there a fellow hurrying along with a big roll of parchments under his arm and a sketchboard slung across his back, a knife-sharpener oiling the shaft of his grinding wheel on its barrow. Two women walked by, headed the other way, one with downcast eyes and a silver collar around her neck, the other, in a dress worked with lightning bolts, holding a coiled silver leash.

Rand's breath caught; it was an effort not to look back at them.

"Was that. . . ?" Mat's eyes were open wide, staring out of the hollows of his eye sockets. "Was that a *damane?*"

"That is the way they were described," Ingtar said curtly. "Hurin, are we going to walk every street in this Shadow-cursed town?"

"He's been everywhere, Lord Ingtar," Hurin said. "His stench is everywhere." They had come into an area where the stone houses were three and four stories high, as big as inns.

They rounded a corner, and Rand was taken aback by the sight of a score of Seanchan soldiers standing guard in front of a big house on one side of the street—and by the sight of two women in lightning-marked dresses talking on the doorsteps of another across from it. A banner flapped in the wind over the house the soldiers protected; a golden hawk clutching lightning bolts. Nothing marked out the house where the women talked except themselves. The officer's armor was resplendent in red and black and gold, his helmet gilded and painted to look like a spider's head. Then Rand saw the two big, leathery-skinned shapes crouched among the soldiers and missed a step.

*Grolm.* There was no mistaking those wedge-shaped heads with their three eyes. *They can't be.* Perhaps he was really asleep, and this was all a nightmare. *Maybe we haven't even left for Falme, yet.*

The others stared at the beasts as they walked past the guarded house. "What in the name of the Light are they?" Mat asked.

Hurin's eyes seemed as big as his face. "Lord Rand, they're. . . . Those are. . . ."

"It doesn't matter," Rand said. After a moment, Hurin nodded.

"We are here for the Horn," Ingtar said, "not to stare at Seanchan monsters. Concentrate on finding Fain, Hurin."

The soldiers barely glanced at them. The street ran straight down to the round harbor. Rand could see ships anchored down there; tall, square-looking ships with high masts, small in that distance.

"He's been here a lot." Hurin scrubbed at his nose with the back of his hand. "The street stinks of layer on layer on layer of him. I think he might have been here as late as yesterday, Lord Ingtar. Maybe last night."

Mat suddenly clutched his coat with both hands. "It's in there," he whispered. He turned around and walked backwards, peering at the tall house with the banner. "The dagger is in there. I didn't even notice it before, because of those—those things, but I can feel it."

Perrin poked a finger in his ribs. "Well, stop that before they start wondering why you're goggling at them like a fool."

Rand glanced over his shoulder. The officer was looking after them.

Mat turned back around sullenly. "Are we just going to keep on walking? It's in there, I tell you."

"The Horn is what we are after," Ingtar growled. "I mean to find Fain and make him tell me where it is." He did not slow down.

Mat said nothing, but his entire face was a plea.

*I have to find Fain, too,* Rand thought. *I have to.* But when he looked at Mat's face, he said, "Ingtar, if the dagger is in that house, Fain likely is, too. I can't see him letting the dagger or the Horn, either one, far out of his sight."

Ingtar stopped. After a moment, he said, "It could be, but we will never know from out here."

"We could watch for him to come out," Rand said. "If he comes out at this time of the morning, then he spent the night there. And I'll wager where he sleeps is where the Horn is. If he does come out, we can be back to Verin by midday and have a plan made before nightfall."

"I do not mean to wait for Verin," Ingtar said, "and neither will I wait for night. I've waited too long already. I mean to have the Horn in my hands before the sun sets again."

"But we don't know, Ingtar."

"I know the dagger is in there," Mat said.

"And Hurin says Fain was here last night." Ingtar overrode Hurin's attempts to qualify that. "It is the first time you have been willing to say anything closer than a day or two. We are going to take back the Horn now. Now!"

"How?" Rand said. The officer was no longer watching them, but there were still at least twenty soldiers in front of the building. And a pair of *grolm. This is madness. There can't be* grolm *here.* Thinking it did not make the beasts disappear, though.

"There seem to be gardens behind all these houses," Ingtar said, looking around thoughtfully. "If one of those alleys runs by a garden wall. . . . Sometimes men are so busy guarding their front, they neglect their back. Come." He headed straight for the nearest narrow passage between two of the tall houses. Hurin and Mat trotted right after him.

Rand exchanged looks with Perrin—his curly-haired friend gave a resigned shrug—and they followed, too.

The alley was barely wider than their shoulders, but it ran between high garden walls until it crossed another alley big enough for a pushbarrow or small cart. That was cobblestoned, too, but only the backs of buildings looked down on it, shuttered windows and expanses of stone, and the high back walls of gardens overtopped by nearly leafless branches.

Ingtar led them along that alley until they were opposite the waving banner. Taking his steel-backed gauntlets from under his coat, he put them on and leaped up to catch the top of the wall, then pulled himself up enough to peek over. He reported in a low monotone. "Trees. Flower beds. Walks. There isn't a soul to be— Wait! A guard. One man. He isn't even wearing his helmet. Count to fifty, then follow me." He swung a boot to the top of the wall and rolled over inside, disappearing before Rand could say a word.

Mat began to count slowly. Rand held his breath. Perrin fingered his axe, and Hurin gripped the hilts of his weapons.

". . . fifty." Hurin scrambled up and over the wall before the word was well out of Mat's mouth. Perrin went right beside him.

Rand thought Mat might need some help—he looked so pale and drawn—but he gave no sign of it as he scrambled up. The stone wall provided plenty of handholds, and moments later Rand was crouched on the inside with Mat and Perrin and Hurin.

The garden was in the grip of deep autumn, flower beds empty except for a few evergreen shrubs, tree branches nearly bare. The wind that rippled the banner stirred dust across the flagstone walks. For a moment Rand could not find Ingtar. Then he saw the Shienaran, flat against the back wall of the house, motioning them on with sword in hand.

Rand ran in a crouch, more conscious of the windows blankly peering down from the house than of his friends running beside him. It was a relief to press himself against the house beside Ingtar.

Mat kept muttering to himself, "It's in there. I can feel it."

"Where is the guard?" Rand whispered.

"Dead," Ingtar said. "The man was overconfident. He never even tried to raise a cry. I hid his body under one of those bushes."

Rand stared at him. *The* Seanchan *was overconfident?* The only thing that kept him from going back right then was Mat's anguished murmurs.

"We are almost there." Ingtar sounded as if he were speaking to himself, too. "Almost there. Come."

Rand drew his sword as they started up the back steps. He was aware of Hurin unlimbering his short-bladed sword and notched sword-breaker, and Perrin reluctantly drawing his axe from the loop on his belt.

The hallway inside was narrow. A half-open door to their right smelled like a kitchen. Several people were moving about in that room; there was an indistinguishable sound of voices, and occasionally the soft clatter of a pot lid.

Ingtar motioned Mat to lead, and they crept by the door. Rand watched the narrowing opening until they were around the next corner.

A slender young woman with dark hair came out of a door ahead of them, carrying a tray with one cup. They all froze. She turned the other way without looking in their direction. Rand's eyes widened. Her long white robe was all but transparent. She vanished around another corner.

"Did you see that?" Mat said hoarsely. "You could see right through—"

Ingtar clapped a hand over Mat's mouth and whispered, "Keep your mind on why we are here. Now find it. Find the Horn for me."

Mat pointed to a narrow set of winding stairs. They climbed a flight, and he led them toward the front of the house. The furnishings in the hallways were sparse, and seemed all curves. Here and there a tapestry hung on a wall, or a folding screen stood against it, each painted with a few birds on branches, or a flower or two. A river flowed across one screen, but aside from rippling water and narrow strips of riverbank, the rest of it was blank.

All around them Rand could hear the sounds of people stirring, slippers scuffing on the floor, soft murmurs of speech. He did not see anyone, but he could imagine it all too well, someone stepping into the hall to see five slinking men with weapons in their hands, shouting an alarm. . . .

"In there," Mat whispered, pointing to a big pair of sliding doors ahead, carved handholds their only ornamentation. "At least, the dagger is."

Ingtar looked at Hurin; the sniffer slid the doors open, and Ingtar leaped through with his sword ready. There was no one there. Rand and the others hurried inside, and Hurin quickly closed the doors behind them.

Painted screens hid all the walls and any other doors, and veiled the light coming through windows that had to overlook the street. At one end of the big room stood a tall, circular cabinet. At the other was a small table, the lone chair on the carpet turned to face it. Rand heard Ingtar gasp, but he only felt like heaving a sigh of relief. The curling golden Horn of Valere sat on a stand on the table. Below it, the ruby in the hilt of the ornate dagger caught the light.

Mat darted to the table, snatching Horn and dagger. "We have it," he crowed, shaking the dagger in his fist. "We have both of them."

"Not so loud," Perrin said with a wince. "We don't have them out of here, yet." His hands were busy on the haft of his axe; they seemed to want to be holding something else.

"The Horn of Valere." There was sheer awe in Ingtar's voice. He touched the Horn hesitantly, tracing a finger along the silver script inlaid around the bell and mouthing the translation, then pulled his hand back with a shiver of excitement. "It is. By the Light, it is! I am saved."

Hurin was moving the screens that hid the windows. He shoved the last out of his way and peered into the street below. "Those soldiers are all still there, looking like they've took root." He shuddered. "Those . . . things, too."

Rand went to join him. The two beasts were *grolm;* there was no denying it. "How did they. . . ." As he lifted his eyes from the street, words died. He was looking over a wall into the garden of the big house across the street. He could see where further walls had been torn down, joining other gardens to it. Women sat on benches there, or strolled along the walks, always in pairs. Women linked, neck to wrist, by silver leashes. One of the women with a collar around her neck looked up. He was too far to make out her face clearly, but for an instant it seemed that their eyes met, and he knew. The blood drained from his face. "Egwene," he breathed.

"What are you talking about?" Mat said. "Egwene is safe in Tar Valon. I wish I were."

"She's here," Rand said. The two women were turning, walking toward one of the buildings on the far side of the joined gardens. "She is there, right across the street. Oh, Light, she's wearing one of those collars!"

"Are you sure?" Perrin said. He came to peer from the window. "I don't see her, Rand. And—and I could recognize her if I did, even at this distance."

"I am sure," Rand said. The two women disappeared into one of the houses that faced the next street over. His stomach was twisted into a knot. *She is supposed to be safe. She's supposed to be in the White Tower.* "I have to get her out. The rest of you—"

"So!" The slurring voice was as soft as the sound of the doors sliding in their tracks. "You are not who I expected."

For a brief moment, Rand stared. The tall man with the shaven head who had stepped into the room wore a long, trailing blue robe, and his fingernails were so long that Rand wondered if he could handle anything. The two men standing obsequiously behind him had only half their dark hair shaved, the rest hanging in a dark braid down each man's right cheek. One of them cradled a sheathed sword in his arms.

It was only a moment he had for staring, then screens toppled to reveal, at either end of the room, a doorway crowded with four or five Seanchan soldiers, bareheaded but armored, and swords in hand.

"You are in the presence of the High Lord Turak," the man who carried the sword began, staring at Rand and the others angrily, but a brief motion of a finger with a blue-lacquered nail cut him short. The other servant stepped forward with a bow and began undoing Turak's robe.

"When one of my guards was found dead," the shaven-headed man said calmly, "I suspected the man who calls himself Fain. I have been suspicious of him since Huon died so mysteriously, and he has always wanted that dagger." He held out his arms for the servant to remove his robe. Despite his soft, almost-singing voice, hard muscles roped his arms and smooth chest, which was bare to a blue sash holding wide, white trousers that seemed made of hundreds of pleats. He sounded uninterested, and indifferent to the blades in their hands. "And now to find strangers with not only the dagger, but the Horn. It will please me to kill one or two of you for disturbing my morning. Those who survive will tell me of who you are and why you came." He stretched out a hand without looking—the man with the scabbarded sword laid the hilt in the hand—and drew the heavy, curved blade. "I would not have the Horn damaged."

Turak gave no other signal, but one of the soldiers stalked into the room and reached for the Horn. Rand did not know whether he should laugh, or not. The man wore armor, but his arrogant face seemed as oblivious to their weapons as Turak was.

Mat put an end to it. As the Seanchan reached out his hand, Mat slashed it with the ruby-hilted dagger. With a curse, the soldier leaped back, looking surprised. And then he screamed. It chilled the room, held everyone where they stood in astonishment. The trembling hand he held up in front of his face was turning black, darkness creeping outwards from the bleeding gash that crossed his palm. He opened his mouth wide and howled, clawing at his arm, then his shoulder. Kicking, jerking, he toppled to the floor, thrashing on the silken carpet, shrieking as his face grew black and his dark eyes bulged like overripe plums, until a dark, swollen tongue gagged him. He twitched, choking raggedly, heels drumming, and did not move again. Every bit of his exposed flesh was black as putrid pitch and looked ready to burst at a touch.

Mat licked his lips and swallowed; his grip shifted uneasily on the dagger. Even Turak stared, openmouthed.

"You see," Ingtar said softly, "we are no easy meat." Suddenly he leaped over the corpse, toward the soldiers still goggling at what was left of the man who had stood at their shoulders only moments before. "Shinowa!" he cried. "Follow me!" Hurin leaped after him, and the soldiers fell back before them, the sounds of steel on steel rising.

The Seanchan at the other end of the room started forward as Ingtar moved, but then they were falling back, too, before Mat's thrusting dagger even more than from the axe Perrin swung with wordless snarls.

In the space of heartbeats, Rand stood alone, facing Turak, who held his blade upright before him. His moment of shock was gone. His eyes were sharp on Rand's face; the black and swollen body of one of his soldiers might as well not have existed. It did not seem to exist for the two servants, either, any more than Rand and his sword existed, or the sounds of fighting, fading now from the rooms to either side out into the house. The servants had begun calmly folding Turak's robe as soon as the High Lord took his sword, and had not looked up even for the dead soldier's shrieks; now they knelt beside the door and watched with impassive eyes.

"I suspected it might come to you and me." Turak spun his blade easily, a full circle one way, then the other, his long-nailed fingers moving delicately on the hilt. His fingernails did not seem to hamper him at all. "You are young. Let us see what is required to earn the heron on this side of the ocean."

Suddenly Rand saw. Standing tall on Turak's blade was a heron. With the little training he had, he was face-to-face with a real blademaster. Hastily he tossed the fleece-lined cloak aside, ridding himself of weight and encumbrance. Turak waited.

Rand desperately wanted to seek the void. It was plain he would need every shred of ability he could muster, and even then his chances of leaving the room alive would be small. He had to leave alive. Egwene was almost close enough for him to shout to her, and he had to free her, somehow. But *saidin* waited in the void. The thought made his heart leap with eagerness at the same time that it turned his stomach. But just as close as Egwene were those other women. *Damane.* If he touched *saidin,* and if he could not stop himself channeling, they would know, Verin had told him. Know and wonder. So many, so close. He might survive Turak only to die facing *damane,* and he could not die before Egwene was free. Rand raised his blade.

Turak glided toward him on silent feet. Blade rang on blade like hammer on anvil.

From the first it was clear to Rand that the man was testing him, pushing only hard enough to see what he could do, then pushing a little harder, then just a little harder still. It was quick wrists and quick feet that kept Rand alive as much as skill. Without the void, he was always half a heartbeat behind. The tip of Turak's heavy sword made a stinging trench just under his left eye. A flap of coat sleeve hung away from his shoulder, the darker for being wet. Under a neat slash beneath his right arm, precise as a tailor's cut, he could feel warm dampness spreading down his ribs.

There was disappointment on the High Lord's face. He stepped back with a gesture of disgust. "Where did you find that blade, boy? Or do they here truly award the heron to those no more skilled than you? No matter. Make your peace. It is time to die." He came on again.

The void enveloped Rand. *Saidin* flowed toward him, glowing with the promise of the One Power, but he ignored it. It was no more difficult than ignoring a barbed thorn twisting in his flesh. He refused to be filled with the Power, refused to be one with the male half of the True Source. He was one with the sword in his hands, one with the floor beneath his feet, one with the walls. One with Turak.

He recognized the forms the High Lord used; they were a little different from what he had been taught, but not enough. The Swallow Takes Flight met Parting the Silk. Moon on the Water met The Wood Grouse Dances.

Ribbon in the Air met Stones Falling From the Cliff. They moved about the room as in a dance, and their music was steel against steel.

Disappointment and disgust faded from Turak's dark eyes, replaced by surprise, then concentration. Sweat appeared on the High Lord's face as he pressed Rand harder. Lightning of Three Prongs met Leaf on the Breeze.

Rand's thoughts floated outside the void, apart from himself, hardly noticed. It was not enough. He faced a blademaster, and with the void and every ounce of his skill he was barely managing to hold his own. Barely. He had to end it before Turak finally did. *Saidin? No! Sometimes it is necessary to Sheath the Sword in your own flesh.* But that would not help Egwene, either. He had to end it now. Now.

Turak's eyes widened as Rand glided forward. So far he had only defended; now he attacked, all out. The Boar Rushes Down the Mountain. Every movement of his blade was an attempt to reach the High Lord; now all Turak could do was retreat and defend, down the length of the room, almost to the door.

In an instant, while Turak still tried to face the Boar, Rand charged. The River Undercuts the Bank. He dropped to one knee, blade slashing across. He did not need Turak's gasp, or the feel of resistance to his cut to know. He heard two thumps and turned his head, knowing what he would see. He looked down the length of his blade, wet and red, to where the High Lord lay, sword tumbled from his limp hand, a dark dampness staining the birds woven in the carpet under his body. Turak's eyes were still open, but already filmed with death.

The void shook. He had faced Trollocs before, faced Shadow spawn. Never before had he confronted a human being with a sword except in practice or bluff. *I just killed a man.* The void shook, and *saidin* tried to fill him.

Desperately he clawed free, breathing hard as he looked around. He gave a start when he saw the two servants still kneeling beside the door. He had forgotten them, and now he did not know what to do about them. Neither man appeared armed, yet all they had to do was shout. . . .

They never looked at him, or at each other. Instead, they stared silently at the High Lord's body. They produced daggers from under their robes, and he tightened his grip on the sword, but each man placed the point to his own breast. "From birth to death," they intoned in unison, "I serve the Blood." And plunged the daggers into their own hearts. They folded forward almost peacefully, heads to the floor as if bowing deeply to their lord.

Rand stared at them in disbelief. *Mad,* he thought. *Maybe I will go mad, but they already were.*

He was getting to his feet shakily when Ingtar and the others came

running back. They all bore nicks and cuts; the leather of Ingtar's coat was
stained in more than one place. Mat still had the Horn and his dagger, its
blade darker than the ruby in its hilt. Perrin's axe was red, too, and he
looked as if he might be sick at any moment.

"You dealt with them?" Ingtar said, looking at the bodies. "Then we're
done, if no alarm is given. Those fools never cried for help, not once."

"I will see if the guards heard anything," Hurin said, and darted for the
window.

Mat shook his head. "Rand, these people are crazy. I know I've said that
before, but these people really are. Those servants. . . ." Rand held his
breath, wondering if they had all killed themselves. Mat said, "Whenever
they saw us fighting, they fell on their knees, put their faces to the floor,
and wrapped their arms around their heads. They never moved, or cried
out; never tried to help the soldiers, or give an alarm. They're still there, as
far as I know."

"I would not count on them staying on their knees," Ingtar said dryly.
"We are leaving now, as fast as we can run."

"You go," Rand said. "Egwene—"

"You fool!" Ingtar snapped. "We have what we came for. The Horn of
Valere. The hope of salvation. What can one girl count, even if you love
her, alongside the Horn, and what it stands for?"

"The Dark One can have the Horn for all I care! What does finding the
Horn count if I abandon Egwene to this? If I did that, the Horn couldn't
save me. The Creator couldn't save me. I would damn myself."

Ingtar stared at him, his face unreadable. "You mean that exactly, don't
you?"

"Something's happening out here," Hurin said urgently. "A man just
came running up, and they're all milling like fish in a bucket. Wait. The
officer is coming inside!"

"Go!" Ingtar said. He tried to take the Horn, but Mat was already
running. Rand hesitated, but Ingtar grabbed his arm and pulled him into
the hall. The others were streaming after Mat; Perrin only gave Rand one
pained look before he went. "You cannot save the girl if you stand here and
die!"

He ran with them. Part of him hated himself for running, but another
part whispered, *I'll come back. I'll free her somehow.*

By the time they reached the bottom of the narrow, winding staircase,
he could hear a man's deep voice raised in the front part of the house,
angrily demanding that someone stand up and speak. A serving girl in her
nearly transparent robe knelt at the bottom of the stairs, and a gray-haired
woman all in white wool, with a long floury apron, knelt by the kitchen

door. They were both exactly as Mat had described, faces to the floor and arms wrapped around their heads, and they did not stir a hair as Rand and the others hurried by. He was relieved to see the motions of breathing.

They crossed the garden at a dead run, climbing over the back wall rapidly. Ingtar cursed when Mat tossed the Horn of Valere ahead of him, and tried again to take it when he dropped outside, but Mat snatched it up with a quick, "It isn't even scratched," and scampered up the alley.

More shouts rose from the house they had just left; a woman screamed, and someone began tolling a gong.

*I will come back for her. Somehow.* Rand sped after the others as fast as he could.

# CHAPTER
# 46

## To Come Out of the Shadow

Nynaeve and the others heard distant shouts as they approached
the buildings where the *damane* were housed. The crowds were
beginning to pick up, and there was a nervousness to the people
in the street, an extra quickness to their step, an extra wariness in the way
they glanced past Nynaeve, in her lightning-paneled dress, and the woman
she held by a silver leash.

Shifting her bundle nervously, Elayne peered toward the noise of shouts,
one street over, where the golden hawk clutching lightning rippled in the
wind. "What is happening?"

"Nothing to do with us," Nynaeve said firmly.

"You hope," Min added. "And so do I." She increased her pace, hurrying up the steps ahead of the others, and disappeared inside the tall stone
house.

Nynaeve shortened her grip on the leash. "Remember, Seta, you want us
to make it through this safely as much as we do."

"I do," the Seanchan woman said fervently. She kept her chin on her
chest, to hide her face. "I will cause you no trouble, I swear."

As they turned up the gray stone steps, a *sul'dam* and a *damane* appeared
at the head of the stairs, coming down as they went up. After one glance to
make sure the woman in the collar was not Egwene, Nynaeve did not look

at them again. She used the *a'dam* to keep Seta close by her side, so if the *damane* sensed the ability to channel in one of them, she would think it was Seta. She felt sweat trickling down her spine, though, until she realized they were paying her no more attention than she gave them. All they saw was a dress with lightning panels and a gray dress, the women wearing them linked by the silver length of an *a'dam*. Just another Leash Holder with a Leashed One, and a local girl hurrying along behind with a bundle belonging to the *sul'dam*.

Nynaeve pushed open the door, and they went in.

Whatever the excitement beneath Turak's banner, it did not extend here, not yet. There were only women moving about in the entry hall, all easily placed by their dress. Three gray-dressed *damane*, with *sul'dam* wearing the bracelets. Two women in dresses paneled with forked lightning stood talking, and three crossed the hall alone. Four dressed like Min, in plain dark woolens, hurried on their way with trays.

Min stood waiting down the entry hall when they went in; she glanced at them once, then started deeper into the house. Nynaeve guided Seta down the hall after Min, with Elayne scurrying along in their wake. No one gave them a second glance, it seemed to Nynaeve, but she thought the trickle of sweat down her backbone might become a river soon. She kept Seta moving quickly so no one would have a chance for a good look—or worse, a question. With her eyes fixed on her toes, Seta needed so little urging that Nynaeve thought she would have been running if not for the physical restraint of the leash.

Near the back of the house, Min took a narrow stairs that spiraled upwards. Nynaeve pushed Seta up it ahead of her, all the way to the fourth floor. The ceilings were low, there, the halls empty and silent except for the soft sounds of weeping. Weeping seemed to fit the air of the chilly halls.

"This place . . ." Elayne began, then shook her head. "It feels. . . ."

"Yes, it does," Nynaeve said grimly. She glared at Seta, who kept her face down. A pallor of fear made the Seanchan woman's skin paler than it was normally.

Wordlessly, Min opened a door and went in, and they followed. The room beyond had been divided into smaller rooms by roughly made wooden walls, with a narrow hallway running to a window. Nynaeve crowded after Min as she hurried to the last door on the right and pushed in.

A slender, dark-haired girl in gray sat at a small table with her head resting on folded arms, but even before she looked up, Nynaeve knew it was Egwene. A ribbon of shining metal ran from the silver collar around

Egwene's neck to a bracelet hanging on a peg on the wall. Her eyes widened at the sight of them, her mouth working silently. As Elayne closed the door, Egwene gave a sudden giggle, and pressed her hands to her mouth to stifle it. The tiny room was more than crowded with all of them in it.

"I know I'm not dreaming," she said in a quivering voice, "because if I was dreaming, you'd be Rand and Galad on tall stallions. I have been dreaming. I thought Rand was here. I couldn't see him, but I thought. . . ." Her voice trailed off.

"If you'd rather wait for them . . ." Min said dryly.

"Oh, no. No, you are all beautiful, the most beautiful thing I've ever seen. Where did you come from? How did you do it? That dress, Nynaeve, and the *a'dam,* and who is. . . ." She gave an abrupt squeak. "That's Seta. How. . . ?" Her voice hardened so that Nynaeve barely recognized it. "I'd like to put *her* in a pot of boiling water." Seta had her eyes squeezed shut, and her hands clutched her skirts; she was trembling.

"What have they done to you?" Elayne exclaimed. "What could they do to make you want something like that?"

Egwene never took her eyes off the Seanchan woman. "I'd like to make her feel it. That's what she did to me, made me feel like I was neck deep in. . . ." She shuddered. "You do not know what it is like wearing one of these, Elayne. You don't know what they can do to you. I can never decide whether Seta is worse than Renna, but they're all hateful."

"I think I know," Nynaeve said quietly. She could feel the sweat soaking Seta's skin, the cold tremors that shook her limbs. The yellow-haired Seanchan was terrified. It was all she could do not to make Seta's terrors come true then and there.

"Can you take this off of me?" Egwene asked, touching the collar. "You must be able to if you could put that one on—"

Nynaeve channeled, a pinpoint trickle. The collar on Egwene's neck provided anger enough, and if it had not, Seta's fear, the knowledge of how deserved it truly was, and her own knowledge of what she wanted to do to the woman, would have done it. The collar sprang open and fell away from Egwene's throat. With an expression of wonder, Egwene touched her neck.

"Put on my dress and coat," Nynaeve told her. Elayne was already unbundling the clothes on the bed. "We will walk out of here, and no one will even notice you." She considered holding her contact with *saidar*—she was certainly angry enough, and it felt so wonderful—but, reluctantly, she let it go. This was the one place in Falme where there was no chance of a *sul'dam* and *damane* coming to investigate if they sensed someone channeling, but they would certainly do so if a *damane* saw a woman she thought was a *sul'dam* with the glow of channeling around her. "I don't know why you aren't gone already. Alone here, even if you could not figure out how to get that thing off you, you could have just picked it up and run."

As Min and Elayne hurriedly helped her change into Nynaeve's old dress, Egwene explained about moving the bracelet from where a *sul'dam* left it, and how channeling made her sick unless a *sul'dam* wore the bracelet. Just that morning she had discovered how the collar could be opened without the Power—and found that touching the catch with the intention of opening it made her hand knot into uselessness. She could touch it as much as she wanted so long as she did not think of undoing the catch; the merest hint of that, though, and. . . .

Nynaeve felt sick herself. The bracelet on her wrist made her sick. It was too horrible. She wanted it off her wrist before she learned more about *a'dam,* before she perhaps learned something that would make her feel soiled forever for having worn it.

Unfastening the silver cuff, she pulled it loose, snapped it closed, and hung it on one of the pegs. "Don't think that means you can shout for help now." She shook a fist under Seta's nose. "I can still make you wish you were never born if you open your mouth, and I do not need that bloody . . . thing."

"You—you do not mean to leave me here with it," Seta said in a whisper. "You cannot. Tie me. Gag me so I cannot give an alarm. Please!"

Egwene gave a mirthless laugh. "Leave it on her. She won't call for help even without a gag. You had better hope whoever finds you will remove the *a'dam* and keep your little secret, Seta. Your dirty secret, isn't it?"

"What are you talking about?" Elayne said.

"I have thought about it a great deal," Egwene said. "Thinking was all I could do when they left me alone up here. *Sul'dam* claim they develop an affinity after a few years. Most of them can tell when a woman is channeling whether they're leashed to her or not. I wasn't sure, but Seta proves it."

"Proves what?" Elayne demanded, and then her eyes widened in sudden realization, but Egwene went on.

"Nynaeve, *a'dam* only work on women who can channel. Don't you see? *Sul'dam* can channel the same as *damane.*" Seta groaned through her teeth, shaking her head in violent denial. "A *sul'dam* would die before admitting she could channel, even if she knew, and they never train the ability, so they cannot do anything with it, but they can channel."

"I told you," Min said. "That collar shouldn't have worked on her." She was doing up the last buttons down Egwene's back. "Any woman who couldn't channel would be able to beat you silly while you tried to control her with it."

"How can that be?" Nynaeve said. "I thought the Seanchan put leashes on any woman who can channel."

"All of those they find," Egwene told her. "But those they can find are like you, and me, and Elayne. We were born with it, ready to channel whether anyone taught us or not. But what about Seanchan girls who aren't born with the ability, but who could be taught? Not just any woman can become a—a Leash Holder. Renna thought she was being friendly telling me about it. It is apparently a feastday in Seanchan villages when the *sul'dam* come to test the girls. They want to find any like you and me, and leash them, but they let all the others put on a bracelet to see if they can feel what the poor woman in the collar feels. Those who can are taken away to be trained as *sul'dam*. They are the women who could be taught."

Seta was moaning under her breath. "No. No. No." Over and over again.

"I know she is horrible," Elayne said, "but I feel as if I should help her somehow. She could be one of our sisters, only the Seanchan have twisted it all."

Nynaeve opened her mouth to say they had better worry about helping themselves, and the door opened.

"What is going on here?" Renna demanded, stepping into the room. "An audience?" She stared at Nynaeve, hands on hips. "I never gave permission for anyone else to link with my pet, Tuli. I do not even know who you—" Her eyes fell on Egwene—Egwene wearing Nynaeve's dress instead of *damane* gray. Egwene with no collar around her throat—and her eyes grew as big as saucers. She never had a chance to yell.

Before anyone else could move, Egwene snatched the pitcher from her washstand and smashed it into Renna's midriff. The pitcher shattered, and the *sul'dam* lost all her breath in a gurgling gasp and doubled over. As she fell, Egwene leaped on her with a snarl, shoving her flat, grabbing for the collar she had worn where it still lay on the floor, snapping it around the other woman's neck. With one jerk on the silver leash, Egwene pulled the bracelet from the peg and fitted it to her own wrist. Her lips were pulled back from her teeth, her eyes fixed on Renna's face with a terrible concentration. Kneeling on the *sul'dam*'s shoulders, she pressed both hands over the woman's mouth. Renna gave a tremendous convulsion, and her eyes bulged in her face; hoarse sounds came from her throat, screams held back by Egwene's hands; her heels drummed on the floor.

"Stop it, Egwene!" Nynaeve grabbed Egwene's shoulders, pulling her off of the other woman. "Egwene, stop it! That isn't what you want!" Renna lay gray-faced and panting, staring wildly at the ceiling.

Suddenly Egwene threw herself against Nynaeve, sobbing raggedly at her breast. "She hurt me, Nynaeve. She hurt me. They all did. They hurt me, and hurt me, until I did what they wanted. I hate them. I hate them for hurting me, and I hate them because I couldn't stop them from making me do what they wanted."

"I know," Nynaeve said gently. She smoothed Egwene's hair. "It is all right to hate them, Egwene. It is. They deserve it. But it isn't all right to let them make you like they are."

Seta's hands were pressed to her face. Renna touched the collar at her throat disbelievingly, with a shaking hand.

Egwene straightened, brushing her tears away quickly. "I'm not. I am not like them." She almost clawed the bracelet off of her wrist and threw it down. "I'm not. But I wish I could kill them."

"They deserve it." Min was staring grimly at the two *sul'dam*.

"Rand would kill someone who did a thing like that," Elayne said. She seemed to be steeling herself. "I am sure he would."

"Perhaps they do," Nynaeve said, "and perhaps he would. But men often mistake revenge and killing for justice. They seldom have the stomach for justice." She had often sat in judgment with the Women's Circle. Sometimes men came before them, thinking women might give them a better hearing than the men of the Village Council, but men always thought they could sway the decision with eloquence, or pleas for mercy. The Women's Circle gave mercy where it was deserved, but justice always, and it was the Wisdom who pronounced it. She picked up the bracelet Egwene had discarded and closed it. "I would free every woman here, if I could, and destroy every last one of these. But since I cannot. . . ." She slipped the bracelet over the same peg that held the other one, then addressed herself to the *sul'dam*. *Not Leash Holders any longer,* she told herself. "Perhaps, if you are very quiet, you will be left alone here long enough to manage to remove the collars. The Wheel weaves as the Wheel wills, and it may be that you've done enough good to counterbalance the evil you have done, enough that you will be allowed to remove them. If not, you will be found, eventually. And I think whoever finds you will ask a great many questions before they remove those collars. I think perhaps you will learn at first hand the life you have given to other women. That is justice," she added, to the others.

Renna wore a fixed stare of horror. Seta's shoulders shook as she sobbed into her hands. Nynaeve hardened her heart—*It is justice,* she told herself. *It is*—and herded the others out of the room.

No one paid any more attention to them going out than they had coming in. Nynaeve supposed she had the *sul'dam* dress to thank for that, but she could not wait to change into something else. Anything else. The dirtiest rag would feel cleaner on her skin.

The girls were silent, walking close behind her, until they were out on the cobblestone street again. She did not know if it was what she had done or the fear that someone might stop them. She scowled. Would they have felt better if she had let them work themselves up to cutting the women's throats?

"Horses," Egwene said. "We will need horses. I know the stable where they took Bela, but I don't think we can get to her."

"We have to leave Bela here," Nynaeve told her. "We are leaving by ship."

"Where is everybody?" Min said, and suddenly Nynaeve realized the street was empty.

The crowds were gone, not a sign of them to be seen; every shop and window along the street were shuttered tight. But up the street from the harbor came a formation of Seanchan soldiers, a hundred or more in ordered ranks, with an officer at their head in his painted armor. They were still halfway down the street from the women, but they marched with a grim, implacable step, and it seemed to Nynaeve that every eye was fixed on her. *That's ridiculous. I can't see their eyes inside those helmets, and if anybody had given an alarm, it would be behind us.* She stopped anyway.

"There are more behind us," Min murmured. Nynaeve could hear those boots, now. "I don't know which will reach us first."

Nynaeve took a deep breath. "They are nothing to do with us." She looked beyond the approaching soldiers, to the harbor, filled with tall, boxy Seanchan ships. She could not make out *Spray;* she prayed it was still there, and ready. "We will walk right past them." *Light, I hope we can.*

"What if they want you to join them, Nynaeve?" Elayne asked. "You are wearing that dress. If they start asking questions. . . ."

"I will not go back," Egwene said grimly. "I'll die first. Let me show them what they've taught me." To Nynaeve's eye, a golden nimbus suddenly seemed to surround her.

"No!" she said, but it was too late.

With a roar like thunder, the street under the first ranks of Seanchan erupted, dirt and cobblestones and armored men thrown aside like spray from a fountain. Still glowing, Egwene spun to stare up the street, and the thunderous roar was repeated. Dirt rained down on the women. Shouting Seanchan soldiers scattered in good order to shelter in alleys and behind stoops. In moments they were all out of sight, except for those who lay around the two large holes marring the street. Some of those stirred feebly, and moans drifted along the street.

Nynaeve threw up her hands, trying to look in both directions at once. "You fool! We are trying *not* to attract attention!" There was no hope of that now. She only hoped they could manage to work their way around the soldiers to the harbor through the alleys. *The* damane *must know, too, now. They could not have missed that.*

"I won't go back to that collar," Egwene said fiercely. "I won't!"

"Look out!" Min shouted.

With a shrill whine, a fireball as big as a horse arched into the air over the rooftops and began to fall. Directly toward them.

"Run!" Nynaeve shouted, and threw herself into a dive toward the nearest alleyway, between two shuttered shops.

She landed awkwardly on her stomach with a grunt, losing half her breath, as the fireball struck. Hot wind washed over her down the narrow passage. Gulping air, she rolled onto her back and stared back into the street.

The cobblestones where they had been standing were chipped and cracked and blackened in a circle ten paces across. Elayne was crouched just inside another alley on the other side of the street. Of Min and Egwene, there was no sign. Nynaeve clapped a hand to her mouth in horror.

Elayne seemed to understand what she was thinking. The Daughter-Heir shook her head violently and pointed down the street. They had gone that way.

Nynaeve heaved a sigh of relief that immediately turned to a growl. *Fool girl! We could have gotten by them!* There was no time for recriminations, though. She scooted to the corner and peered cautiously around the edge of the building.

A head-sized fireball flashed down the street toward her. She leaped back just before it exploded against the corner where her own head had been, showering her with stone chips.

Anger had her awash in the One Power before she was aware of it. Lightning flashed out of the sky, striking somewhere up the street with a crash near the origin of the fireball. Another jagged bolt split the sky, and then she was running down the alley. Behind her, lightning lanced the mouth of the alley.

*If Domon doesn't have that ship waiting, I'll. . . . Light, let us all reach it safely.*

Bayle Domon jerked erect as lightning streaked across the slate-gray sky, striking somewhere in the town, then again. *There do no be enough clouds for that!*

Something rumbled loudly up in the town, and a ball of fire smashed into a rooftop just above the docks, throwing splintered slates in wide arcs. The docks had emptied themselves of people a while back, except for a few Seanchan; they ran wildly, now, drawing swords and shouting. A man appeared from one of the warehouses with a *grolm* at his side, running to keep up with the beast's long leaps as they vanished into one of the streets leading up from the water.

One of Domon's crewmen jumped for an axe and swung it high over a mooring cable.

In two strides, Domon seized the upraised axe with one hand and the man's throat with the other. "*Spray* do stay till *I* do say sail, Aedwin Cole!"

"They're going mad, Captain!" Yarin shouted. An explosion sent echoes rumbling across the harbor, sending the gulls into screaming circles, and lightning flickered again, crashing to earth inside Falme. "The *damane* will kill us all! Let us go while they're busy killing one another. They will never notice us till we are gone!"

"I did give my word," Domon said. He wrenched the axe from Cole's hand and threw it clattering onto the deck. "I did give my word." *Hurry, woman,* he thought, *Aes Sedai or whatever you be. Hurry!*

Geofram Bornhald eyed the lightning flashing over Falme and dismissed it from his mind. Some huge flying creature—one of the Seanchan monsters, no doubt—flew wildly to escape the bolts. If there was a storm, it would hinder the Seanchan as much as it did him. Nearly treeless hills, a few topped by sparse thickets, still hid the town from him, and him from it.

His thousand men lay spread out to either side of him, one long, mounted rank rippling along the hollows between hills. The cold wind tossed their white cloaks and flapped the banner at Bornhald's side, the wavy-rayed golden sun of the Children of the Light.

"Go now, Byar," he commanded. The gaunt-faced man hesitated, and Bornhald put a snap into his voice. "I said, go, Child Byar!"

Byar touched hand to heart and bowed. "As you command, my Lord Captain." He turned his horse away, every line of him shouting reluctance.

Bornhald put Byar out of his mind. He had done what he could, there. He raised his voice. "The legion will advance at a walk!"

With a creak of saddles the long line of white-cloaked men moved slowly toward Falme.

Rand peered around the corner at the approaching Seanchan, then ducked back into the narrow alley between two stables with a grimace. They would be there soon. There was blood crusted on his cheek. The cuts he had from Turak burned, but there was nothing to be done for them now. Lightning flashed across the sky again; he felt the rumble of its plummet through his boots. *What in the name of the Light is happening?*

"Close?" Ingtar said. "The Horn of Valere must be saved, Rand." Despite the Seanchan, despite the lightning and strange explosions down in the town proper, he seemed preoccupied with his own thoughts. Mat and Perrin and Hurin were down at the other end of the alley, watching another Seanchan patrol. The place where they had left the horses was close, now, if they could only reach it.

"She's in trouble," Rand muttered. Egwene. There was an odd feeling in his head, as if pieces of his life were in danger. Egwene was one piece, one thread of the cord that made his life, but there were others, and he could feel them threatened. Down there, in Falme. And if any of those threads was destroyed, his life would never be complete, the way it was meant to be. He did not understand it, but the feeling was sure and certain.

"One man could hold fifty here," Ingtar said. The two stables stood close together, with barely room for the pair of them to stand side by side between them. "One man holding fifty at a narrow passage. Not a bad way to die. Songs have been made about less."

"There's no need for that," Rand said. "I hope." A rooftop in the town exploded. *How am I going to get back in here? I have to reach her. Reach them?* Shaking his head, he peeked around the corner again. The Seanchan were closer, still coming.

"I never knew what he was going to do," Ingtar said softly, as if talking to himself. He had his sword out, testing the edge with his thumb. "A pale little man you didn't seem to really notice even when you were looking at him. Take him inside Fal Dara, I was told, inside the fortress. I did not want to, but I had to do it. You understand? I had to. I never knew what he intended until he shot that arrow. I still don't know if it was meant for the Amyrlin, or for you."

Rand felt a chill. He stared at Ingtar. "What are you saying?" he whispered.

Studying his blade, Ingtar did not seem to hear. "Humankind is being swept away everywhere. Nations fail and vanish. Darkfriends are everywhere, and none of these southlanders seem to notice or care. We fight to hold the Borderlands, to keep them safe in their houses, and every year, despite all we can do, the Blight advances. And these southlanders think Trollocs are myths, and Myrddraal a gleeman's tale." He frowned and shook his head. "It seemed the only way. We would be destroyed for nothing, defending people who do not even know, or care. It seemed logical. Why should we be destroyed for them, when we could make our own peace? Better the Shadow, I thought, than useless oblivion, like Carallain, or Hardan, or. . . . It seemed so logical, then."

Rand grabbed Ingtar's lapels. "You aren't making any sense." *He can't mean what he's saying. He can't.* "Say it plain, whatever you mean. You are talking crazy!"

For the first time Ingtar looked at Rand. His eyes shone with unshed tears. "You are a better man than I. Shepherd or lord, a better man. The prophecy says, 'Let who sounds me think not of glory, but only salvation.' It was my salvation I was thinking of. I would sound the Horn, and lead the heroes of the Ages against Shayol Ghul. Surely that would have been enough to save me. No man can walk so long in the Shadow that he cannot come again to the Light. That is what they say. Surely that would have been enough to wash away what I have been, and done."

"Oh, Light, Ingtar." Rand released his hold on the other man and sagged back against the stable wall. "I think. . . . I think wanting to is enough. I think all you have to do is stop being . . . one of them." Ingtar flinched as if Rand had said it out. Darkfriend.

"Rand, when Verin brought us here with the Portal Stone, I—I lived other lives. Sometimes I held the Horn, but I never sounded it. I tried to escape what I'd become, but I never did. Always there was something else required of me, always something worse than the last, until I was. . . . You were ready to give it up to save a friend. Think not of glory. Oh, Light, help me."

Rand did not know what to say. It was as if Egwene had told him she had murdered children. Too horrible to be believed. Too horrible for anyone to admit to unless it was true. Too horrible.

After a time, Ingtar spoke again, firmly. "There has to be a price, Rand. There is always a price. Perhaps I can pay it here."

"Ingtar, I—"

"It is every man's right, Rand, to choose when to Sheathe the Sword. Even one like me."

Before Rand could say anything, Hurin came running down the alley. "The patrol turned aside," he said hurriedly, "down into the town. They seem to be gathering down there. Mat and Perrin went on." He took a quick look down the street and pulled back. "We'd better do the same, Lord Ingtar, Lord Rand. Those bug-headed Seanchan are almost here."

"Go, Rand," Ingtar said. He turned to face the street and did not look at Rand or Hurin again. "Take the Horn where it belongs. I always knew the Amyrlin should have given you the charge. But all I ever wanted was to keep Shienar whole, to keep us from being swept away and forgotten."

"I know, Ingtar." Rand drew a deep breath. "The Light shine on you,

Lord Ingtar of House Shinowa, and may you shelter in the palm of the Creator's hand." He touched Ingtar's shoulder. "The last embrace of the mother welcome you home." Hurin gasped.

"Thank you," Ingtar said softly. A tension seemed to go out of him. For the first time since the night of the Trolloc raid on Fal Dara, he stood as he had when Rand first saw him, confident and relaxed. Content.

Rand turned and found Hurin staring at him, staring at both of them. "It is time for us to go."

"But Lord Ingtar—"

"—does what he has to," Rand said sharply. "But we go." Hurin nodded, and Rand trotted after him. Rand could hear the steady tread of the Seanchan's boots, now. He did not look back.

# CHAPTER
## 47

### *The Grave Is No Bar to My Call*

**M**at and Perrin were mounted by the time Rand and Hurin reached them. Far behind him, Rand heard Ingtar's voice rise. "The Light, and Shinowa!" The clash of steel joined the roar of other voices.

"Where's Ingtar?" Mat shouted. "What's going on?" He had the Horn of Valere lashed to the high pommel of his saddle as if it were just any horn, but the dagger was in his belt, the ruby-tipped hilt cupped protectively in a pale hand that seemed made of nothing but bone and sinew.

"He's dying," Rand said harshly as he swung onto Red's back.

"Then we have to help him," Perrin said. "Mat can take the Horn and the dagger on to—"

"He is doing it so we can all get away," Rand said. *For that, too.* "We will all take the Horn to Verin, and then you can help her take it wherever she says it belongs."

"What do you mean?" Perrin asked. Rand dug his heels into the bay's flanks, and Red leaped away toward the hills beyond the town.

"The Light, and Shinowa!" Ingtar's shout soared after him, sounding triumphant, and lightning crashed across the sky in answer.

Rand whipped Red with his reins, then lay against the stallion's neck as the bay laid out in a dead run, mane and tail streaming. He wished he did not feel as if he were running away from Ingtar's cry, running from what he was supposed to do. *Ingtar, a Darkfriend. I don't care. He was still my friend.* The bay's gallop could not take him away from his own thoughts. *Death is lighter than a feather, duty heavier than a mountain. So many duties. Egwene. The Horn. Fain. Mat and his dagger. Why can't there just be one at a time? I have to take care of all of them. Oh, Light, Egwene!*

He reined in so suddenly that Red slid to a halt, sitting back on his haunches. They were in a scanty copse of bare-branched trees atop one of the hills overlooking Falme. The others galloped up behind him.

"What do you mean?" Perrin demanded. "*We* can help Verin take the Horn where it's supposed to go? Where are *you* going to be?"

"Maybe he's going mad already," Mat said. "He wouldn't want to stay with us if he was going mad. Would you, Rand?"

"You three take the Horn to Verin," Rand said. *Egwene. So many threads, in so much danger. So many duties.* "You do not need me."

Mat caressed the dagger's hilt. "That's all very well, but what about you? Burn me, you can't be going mad yet. You can't!" Hurin gaped at them, not understanding half of it.

"I'm going back," Rand said. "I should never have left." Somehow, that did not sound exactly right in his own ears; it did not feel right inside his head. "I have to go back. Now." That sounded better. "Egwene is still there, remember. With one of those collars around her neck."

"Are you sure?" Mat said. "I never saw her. Aaaah! If you say she is there, then she's there. We'll all take the Horn to Verin, and then we will all go back for her. You don't think I would leave her there, do you?"

Rand shook his head. *Threads. Duties.* He felt as if he were about to explode like a firework. *Light, what's happening to me?* "Mat, Verin must take you and that dagger to Tar Valon, so you can finally be free of it. You don't have any time to waste."

"Saving Egwene isn't wasting time!" But Mat's hand had tightened on the dagger till it shook.

"We aren't any of us going back," Perrin said. "Not yet. Look." He pointed back toward Falme.

The wagon yards and horse lots were turning black with Seanchan soldiers, thousands of them rank on rank, with troops of cavalry riding scaled beasts as well as armored men on horses, colorful gonfanons marking the officers. *Grolm* dotted the ranks, and other strange creatures, almost but not quite like monstrous birds and lizards, and great things like nothing he could describe, with gray, wrinkled skin and huge tusks. At intervals along the lines stood *sul'dam* and *damane* by the score. Rand wondered if Egwene were one of them. In the town behind the soldiers, a rooftop still exploded now and again, and lightning still streaked the sky. Two flying beasts, with leathery wings twenty spans tip to tip, soared high overhead, keeping well away from where the bright bolts danced.

"All that for us?" Mat said incredulously. "Who do they think we are?"

An answer came to Rand, but he shoved it away before it had a chance to form completely.

"We aren't going the other way either, Lord Rand," Hurin said. "Whitecloaks. Hundreds of them."

Rand wheeled his horse to look where the sniffer was pointing. A long, white-cloaked line rippled slowly toward them across the hills.

"Lord Rand," Hurin muttered, "if that lot lays an eye on the Horn of Valere, we'll never get it close to an Aes Sedai. We'll never get close to it again ourselves."

"Maybe that's why the Seanchan are gathering," Mat said hopefully. "Because of the Whitecloaks. Maybe it doesn't have anything to do with us at all."

"Whether it does or not," Perrin said dryly, "there is going to be a battle here in a few minutes."

"Either side could kill us," Hurin said, "even if they never see the Horn. If they do. . . ."

Rand could not manage to think about the Whitecloaks, or the Seanchan. *I have to go back. Have to.* He was staring at the Horn of Valere, he realized. They all were. The curled, golden Horn hung at Mat's pommel, the focus of every eye.

"It has to be there at the Last Battle," Mat said, licking his lips. "Nothing says it can't be used before then." He pulled the Horn free of its lashings and looked at them anxiously. "Nothing says it can't."

No one else said anything. Rand did not think he could speak; his own thoughts were too urgent to allow room for speech. *Have to go back. Have to go back.* The longer he looked at the Horn, the more urgent his thoughts became. *Have to. Have to.*

Mat's hand shook as he raised the Horn of Valere to his lips.

It was a clear note, golden as the Horn was golden. The trees around them seemed to resonate with it, and the ground under their feet, the sky overhead. That one long sound encompassed everything.

Out of nowhere, a fog began to rise. First thin wisps hanging in the air, then thicker billows, and thicker, until it blanketed the land like clouds.

Geofram Bornhald stiffened in his saddle as a sound filled the air, so sweet he wanted to laugh, so mournful he wanted to cry. It seemed to come from every direction at once. A mist began to rise, growing even as he watched.

*The Seanchan. They are trying something. They know we are here.*

It was too soon, the town too far, but he drew his sword—a clatter of scabbards ran down the rank of his half legion—and called, "The legion will advance at a trot."

The fog covered everything, now, but he knew Falme was still there, ahead. The pace of the horses picked up; he could not see them, but he could hear.

Abruptly the ground ahead flew up with a roar, showering him with dirt and pebbles. From the white blindness to his right he heard another roar, and men and horses screamed, then from his left, and again. Again. Thunder and screams, hidden by the fog.

"The legion will charge!" His horse leaped forward as he dug in his heels, and he heard the roar as the legion, as much of it as still lived, followed.

Thunder and screams, wrapped in whiteness.

His last thought was regret. Byar would not be able to tell his son Dain how he had died.

Rand could not see the trees around them any longer. Mat had lowered the Horn, eyes wide with awe, but the sound of it still rang in Rand's ears. The fog hid everything in rolling waves as white as the finest bleached wool, yet Rand could see. He could see, but it was mad. Falme floated somewhere beneath him, its landward border black with the Seanchan ranks, lightning ripping its streets. Falme hung over his head. There Whitecloaks charged and died as the earth opened in fire beneath their horses' hooves. There men ran about the decks of tall, square ships in the harbor, and on one ship, a familiar ship, fearful men waited. He could even recognize the face of the captain. Bayle Domon. He clutched his head with both hands. The trees were hidden, but he could still see each of the others clearly. Hurin anxious. Mat muttering, fearful. Perrin looking as if he knew this was meant to be. The fog roiled up all around them.

Hurin gasped. "Lord Rand!" There was no need for him to point.

Down the billowing fog, as if it were the side of a mountain, rode shapes on horses. At first the dense mists hid more than that, but slowly they came closer, and it was Rand's turn to gasp. He knew them. Men, not all in armor, and women. Their clothes and their weapons came from every Age, but he knew them all.

Rogosh Eagle-eye, a fatherly looking man with white hair and eyes so sharp as to make his name merely a hint. Gaidal Cain, a swarthy man with the hilts of his two swords sticking above his broad shoulders. Golden-haired Birgitte, with her gleaming silver bow and quiver bristling with silver arrows. More. He knew their faces, knew their names. But he heard a hundred names when he looked at each face, some so different he did not recognize them as names at all, though he knew they were. Michael instead of Mikel. Patrick instead of Paedrig. Oscar instead of Otarin.

He knew the man who rode at their head, too. Tall and hook-nosed, with dark, deep-set eyes, his great sword Justice at his side. Artur Hawkwing.

Mat gaped at them as they reined in before him and the others. "Is this. . . ? Is this all of you?" They were little more than a hundred, Rand saw, and realized that somehow he had known that they would be. Hurin's mouth hung open; his eyes bulged almost out of his head.

"It takes more than bravery to bind a man to the Horn." Artur Hawkwing's voice was deep and carrying, a voice used to giving commands.

"Or a woman," Birgitte said sharply.

"Or a woman," Hawkwing agreed. "Only a few are bound to the Wheel, spun out again and again to work the will of the Wheel in the Pattern of the Ages. You could tell him, Lews Therin, could you but remember when you wore flesh." He was looking at Rand.

Rand shook his head, but he would not waste time with denials. "Invaders have come, men who call themselves Seanchan, who use chained Aes Sedai in battle. They must be driven back into the sea. And—and there is a girl. Egwene al'Vere. A novice from the White Tower. The Seanchan have her prisoner. You must help me free her."

To his surprise, several of the small host behind Artur Hawkwing chuckled, and Birgitte, testing her bowstring, laughed. "You always choose women who cause you trouble, Lews Therin." It had a fond sound, as between old friends.

"My name is Rand al'Thor," he snapped. "You have to hurry. There isn't much time."

"Time?" Birgitte said, smiling. "We have all of time." Gaidal Cain dropped his reins and, guiding his horse with his knees, drew a sword in either hand. All along the small band of heroes there was an unsheathing of swords, an unlimbering of bows, a hefting of spears and axes.

Justice shone like a mirror in Artur Hawkwing's gauntleted fist. "I have fought by your side times beyond number, Lews Therin, and faced you as many more. The Wheel spins us out for its purposes, not ours, to serve the Pattern. I know you, if you do not know yourself. We will drive these invaders out for you." His warhorse pranced, and he looked around, frowning. "Something is wrong here. Something holds me." Suddenly he turned his sharp-eyed gaze on Rand. "You are here. Have you the banner?" A murmur ran through those behind him.

"Yes." Rand tore open the straps of his saddlebags and pulled out the Dragon's banner. It filled his hands and hung almost to his stallion's knees. The murmur among the heroes rose.

"The Pattern weaves itself around our necks like halters," Artur Hawkwing said. "You are here. The banner is here. The weave of this moment is set. We have come to the Horn, but we must follow the banner. And the Dragon." Hurin made a faint sound as if his throat had seized.

"Burn me," Mat breathed. "It's true. Burn me!"

Perrin hesitated only an instant before swinging down off his horse and striding into the mist. There came a chopping sound, and when he returned, he carried a straight length of sapling shorn of its branches. "Give it to me, Rand," he said gravely. "If they need it. . . . Give it to me."

Hastily, Rand helped him tie the banner to the pole. When Perrin remounted, pole in hand, a current of air seemed to ripple the pale length of the banner, so the serpentine Dragon appeared to move, alive. The wind did not touch the heavy fog, only the banner.

"You stay here," Rand told Hurin. "When it's over. . . . You will be safe, here."

Hurin drew his short sword, holding it as if it might actually be of some use from horseback. "Begging your pardon, Lord Rand, but I think not. I don't understand the tenth part of what I've heard . . . or what I'm seeing"—his voice dropped to a mutter before picking up again—"but I've come this far, and I think I'll go the rest of the way."

Artur Hawkwing clapped the sniffer on the shoulder. "Sometimes the Wheel adds to our number, friend. Perhaps you will find yourself among us, one day." Hurin sat up as if he had been offered a crown. Hawkwing bowed formally from his saddle to Rand. "With your permission . . . Lord Rand. Trumpeter, will you give us music on the Horn? Fitting that the Horn of Valere should sing us into battle. Bannerman, will you advance?"

Mat sounded the Horn again, long and high—the mists rang with it— and Perrin heeled his horse forward. Rand drew the heron-mark blade and rode between them.

He could see nothing but thick billows of white, but somehow he could still see what he had before, too. Falme, where someone used the Power in the streets, and the harbor, and the Seanchan host, and the dying White-cloaks, all of it beneath him, all of him hanging above, all of it just as it had been. It seemed as if no time at all had passed since the Horn was first blown, as though time had paused while the heroes answered the call and now resumed counting.

The wild cries Mat wrung from the Horn echoed in the fog, and the drumming of hooves as the horses picked up speed. Rand charged into the mists, wondering if he knew where he was headed. The clouds thickened, hiding the far ends of the rank of heroes galloping to either side of him, obscuring more and more, till he could see only Mat and Perrin and Hurin clearly. Hurin crouched low in his saddle, wide-eyed, urging his horse on. Mat sounding the Horn, and laughing between. Perrin, his yellow eyes glowing, the Dragon's banner streaming behind him. Then they were gone, too, and Rand rode on alone, as it seemed.

In a way, he could still see them, but now it was the way he could see Falme, and the Seanchan. He could not tell where they were, or where he was. He tightened his grip on his sword, peered into the mists ahead. He charged alone through the fog, and somehow he knew that was how it was meant to be.

Suddenly Ba'alzamon was before him in the mists, throwing his arms wide.

Red reared wildly, hurling Rand from his saddle. Rand clung to his sword desperately as he soared. It was not a hard landing. In fact, he thought with a sense of wonder that it was very much like landing on . . . nothing at all. One instant he was sailing through the mists, and the next he was not.

When he climbed to his feet, his horse was gone, but Ba'alzamon was still there, striding toward him with a long, black-charred staff in his hands. They were alone, only they and the rolling fog. Behind Ba'alzamon was shadow. The mist was not dark behind him; this blackness excluded the white fog.

Rand was aware of the other things, too. Artur Hawkwing and the other heroes meeting the Seanchan in dense fog. Perrin, with the banner, swinging his axe more to fend off those who tried to reach him than harm them. Mat, still blowing wild notes on the Horn of Valere. Hurin down from his saddle, fighting with short sword and sword-breaker in the way he knew. It seemed as if the Seanchan numbers would overwhelm them in one rush, yet it was the dark-armored Seanchan who fell back.

Rand went forward to meet Ba'alzamon. Reluctantly, he assumed the void, reached for the True Source, was filled with the One Power. There was no other way. Perhaps he had no chance against the Dark One, but whatever chance he did have lay in the Power. It soaked into his limbs, seemed to suffuse everything about him, his clothes, his sword. He felt as if he should be glowing like the sun. It thrilled him; it made him want to vomit.

"Get out of my way," he grated. "I am not here for you!"

"The girl?" Ba'alzamon laughed. His mouth turned to flame. His burns were all but healed, leaving only a few pink scars that were already fading.

He looked like a handsome man of middle years. Except for his mouth, and his eyes. "Which one, Lews Therin? You will not have anyone to help you this time. You are mine, or you are dead. In which case, you are mine anyway."

"Liar!" Rand snarled. He struck at Ba'alzamon, but the staff of charred wood turned his blade in a shower of sparks. "Father of Lies!"

"Fool! Did those other fools you summoned not tell you who you are?" The fires of Ba'alzamon's face roared with laughter.

Even floating in emptiness, Rand felt a chill. *Would they have lied? I don't want to be the Dragon Reborn.* He firmed his grip on his sword. Parting the Silk, but Ba'alzamon beat every cut aside; sparks flew as from a blacksmith's forge and hammer. "I have business in Falme, and none with you. Never with you," Rand said. *I have to hold his attention until they can free Egwene.* In that odd way, he could see the battle rage among the fog-shrouded wagon yards and horse lots.

"You pitiful wretch. You have sounded the Horn of Valere. You are linked to it, now. Do you think the worms of the White Tower will ever release you, now? They will put chains around your neck so heavy you will never cut them."

Rand was so surprised he felt it inside the void. *He doesn't know everything. He doesn't know!* He was sure it must show on his face. To cover it, he rushed at Ba'alzamon. Hummingbird Kisses the Honeyrose. The Moon on the Water. The Swallow Rides the Air. Lightning arched between sword and staff. Coruscating glitter showered the fog. Yet Ba'alzamon fell back, his eyes blazing in furious furnaces.

At the edge of his awareness, Rand saw the Seanchan falling back in the streets of Falme, fighting desperately. *Damane* tore the earth with the One Power, but it could not harm Artur Hawkwing, nor the other heroes of the Horn.

"Will you remain a slug beneath a rock?" Ba'alzamon snarled. The darkness behind him boiled and stirred. "You kill yourself while we stand here. The Power rages in you. It burns you. It is killing you! I alone in all the world can teach you how to control it. Serve me, and live. Serve me, or die!"

"Never!" *Have to hold him long enough. Hurry, Hawkwing. Hurry!* He launched himself at Ba'alzamon again. The Dove Takes Flight. The Falling Leaf.

This time it was he who was driven back. Dimly, he saw the Seanchan fighting their way back in among the stables. He redoubled his efforts. The Kingfisher Takes a Silverback. The Seanchan gave way to a charge, Artur Hawkwing and Perrin side by side in the van. Bundling Straw. Ba'alzamon caught his blow in a fountain like crimson fireflies, and he had to leap away before the staff split his head; the wind of the blow ruffled his hair. The Seanchan surged forward. Striking the Spark. Sparks flew like hail, Ba'alzamon jumped from his stroke, and the Seanchan were driven back to the cobblestone streets.

Rand wanted to howl aloud. Suddenly he knew that the two battles were linked. When he advanced, the heroes called by the Horn drove the Seanchan back; when he fell back, the Seanchan rose up.

"They will not save you," Ba'alzamon said. "Those who might save you will be carried far across the Aryth Ocean. If ever you see them again, they will be collared slaves, and they will destroy you for their new masters."

*Egwene. I can't let them do that to her.*

Ba'alzamon's voice rode over his thoughts. "You have only one salvation, Rand al'Thor. Lews Therin Kinslayer. I am your only salvation. Serve me, and I will give you the world. Resist, and I will destroy you as I have so often before. But this time I will destroy you to your very soul, destroy you utterly and forever."

*I have won again, Lews Therin.* The thought was beyond the void, yet it took an effort to ignore it, not to think of all the lives where he had heard it. He shifted his sword, and Ba'alzamon readied his staff.

For the first time Rand realized that Ba'alzamon acted as if the heron-mark blade could harm him. *Steel can't hurt the Dark One.* But Ba'alzamon watched the sword warily. Rand was one with the sword. He could feel every particle of it, tiny bits a thousand times too small to be seen with the eye. And he could feel the Power that suffused him running into the sword, as well, threading through the intricate matrices wrought by Aes Sedai during the Trolloc Wars.

It was another voice he heard then. Lan's voice. *There will come a time when you want something more than you want life.* Ingtar's voice. *It is every man's right to choose when to Sheathe the Sword.* The picture formed of Egwene, collared, living her life as a *damane. Threads of my life in danger. Egwene. If Hawking gets into Falme, he can save her.* Before he knew it, he had taken the first position of Heron Wading in the Rushes, balanced on one foot, sword raised high, open and defenseless. *Death is lighter than a feather, duty heavier than a mountain.*

Ba'alzamon stared at him. "Why are you grinning like an idiot, fool? Do you not know I can destroy you utterly?"

Rand felt a calmness beyond that of the void. "I will never serve you, Father of Lies. In a thousand lives, I never have. I know that. I'm sure of it. Come. It is time to die."

Ba'alzamon's eyes widened; for an instant they were furnaces that put sweat on Rand's face. The blackness behind Ba'alzamon boiled up around him, and his face hardened. "Then die, worm!" He struck with the staff, as with a spear.

Rand screamed as he felt it pierce his side, burning like a white-hot poker. The void trembled, but he held on with the last of his strength, and drove the heron-mark blade into Ba'alzamon's heart. Ba'alzamon screamed, and the dark behind him screamed. The world exploded in fire.

# CHAPTER 48

## First Claiming

Min struggled up the cobblestone street, pushing through crowds that stood white-faced and staring, those who were not screaming hysterically. A few ran, seemingly without any idea of where they were running, but most moved like poorly handled puppets, more afraid to go than to stay. She searched the faces, hoping to find Egwene, or Elayne, or Nynaeve, but all she saw were Falmen. And there was something drawing her on, as surely as if she had a string tied to her.

Once she turned to look back. Seanchan ships burned in the harbor, and she could see more in flames off the harbor mouth. Many squarish vessels were already small against the setting sun, sailing west as fast as *damane* could make the winds drive them, and one small ship was beating away from the harbor, tilting to catch a wind to take it along the coast. *Spray.* She did not blame Bayle Domon for not waiting longer, not after what she had seen; she thought it a wonder he had remained so long.

There was one Seanchan vessel in the harbor not burning, though its towers were black from fires already extinguished. As the tall ship crept toward the harbor mouth, a figure on horseback suddenly appeared around the cliffs skirting the harbor. Riding across the water. Min's mouth fell open. Silver glittered as the figure raised a bow; a streak of silver lanced to the boxy ship, a gleaming line connecting bow and ship. With a roar she could hear even at that distance, fire engulfed the foretower anew, and sailors rushed about the deck.

Min blinked, and when she looked again, the mounted figure was gone. The ship still slowly made way toward the ocean, the crew fighting the flames.

She gave herself a shake and started to climb the street again. She had seen too much that day for someone riding a horse across water to be more than a momentary distraction. *Even if it really was Birgitte and her bow. And Artur Hawkwing. I did see him. I did.*

In front of one of the tall stone buildings, she stopped uncertainly, ignoring the people who brushed past her as if stunned. It was in there, somewhere, that she had to go. She rushed up the stairs and pushed open the door.

No one tried to stop her. As far as she could tell, there was no one in the house. Most of Falme was out in the streets, trying to decide whether they had all gone mad together. She went on through the house, into the garden behind, and there he was.

Rand lay sprawled on his back under an oak, face pale and eyes closed, left hand gripping a hilt that ended in a foot of blade that appeared to have been melted at the end. His chest rose and fell too slowly, and not with the regular rhythm of someone breathing normally.

Taking a deep breath to calm herself, she went to see what she could do for him. First was to get rid of that stub of a blade; he could hurt himself, or her, if he started thrashing. She pried his hand open, and winced when the hilt stuck to his palm. She tossed it aside with a grimace. The heron on the hilt had branded itself into his hand. But it was obvious to her that that was not what had him lying there unconscious. *How did he come by that? Nynaeve can put a salve on it later.*

A hasty examination showed that most of his cuts and bruises were not new—at least, the blood had had time to dry in a crust, and the bruises had started to turn yellow at the edges—but there was a hole burned through his coat on the left side. Opening his coat, she pulled up his shirt. Breath whistled through her teeth. There was a wound burned into his side, but it had cauterized itself. What shook her was the feel of his flesh. It had a touch of ice in it; he made the air seem warm.

Grabbing his shoulders, she began to drag him toward the house. He hung limp, a dead weight. "Great lummox," she grunted. "You couldn't be short, and light, could you? You have to have all that leg and shoulder. I ought to let you lie out here."

But she struggled up the steps, careful not to bump him any more than she could avoid, and pulled him inside. Leaving him just within the door, she knuckled the small of her back, muttering to herself about the Pattern, and made a hasty search. There was a small bedroom in the back of the house, perhaps a servant's room, with a bed piled high with blankets, and logs already laid on the hearth. In moments, she had the blankets thrown back and the fire lit, as well as a lamp on the bedside table. Then she went back for Rand.

It was no small task getting him to the room, or up onto the bed, but she managed it with only a little hard breathing, and covered him up. After a moment, she stuck a hand under the blankets; she winced and shook her head. The sheets were icy cold; he had no body warmth for the blankets to hold. With a put-upon sigh, she wriggled under the covers beside him. Finally, she put his head on her arm. His eyes were still closed, his breathing ragged, but she thought he would be dead by the time she came back if she left to find Nynaeve. *He needs an Aes Sedai,* she thought. *All I can do is try to give him a little warmth.*

For a time she studied his face. It was only his face she saw; she could never read anyone who was not conscious. "I like older men," she told him. "I like men with education, and wit. I have no interest in farms, or sheep, or shepherds. Especially boy shepherds." With a sigh, she smoothed back the hair from his face; he had silky hair. "But then, you aren't a shepherd, are you? Not anymore. Light, why did the Pattern have to catch me up with you? Why couldn't I have something safe and simple, like being shipwrecked with no food and a dozen hungry Aielmen?"

There was a sound in the hall, and she raised her head as the door opened. Egwene stood there, staring at them by the light of the fire and the lamp. "Oh," was all she said.

Min's cheeks colored. *Why am I behaving like I've done something wrong? Fool!* "I . . . I'm keeping him warm. He is unconscious, and he's as cold as ice."

Egwene did not come any further into the room. "I—I felt him pulling at me. Needing me. Elayne felt it, too. I thought it must be something to do with—with what he is, but Nynaeve didn't feel anything." She drew a deep, unsteady breath. "Elayne and Nynaeve are getting the horses. We found Bela. The Seanchan left most of their horses behind. Nynaeve says we should go as soon as we can, and—and. . . . Min, you know what he is, don't you, now?"

"I know." Min wanted to take her arm from under Rand's head, but she could not make herself move. "I think I do, anyway. Whatever he is, he is hurt. I can do nothing for him except keep him warm. Maybe Nynaeve can."

"Min, you know . . . you do know that he cannot marry. He isn't . . . safe . . . for any of us, Min."

"Speak for yourself," Min said. She pulled Rand's face against her breast. "It's like Elayne said. You tossed him aside for the White Tower. What should you care if I pick him up?"

Egwene looked at her for what seemed a long time. Not at Rand, not at all, only at her. She felt her face growing hotter and wanted to look away, but she could not.

"I will bring Nynaeve," Egwene said finally, and walked out of the room with her back straight and her head high.

Min wanted to call out, to go after her, but she lay there as if frozen. Frustrated tears stung her eyes. *It's what has to be. I know it. I read it in all of them. Light, I don't want to be part of this.* "It's all your fault," she told Rand's still shape. "No, it isn't. But you will pay for it, I think. We're all caught like flies in a spiderweb. What if I told her there's another woman yet to come, one she doesn't even know? For that matter, what would you think of that, my fine Lord Shepherd? You aren't bad-looking at all, but. . . . Light, I don't even know if I am the one you'll choose. I don't know if I want you to choose me. Or will you try to dandle all three of us on your knee? It may not be your fault, Rand al'Thor, but it isn't fair."

"Not Rand al'Thor," said a musical voice from the door. "Lews Therin Telamon. The Dragon Reborn."

Min stared. She was the most beautiful woman Min had ever seen, with pale, smooth skin, and long, black hair, and eyes as dark as night. Her dress was a white that would make snow seem dingy, belted in silver. All her jewelry was silver. Min felt herself bristle. "What do you mean? Who are you?"

The woman came to stand over the bed—her movements were so graceful, Min felt a stab of envy, though she had never before envied any woman anything—and smoothed Rand's hair as if Min were not there. "He doesn't believe yet, I think. He knows, but he does not believe. I have guided his steps, pushed him, pulled him, enticed him. He was always stubborn, but this time I will shape him. Ishamael thinks he controls events, but I do." Her finger brushed Rand's forehead as if drawing a mark; Min thought uneasily that it looked like the Dragon's Fang. Rand stirred, murmuring, the first sound or movement he had made since she found him.

"Who are you?" Min demanded. The woman looked at her, only looked, but she found herself shrinking back into the pillows, clutching Rand to her fiercely.

"I am called Lanfear, girl."

Min's mouth was abruptly so dry she could not have spoken if her life depended on it. *One of the Forsaken! No! Light, no!* All she could do was shake her head. The denial made Lanfear smile.

"Lews Therin was and is mine, girl. Tend him well for me until I come for him." And she was gone.

Min gaped. One moment she was there, then she was gone. Min discovered she was hugging Rand's unconscious form tightly. She wished she did not feel as if she wanted him to protect her.

Gaunt face set with grim purpose, Byar galloped with the sinking sun behind him and never looked back. He had seen all he needed to, all he could with that accursed fog. The legion was dead, Lord Captain Geofram Bornhald was dead, and there was only one explanation for that; Darkfriends had betrayed them, Darkfriends like that Perrin of the Two Rivers. That word he had to carry to Dain Bornhald, the Lord Captain's son, with the Children of the Light watching Tar Valon. But he had worse to tell, and to none less than Pedron Niall himself. He had to tell what he had seen in the sky above Falme. He flogged his horse with his reins and never looked back.

# CHAPTER 49

## *What Was Meant To Be*

Rand opened his eyes and found himself staring up at sunlight slanting through the branches of a leatherleaf, its broad, tough leaves still green despite the time of year. The wind stirring the leaves carried a hint of snow, come nightfall. He lay on his back, and he could feel blankets covering him under his hands. His coat and shirt seemed to be gone, but something was binding his chest, and his left side hurt. He turned his head, and Min was sitting there on the ground, watching him. He almost did not know her, wearing skirts. She smiled uncertainly.

"Min. It is you. Where did you come from? Where are we?" His memory came in flashes and patches. Old things he could remember, but the last few days seemed like bits of broken mirror, spinning through his mind, showing glimpses that were gone before he could see them clearly.

"From Falme," she said. "We're five days east of there, now, and you've been asleep all that time."

"Falme." More memory. Mat had blown the Horn of Valere. "Egwene! Is she. . . ? Did they free her?" He held his breath.

"I don't know what 'they' you mean, but she's free. We freed her ourselves."

"We? I don't understand." *She's free. At least she is—*

"Nynaeve, and Elayne, and me."

"Nynaeve? Elayne? How? You were *all* in Falme?" He struggled to sit up, but she pushed him back down easily and stayed there, hands on his shoulders, eyes intent on his face. "Where is she?"

"Gone." Min's face colored. "They're all gone. Egwene, and Nynaeve, and Mat, and Hurin, and Verin. Hurin didn't want to leave you, really. They're on their way to Tar Valon. Egwene and Nynaeve back to their training in the Tower, and Mat for whatever the Aes Sedai have to do about that dagger. They took the Horn of Valere with them. I can't believe I actually saw it."

"Gone," he muttered. "She didn't even wait till I woke up." The red in Min's cheeks deepened, and she sat back, staring at her lap.

He raised his hands to run them over his face, and stopped, staring at his palms in shock. There was a heron branded across his left palm, too, now, to match the one on his right, every line clean and true. *Once the heron to set his path; Twice the heron to name him true.* "No!"

"They are gone," she said. "Saying 'no' won't change it."

He shook his head. Something told him the pain in his side was important. He could not remember being injured, but it was important. He started to lift his blankets to look, but she slapped his hands away.

"You can't do any good with that. It isn't healed all the way, yet. Verin tried Healing, but she said it didn't work the way it should." She hesitated, nibbling her lip. "Moiraine says Nynaeve must have done something, or you wouldn't have lived till we carried you to Verin, but Nynaeve says she was too frightened to light a candle. There is . . . something wrong with your wound. You will have to wait for it to heal naturally." She seemed troubled.

"Moiraine is here?" He barked a bitter laugh. "When you said Verin was gone, I thought I was free of Aes Sedai again."

"I am here," Moiraine said. She appeared, all in blue and as serene as if she stood in the White Tower, strolling up to stand over him. Min was frowning at the Aes Sedai. Rand had the odd feeling that she meant to protect him from Moiraine.

"I wish you weren't here," he told the Aes Sedai. "As far as I am concerned, you can go back to wherever you've been hiding and stay there."

"I have not been hiding," Moiraine said calmly. "I have been doing what I could, here on Toman Head, and in Falme. It was little enough, though I learned much. I failed to rescue two of my sisters before the Seanchan herded them onto the ships with the Leashed Ones, but I did what I could."

"What you could. You sent Verin to shepherd me, but I'm no sheep,

Moiraine. You said I could go where I wanted, and I mean to go where you are not."

"I did not send Verin." Moiraine frowned. "She did that on her own. You are of interest to a great many people, Rand. Did Fain find you, or you him?"

The sudden change of topic took him by surprise. "Fain? No. A fine hero I make. I tried to rescue Egwene, and Min did it before me. Fain said he would hurt Emond's Field if I didn't face him, and I never laid eyes on him. Did he go with the Seanchan, too?"

Moiraine shook her head. "I do not know. I wish I did. But it is as well you did not find him, not until you know what he is, at least."

"He's a Darkfriend."

"More than that. Worse than that. Padan Fain was the Dark One's creature to the depths of his soul, but I believe that in Shadar Logoth he fell afoul of Mordeth, who was as vile in fighting the Shadow as ever the Shadow itself was. Mordeth tried to consume Fain's soul, to have a human body again, but found a soul that had been touched directly by the Dark One, and what resulted. . . . What resulted was neither Padan Fain nor Mordeth, but something far more evil, a blend of the two. Fain—let us call him that—is more dangerous than you can believe. You might not have survived such a meeting, and if you had, you might have been worse than turned to the Shadow."

"If he is alive, if he did not go with the Seanchan, I have to—" He cut off as she produced his heron-mark sword from under her cloak. The blade ended abruptly a foot from the hilt, as if it had been melted. Memory came crashing back. "I killed him," he said softly. "This time I killed him."

Moiraine put the ruined sword aside like the useless thing it now was, and wiped her hands together. "The Dark One is not slain so easily. The mere fact that he appeared in the sky above Falme is more than merely troubling. He should not be able to do that, if he is bound as we believe. And if he is not, why has he not destroyed us all?" Min stirred uneasily.

"In the sky?" Rand said in wonder.

"Both of you," Moiraine said. "Your battle took place across the sky, in full view of every soul in Falme. Perhaps in other towns on Toman Head, too, if half what I hear is to be believed."

"We—we saw it all," Min said in a faint voice. She put a hand over one of Rand's comfortingly.

Moiraine reached under her cloak again and came out with a rolled parchment, one of the large sheets such as the street artists in Falme used. The chalks were a little smudged when she unfurled it, but the picture was still clear enough. A man whose face was a solid flame fought with a staff against another with a sword among clouds where lightning danced, and behind them rippled the Dragon banner. Rand's face was easily recognizable.

"How many have seen that?" he demanded. "Tear it up. Burn it."

The Aes Sedai let the parchment roll back up. "It would do no good, Rand. I bought that two days gone, in a village we passed through. There are hundreds of them, perhaps thousands, and the tale is being told everywhere of how the Dragon battled the Dark One in the skies above Falme."

Rand looked at Min. She nodded reluctantly, and squeezed his hand. She looked frightened, but she did not flinch away. *I wonder if that's why Egwene left. She was right to leave.*

"The Pattern weaves itself around you even more tightly," Moiraine said. "You need me now more than ever."

"I don't need you," he said harshly, "and I don't want you. I will not have anything to do with this." He remembered being called Lews Therin; not only by Ba'alzamon, but by Artur Hawkwing. "I won't. Light, the Dragon is supposed to Break the World again, to tear everything apart. I will not be the Dragon."

"You are what you are," Moiraine said. "Already you stir the world. The Black Ajah has revealed itself for the first time in two thousand years. Arad Doman and Tarabon were on the brink of war, and it will be worse when news of Falme reaches them. Cairhien is in civil war."

"I did nothing in Cairhien," he protested. "You can't blame that on me."

"Doing nothing was always a ploy in the Great Game," she said with a sigh, "and especially as they play it now. You were the spark, and Cairhien exploded like an Illuminator's firework. What do you think will happen when word of Falme reaches Arad Doman and Tarabon? There have always been men willing to proclaim for any man who called himself the Dragon, but they have never before had such signs as this. There is more. Here." She tossed a pouch on his chest.

He hesitated a moment before opening it. Within lay shards of what seemed to be black-and-white glazed pottery. He had seen their like before. "Another seal on the Dark One's prison," he mumbled. Min gasped; her grip on his hand sought comfort, now, rather than offering it.

"Two," Moiraine said. "Three of the seven are broken now. The one I had, and two I found in the High Lord's dwelling in Falme. When all seven are broken, perhaps even before, the patch men put over the hole they drilled into the prison the Creator made will be torn asunder, and the Dark One will once more be able to put his hand through that hole and touch the world. And the only hope of the world is that the Dragon Reborn will be there to face him."

Min tried to stop Rand from throwing back the blankets, but he pushed her gently aside. "I need to walk." She helped him up, but with a great many sighs and grumbles about him making his wound worse. He discovered that his chest was wrapped round with bandages. Min draped one of the blankets about his shoulders like a cloak.

For a moment he stood staring down at the heron-mark sword, what was left of it, lying on the ground. *Tam's sword. My father's sword.* Reluctantly, more reluctantly than he had ever done anything in his life, he let go of the hope that he would discover Tam really was his father. It felt as if he were tearing his heart out. But it did not change the way he felt about Tam, and Emond's Field was the only home he had ever known. *Fain is the important thing. I have one duty left. Stopping him.*

The two women had to support him, one on either arm, down to where the campfires were already burning, not far from a road of hard-packed dirt. Loial was there, reading a book, *To Sail Beyond the Sunset,* and Perrin, staring into one of the fires. The Shienarans were making preparations for their evening meal. Lan sat under a tree sharpening his sword; the Warder gave Rand a careful look, then a nod.

There was something else, too. The Dragon banner rippled on the wind over the middle of the camp. Somewhere they had found a proper staff to replace Perrin's sapling.

Rand demanded, "What is that doing out where anybody who passes by can see it?"

"It is too late to hide, Rand," Moiraine said. "It was always too late for you to hide."

"You don't have to put up a sign saying 'here I am,' either. I'll never find Fain if somebody kills me because of that banner." He turned to Loial and Perrin. "I'm glad you stayed. I would have understood if you hadn't."

"Why would I not stay?" Loial said. "You are even more *ta'veren* than I believed, true, but you are still my friend. I hope you are still my friend." His ears twitched uncertainly.

"I am," Rand said. "For as long as it's safe for you to be around me, and even after, too." The Ogier's grin nearly split his face in two.

"I'm staying as well," Perrin said. There was a note of resignation, or acceptance, in his voice. "The Wheel weaves us tight in the Pattern, Rand. Who would have thought it, back in Emond's Field?"

The Shienarans were gathering around. To Rand's surprise, they all fell to their knees. Every one of them watched him.

"We would pledge ourselves to you," Uno said. The others kneeling with him nodded.

"Your oaths are to Ingtar, and Lord Agelmar," Rand protested. "Ingtar died well, Uno. He died so the rest of us could escape with the Horn." There was no need to tell them or anyone else the rest. He hoped that Ingtar had found the Light again. "Tell Lord Agelmar that when you return to Fal Dara."

"It is said," the one-eyed man said carefully, "that when the Dragon is Reborn, he will break all oaths, shatter all ties. Nothing holds us, now. We would give our oaths to you." He drew his sword and laid it before him, hilt toward Rand, and the rest of the Shienarans did the same.

"You battled the Dark One," Masema said. Masema, who hated him. Masema, who looked at him as if seeing a vision of the Light. "I saw you, Lord Dragon. I saw. I am your man, to the death." His dark eyes shone with fervor.

"You must choose, Rand," Moiraine said. "The world will be broken whether you break it or not. Tarmon Gai'don will come, and that alone will tear the world apart. Will you still try to hide from what you are, and leave the world to face the Last Battle undefended? Choose."

They were all watching him, all waiting. *Death is lighter than a feather, duty heavier than a mountain.* He made his decision.

# CHAPTER 50

## *After*

By ship and horse the stories spread, by merchant wagon and man on foot, told and retold, changing yet always alike at the heart, to Arad Doman and Tarabon and beyond, of signs and portents in the sky above Falme. And men proclaimed themselves for the Dragon, and other men struck them down and were struck down in turn.

Other tales spread, of a column that rode from the sinking sun across Almoth Plain. A hundred Bordermen, it was said. No, a thousand. No, a thousand heroes come back from the grave to answer the call of the Horn of Valere. Ten thousand. They had destroyed a legion of the Children of the Light entire. They had thrown Artur Hawkwing's returned armies back into the sea. They were Artur Hawkwing's armies returned. Toward the mountains they rode, toward the dawn.

Yet one thing every tale had the same. At their head rode a man whose face had been seen in the sky above Falme, and they rode under the banner of the Dragon Reborn.

*And men cried out to the Creator, saying, O Light of the Heavens, Light of the World, let the Promised One be born of the mountain, according to the Prophecies, as he was in Ages past and will be in Ages to come. Let the Prince of the Morning sing to the land that green things will grow and the valleys give forth lambs. Let the arm of the Lord of the Dawn shelter us from the Dark, and the great sword of justice defend us. Let the Dragon ride again on the winds of time.*

—*from* **Charal Drianaan te Calamon, The Cycle of the Dragon,**
Author unknown, the Fourth Age

# The End
# of the Second Book of
# *The Wheel of Time*

# GLOSSARY

**A Note on Dates in This Glossary.** Three systems of recording dates have been in general use since the Breaking of the World. The first recorded years After the Breaking (AB). Since the years of the Breaking and immediately after were years of almost total chaos, and since this calendar was adopted a good hundred years after the end of the Breaking, its starting point was arbitrarily assigned. At the end of the Trolloc Wars many records had been lost, so much so that there was argument about the exact year under the old system. A new calendar was therefore established, dating from the end of the Wars and celebrating the supposed freedom of the world from the Trolloc threat. This second calendar recorded each year as Free Year (FY). After the disruption, death, and destruction caused by the War of the Hundred Years, a third calendar came into being. This calendar, of the New Era (NE), is currently in use.

*a'dam* (AYE-*dam*): A device, consisting of a collar and a bracelet linked by a silvery metal leash, that may be used to control, against her will, any woman who can channel. The collar is worn by the *damane*, the bracelet by the *sul'dam*. **See also** *damane; sul'dam.*

*Aes Sedai* (EYEZ seh-DEYE): Wielders of the One Power. Since the Time of Madness, all surviving Aes Sedai are women. Widely distrusted and feared, even hated, they are blamed by many for the Breaking of the World, and are thought to meddle in the affairs of nations. At the same time, few rulers will be without an Aes Sedai adviser, even in lands where the existence of such a connection must be kept secret. *See also* Ajah; Amyrlin Seat; Time of Madness.

**Agelmar; Lord Agelmar of House Jagad** (*AGH-el-mar;* JAH-gad): Lord of Fal Dara. His sign is three running red foxes.

**Age of Legends:** The Age ended by the War of the Shadow and the Breaking of the World. A time when Aes Sedai performed wonders now only dreamed of. *See also* Wheel of Time; Breaking of the World; War of the Shadow.

**Aiel** (eye-EEL): The people of the Aiel Waste. Fierce and hardy. Also called Aielmen. They veil their faces before they kill, giving rise to the saying "acting like a black-veiled Aiel" to describe someone who is being violent. Deadly warriors with weapons or with nothing but their bare hands, they will not touch a sword. Their pipers play them into battle with the music of dances, and Aielmen call battle "the Dance." *See also*. Aiel warrior societies; Aiel Waste.

**Aiel warrior societies:** Aiel warriors are all members of one of the warrior societies, such as the Stone Soldiers, the Red Shields, or the Maidens of the Spear. Each society has its own customs, and sometimes specific duties. For example, Red Shields act as police. Stone Soldiers often vow not to retreat once battle has been joined, and will die to the last man if necessary to fulfill this vow. The clans of the Aiel frequently fight among themselves, but members of the same society will not fight one another even if their clans are doing so. In this way, there are always lines of contact between the clans even when they are in open warfare. *See also* Aiel; Aiel Waste; *Far Dareis Mai.*

**Aiel Waste:** The harsh, rugged, and all-but-waterless land east of the Spine of the World. Few outsiders venture there, not only because water is almost impossible to find for one not born there, but because the Aiel consider themselves at war with all other peoples and do not welcome strangers.

**Ajah** (AH-jah): Societies among the Aes Sedai to which all Aes Sedai except the Amyrlin Seat belong. They are designated by colors: Blue, Red, White, Green, Brown, Yellow, and Gray. Each follows a specific philosophy of the use of the One Power and the purposes of the Aes Sedai. For example, the Red Ajah bends all its energies to finding men who are attempting to wield the Power and to gentling them. The Brown Ajah, on the other hand, forsakes involvement with the mundane world and dedicates itself to seeking knowledge. There are rumors (hotly denied, and never safely mentioned in front of any Aes Sedai) of a Black Ajah, dedicated to serving the Dark One.

**Alanna Mosvani** (ah-LAN-nah mos-VANH-nie): An Aes Sedai of the Green Ajah.

*alantin* (*ah-LANH-tin*): In the Old Tongue, "Brother"; short for *tia avende alantin,* "Brother to the Trees"; "Treebrother."

**Alar** (AYE-lahr): Eldest of the Elders of Stedding Tsofu.

**Aldieb** (ahl-DEEB): In the Old Tongue, "West Wind," the wind that brings the spring rains.

**al'Meara, Nynaeve** (ahl-MEER-ah, NIGH-neev): A woman from Emond's Field, in the Two Rivers district of Andor (AN-door).

**al'Thor, Rand** (ahl-THOR, RAND): A young man from Emond's Field, once a shepherd.

**al'Vere, Egwene** (ahl-VEER, eh-GWAIN): A young woman from Emond's Field.

**Amalisa, Lady** (ah-mah-LEE-sah): Shienaran of House Jagad; Lord Agelmar's sister.

**Amyrlin Seat** (AHM-ehr-lin SEAT): (1) The title of the leader of the Aes Sedai. Elected for life by the Hall of the Tower, the highest council of the Aes Sedai, which consists of three representatives (called Sitters) from each of the seven Ajahs. The Amyrlin Seat has, theoretically at least, almost supreme authority among the Aes Sedai, and ranks socially as the equal of a king or queen. A slightly less formal usage is simply the Amyrlin. (2) The throne upon which the leader of the Aes Sedai sits.

**Anaiya** (ah-NYE-yah): An Aes Sedai of the Blue Ajah.

*angreal* (anh-gree-AHL): A very rare object that allows anyone capable of channeling the One Power to handle a greater amount of the Power than would be safely possible unaided. Remnants of the Age of Legends, the means of their making is no longer known. Few remain in existence. *See also* sa'angreal; ter'angreal.

**Arad Doman** (AH-rahd do-MAHN): A nation on the Aryth Ocean.

**Arafel** (AH-rah-fehl): One of the Borderlands.

*Avendesora* (*AH-vehn-deh-SO-rah*): In the Old Tongue, "the Tree of Life." Mentioned in many stories and legends.

**Aybara, Perrin** (ay-BAHR-ah, PEHR-rihn): A young man from Emond's Field, formerly a blacksmith's apprentice.

**Ba'alzamon** (bah-AHL-zah-mon): In the Trolloc tongue, "Heart of the Dark." Believed to be the Trolloc name for the Dark One. *See also* Dark One; Trollocs.

**Barthanes, Lord, of House Damodred** (bahr-THAN-nehs): Cairhienin lord, second only to the king in power. His personal sign is the Charging Boar. The sign of House Damodred is the Crown and Tree.

**Bel Tine** (BEHL TINE): Spring festival celebrating the end of winter, the first sprouting of crops, and the birth of the first lambs.

**Betrayer of Hope:** *See* Ishamael.

**Birgitte** (ber-GEET-teh): Golden-haired heroine of legend and a hundred gleemen's tales, she had a silver bow and silver arrows, with which she never missed.

**bittern** (BIHT-tehrn): A musical instrument that may have six, nine, or twelve strings, and is held flat on the knees and played by plucking or strumming.

**Blasted Lands:** Desolated lands surrounding Shayol Ghul, beyond the Great Blight.

**Blight, the:** *See* Great Blight, the.

**Borderlands, the:** The nations bordering the Great Blight. Saldaea, Arafel, Kandor, and Shienar.

**Bornhald, Geofram** (BOHRN-hahld, JEHF-rahm): A Lord Captain of the Children of the Light.

**Breaking of the World, the:** During the Time of Madness, male Aes Sedai who had gone insane, and who could wield the One Power to a degree now unknown, changed the face of the earth. They caused great earthquakes, leveled old mountain ranges and raised new mountains, lifted dry land where seas had been and made the ocean rush in where dry land had been. Many parts of the world were completely depopulated, and the survivors were scattered like dust on the wind. This destruction is remembered in stories, legends, and history as the Breaking of the World. *See also* Time of Madness.

**Byar, Jaret** (BY-ahr, JAH-ret): An officer of the Children of the Light.

**Caemlyn** (KAYM-lihn): The capital city of Andor.

**Cairhien** (KEYE-ree-EHN): Both a nation along the Spine of the World and the capital city of that nation. The city was burned and looted during the Aiel War (976–978 NE). The sign of Cairhien is a many-rayed golden sun rising from the bottom of a field of sky blue.

**Carallain** (KAH-rah-layn): One of the nations wrung from Artur Hawkwing's empire during the War of the Hundred Years. It weakened thereafter, and the last traces vanished about 500 NE.

**Cauthon, Mat** (CAW-thon, MAT): A young man from the Two Rivers. Full name: Matrim (MAT-rihm) Cauthon.

**channel:** (verb) To control the flow of the One Power. *See also* One Power.

**Children of the Light:** A society holding strict ascetic beliefs, dedicated to the defeat of the Dark One and the destruction of all Darkfriends. Founded during the War of the Hundred Years by Lothair Mantelar (LOH-thayr MAHN-tee-LAHR) to proselytize against the increasing numbers of Darkfriends, they evolved during the war into a completely military organization, extremely rigid in their beliefs, and completely certain that only they know the truth and the right. They hate Aes Sedai, considering them, and any who support or befriend them, Darkfriends. They are known disparagingly as Whitecloaks. Their sign is a golden sunburst on a field of white.

**Chronicles, Keeper of the:** Second in authority to the Amyrlin Seat among the Aes Sedai, she also acts as secretary to the Amyrlin. Chosen for life by the Hall of the Tower, and usually of the same Ajah as the Amyrlin. *See also* Amyrlin Seat; Ajah.

**Corenne** (*koh-REEN-neh*): In the Old Tongue, "Return," or "the Return."

**Covenant of the Ten Nations:** A union formed in the centuries after the Breaking of the World when nations were first re-created (circa 300

AB). Dedicated to the defeat of the Dark One. Broken apart by the Trolloc Wars. *See also* Trolloc Wars.

*cuendillar* (CWAIN-der-yar): Also known as heartstone. *See* heartstone.

*Daes Dae'mar* (DAH-ess day-MAR): The Great Game, also known as the Game of Houses. Name given the scheming, plots, and manipulations for advantage by the noble Houses. Great value is given to subtlety, to aiming at one thing while seeming to aim at another, and to achieving ends with the least visible effort.

**Dai Shan:** (DYE SHAN): A title in the Borderlands meaning Diademed Battle Lord. *See also* Borderlands.

*damane* (*dah-MAHN-ee*): In the Old Tongue, "Leashed Ones." Women who can channel who are held prisoner by *a'dam* and used by the Seanchan for many purposes, chiefest of these being as weapons in battle. *See also* Seanchan; *a'dam; sul'dam.*

**Damodred, Lord Galadedrid** (DAHM-oh-drehd, gah-LAHD-eh-drihd); Half-brother to Elayne and Gawyn. His sign is a winged silver sword, point down.

**Darkfriends:** Those who follow the Dark One and believe they will gain great power and rewards, and even immortality, when he is freed from his prison.

**Dark One:** Most common name, used in every land, for Shai'tan. The source of evil, antithesis of the Creator. Imprisoned by the Creator at the moment of Creation in a prison at Shayol Ghul. An attempt to free him from that prison brought about the War of the Shadow, the tainting of *saidin,* the Breaking of the World, and the end of the Age of Legends.

**Dark One, naming the:** Saying the true name of the Dark One (Shai'tan) draws his attention, inevitably bringing ill fortune at best, disaster at worst. For that reason, many euphemisms are used, among them the Dark One, Father of Lies, Sightblinder, Lord of the Grave, Shepherd of the Night, Heartsbane, Heartfang, Grassburner, and Leafblighter. Someone who seems to be inviting ill fortune is often said to be "naming the Dark One."

**Daughter-Heir:** Title of the heir to the throne of Andor. The eldest daughter of the queen succeeds her mother on the throne. Without a surviving daughter, the throne goes to the nearest female blood relation of the queen.

**Daughter of the Night:** *See* Lanfear.

**Dome of Truth:** Great audience hall of the Children of the Light, located in Amador (AH-mah-door), the capital of Amadicia (AH-mah-DEE-cee-ah). There is a King of Amadicia, but the Children rule in all but name. *See also* Children of the Light.

**Do Miere A'vron** (DOH me-EHR a-VRAWN): *See* Watchers Over the Waves.

**Domon, Bayle** (DOH-mon, BAIL): The captain of the *Spray,* who collects old things.

**Draghkar** (DRAGH-kahr): A creature of the Dark One, made originally by twisting human stock. A Draghkar appears to be a large man with bat-like wings, whose skin is too pale and whose eyes are too large. The Draghkar's song can draw its prey to it, suppressing the victim's will. There is a saying: "The kiss of the Draghkar is death." It does not bite, but its kiss will consume first the soul of its victim, and then its life.

**Dragon, false:** Occasionally men claim to be the Dragon Reborn, and sometimes one of them gains following enough to require an army to put it down. Some have begun wars that involved many nations. Over the centuries most of these have been men unable to channel the One Power, but a few could do so. All, however, either disappeared or were captured or killed without fulfilling any of the Prophecies concerning the Rebirth of the Dragon. These men are called false Dragons. Among those who could channel, the most powerful were Raolin Darksbane (335–36AB), Yurian Stonebow (circa 1300–1308 AB), Davian (FY 351), Guaire Amalasan (FY 939–43), and Logain (997 NE). *See also* Dragon Reborn.

**Dragon, Prophecies of the:** Little known and seldom spoken of, the Prophecies, given in *The Karaethon Cycle,* foretell that the Dark One will be freed again to touch the world. And that Lews Therin Telamon, the Dragon, Breaker of the World, will be reborn to fight Tarmon Gai'don, the Last Battle against the Shadow. *See also* Dragon, the.

**Dragon, the:** The name by which Lews Therin Telamon was known during the War of the Shadow. In the madness that overtook all male Aes

Sedai, Lews Therin killed every living person who carried any of his blood, as well as everyone he loved, thus earning the name Kinslayer. *See also* Dragon Reborn; Dragon, Prophecies of the.

**Dragon Reborn:** According to prophecy and legend the Dragon will be born again at mankind's greatest hour of need to save the world. This is not something people look forward to, both because the Prophecies say the Dragon Reborn will bring a new Breaking to the world and because Lews Therin Kinslayer, the Dragon, is a name to make men shudder, even more than three thousand years after his death. *See also* Dragon, the; Dragon, false; Dragon, Prophecies of the.

**Dragon's Fang, the:** A stylized mark in the shape of a teardrop balanced on its point. Scrawled on a door or a house, it is an accusation of evil against the people inside, or an attempt to bring the Dark One's attention, and thus harm, to them.

**Dreadlords:** Those men and women who, able to channel the One Power, went over to the Shadow during the Trolloc Wars, acting as commanders of the Trolloc forces.

**Elaida** (eh-LY-da): An Aes Sedai of the Red Ajah who advises Queen Morgase of Andor. She sometimes has the Foretelling. *See also* Foretelling.

**Elayne** (ee-LAIN): Queen Morgase's daughter, the Daughter-Heir to the Throne of Andor. Her sign is a golden lily.

**Fain, Padan** (FAIN, PAHD-ahn): A man imprisoned as a Darkfriend in Fal Dara keep.

*Far Dareis Mai* (FAHR DAH-rize MY): Literally "Maidens of the Spear." A warrior society of the Aiel, which, unlike any of the others, admits women and only women. A Maiden may not marry and remain in the society, nor may she fight while carrying a child. Any child born to a Maiden is given to another woman to raise, in such a way that no one knows who the child's mother was. ("You may belong to no man, nor may any man belong to you, nor any child. The spear is your lover, your child, and your life.") These children are treasured, for it is prophesied that a child born of a Maiden will unite the clans and return the Aiel to the greatness they knew during the Age of Legends. *See also* Aiel; Aiel warrior societies.

**Five Powers, the:** There are threads to the One Power, and each person who can channel can usually grasp some threads better than others.

These threads are named according to the sorts of things that can be done using them—Earth, Air, Fire, Water, and Spirit—and are called the Five Powers. Any wielder of the Power will have a greater degree of strength with one, or possibly two, of these, and lesser strength in the others. Some few may have great strength with three, but since the Age of Legends no one has had great strength with all five. Even then this was extremely rare. The degree of strength can vary greatly between individuals, so that some who can channel are much stronger than others. Performing certain acts with the One Power requires ability in one or more of the Five Powers. For example, starting or controlling a fire requires Fire, and affecting the weather requires Air and Water, while Healing requires Water and Spirit. While Spirit was found equally in men and in women, great ability with Earth and/or Fire was found much more often among men; with Water and/or Air among women. There were exceptions, but it was so often so that Earth and Fire came to be regarded as male Powers, Air and Water as female. Generally, no ability is considered stronger than any other, though there is a saying among Aes Sedai: "There is no rock so strong that water and wind cannot wear it away, no fire so fierce that water cannot quench it or wind snuff it out." It should be noted this saying came into use long after the last male Aes Sedai was dead. Any equivalent saying among male Aes Sedai is long lost.

**Flame of Tar Valon:** The symbol of Tar Valon, the Amyrlin Seat, and the Aes Sedai. A stylized representation of a flame; a white teardrop with the point upward.

**Forsaken, the:** Name given to thirteen of the most powerful Aes Sedai ever known, who went over to the Dark One during the War of the Shadow in return for the promise of immortality. According to both legend and fragmentary records, they were imprisoned along with the Dark One when his prison was resealed. Their names are still used to frighten children.

**Gaidin** (GYE-deen): Literally, "Brother to Battles." A title used by Aes Sedai for the Warders. *See also* Warder.

**Galad** (gah-LAHD): *See* Damodred, Lord Galadedrid.

**Galldrian su Riatin Rie** (GAHL-dree-ahn soo REYE-ah-tin REE) : Literally, Galldrian of House Riatin, King. King of Cairhien. *See also* Cairhien.

**Game of Houses, the:** *See Daes Dae'mar.*

**Gawyn** (GAH-wihn): Queen Morgase's son, and Elayne's brother. His sign is a white boar.

**gentling:** The act, performed by Aes Sedai, of shutting off a male who can channel from the One Power. This is necessary because any man who learns to channel will go insane from the taint on *saidin* and will almost certainly do horrible things with the Power in his madness. A man who has been gentled can still sense the True Source, but he cannot touch it. Whatever madness has come before gentling is arrested by the act of gentling, but not cured by it, and if it is done soon enough death can be averted. *See also* One Power, the; stilling.

**gleeman:** A traveling storyteller, musician, juggler, tumbler, and all-around entertainer. Known by their trademark cloaks of many-colored patches, they perform mainly in the villages and smaller towns.

**Goaban** (GO-ah-banh): One of the nations wrung from Artur Hawkwing's empire during the War of the Hundred Years. It weakened, and faded away approximately 500 NE. *See also* Artur Hawkwing; War of the Hundred Years.

*Great Blight, the:* A region in the far north, entirely corrupted by the Dark One. A haunt of Trollocs, Myrddraal, and other creatures of the Shadow.

**Great Game, the:** *See Daes Dae'mar.*

**Great Hunt of the Horn, the:** A cycle of stories concerning the legendary search for the Horn of Valere, in the years between the end of the Trolloc Wars and the beginning of the War of the Hundred Years. If told in its entirety, the cycle would take many days.

**Great Lord of the Dark:** The name by which Darkfriends refer to the Dark One, claiming that to use his true name would be blasphemous.

**Great Serpent:** A symbol for time and eternity, ancient before the Age of Legends began, consisting of a serpent eating its own tail. A ring in the shape of the Great Serpent is awarded to women who have been raised to the Accepted among the Aes Sedai.

*Hailene* (heye-LEE-neh): In the Old Tongue, "Those Who Come Before," or "Forerunners."

**Halfman:** *See* Myrddraal.

**Hardan:** One of the nations wrung from Artur Hawkwing's empire, now long forgotten. It lay between Cairhien and Shienar.

**Hawkwing, Artur:** A legendary king (ruled FY 943–994) who united all the lands west of the Spine of the World, as well as some lands beyond the Aiel Waste. He even sent armies across the Aryth Ocean (FY 992), but all contact with these was lost at his death, which set off the War of the Hundred Years. His sign was a golden hawk in flight. *See also* War of the Hundred Years.

**heartstone:** An indestructible substance created during the Age of Legends. Any force used in an attempt to break it is absorbed, making heartstone stronger.

**hide:** A unit of area for measuring land, equal to 100 paces by 100 paces.

**Horn of Valere** (vah-LEER): The legendary object of the Great Hunt of the Horn. The Horn supposedly can call back dead heroes from the grave to fight against the Shadow.

**Hundred Companions, the:** One hundred male Aes Sedai, among the most powerful of the Age of Legends, who, led by Lews Therin Telamon, launched the final stroke that ended the War of the Shadow by sealing the Dark One back into his prison. The Dark One's counterstroke tainted *saidin;* the Hundred Companions went mad and began the Breaking of the World. *See also* Time of Madness; Breaking of the World; True Source; One Power.

**Hurin** (HEW-rhin): A Shienaran who has the ability to smell where violence has been done, and to follow the scent of those who did it. Called a "sniffer," he serves the King's justice in Fal Dara, in Shienar.

**Illian** (IHL-lee-ahn): A great port on the Sea of Storms, capital city of the nation of the same name.

**Ingtar, Lord, of House Shinowa** (IHNG-tahr); (shih-NOH-wah): A Shienaran warrior. His sign is the Gray Owl.

**Ishamael** (ih-SHAH-may-EHL): In the Old Tongue, "Betrayer of Hope." One of the Forsaken. Name given to the leader of the Aes Sedai who went over to the Dark One in the War of the Shadow. It is said that even he forgot his true name. *See also* Forsaken.

*Karaethon Cycle, the* (ka-REE-ah-thon): See Dragon, Prophecies of the.

**kith:** Close friends and acquaintances.

**Laman** (LAY-mahn): A king of Cairhien, of House Damodred, who lost his throne and life in the Aiel War.

**Lan; al'Lan Mandragoran** (AHL-LAN man-DRAG-or-an): A Warder, bonded to Moiraine. Uncrowned King of Malkier, Dai Shan, and the last surviving Malkieri lord. *See also* Warder; Moiraine; Malkier; Dai Shan.

**Lanfear** (LAN-fear): In the Old Tongue, "Daughter of the Night." One of the Forsaken, perhaps the most powerful next to Ishamael. Unlike the other Forsaken, she chose this name herself. She is said to have been in love with Lews Therin Telamon. *See also* Forsaken; Dragon, the.

**league:** *See* Length, units of.

**Leane** (lee-AHN-eh): An Aes Sedai of the Blue Ajah, and Keeper of the Chronicles. *See also* Ajah; Chronicles, Keeper of the.

**Leashed Ones:** *See damane.*

**Length, units of:** 10 inches = 3 hands = 1 foot; 3 feet = 1 pace; 2 paces = 1 span; 1000 spans = 1 mile; 4 miles = 1 league.

**Lews Therin Telamon; Lews Therin Kinslayer:** *See* Dragon, the.

**Liandrin** (lee-AHN-drihn): An Aes Sedai of the Red Ajah, from Tarabon.

**Logain** (loh-GAYN): A false Dragon, gentled by the Aes Sedai.

**Loial** (LOY-ahl): An Ogier from Stedding Shangtai.

**Luc; Lord Luc of House Mantear** (LUKE; MAN-tee-ahr): Tigraine's brother. His disappearance in the Great Blight (971 NE) is believed to be connected to Tigraine's later disappearance. His sign was an acorn.

**Luthair:** See Mondwin, Luthair Paendrag.

**Malkier** (mahl-KEER): A nation, once one of the Borderlands, now consumed by the Blight. The sign of Malkier was a golden crane in flight.

**Manetheren** (mahn-EHTH-ehr-ehn): One of the Ten Nations that made the Second Covenant, and also the capital city of that nation. Both city and nation were utterly destroyed in the Trolloc Wars.

**marath'damane** (MAH-rahth'dah-MAHN-ee): In the Old Tongue, "Those Who Must Be Leashed." Term used by the Seanchan for women who can channel, but who have not yet been captured and collared. *See also damane; a'dam;* Seanchan.

**Masema** (mah-SEE-mah): A Shienaran soldier who hates Aiel.

*mashiara* (*mah-shee-AH-rah*): In the Old Tongue, "beloved," but meaning a love that is lost beyond redeeming.

**Merrilin, Thom** (MER-rih-lihn, TOM): A gleeman.

**mile:** *See* Length, units of.

**Min** (MIN): A young woman with the ability to read the auras she sometimes sees surrounding people.

**Moiraine** (mwah-RAIN): An Aes Sedai of the Blue Ajah.

**Mondwin, Luthair Paendrag** (LEW-thair PAY-ehn-DRAG MONdwihn): Son of Artur Hawkwing, he commanded the armies Hawkwing sent across the Aryth Ocean. His banner was a golden, spreadwinged hawk clutching lightning bolts. *See also* Hawkwing, Artur.

**Mordeth** (MOOR-death): Councilor who turned the city of Aridhol to use Darkfriends' ways against the Darkfriends, thus bringing its destruction and earning it a new name, Shadar Logoth ("Where the Shadow Waits"). Only one thing survives in Shadar Logoth beside the hate that killed it, and that is Mordeth himself, bound in the ruins for two thousand years, waiting for someone to come whose soul he can consume and so take on new flesh.

**Morgase** (moor-GAYZ): Queen of Andor, High Seat of House Trakand (TRAHK-ahnd).

**Myrddraal** (MUHRD-draal): Creatures of the Dark One, commanders of the Trollocs. Twisted offspring of Trollocs in which the human stock used to create the Trollocs has resurfaced, but tainted by the evil that made the Trollocs. Physically they are like men except they have no eyes, but can see like eagles in light or dark. They have certain powers stemming from the Dark One, including the ability to cause paralyzing fear with a look and the ability to vanish wherever there are shadows. One of their few known weaknesses is that they are reluctant to cross running water. In different lands they are known by many names, among them Halfmen, the Eyeless, Shadowmen, Lurks, and Fades.

**Niall, Pedron** (NEYE-awl, PAY-drohn): Lord Captain Commander of the Children of the Light. *See also* Children of the Light.

**Nisura, Lady** (nih-SOO-rah): A Shienaran noblewoman, and one of the Lady Amalisa's attendants.

**One Power, the:** The power drawn from the True Source. The vast majority of people are completely unable to learn to channel the One Power. A very small number can be taught to channel, and an even tinier number have the ability inborn. For these few there is no need to be taught; they will touch the True Source and channel the Power whether they want to or not, perhaps without even realizing what they are doing. This inborn ability usually manifests itself in late adolescence or early adulthood. If control is not taught, or self-learned (extremely difficult, with a success rate of only one in four), death is certain. Since the Time of Madness, no man has been able to channel the Power without eventually going completely, horribly mad, and then, even if he has learned some control, dying from a wasting sickness that causes the sufferer to rot alive, a sickness caused, as is the madness, by the Dark One's taint on *saidin*. For a woman the death that comes without control of the Power is less horrible, but it is death just the same. Aes Sedai search for girls with the inborn ability as much to save their lives as to increase Aes Sedai numbers, and for men with it in order to stop the terrible things they inevitably do with the Power in their madness. *See also* channel; Time of Madness; True Source.

**Pattern of an Age:** The Wheel of Time weaves the threads of human lives into the Pattern of an Age, often called simply the Pattern, which forms the substance of reality for that Age. *See also ta'veren.*

**Powers, the Five:** *See* Five Powers.

**Questioners, the:** An order within the Children of the Light. Their avowed purposes are to discover the truth in disputations and to uncover Darkfriends. In the search for truth and the Light, their normal method of inquiry is by torture; their normal attitude that they know the truth already and must only make their victim confess to it. The Questioners refer to themselves as the Hand of the Light, the Hand that digs out truth, and at times act as if they were entirely separate from the Children and the Council of the Anointed, which commands the Children. The head of the Questioners is the High Inquisitor, who sits on the Council of the Anointed. Their sign is a blood-red shepherd's crook.

**Ragan** (rah-GAHN): A Shienaran warrior.

**Red Shields:** *See* Aiel warrior societies.

**Renna** (REEN-nah): A Seanchan woman; a *sul'dam*. *See also* Seanchan; *sul'dam*.

**Rhyagelle** (*rheye-ah-GEHL*): In the Old Tongue, "Those Who Come Home," or "Homecomers."

*sa'angreal* (*SAH-ahn-GREE-ahl*): Any one of a number of objects that allow an individual to channel much more of the One Power than would otherwise be possible or safe. A *sa'angreal* is like unto, but much more powerful than, an *angreal*. The amount of the Power that can be wielded with a *sa'angreal* compares to the amount of the Power that can be handled with an *angreal* as the power wielded with the aid of an *angreal* does to the amount of the Power that can be handled unaided. Remnants of the Age of Legends, the means of making *sa'angreal* is no longer known. Only a handful remain, far fewer even than *angreal*.

*saidar* (*sah-ih-DAHR*): *saidin* (sah-ih-DEEN): *See* True Source.

**Saldaea** (sahl-DAY-ee-ah): One of the Borderlands.

**Sanche, Siuan** (SAHN-chay, swahn): An Aes Sedai formerly of the Blue Ajah. Raised to the Amyrlin Seat 985 NE. The Amyrlin Seat is of all Ajahs, and of none.

**Sea Folk:** More properly, the Atha'an Miere (a-tha-AHN mee-AIR), the People of the Sea. Inhabitants of islands in the Aryth (AH-rihth) Ocean and the Sea of Storms, they spend little time on those islands, living most of their lives on their ships. Most seaborne trade is carried by the Sea Folk's ships.

**Seanchan** (SHAWN-CHAN): (1) Descendants of the armies Artur Hawkwing sent across the Aryth Ocean, who have returned to reclaim the lands of their forefathers. (2) The land from which the Seanchan come. *See also Hailene; Corenne; Rhyagelle.*

**Seandar** (shawn-DAHR): Capital city of Seanchan, where the Empress sits on the Crystal Throne in the Court of the Nine Moons.

**Selene** (seh-LEEN): A woman met on the journey to Cairhien.

**Seta** (SEE-tah): A Seanchan woman; a *sul'dam*. *See also* Seanchan; *sul'dam*.

**Shadar Logoth** (SHAH-dahr LOH-goth): A city abandoned and shunned since the Trolloc Wars. It is tainted ground, and not a pebble of it is safe. *See also* Mordeth.

**Shai'tan** (SHAY-ih-TAN): *See* Dark One.

**Shayol Ghul** (SHAY-ol GHOOL): A mountain in the Blasted Lands, the site of the Dark One's prison.

**Sheriam** (SHEER-ee-ahm): An Aes Sedai of the Blue Ajah. The Mistress of Novices in the White Tower.

**Shienar** (shy-NAHR): One of the Borderlands. The sign of Shienar is a stooping black hawk.

*shoufa* (SHOO-fah): A garment of the Aiel, a cloth, usually the color of sand or rock, that wraps around the head and neck, leaving only the face bare.

**span** *See* Length, units of.

**Spine of the World, the:** A towering mountain range, with only a few passes, which separates the Aiel Waste from the lands to the west.

*stedding* (STEHD-ding): An Ogier (OH-geer) homeland. Many *stedding* have been abandoned since the Breaking of the World. They are shielded in some way, no longer understood, so that within them no Aes Sedai can channel the One Power, nor even sense that the True Source exists. Attempts to wield the One Power from outside a *stedding* have no effect inside a *stedding* boundary. No Trolloc will enter a *stedding* unless driven, and even a Myrddraal will do so only at the greatest need and then with the greatest reluctance and distaste. Even Darkfriends, if truly dedicated, feel uncomfortable within a *stedding*.

**stilling:** the act, performed by Aes Sedai, of shutting off a woman who can channel from the One Power. A woman who has been stilled can sense the True Source, but she cannot touch it.

**Stone Soldiers:** *See* Aiel warrior societies.

*sul'dam* (SUHL-DAHM): A woman who has passed the tests to show that she can wear the bracelet of an *a'dam* and thus control a *damane*. *See also:* a'dam; damane.

**Sunday:** A feastday and festival in midsummer, celebrated in many parts of the world.

**sung wood:** *See* Treesinger.

**Suroth, High Lady** (SUE-roth): A Seanchan noblewoman of high degree.

*Tai'shar* (*TIE-SHAHR*): In the Old Tongue, "True blood of."

**ta'maral'ailen** (*tah-MAHR-ahl-EYE-lehn*): In the Old Tongue, "Web of Destiny." A great change in the Pattern of an Age, centered around one or more people who are *ta'veren*. *See also* Pattern of an Age; *ta'veren*.

**Tanreall, Artur Paendrag** (tahn-REE-ahl, AHR-tuhr PAY-ehn-DRAG): *See* Hawkwing, Artur.

**Tarmon Gai'don** (TAHR-mohn GAY-dohn): The Last Battle. *See also* Dragon, Prophecies of the; Horn of Valere.

**Tar Valon** (TAHR VAH-lon): A city on an island in the River Erinin. The center of Aes Sedai power, and location of the White Tower.

**ta'veren** (*tah-VEER-ehn*): A person around whom the Wheel of Time weaves all surrounding life-threads, perhaps *all* life-threads, to form a Web of Destiny. *See also* Pattern of an Age.

**Tear** (TEER): A great seaport on the Sea of Storms.

**Telamon, Lews Therin** (TEHL-ah-mon, LOOZ THEH-rihn): See Dragon, the.

*ter'angreal* (*TEER-ahn-GREE-ahl*): Any one of a number of remnants of the Age of Legends that use the One Power. Unlike *angreal* and *sa'angreal,* each *ter'angreal* was made to do a particular thing. For example, one makes oaths taken within it binding. Some are used by Aes Sedai, but their original purposes are largely unknown. Some will kill or destroy the ability to channel of any woman who uses them. *See also angreal; sa'angreal.*

*tia avende alantin* (*TEE-ah ah-VEN-day ah-LANH-tin*): "Brother to the Trees."

*Tia mi aven Moridin isainde vadin:* In the Old Tongue, "The grave is no bar to my call." Inscription on the Horn of Valere. *See also* Horn of Valere.

**Tigraine** (tee-GRAIN): As Daughter-Heir of Andor, she married Taringail

Damodred and bore his son Galadedrid. Her disappearance in 972 NE, shortly after her brother Luc vanished in the Blight, led to the struggle in Andor called the Succession, and caused the events in Cairhien that eventually brought on the Aiel War. Her sign was a woman's hand gripping a thorny rose stem with a white blossom.

**Time of Madness:** The years after the Dark One's counterstroke tainted the male half of the True Source, when male Aes Sedai went mad and Broke the World. The exact duration of this period is unknown, but it is believed to have lasted nearly one hundred years. It ended completely only with the death of the last male Aes Sedai. *See also* Hundred Companions; True Source; One Power; Breaking of the World.

**Tinkers:** *See* Tuatha'an.

**Traveling People:** *See* Tuatha'an.

**Tree, the:** *See Avendesora.*

**Treekillers:** An Aiel name for the Cairhienin, always said in tones of horror and disgust.

**Treesinger:** An Ogier who has the ability to sing to trees (called "treesong"), either healing them, or helping them to grow and flower, or making things from the wood without damaging the tree. Objects made in this manner are called "sung wood" and are highly prized. Few Ogier remain who are Treesingers; the Talent seems to be dying out.

**treesong:** *See* Treesinger.

**Trollocs (TRAHL-lohks):** Creatures of the Dark One, created during the War of the Shadow. Huge in stature, they are a twisted blend of animal and human stock. Vicious by nature, they kill for the pure pleasure of killing. Deceitful in the extreme, they cannot be trusted unless coerced by fear. They are divided into tribe-like bands, among them the Dha'vol, the Ko'bal, and the Dhai'mon.

**Trolloc Wars:** A series of wars, beginning about 1000 AB and lasting more than three hundred years, during which Trolloc armies ravaged the world. Eventually the Trollocs were slain or driven back into the Great Blight, but some nations ceased to exist, while others were almost depopulated. All records of the time are fragmentary. *See also* Covenant of the Ten Nations.

**True Source:** The driving force of the universe, which turns the Wheel of

Time. It is divided into a male half (*saidin*) and a female half (*saidar*), which work at the same time with and against each other. Only a man can draw on *saidin,* only a woman on *saidar.* Since the beginning of the Time of Madness, *saidin* has been tainted by the Dark One's touch. *See also* One Power.

**Tuatha'an** (too-AH-thah-AHN): A wandering folk, also known as the Tinkers and as the Traveling People, who live in brightly painted wagons and follow a totally pacifist philosophy called the Way of the Leaf. Things mended by Tinkers are often better than new. They are among the few who can cross the Aiel Waste unmolested, for the Aiel strictly avoid all contact with them.

**Turak, High Lord of House Aladon** (TOO-rak; AL-ah-dohn): A Seanchan of high degree, commander of the *Hailene. See also* Seanchan; *Hailene.*

**Verin** (VEHR-ihn): An Aes Sedai of the Brown Ajah.

**Warder:** A warrior bonded to an Aes Sedai. The bonding is a thing of the One Power, and by it he gains such gifts as quick healing, the ability to go long periods without food, water, or rest, and the ability to sense the taint of the Dark One at a distance. So long as a Warder lives, the Aes Sedai to whom he is bonded knows he is alive however far away he is, and when he dies she will know the moment and manner of his death. The bonding does not tell her how far he is, though, nor in what direction. While most Ajahs believe an Aes Sedai may have one Warder bonded to her at a time, the Red Ajah refuses to bond any Warders at all, while the Green Ajah believe an Aes Sedai may bond as many Warders as she wishes. Ethically the Warder must accede to the bonding, but it has been known to be done involuntarily. What the Aes Sedai gain from the bonding is a closely held secret. *See also* Aes Sedai.

**War of Power:** *See* War of the Shadow.

**War of the Hundred Years:** A series of overlapping wars among constantly shifting alliances, precipitated by the death of Artur Hawkwing and the resulting struggle for his empire. It lasted from FY 994 to FY 1117. The war depopulated large parts of the lands between the Aryth Ocean and the Aiel Waste, from the Sea of Storms to the Great Blight. So great was the destruction that only fragmentary records of the time remain. The empire of Artur Hawkwing was pulled apart in the wars, and the nations of the present day were formed. *See also* Hawkwing, Artur.

**War of the Shadow:** Also known as the War of Power, it ended the Age of Legends. It began shortly after the attempt to free the Dark One, and soon involved the whole world. In a world where even the memory of war had been forgotten, every facet of war was rediscovered, often twisted by the Dark One's touch on the world, and the One Power was used as a weapon. The war was ended by the resealing of the Dark One into his prison. *See also* Hundred Companions, the; Dragon, the.

**Watchers Over the Waves:** A group who believe that the armies Artur Hawkwing sent across the Aryth Ocean will one day return, and so keep watch from the town of Falme (FAHL-may) on Toman Head.

**Web of Destiny:** *See ta'maral'ailen.*

**Weight, units of:** 10 ounces = 1 pound; 10 pounds = 1 stone; 10 stone = 1 hundredweight; 10 hundredweight = 1 ton.

**Wheel of Time, the:** Time is a wheel with seven spokes, each spoke an Age. As the Wheel turns, the Ages come and go, each leaving memories that fade to legend, then to myth, and are forgotten by the time that Age comes again. The Pattern of an Age is slightly different each time an Age comes, and each time it is subject to greater change, but each time it is the same Age.

**Whitecloaks:** *See* Children of the Light.

**White Tower:** The palace of the Amyrlin Seat in Tar Valon, and the place where Aes Sedai are trained.

**Wisdom:** In villages, a woman chosen by the Women's Circle for her knowledge of such things as healing, and foretelling the weather, as well as for common good sense. A position of great responsibility and authority, both actual and implied. She is generally considered the equal of the mayor, just as the Women's Circle is the equal of the Village Council. Unlike the mayor, the Wisdom is chosen for life, and it is very rare for a Wisdom to be removed from office before her death. Depending on the land, she may instead have another title, such as Guide, Healer, Wise Woman, or Reader.